THE
BINDINGS
OF WOE

– Chain of Worlds –

CONNOR JACKSON

◆ FriesenPress

One Printers Way
Altona, MB R0G 0B0
Canada

www.friesenpress.com

Copyright © 2022 by Connor Jackson
First Edition — 2022

Cover illustration by David Bou
Map illustrations by Paul Schultz

ISBN
978-1-03-912844-6 (Hardcover)
978-1-03-912843-9 (Paperback)
978-1-03-912845-3 (eBook)

1. FICTION, FANTASY, EPIC

Distributed to the trade by The Ingram Book Company

The Coastlands

Brienenwood

Mountains of Fire

Ebbenwood

TERRALAND

The Gr

Brienen Lake

Valley of Aol

Dip of Ebbenwood

Sea of Dread

The Isles

Audria Channel

Splitland

The Lowlands

Webwood

Keldaria

The Great Ocean

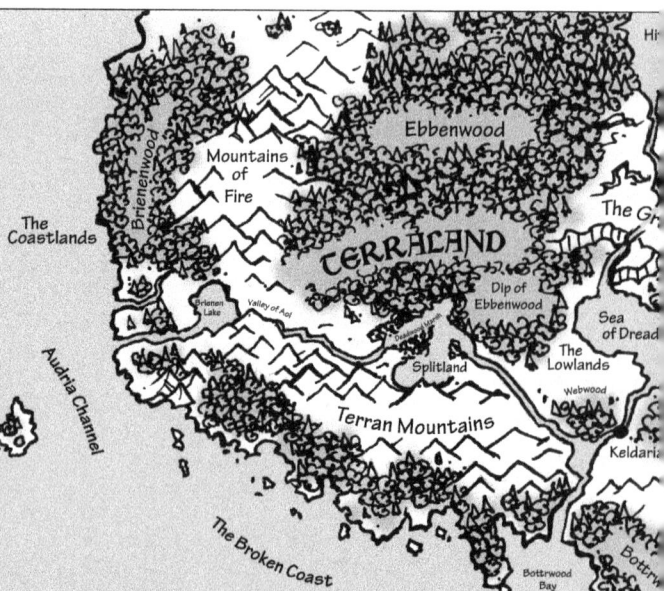

The Broken Coast

Bottrwood Bay

Bottr

PEEK

Peeken

Gulf of Blades

Wegwag Forest

Kelm

FRAAGG

Mahkouan Peninsula
Realm of the Goblin Colony Kingdoms

Bruntol Forest

Divide Mountains

DOKKIC

SHAUL

LABLIK

Binniksar

Credal

Maigina Wood

Nakuna

Chaulup Isles

Gishbar

The Great Greenwood

Red Mountains

Craggon's

UPERIN

Higidolish

Gorlaist Prairie

Jugana Forest

HOPKI

Jikket

MISHIC

Bay of Teeth

Maelstrom Bay

N
W E
S

Hopki Islands

Miathema Swamp

Serpent Gulf

South to BELDAR

NORTHERN GAIA

and the realms of
the Dwarven Commonwealth,
the Goblin Colony Kingdoms,
and the Northern Kingdom
of Humanity.

Pegasus
Mountains
"Worlds End North"

The
hlands

Cliff

Territore

WORLDS END MOUNTAINS

Forest

ntains of Craldorik

DITHRAINE

Ket
Lake

Dithallin

Tyedmur

CORWEN

Larthelan

Loden
Lake

Thegefferan

Heartwood

Telladar

Anvil
Forest

Dunewane Sea

Dunewane Delta

Bay
of Blades

The Korochuspian

Thegefferan's Scar

Dulenbelt Islands

Qortllibron

DULENGAR

Fang Forest

YODMERE

Mikrundor

Daegor Sea

Ironcleft

CHRAK

Attoauwy Swamp

Udalen

Brithmor
Lake

Somnenwood

Hegaranath

The
Drearlands

Thithilin

UBINON MOUNTAINS

Urubinon Desert

South to XAIDAR and the Sovereign Lands

Isles Not To Scale

The Far Isle

Farwood
Forest

The Isles

The North Isle

Crall

Gieme

Wester Forest

Crall Cove

Leydes

Fort Audrin

The West Isle

Furik
Forest

Furik Hills

Muyer

Furik River

Souten River

Muyer River

Rudenhull

Souten

Quinredal

Vellum Forest

Verrel

Caswen

Fort Audrik

Keldrid
Lake

Quinic Reef

Gale

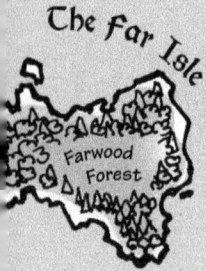

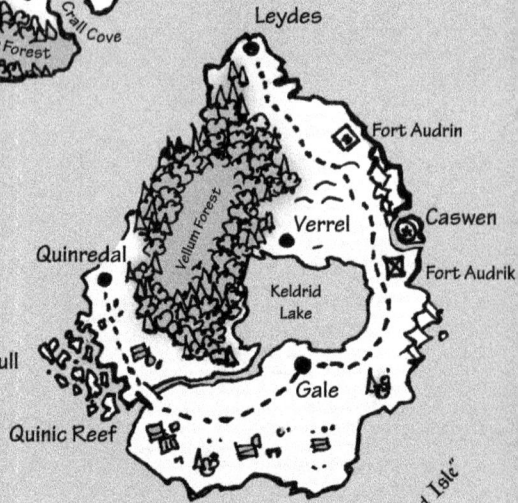

The East Isle "The Grand Isle"

Legend
- Minor Settlement
- ◎ Major Settlement
- ✪ Provincial Capital
- ◈ Military Fort
- ⊠ Ruins

The
Coastlands

Ledid

New
Brienen

Kikilet
Woods

Brienen
Lake

Old
Brienen

Valley
of Aol

Sader

Sternn

Brienen River

Fort
Eageran

Eageran Forest

The Broken Path

Fort Burul

Audria Channel

N

E

S

Chapter 1

"Carver! Carver, where are you?"

Where is that boy? she wondered. *He's never around when I need him.*

"Carver!" she shouted again as she walked briskly through the silent village, scanning her eyes from side to side.

It was cold outside, but she didn't mind. It was the cold she expected from an early morning walk. The grass was still damp after the previous night's rain, creating faint shimmers of reflected sunlight from the water that clung to each blade of green. She continued through the village, passing the small wooden cottages with thatched roofs that lined the sides of the wide, grassy avenue, and smiled at her fellow pale-skinned villagers who occasionally crossed her path on the way to start their day.

"Carver!"

Though the village was small, and she knew she would find him eventually, she still disliked shouting all around so early in the morning. Keeping on, she strode through the thin morning fog, kicking up spits of water from the grass with each step of her worn cowhide boots.

"Good morning, Velanna," a calm voice called out from behind her.

Velanna stopped and turned around. Behind her, having just emerged from a different avenue of wet grass going elsewhere into the village, stood a short, gray-haired woman with her wrinkled hands clasped together.

"Oh, morning, Direne. How are you doing this morning?"

"I'm doing fine, dear. Thank you for asking. I'm just having my morning stroll through the village."

Direne turned her head and looked up and down the wide stretch of grass between the rows of small, slightly disheveled cottages, then took a deep, calming breath before looking back at Velanna.

"Can't find that boy of yours, eh? I'm surprised he's up and about so soon after Agon returned Aol to the sky," she said with a soft chuckle.

Velanna gave the eastern sun a quick glance before looking back to Direne. "As am I. I want him to help Bran load the wagons for the trip today, but he seems to have disappeared. He probably knows he's going to be helping and is avoiding me on purpose."

"Sixteen-year-olds are often trouble that way, dear. I still remember searching for you when you were a young girl, usually finding you out with Bran." Direne smiled at the memory.

Velanna grinned and lowered her eyes, blushing. "Hmm ... I usually find him out with Helena."

"Oh ..." Direne's eyes widened, followed by a small, knowing smile.

Velanna looked back up. "No, not like that. They're just friends, though I think they would be great together. Mostly because Helena actually pays attention to all the schoolhouse lessons and not just the ones about learning to fight or how to ride a horse, and she keeps him out of trouble. Well, most of the time, anyway."

Direne laughed as she casually closed the distance between herself and Velanna. "He's a good boy. You and Bran have done a wonderful job raising him, especially for such a young couple. It's hard to think that the two of you were younger than Carver is now when you had him."

Velanna grinned at the memory, but her faint smile quickly darkened. Direne noticed the sudden change in the young woman's face.

"Oh, don't let yourself be bothered at your young age of motherhood. It can happen to any—"

"No, it's not that. I, oh, um, never mind."

"Don't you keep secrets from me, young woman. I practically raised you after your parents died, so you don't get to hide bothersome feelings from me," the old woman said sternly, though still in a pleasant tone.

Velanna felt foolish as she looked at Direne and let out a short exhale through her nose. "That's just it. I barely remember my parents, and Bran never met his father, while his mother was apparently so awful that he fled the whorehouse she worked and lived at while he was still a boy. Neither of us truly had our own parents, so how can we know if we're good parents ourselves?"

"Velanna." Direne placed a soft hand on Velanna's arm. "Do you and Bran truly think as such?"

"Bran doesn't. Just me. Well, not all the time, though. I don't know. I just feel like I didn't do the right things with him when I was supposed to— Carver, I mean." Velanna's eyes trailed down to the grass as she finished.

Direne released Velanna's arm and snapped her wrinkled fingers. "Look at me."

Velanna's eyes shot up at the old woman.

"You don't deserve these horrid thoughts you're putting through your mind. You're a great mother, and Bran is a great father, and it shows through your son. The loss of your parents was a tragedy, and Bran's upbringing before he stumbled into this village as a lad was dreadful by his recounting, but the loss and abuses you two suffered didn't make you weak; they made you both strong."

Velanna let out an embarrassed sigh. "I know, I know. I shouldn't have said—"

"I'm not finished, girl."

Velanna held her tongue while her frustration at herself for her insistence on speaking without thinking grew.

"And I understand that while I took you in and watched over you growing up, I was not your mother. I never tried to replace her. But—"

"That's not what I—"

Direne snapped her fingers again. "But having a mother or not, or someone who takes care of you in a similar way, doesn't determine if you will be a good one yourself when the time comes. Who you are and who you take as a partner decide what kind of parent you'll be. And while I must admit I didn't think much of Bran in his early teenage years ..."

Direne stopped and thought for a moment, then she let out a quick laugh. "And my opinion of the boy couldn't have gotten any lower when I found out you stopped bleeding and had a belly bigger than a girl of fourteen of Cosom's winters should have had. By the stars, I wanted to drown that Bran in the lake when I found out."

Velanna joined Direne in a laugh.

"But he didn't run, even when he had every chance to. He could have left the moment your belly began to swell, but he stayed at your side and didn't look at any other girl, from what I remember. He was dedicated to you, and I saw that you were to him as well, and both of you have extended that dedication and love to Carver."

Velanna couldn't think of what to say in reply.

"Oh my, I went off a bit there, didn't I? Sorry, dear. I didn't mean to ramble so much, but you should listen to what I said. You're a—"

Velanna stepped forward and hugged Direne. Direne held her tongue and hugged back.

The warm touch of Direne made the chilly air that caressed Velanna's face and hands more noticeable.

"Thank you, Direne," Velanna said as she broke the hug and stepped back.

The edges of Direne's mouth rose into a warm smile. "Think nothing of it, dear. And before my old mind forgets, I believe I saw your boy heading over toward the archery range during my walk. Give him a hug for me when you see him." Direne stepped back and made to turn and head down the way Velanna had come from.

"I will. Thanks, Direne," Velanna said as she nodded with a smile of appreciation, then turned toward the village archery range.

It only took a minute at her quickened pace for her to reach the range: a small field on the north end of the village with targets laid about a few dozen feet away on the northern side. It was a small range, but it was all the people of the tiny village needed.

Velanna stood still for a moment and peered out at the targets on the opposite end of the field. They were all small wooden disks with painted white rings around their flat surfaces, held up by a tripod stand of thick sticks and worn rope, stationed in a line of decreasing size from right to left along the field's edge.

Suddenly, something caught her eye. One of the targets was missing from its stand, and there, sitting against the empty wooden support, was a boy. He was facing away from her, toward the northern hills that stretched out far after the brief flatness of the range ended.

"There you are," Velanna said to herself.

Even at this distance, she could recognize her son from just the back of his head. He had thick, scruffy hair that covered his ears and ran down the back of his neck just shy of touching the base. Instead of matching his mother's auburn hair, his was a dark brown.

Velanna started toward him, feeling frustrated after the hunt she had been forced to embark on just to find him. He didn't notice her approach, and as she got closer, she realized why. He was fiddling with something in his lap, something that made a scraping sound. She walked up behind him and looked down. On his lap was a painted wooden disk that he was proceeding to carve lines into with a small, curved dagger.

"What are you doing?"

Carver's head snapped back as he let out a gasp. Despite his age, his face showed no signs of facial hair.

"Gah! You scared me. I didn't hear you walk up."

Velanna folded her arms and stared down at her son's surprised face. He may not have shared her auburn hair, but he had her dark-green eyes, almost brown from a distance. Velanna grabbed the target from her son's lap.

Carver remained silent as he watched her inspect it with a look of distaste on her face.

"What are you doing to this? You're wrecking it," Velanna said as she lowered the target and glared down at her son.

"No, I'm not. It's just some marks. I'm not cutting through it."

"Why are you doing it at all?"

"I don't know. I just felt like it. There's nothing to do right now," Carver explained as he slid his dagger into a small sheath that was buckled to his belt.

"Actually, there is. I want you to help your father prepare the wagons for Caswen, and once that's done, you'll be coming with us to deliver the tax and then sell the remaining goods."

Carver's expression contorted immediately. "Why do I have to come?" he complained.

Velanna turned her body to the empty stand and placed the defaced disk back where it belonged, frowning at the realization that an argument was needed. "Because I want you to. Now go help your father. He's over by the stables, and no more of this." Velanna pointed to the damaged target. "They're for archery practice, not carving out of boredom. Okay?"

"Okay, I won't. But it's not wrecked; it's fine. Besides, arrows make marks in them anyway, so it doesn't really matter," Carver said, trying to get the last word as he rose from the wet grass that left the legs of his wool trousers slightly damp.

"Carver, this isn't a debate. I don't care what you think about it, just no more. Now go help your father."

With that, Velanna turned and walked back into the village with renewed frustration.

✠ ✠ ✠

Carver followed his mother back into the village before he split off and headed his own way, now also feeling frustrated. He had known for days that his parents were among those chosen to go to the city, which meant he was to go too. Carver bit his lip. He had hoped that if he got up early enough he could hide until his parents had left and avoid being dragged along, but it hadn't worked. His mother had found him and made it clear he would be helping, just as he had dreaded.

He trudged through the heart of the village, heading south through the wide paths of grass between the many wooden cottages. He knew the layout of the village enough that his attention was not needed to traverse to the other side. Instead, he turned his attention inward, his eyes glazing over as he stared at the wet grass and daydreamed about battles and fighting. Such was common for him, as his mind would regularly drift out of the real world and into his own: a world full of combat, battles where he was the hero who single-handedly won the day against all odds or was the lone survivor after a great show of bloodshed.

He loved fighting, and though he had never been in a real fight before, he imagined he would be quite good at it. After all, training to fight was the only part of his limited schooling that he enjoyed and paid any real attention to besides learning how to ride a horse.

He figured himself to be the best youth in the village when it came to combat exercises. From hand-to-hand grappling to sparring with dull practice blades, he almost always came out ahead of the others his age, and when he didn't, it was only by a small margin.

He delighted in combat training. Straining himself in combative exercises made him feel alive and strong. It filled him with a feeling of power, manifesting over the years into a confidence that he could take on anything the world could threaten him with, whether it be a human, dwarf, goblin, or a beast such as a giant forest spider, malicious harpy, or any other creature that a sharp blade could end.

A large part of his success in combat training was due to his mother, the most skilled fighter he knew.

Carver thought back to an event that occurred five years ago, the long, festive winter celebration during the last night before spring and the ending of the year 199. The night sky above his village had been filled with orange light from the roaring bonfires that many of his fellow villagers danced and sang around. The adults were drinking merrily and laughing, and the children were playing and fighting, as children do.

Then, at the last hour of the last night before the new century, the adults formed a grand circle in the center of the village, and the celebration of might commenced: a rapid succession of one-on-one, hand-to-hand matches where any man or woman of the village could show off their fighting prowess to a cheering crowd of friends and family.

It was then that Carver saw for the first time the splendor that combat could be, for when his mother stepped into the circle with those behind her chanting her name, Carver felt a surge of pride just for being her child. Carver had watched in awe and shock as his mother beat every man and woman who stepped into the circle, one after another. She was as quick as she was strong, easily able to outmaneuver all the challengers she faced and wear them down. It was amazing to behold.

He thought back to the end of his mother's last match of that night, remembering how bruised and drenched in sweat her skin was. Her face was splattered in blood from her opponents' broken noses and torn lips, blanketing much of her pale skin under a crimson veil. Despite her battered appearance, she looked like she was ready to do it all again, standing there with her head held up and her fists at the ready for anyone else who thought to step into the circle and challenge her. Carver had never seen his mother like that before.

At that moment he had thought his mother looked like how he imagined the human warriors of old did in the lessons he was forced to sit through at the village schoolhouse; stories about the brave men and women, beaten and bloody, fighting tooth and nail against the invading armies of the tartaruns from the far south, who sought to conquer and enslave the known world.

He remembered the sound of the villagers cheering his mother's name and the sight of her opponents congratulating her on her hard-fought wins while cupping their bleeding noses and rubbing their bruised chins. They all respected her, admiring her strength and skill.

Carver wanted that. He wanted to be a remarkable fighter like his mother. An unbeatable force of strength and speed. His mother knew this about him and did her best to teach him. With the training he'd received from his limited schooling between chores and village work, combined with the extra lessons from his mother, Carver was growing into an impressively skilled fighter for his young age. Though only sixteen, he felt like he could compete with a well-trained soldier in the queen's army. He knew he could.

Carver's daydreaming was halted as something smashed into his side, knocking him to the ground. His back hit the grass hard, smearing dirt onto the shoulders of his wool tunic and knocking the air out of him, and his head slammed into the ground, making his vision swim. He attempted to pull his head up to see what had struck him, but the fuzziness in his head and the strain on his lungs made him too slow. Before he could grasp his situation, something heavy landed on his stomach.

What little air remained in his lungs was forced out with a painful wheezing sound as his head slammed back down, causing his eyes to shut. Hands grabbed his wrists, forcing them down to his sides, and it was only then that he realized someone was on top of him. With a rush of adrenaline and anger, Carver tensed his muscles in preparation for a fight. Then he opened his eyes, and his adrenaline rushed away almost as quickly as it had arrived.

He was staring up at the face of a smiling young girl with large brown eyes. Her light-brown hair hung over her left shoulder and down into his face in a long, thick braid.

"Hey, Carver!" she shouted with a wide grin.

After taking a second to catch his breath, Carver opened his mouth. "Helena! What the hell are you doing?" His words were accompanied with a cough.

"Pinning you down, apparently!" she said with a laugh.

"Get off me!" Carver barked through a second cough as air surged back into his lungs.

Helena giggled and released Carver's wrists. Then she sat up on his stomach and pushed herself off him.

Carver coughed again as he stood up.

"What the hell was that?" he demanded as he brushed dirt off his tunic and the backside of his trousers.

"I saw you walking with your head down and could tell you weren't paying attention. So, I decided to tackle you," Helena replied with a shrug.

Carver looked up from cleaning off his trousers. "That really hurt, you know," he said before a fourth cough.

"Oh, poor little baby," Helena jibed as she leaned forward, placing her hands on her knees.

"Piss off," Carver said with a grin.

Helena let out a short laugh. "So, what are you doing?"

Carver resumed his trek through the village as Helena strode beside him.

"My mom wants me to help my dad prepare for the trip to Caswen. Then I'm going with them to offload all day," Carver said with some grievance to his tone.

"Oh, I'm going too, actually," Helena replied cheerfully. "My parents are going to set up a stall and sell some of the things they've made in our smithy. They want me to come along and help. I actually made a few of the things we'll be selling," she added with excitement.

Carver turned to face Helena as they walked. She looked as she always did, upbeat and joyful. Helena always seemed to be in a good mood, no matter what she was doing.

She was wearing what everyone in the village typically wore, Carver included: a plain white woolen tunic paired with equally plain brown wool pants and simple, cheaply made cowhide boots. Helena's tunic was stained black with grime along the sleeves and collar from her parents' workshop, as were her trousers. The apron she wore while smithing did a decent job of protecting her garments, but it wasn't perfect. The dirty clothes made her look tough, like a girl who wasn't afraid to get her hands dirty, which was exactly the type of girl she was.

"Really? You sound as if you like the idea of wasting your whole day dealing with city people."

"It's not a waste. I get to practice my bartering, help my parents out, and see the city."

"You won't get to see the city. We'll be at the Outer Market. All you'll be able to see is the gate and the walls. The Inner Market is only for the city merchants. You know that."

"Don't be so damn negative, Carver," Helena said as she punched him lightly in the shoulder. "We won't be selling all day. We'll have time to go in and look around, I'm sure."

Carver looked over at Helena again, wondering how much more physical abuse he would suffer from her before the day's end.

They'd been friends for as long as either of them could remember. Being the same age and growing up in the same small village meant they spent almost all their free time together. They were close friends, and they were quite physical with each other. They often practiced their fighting skills, sparring with practice blades when they weren't attending class, performing their village chores and duties, or wrestling to settle even the slightest disagreements that sparked between them.

Carver usually won in the end, though not by a huge margin. Helena was remarkably strong for a person of her gender and size. Years spent helping her parents run the village blacksmith shop had built up her muscles considerably, despite her small frame.

"Don't be so damn positive," Carver joked in response to Helena's previous comment.

Helena smiled as she kept pace with Carver. They continued walking in comfortable silence, taking in the serene scenery of their village as people prepared for the day.

After a few short minutes, they passed the last cottage at the south end of the village and stood before a large field much like the archery range to the north, but instead of targets stationed at the end there was a rough-looking stable with a handful of horses grazing over hay-filled troughs inside. Scattered throughout the field were carts and wagons of varying sizes. Carver could see his father, already loading some crates into one of the wagons.

Carver's father was a tall, clean-shaven man with short, dark-brown hair. He had a fit build developed from years of challenging work as a hunter for the village. As if somehow sensing his son's arrival, the man looked up from the wagon and spotted Carver and Helena almost instantly.

"Well, look who it is. You're just in time to help me load these wagons," he called out, smiling.

"Hi, Bran," Helena said, waving as she and Carver approached.

"Hello, Helena, how are you doing?" Bran asked as he stepped down from the back of the wagon, causing it to creak and rock.

"I'm doing good. I'm excited to go to Caswen."

"Oh, you'll be coming too? I thought it was just your parents and us." Bran gestured to his son.

"Nope," Helena said with a smile. "I'm coming to help my parents out. Plus, they want me to try and sell the things I made in the smithy."

Bran raised his eyebrows. "Really? That's great. What have you made so far?"

"Nothing too special. Just a couple of knives and daggers, a decent arming sword, and a hand axe. The axe is okay. I couldn't get the edge to curve right, so it looks a little off. But it's still decent quality."

"Knives and daggers? What's the difference?" Carver asked.

Helena rolled her eyes at her friend. "How can you not know the difference? Knives are meant as tools and only have one bladed edge. Daggers," Helena pointed to the dagger sheathed on Carver's belt, "are meant as weapons and are bladed on both edges."

Carver raised his open palms and made a face that said he was sorry for asking. His sarcastic expression caused Helena to quickly exhale through her nose in amusement.

Bran chuckled. "That's quite impressive, Helena. I'm sure your parents are proud of you."

"Thanks, Bran," Helena said as Carver ended his exaggerated mannerisms.

Bran turned his attention back to his son. "I assume your mother sent you to help me prepare the wagons for the trip?"

"Yes, but do I have to come? I'd really rather stay here."

Bran gave his son a look of pity. "Yes, you have to come. Your mother and I want you to get more experience outside the village other than hunting and fishing, Carver."

"It's not hard, Dad. I know how to lift crates and sacks on and off a wagon. I've gone with you guys once before, remember? Why don't I just go hunting for the day instead? I'll find something for dinner tonight; I'll even prepare and cook it by myself."

"No, Carver, you're not going hunting by yourself. It's too dangerous for someone your age to be hunting alone in Vellum Forest. The vells might seem harmless when you're hunting in armed groups, but alone they would see you as easy prey and swarm you, if a cougar or giant spider doesn't get you first, that is."

Carver opened his mouth to say that he would have someone else accompany him, but he never got the chance.

"And it's not just about moving goods, you know. You'll be helping with the setup once we get there, as well as chipping in to trade our merchandise. Besides, having you help me offload the tax to the city's soldiers will leave your mother and Helena's parents free to get started on setting up the stalls and preparing the goods. Your mother wants to get there early as well, so we can get a good spot and attract more attention."

"But why do we have to leave this early? The sun's barely returned, and the tax isn't supposed to be gathered until midday, isn't it?"

Bran let out a small sigh and changed his tone to be more strict. "Because, Carver, it's a three-hour ride to Caswen, and the hills between us and the city mean we have to ride at a slower pace than we'd like, especially since the horses are hauling such heavy loads. By the time we finish preparing and get there it'll be closer to noon than it is to morning, which gives us only a couple hours' advance to deal with the soldiers when it comes to paperwork and the tax, then set up the stalls and offload the goods. We aren't worried about being late for noon; we're worried about not being early enough to get a clear spot near the city gate."

Carver let out a sigh of disappointment. "Fine," he muttered, looking down toward the grass. He walked past his father to a hefty sack of grain and heaved it onto his shoulder. In his frustration he tried to lift the sack up harshly in an attempt to show his displeasure, but he misjudged the weight and stumbled, nearly falling before he got the sack over his shoulder. Carver's face reddened with a wave of embarrassment.

"You'll be fine, son, it's not that bad," Bran said, switching back to a gentler voice. "At least you'll have Helena to talk to," he added with a chuckle. He turned to her and smiled. "You want to lend your friend and his father a hand, blacksmith?"

"Sure. My parents already loaded their wagon last night, so I'm just killing time before we go," Helena said, already marching toward some crates and sacks that needed to be loaded.

"Look at that," Bran said. "Helena's more than happy to help your father lift these heavy goods."

Helena shot Carver an antagonizing grin.

Carver couldn't help but grin in return despite his frustration. "I didn't know you had gotten so old that you couldn't load a wagon, Dad," he said with levity.

"Ha. I wouldn't call myself old yet. I'm pretty much only twice your age, you brat."

"Then you'd think you should have twice the wisdom. Strange."

Bran chuckled and ran his fingers through his short brown hair, smiling at his son's quick wit.

Between the three of them, the job was done in little less than half an hour. They had filled two large wagons with an assortment of goods. Large sacks of grain, well-sealed barrels containing a range of goods from dried and salted meats to animal hides and lumber, and wooden crates with miscellaneous tools and equipment were packed inside. However, one of the wagons had something of much more value stashed within it. Tucked away in the back was a smaller wooden crate containing an assortment of pouches filled with coins.

Once the loading was finished, Carver and Helena stood back and watched as Bran hitched two horses to each of the wagons and made sure each horse was comfortable and ready to pull a heavy burden.

"Thanks, you two. You've both been a great help. However, we're short two barrels of salted cod. That Duncan fellow was supposed to show up this morning with them. I guess he's running late. Oh well. You two can run off now. I'll go get the third wagon from Helena's parents ready and hope that Duncan shows up by then. If not, he'll have Velanna to deal with," Bran said with a grin. "I'll come find you both when we're ready to head out. Go do whatever until then," Bran added as he made sure the last horse was fitted properly in its harness to the front of the second wagon.

"Alright, see you, Dad."

Helena waved goodbye to Bran and gave him a wide smile, feeling good after a job well done, then turned and jogged to catch up to Carver, who was already strolling back into the village.

The temperature had warmed up during the last half hour. The light fog from earlier had dissipated into the warmer air, and the village was fully awake, with people all around. Some were readying their gear for hunting and gathering out in the western forest or the northern hills alongside their trained dogs. Others carried nets and fishing poles while heading to the great lake to the south. Many others scooped up hoes and rakes to tend to their small fields scrunched in the flat areas between the village and the eastern hills. A handful got to work in their shops, creating tools and preparing food. The rest went to care for the penned livestock around the village, including sheep, pigs, chickens, and cattle.

It was a small yet busy village, situated in a low dip in the earth, encircled from the north and east by hills that went on for miles. The sunken area and isolation the land provided made day-to-day life in the village quiet and calm, but it left little space needed for farming. To counter their lack of agriculture, the villagers relied heavily on crafting tools for trade, fishing, and hunting and gathering.

Vellum Forest, as the western woods were called, was a massive expanse of trees that filled the heart of the large island with tall trees and heavy shadows. The forest was named after the vellums that infested it: reptilian hound-like creatures introduced to the area from distant southern lands in times long past, now mainly referred to as "vells" or "goblin wolves" by the locals. Apart from these creatures, the deep forest was a pristine location for the village hunters. Carver often spent his days in those woods, hunting with his mother and father until the two moons replaced the sun.

"How many times have you been to Caswen, Helena?"

Helena looked surprised, as if she had been startled by the sudden question. "Um ... a few times, maybe like three or four. I don't know, why?"

"Just curious. You seem really excited to go is all."

"I like going. I think it's incredible. The huge stone wall that surrounds the city, the sheer amount of people living inside, and the things you can buy at the Inner Market are amazing. Like last time I went, when my parents took me along for their business with some of the city blacksmiths, I found that book about the invasion of the tartaruns. Remember, the one made up of old translated journal entries from soldiers? You can't get that kind of stuff unless you go to the city."

"Yeah, I remember. Did you ever finish reading it?"

"No. I stopped about halfway through. I kept thinking the journal entries would get better, but they just kept getting sadder and more depressing. Nearly every entry was about how the tartaruns captured another city or butchered another army. Besides, I already know how it ended. We all learned the history of the Tartarun Invasion from our lessons, so unless I wanted to read more firsthand accounts of how horrible it was, there wasn't really any point of continuing."

"Well, what did you expect to read?" Carver asked with a chuckle. "They were combat diaries from people who actually fought in the war, which we were pretty much losing for the most part until everyone signed that treaty at the end."

"The Stalemate Treaty, Carver. Because both sides were stuck in a stalemate that neither could break. And everyone didn't just sign a treaty all at once at the end. The goblins signed it on their own first, and it was only the liberated colony kingdoms of Mahkoua that broke away from the rest of the Old Goblin Empire, which was still held by the tartaruns, and even then some of the current colony kingdoms were left out of it."

"Okay, sure, whatever. But everyone did sign it in the end."

"The humans signed it quickly after the goblins did, yeah, but it took the dwarves a while after that until they signed it too and left a fifth of their lands under tartarun control. The Stalemate Treaty wasn't a collective choice by the northern races, Carver. The humans signing it and leaving the dwarves on their own is a big reason why Terraland isn't part of the Dwarven Commonwealth anymore. Don't you pay attention to anything we learn at the schoolhouse?"

"I don't care about the details of changing kingdom borders or treaty signing stuff. It was forever ago, anyway. Back before people started to count the years. Who cares what happened back then?"

Helena gave Carver a disgruntled glare. "It was somewhere close to three hundred years ago. And people did count the years back then. The dwarves had a calendar for who knows how many centuries during the Lost Years, before it was reset by—" Helena stopped and rubbed her face. "Oh, you don't care, whatever. But it is interesting. And it's important to learn what happened in the past, so it doesn't happen again in the future—at least not the bad things."

"Pfft," Carver waved his hand toward Helena as if to deflect her words back at her face. "I don't think we need to worry about tartaruns attacking us, seeing as the sovereigns wiped them all out. So, we can't make sure it doesn't happen again since it literally can't happen again," he stated with confidence.

Helena rolled her eyes. "Whatever. It's still sad to read about it. Hearing what happened from the history tome in class is one thing, but reading the individual notes of people who were actually in the war was too much. I thought the book would be like an in-depth history tome, with facts and secrets I didn't know, but it was just depressing letters to loved ones and reports about defeats and pyrrhic victories. Nothing happy at all."

Helena crossed her arms as if attempting to guard herself from the memory of the pages.

A moment of silence sprouted between the two friends as they strolled deeper into the village, but then Carver erupted with a mocking voice. "Oh, well, today all my friends were torn apart by ten-foot-tall, gray-scaled monster men, but I sure do love this fresh air. I think I'll go carve a statue using the wood from my ruined home. Oh, look, there's a horde of tartaruns coming to kill me. At least it's a nice day." He gave Helena a smug grin.

"Piss off," Helena joked, giving Carver a push. He laughed as he retained his balance and found his place back beside Helena.

"Hey, guys!" a young male voice called from behind them.

Carver and Helena stopped and looked back, both of them recognizing the voice. A teenage boy of a similar age to themselves was jogging toward them. His cheeks and upper lip showed the faint signs of hair growth that Carver's lacked, and his dirty blond hair would have hung down to his shoulders were it not tied into a thick ponytail. Beside him, matching his speed, was a girl of similar age. She had short hair, the same dirty blond as the boy's, that barely passed her ears, with bangs down to her eyebrows. They stopped a few feet away from Carver and Helena, both of them out of breath.

"Hey, guys, what's going on?" Carver asked.

The boy met Carver's gaze with his bright-blue eyes. "Guess what we just heard?" he said, huffing.

"What?" Helena asked, looking from the boy to the girl, not quite sure if she should be excited or worried.

The boy looked over at Helena. "So, we heard you'll both be in the city today, delivering the tax and trading, right? Well, guess what?"

Carver and Helena both shot the boy a look of annoyance, waiting for him to get on with it.

"There's going to be sovereigns there!" the girl blurted out, stealing the boy's thunder.

Helena gasped with a look of equal parts disbelief and excitement. "For real?"

"Yeah!" the boy said. "Our grandfather just dropped off some barrels of fish from his fishery in Leydes—"

"For your trip to Caswen today," the girl butted in.

"They know that, sis. Anyway, traders from Caswen told him a sovereign ship has been docked in the Caswen port for the last few days!"

"We made him tell us all the details before he took the barrels to the stables," the girl added with a bright smile.

At that, Carver and Helena shot each other a look.

"I guess we know why the barrels were late," Carver said, voicing what they were both thinking.

Helena grinned, then turned her attention back to the others. "Why would sovereigns be at Caswen? They're not supposed to collect the tax until it's been sailed over to the mainland and joined with the rest of Terraland's taxes."

"We don't know. All we know is there's apparently a sovereign ship there," the girl answered.

Carver turned once again to Helena. "Do you think we'll see any? Actual sovereigns, I mean?"

"I hope so. I've always wanted to see one. So far, Seb is the only one of us to have seen one, and that was years ago," Helena said, directing her hand toward the blue-eyed boy.

"Yeah, but I didn't get to see it close up, though. I already told you guys the story after it happened. I saw a huge ship sailing by while I was out fishing with my grandfather during a visit, and I saw one of them standing on the deck. It was pretty far away, and all I could see was a tall, blurry figure, but I could tell it wasn't a human or a dwarf, and it definitely wasn't a goblin."

"That's still better than any of us. We've only heard about them in our teachings," Helena said.

"Nina would have seen it too if she hadn't been sick with a fever at home," Sebastian said, nudging his sister with his elbow.

"I'm glad I missed it," Nina replied. "They sound awful from what we've been told about them. Seven feet tall, always bald, with no ears or nose, weird X-shaped bone feet with claws. I can't imagine having them patrolling around the village, hunting for people who develop sorcery like we hear they do on the mainland and the bigger towns around here. It sounds so creepy." She shivered and gave Sebastian a sharp glance with her matching blue eyes.

Sebastian received Nina's glance and chuckled. "You sound like you think the sovereigns are going to come and take you away. They only take people who develop sorcery, like you just said, and since sorcery apparently only shows up in a person during the beginnings of puberty, if they develop it at all, I think we're all going to be fine. The four of us are well past the point of sorcery and the power to use magic unlocking in ourselves. Unless one of us developed sorcery, learned how to channel it into magic, and has been hiding it," Sebastian finished with a jesting look toward Carver and Helena.

Carver threw up his hands and grinned. "Yep, you caught us! We're secret sorcerers. I can shoot fire from my hands, and Helena can heal wounds with her mind." Carver lowered his hands and nudged Helena's shoulder with his elbow. "She had to get good at healing herself since I always kick her ass when we practice fighting together."

Helena jabbed her elbow into Carver's arm with much more force than he had to hers. "I'm sorry, but who knocked your ass down and pinned you to the dirt earlier?"

"That doesn't count. I wasn't paying attention."

"I know. You don't pay attention to anything, Carver," Helena said with a smile. "But anyways, I bet that's why the sovereigns are at Caswen right now. They're looking for people in the city who developed sorcery and haven't turned themselves in."

"Maybe. But that seems like a weird coincidence that they'd be looking on the same day as the taxes are supposed to be collected."

"If you guys see any sovereigns up close in the city, you have to tell us about it, especially about the bone-claw feet, whatever that means," Sebastian said.

Carver shrugged. "We'll try our best, but we probably won't see any. We're going to be stuck at the Outer Market all day. I seriously doubt the sovereigns would go anywhere near there."

Sebastian tilted his head. "Why wouldn't they? It's where the taxes are coming in from all the settlements, and they could check everyone who shows up for sorcery—however it is they check for it."

"If that's the reason then why don't we hear about them being at the Outer Market every year? I think they'll only be inside the city," Carver said.

Helena gave Carver a quick smack to the shoulder. "Well, then that's even more reason for us to do a good job. If we finish early, we can go into the city and try to see one."

"Maybe," Carver said, rubbing his shoulder.

"It's about time we actually saw a sovereign," Helena continued. "We hear about them all the time—how they wiped out the tartaruns with their sorcery and conquered the world, making everyone learn and speak their language as well as making us pay them these taxes once a year, but we never see them. It's crazy. Why do we almost never hear of them coming to our islands? And when they do, why have we never had one come to our village and look around for people who develop sorcery? It's like they don't exist, or we don't exist to them."

Sebastian opened his mouth. "I think—"

"Hey, Carver!" another voice called out from behind the siblings, cutting Sebastian off.

Carver looked up and saw that it was his father waving at him and Helena. "You two ready?"

"Already?" Carver called back in confusion.

"Yep. Helena's parents already loaded their wagon, remember? I just had to hitch it to the horses and get everyone else ready for the ride. And Duncan showed up right after the two of you left. So, let's go."

"Alright, see you guys," Carver said to Sebastian and Nina, then walked toward his father.

"Bye," Helena said, following Carver.

"Bye," Sebastian and Nina said, waving.

"Make sure to look out for any sovereigns!" Sebastian added.

"We will, don't worry," Carver replied without turning around.

Chapter 2

The journey to the east was painfully slow for Carver, as the hill-infested land between his village and the city made a straight, smooth ride impossible. The road he and his group followed was little more than a dirt path, an indentation of past inconvenient travels, winding around the hills like a python searching for prey in the grass. The group was forced repeatedly to slow their horses' already slow trot to an even slower walk, as the bumpy ground required a steady control to climb and descend safely with the loaded wagons. Often, the shoddy dirt road would end at the base of a large grassy hill, only continuing on the other side, forcing the group to ascend the hill carefully and slowly. Whenever the group encountered a great mound of earth that was too steep for their horses to climb with the wagons, the procession was forced to spend substantial time going around it.

Rarely, a wide area of relatively flat ground would be waiting for them beyond one of the hills, allowing for a short increase of pace along the dirt path, which was slowly thinning at the sides due to the grass that seemed determined to overtake the trail once again. Each time such a flat stretch appeared, Carver would relax in the seat of his wagon and enjoy the faster speed at which the horses pulled him along. The enjoyable pace never lasted long, though. Eventually, another hill or stretch of uneven terrain would arrive, each time feeling like more of a hindrance than the last, renewing Carver's feeling of frustration. What could have been a leisurely journey if there had been a regularly maintained road was a grueling three-hour excursion.

As the third hour crept up, so did the city. Caswen, the capital of the Isles. Its tall stone walls climbed into view and stretched into the distance as their wagons passed over the last grassy hill.

Carver had seen the city only a few times in his life, but since Caswen was the only city amid the islands, and it had such a massive scale, the sight never lost its power. Every other settlement throughout the islands that formed the province of the Isles was either a lone farm or collection of hamlets that couldn't be found on a map, a village of minor standing, or a town of decent population and size but well under the capital's grandeur, which made Caswen an intimidating place for most Islers.

Those ruling across the sea had nicknamed the city "Terraland's Stamp" as a reminder to the isolated island chain inhabitants that they were merely a single piece of a larger realm, a province within the kingdom of Terraland, the northern kingdom of humanity, which was itself only a portion of a much greater realm, the Sovereign Empire.

Carver had never been to mainland Terraland before. He had never even ventured to the other nearby islands that made up the rest of the Isles. He had spent his whole existence isolated from the rest of the world. What little Carver did know about the grander world and his place within it was what he learned during his limited time within his village schoolhouse between his chores and work.

He was taught that the world he lived in was called Gaia and that the island his village called home was the easternmost island of the four that made up the province of the Isles. He knew that the eastern island was the closest to the mainland, the massive continent that made up most of Gaia's known lands, and that it was also the largest of those islands. It was formally named the Eastern Isle, but many of the locals referred to it as the Grand Isle due to its size and the presence of the capital on its eastern coast.

Carver was also told how the mainland of Gaia was larger than the Isles a thousand times over and that it contained the many kingdoms of the world's races: the five dwarf kingdoms that made up the Dwarven Commonwealth;

the many goblin realms, which varied widely in size, title, and power; the two kingdoms of humanity, one being Terraland at the northernmost point of the explored world, while the other laid far to the south, its name unknown to him and his village, though rumored to be a land of deserts and scorching heat. There was also the race of the sovereigns, whom Carver was told were the lords of all Gaia and its races, originating from a land so far to the south that nothing was known about it to anyone but the sovereigns themselves.

Carver had heard that each of these distant lands had many cities that outdid even Caswen, though he could not imagine what such a city could look like. Other than the basic tales and history of Gaia and its single continent, Carver knew next to nothing about it, and he didn't much care to.

"Well, there it is," Carver said after a long period of silence, nudging Helena with his left knee. He sat beside her at the front of the wagon while she held the reins of the horses that pulled them along.

Helena looked at him. "It's weird how we can't see Caswen from the village. It's so big that you'd think it would always be visible from home, but the hills block it out."

Carver made a low-effort hum in response.

They rode at the back of the group, their wagon holding the smallest number of crates, barrels, and sacks filled with goods and supplies. In front of them rode Helena's parents, hauling a wagon of similar stock yet in more abundance, but also loaded with arms, armor, and metal tools they had crafted in their smithy. At the front of the group rode Velanna and Bran, their wagon carrying a nearly identical batch of trade goods, albeit with even more value due to the bags of coins hidden within one of the crates.

The adults all had sheathed swords buckled to their belts, which hung out over the side of their seats, while Helena had only a simple dagger similar to the one Carver had sheathed at his belt. They carried weapons in case their caravan was beset by bandits, thugs, or menacing creatures along the path, as their small village could not afford an armed escort, which would have been proper for such a journey. However, such a happening was unlikely to unfold, as brigands and beasts were not common amid the hills and dips separating Caswen from their village.

The sun sat high in the cloudless blue sky, covering the grassy hills of the Eastern Isle with warm light. As Carver and his group traveled over the last hill, the entrance of the city came into view. A huge portcullis hung open, giving a small glimpse of what lay behind the city's towering gray stone walls. The only thing still between their group and the city was a large array of farms and cottages.

The area was home to a big town that had grown around the perimeter of the city's walls along with vast patches of farmland. Fenced fields spanned the outskirts of the town and filled every space between the outer structures that wasn't being used for trails and roads. Cows, pigs, goats, chickens, horses, and sheep grazed throughout while handfuls of human and goblin farmers worked the fields.

The goblins made up nearly half of the people whom Carver saw busying about the town's outer regions, and he found himself watching them more than he did the humans as Helena guided the wagon past the first few farms.

Each goblin looked similar to the others of their same sex, and Carver found it difficult to tell many of them apart from the distance. Each stood at a height ranging from four feet five inches to four feet ten inches and had green skin that varied slightly between light and dark shades. While the goblins were smaller than the average human in stature, their heads and faces were disproportionately large, which Carver thought odd.

Their ears were long and pointed, stretching off the sides of their heads up to a foot in length. Their eyes were twice the size of a human's and had yellow sclera with large black pupils, shaped like vertical ovals and without visible irises, in the center. Their mouths were also distinctly wider than a human's and were filled with small white teeth that only made the mouths look larger when open.

Most appeared to be males, all with fat, sharp, pointed green noses and shaved heads. The few female goblins Carver saw had much smaller noses, more akin to a human's in size but still with a sharp point, and the females all had long black hair that varied widely in style, with some of the small green women wearing it down to their lower back while others had multiple pony-tails or intricately braided hairstyles.

Carver did not often see goblins, as none lived in his village, but he was aware that the race made up a large portion of the province's population.

Carver turned his focus away from the green denizens and sat up straight in his seat. "It always amazes me how small our home is compared to the farming quarter of Caswen," he said as he peered at a wide fenced field of wheat that was the size of his village's entire farming area.

"It's crazy, yeah. Sometimes I forget that we're the smallest mapped settlement in the Isles, but then I see this place."

Their trio of wagons made its way deeper into the outer town of Caswen, the constant sound of barking dogs and voices all around them, following the dirt path that now resembled a proper road. They had to slow down at times to avoid free-ranging chickens and the careless, scrappy looking children who chased the fat birds across their path.

Letting Helena deal with the navigating, Carver leaned back and gazed at the buildings they passed while they moved through the heart of the town. Most were standard shacks or cottages, all with thatched roofs and with walls ranging from wood to brick to a mix of both, but a few unique establishments here and there caught Carver's eye. A small weaving house with colorful garments on display sat between two filthy wood shacks, looking out of place with its mostly clean brick walls next to its mud-splattered neighbors. A tavern the size of at least six of Verrel's cottages bustled with commotion and faint music, and a blacksmith's workshop sent loud clangs into the air as a man hammered a hot, glowing rod of metal over a black anvil.

Carver watched the blacksmith work for a moment and then nudged Helena. "You ever make something like that at your smithy?"

"Like what?" Helena asked.

Carver pointed to the entrance of the smithy. "That fancy long-sword there."

Helena's gaze followed Carver's finger to a sword hung horizontally above the doorway to the smithy. The blade was nothing special to her notice, but the weapon's hilt, from guard to pommel, was adorned with intricate markings and curved inlays. Helena would have been impressed had the whole sword not been carved out of wood. It was a claim of skill with metal, not a show of it, and to her that meant nothing.

Helena turned her attention back to the horses. "No, we've never made something so fancy, and that's an arming sword, not a longsword."

"What's the difference?"

"Wow, you really don't pay attention to anything, do you? I know I've explained this to you before. Including the blade and the hilt, a longsword averages around three and a half feet long. So, basically from the bottom of your leg to the top of your hip, and you wield it with both hands. An arming sword, that one," she gestured her eyebrows back toward the smithy, which was almost out of view, "is only about two and a half feet long, basically an arm's length, and it's one handed. It's easy to remember since longsword starts with "L," as in leg-to-hip-length, and arming sword has its length in the name: arm. My parents taught me that. It's quite simple," she said, finishing her lecture with slight lip to her tone.

"Oh, whatever," Carver replied, waving his hand dismissively. "I'll just call them all swords. Then I'll never be wrong."

"You'll also never be right, either."

The noise of wooden wheels rolling over dirt suddenly morphed into a louder smacking sound as the group's wagons passed the last of the outer town's cottages and rolled onto a narrow stone bridge. The water beneath formed a great moat, wide enough to be considered a manmade river, that encircled the city's walls and met the ocean at both ends, leaving the entire city on an island of its own. On the other side of the bridge was a wide patch of flat, grassy ground that led up to the great portcullis and went far along the wall's exterior in both directions.

People, tents, wagons, and small stalls were scattered around the grass just before the entrance to Caswen, though the current display was minor compared to what Carver knew it would be in an hour or two.

Groups of humans and goblins ran about, claiming spots to station their wagons and begin setting up temporary stalls and tents. Carver also saw handfuls of humans in armored uniforms pointing others around and trying to keep the main path to the portcullis clear.

These figures of authority all wore the same set of armaments: a sleeved brown gambeson, which had a short collar that climbed up the lower half of the neck, a thin shirt of sleeved chainmail overtop of the gambeson that added an extra layer of protection and ended a bit below the waist and just after the elbows, where leather gauntlets with hide bracers were worn, and a set of mail leggings that extended down the legs and ended at tall, laced hide boots that covered their legs to a few inches below the knee.

Atop the suit of chainmail that covered the gambeson was a plain, short-sleeved, pocketed gray surcoat that hung just past the hips and displayed the profile of a bear's head in the center and a small insignia of a hexagon with a wide triangular chip filling a sixth of the shape sewn over the right breast. Atop each of their heads was a round-topped helmet that covered a portion of the ears with iron guards but left the face visible from the chin to just above the eyes.

Carver knew these persons to be the soldiers that made up the Caswen Guard, a large force of trained men and women—composed only of humans, from what Carver had seen—who enforced law and order within the great city. In times of war they would be called upon, along with the guards from the other settlements, to form the province's army.

Carver almost never saw these soldiers since his own village, being such a small and close-knit community, rarely had disputes or crimes that couldn't be handled by the locals alone and ultimately lacked the population and resources to outfit a standing guard. As such, the inhabitants of his village trained to defend themselves and expected everyone to enforce the village standard of decency at all times.

When Carver did see any soldiers, it was either during his few trips to the city with his family or when patrolling bands of soldiers came by his village for supplies or to inquire about things that he was not informed about.

The Caswen soldiers tried desperately to maintain order amongst the chaos, keeping people off the road and away from the approaching wagons. A line of wagons was forming off to the side of the road in front of a group of guardsmen who were manning a table with papers and inkwells. Helena shifted the horses toward the line, following her and Carver's parents.

"Here we go," Carver said, as if anticipating a struggle.

Helena gave him a quick smile.

Her father leaned out from his wagon and looked back at them. His face was weathered with age but still young enough that no gray was visible in his brown mop of hair or his patchy beard.

"Alright, you two, make sure you've got your pins on."

"Got it, Damath," Carver replied.

Damath gave a quick nod and then leaned back in his seat.

Carver reached back toward the top of a crate just behind the thin wood divider between the seats and the wagon's storage area.

"Shit!"

"What is it, Carver?" Helena asked calmly.

"The pins are gone. Shit, they must have fallen off." Carver looked over the wooden barrier, peering down into the tight gaps between the crates, barrels, and sacks. "They must have fallen in between."

"That sucks. You can borrow one of mine if you want."

Carver looked at Helena, first seeing the large grin pinned to her face, then the two metal shapes pinned on her wool tunic.

Each of the pins was a simple square of iron with three capital "I's" inlaid into the face of the metal.

Carver frowned. "You idiot."

Helena let out a gleeful chuckle. "I told you the pins would fall off if you just left them on that crate."

"They didn't fall off; you took them. How did you do that without me noticing?"

"Like I keep saying, you don't pay attention to anything." She continued to giggle.

Carver reached for one of the pins on her chest. "Give me that."

Helena turned away from his hand and chuckled. "Don't you get grabby with me, Carver. If you want to touch my breasts, you need to at least buy me something first."

Carver halted and shot her a puzzled look. Helena's giggle ended abruptly when she saw Carver's face. "That came out wrong. It was a joke," she said, blushing.

Feeling awkward about the situation himself, Carver flicked Helena's ear with his left hand. As she turned and slapped at his hand in reflex, his right hand darted in and yanked one of the pins from her grime-stained tunic, taking a small bit of wool along with it.

Helena gasped. "You little …" She reached to grab the pin from his hand.

"Nope!" Carver laughed as he held the pin out of reach.

The left side of the wagon suddenly dipped down, causing its inventory to jumble around.

Helena realized she hadn't been paying attention and had let the horses pull the wagon slightly off the road and onto the grass. She grabbed the reins in both hands and corrected their course, but not before her father looked back from his wagon again.

"What's going on back there?"

"Sorry, Dad."

"Don't wreck anything, and keep your eyes on the road, Helena. We're just about to the line."

Carver laughed. "Now look who's not paying attention to anything," he said while pinning the iron pin to his own wool tunic.

Helena glared at Carver but was unable to hold back her grin.

Carver and Helena waited silently once their wagon was stopped in the line. It only took a few minutes until Velanna and Bran's wagon was in front of the guards' table.

"Settlement name and number," the soldier sitting at the table said without looking up from his papers. He had the same hexagon insignia sewn on his gray surcoat over the right breast, but unlike the others Carver had seen, his had a second triangular chip below the first, which left his insignia a third filled in.

"Verrel, settlement number three," Velanna said in a clear, formal voice.

The soldier looked up from his papers and eyed the pins that Velanna and her husband wore, then looked back down at his papers. "How many with you, and how many stalls are you planning to set up?" he asked while writing something with a feather pen.

"Three wagons. Six people, including me. We have two stalls we'd like to put up."

A soldier stood at each side of the table, one male and the other female, each with an iron-tipped spear in hand that pointed toward the open sky. They both eyed the group, glaring from Velanna's wagon down to the one in which Carver and Helena sat. The soldier on the right looked at the one who was sitting at the table and gave him a tired nod.

"Three wagons, six people, and two stalls from Verrel, settlement number three," the seated soldier repeated as he finished writing. He looked up at Velanna while gesturing to his left with his elbow. "Go to your right and find yourself a spot. I'll send someone to assess and collect your tax when available."

Velanna nodded and started moving her wagon to the right, followed by the rest of the group.

As they maneuvered through the crowds and stalls, Carver watched the people around them scurry about with their own wagons and goods. A man held up the side of a newly constructed stall while a woman frantically searched for something in the grass by his feet. He saw a flash of the letter "V" on the small iron square pinned to her brown tunic.

The "V" was the sovereign numeral assigned to Quinredal, if Carver remembered correctly, a large town on the west coast of the Eastern Isle. He felt a quick urge to ask Helena if he was correct, but he held his tongue in case he was wrong. He'd had enough of Helena gloating about her knowledge for one day. *That'll be us soon,* Carver thought.

As their wagon rolled on, Carver shifted his view to the other side of the wagon, looking past Helena, who was utterly focused on guiding the horses through the mess of obstacles. He spotted a male goblin whose brown tunic was pinned with an iron square holding an "I" followed by an "X." It took Carver a few seconds to remember that "IX" indicated nine in sovereign numerals, after which he realized he had no idea which settlement the number belonged to. He wondered if Helena knew.

"Alright, we're here!" Carver heard his mother shout from up front.

Helena pulled the reins, bringing the horses to a stop. Then everyone climbed out of their wagons and got to work pulling boards and tools out of the wagons and assembling two small stalls side by side.

Carver hated the speed at which it all needed to be done – hastily hammering boards together, carrying heavy sacks back and forth, and unloading crates and barrels from the wagons while his parents called him over repeatedly for another interrupting task. He also knew this was just the beginning. Soon there would be dozens of stalls and wagons sprawled out across the grassy area between the wide moat and Caswen's walls, each manned by screaming country folk trying to catch the eye of Caswen's locals. The day was going to be hectic, as it was every August first: Taxation Day.

Chapter 3

"Done," Bran said to the group as he and Helena's father raised the second stall.

The stalls were simple and sturdy, with enough room to display a decent amount of product. To allow them to display more items, Velanna had hung S-shaped double-sided iron hooks onto one side of each wagon, from which more goods could be hung.

Bran looked at Carver, who was removing an assortment of small weapons from a barrel and placing them on the wagons' hooks. He was pleased to see his boy working hard.

"Carver."

Carver turned toward his father as he placed an iron axe with an unevenly curved edge on one of the hooks. "Yeah?"

"A collector should probably be here any minute. Let's start preparing the tax." He nodded toward one of their wagons.

Carver gave the axe he had just placed one last look, feeling good about its placement, then headed over to his father. "Weren't we supposed to get the taxes ready first?"

Bran stopped and looked back at his boy. "Well, yes, we were. But your mother and I changed our minds. Better to get everyone working on the stalls and trade goods first, so we don't miss a chance to sell something. If the taxes aren't ready to be inspected quite on time, what are they going to do, not take them and send us away? It'll be fine."

Carver nodded in agreement.

"So, how are you doing?" Bran asked as Carver walked to his side.

"I'm okay. So far it's not so bad."

"I know it sucks, and I hate being stuck in this crowded mess as much as you do. But it's only once a year during the harvest season, and it needs to be done. Besides, it's not like we're the ones picked to come here every time," he added, giving his son a pat on the back.

"I know, Dad. It's fine, really," Carver said as the two of them reached the back of the farthest wagon.

Bran smiled at Carver, then climbed into the wagon. "Alright, this is the wagon with the taxes. I'll pass you the goods, and you pile them based on their markings. The ones marked with an "X" are for the sovereigns, and those with a single line go to Caswen," Bran said as he reached down and lifted a small wooden crate. He spun around and passed it down into his son's waiting hands.

"An "X" for the sovereigns? Is that because of the feet thing?"

Bran looked down at his son in confusion. "What? Oh, um, huh. I hadn't thought about that. No, we just used an "X." Coincidence, I guess. But I've still never seen a sovereign, so I wouldn't know if them having X-shaped feet is true or not."

Carver nodded to his father before looking down at the top of the crate he was holding. On the side facing him he saw a small "X" marked in white paint. Carver placed the crate on the grass, then reached to grab the sack of grain being passed down to him.

Another white "X."

Carver placed the sack beside the crate. Before he was ready, his father was already offering him another small crate. Carver took it and saw a white line painted diagonally across the same spot where the "X" was on the last one. He set it down, then turned back to his father.

Bran continued handing his son the goods at a steady pace, Carver keeping up as best as he could. After a few minutes, the pile marked with "X's" was noticeably larger than the one made up of goods marked with a lone white line. Carver looked past his father at the last few sacks and crates still within the wagon. Most of them were marked with an "X," from what Carver could see.

"Hey, Dad," Carver said as he received the next sack of grain from his father. It was marked with a white line, so he placed it down to his right as his father looked down at him. "Why is so much of this for the sovereigns?"

Bran wiped the sweat from his forehead with the back of his hand. "I'm not sure. The letter we received from Caswen stated that this is the required amount, though." Bran passed down an X-marked sack. "The tax has shifted from sixty-forty to almost seventy-thirty in favor of the sovereigns. If this keeps up, the Magistrate is going to probably increase the base tax in general just to keep the city stocked and the province running."

Carver added the sack to the growing pile of sovereign-marked tax, wondering how much of his village's resources had been lost to these taxes over the years. Compared to the other villages and towns of the Isles, which were large enough to be on a map, Verrel's contribution was quite small.

The perks of Verrel being such a small settlement in a system of taxation based on settlement size and population meant their expected resources were reduced, allowing them to stock more heavily with goods to trade for profit. But to Carver it still felt like his village was losing more than anyone else. He hated the idea of giving away their hard-earned resources to people he never saw. People who took and never seemed to give back, at least in his eyes.

Carver felt that the system left the countryside to fend for itself year after year to survive off arduous work while Caswen got to sit back and drink in the taxes to fuel itself and stay stocked for the harsh winters, sending the rest across the sea to the Terraland Crown on the mainland.

What was given to the sovereigns was even worse to him, however, because the never-present ruling creatures took more now than ever, it seemed, and had it sent to them by Caswen's ships along with the pitiful share meant for mainland Terraland.

That was how the world worked, though, and Carver knew there was nothing he could do to stop it, so he tried to stop thinking about it. But seeing how much more was being taken from Caswen frustrated Carver. He agreed with his father that soon the magistrate of the Isles, who lorded over the province from his manor within Caswen's mighty walls, would raise the tax to compensate for the amount the province and the Terraland Crown lost to the sovereigns. Carver was angry at the thought of how much his village was losing due to these taxes, regardless of who it went to and for what reason.

Suddenly, he heard another wagon approaching. He and Bran stopped unloading and looked over toward the noise. A pair of horses appeared from around the corner of an empty wagon, pulling their own wagon behind them. It was different from the ones from Verrel. Instead of the open-topped wooden wagons Carver's group and the other settlements had arrived with, this wagon had a roof, and its wooden sides were reinforced with iron plating. It was an armored crate on wheels, accompanied by three male Caswen soldiers, two of whom were sitting up front, one holding a spear and the other appearing to have no weapon at all. A third guard was holding onto the metal bars of a door at the back of the wagon with one hand while maintaining his grip on a spear with the other, his feet balancing on an iron step below the door.

"Verrel, settlement three?" the driver asked as he pulled the wagon up beside theirs. Unlike his fellow soldiers, who were both dismounting from the reinforced wagon, each with a single triangular chip detailed within their hexagonal insignia, the soldier who addressed Bran had two fractions filled in.

"That's us," Bran replied, tapping the pin on his tunic. He hopped down from the back of the wagon and approached the soldier.

Dismounting from his wagon, the driver removed a black journal and an inked feather from the small leather satchel attached to his belt. "Alright, let's see what you have for us."

As the soldier stepped around the horses, Carver saw that he was indeed armed. A sword that was the length of his arm, a detail Carver subconsciously noted thanks to Helena's brief lesson, was hanging from his belt in a sheath.

The two other soldiers took their places, with one opening the armored wagon's door and waiting by it while the other stood between the two wagons and watched the situation unfold.

Bran and the head soldier slowly went through all of the goods and took stock, the soldier writing down all of the details in his journal as they went. Once the lead soldier established that each barrel, crate, and sack contained the appropriate amount and weight of goods that Verrel was expected to surrender as tax, Carver handed them one by one to the soldier standing near him, who handed them off to the soldier by the armored wagon, who placed them inside. The process went on for some time, requiring the two soldiers to leave their spears propped against the armored wagon while they worked.

Once the last of the stock made its way inside the armored wagon, Bran and the lead soldier stood off to the side and discussed the final details.

As he waited for his father to finish, Carver inspected the other soldiers from a comfortable distance. He noted how each guard's neck was partially exposed between the collar of the gambeson and their chins, as well as the obvious vulnerability of their faces above. He also looked at their hide gauntlets, which stretched up their forearms as bracers. The leather seemed thin and had no mail underneath, and the gauntlets themselves did not cover the fingers of either hand. The mail armor they wore also appeared to be thin and light, and even with the gambeson underneath Carver doubted it could prevent a proper thrust from a spear or a thin sword from piercing the soldiers' flesh.

This was one of the main components of Carver's limited martial training back at home, finding weaknesses in an opponent's defenses. He had been instructed repeatedly that understanding an opponent's weaknesses, whether through fault of themselves or their equipment, mixed with practiced speed and precision, was the key to taking someone down who had better gear than himself.

Being from a small, self-reliant village in the hills, Carver had been taught that he would most likely be the underequipped party if he ever found himself in a life-or-death conflict with another person, despite the unlikelihood of him ever actually being in such a fight. So, he was trained without the comfort of being protected by expensive armor or a sturdy shield. He would either dodge the hit, block it with his own blade, or prevent the opponent from having time to attack. If all those failed, he was told he would be killed by his assailant. That didn't stop Carver from fantasizing about wearing armor, however. He thought it would make him look like a better fighter.

"Everything seems to be here," the soldier standing with Carver's father said. He gave the open page of his journal a thorough second glance before closing its thick parchment binding and exchanging nods with Bran.

The soldier and his companions returned to their wagon. The driver stirred the horses into motion and continued on to the next group.

"There it goes," Carver said to his father, disappointment in his voice.

"Yeah. It would be nice if they finally build a proper road from here to home after all of Verrel's contributions. Riding over all those steep hills is a time-consuming pain, and the road is a joke," Bran said as he watched the armored wagon disappear into the fast-growing makeshift market.

Most of the other settlement representatives had shown up by then, arriving either in wagons coming over the bridge to the west or by ship on the beach to the east. The havoc was erupting predictably, with more frequency as well. People raced to claim any remaining unoccupied patches of grass, setting up their stalls before someone else did, and wagons piled up behind each other to register with the city guards.

More of Caswen's soldiers arrived from inside the city to keep things calm and orderly. The soldiers were outnumbered, however, by the droves of citizens flowing out from the main gate and rushing around the market in search of cheap goods and rare items.

The Outer Market, as the locals called it, was born anew: ambassadors from every substantial settlement and irrelevant hamlet in the Isles trying to make back in trade what they were forced to give away in taxes to the city, the Crown, and the sovereigns.

Caswen's citizens used the event to buy all kinds of goods from the smaller settlements. To those in the city, the gathering outside their city's gate was like a yearly sale at a shop that had everything.

The Outer Market sold its wide variety of goods at prices far cheaper than the Inner Market, filling the pockets of the outer settlements with coin and decent trade while also allowing the city's locals to recoup some of their lost goods without going broke in the process. It was an Isler tradition, from what Carver had been told, as the rest of Terraland instead relied on tax collectors coming to each settlement and taking the taxes to each province's capital themselves, with a large portion of each province's share going to the kingdom's capital.

Bran placed a hand on his son's shoulder. "Come on, Carver, let's get this over with." With that, he rejoined the rest of the group.

Carver attempted to think of one last idea that could get him out of helping, but it was useless; he was already there, so he placed his hands in the pockets of his trousers and followed his father.

The first two hours were a strain, a never-ending stream of humans and goblins clumping together in what no one could even pretend was an organized line, all saying the same things.

"How much for this?"

"I'll only pay this much."

Carver was glad he wasn't the one dealing with the locals; he couldn't handle it. *Oh, you'll only pay less than its price? Well, you can't have it then. Get lost,* Carver thought, wishing his mother would say just that.

Instead, Velanna spent her time bartering with the locals, trying to strike a deal with each person who haggled with her. She was manning the main stall, mostly selling animal hides, sacks of grains and seeds, freshly killed game, and salted salmon and cod.

Carver and Bran had the honorary title of laborers. They moved the goods around, restocked their stalls, and kept the empty crates and barrels from cluttering their area.

While sliding an empty crate back into one of their wagons, Carver looked over at the second stall they had erected. Helena had been manning the stall for the last half hour, selling the armaments and miscellaneous metal items and tools that she and her parents had made in their smithy. Her father was helping from the side, giving advice and support to his daughter when needed.

Helena's blond-haired, silken-faced mother was laboring behind the stall, keeping the goods organized and flowing. Her muscles strained as she worked, but she did not slow down. Just like her daughter, years of working in the smithy had crafted her into a remarkably strong woman. She looked to be at least a decade younger than her grizzled husband, which to Carver, whose parents were of nearly the same age and both still had youthful features, always seemed odd. Carver had asked his parents about it once and was told he should not concern himself with the relationships of others.

Carver looked back at the wagon he and his father were working with. Seeing how much unsold merchandise remained disheartened him, partly because the thought of the goods returning home with them meant that his village would be more harshly affected by the tax and partly because each crate, barrel, and sack still in the wagon meant more time toiling at the Outer Market. He wanted to go home.

While he was restocking Helena's stall with horseshoes and iron knives, Helena had reminded him that once they were finished, they could go inside the city to peruse the Inner Market and maybe see a sovereign.

When first told at Verrel about the chance of seeing sovereigns while in Caswen, Carver found himself not hating the idea of coming to the city so much, but now he didn't care. Even if they went to the Inner Market, he doubted he and Helena would see a sovereign shopping there alongside the goblins and humans. He just wanted to finish the job so they could all ride home and be done with the whole event.

Despite his desire to return home, Carver knew that what his father said to him earlier about his village's involvement in the Outer Market was true, that it needed to be done, but he kept wondering why it had to be him who did it.

Carver tried to stop thinking about it. He realized how whiny his thoughts sounded, and he hated when he made himself look and feel like a whiny kid.

Over the next two hours, things began to quiet down, but it remained busy and irritating. Carver's attempts to avoid looking miserable failed repeatedly, having him constantly resetting his face when his parents told him to cheer up or to stop looking so down. They didn't want the customers to see him like that.

It was driving Carver mad. He wasn't trying to look upset, but he couldn't stop his face from returning to a naturally bored and unenthusiastic expression as he worked. Finally, after what felt like forever, Helena came over to him.

"Hey, mopey. Do you need a hug?" she teased.

Her voice lifted Carver's mood despite the clear note of antagonism it carried. He looked up from trying to open a crate that refused to comply. "I need a damn excuse to get out of here," he said, sounding more bitter than he wanted to. He quickly changed the subject. "How's it going for you?"

Helena smiled. Whether her smile was at his obvious displeasure or the reminder of her success at the stall, Carver wasn't sure.

"It's going well. My dad said I'm actually doing a really good job haggling."

Carver pretended to be surprised at her statement, since he had already observed her doing a fine job as he labored behind her. "Really? That's good. So, what's going on?"

"Our parents said we can take a break since things have died down a fair bit." She gestured with her thumb over toward the stalls. "We get one hour, they said. You want to go look around the Inner Market? We might see a sovereign there, and if not we can still check out the stuff for sale."

"You want to spend your break going from a crowded market to an even more crowded market?" He didn't understand how Helena could still be so full of energy and excitement.

Helena gave Carver a frown that said, *"Just shut up and stop complaining."*

Carver wondered if he was going to hear Helena's famous line again: *"Don't be so damn negative, Carver,"* to which he would give his usual response: *"Don't be so damn positive then."* But Helena didn't say it.

"I want to go look around. And I want you to come with me. So, let's go. What else are you going to do? Stay in this crowded market for your break?"

Carver realized that Helena was right. He could go with her and have an hour of relative freedom or stay behind and probably be called in to help during his break anyway.

"Alright. Let's go," Carver said, abandoning his failing efforts to open the rebellious crate.

"That's better," Helena said, smiling. She had a particular smile for when she got her way – one that Carver saw often.

They traversed the alley-like paths created by the constructed market, maneuvering through the crowds that filled the tight avenues. Once they were clear of the mass of tents, wagons, and canopied stalls that shadowed the ground from the midday sun, they headed toward the city's massive entrance.

A handful of male and female soldiers wielding tall, iron-tipped spears stood at attention near the high opening in the wall and under the shadowed arch it created. Some of the soldiers guarding the way glanced at the two teens but otherwise paid them no mind.

Carver and Helena nodded and smiled at the soldiers who happened to make eye contact with them, and then they merged with the rest of the commoners entering the city while trying not to bump into those coming out. They entered the shadow of the arch and passed beneath the grand portcullis that hung above their heads. When the sun hit their shoulders again, they were in Caswen.

Chapter 4

The city was massive, outdoing their village a hundred times over. Buildings stretched out in every direction, some so tall they shadowed long stretches of the cobblestone street from the sun.

Carver and Helena were out of their element as they walked down the main road, trying to follow the signs stationed at the intersections and the narrow streets that branched off in every direction. The Inner Market was not far from the gate, but they walked at a slow pace, staring in wonder at the towering buildings that loomed over them.

Where they lived, no building was high enough that they couldn't throw a stone onto its roof, but in Caswen it would be hard to hit the shutters of the highest windows.

The buildings formed a wide-ranging array of architectural styles and were built of various materials. Some of the homes were small and simple, with wooden walls and thatched roofs like most of the homes outside Caswen's walls and all the dwellings in Verrel. Other homes were made of bricks, with tiled roofs, and rose up multiple floors. Sometimes two brick homes were attached together to form a single wide building.

Scattered amongst the brick and wood buildings were large rectangular stone towers that climbed into the sky, each ending in a flat roof. Each tower was dotted with small square gaps for windows and surrounded by wooden stairs and catwalks, but only up to the halfway mark, which still surpassed most of the other buildings. While being the tallest and most imposing structures in the city, these grand housing towers were not desirable to most.

Each tower held within it nearly a dozen floors, each one a single room. Any room below the halfway mark of each tower was accessible from the scaffold staircase that climbed up the rectangular stone tower to each room's door. Those above the halfway mark had no doors to the outside and relied on a staircase within each room to lead above or below, requiring the residents to pass through each other's cramped rooms to reach their own.

On the outside, the towers were incredible marvels of construction, but in reality, they were nothing more than efficient uses of space to pack in as many people as possible, de-crowding the streets of the poor.

Carver couldn't imagine living in such a building. What if the floor above gave way? What if the floor below that gave way? He preferred the wooden cottages he grew up around back at his village, as he had no fear of falling through the dirt floor or being crushed by the thatched roof. He was curious as to how these large stone towers were constructed, however. How long did it take to erect one? How many builders fell and perished during each tower's construction? Did people move into the bottom floors while the top ones were being added?

"Here we are," Helena announced, interrupting Carver's pondering.

Carver pulled his gaze away from the closest tower and saw the city's great market, known as the Inner Market to the Islers who lived outside Caswen's stone walls but merely the Market to those within.

They stopped and scanned the grand expanse of shops and stalls. The cobblestone road the two of them had been following widened into a large, circular courtyard of flat stone. The enclosure was filled with booths and canopy-topped stalls, similar to those of the Outer Market, which shaded the ground from the looming sun. Unlike the Outer Market, however, the booths and stalls here were arranged in rings, facing inward with one wide opening into each grouping.

The perimeter of the stone courtyard was made up of one-story brick buildings acting as larger and more permanent shops. The brick shops were all connected to each other, acting as a wall that had only four wide gaps where the road led out of the market and into the capital city's four main districts.

The east exit led to Caswen's Port District, where most of the city's industry and trade with other lands occurred. The great docks of the Port District saw a never-diminishing procession of ships sailing across the Audria Channel, the wide stretch of water that separated the Isles from the coast of mainland Terraland's westernmost province.

The south exit wound up into the elevated High District, which housed the wealthy and influential, and at the very top, on a hill overlooking the city and almost always in view from below, stood the great manor where the magistrate of the Isles resided with his family and council.

The north exit brought one to the poorer side of the city, known as the First District or, more commonly, the Goblin District, though plenty of humans resided there. The First District was where the original town of Caswen had started when the Isles were under goblin rule long ago. It was a tight, cramped district built primarily of lumber. The district began when the cobblestone road turned into a muddy dirt path that branched into alleys of structural decay.

The west exit, where Carver and Helena stood, led to Caswen's gate through the Common District, or Low District, as it was also called, the city's largest and most populated district. It was made up of residences, taverns, and small shops.

Each of the four districts had many paths and multiple branches that led to housing areas, the Common District most of all, creating a city full of alleys and tight streets with homes on both sides. The Inner Market was at the center of it all.

The market was roaring with activity. Humans and goblins marched in every direction, busily heading toward the beckoning calls from those manning the shops and stalls. Many armored guards were also present within the market, easily noticeable as they stood motionless at their posts amidst the wave of movement that spread around them. Each had a sword buckled to his or her belt and also held a tall, iron-tipped spear.

Carver looked over at Helena, who was much more infatuated with the sight than he was.

Helena enjoyed the look of the stalls being grouped in rings, which gave the market a sense of organization while also appearing sporadic and bizarre, which she found appealing. Each of the canopied booths and stalls within the inward-facing rings had a sign hanging from it that advertised what one could purchase there. The number of categories made Helena's head spin: baked goods, fresh produce, tools, weapons, armor, trinkets, clothes, housewares.

Helena pointed as she grabbed Carver by his shoulder. "There!"

Before Carver could even look, he felt himself being pulled in that direction. "Wait, what?" he asked, his feet already beginning to move. Carver found a brief second between keeping his footing and avoiding collision with the people of the market to look up and see where he was being pulled toward: a small ring of stalls and booths laden with signs advertising their contents. Nothing about it appeared out of the ordinary. But then something caught his eye. One of the signs displayed the neatly illustrated word "Books."

Carver realized he should have known that Helena would choose there first. She loved to read, as Carver well knew. When she wasn't working at her parents' forge, busy with schooling or chores, or spending time with him, Helena spent her idle hours reading whatever she could find. It was a difficult hobby for her to indulge, however, as books were not a common sight in the Isles.

Carver and Helena had been told that the making of books was a dwarf art and that the race took great pride in writing everything down and keeping track of the world through endless installments of histories. The dwarves had invented some kind of device that could copy and replicate any page placed into it, allowing copies of a book to be made in a fraction of the time it would have taken to replicate the pages by hand.

From what the two teens understood, most books were housed in great libraries, the grandest of which were known as historiums, built within the dwarf kingdoms and other great cities of the world, but no such library or historium existed within Caswen's walls. Any books that did arrive to Terraland from the southern trade routes or that had been created in the kingdom itself were rarely sent across the sea to the Isles. On the rare occasion of books making it to the far islands, or even being created within their small borders, they could almost always be found within Caswen's Inner Market.

Carver started to wonder how much of "his" break would be spent looming over these bricks of inked paper, but his thoughts were quickly interrupted as a falling sensation suddenly overtook his senses. Before he knew what was happening, Carver found that the soles of his cowhide boots no longer had contact with the cobblestone street. This realization was followed by a cold pain as the side of his face crashed against the cobblestones, followed by the rest of his body.

In a state of dizzy confusion, Carver managed to raise his head, only to see the back of Helena disappearing through a crowd of citizens, appearing not to have noticed his fall or that she had caused it.

The cold pain on Carver's cheek abruptly morphed into a sore, burning ache, filling him with a bout of frustration rather than agony. Then he noticed that people were beginning to stare at him. Before he drew a larger audience Carver pushed himself to his feet, and, rubbing his cheek and rotating his jaw, hurried after his companion.

It wasn't hard to spot Helena in a crowd. She stood out like a flowered branch on a withering tree, youthful and full of life amidst her drab surroundings. She was standing in front of a small wooden booth that looked more like a cluttered desk under a dark cloth canopy than a shop.

Displayed on the desk was an arrangement of books piled in chaotic rows. This was Helena's reason for charging through the crowded market without care. This was why her excitement throughout the day never dampened despite the lack of seeing a sovereign.

Carver approached her from behind, completely unnoticed, as Helena directed all of her attention to the open book she held in her hands.

On the other side of the desk sat a balding man in a stained brown coat. He watched Helena with interest as he twiddled his thumbs together. When he noticed Carver approach, he stood up, but he didn't seem to rise more than an inch. Had Carver not clearly seen the man get off his chair, he would have assumed he was still sitting.

A dwarf, then, Carver realized.

Much like the books they were known to craft, dwarves were a rare sight in the Isles. Most lived on Gaia's mainland within their five kingdoms south of Terraland and didn't tend to venture out of them. While the dwarf lands included a heavy population of humans, the reverse could not be said about Terraland. Though a few dwarves resided in the northern human kingdom, they rarely came across the sea to the Isles, and any who did were a small minority among the humans and goblins who called the province home. For these reasons Carver was always surprised when he saw a dwarf. He could count the number of experiences on one hand.

The dwarf, standing at a height of four feet three inches, as was the average height for his people, leaned forward and smiled while resting his elbows on the edge of the desk, which Carver also now realized was lower to the ground than was typical to account for the dwarf's short stature. "Greetings, sir. Please, take a look at my books. I'm sure you'll find one that will interest you."

The dwarf's words broke Helena's focus on the book she was so engrossed in, and she turned to see whom the dwarf was speaking to. Upon seeing Carver, however, she turned her head back and resumed her study of the tome in her hands.

Carver was slightly miffed at Helena's nonchalant attitude. He was expecting a "Hey, are you okay? I saw you fall," or at least a "Where were you?" But what he received instead was a quick glance and an "Oh, there you are." He let the feeling pass. He knew she meant no ill by it, so he met the dwarf's eyes with a friendly smile.

The dwarf had a rough appearance, with a patchy beard and dark bags under his blue eyes.

"Is there anything in particular I can help you find?" he asked Carver.

"No, just looking, thanks," Carver said as he eyed the tomes on display.

The dwarf looked at the identification pin on Carver's tunic and then at Helena's. "Ah, I get it," he said with a grin as he nodded toward Helena. "Your woman is the reader of the couple. My wife is the same way. I can only sell the books after she has read them first," he said with a laugh.

Carver looked over at Helena, who didn't seem to have heard what the dwarf said. She simply flipped the page she was on and examined the next one.

"Oh, no, we're not together. But yes, she's the reader."

Carver picked up a book from the pile and looked at its cover. "The Sovereign Rescue, A History by Dolie Pith," was written across the front of the tome in tilted lettering.

"Pith." Carver chuckled under his breath, then opened the book to its first page and skimmed the introduction, though he read slowly and struggled with some of the words, reading not being something he practiced or found interesting.

> Without the arrival of the sovereigns, the world would likely have turned into a dark place, unrecognizable to us living today. Every person, whether dwarf, human, or goblin, has heard of the Tartarun Invasion from times past, and even those who know the least of that time still know that our entire world was under the threat of great and far-reaching doom.
>
> The tartaruns, taller than the tallest human by at least three feet, with gray-scaled skin as hard and durable as even the most thickly skinned dwarf, brought a wave of death and enslavement from the far southern jungles of Beldar and across the Serpent Gulf. The war was a massacre of the three northern races, lasting nearly a decade, and ending in a bitter peace brought forth by the signing of the Stalemate Treaty, which saw the loss of the dwarf kingdom of Hathrak and more than half of the Old Goblin Empire to the invaders.
>
> Many of us today may think that the treaty signed between the northern races and the southern tartaruns was the end of the conflict, but that was not the case. The

decades that followed were ripe with building tensions left by the horrid war.

The dwarf people did not live comfortably in their vastly weakened realms knowing that just over the Hathrak/ Dulengar border, the Attoauwv Swamp, which may as well have been the Urubinon Mountains due to the barrier it posed at that time, many of their people were living in slavery to a foreign realm.

The seceded territories of the Old Goblin Empire in the Mahkouan Peninsula, now known as the Colony Kingdoms, though even Mahkoua's colony realms Mishil and Hopki remained part of the Goblin Empire and lost to the tartaruns, fell into constant war with each other. Each of Mahkoua's seceded territories claimed to be a new kingdom and desired to found a new empire in the north while the remaining Goblin Empire in Beldar and southern Mahkoua never stopped their guerrilla warfare against their conquerors.

And finally, the relations between the Dwarven Commonwealth and the young realm of Terraland were strained. The remaining dwarf realms saw the human queen's actions in signing the Stalemate Treaty as a treacherous stab in the back by their ally. They told that it was against the wishes of the Commonwealth, which Terraland was a part of at the time and to this day has been the only non-dwarf realm to have been counted amongst the power of the Commonwealth. These relations only worsened in the aftermath of the Terraland Civil War, where the two children of Terraland's first king, Keldar Coshrune, who was slain in battle against the tartaruns, turned their father's newly formed kingdom into a battleground as each child claimed ownership of the throne.

The war with the tartaruns wounded the world, and rather than heal with time, the wounds festered into chaos and distrust. Decades later, when the lands shook under the footsteps of marching armies once again, all those in the north assumed the worst, that the tartaruns had returned with new strength against our lands, which were at that point weaker than ever before.

However, it was not the savage tartaruns who marched into Dulengar from the long-abandoned southwest of Gaia but the liberated armies of Beldar and Hathrak alongside a vast army of Xaidaran humans, all of them marching under the banner of the Sovereign Empire, along with the sovereigns who led them forward.

The sovereigns launched a noble campaign to bring order to the northern lands, bringing the warring Colony Kingdoms of Mahkoua to heel under their banner, reuniting the Dwarven Commonwealth with the lost kingdom of Hathrak within their mighty empire, and conquering the Northern Kingdom of Humanity so that they could turn it away from its path of treachery and violence and toward peace and prosperity.

The sovereigns not only eradicated the tartarun race but also saved us from ourselves and brought the world into a golden age of peace and order. This tome is the first in a set of three that delves into the details of these times and hopes to educate all who read it to understand just how grateful we all are—

Carver shut the parchment-bound book with a clench of his hand and placed it back on the table. Of the few books he had seen in his life, almost all of them were somehow related to how the sovereigns had saved the people of the known world or how the lands of Gaia were a dystopia of war and infighting before the sovereigns arrived. He hated it.

"That one's new," the dwarf merchant said, gesturing at the book Carver had just set down. "Written last year, actually, by Dolie Pith. Fresh from the printing presses of the Hathrak Publishers Guild. The rest are translations of preexisting texts from the Dulengar Publishers Guild. Still good, though; good condition and approved by the sovereigns for distribution."

Before Carver could respond, the dwarf looked over at Helena. "Hey, you going to read the whole thing before you buy it?" he asked in a stern yet still friendly tone.

Surprisingly, Helena heard the dwarf and looked up from her reading. "Oh, sorry," she said as she closed the book and handed it back to him.

The dwarf took the tome and placed it back atop the cluttered desk.

Carver looked at the book's title as it passed hands, seeing that "Empire to Commonwealth: The Dividing of the Old Dwarven Empire. Volume II," took up most of the cover's face.

Helena looked at the other tomes, her eyes leaping eagerly from book to book. "What can I get with this?" she asked as she pulled a small cloth pouch from her trouser pocket and carefully spilled its contents into her palm. Four small round coins clinked together in her hand. Each one was made from tiny copper shards that were held in place by a thin, decagon iron frame. Three of the coins had the full ten shards in the frame, giving the coins the appearance of being solid copper, while one had only four shards, leaving most of the coin as a hollow frame.

The dwarf looked at the offering. From the way he bit his bottom lip, Carver could see that his answer would not be pleasing to Helena.

"I'm sorry to say, but each of these tomes sells for four silver absol shards a piece."

Carver saw the energy drain from Helena's face.

"What? The last time I was here I was able to buy a book for just two silver shards. I have the equivalent here with two full copper absols," Helena said, distress in her voice.

The dwarf frowned. "Well, it wasn't at my shop. If you found a tome for that price then you probably got it from someone who stole it and didn't know its true worth. Books aren't easy to make. Even with the printing presses, they take time and effort to craft."

The dwarf looked back at the offering of coins Helena still held out. "Three full copper absols and four shards just doesn't cover the cost of these books. I need to make a profit for my employers, or they take the absols out of my end."

Helena closed her palm over the coins and lowered her hand to her side. "But you have so many. Isn't there anything here I can afford with thirty-four shards?"

The dwarf huffed. "I have so many because folk, if they can even read to begin with, don't spend their absols on books when they're hungry and cold. Times are harder than usual lately, and most of you humans don't value books even on a good day."

"Then why are you trying to sell them at all?" Carver asked, feeling a great deal of pity for Helena.

The book merchant shot Carver a frustrated glance, clearly offended by his question. "Because they're all I have, young man. I don't have a farm or a craftsmen's shop. What I have is a hungry family, a useless collection of my late father's unsold tomes, and a contract of which six years remain to continue selling whatever books his old employers send over. I inherited this business from my old man, along with the contract. Believe me, if I could make absols by burning these things, I gladly would."

Carver crossed his arms and furrowed his brow. "So, no one buys your books, but when someone wants to, you don't sell them because they don't have enough absols? It sounds like any coin is better than what you're getting, whether full absols or just shards."

"Just because they don't sell often doesn't mean I'm going to just give them away. And like I said, it's not up to me. I'm under contract to sell whatever tomes my employers send me, and they expect a certain threshold of profit sent back. If I'm under that threshold, they take it out of my pay."

With a sigh of disappointment, Helena deposited the coins back into her pouch. "It's alright, Carver. You want to go look around somewhere else?"

"Sure," he said, trying to sound less frustrated than he was.

Helena looked back at the book merchant and nodded. "Thanks anyway," she said, then turned away from the booth.

Carver saw the dwarf's face shift from frustration to what appeared to be sadness. "I'm sorry I have nothing for you, young lass."

Carver glared at the dwarf, then turned to follow Helena; he wasn't as forgiving as she was. He had to hurry to catch up to her as she drifted out of the ring of stalls and headed toward another, apparently uninterested in what the other shops within the current ring had to offer.

"I'm sorry you couldn't afford any of those books, Helena."

"It's okay. Maybe next time I'll have enough absols to get one. Let's just go look at the other stalls. I'm not leaving without something from this market."

"Well, okay then. How about over there?" Carver gestured toward another ring.

Helena looked over at where he indicated. "Sure."

As they entered the next ring of stalls, something grabbed Carver's attention.

"Helena, look. There's a potion booth," he said with an excitement Helena did not often hear from him.

The booth had a variety of small to medium glass bottles and vials filled with liquids ranging from dark red to black strewn about it. Behind the booth stood a tall, thin man. He was young and had a head of short, jet-black hair that seemed purposely messy. His face was clean shaven, aside from the thin sideburns that descended from his hair down to his jawline. He wore a faded blue jerkin, which was unbuttoned over a white cloth tunic. He also wore matching faded blue gloves that left his fingers visible past the knuckles. Below it all he had on black trousers and even blacker boots. The outfit made him stand out like a sparrow amongst crows.

As Carver and Helena approached his booth, he smiled widely and held his arms out to his sides. "You two! Young lad and lady. Have you ever been unable to sleep? Have you ever been cut or broken a bone? Have you ever been unable to compete with a stronger individual or wanted to impress your friends with your tolerance for pain? Have you ever come home from a hunt empty handed and were left hungry as a result? Well, I have the solution to all that and more. Come over and be delighted by these fantastic potions and poultices from overseas, courtesy of Gillian's Potions!"

Carver looked above the merchant's head to see a dark-blue banner with the name "Gillian's Potions" scrawled across it in bright-orange lettering, although the font was strange and hard for Carver to read.

"I'm assuming you're Gillian, then?" Carver asked as he and Helena stopped in front of the booth.

"My young friend," the potion merchant said as he leaned over the booth's counter, his smile growing larger, "you flatter me with your words. Being mistaken or even compared to Master Gillian is both a delight and an inspiration. But no, I am merely Gillian's employee. My name is Paalen, Pal to my friends, and all my customers are friends, so please, call me Pal, friend."

Carver heard Helena giggle.

"I like him," she whispered.

Carver felt a slight bit overwhelmed by Paalen's personality and immediately found him somewhat irritating, but his curiosity about the man's stock forced him to be sociable in return.

"Okay, then. Are these real potions you have for sale? With magic, I mean," Carver asked, hoping to skip the introductions and get straight to his interest.

"Oh, by the moons, no. Such things are illegal, as you should very well know. Under sovereign law, magic is forbidden and those of us humans who develop sorcery are to be handed over to them, such as I also assume you know already. As such, no potions of our making may be enhanced with said magic. Though pay close attention to the word enhanced, my friend, as such a word is exactly suited for what I'm saying." Pal appeared to be incredibly pleased with himself.

"Um. Sorry, what?" Carver tried to speak politely. He heard Helena giggle again beside him.

"No apology needed, my friend," Paalen said as he stood up tall and clapped his gloved hands together. "While we humans at one time used sorcery to boost the effectiveness of our potions, it's not sorcery and magic that makes or breaks the potion. Our kind crafted potions without the aid of sorcery for untold years with only the knowledge gifted to us by Lilberith, Goddess of the Woods, amid the Age of Creation." Paalen flashed his hands in a gesture of excitement as he continued. "And of that variety I have now here before you both. Potions and poultices too, if you so desire, of honest make and potent effect through no forbidden means." Paalen finished with his hands on his hips, looking as proud as could be.

Carver was quickly growing weary of Paalen's manner of speaking, but he maintained a pleasant face and tried to act as if he were enjoying the exchange so that he might finally get to his desire. Before Carver or Helena could speak, however, Paalen beat them to the punch, much to Carver's frustration.

"Can I ask my friend his name and the name of his partner, who has, if I may say, a truly heartwarming chuckle." Paalen bowed slightly toward Helena.

Carver looked over at Helena, who was now wearing a grin similar to Paalen's, then back at the merchant. "My name is Carver, and this is He—"

"My name is Helena," she interrupted, mimicking the bow Paalen had performed, though with an added giggle and a blush.

"Ah, now we're properly acquainted. I wouldn't have it any other way. Now, might I inquire as to what kind of potions the two of you are looking for amongst my humble stock?"

Carver jumped at the chance to speak again, especially now that the topic had finally landed on the specifics of the potions themselves. "Anything, really. What kinds of potions do you have, and how do you make them?" Carver asked while examining the array of bottles and vials on the counter.

Paalen grinned and straightened his posture. "This one here is of the enhancement variety," he said as he picked up a small, corked, rectangular bottle with a black liquid inside and uncorked it with a flick of his thumb. "Here, take a whiff."

Carver leaned forward, placing his nose just over the bottle, and sniffed. Helena was about to do the same until she saw how Carver reacted.

"Gah! Shit! That's awful!" Carver pulled his head away and clasped a hand over his nose as a vile, sulfur-like burnt smell traveled up his nostrils.

"As it should be," Paalen said in a pleasantly calm voice. "Ragewhirl is the proper name, though many also call it ragerum due to one of its staple ingredients. The pollen from crushed berserkerweed mixed with dwarf black rum and boiled marrowstalk marrow. Simple to make if you can find the ingredients yet very effective."

Carver, only now recovering from the lingering sulfuric scent of the berserkerweed mix, returned his attention to the bottle in Paalen's hand. "Do people actually drink that stuff? Why?"

"They most certainly do. Downing this potion will put you into a state of heightened aggression after only a few minutes. You felt a burst of anger from just the smell, did you not? Not only does drinking it make you angry, it also dulls the sense of pain throughout the body, boosts your adrenaline and energy, and strips away the burden of fear from your mind, all things that someone entering combat will benefit from." Paalen recorked the small bottle and returned it to the shelf. "It is most often purchased by mercenaries and soldiers, but even a farmer or a merchant can benefit from ragewhirl should bandits, beasts, or monsters make themselves present at one's home or farm. Though one must be cautious, as ingesting too much can cause you to be overwhelmed by rage and lose self-control."

"How much is too much?" Carver asked.

Paalen shrugged. "It depends on the person and the amount of aggression they already have in their personality. A man with a naturally short temper may find that a quarter of a standard bottle or vial is enough. Any more would push him into a dangerous frenzy, whereas a calm and collected man might need the whole amount to achieve the same effect. In most cases, ingesting a quarter or half of a standard-size ragewhirl potion is enough to benefit safely from the potion's effects, though it's best for one new to ragewhirl to partake of it first in a calm environment to get used to its effects."

"I think a single sip would send Carver over the edge then," Helena said, chuckling.

"What else do you have?" Carver asked, ignoring Helena's jibe.

"Oh, many things that you're sure to wonder at." Paalen tapped his index finger on a stubby glass vial of dark-red liquid. "This here is hound sense. It's a wonderfully practical potion, but far more than practically wonderful, let me tell you. This potion, when drunk but fifteen minutes before a hunt, will give the hunter keen eyes and sharp hearing, much like those of a trusty hunting hound, for nearly an hour. Though I must inform that after the hour of heightened perception comes drowsiness, dulled senses, and a headache. An undesirable side effect, I know, but it can be postponed by consuming more of the potion until the hunt is finished."

Paalen moved his hand to a different, taller vial filled with dark liquid, though not as black as the ragewhirl. "And this here is nymph tears. Not made from real nymph tears, mind you. Not all the absols in Terraland could make me try and force tears from a nymph, be they naiads, dryads, or harpies. It—" Paalen cut himself off as his eyes shifted across the booth and focused in on a fat square bottle full of dark-red liquid.

"Oh, but this one. This one is the most widely useful. This here is a healing potion, made from the waters collected from the stems and leaves of healer's stalk as well as the leaves themselves, combined with a smooth mixture of dwarf moonshine and, of course, the boiled marrow from marrowstalk plants, as is standard for all potions. It's called what it is, healing potion, or healer's potion, depending on your preference. It can be applied directly to small wounds, but it is more effectively used through ingestion to work on greater ailments, such as internal bleeding, broken bones, and deep or multiple injuries."

Carver's eyes lit up. "And it really works? It can heal you as good as new?"

"Well, the potion doesn't itself do the healing; it merely boosts your body's healing rate and leaves you to do the rest. And by no means does one sip cure all ailments. With regular consumption over a period of time, a wound that would take a month or more to heal will only take a few short weeks. And a wound of a few weeks merely a few days. However, the potion does have the immediate effect of reducing the pain."

Carver listened to Paalen's every word, though he did not take his eyes off the fat, square bottle of dark-red liquid. Noticing Carver's intense interest in the potion, he leaned forward over the counter. "Carver and Helena, my new friends, might I ask you an innocent question?"

Carver and Helena looked at each other for a moment before looking back to Paalen and nodding.

Paalen scanned his eyes over the area behind the two teens and then to the sides where his fellow merchants busied themselves with distracted customers. "Okay," he said finally, "might I ask you both your opinion on the sovereigns and their decree regarding sorcery?"

Carver and Helena looked at each other again, though this time they both had concern on their faces. Helena was the first to turn back to Paalen. "I don't really think about them or their law that forbids humans to wield magic through sorcery. I've—"

"Please, my friend, speak a little more quietly," Paalen said, leaning closer. "This is a conversation between us friends. No need to involve those around us."

Helena nodded slightly. "I've never even seen a sovereign before," she whispered.

Paalen turned his gaze to Carver. "And what about you, friend?"

Carver opened his mouth to speak but then hesitated, as he remembered that he was supposed to speak quietly. "I hate them," he whispered. "I've never seen one, but I've been told all my life that I'm supposed to fear and respect them, but I don't. All they do is take from us, and their law on sorcery is—"

Paalen held up a gloved hand, cutting Carver off. "That's enough, my young friend," he said as he glanced around. "I think I've heard enough to get a sense of your standing when it comes to such things."

Paalen brought his hands back to his side of the booth and then appeared to be using them for something that neither Carver nor Helena could properly see. After a couple of seconds, they heard a metal latch tapping onto wood, a sliding noise, and then a brief clink.

Before Carver or Helena could look at each other again, wondering what was going on, Paalen brought his hands back up, now holding a square glass bottle of dark-red liquid the same size as the square bottle of healer's potion on the counter. He placed it in the center of the counter.

"Now this, Carver, will heal any wound in but an instant."

"How? You mean ..."

Paalen grinned and nodded his head ever so slightly.

Carver took a step forward so he could be as close to the booth as possible. "I thought you said you didn't sell mag—I mean enhanced potions."

"I said no such thing. I only stated that none of what you saw before you were of such make. But I never said I didn't have other products, products that I would gladly sell to my dear friends, such as you two."

Helena put a hand on Carver's shoulder. "Carver, if that's real, then we should go. Magic is forbidden in all forms to us. If we got caught with a potion like that we'd be in who knows how much trouble."

Paalen turned to Helena and addressed her with a calm look in his eyes. "That's just it, Helena. Take a look at this bottle and the liquid inside, and tell me if you can tell the difference between it and the others."

Helena studied the square bottle, as did Carver, realizing that the contents of the supposedly magic-enhanced potion appeared identical to the others.

Helena kept her hand on Carver's shoulder but turned her attention to Paalen. "It looks exactly the same. Is there no difference?"

"Aside from the potency of the potion's effects and the taste of sheep's blood, no, there is not.

"Sheep's blood?" Helena and Carver exclaimed, though still somewhat quietly despite the fact that no one around them seemed to be paying attention to them.

"Yes. Though it doesn't have to be sheep's blood. The blood of any animal will do."

Carver gently pushed Helena's hand off his shoulder. "No, I mean why is there sheep blood in it?"

"Ah, I see. Yes, I suppose blood isn't the most pleasant ingredient. I'm no expert as to the details of such a reason, but I do know that blood is required for amplified potions due to its ability to hold a magical charge."

"Blood can hold magic?" Helena asked, somewhat forgetting her concern for their safety as curiosity got the better of her young mind.

"Apparently so. That's why blood is needed when crafting any potion of magical variety, but as a result the color becomes red, as if the potion were made with marrowstalk marrow instead."

"Gross," Helena said with a shiver.

Carver too felt a slight degree of disgust in the learning of such a detail, but then his mind burst with a new question. "Then how can we know if what you're selling is real? It could just be a marrowstalk potion of healing, since it looks the same."

"Carver, you wound me more than this potion could heal. I would never lie to a friend. However, I understand your skepticism. Absolutely, I do. So, why don't you let me prove my words with a little demonstration?"

Paalen pulled out a sharp knife while simultaneously pulling off his right glove with his teeth. Then, without hesitation, he dragged the knife's edge along the back of his hand. Blood immediately surfaced and clung to the edge of the knife as Paalen pulled it away from his skin and set it down.

Carver and Helena both took a step back, wide eyed.

"Ah, no, please, don't let me frighten you. Just watch and be amazed, my young friends."

Maintaining his friendly energy and smile, Paalen uncapped the bottle and poured some of its thick red contents onto his bleeding hand.

Helena and Carver leaned in close to watch as the syrupy red liquid seeped into the shallow cut on Paalen's hand. After a few seconds they noticed that the bleeding had stopped. A few seconds later they watched in amazement as the cut became harder and harder to see until it closed and only a scar remained. Then it also faded away.

"By the stars!" Helena gasped, her eyes riveted to Paalen's hand.

Carver's eyes also remained fixed on the spot. The blood around the area was still wet and dripping, but the source of the blood was completely gone.

"That's amazing! Can you do me?" Carver asked with heightened excitement.

"Your voice, Carver. Please keep it low. But of course. Give me your hand."

Paalen set the bottle on the table and then grabbed Carver's outstretched arm.

Helena gave Carver a concerned look, but his calmness reassured her that everything was fine.

Paalen made a small cut on the side of Carver's arm. Carver hissed from the pain and pulled his arm away slightly. A trail of bright blood ran down the edge of his arm and dripped onto the cobblestone next to his boots. Paalen poured a series of thick red drops onto Carver's cut.

Helena watched as, just like Paalen's, Carver's cut closed up and faded away before the last of the blood could trail off the side of his arm.

"Ow! That stings," Carver hissed as he watched the wound close up and disappear.

"That it does, my friend. I'm used to it, but to the unaccustomed it can be an unpleasant experience, though not without results, as you two can see."

"Helena, check it out! You can't even tell there was a cut there at all," Carver said, holding his arm up to her face.

Paalen flinched at the volume of Carver's voice. "Must I reiterate?"

"What?" Carver asked as he looked back at Paalen.

Before Paalen could clarify, Helena pushed his arm away from her face. "I did see. It's amazing. But Paalen, how—"

"Please, Helena, call me Pal."

"Pal. Sorry. But how do you have potions like this if ... you know?"

Paalen corked the bottle of enhanced healer's potion and placed it back in its hidden compartment on his side of the booth. "Now, Helena, that question is best left unanswered for all parties involved. What matters is that I have them and am willing to sell them to you."

"How much then?" Carver asked.

Paalen smiled. "Well, for the bottle you were just shown, six silver shards, or six whole copper absols, or sixty copper shards if you are without absol frames entirely. Though carrying sixty copper shards would be quite a bother, I can imagine," he concluded with a chuckle.

Helena and Carver did not join in with the laugh as they looked at each other once more. This time Carver was the one who looked disappointed.

"Do you have anything cheaper?" Helena asked for Carver.

"If you have little in the way of absols or shards, then by all means, buy less potion," Paalen said as he set a small square vial on the display counter. The vial was half the size of the previous bottle but was full of the same red liquid.

"This here is the same thing, though only half as much, and the price is half as much as well. Three silver shards or three full copper absols will do nicely."

Helena looked at Carver with a worried face. "That's basically all we have, Carver. We haven't even looked at the rest of the market yet."

Carver bit his lip, but before he could respond, Paalen interjected. "I'll tell you what. As the two of you have been friendlier than most and delighted me with conversation, I would, just for the two of you, be willing to knock the price of this potion down from three whole copper absols to two absols and eight shards."

Carver knew better than to barter with coin that wasn't his, so he waited for Helena to answer.

"Could we come back later?" she asked. "I want to see what else is here before we buy anything."

"Why of course, my friends. Take your time. Your private discount will last until the market closes tonight, after which I'll be packing up and heading back home across the sea."

"Awesome. Thanks, Pal," Helena said, smiling.

"Yeah. Thanks," Carver added.

"Think nothing of it. Though I do suggest you keep our business arrangement private, as well as our pleasant conversation."

"We will," Helena assured him as she tugged Carver by the shoulder. With a quick nod to Paalen, Carver turned and followed Helena.

"You two have a wonderful time browsing this here market and its wares. You both know where to find me!" Paalen called as they headed back into the heart of the busy market.

As their hour of freedom wound down, Helena stopped frequently to inspect many of the different stalls and booths. Carver pretended to pay attention as she showed him random trinkets from each shop, reacting to each pause in her voice with a "Hmm," or "Cool."

Other than Paalen's potion booth, nothing piqued Carver's interest. He was much more focused on how bare bones the market seemed to be. He thought back to the last time he had visited it.

His parents had brought him there a few years earlier. He remembered many more shops, and he didn't recall the wares being so lackluster. Now the trinkets looked cheap, the clothes looked worn, the ironwork looked shoddily crafted, and the food had little smell or color to entice the senses.

Carver wondered what happened to the quality of it all, but then it hit him: the sovereigns and their steep taxes. To Carver, the market no longer seemed to be a place to purchase luxuries or acquire items with ease. Instead, it was a shamble of people trying to barter for necessities and make back what was stolen from them in the yearly taxes.

"Carver!" Helena's voice rang into his ears, pulling him out of his angry thoughts. He realized he was staring directly into Helena's brown eyes, which were looking at him with an expectant glare.

"What do you think?" she asked in a way that told him she had already asked the question.

He looked at what she was holding up to his face. It was a necklace, a thin, white rope of steel that hung from her fingers. Attached to the delicate white metal chain was a small charm shaped like a winged horse.

"Yeah, sure."

"What?"

Not a yes or no question then, Carver realized.

"You weren't even listening, were you?"

Before Carver could lie, Helena spoke again. "I'm thinking about buying it, and it's six copper shards, so we'd have exactly enough left over to get that healing potion you want from Pal afterwards, if you still think that's a good idea. What do you think of it?"

Carver gave Helena an apologetic look, then reached out and took the necklace in his hands, giving it a delicate inspection. The winged horse was smooth yet bumpy where the details rose, and the chain was light and felt soft when piled in the palm of the hand. It was too nice to be in the same market that sold such degraded and shoddy items. He looked up as he handed the necklace back to Helena. "It's actually quite nice," he said, hoping she would drop the fact that she had just caught him ignoring her.

"Yeah, I really like it," Helena said as she played with the necklace with her fingers.

Carver knew that his opinion on the necklace didn't actually matter. Helena would do what she wanted regardless of what he thought. He did think it was nice, though.

Without another word to him, Helena turned her attention to a woman behind the counter of the stall. She was tall and skinny, wearing a dirty gray tunic with wrinkled brown trousers and an overly wide bonnet. The bonnet stood out even more due to her boney face and dirty clothes.

The necklace is probably hers, Carver thought. *She's probably selling it so she can afford to buy some food from the very same market she's working at.* This realization sparked more angry thoughts about the sovereigns.

Helena took the small cloth pouch out of her pocket again and reached inside. She pulled out the iron frame with four copper shards held within and then one full copper coin. Helena placed the nearly empty-framed coin on the booth's counter and then turned the full coin sideways and pushed her thumb into the bottom. A single copper shard popped out of the frame and fell onto the counter next to the mostly framed coin. Helena moved her thumb over and pushed into the coin again, which caused another copper shard to pop out of the iron frame and land on the counter. Helena gave the remaining shards in the coin a firm squeeze to make sure they were still locked in place before putting the coin back in the cloth pouch.

Carver guessed the necklace was probably more expensive than it was being sold for, since it seemed to be of fine quality. He assumed that if Helena could afford it and still have absols left to buy a discounted potion from Paalen then the necklace's worth had to have been lowered to entice poor, hungry people to purchase it over food and extra clothing.

Carver turned around and leaned against the side of the stall, staring out into the market, unable to ignore its depressing state.

How long until Verrel shares this fate? he wondered.

Carver began to regret not hiding better when his mother came searching for him that morning. He wished he had fought harder to get out of coming or stayed at their own stall instead of following Helena inside of Caswen's walls. The sullen state of the city and its market made him angry, angrier than most things. Carver felt like he was looking at the future of his village and the rest of the Isles. The knowledge that he could do nothing to change it lit a fire in his blood.

Carver's angry, wandering thoughts fled to the back of his mind as the sound of raised voices from farther off reached his ears. He looked over toward the commotion, which was a good distance to his left, on the south side of the market. A crowd of people was creating a wide lane into the market for an armored wagon manned by two soldiers and pulled by two horses. Carver recognized the type of wagon as the same kind that had taken his village's tax contribution earlier. This metal wagon was not alone, however. More armored wagons turned into the market from around the corner of a brick building at the south exit, each manned by two human soldiers and pulled by two horses. Other soldiers trotted on impressive steeds alongside the procession, two per wagon, one on each side. The wagon drivers and the mounted escorts kept their eyes forward, not paying any heed to the looks or nervous chatter coming from the seemingly frightened market folk.

Carver wasn't sure why the people nearest to the procession seemed so frightened, but as the mounted soldiers continued to round the corner alongside more armored wagons and headed deeper into the market, three mounted figures suddenly came into Carver's view, freezing him in place.

Chapter 5

❧

The first thing that drew Carver's immediate attention to the three figures riding amongst the rest was their mounts. The creatures didn't resemble horses but rather large, muscular felines of some kind. Carver thought the beasts similar to the cougars he had seen prowling the hills and Vellum Forest every now and again, but even that was too far a stretch.

The cougar-like mounts were nearly the size of the horses around them, though with shorter legs that kept them lower to the ground, and instead of fur they were covered in dark-purple scales. Their lipless mouths stretched far around the sides of their wide heads, ending at flat, pointed ears, exposing 180 degrees of thin, razor teeth. Their eyes, entirely bright blue with no visible pupils or irises, glared at the crowds of people who were staring intently at the scaled beasts.

The horses closest to the creatures showed clear signs of unease and agitation, frequently pulling their heads back and turning slightly with displeased neighs, causing their riders, some of whom looked nervous of the creatures, to adjust their course as they tried to calm their mounts.

Riding atop each of the wide-mouthed, purple-scaled beasts were humanoid creatures who looked just as strange to Carver as the animals they rode. Even sitting on their beasts, Carver could tell that they were at least a foot taller than the human soldiers riding amongst them.

Each wore a matching set of bright metal armor, impressive not only for its pearl-like color, but also for its extravagant detail, with turquoise grooves and inlays across the metal. The armor was sleek and thin in most places, looking like it was more for ceremonial purposes than actual combat. The armor covered the beings from their shoulders to their hips, where each had what looked to be a long sheathed sword buckled to their waist, though from a distance Carver could not make out the true shape or length of the blades.

The armor disappeared at the joints, replaced with black mail that kept it tight and together, while also leaving their arms unrestricted. Where the armor stopped at the waist, tight white robes began, seeming to come from under the armor as if part of a covered layer of fine clothing. The white robes covered their long legs but left their feet exposed.

Carver wasn't sure what was stranger, their heads or their feet.

Their feet, if one could call them that, hanging to the sides of their mounts, looked as if they were entirely exposed bone. Each bone foot began as a thick gray stalk that split into four thinner bone-like stalks a little way down, looking like an "X." Each of the thinner stalks ended in a sharp claw that pointed downwards. The creatures' heads did little to normalize their appearance either.

They were entirely bald, almost smooth looking, with beige skin from neck to scalp. Where their ears and noses should have been there were only slits, one large slit for each ear and two smaller slits in place of the nose, each resembling gills more than traditional sensory orifices, giving their heads a dented shape.

Below the gill-like nose slits was a fairly human-looking mouth, though with flat, beige lips that nearly blended into the skin, and above the nose slits were two human-like eyes, though slightly larger and lacking hair over the brow ridges. Their cheekbones were overly prominent, giving each creature's face a sharp perimeter before ending in a narrow chin.

The foreign features of each creature's face was enhanced by an equally foreign design that was imprinted into their skin. Thick black lines curved under their large eyes and shot down their sharp cheeks, meeting in a dual-pointed design along the chin. Two thinner inked lines rose from their chins up over the lips, ending just before their noses, creating a kind of pitch-fork design.

While the purple-scaled mounts were completely unknown to him, Carver had heard enough descriptions of the sovereigns from his schooling to know one when he saw one, or three, for that matter.

"Sovereigns ..." Carver said under his breath in an attempt to gain Helena's attention, as he was too enraptured with the sight to look away.

When Carver did not hear Helena respond or react, he reached back with his left hand, not taking his eyes off the sovereigns or their mounts, and felt around for Helena's arm. Once he felt it in his grasp, he squeezed it tight and gave it a pull.

"Hey! What are y—"

Helena froze.

All the people near the line of wagons either backed away or stepped closer to get a better look, though the faces of everyone spoke of tense nerves. No more wagons or riders entered the market from the south exit, and all those riding at the front of the procession were now deep in the market and surrounded by at least a hundred bystanders on each side. Despite the massive crowd building up, no one dared to get in the way of the line of wagons.

Only a few times did the soldiers at the front of the procession have to call out for those around them to move back, and each shout may as well have been a physical blow as those addressed jumped back as if being struck with force.

At that moment Carver lost all his hatred for the sovereigns, so caught up in the strangeness of their appearance that he totally forgot everything else on his mind.

Then, just as the wagon at the head of the procession was beginning to turn right, rounding a wide corner of canopied stalls and booths toward the east, something caught Carver's eye between the gaps of the crowd ahead of him and Helena.

A wooden barrel rolled out from the crowd on the other side of the open space made for the wagons, passed under the closest mounted soldier before he noticed it, and bumped into the front-left wheel of the middle-most armored wagon, which was passing by just six feet ahead of Carver.

Carver lost his view of the barrel almost as quickly as he noticed it, and as he stretched his neck to the side and took a half step forward to see if he could spot it again through the crowd, he was greeted by a bright flash, followed by a deafening boom.

A wave of heat struck Carver's face and chest, knocking him off his feet. When he opened his eyes a moment later, he felt utterly disoriented and noticed that he was staring up at the sky, which had turned grayish and slightly cloudy since he had last looked at it. All sounds had vanished from Carver's notice as well, replaced instead by a single loud, heavy, all-encompassing hum of nothingness that further disoriented him.

Lost in confusion, all Carver could do was lie still and breathe while staring up at the cloudy sky. After a few seconds, however, the overbearing silence that seemed to emanate from inside his own head began to dissipate, replaced by a sudden, steadily increasing ringing in his ears. Other sounds quickly became audible alongside the ringing, and although these new sounds were hard for Carver to discern at first, after a handful of seconds, they became clear enough for him to make out.

Shouting. Screaming. Running.

Carver wanted to move and look around, but in that strange moment he couldn't seem to remember how to use his arms or legs. He tried to regain a sense of where his limbs were and how to control them, which, to his surprise, took him a few seconds to achieve. Once his mind reconnected to his extremities, he pulled his arms in and pushed his hands against the cobblestones beneath him.

He raised his torso off the ground with difficulty, the act of sitting up feeling like he was falling out of bed while half asleep. His depth perception flew away from his eyes, then boomeranged back into his skull, making him feel as if he had been struck in the forehead. Carver's stomach clenched, making him want to vomit as a surge of dizziness arrived behind his eyes and made him want to fall back to the ground.

His vision cleared just enough for him to focus, giving him a brief view of another bright flash that blinked into existence alongside another boom from the line of scattering armored wagons, some of which were obscured in thick gray smoke, one having been knocked over onto its side.

The wooden wheels of the armored wagon closest to the second flash blew apart and sent shrapnel in every direction while the wagon itself was flipped over, unseating the driver and pulling the tethered horses to the ground.

Carver managed to remain sitting while shielding his face from the heat that followed the bright flash, and the boom was softened somewhat by the ringing in his ears. After the second heatwave pushed past him, Carver turned his attention behind him, suddenly remembering he was with Helena.

Like him, she was on the ground, though she was arched up on her side. She looked just as dazed as he felt, her eyes wide in confusion as she scanned the area around them.

Carver grabbed the trinket booth's edge and hoisted himself to his feet. The rise in elevation made his dizziness worse for a moment, but he gripped the booth to prevent himself from collapsing and forced his mind to focus on balancing. The hum that dominated his hearing continued to dissipate, making way for a high-pitched ringing along with a symphony of muffled screams and shouts from all around him.

At that instance, Carver actually preferred the strange, deafening silence. Trying to ignore the violent commotion erupting behind him, and still not entirely registering what was going on due to his shaken perception, Carver reached down to his distressed friend.

At first Helena recoiled from his hands, as if startled by them. Then, upon realizing they were attached to her friend, she reached up and grabbed them, allowing Carver to pull her to her feet.

"Wha—"

Before she could even begin her question, Carver slammed into her, pushed forward by another blast behind him. Helena caught him, wrapping her arms around his back as he crashed against her, nearly knocking her over. Carver's body shielded her from the heatwave that followed the cracking boom.

Before Helena could look at Carver and see if he was hurt, Carver broke away from her grip with a drunken shuffle. He placed his hand on her shoulder for balance as he turned to look back.

Large clouds of thick gray smoke were blowing through the market, emanating from shallow craters in the cobblestone that were multiple feet in diameter, surrounded by black scorch marks. Dozens of booths and stalls had been knocked over, shattered to bits or in flames, adding black smoke to the billowing gray smoke that already covered much of the area. People were scattering in every direction, pushing and stepping over one another as they fled the scene. Riderless horses galloped through the market, trampling anyone in their way. Those that were still hitched to the wagons broke from the procession and pulled the wagons in different directions, knocking over stalls and colliding with pedestrians.

But worst of all, beside and ahead of Carver, some partially hidden by smoke and some in clear view, were humans and goblins splattered in red, lying on the ground around the black, smoking craters. Some were missing limbs; some had large portions of their clothing missing, which revealed terrible burns all over their flesh; and some had large bits of wood or metal sticking out of their bodies. Many lay perfectly still and didn't make a sound while others writhed in place and screamed in agony.

The Caswen soldiers who were still mounted were trying to get ahold of their panicked horses. Those who could not were bucked off. The soldiers who were already stationed in the market struggled to run against the flow of fleeing civilians toward the quickly scattering procession of wagons, some being knocked over or having their weapons torn from their hands. Many of the soldiers threw down their spears and drew their swords instead as they tried to pass through the smoke and the flow of people.

Carver's attention was suddenly caught by the sight of a male soldier pinned under an overturned wagon with a pool of blood leaking out from where his legs should have been. A female soldier was yanking on his arms, attempting to rescue her injured comrade. Before she realized there was no hope for the pinned man, an iron-tipped bolt exploded through her neck. A shower of red rained down from the protruding shaft, mixing with the enlarging pool of blood from the man's crushed legs.

The woman released her grip on the trapped man and clutched at the wooden shaft that stuck out past her chin just above her gambeson. She wrapped her hands around it as if expecting to remove the bolt by pulling it through her neck, but mere seconds later, she fell to the ground alongside her comrade.

Carver suddenly found himself experiencing déjà vu as he realized his feet were moving without his consent. It took him a moment to realize Helena was pulling him by his wrist. Carver surrendered to her grip, stumbling along behind her.

Helena's grip on Carver's wrist caused the tips of his fingers to grow numb as his blood flow struggled to move up his arm. Carver didn't understand. He could have sworn he had been listening to Helena prattle on about some necklace mere seconds ago, but now he couldn't decipher if that had actually happened at all.

Suddenly, he felt his feet leave the ground at the same time as Helena's grip disappeared from his wrist. He felt his direction change, and a moment later, he smashed down onto the cobblestone, landing on his right arm.

The pain that shot through his arm was strong, but he barely had time to register it as the right side of his head smacked against the ground. His vision swam, making him so dizzy he had to close his eyes once more. A deep silence strangled his hearing and left him completely disoriented, but Carver managed to force himself into a sitting position and tried to look around.

Helena was nowhere to be seen amidst the gray and black smoke.

A sudden spike of pain called to Carver from his left leg. He pulled the throbbing leg closer to him and paled in shock as he saw a piece of wood, two fingers thick and nearly as long, plunged through his trousers and sticking into his left calf. A dark stain was spreading beneath his trousers around the large splinter, and rivulets of red dripped onto the ground.

Carver pulled his leg closer and reached for the splinter, but the motion only made the pain worse. Grinding his teeth and letting out a dreadful hiss, Carver wrapped his hand around the thick piece of wood, took a deep breath, and pulled, slowly at first due to hesitation, but the pain proved too great. So, with a teeth-clenched scream, Carver ripped the foreign object out of his left calf. A spurt of blood followed, splashing onto the ground as he howled in agony. The pain made his eyes water, and wrapping his hands around the fresh hole did nothing to dull the throbbing. Carver squeezed the wound and looked around desperately for any sign of aid as sound began to return to him once again over the drowning hum in his ears.

Smoke swirled around him, obscuring his view. Despite the smoke, however, Carver saw the orange glow of flames burning brightly around him. He also heard footsteps on all sides, as if dozens of people were running all around him, but he couldn't see any of them.

A surge of pain in his calf pulled his attention away from his poorly perceived surroundings, and Carver tried to squeeze his hands over the wound even tighter. Bright blood continued to seep through his fingers and drip onto the ground, but Carver couldn't think of anything else to do in order to stop the bleeding. His eyes watered from the pain as he tried to get a handle on himself and think, but before he could come up with a plan, another resounding boom erupted nearby.

The sudden boom startled Carver as his instincts predicted another blast of heat to follow. However, as he turned to face the blast, he was greeted not by a wave of heat but by the sight of the smoke blowing away, revealing a wide area of the market.

The majority of the nearby stalls were either in flames or smashed apart, with thick clouds of dark smoke billowing upwards from the flaming piles of wood and merchandise, swallowing parts of the sky and obscuring the distant edges of the market. Soldiers were scattered throughout the area, their blades clashing with handfuls of civilians.

The sight not only shocked Carver but also filled him with fear. He had no idea what was going on or how he had wound up in the center of it, but he realized immediately that he was in serious danger. Cries of death and panic came from every direction, yet despite all that was unfolding around him, Carver's mind latched onto a single thought: Helena.

Where did she go? How did we get separated? Is she hurt? Is she dead? His mind raced with worry.

Carver tried to look at where he remembered being pulled by Helena only a moment ago, but to his dismay, he no longer had any bearing on where that was. Everything looked completely different or was obscured by smoke and flames, leaving him utterly lost.

As he looked around, he was able to make out the shapes of people fighting nearby within the smoke. He also saw more flames piercing the dense smoke, like torches in the early morning fog. Every fiber in Carver's body screamed at him to get up and run, but he was frozen in place. Every direction seemed to lead to the same thing: smoke, flames, and battles between soldiers and strangers. Nowhere seemed safe.

Carver felt his heart race inside his chest. Even though his mind was still struggling to focus after striking the hard cobblestone ground, a wave of adrenaline surged through his body and crushed his hesitation beneath a call for self-preservation.

Carver released the wound in his leg and leaped to his feet. The quick rise filled him with nausea, made worse by the ringing in his ears and the fogginess in his head, but Carver's hammering heart pushed the sensation away, seeming to beat even faster in his chest.

With his adrenaline-fueled panic blocking out the worst of the pain from his punctured left calf, Carver broke into a run, straight into the heavy smoke.

He held his breath within the dense cloud that was all around him. As he ran, he tried to ignore the dizziness that still clung to his mind as well as the pain in his left leg. The process was a balancing act that left him with little time to look around and plan a proper route out of the chaos.

Within a matter of seconds, Carver emerged from the thick wall of gray smoke into a clear area. He tried to stop once he realized he could see again, so he could figure out a plan, but in attempting to halt so quickly he stumbled, and the pain from his leg snuck through his adrenaline. Carver's left leg spasmed from the sudden renewal of agony and turned his stumble into a hard fall to the ground.

His elbows scraped along the cobblestones. Then he forced himself back to his feet. His leg spiked in pain once again and tried to bring him back down, but Carver clenched his teeth and stiffened his leg in order to keep his balance. Standing once again on his own two feet, Carver looked around for Helena, one of the market's exits, or any threat that might endanger him.

What he saw was the third of his immediate concerns. All around him were groups of people pushing past each other, flaming stalls surrounded by sharp piles of ruined wood, blinding smoke blowing in every direction, and soldiers clashing blades with human and goblin civilians who wielded arming swords and daggers.

To Carver's further surprise and confusion, when he witnessed one of the human civilians get the better of a soldier and run him through with an arming sword, the civilian did not try to flee. Instead, he charged another soldier who was in the midst of skewering a goblin assailant.

Who am I supposed to be avoiding? The soldiers? The people fighting the soldiers? Why are people attacking each other? What made all this smoke and fire? Carver's mind jumped from thought to thought as he watched the battle play out.

Unclear as to whom his foe was, Carver decided to avoid everyone and turned to run through the next patch of smoke, hoping to either find Helena or an escape from the area.

As Carver passed from one cloud of smoke to the next, all the while fighting through the pain in his left leg, he noticed that the number of people engaged in combat with the soldiers seemed to be growing. The soldiers were outnumbered and surrounded by dagger or sword-wielding attackers. Still, not everyone was fighting. Carver saw many people trying to flee just as he was. Human and goblin men, women, and children were scrambling around, many of them injured and all of them terrified.

Carver ran as fast as he could manage, each step sending a fresh stream of blood down the back of his leg. However, he never managed to get far before a group of soldiers and armed civilians would appear from the smoke and begin murdering each other right in front of him. Each time it happened Carver was forced to halt and retreat in search of another way to reach one of the market's four exits. Each time he had to stop and turn around, however, Carver found it more difficult to keep going as the pain in his leg increased with every movement.

Carver struggled to maintain his stamina and overcome his pain, which threatened to bring him down, until he ran out of breath. He dropped to the ground for a moment's reprieve and crawled under a stall that had been knocked onto its side. At that moment he wasn't sure what was worse, the constant screams, the blinding and suffocating smoke, the pain that racked his leg, or the overwhelming stench of blood.

Trying to ignore everything that assailed his senses and pained his body, Carver focused on scanning the area, trying desperately to glimpse a route that would lead him away from this madness. Instead, his attention was drawn to a fleeing human woman with her two small boys.

One boy struggled to maintain his hold on his mother's waist as she pulled him along. The other was limp in her arms.

As Carver watched them run through the violent scene, he realized the woman's eyes were fixed in a certain direction. He followed her gaze and saw a wide street that led out of the market with brick homes on both sides, only partially obscured with smoke.

There it is! That's my way out! Carver's mind screamed.

He crawled out from under the stall and leaped to his feet with a fresh burst of adrenaline, running after the fleeing woman as fast as he could manage with his injured leg.

The woman and her children had just about made it to the opening, Carver not far behind, when one of the large, scaled feline creatures, now riderless, leapt out of the smoke near the exit and landed in the clear space just before the street began.

The woman let out a terrified scream and spun around, yanking her son while struggling to keep her second child secured in her other arm. Her eyes locked with Carver's, who skidded to a halt a few feet away from her.

Before the woman could make it three steps, the feline creature lifted its paw, revealing a scaleless palm of soft black tissue with a short, wet spike that extended from the center of it.

The woman screamed as the beast struck her, driving the wet spike through her back and slapping her to the ground, pinning her on top of the child in her arms. The woman's other child was pulled down to the ground with her.

The feline beast opened its freakishly wide maw to the point where its jaw looked to be unhinged, exposing a second row of thin, needle-like teeth hiding behind the first. The woman and her child's screams echoed behind Carver as he turned and ran the other way before they were abruptly silenced a second later.

Every fiber of Carver's being wanted to look back to see if the creature was chasing him next, but he refrained. He knew that if the beast were after him, turning around to look would only slow him down. Carver kept running through the smoke and over the carnage, hoping beyond measure that the creature was not right behind him. With a burst of terror induced from the suspense of whether or not the creature's wet paw-spike was going to burst through his chest and pin him to the ground too, Carver dove behind the first display of cover he saw.

He landed on his hands and knees, eyes closed, teeth clenched, heart racing, and waited to live or die. At that moment, all the chaos and noise, the screaming and fighting, the smell of smoke and blood, the pain in his leg, it all disappeared. Nothing existed to Carver except the mental image of that horrible creature.

Carver opened his eyes.

His surroundings returned to his senses, and so did his pain. He shifted himself over to a sitting position, only to realize he had taken cover under one of the armored wagons, which had been overturned. His heart began to slow with the realization that the creature had seemingly ignored him or lost his trail through the smoke, but he knew that he was still far from safe.

Carver assessed the battlefield for any glimpse of escape. His focus was partially interrupted, however, as his punctured calf continued to throb with pain. Upon rubbing the still-pulsing right side of his head, he was unsettled by the sight of the fresh blood that returned on his wrist and forearm.

Carver had never given the idea that he could actually die any real thought before, always thinking of death as some faraway thing that could never happen to him, but now the hard truth seemed to be all he could think of. He was unable to focus on searching for an escape route, as thoughts of his home and parents rushed to his mind. Now more than ever he wished he had succeeded in avoiding his mother that morning.

Carver's attention was torn away from his scrambling thoughts when his vision landed on a frightening figure in the distance. The abnormally tall figure stood almost calm amidst the chaotic battle, looming over the men and women around it by a foot of height, if not more.

Had the moment not been what it was, Carver would have been thrilled to see a sovereign so close up, but the threat of death overwhelmed his awe. His fear was replaced with absolute terror as Carver watched the sovereign raise its long-fingered hand and fire a white bolt of energy from its palm.

The bolt of white light struck the back of a man who was clashing blades with a Caswen soldier. The man's head shot back as his limbs went stiff, causing his grasp on his sword to tighten beyond reason. The soldier whom the man was fighting stepped back in horror, turning his head to see the source of his opponent's state. Without so much as a sound, the struck man fell to the ground, dead before he made contact.

Carver watched as another blast of white energy shot out of the sovereign's hand, this time striking a woman who was fending off two soldiers by herself in a losing struggle. Just like the previous person, the woman's body went rigid at the moment of impact. Instead of slumping to the ground, however, her stiff, upright body was impaled by her two attackers' swords. Black smoke rushed out of her wounds as the soldiers pulled their blades from her gut. Instead of blood spilling out onto the ground, the black smoke rose up and faded into the air. When they removed their blades, the woman's body fell backwards onto the cobblestone street, black smoke continuing to escape her insides as if she were hollow.

Carver was stunned and horrified by the sight.

The sovereign continued to unleash bolt after bolt of pallid energy into the bodies of those who crossed blades with the soldiers. The bodies fell in the same way when struck by the bolts, tense and motionless, followed by black smoke pouring from their mouths and wounds.

"Hurry up!" a voice demanded from Carver's right.

Carver turned his attention away from the massacre to see who was speaking. Distracted by the horrific display of sovereign sorcery at work, the thought that the owner of the voice could be an enemy did not cross his mind.

Looking to his right, Carver saw a group of people snatching up the wagon's spilled collection of small crates and sacks a mere three feet away from him. He didn't need to wonder what was in those crates and sacks, as their contents were spilling out into piles as they were grabbed off the ground.

Grain, strips of salted meat, and absol coins of copper, silver, and even a few of gold littered the cobblestones, with many of the absols having had their shards dislodged from their frames and scattered in a mess of wealth.

Carver had no idea how he didn't immediately notice the piles of absols and shards when he scrambled up next to them.

"Grab as much as you can run with! We need to make this worth it!" a woman's voice ordered.

Carver counted eight of them, five men and three women, humans all, with swords and daggers buckled to their belts in leather sheaths, all scrambling to gather the spilled goods that had been expelled from a smoking hole on the wagon's far end.

Still sitting there, motionless and in shock, Carver watched as the band of armed citizens rounded up a small array of mostly intact crates and sacks and stuffed their pockets with handfuls of loose grain, absols, and shards.

The man closest to Carver suddenly became aware of the boy's presence. He dropped the crate he was holding and drew his short dagger from its sheath as the corner of the wooden crate split against the cobblestones.

A woman standing behind the man looked up from her task at the sound of the wooden crate smashing. She locked eyes with Carver, but instead of pulling out a weapon, as the man had done, she frowned in frustration. "Ignore him! He's not a problem!" she barked at the man holding the dagger.

"But we're supposed to leave civilian bodies behind!" the man replied.

"Only us working within the guard are! Now help us get these out of here, you fool!"

With agonizing hesitation, the man placed his dagger back in its sheath and then accepted a new crate from the woman. Then he turned and hurried off, following others who were running away from the wagon with whatever they could carry.

The woman and another man remained near the wagon, both picking up the last of the mostly intact crates and untorn sacks, along with any handfuls of absols they could find. The woman turned to face Carver again, but this time she gave him a sad look. She reached into the broken top of the crate she was holding and pulled out a small cloth pouch.

"Here."

She tossed it to him, and Carver caught it in an awkward grip.

"Now get yourself out of here. And I'm sorry," the woman said, then turned away from Carver and ran after her group.

Carver looked down at the pouch in his hands. It was slightly heavy and clinked from within, telling him in an instant that it was full of absols. Confused, he looked up to see where the group of thieves were going. They headed toward one of the brick buildings on the market's perimeter. Its windows and door were boarded up, indicating that it was abandoned.

Carver did not understand what the thieves were thinking by running up to a building they would not be able to enter, but then, to Carver's complete bewilderment, the leading man stopped, held out his hand, and after a handful of seconds, a bright white bolt of energy shot from his palm. The door and the boards that kept it shut shattered inward, collapsing to the ground in large, smoldering pieces.

The first six thieves ran through the doorway and disappeared into the abandoned building.

"They're taking the shipment! Stop them!" a loud male voice bellowed to Carver's left.

Carver looked up and saw the tall sovereign, who had ceased firing magical bolts, pointing a long finger at the shattered door and the thieves who had yet to run inside.

A small band of soldiers rallied around the towering sovereign, seven in all, with swords drawn and surcoats speckled in blood. Five of them ran after the thieves while two broke off and ran toward Carver.

The moment he saw the two soldiers abandon their fellows and charge toward him, Carver hadn't a clue what they were thinking, but in the next second, his mind clicked, and he looked down at his hands. To his immediate panic he realized that he was still holding the pouch of what he assumed to be absols. At that moment Carver lost all sense of feeling in his body as his mind switched from confused panic to total fight-or-flight instinct.

In the briefest of seconds Carver's mind came up with a three-step plan: drop the pouch, stand up, and run.

Carver threw the pouch to the side and quickly pulled himself up to his feet using the tipped wagon's wooden wheel that jutted out above his head. As soon as he was balanced he bolted forward as a new surge of adrenaline shot through his body. He only had one goal in mind: to reach the open doorway of the abandoned building before the soldiers did.

Carver forced his legs to propel him faster than they had energy to do. He knew that this was it, that if he failed now, he would die. One slip on the cobblestone, one trip over anything, one error in footing, and Carver knew he would never see his home or his family again.

The last of the fleeing thieves disappeared through the doorway. The soldiers who pursued them were but two dozen feet from the doorway themselves, nearly between Carver and his only foreseeable escape from death. The other two soldiers who were coming straight for him turned to maintain their pursuit as he crossed the smokeless stretch of courtyard.

Carver noticed the two soldiers pass out of his peripheral vision. He wanted to look over his shoulder to see how close they were, but instead he kept his attention fixed on the door and the larger group of soldiers, who were about to block his access to it. Carver lowered his head and pushed his stamina even further in a desperate attempt to outrun them.

"There's another coming! Don't let him get inside!" a man's voice called from ahead. The voice sounded so close that for a brief instant Carver thought he might crash straight into the group of soldiers, but before he knew it, the smoky daylight turned dark, and the thudding of his boots on the cobblestone turned to the creaking of old wood.

He was inside.

Looking up from his blind charge, Carver was lost for what to do next, as his three-step plan was now over. His immediate thought was that he had won; he had escaped the market and was safe. Carver's delusional comfort was ripped away as soon as it arrived, replaced with a panicked realization that a new plan was needed for escaping the building and the soldiers who had followed him inside.

The speed at which Carver ran gave him no time to formulate another plan, for when he tried to slow down to assess the building's layout, his legs kept going. Unable to stop in time, Carver ran straight into a dusty table in the center of the room.

The heavy table crashed onto its side, with Carver tumbling over it. A cloud of dust and cobwebs flew up, straight into his face and into his eyes and mouth. The thud of the table hitting the old floor was complemented by a barrage of smaller thuds as the soldiers flooded into the building.

Wiping the dust and cobwebs from his face, Carver grabbed the side of the table and pulled himself up. It was dark inside the building, with the only light coming in through the doorway and through a large window at the back of the room, its shutters wide open.

Carver's attention snapped to the window. He didn't know where it led, but he didn't care. It offered a way out, and that was enough for him at that moment.

With fresh pain coming from his hip and foot after his collision with the table, Carver launched himself toward his new goal. His left calf spiked with pain, having snuck through his adrenaline once again, tipping him off balance just enough for him to bump into a large wooden support beam but not enough to cause him to fall. Without a second thought, Carver threw himself out the open window and crashed onto a stretch of dirt three feet below.

Not allowing himself to come to a complete stop, Carver scrambled to his feet and ran as fast as he could. He found himself running down a small alley formed of brick buildings on both sides, with the occasional door or window facing the narrow path.

The sunlight from the gray sky above illuminated the alley well enough for Carver to see ahead, though many shadows climbed up the walls and obscured parts of the path. As he looked ahead he saw the two straggler thieves running ahead of him. However, just as Carver noticed them, they turned right and disappeared.

They knew a way out of the market. Maybe they know a way out of here too, Carver thought in desperation.

It was not as if he felt he had any other choice but to follow them, however, as he could already hear the clinking of chainmail behind him. This time Carver did look back, and he saw the soldiers vaulting through the open window one by one, thankfully slowed by the weight of their armor.

Carver turned his attention forward again. As soon as he reached the spot where the thieves had vanished he turned right as well, immediately finding himself on another narrow street, more akin to an alley, though nearly three times as long as the previous one, with homes forming the walls on each side.

Carver saw all eight thieves up ahead. He ran after them in the hope of being guided to an escape, and for a moment he felt like he was making good progress, but the sudden sound of many running boots from behind him crushed his optimism.

Further crushing Carver's hopes, the thieves broke off into smaller groups and split up down different tight streets that branched off from the alley.

Now who do I follow? Carver wondered as his panic increased.

The exhaustion in his legs was becoming unbearable, and he could feel his pace slowing as the pain in his left calf continued to surpass his draining adrenaline. Without much thought, Carver banked a hard left down a new path and pursued a random pair of the thieves.

"Pair up and go after them! Take them alive if you can!" a male voice shouted behind him.

Carver heard a parade of footsteps pass by the alley he had turned down. Though the sound of heavy boots faded, it did not vanish entirely. What remained was a small collection of thuds. Without turning to see for himself, Carver guessed that two soldiers were still pursuing him.

As Carver felt his speed reducing, the approaching footsteps grew louder from behind. The two thieves ahead of him got farther and farther away, until they too separated down different streets and vanished from his sight. Carver struggled to keep moving, desperately trying to ignore the pain in his left calf, which slowly turned his run into a fast hobble, and the wave of dizziness that was growing behind his eyes. He told himself that if he could just make it to the intersection where the two thieves had split up that he would be safe, thinking the two soldiers behind him would choose the path with only one thief rather than two.

However, Carver quickly realized that he was not going to make it to either alley in time, as his legs wobbled and he heard the running footsteps behind him get even closer. The tiny reserve of adrenaline that still remained in Carver's body was suddenly released when he felt a boot clip the back of his left heel and a hand grab his right shoulder.

In an act of pure panic, Carver threw himself against the alley's left wall and stopped running. The soldier who had attempted to grab his shoulder stumbled past him. Using the brief window of time it took for the soldier to bring himself to a stop, Carver spun around and tried to run back the way he had come from.

"Stop him!" the soldier shouted.

Just as Carver heard the man's words from behind, he found himself faced with the other soldier only a few feet ahead, blocking his attempt at escape. The second soldier drew his sword in a quick yet clumsy motion and held the blade in a threatening manner toward Carver.

Carver stopped his hobbling run and tried to step to the side in order to find some kind of opening to get past the soldier. The man took a half step back but did not lower his weapon. His face looked uneasy, his eyes hesitant.

Realizing he would not be able to slip past the soldier, Carver reached for his dagger, which was still sheathed to his belt. Due to his panic, however, Carver's hand missed its mark and passed by the dagger's grip. He grabbed at the dagger again, this time wrapping his fingers around its grip and drawing the blade quickly, but in the brief time it took him to correct his fumble and arm himself, the soldier behind him was upon him.

Before Carver could react, he felt hands wrap tightly around his upper arms and pull him back. Carver tried to turn his body into his attacker, so he might face him, but the soldier was too fast, slamming him into the brick wall.

Carver managed to hold onto his dagger, but his arms were pushed forward and held against the cold bricks by the soldier behind him, preventing him from retaliating. Despite the soldier's firm hold, however, Carver managed to bend his elbows and push his knuckles into the wall, breaking free.

As Carver spun around, he lowered his dagger and angled the blade upwards, then jabbed the dagger up at the soldier's chest. Due to Carver's haste and his close proximity to the soldier, his strike was awkward and lacked the power he had intended. The dagger stabbed through the man's surcoat but was stopped by the chainmail and gambeson beneath.

Carver attempted to pull his dagger away and stab again, but the soldier grabbed his wrist and held it still.

Carver swung his other fist at the man, but the soldier pushed his open hand against Carver's face and shoved his head into the brick wall behind him. As Carver's head struck the wall, the soldier grabbed his throat, pinning him against the wall while maintaining his grip on Carver's wrist.

As Carver felt his head swell with pain and his throat tighten, his instincts forced him to grab at the soldier's arm with both hands to try to tear it away from his neck. The soldier allowed Carver to retract his dagger-wielding hand, and in doing so pulled the dagger from Carver's hand and threw it to the ground.

As Carver squeezed the soldier's arm and squirmed in an effort to break free, the soldier punched him hard in the ribs. The blow was too fast to carry any substantial force, but it made Carver gasp.

"You bastards!" the soldier screamed in Carver's face.

Carver saw another punch coming, this time with more wind up. He tried to grab the soldier's incoming fist, but he was too slow, and it slammed into his ribs once again.

"Do you have any idea how many people you just killed, you Aethi'ziton terrorist!"

The soldier punched Carver in the ribs a third time, sending a spike of pain through his side that forced him to gasp again, though now even less air reached his lungs as the man squeezed his throat tighter. Carver continued his struggle to pull the man's hand off his throat.

"What kind of sorcery did you monsters unleash back there? You murderers just butchered innocents!"

Carver felt another punch in the ribs as he strained to keep the soldier's hand from strangling him. His strength was waning as the blows to his side kept coming, the pain from each strike growing exponentially. His punctured left leg continued to spasm and bleed as he tried to remain standing during the struggle.

"How can you rebels claim to be fighting for people's freedom—"

The soldier punched Carver in the ribs again.

"—when you murder them like animals!"

He hit Carver again.

"Stop! He's had enough. You'll kill him!"

The soldier stopped his next punch mid-swing and looked to his right. "I should kill him! Look at what he and his comrades did! All that killing just so they could steal a handful of absols and food to continue their rebellion!"

Carver barely heard the man's words as he struggled to prevent himself from being strangled against the wall. His ribs pulsed with throbbing agony, and his left leg threatened to give out amidst the pain from his wound. Carver's thoughts turned to his home and his family and the thought that he might never see either of them again if he could not break free from the soldier's grip. His mind raced for any idea that might save him as his eyes looked straight ahead at the man who was his enemy.

It was then that Carver remembered how the armor of Caswen soldiers left their necks exposed. With that recollection, his eyes focused in on the man's neck, which was indeed visible above the collar of his gambeson.

The soldier looked back at Carver, then wound up for another punch. As the eyes of his attacker locked onto his own, a sudden rush of anger overwhelmed Carver, filling him with the feeling that all he wanted in life was to kill this man.

Before the soldier could swing his fist, Carver growled through clenched teeth, then slid across the wall to his right, shifting his balance and forcing the soldier to turn slightly in order to maintain the pressure on his throat. Then Carver swung his legs up to the left, allowing himself to fall, and the soldier was forced to either hold Carver's entire weight by the throat with one hand or let him fall to the ground.

The soldier chose the latter, releasing Carver's throat as the boy slipped and fell to the ground, but Carver kept both his hands wrapped around the soldier's arm as he fell and heaved with a surge of energy. The soldier was pulled down with Carver, landing on top of him, crushing him with the weight of his body and his armor. He cursed loudly as he was brought down, then started pushing himself up over Carver.

When Carver felt the soldier's weight shift, he realized he was about to lose his chance to make a move. He scrambled to concoct a plan of attack, but in the few brief seconds Carver had, the only exploitable weakness he could see was the soldier's neck. He also realized he had no weapon or even an angle that would allow him to use his hands.

The soldier rose another inch above Carver's body, and Carver panicked. His utter terror of being killed overwhelmed him, and an almost animal instinct took over. He released the soldier's arm and reached out with both hands. He grabbed the soldier by the back of the head and then yanked the man's face back closer to his own. Then Carver sank his teeth into the side of the man's neck.

The man shouted in pain and tried to pull his head away, but Carver clenched his jaw harder, feeling his teeth punch through flesh and sinew. The man screamed again and frantically tried to remove himself from Carver. At that moment, Carver pushed the man's head away while pulling his own head back, his teeth still clenched.

An eruption of blood burst forth from the man's neck as Carver tore out a chunk of fleshy matter with his teeth. The man's blood sprayed Carver's face and neck as well as the ground around his head, and Carver turned his face away to shield his eyes.

The man rolled off Carver and landed on his back. He clutched his neck with both hands as he awkwardly kicked and squirmed on the ground. Blood poured through his fingers and down the back of his hands, and his eyes turned to Carver with pure terror emanating from them.

Carver spat a chunk of red meat from his mouth and rolled over to his stomach. He pushed himself to his feet, feeling a total rush of instinct and violent rage take over, and spun himself around to face the other soldier. The second man was standing but a few feet away, staring in utter shock at Carver and the soldier squirming by his feet. His sword was relaxed in his hand, held down by his side as he looked at Carver with terrified eyes.

Carver screamed with rage and charged the stunned soldier.

The soldier did not raise his sword to protect himself. Instead, he let the weapon fall from his fingers and took a step back.

Carver crashed into the soldier just as the sword hit the ground, sending him toppling backwards. The soldier cried out in fear and covered his throat with his hands as his helmet flew off, revealing a head of short, scruffy blond hair.

Carver pushed himself up from the soldier's chest and began to pummel his exposed face.

"Wai—"

Carver's fists smashed into the man's face.

"Sto—"

Again, Carver's knuckles struck the man's face.

"Plea—"

Carver's assault did not relent.

The soldier let go of his throat and pushed and clawed at Carver's chest, trying desperately to knock or pull him off, but he failed each time.

Again and again Carver hammered his fists into his final challenger's face. He only stopped when his knuckles hurt too much to continue.

Taking advantage of the moment's reprieve, the blond-haired soldier took in a short, pyrrhic breath.

At the sound of the soldier's insistence on survival, Carver raised his aching, bloody fists to continue the beating.

"Wait!"

The sound of the beaten man's voice caught Carver off guard, as it sounded less like a man and more like a teenage boy. Freezing his fists above the soldier's face, Carver waited for another word, despite his instincts telling him otherwise.

A painful-sounding, rasping cough exited the blond soldier's mouth, followed by a spit of blood. His nose was bleeding from both nostrils, sending a stream of blood over his lips, the bottom of which was torn and bleeding heavily.

"Please ... Let me go ... I wasn't going to attack you ..."

Focusing more closely on the soldier's face, beaten and bloody as it was, Carver saw that he appeared much closer to Carver's age than the other soldier, who now lay completely still behind him.

"I was just ... following orders ... I've only been a soldier ... for a month ... I needed the absols ... My family ... I ... I didn't want this ..." the older boy tried to explain through his panicked wheezing and blood-sprinkling coughs.

Carver was unsure if all these excuses were true or not, but then he realized the boy's voice was the same one that had called for the other soldier to stop his beating. He also realized the older boy had not joined his companion in beating him even when he had the opening to do so.

Carver didn't know what he was feeling, and he didn't like it. What he did know, however, was that the pain in his body was coming back as his adrenaline drained from his system. The returning presence of his injuries, now joined by a strong pain that spread across his lower-right ribs and side, reignited Carver's fear and anger, driving him to act without thinking. He grabbed the older boy by the throat with both hands and squeezed.

"I didn't do anything! I'm not part of this! Leave me alone!" Carver screamed into the boy's face as he strangled him.

The helpless boy pushed his hands into Carver's chest and opened his cut lips to speak, but only a desperate choking sound came out.

Carver suddenly released the boy's throat and pushed himself off him, standing up.

The boy coughed and groaned as Carver stepped away from him. After a few seconds of pitiful struggling, the boy looked at Carver and opened his mouth to speak yet again, but Carver was already limping off down the street.

Chapter 6

The evening wind that blew into the manor's high-ceilinged hallway through the open windows on the left wall brought a slight chill to his old bones despite the August heat keeping the wind warmer than most times of the year. He noted to himself that he would need to remember to close the shutters on his way back. Rubbing his arms beneath his gray robe to keep warm, he continued down the long stone hallway toward the large double doors at its end.

The doors were quite impressive, carved from solid oak, with the emblem of a great bear spanning from one side to the other. As he reached the doors, however, he found himself frozen in place, though not from the cooling summer air in the stone hallway. He didn't want to open the doors.

While standing there, his mind wandered to the idea that if there had been any soldiers standing guard in the great hall, they would surely be suspicious of him standing in silence by the doors, or perhaps they would just assume he was a senile old man who had forgotten where he was going.

With a disheartening sigh, he adjusted his gray robe and ran a hand through his receding gray hair. Then he braced his body, and with both hands placed firmly on the center of the wood, he pushed the great doors open.

As the heavy doors, though not so mighty that an old man such as himself couldn't open them, pushed open, the chamber beyond was revealed. It was large and composed mostly of stone. It was nearly a perfect square, with three tall stone pillars on the left and right sides, adding a remarkable look of symmetry.

A human soldier was stationed at the base of each pillar, standing straight and focused with a spear gripped firmly in hand. High above each soldier's helmeted head, chains embedded into the pillars spanned into the center of the room, meeting in a single loop that held a large brazier in place high above the floor. The fire from the brazier illuminated the chamber, save for the spots behind the pillars, which danced with shadows. Beneath the hanging brazier, the stone floor was lacking any rugs or furniture, making the room feel empty and drab despite its grand appearance.

The only other standout in the chamber was the high-backed wooden throne at the far end. The throne's presence was made larger due to the circular dais of stone steps on which it sat. Looming over the impressive seat from behind was a great glass window that took up nearly a third of the back wall and gave a northern view over the city of Caswen and the darkening sky above it.

A middle-aged man was sitting in the large wooden chair. He was dressed finely, sporting a faded yellow doublet with white embroidery down the arms and thick brown fur covering the shoulders. His trousers were dark blue and had similar white embroidery going down the sides until they reached black laced boots. His eyes were deep blue, almost matching his trousers, and stood out on his thin, pale face. Above them was graying brown hair that was combed back and appeared to have been cut recently.

The elegantly dressed man sat in a slumped position with his right arm leaned against the chair's arm, propping his head up. He wore a small silver crown atop his graying head. The silver crown was plain, merely a thick loop with flat sides, but it still gave off a shine when the light of the brazier reflected off it. The crown's aura of majesty was overshadowed by the expression of misery that its wearer wore on his thin face.

At the sound of the large doors opening, the silver-crowned man looked up. "Ah. Hello, Adaman. Come in," he said with a noticeable lack of energy.

Having already entered the chamber, Adaman met the verbal invitation with a small nod as he approached. "Greetings, Magistrate Julius."

Julius did not move a muscle as Adaman approached. "No doubt you have come to tell me about the attack on the market."

Adaman lowered his gaze. "I have, sir. Though, it seems you have already been made aware of the incident."

"Renneil informed me that the Lost Seekers attacked the market, though the rising smoke I saw from the manor had already told me that." Julius gestured his thumb back toward the great window behind his throne. "He told me that you would have more information. Would you be so kind as to inform me of the details?"

"And where is Renneil, if I might ask? Should he not be present in this briefing, since, after all, it is one of his duties as spymaster to help handle these Aethi'ziton insurrections, not just mine as chancellor." Adaman bit his lip, realizing too late that he had let his anxiety and frustration get the better of him.

"Renneil assured me that he is looking into the matter in his own way, as he always does."

Adaman redirected his uncomfortable gaze from Julius to the stone floor, took a deep breath, then looked back up toward the throne. "It was as we expected, my lord," Adaman began. "The rebels ambushed the tax convoy on its way to the docks, just as the intelligence said they would. It seems, however, that the rebels either learned of our acquisition of their plans or, more likely, knew all along, and the plans were intentionally false to misguide us, because despite the information that they would launch the attack somewhere beyond the market to avoid civilian casualties, most of the assault was directed exactly there. Our forces were spread throughout the checkpoints around the city's districts, along the decoy routes, and stationed at the Outer Market to keep things in order there, so those left to guard the city market were left ill prepared and lacking in numbers for such an assault."

Julius's seemingly uninterested face did not change in expression. When it became clear to Adaman that Julius was not going to speak, he reluctantly continued his briefing. "From the brief report I received, it appears the rebels did indeed plan on using the market as the strike point, for when they struck they did so wearing no armor. Instead they wore peasant garb and were armed with small concealed blades. They used the area's high density of civilians and the mass panic the attack created to their advantage. Our soldiers were unable to discern their assailants from the fleeing civilians, and because of this the rebels were able to strike a great many of our soldiers down. When the chaos began, the soldiers stationed at nearby checkpoints heard the commotion and came running to reinforce. The perimeter of the scene was quickly blockaded, and attempts were made to get the civilians out before ... before a massacre unfolded."

Again Adaman paused to allow Julius a chance to respond, but once more he kept silent and waited for more.

"The rebels attacked with a weapon we have not seen or heard of before. As it was described to me by the soldiers who witnessed it, it sounds as if it were some kind of magic, sending out waves of force alongside a loud, crashing bang, essentially out of thin air, spreading flames and leaving smoldering pits in the ground. Many civilians were caught in these sudden, strange blasts, as whatever caused those craters began around the procession of wagons while it was traveling through the center of the market with a large crowd around it. More blasts occurred during the assault, and with the smoke and flames spreading quickly, many people lost their lives in the confusion."

Adaman felt a sickness in his stomach trying to prevent him from continuing. Swallowing uncomfortably, he suppressed the powerful sensation and forced his next words out. "It also appears that many rebels had infiltrated the Caswen Guard and went out of their way to strike fleeing civilians."

"Are you certain?" Julius asked in disbelief as a jolt of energy caused him to sit forward slightly.

Adaman nodded wearily. "Reports indicate that handfuls of our soldiers fled the battle with the rebels as the smoke cleared, and many of our soldiers spoke of their fellows ignoring commands and slaughtering innocents."

The room filled with an excruciating silence.

"Why?" Julius asked, more to himself than to Adaman, and leaned back into his seat. "Why would they do that? Aren't these rebels supposedly fighting to free the people from sovereign rule? If so, why would they target the innocents they claim they want to liberate? To steal the taxes? Is such a meaningless goal worth the death of innocents?"

"I do not think their main goal was to steal from the Sovereign Empire or Terraland Crown, my lord, although such an act will surely help fund and supply their cause. I believe their primary objective was to create a large-scale public incident that would drive a wedge between the people and the ruling authority."

Julius gave Adaman a look that asked him to clarify. Adaman cleared his throat, making a louder sound than he had anticipated due to the utter silence of the large chamber, and thought of how he could explain himself. "It is my assumption that the rebels intended to make it look like our loyal city soldiers were the ones who acted as such, killing innocents without mercy. And due to the manner in which the rebels struck, garbed like commoners and striking at soldiers while acting like bystanders fleeing for their lives, many of our loyal soldiers did strike true civilians out of fear. It was relayed to me that many of our men and women couldn't tell a Lost Seeker from a true commoner and that they saw too many of their comrades fall while attempting to help a fleeing citizen who then suddenly plunged a blade into their back. The situation was chaos, a chaos the rebels played into."

Adaman stopped for a moment to allow Julius to digest the information. When the magistrate appeared to be waiting for more, Adaman continued. "We are caught in a difficult situation, my lord. The people may think we are responsible for this—the soldiers of the Caswen Guard, I mean to say. Without a doubt many of those who escaped are fueling the stories that the City Guard ruthlessly slaughtered everyone to either protect themselves or to ensure no rebels escaped, a brutal justification to be sure, if it were the case, and I'm sure it might have been in some instances. But if we try to discredit this falsehood and lead with the evidence that these actions were primarily carried out by the Lost Seekers, operating within the ranks of the City Guard to sow dissent between our soldiers and the people, we would only be telling our citizens that their protectors have been infected with terrorists, that the City Guard is plagued by the very rebels it is supposed to be eradicating. Not everyone would believe this explanation, however, and those who did would lose trust in us."

Another long silence fell over the room.

"How many?" Julius inquired dryly, shattering the overbearing silence.

"Sir?"

"How many are dead? How many lives were lost to this failure?"

"It's too soon for an accurate count, but from the first reports they've rounded the suspected number of bodies within the market to around two hundred, with close to forty confirmed as Lost Seekers so far by those who saw them draw blades or fought them themselves. Our soldiers are still counting, however." Adaman found it impossible not to return his gaze to the stone floor.

Once again the chamber was silent. The only proof to Adaman that he had not gone deaf was the sound of his own teeth grinding together inside his head.

"Two hundred dead, with less than half being actual rebels," Julius said, as if speaking to himself again.

Adaman wanted to leave, to resign as chancellor, if only to escape this horrid ordeal, but he couldn't. He knew he had to continue. "There is more, sir." Adaman decided it best not to look at Julius as he continued. "Of the three sovereigns accompanying the tax convoy, one ... one of them was killed during the ambush."

The silence in the room seemed to enhance tenfold, leaving only the sound of Adaman's heartbeat to comfort him.

"When will they be here?" Julius asked.

Adaman forced himself to look back up at the magistrate, who was now holding his face in his other hand. "They should arrive any minute, sir."

Not another word was spoken between them. They both remained motionless and silent. The soldiers stationed at each pillar also kept quiet, with only a single cough interrupting the silence from a female soldier standing at the pillar closest to the chamber's open door.

Moments later, the solemn silence of the empty chamber was interrupted by the sound of clacking steps coming down the cold stone hallway behind Adaman.

Without taking his eyes off the floor, Adaman ascended the dais and took his place next to the throne.

The clacks became louder and louder, each one causing the white wisps of hair on the back of Adaman's neck to stand up. Then the sound suddenly ceased.

Adaman felt like he was no longer in control of his body as his head rose to view that which stood before him as he struggled to keep his focus on the floor. He heard the newcomer speak before his eyes were able to focus.

"Why did this happen?" a deep male voice asked. The voice was loud and powerful, filling the empty chamber.

There, standing in the very spot Adaman had just vacated, were two towering beings. Their skin was pale, much like his own, though a little darker in complexion. Their eyes were large and strange, and their lack of lips, ears, and noses made it impossible to mistake them for anything else. Their foreign, black-inked facial markings further amplified their strange appearance.

Each was wearing a matching set of pearl-tinted armor with black mail covering the joints. Their armor gleamed as the light of the brazier bounced off the folds of polished metal, while the black mail seemed to drink in the light. Turquoise grooves and inlays were visible all along the armor, running over the shoulders and across the smooth chest plate, looking like fine penmanship. The armor reached down to their waists where their sheathed swords were buckled, and their robes beneath their armor hung down to cover their legs.

Adaman knew, however, that the robes were no mere wool garb like he wore but rather a fine linen that also covered their torsos under the armor, a garment known as chiton. The white linen chiton hung down to just above their feet, secured to their legs with fine lace, allowing their bare feet, though they looked like anything but feet, to be fully visible.

Adaman was always disturbed by the appearance of the sovereigns' gray, X-shaped feet and the sharp, inch-long claw at each of the four ends. What he found even stranger was the fact that their feet seemed to be bone-like, almost metallic in nature due to their gray color, causing an eerie clinking noise to accompany each step they took, like a hammer striking stone.

Adaman heard a sad sigh come from Julius beside him, followed by the same monotone voice as before. "What do you mean?" Julius asked, though it was clearly not a real question.

"You and those in your command told us that everything was under control, that the intelligence you acquired ensured no harm would befall the shipment as it passed through the city toward the harbor," the sovereign said. "It seems you are either a liar or a fool, each of which is equally concerning to us."

"You fully blame us, do you? Were you not told that three sovereigns and your monstrous scaly mounts escorting the real convoy would draw attention to it? That the whole plan was to shift the danger onto the decoys in controlled paths? Had the three of you not disregarded our warnings, perhaps this disaster could have been avoided."

Adaman cringed at the way the silver-crowned magistrate addressed the two sovereigns.

"You dare try to blame us!" the sovereign roared. "You humans are under no authority to instruct us about anything, especially one such as you, who has been a constant and consistent disappointment to us. You're the magistrate of this province, and it is you who is responsible for this critical failure by your people. These rebellious Lost Seekers, or Aethi'ziton, as they call themselves in your dead language, are citizens within your province, citizens who took up arms against the empire to which you owe fealty. Worse yet, their assault was aided by the forbidden use of sorcery, revealing that sorcerers are running free within your lands, violating one of the empire's greatest laws. Much of the tax shipment was also taken by these rebels, and we expect the lost amount to be replaced without delay."

Adaman was surprised that the sovereign did not mention his fallen comrade among his list of grievances.

Julius finally sat up straight and shuffled his body as if to get comfortable. "And how are we to remedy the amount lost?" he asked, his tone betraying a hint of frustration. "With the current tax increase in the empire's favor, we barely have enough for the Isles as it is, and even less once we send what is expected of us to the Crown in Keldaria. How am I supposed to keep this province running with so few absols in its treasury and the lack of harvest in its granaries? Times are strained more than ever, and winters do not get any easier with stockpiles as low as they are now. The people you expect to supply these yearly taxes are poor, hungry, and terrified, even more so now after such a massacre."

"The civilian deaths in the market were not our wish," the same sovereign replied, "but neither are they our concern, nor should they be yours. Your focus should be the eradication of the Lost Seekers, as it should be with all Terraland's magistrates to erase these rebels from every corner of this land. To maintain the prosperity and order of each realm, sacrifices from its leaders and citizens must be made, sacrifices that you too are expected to make so that the empire to which you are a part of shall continue to be one of peace and security. We do not care how you manage your responsibilities, only that you do. If these incidents continue, we shall be forced to deem the Isles as lost, after which we will deal with it severely, along with everyone who lives here, to ensure the total eradication of the rebel threat that these islands pose to the empire."

After a great sigh, Julius's voice devolved back into its normal, solemn state. "And with what resources am I to purge this rebel threat? I lack the funds to outfit and supply a proper provincial army, which leaves me lacking the manpower needed to protect and patrol the whole of the Isles, let alone Caswen. I am without the support of my people, many of whom go as silent as the grave at inquiries about the Lost Seekers. Those that know something about the Lost Seekers or their activities fear their ire should they cooperate with the soldiers, or the executioner's axe if they are suspected of knowing too much to not be involved themselves. Those that know nothing fear being dragged into the chaos by either side and wish to simply live their lives and work their lands, though each day more of the common folk find that goal unachievable. Of those slain at the market today, I hear not even a fourth were among the rebels responsible for the attack." Julius's words echoed the impression of defiance, but the tone in which they were used diminished that effect, sounding more like defeated excuses than a justified argument.

The sovereign who had previously remained silent spoke up, having a much calmer, though still deep, voice. "If you claim your position as magistrate of the Isles ineffective and your province lost to treason and rebellion, then the empire will have no choice but to wipe the Isles from existence, both physically and from history, just as it did to the tartaruns that plagued your lands so long ago. The stability of Terraland, as well as all other kingdoms within Gaia and the Sovereign Empire, will not suffer the spread of these rebels due to your impotence."

"Will not suffer the spread?" Julius said, though it was clearly not a question. "To my knowledge, the Lost Seekers and their rebellion originated on mainland Terraland, a rebellion that has already grown ripe within the seams of even the Dwarven Commonwealth and the Mahkouan Colony Kingdoms, just as it has in Terraland. So much so that you have taken to transporting the Isles' tax across the Audria Channel to the mainland of Gaia under the escort of your ships for fear of rebel piracy."

"The Sovereign Empire fears nothing!" the first sovereign shouted while clenching his right foot in anger, the gray talons piercing the chamber's stone floor and kicking up specks of rubble. "Especially not some rebellion led by misguided terrorists hell bent on plunging its own realms and people into chaos and disorder. We sovereigns graced you lesser races with knowledge and safety within the rule of our vast empire, an empire that blankets all of Gaia and your existence with protection and order. Only beasts fight against peace and law, and the Sovereign Empire does not fear beasts. Whether or not humanity reveals itself to be nothing but unworthy beasts or grateful, obedient citizens, the emperor and the Council will be greatly reconsidering the role you northern humans have in the empire's future!"

"That won't be necessary!" a female voice called out from the hall behind the two sovereigns.

Everyone but Julius turned toward the source of the voice. Instead, he seemingly ignored it and resumed his slumped position on his throne, leaning his head against the knuckles of his hand.

From the long hall strode a tall young woman with bright brown eyes and shoulder-length hair that warmed the cold feel of the room with its light, coppery-brown color.

Beside her walked a young man with a clean-shaven face and a head of short blond hair who could not have been more than eighteen. The young man was wearing a soldier's uniform, minus the iron helmet. All of his other qualities were overshadowed by his bruised and bloody face.

The wounded soldier stopped at the sight of the sovereigns, too terrified to approach them, but the woman grabbed him by the shoulder of his surcoat and pulled him along.

The woman also wore the uniform of a soldier, also minus the helmet, but hers was much more intricate, with iron pauldrons strapped over her surcoat's shoulders, and iron plates that reinforced the mail that covered her knees and wrists. Her surcoat also stood out amongst those worn by the other soldiers in the room. Instead of gray, hers was a faded crimson. Over her right breast, just above the bear's head profile emblem in the center of her surcoat, was a black hexagon sewn into the wool, with five pieces of six filled.

"Aellia, I was wondering when my marshal would arrive," Julius said, his eyes resting on her. "What is it you say?"

Aellia stopped just ahead of the sovereigns, standing off to the left side of the room. The terrified young soldier trembled beside her.

"We have uncovered the location of a base of operations for the Lost Seekers," she announced. "While nothing found on the slain rebels in the heart of the market revealed any substantial information, this young soldier followed a group of the Lost Seekers out of the area and learned that at least some of them came from Verrel."

The room fell silent for a moment.

"Verrel?" Julius asked. "If I'm not mistaken, after having spent considerable time with the treasurer last month going over the province's records in preparation for today, Verrel is that hunting village on the eastern border of Vellum Forest? It's the smallest mapped settlement within the Isles, barely able to be called a village, let alone be a base of operations for the Lost Seekers. Based on the treasurer's reports, the population wasn't more than a hundred."

Julius looked down at the young soldier next to Aellia, unable to discern if his face was redder from fright or bluer from bruises. "What is your name, boy? And what evidence did you find that links such a small village to this attack?"

The boy took a second to respond, first trying to contain his nervous trembling. "My name is Kieran, my lord. One ... one of the rebels, sir ... he ... I pulled this from him while he was on top of me."

Kieran extended his arm and opened his hand, revealing a small square pin made of iron with three "I's" inlaid on it. He looked up at Aellia and received a piercing glare from her brown eyes, then looked away as he continued. "He murdered my comrade and beat me, sir. A group of the Lost Seekers looted one of the convoy wagons near the market's south exit and used a series of back streets and abandoned buildings to escape. A detachment of us chased them, but they planned their escape well. They split up down individual alleys and streets, forcing us to divide our efforts and pursue them in smaller groups."

"And the Lost Seeker who you got this identification pin from, he killed your comrade and beat you this badly? Why did he or his comrades not kill you as he did your companion?" Julius inquired.

"He fell behind the others, my lord. By the time we caught up to him he was alone. He didn't kill me because ... I ... I don't rightly know, my lord."

"Did he say anything to you? Make any claims or let slip any information that further connects him to Verrel besides an Outer Market identification pin?"

Again, Kieran looked up at Aellia and received the same stern glare. He turned back to Julius. "No. No, he never said a word to me, my lord."

"The boy speaks the truth, my lord," Aellia said. "We have confirmation of this from multiple soldiers who pursued the same group of rebel thieves. It seems that Verrel has been harboring terrorists who are against Terraland and the Sovereign Empire for some time." She gestured toward the sovereigns as she mentioned the empire, each of whom was listening intently. "With your permission, my lord, I will lead a detachment of Caswen's finest to purge the village of Lost Seekers and wipe out any threat therein. It is my hope that we shall find further information there that will lead us to the heart of these traitors' operations within our province." She directed each word to the silver-crowned lord with acute focus.

Julius leaned forward, showing a concern unfitting of his weak tone. "Just like that? You would put a village to the sword based on an identification pin and nothing more? Could the Lost Seekers not be wearing such pins in order to give us misinformation, to escape under the blame of another or even to sow paranoia and confusion by falsely linking settlements to themselves? It seems the Lost Seekers are already in the business of surrendering false intelligence, if what happened today is any indication. Was it not you and your soldiers who discovered the rebel plans surrounding today's attack, the plans that, as I was informed, set us up to prepare for the exact opposite of what happened today?"

He eyed Aellia intently. She returned Julius's gaze, although she said nothing in reply. After a moment of silence, Julius leaned back in his seat and turned his attention toward the two sovereigns. "What do you two think on this matter? For as we all know, the decisions of humanity are not made by humans."

After a second passed, the sovereign who had been leading the discussion turned to the marshal. "Burn it to the ground. Learn what you can from its inhabitants and then eliminate them, all of them. An example must be set. It is the responsibility of each settlement to root out any traitors within and staunch the threat of rebellion. Failure to do so indicates the people there are knowingly harboring these rebels or actively involved in the rebellion themselves."

The sovereign turned back to Julius. "We shall not allow such hideous acts of treason to flower in these lands. We shall depart tonight, along with the navel escort for the tax ships to the continent, which will have the entirety of the empire's tribute. The amount you failed to deliver will be taken from the province's share. It is the sacrifice you will make to sustain the peace and order we provide you."

The sovereign looked at Aellia with a cold glare that almost made her take a step back, but she held steady, waiting for the sovereign's next words.

"Do not fail in this task."

Without another word, both sovereigns turned and walked out, neither desiring a response nor addressing the magistrate's previous concern, leaving behind only a softening echo of hard clacks from each step they made down the stone hall until only dreadful silence remained.

Chapter 7

❧

Carver awoke to a comforting sight: the thatched ceiling of his small bedroom. He was lying in his bed, which was little more than a straw-stuffed mattress on the dirt floor, tucked beneath a thin sheet. He stared up at the familiar ceiling for a moment, allowing his eyes to adjust to the dim light that came from a nearly consumed candle on the floor to his left. As the haziness of waking up began to subside, Carver sat up.

His calm effort was abruptly ceased as a sharp pain erupted from his mid-section. Wincing in pain, he tore off the sheet that covered his body to see what had caused him such pain.

To Carver's surprise he saw that he was wearing only his pair of knee low braies along with a thick layer of bandaging wrapped around the middle of his left leg. His exposed torso revealed a large bruise, surrounded by lesser bruises, that stretched over much of the area around his lower-right ribs, reaching around part of his back and climbing as high as his breast with dark-blue and purple discoloration.

The area of bandaging that covered his left calf was stained dark red and had allowed trace amounts of red to seep through into the straw of his bed.

Remaining still for a moment, Carver checked himself over with his eyes and his hands, looking for any signs of further bandaging or bruises. He found no more bruises, but he found more bandages wrapped around his head, pinning his semi-long brown hair to his scalp. The bandage around his head was lighter than that around his left leg, and it only felt slightly damp on the right side just above his temple.

It all came flooding back to him at once: the chaos at the market, running for his life, and, worst of all, the pain. A horrible ache boomed beneath Carver's bruises, and a splitting headache came to life, emanating from the right side of his head. His left calf also began to pulse with sharp pain, and one of his lower-right ribs hurt intensely above the others.

Carver fell back onto his mattress, his head striking his straw-filled pillow. As he fought the pain returning to his body, he realized he had no memory of how he got there. A burst of confusion and fear barged into Carver's head, but his horrible headache prevented him from even trying to remember any of the details.

"Carver?" a weary voice asked from the left side of his room.

Carver turned toward it, pulling the sheet over his legs and lower torso at the realization that someone else was in the room.

There, lifting her head from its sleeping position on a small, thin table against the far wall, was Helena. Her sleepy eyes opened wide with shock when she saw him.

"Helena?" Carver exclaimed, his voice strained.

She sprang up from the stool she had been sitting on and dashed over to Carver's bed. She dropped to her knees and hugged him tightly from his left side. A small pop came from Carver's lower-right side as Helena squeezed his aching body.

"Augh! Off me!" Carver wheezed, feeling as if one of his ribs had moved.

Helena pushed herself off from Carver, suddenly remembering the fragile state he was in.

"Oh, shit, I'm sorry!" she gasped. "Are you okay?"

Carver took a moment to respond, letting the pain that emanated from his lower-right side pass from excruciating to mild. After a fit of groans and deep breaths, Carver found the strength to speak again.

"What happened ... How did I get here?"

"You don't remember?"

Carver returned his gaze to the ceiling. "I remember limping down an alley in the city. I was lost, I think. I felt like I was going to pass out. I think I did pass out. Then I woke up here." He turned back to Helena, who had gotten up and brought over the small stool from the other side of the room. "Wait. Helena … how did you get here?"

Helena placed the small stool next to Carver's bed and sat down. "Some kind of … I don't know what to call it. A force like a strong wind separated us. It came from whatever was creating those loud bangs and destroying everything, I think. It knocked us apart, and I hit my head." Helena tilted her head and showed Carver a purple bruise stretching past her temple and onto her forehead. "By the time I recovered my senses and got up, I realized you weren't with me. Everything was going crazy. There was fire and smoke and people fighting all over the place. I couldn't see you anywhere with all the smoke blowing around, and I didn't know what to do. I panicked and just ran."

Helena looked at the floor for a moment in shame before she returned her gaze to Carver. "I ran back to the Outer Market as fast as I could to find our parents and get help. Everyone in the Outer Market was just catching wind of what was happening and were starting to panic. I found our parents and told them that I lost you in the Inner Market, and then we all ran into Caswen to find you. Or rather, we would have, if you hadn't appeared when you did. Before we made it to the gate, we saw you hobble out from within. You were covered in blood and limping, so you immediately stood out amongst the crowd that was running out of the city. When you saw us, you collapsed. We picked you up and fled back home. Your mom raced here with you on a horse while the rest of us stayed behind to pack up and follow. She got back to Verrel way before us. I heard that when she arrived, her horse nearly collapsed from exhaustion. She must have had it in full gallop the whole way back. You were still unconscious when the rest of us got back hours later. I thought you were going to die."

Carver could not recall anything past limping through the dark alleyways and tight streets behind and between Caswen's tall brick and stone buildings. It all felt so far away in time. Becoming aware of the growing silence caused from his deep thinking, Carver brushed the fuzzy memories from his mind and looked back at Helena.

"Where's my mom and dad?"

"They're asleep. Everyone except those on watch tonight are. Like I said, you've been out for a long time. Agon pulled Aol down a few hours ago."

"Then what are you doing here?"

Helena tried to hide it by looking down, but Carver was still able to see the clever smirk formed by her lips. "I snuck in."

Looking back up at Carver, her smirk evaporated into concern. "I couldn't sleep not knowing if you would still be alive in the morning. I've been sitting here next to you since our wagons got back. My parents wanted me home after dark, saying that you needed privacy and rest and that you were going to be fine, but I couldn't do it. So yeah, I snuck back in and have been waiting for you to wake up. What happened to you, Carver? You were covered in blood when we found you. How did you end up like that, and like this?" Helena placed a concerned hand against Carver's chest.

Carver hissed in pain at her touch, causing her to recoil.

"Sorry," she said, giving an apologetic smile.

Carver waited for the pain to subside before speaking. He wondered if he should kick Helena out of his room to prevent her from causing him even more pain, but he knew that she would not listen. So, preparing his wounds for a few more pokes and prods from his concerned friend, Carver transitioned some of his energy to his vocal muscles.

"That force that separated us, whatever it was, well, it knocked me farther into the market. My head hit the ground so hard that I'm surprised I didn't get knocked out. I tried to find you, but I couldn't. There was too much smoke and chaos. I didn't even know where I was. I tried to find my own way out through all the fighting, but every time I tried, soldiers and the people they were fighting got in the way. Eventually, I was able to escape through an abandoned building that some of the thieves went through."

"Thieves?" Helena asked.

"A group of people were stealing bags of absols and other things that spilled from one of those armored wagons. I saw them run into a building, like they knew it led out of the market. I think one of them was a sorcerer. I saw a man in the lead hold up his hand and shoot some kind of light out of his palm, just like one of the sovereigns was doing. The building's boarded-up door shattered, and they all ran inside. I figured that was my only way out, so I followed them, but I ended up getting chased by soldiers who were after the thieves. Two of the soldiers caught me. One of them ... He's the one who did this." Carver hovered his hand over top of his bruised right side.

Helena made to reach forward and touch Carver's torso again, as if his gesture was somehow an invitation, but Carver grabbed her wrist to prevent another incident. He released it when he saw her eyes open in realization of what she was doing and was grateful to see Helena pull her hand back to her side.

"How did you get away from him?" Helena asked with dire interest.

Carver paused for a second, allowing his mind to recall the answer. "I ... I killed him. Most of the blood I was covered in was probably his. I ... ripped his throat out with my teeth. The other one I beat and left behind when I ran." He spoke slowly, seemingly shocked by his own words and recollection.

Helena's body went still, and her eyelids seemed to disappear as her eyes widened. "You ... killed him?" she whispered. Before Carver could confirm his answer, Helena continued. "I can't believe ... I mean ... Carver ... By Cosom." The muscles in her face relaxed, and her shocked expression returned to one of concern. "Well, I'm glad you did. He would have killed you if you hadn't; I'm sure of that," she said, albeit uncomfortably, then grabbed Carver's left hand and lifted it up slightly from the bed.

Carver reacted with a jolt, expecting Helena to place her other hand on one of his injured areas again. He calmed at the realization that it was only his hand she wanted, which made him feel rather strange. A hot tingle ran through his fingers and down his spine as Helena's hand wrapped around his, causing him to experience anxiety, relief, and an odd sensation of happiness.

"How do you feel?" she asked, holding his left hand a few inches above his chest.

Letting the feeling of strangeness pass from his mind, Carver focused on the comforting touch from Helena's hand around his. "I feel fine," he lied.

Helena smiled with a look that suggested she actually believed him. Then her eyes panned down to where she firmly held Carver's hand and she abruptly released it as an expression of surprise washed over her face, causing his hand to drop to his chest.

Carver winced as his hand smacked the edge of his bruises, holding back the urge to curse at Helena for adding to his pain.

"Oh, by Dema's ass. I—ah, I'm sorry, Carver. I, um. I didn't mean to …"

With much effort, Carver formed a pleasant smile, trying to ignore the sting from his bruises among the pain from his other injuries. "It's fine, Helena. You should probably go get some sleep. I'm sure I'll still be alive in the morning." A kinder way of telling her to get out and stop hurting him, Carver did not know. Helena took his request at face value and rose from the stool. "Okay, goodnight, Carver," she said, seemingly embarrassed by her actions, though still showing relief. "I'll see you in the morning."

Helena opened the door to Carver's room and slipped out, pulling it closed behind her. Before the door came to a complete close, however, she stuck her head through the gap. "Don't tell your or my parents that I snuck in here, okay?" she whispered. "They'll probably get really mad at me."

Carver, who already had his eyes closed and his bedsheet brought up to his collarbone, replied with a simple thumbs-up, then pulled his hand back under the sheet. His gesture was followed by the sound of the door clicking shut.

With Helena gone, Carver had only the dim light of the bedside candle and his aching body to share the room with. The pain and soreness throughout his body was bothersome as he tried to relax, but his exhaustion was greater, and after only a short time of painful discomfort, he fell into a deep, fatigued sleep.

Chapter 8

❧

The uncomfortable heat was the first thing Carver noticed as he opened his eyes. It was only after he tried to take a breath that he also noticed the lack of air in his room. Inhaling naught but a thick cloud of smoke, his lungs contracted violently, forcing him to sit up in his bed and burst into a fit of harsh coughing before he was even fully awake. While failing to achieve any relief, Carver was suddenly confronted by another hindrance: he couldn't see.

With an unintentional second breath brought forth by his shriveling lungs, Carver felt even more thick smoke funnel down his windpipe. Carver tossed himself from his bed, meeting the packed dirt floor with a thud. The forgotten pain from his injuries resurfaced in an instant, spreading throughout his body.

Unable to shout due to the lack of oxygen in his lungs, Carver responded to the pain with a fit of coughing. Each cough sent a surge of agony into his bruised side. Forcing his coughing to cease with excruciating effort, Carver managed to hold what little of his breath he had remaining.

Looking around frantically, Carver could see almost nothing but heavy smoke. His eyes stinging, he had enough sense to remember where the door to his room was in relation to his bed. He crawled awkwardly toward it.

He was met with confirmation of his judgment by the crack beneath his door as well as the feeling of hot air flowing from it. Carver reached up to where he knew the handle should be and pulled.

As the door creaked open, a wave of intense heat assaulted Carver's face, reminding him of the fiery blasts from the market. He closed his eyes and braced himself as the painful heat pushed against his face.

What's going on? The front door! I need to get outside! his mind screamed. Once accustomed to the heat that assaulted him, Carver opened his eyes to assess his situation.

Fire.

It was the only word Carver could think of upon seeing his home's common room. The heavy smoke was less prevalent due to the two windows on the south wall that, despite having their shutters closed, allowed much of the smoke to slip through, though most of the ceiling was still obscured. The lack of smoke compared to what he had suffered from in his bedroom allowed Carver to see the utter chaos his home was in.

Fire climbed up the room's walls, the kitchen hearth and the large pot held within were blocked by a stretch of flame, and the old table and chairs in the center of the room were covered in burning thatch, as was much of the dirt floor. Carver looked across the room to where the door of his parents' room was, but a great pile of burning thatch blocked it with rising smoke.

Unable to bear the burning in his lungs any longer, Carver released his hold on his respiratory muscles and took a deep breath. This time instead of smoke, Carver felt air going into his lungs. Though the relief of oxygen was great, the burning he felt in his throat quickly seized his attention. Carver cut his breath short as the hot air entering his body brought with it too much pain for him to continue inhaling.

Now refueled with a less than adequate half breath, Carver scrambled across the dirt floor, avoiding the patches of burning thatch but still feeling hot tips of flame whip his exposed skin as he brushed past. He hurried under the table and tried to take another breath. Once again, hot air came into his lungs, and he cut the breath short.

Just as Carver was about to begin crawling again, he heard a loud cracking sound from above, and a chunk of burning wood and thatch crashed onto the dirt floor just ahead of him. A flurry of embers shot out of the pile and struck Carver's face. He recoiled and fell to the side as the embers pricked his skin.

He bared his teeth and forced himself back to his knees and hands. The path directly ahead of him was now blocked, so he dragged himself around the burning obstacle.

Popping and crackling was all Carver could hear as he pulled his knees across the floor. A moment later he found himself exactly where he wanted to be: at the front door of the common room. He battled intense pain along his side as he reached up for the handle. This time, however, he was spared the wave of heat when the door flew open. Instead, a gust of cold air cooled his face.

Had Carver's eyes been closed, he would have been relieved to have access to fresh air, but what he saw diminished his victory almost instantly.

Verrel was in chaos.

Flames engulfed many of the nearby cottages, and handfuls of bodies were scattered around the blood-splattered grass. Carver felt like he was back at the Inner Market. Further resembling his past experience, he saw groups of soldiers, each wearing the armor of the Caswen Guard, running through the area and clashing blades with villagers. The brightness caused by the massive fires throughout the village gave Carver the impression that it was the middle of the day, with the sky only appearing black because of the thick smoke, but the stars that looked down at him, along with the two full moons nearly side by side in the black sky, stated otherwise.

After taking in another much-needed breath, Carver fought back the shock that threatened to lock him in place and stood up. The events unfolding before him distracted him from the pain in his left calf. Instead of pain, Carver was filled with horror.

He stepped away from the burning cottage that used to be his family's home and tried to figure out what the next second would bring. He was snapped out of his daze when he noticed his mother's auburn hair whipping violently from side to side two dozen feet away from him. Turning his attention to what he recognized to be his mother's back, Carver paled when he processed the sight.

Two male soldiers were swinging short blades in wide arcs at Velanna, barely missing her each time. Lying behind and around Velanna were the bodies of several villagers, along with their dropped weapons or farming tools, which they had used as weapons.

Among the scattered bodies was one that stood out to Carver: a man with short brown hair who was still gripping a blood-drenched sword in his left hand.

Carver had never seen his father so still before.

At that moment Carver felt more pain than all of his wounds combined. His heart filled with a sensation of deep despair, sending a cold chill through his veins.

Just then, he heard a scream. He looked up in time to see his mother's large dagger exiting the throat of one of the two men attacking her.

The wounded man collapsed to his knees and clutched his throat, dropping his sword as his eyes opened wide in horror. The remaining man ignored his comrade's fall and continued to slash at Velanna. His swings were fast but clumsy. Velanna was able to predict where each swing would end and stepped out of the way each time while she slashed at her assailant with fast cuts. Most of her dagger's strikes landed uselessly against the soldier's chainmail, cutting through his surcoat each time, but some well-timed lunges landed a few cuts across his exposed face.

The soldier was unable to maintain his position against Velanna's fast maneuvers without his partner, and he began to back up, his strikes becoming defensive rather than offensive. Velanna did not let up, jabbing and slashing at him with much more power and momentum.

Carver was transfixed by his mother's struggle. His instincts told him to run to her aid, but he did not want to startle her and cause a lapse in her focus. If he made his presence known, he knew she would change her priorities from fending off her enemy to protecting Carver, and he did not want to take up any of his mother's fighting energy. Instead, he made to run toward his motionless father. He made it only a handful of steps, however, before his left leg spasmed in pain, and he tumbled into the grass. Carver pushed himself to his knees and saw a dark-red blotch expanding from under the bandages that covered his left calf.

Carver turned away from his injury and forced himself to crawl toward his father, his mind racing with thoughts of what he would have to do depending on his father's condition.

First, I'll pull him to safety. Then I'll check and see if he's injured. If he is, I'll get bandages from the cottage and help him.

Upon reaching his father, however, Carver found himself with no memory of how to apply the aid that he had just planned to perform. As if some unnatural force had wiped away his knowledge, his plan was suddenly gone. Seeing that his father's eyes were open, staring blankly into the sky, gave Carver a burst of frightful adrenaline. He pushed himself to his knees next to his father, panic surging within.

"Dad! Dad!" Carver cried as he grabbed his father by the shoulders and shook him.

Bran did not respond. Carver's panic increased, and he decided he needed to get his father somewhere safe. He stood up as best as he could, gripped his father under the arms, and attempted to drag his body away, but he only managed to move it a few steps before collapsing to the ground with a loud cry as a jolt of pain stabbed into his left calf.

Ignoring the pain, he tried to stand up, but the pain in his calf spiked again, and he fell forward. His hands lunged out to catch himself and ended up landing on his father's chest, only for his right hand to slip forward along the blood and plunge into a deep wound in his father's gut.

Removing his hand in horror, Carver was forced to acknowledge the chasm of a wound that expanded across his father's belly. He wanted to scream, cry, break something, and pass out all at once, but he was unable to accomplish any of those things. All Carver could do was stare at the horrific split in his father's gut and the river of red that escaped from it, further drowning the grass in blood.

"Carver?"

The voice barely made it into Carver's ears.

Somehow tearing his gaze from his father's wound, Carver saw his mother running toward him, her dagger dripping with blood and her eyes a mixture of panic and anger. As she got closer, Carver saw her face go pale.

"No!" Velanna screamed.

Carver realized the soldier she had been fighting was lying motionless on the ground a few feet from his motionless partner. The comfort of knowing that his mother had survived the two-on-one assault was insignificant compared to the unwanted truth that Carver was now looking for any way to deny.

He did not know what to do with his eyes. He found it painful to watch his mother's approach, her face confirming what Carver's brain fought to deny. At the same time, he found the thought of returning his eyes to the source of his grief even more painful, so he kept them locked on his mother.

Velanna opened her mouth to scream once more, but only a drained gasp came forth. She fell to her knees, dropped her dagger in the grass, and placed her hands on the sides of her husband's face.

Bran's skin was warm to Velanna's touch, but his frozen stare into the nothingness beyond her ear chilled her palms. Velanna's mouth remained open as she stared into her husband's lifeless eyes. Tears streamed down her face in rivulets. Then she looked up at the sky and let out a scream of rage. The sound caught Carver off guard, filling him with fear.

Velanna turned toward her son, her face full of emotion. "Carver! We need to—" Velanna's words ceased as her gaze fixed on something behind her son.

Carver looked over his shoulder and saw that their cottage was now engulfed in flames and collapsing at the east end.

"By Cosom!" his mother cried. "It wasn't on fire when—"

As Carver stared at the burning ruins of his home, hands gripped him from under his arms and hoisted him to his feet, sending pain through his calf and his ribs. Carver turned his attention back to his mother and saw that it was her who had pulled him to his feet. She squeezed his upper arms and stared him in the face with a look of grief and anger.

"Carver! We need to go, now!" Velanna shouted as she released Carver's arms, scooped up her dagger, then pulled him forward.

Carver didn't make it more than a few steps before his left leg burst with pain and he fell to the ground, breaking his mother's grip on his arm. He heard her growl and then felt her hand wrap around his right arm.

"Get up!" she shouted as she dug her fingers into his arm and pulled him up.

Carver gritted his teeth and reached out for his mother's shoulders for support, but she was already moving before he could stabilize himself, and he twisted around and fell onto his back.

"Fuck!" Velanna howled as Carver broke from her grasp a second time.

Carver saw the glint of something metal land on the grass by his head. Then he felt both his mother's arms grab him. One arm wrapped under his legs while the other wrapped under his upper back. She screamed through clenched teeth as she lifted him off the ground. He expected his mother to put him down so he could stand again, but instead she began carrying him as she struggled to run.

"Mom, I can walk! Stop! We can't leave Dad!"

"No, you can't, Carver! Shut up! Bran is gone!"

His mother's harsh words hit Carver like he had drunk something foul, creating a sickening sensation in his stomach.

"He can't be dead! Stop! Mom, we—"

Velanna let out a scream that hurt Carver's ears. Before he could figure out what was going on, she dropped him. As Carver landed on the ground, his mother stumbled past him and slammed against the wall of a wooden cottage.

Carver realized his mother had carried him into a wide grass alley behind a grouping of cottages that were not burning. He could still see the flames of other cottages over the tops of the closest buildings, and the sounds of screaming and fighting echoed all around.

Carver forced himself to his feet, using the wall of the cottage for support, and looked at his mother, who was sweating and taking deep breaths.

"Mom, we have to help him! What if we can get him to a healer? We could—"

Velanna grabbed her son by the shoulders, then slammed his back into the wall he was leaning against. "He's gone, you stupid boy! They killed him! And they'll kill you too if you don't get out of here! Is that what you want? You want me to lose you too?" Velanna screamed, tears streaming down her face.

Not knowing how to react, Carver just stared into his mother's dark-green eyes in utter shock. With her face so close to his, he suddenly noticed a foul smell emanating from her mouth. His mother's breath smelled of sulfur, something oddly metallic, and something burnt. Carver found the strange, unpleasant scent familiar, though he could not recall why.

Velanna looked at where she was digging her nails into Carver's shoulders. Then she looked up at his terror-laden face. "Oh, my boy. My baby boy," she said through tears and a sudden shift into sadness as she pulled Carver into an embrace.

The confusion and fear Carver felt drowned out the pain in his ribs from being hugged, but it also prevented him from hugging his mother back. Velanna released him and reached for a small satchel that was attached to her belt, which Carver had not noticed until that moment.

Velanna flipped the satchel open and pulled out a corked rectangular glass vial that was almost the length and width of her hand. A thick black liquid splashed around inside the vial, though half of it seemed to be missing. Velanna uncorked the vial and held it up to Carver. The pungent smell of sulfur, strong alcohol, and what he thought was rusted iron erupted from the vial's narrow top, causing Carver to wince in disgust.

"Drink this, Carver. It's a potion that will hide your pain long enough for us to get away from here."

Carver choked from the smell but took the vial without questioning his mother. He looked at the dark liquid that sloshed around inside and then brought the vial to his mouth, hesitating before drinking it.

"Now, Carver!"

Carver pressed the glass vial to his lips and tilted his head back. The dark liquid ran over his tongue quickly, despite its thickness. It was warm and tasted like the watery ooze out of something rotten and burnt, but Carver forced himself to finish the vial's contents. After choking down the last of the black liquid, he threw the vial to the side with a gasp. His throat burned, and his tongue writhed, and then he gagged.

Just as the sound of revulsion passed from Carver's lips, his mother's hand slammed over his mouth. "Don't throw it up! It'll kick in fast, and then you won't feel like vomiting. Just keep it down, Carver!"

Carver pushed his mother's hand away from his mouth with a snarl and stepped to the side. "Get off of me!" he barked, then gagged again, which led him into a series of coughing and spitting. The pain of stepping on his injured leg caused him to tense up, but he didn't fall.

The beating of his heart quickly stole his attention away from the pain in his leg and the rest of his body. The beating was irregularly fast and kept increasing in speed until Carver couldn't feel it at all anymore, as if his heart had suddenly stopped beating. Then he noticed that the pain throughout his body, specifically his left calf, was gone. The lack of physical feeling was joined by a feeling of frustration that boiled up from his stomach and made his face twitch.

Carver let out a grunt and then bent over forward, placing his hands on his knees as his temples pulsed, making him feel dizzy. His mother's hands gripped him once again by the shoulders and pulled him to face her.

"Control yourself, Carver. I know it feels strange, but you need to focus and stay in control!"

"I am in control!" Carver snapped, pulling away from his mother's grip.

Velanna slapped her son hard across the face, then grabbed him by the shoulders again and held him much tighter, so he could not break away so easily. "No, you're not! Don't let the anger overtake your senses. Use it as fuel to move. Don't get lost in it!"

Again Carver tried to pull away from his mother's grasp, but her grip was too tight. He felt a strong urge to punch her and shove her away, but something in his mind commanded him to stop. Trying instead to focus on where he was and what was going on, Carver took a series of frantic breaths.

Velanna released Carver's shoulders and grabbed his head, forcing him to look at her face. "Please, son. Listen to my voice. I love you. I love you so much. Just focus on my voice and—"

Carver felt a spray of something warm splatter his bare chest at the same moment that his mother abruptly stopped speaking. He looked down and saw the broken tip of an iron-tipped wooden bolt sticking out of his mother's chest. He looked back up at his mother's face in shock.

Velanna opened her mouth, but before she could speak, her grip loosened on Carver's face and she stumbled to the ground. As she hit the grass, she gasped and grabbed the partially exposed tip of the bolt with her right hand. Blood poured from around the shaft and trailed down her fingers.

Carver felt like he couldn't breathe.

Velanna looked up into her son's eyes. "Run ..."

Carver tore his eyes away from his mother and saw a soldier with a crossbow standing at the end of the cottage they were behind. The soldier had his crossbow pushed into the ground with his foot and was pulling the thick drawstring back with both hands so he could reload.

"Carver ... Run ..."

A flurry of sensations overtook Carver. A burst of heat ran up his spine, a spasm of tingles shot down his fingers, a great pressure swelled in his chest, and the edges of his vision filled with a red haze.

✠   ✠   ✠

Helena struggled to understand what was happening around her.

One second she had been sleeping in her bed, warm in her tunic and trousers under her straw-stuffed bed's single sheet, enwrapped in a dream that was now quickly fading from her memory. The next moment she was being ripped from her dream and her bed by her father.

"Reied Tango!" was the first thing Helena thought she heard as the partial warmth of her sheet disappeared.

"What?" she slurred. Then she felt a tight grip around her arm, followed by a yank.

"We need to go!" her father shouted.

Helena swung herself into a sitting position, surrendering to the momentum of her father's pull, and tried to scan her eyes around her room to understand what was happening. Before she could focus, however, she was pulled off her bed. Now standing, she felt the remaining warmth in her body draining through the bottoms of her bare feet into the cold dirt floor of her bedroom.

"Dad, what are you doing?"

The sound of fighting outside found its way into her ears before her father's answer did.

"The village is under attack!" he barked, giving his daughter little time to react before he turned and pulled her along.

"What? Wait!" Helena gasped as she stumbled forward, just now noticing the arming sword in her father's other hand.

Without answering, Helena's father tightened his grip on her arm and took her around the common-room table.

Helena had not even registered that they had left her room. When her father stopped running, her momentum kept going until her arm locked. Stumbling backwards, Helena clenched her teeth at the burn that shot up her arm.

"Are we clear?" her father asked.

It confused Helena why he would ask her such a question, but then she realized the inquiry was directed at her mother, who stood in the cottage's doorway, also with a blade in hand.

"Feira!" Damath shouted when his wife did not respond.

Flinching, Helena's mother broke her focus from whatever she was watching and turned to face her family. The smell of burning wood and thatch suddenly reached Helena's nostrils.

"Are we clear?" her father asked.

"No, but we need to go now."

When Feira noticed Helena standing next to Damath, she abandoned her post in the doorway and crouched down to the level of her daughter's terrified eyes. "We need to run for the forest, sweetie. Just hold on to your father, and don't stop moving."

Helena was caught off guard by her mother's tone. She sounded like a new parent instructing a toddler during an outing to a crowded area.

"Helena, did you hear me?" Feira's tone suddenly shifted from worried mother to assertive parent.

"Yes, Mom."

"Do you understand?"

Helena nodded, although the truth was that she did not understand; far from it, in fact. Less than a minute ago she had been sleeping, lost in a dream she could no longer remember, and now she was being told by her mother to run into the woods.

"Okay," Feira said as she broke eye contact with Helena and rose to address Damath. She leaned forward and kissed him, and he kissed her back.

Helena saw a tear running down her mother's cheek. Then her parents broke their kiss and darted out the front door, Helena's father pulling her along behind him.

A bright light burned Helena's pupils as she was pulled out of her family's cottage, causing her to shield her eyes. Through her fingers, Helena saw that the bright light came from a roaring fire that had enveloped one of the nearby cottages.

Before her eyes could adjust to the sudden brightness, Helena saw a new sight that chilled her blood: bodies lying in the grass. Some were strangers wearing bear-emblemed surcoats over mail armor. The majority she recognized as her fellow villagers.

Had her father not been holding her arm, Helena would have collapsed in shock. Her father's continual pull, however, kept her staggering forward.

Helena's father stopped dead in his tracks, giving Helena no time to adjust. She stumbled past him and then stopped, her eyes rising up from the ground to what had seized her parents' attention.

A group of horses, each carrying a soldier who wielded either a sword or a spear, was galloping down the wide grassy path toward Helena and her parents. The soldiers swung and stabbed their weapons into anyone who was within range. Those who managed to avoid the killing blows were trampled or knocked aside by the horses.

"Quick!" Feira shouted, darting back the way they had come.

The pain resurfaced in Helena's arm, informing her that her father was pulling her again. The three of them ran back toward their cottage, deeper into the burning village.

Helena wanted to tear her arm away from her father's grip. She disliked being pulled about, but her father's touch also gave her a small sense of security, so she refrained from breaking his grip.

This isn't real, she tried to tell herself as flames flashed all around her, and she kept her eyes on the ground, having to constantly leap over bodies as they ran.

The pain in her arm confirmed that she was not in some awful nightmare, however. One body in particular caught her attention: a small girl with scruffy blond hair who lay face down in the grass with a wide gash across her back, splitting her white tunic in two. The girl quickly vanished from view as Helena was pulled past yet another burning cottage.

Feira had looped them through and around the center of the village, ending up in the spot where the charging horsemen had already been. Scattered bodies of villagers showed that the horsemen had been brutally efficient.

"There!" Feira shouted.

Helena looked away from the corpses toward a large gap between two burning cottages. Far behind the homes stood a massive expanse of trees at the top of a steep incline. Vellum Forest: miles of thick trees that dominated the center of the island.

"Look out!" Damath yelled.

The tightness around Helena's bicep disappeared, along with the false sense of security it provided. Free from her father's grip, she was running without guidance. She looked to her left and saw that her father was no longer running beside her. Instead, he was locking blades with an armored man.

"Dad!" Helena screamed, stopping dead in her tracks.

Her father pushed his blade forward, sending his attacker a step back. Helena made to leap to her father's aid, but a hand grasping her shoulder prevented her from moving.

"Stop!" Feira commanded.

Helena looked up to say something but lost her words when she saw another group of horsemen galloping toward them down the wide grassy avenue.

A second soldier appeared from behind a flaming cottage and swung at Helena's father's back. Damath noticed his approach and lunged to the side. The man swung wide past Damath and stumbled into the soldier Damath had been engaging. Helena's father was relieved for a moment, only to turn and see the horsemen racing toward them. His face contorted with a sad realization.

"Run! I'll meet you there!" he shouted as he raised his sword in preparation to fight.

The distance between Helena and her father increased as Helena's mother pulled her backwards.

"Wait!" she screamed, not taking her eyes off her father, who was now clumsily deflecting a series of blows from the two men. Before she could break free from her mother's grip, a large brown horse suddenly appeared before her.

Looking up in shock, Helena was met with the grim sight of a woman in armor identical to those who were assaulting her father, thrusting a long spear toward her chest.

A blurred flash of gray buzzed by Helena's face.

The spear abruptly changed course and fell to the ground, along with much of the hand that wielded it. The blurred swipe of gray revealed itself to be Feira's sword, which was now wetted by fresh blood from the horsewoman's ruined hand.

The horse did not stop its gallop and carried the woman a few feet away before she fell from her saddle and thudded against the ground, screaming and clutching her bloody hand, which was now missing all its fingers. Before a second rider was able to strike at Helena, Feira heaved her daughter back out of range.

Helena heard a clang of iron followed by her mother shouting violently. Before Helena could get her bearings, her mother appeared in front of her, pulling her by the arm.

A loud barrage of hooves filled the space between Helena and her father. The horses may as well have been a thirty-foot wall, blocking her view of him. No riders made to pursue Helena and her mother. Instead, they broke into two groups. Half continued their charge forward, cutting down anyone in their way, while the other half went deeper into the village, riding through the last spot Helena had seen her father.

The unnatural heat from the flames began to lessen, and Helena found herself being led up a steep hill. Despite her body's insistence to watch where she was being dragged, Helena could not take her eyes off her burning village. From the elevation of the hill, she could see just how dire the situation was.

Multiple groups of cavalry rode in circles around the village, slaying anyone they caught trying to escape. Almost every structure was in flames, sending thick towers of smoke high into the night sky, blocking out many of the stars. The two full moons sat high in the black sky, blanketing the area in pale, bluish glow that mixed with the orange flames from the village.

The horrific sight was obscured by darkness once they reached the trees. The sounds of death and fighting faded away as well, replaced by the crunching of leaves and twigs beneath their feet. Suddenly, Feira stopped, bringing Helena to an abrupt halt.

"Are you okay, Helena?" Feira asked while trying to catch her breath.

As Helena struggled to answer, her mother dropped her sword and grabbed her, spinning Helena around and inspecting her from top to bottom while patting her down. Helena still found it impossible to speak. The best she could do was stare at her mother as she examined her for injuries. Finally, Feira pulled her hands away, looked at them, and saw that there was no blood on them.

"Okay. You're not hurt or bleeding."

The ache in Helena's arm said otherwise.

Seeing the shock in her daughter's eyes, Feira felt even worse for saying what she was about to say. "Look, Helena, I need you to stay here and wait for me."

Helena felt a wave of panic wash over her.

"I have to go back and help your father. I can't leave him down there. I'll find him and come right back. I promise. Just wait here. If you see anyone who isn't me or your father, hide." Feira winced and placed a hand on her lower back as if she had just felt a jolt of pain.

Overcome with shock, Helena tried to speak, but was only able to stand and stare into her mother's tear-filled eyes.

"I love you, baby," her mother said softly. After a long kiss against her daughter's forehead, Feira grabbed her sword and dashed back toward Verrel.

Helena turned around just in time to see her mother vanish through the trees. She missed her chance to say something, but she was just in time to see the large tear in her mother's tunic on the lower-right side of her back, along with a dark-red stain that was growing rapidly from underneath.

✠ ✠ ✠

Before the soldier could finish loading the next bolt into his crossbow, Carver was on him.

The soldier dropped his weapon and stumbled back as Carver pushed him into the wall of a cottage and wrapped his hands around his throat. The soldier gasped as he grabbed Carver's wrists with his leather-gauntleted hands, but the boy did not budge an inch in the struggle.

The soldier reached for his sword at his hip. The blade made it halfway out of its sheath before Carver slammed his forehead into the soldier's face. Blood burst from the man's nose and sprayed down his grizzled face as he released his grip on his sword and grabbed Carver's hair to stop another headbutt.

The effort was wasted, however, as Carver sent his forehead into the man's face again, leaving a chunk of his hair in the man's hand. Carver repeated the process again and again as the soldier tried desperately to free himself. Carver's continuous smashing of his head into the man's bloody face had little effect on himself, as the potion coursing through his body prevented him from noticing the pain caused by slamming his head into another person's skull.

The soldier's legs suddenly gave out, and he slid down the wall of the cottage. Carver lowered himself to his knees and dug his hands into the soldier's throat. After a few seconds of strangling him, he realized the man was unconscious.

Carver released his hold on the man's throat and pushed himself to his feet. An overwhelming rage filled his mind and body, overtaking his thoughts with a violent urge to kill anyone in a suit of chainmail. He grabbed the soldier's sword and pulled it from its sheath so quickly that he almost fell over backwards.

Without a second thought, Carver gripped the blade in both hands and slashed it across the unconscious soldier's throat. Before the man's blood had spilled down his surcoat, Carver turned and dashed around the corner of the cottage.

While before the sight of Verrel burning had frozen him in terror and confusion, now it had no effect, as the potent potion dulled Carver's thoughts and senses, other than a primal aggression that pushed him forward.

Carver scanned the area and saw that most of the fighting had moved away from the east side of the village, where he currently was. Great columns of smoke rose into the air from the burning cottages all around him, and distant shouting and screaming echoed from every direction. Carver growled in frustration at not knowing where to go. He tightened his grip on his newly acquired sword and started forward when a sudden movement caught his eye from the right.

A pair of soldiers appeared from behind a partially collapsed cottage farther down the grassy lane and ran northward. That was all the incentive Carver's mind needed to turn around and run after the two soldiers to the north. The pair vanished past another group of flaming cottages, neither of them seeming to notice Carver.

Carver rounded the corner without hesitation. His mind was saturated with anger and a delusional idea that he could slay every soldier and save his village. The wound on his leg no longer pained him as he ran, nor did his heavy breathing cause his ribs or bruised chest to hurt further. He felt pristine and stronger than ever before.

Once around the corner, Carver saw a corpse-laden path of villagers, with only a soldier or two mixed in. The two soldiers were halfway down the path. One had a spear while the other wielded a sword similar to the one Carver held. Both of them stepped over the bodies as they quickly ran through the village. As Carver chased them, his vision was marred by a hazy red cloud along the edges that pulsed as if trying to grow over his eyes.

The soldiers reached the end of the wide path, which opened into a large, grassy cul-de-sac and then disappeared behind a burning cottage. Carver leaped over the bodies in his way with reckless abandon as he ran after the soldiers. As he neared the opening beyond the row of cottages, he realized the chaotic ringing of metal had become much louder among the constant crackling of flames all around him.

A large horse stepped into Carver's path just as he reached the opening. He couldn't react fast enough and smacked into the side of the animal at full force. Most of Carver's breath was knocked from his lungs as he bounced back and tumbled to the ground. The horse reared onto his hind legs in fright.

Carver looked up in time to see the horse slam its front hooves down into the earth and resist the pull of the soldier in its saddle who tried to steady it. The soldier looked down at Carver with shock on his wide, thickly bearded face as he tried to steady his panicked mount.

The soldier raised his spear, prepared to strike Carver, but the horse shifted to the side in order to distance itself from Carver, taking him out of range.

Carver grabbed his sword and leaped to his feet, causing a stream of blood to push out of his leg, though he didn't notice. By then the soldier had managed to regain control of his horse, and he lowered his spear at him. As the soldier dug his heels into his beast and charged, Carver raised his sword and flung it with both hands.

The blade spun a single rotation through the air before it hit the horse's neck, creating a long, shallow gash before crashing to the ground. The horse ceased its charge and clumsily jumped to the side with a scream. The animal couldn't keep its footing, and fell on its side, taking the rider down with it.

The man howled in agony as his right leg was crushed beneath the horse's weight. The animal kicked and screamed and was only just able to get itself up off the ground. It bolted down the path, leaving its rider behind writhing in the grass.

Carver ran toward the crippled soldier. Seeing Carver's approach, the man reached for his spear to defend himself but only managed to partially raise it by the time Carver was on him. Carver grabbed the spear and pulled it from the soldier's grasp, then spun it around and thrust it into the soldier's gut.

The spear's iron head pierced the man's mail and punched through the gambeson beneath, causing him to howl in pain as it plunged into his flesh. He grabbed the wooden shaft with both hands and tried to stop Carver from pushing it in farther.

Carver responded by yanking the spear back, causing a light spray of red to emerge from the punctured armor, and then tried to thrust it into the man's chest. The soldier caught the spear with both hands and struggled with Carver for control, but the overwhelming pain from his crushed leg and partially punctured gut drained his effort. The spear slid through the soldier's hands toward his chest until the iron tip pushed into his chainmail. The spear's thin iron tip bent a ring of the chainmail and poked into the gambeson before it stopped.

"No! Stop! Wait!" the large bearded man pleaded as he struggled to push the spear away.

Carver ignored the man's words and then shifted himself up over the back end of the spear, slamming his body into the thrust. The soldier's eyes bulged as the spear's head broke through more of the chainmail and ripped through the gambeson, embedding itself into his chest. The soldier gasped and coughed as the spear's shaft slid through his hands. Carver continued to put his full weight behind the weapon until the iron head was submerged in his enemy's chest.

Streams of red escaped from the soldier's mouth and trailed down his bearded cheeks as he choked on the rising blood in his throat. Carver pulled on the spear to dislodge it, but it was stuck. Instead, he left the weapon planted in the dying soldier and ran to where his sword had fallen after striking the horse's neck.

An overwhelming feeling of rage continued to surge through Carver's body and drove him to advance into the cul-de-sac, sword in hand. The cul-de-sac was one of many similar areas of the village, a wide space of grass with small cottages surrounding its circular perimeter. Unlike the other cul-de-sacs within Verrel, however, this one had the village schoolhouse at its center.

The schoolhouse was wider than the average cottage and had a small open field of dirt on its west end with a single row of straw training dummies on thick wooden beams. All around the large schoolhouse were bodies, but also among the freshly dead were the living.

Handfuls of villagers were engaged with soldiers in every direction. Some fled for their lives in panic while others defended themselves with weapons ranging from pitchforks and hammers to swords, spears, and daggers. The fires that engulfed the outer cottages of the cul-de-sac illuminated the battle, bathing the participants in flickering orange light and swirling shadows.

Carver ran into the fray, unable to think about his own safety over the rush of anger that coursed through his body. His hazy red vision locked on a soldier who had his back turned. The soldier was engaged in a struggle of blades with a village man who had a dark-red stain spreading under his tunic. Before Carver could reach them, the soldier ran the wounded villager through with his blade.

The villager's face contorted with pain as the soldier yanked the blade from his belly, and then he collapsed to the ground. The soldier checked his flank just in time to notice Carver running up behind him but not quick enough to turn around fully and ready his sword. Carver swung, connecting the side of his blade with the mail covering the soldier's upper arm.

Carver's blade failed to break the chain or damage the gambeson beneath, but the soldier stumbled to the side and pulled his arm away from Carver's blade. Before Carver could strike again, the soldier leapt back and raised his sword to defend himself, knocking Carver's blade aside. Carver pulled his blade back and recovered before the soldier advanced on him.

The soldier snarled at Carver and swung his weapon at Carver's arm. Carver blocked the swing but was forced to take a step back from the power of the strike. Not leaving Carver more than a second to recover, the soldier swung his weapon again toward Carver's left side.

Carver deflected the strike with his blade, sending the soldier's weapon downwards, but this time he held his footing against his assailant. As the soldier tried to step back and raise his weapon, Carver swung his blade hard into the man's sword. The soldier's weapon was forced farther down from the blow. Carver quickly raised his blade for another strike. His action exposed his right thigh and lower torso to the soldier's blade from below, but the potion in Carver's system overruled his better judgment.

Faster than the soldier could seize the opening, Carver brought down his own blade on the man's sword hand. It chopped through the soldier's leather gauntlet and cut deep into his wrist, forcing the soldier to drop his weapon with a shriek of pain and terror.

The soldier jumped back as Carver pulled his blade from the soldier's nearly severed wrist. A spray of blood erupted from the wound. Carver stepped forward and stabbed his blade into the soldier's chest, but once again his weapon failed to pass through the soldier's chainmail and gambeson. The blow did knock the wounded soldier off balance, though, and he stumbled to the ground with another shriek, his helmet falling off.

The haze of red on the edges of Carver's vision seemed to grow in intensity, almost tunneling his vision onto the soldier on the ground. The soldier looked up at Carver in terror and tried to scramble back, but Carver lunged toward him with bared teeth and swung his blade at the man's head. The edge of Carver's sword crunched deep into the man's exposed face, splitting his left eye and severing his nose.

The man perished instantly, but Carver's rage-muddled mind did not register his demise. Instead of moving on, he pulled his sword from the man's face, slashing the blade down again. It made a crunching sound as it sank further into the man's skull. Carver screamed and pulled the blade out again. He continued to scream and swing his blade into the dead man's face, despite the fact that it was now a red mess of something indistinguishable. Carver was lost in a rage-induced trance that overwhelmed his mind.

The sudden presence of a hand grabbing his shoulder from behind broke him from his violent frenzy, and Carver spun around to fight off the new threat. He slashed at the person behind him with a panicked strike to force distance between them. The attack worked, as the person released Carver's shoulder and leapt back to avoid the swing, giving Carver the space needed to follow up with a thrust.

Carver lunged before he could make out his opponent's face and thrust his sword forward with all his strength so that it might pierce his attacker's armor. The blade met no armor, however, and slid effortlessly into the chest of Carver's attacker, erupting out the person's back with a burst of blood.

Carver froze.

A surge of shock filled his body as he steadied his gaze on the person he had just run through. The shock morphed into utter horror as an abrupt realization struck Carver, and the overwhelming anger seemed to lessen within him as he processed where he was and what he had just done. The horrid realization was joined by a sudden spike of pressure that burst from the back of his head.

An unnatural blankness fell over Carver's senses. The stench of blood and the noise of burning cottages disappeared as a heavy, numb feeling spread across the back of his head. Carver could no longer feel his sword's grip in his hands, nor could he feel his arms, which strangely released the sword without his intention as they fell to his sides. Carver's vision darkened, and his legs gave out from under him. He crashed to the ground without knowing he had done so and felt nothing.

The blackness that flooded his vision and blocked out the face of the person who collapsed in front of him was welcoming at that moment.

Chapter 9

Helena was unsure what she was thinking as she left the safety of the trees and ran down the hill toward the burning village. The paralyzing fear she had felt while being pulled from Verrel only moments earlier seemed to have vanished as she watched the village burn from the tree line. Her mind blocked out the severity of the situation, consumed by worry for her family.

The screams became loud again, though there were fewer of them now. Helena hurried down the hill with an ungraceful flurry of strides, leaving whatever plan she had in the dark woods behind her. Upon reaching the bottom of the hill, Helena realized that she did not know what she would do next. She wanted to find her parents, to find a bucket of water and douse the burning cottages. She wanted it all to stop.

Standing in the open field at the base of the slope, Helena struggled to bring her thoughts to a consensus. Before any such decision could be made, however, a new thought arose in her mind: *Look to see where those footsteps are coming from. No, not footsteps, hoofbeats.*

The late entry in Helena's thoughts reigned supreme, and she whipped her attention to her left, bearing witness to an unfortunately familiar sight. A brigade of soldiers rode around the northern side of the village, hurling blazing torches onto the remaining cottages that had yet to be totally engulfed in flames.

Thankfully, the riders' attention was focused on arson rather than her, but she knew they would spot her soon. She had to make a choice: run back up the hill and make for Vellum Forest, or run into Verrel and put some cottages between her and them. Knowing that the former would no doubt cause her to be spotted and cut down as she ran up the exposed incline, Helena chose the latter.

She put a burning cottage between them and herself. By the time she heard them thunder past the spot where she had just been standing, she had put two more burning cottages and an overturned wagon between them. The ground was littered with even more bodies than she remembered.

Apart from the swaying flames, there was no movement within Helena's view. The few screams she could hear over the crackling fires were coming from the south end of the village. Taking that into account, Helena ran toward the north end of Verrel.

It was increasingly difficult to avoid stepping on the corpses sprawled throughout the village, forcing Helena to play a gruesome game of hopscotch as she ran. When the clusters of dead lessened, Helena took her eyes off the ground, only to find herself standing in front of the village schoolhouse.

The building's tall, angled thatched roof could no longer withstand the parasitic fire, and with a loud, bellowing creak, it collapsed in on itself. A burst of embers exploded over the schoolhouse's oak walls, followed by a hiss as the remaining wooden supports began to crack from the heat.

The sounds around Helena became a symphony of crackling and crunching as more structures buckled and collapsed. Doing her best to ignore it all, Helena hurried past the roofless schoolhouse and searched her ravaged surroundings for any sign of her parents. Then she saw it.

On the blood-soaked dirt that used to be the schoolhouse's training yard, Helena stood completely still. She felt colder than she had ever felt before, despite the heat all around her. At her feet, lying in a bloody pool that turned the dirt into a reddish mud, was her father, an arming sword thrust into his chest and sticking out his back.

Unable to discern what she was feeling, Helena turned her eyes to the body beside her father's. There, adding to the stream of red that continued to drain into the dirt, was Carver, just as motionless as her father.

Carver was face down in the dirt. A large, fresh gash on the back of his head was releasing a flow of blood onto his back and through his long brown hair. The bandages that were wrapped around his head had fallen off, and those covering his leg were soaked in blood, so heavy that they hung off his skin.

Helena fell to her knees.

She reached out for the hilt of the sword that was buried in her father's chest but then retracted her hand as soon as she touched the wooden grip. She couldn't muster the strength to pull it out. The orchestra of burning wood around her seemed to soften, giving way to a dull hum.

Helena began to cry but was unable to muster up even a single tear. Her eyes tensed as the hot air dried them out. A series of dry, hyperventilated weeps was all she could manage. She felt overwhelmed with despair, unable to focus her grief on any specific thing as she was thrown into a whirlpool of trauma. All around her splashed the loss of her father, the loss of her best friend, the loss of her home, and the potential loss of her mother.

Unable to stare at her father any longer, Helena closed her eyes and slumped forward onto the bloody mud that had been soaking into the knees of her trousers. There she lay, her eyes shut, waiting for anything to come and break her away from this horrid reality.

The quiet sound of inhalation was the first thing to answer her request.

Helena opened her eyes and was greeted by the sliced head of her best friend, which lay just inches away from her own. The faint sound of breath that came from Carver contradicted the lethal gash across his head.

Helena remained still, utterly defeated, staring at Carver's body. Then the sound of another breath came from Carver's muddy face.

Helena did not let her mind's insistent denial of the facts deceive her. She closed her eyes tight, trying to ignore the vile tricks her ears were playing on her grief.

A third breath.

Helena's body surged with energy, and she pushed herself up from the bloody ground. Her crippling sadness and despair was blocked out by a powerful burst of adrenaline. She placed her ear next to where Carver's mouth was scrunched into the blood-soaked dirt.

A fourth breath.

Helena slid her hands under Carver's chest and rolled him over. His body flopped with a disheartening limpness. Helena stared at his dirt-covered mouth, which remained slightly open.

He took a fifth breath, his mouth widening as his chest rose slightly.

"Carver!"

A sixth breath.

"Carver!" she screamed again, this time grabbing the sides of his face in her hands.

His skin was warm.

Helena used her thumbs to open Carver's eyelids. His dark-green eyes appeared lifeless.

The sound of galloping horses suddenly came into range.

Helena let Carver's eyes shut and grabbed him by the shoulders as a surge of panic dulled her perception of her surroundings. "Carver! Carver, wake up!"

The stampeding of horses became louder.

Helena placed her ear next to Carver's mouth and listened to make sure she had not gone mad. She felt his warm breath on her ear as the sound of a faint exhalation emerged past his lips.

Voices became discernable amongst the galloping sound.

Helena's senses finally managed to inform her of the approaching danger, and she looked up from her efforts. The sound of charging horses was becoming louder from behind some partially collapsed cottages to the east.

Helena looked down at Carver. Another weak breath but only that.

In desperation, Helena wrapped her arms around Carver's back. With a heave, she lifted him off the schoolhouse's blood-soaked training yard and hoisted him onto her shoulder, then made off toward a small space between two burning cottages to the west. The flames eating the cottages stretched out toward her like hands from each side as she made her way through the tight gap, sending small surges of brief, white pain into her exposed hands, neck, and face. Helena fought through the pain and emerged on the other side of the small gap.

The burned spots on her face and neck began to sting as the cool air struck her. Her adrenaline focused more on giving her the strength to carry Carver than it did toward blocking out the pain. With the heat of the flames now behind her, Helena made off to the west and ascended the steep hill as fast as her body could manage.

Her legs burned with exertion as she struggled with Carver's weight, but she forced herself onward and did not stop for a breath. The large trees seemed to grow thicker and taller as she approached the dark cavalcade of nature at the top of the steep incline. She felt a warm substance run down the back of her neck and pass down the curves of her back. She thought for a second that it was her own blood, but then she clued in to its source, adding to her dread.

The warm trail that dripped down her spine was abruptly countered by the cold interior of Vellum Forest. As she ran, she tried to prevent Carver from bouncing around on her shoulder. The darkness became too much though, and Helena was finally forced to halt in fear of running into a tree or tripping over roots or a rock. The sound of the horses did not follow her into the woods. Only one sound did.

Another breath.

✠   ✠   ✠

Sebastian did his best to quiet Nina's crying, but her wails echoed out of the small forest clearing and far into the dark woods.

"I said shut her up!" an angry voice hissed from the dark.

Sebastian tightened his grip on his sister's shoulders. "Nina! You need to be quiet, please!" His voice was drowned out by her incessant wailing and broken breaths.

Sebastian wanted to join her. He wanted to sit next to his sister on the fallen tree and crumble into tears, but he couldn't. He needed to stay strong for her and bring her loud cries to a halt. "Nina! They'll hear you and find us. You have to stop."

Nina responded with a flurry of ugly, hyperventilated gasps, sounding as if she were choking on her own breath. Her crying eyes were staring straight into Sebastian's, but she was not truly seeing her brother's face amidst the tears and panic.

Suddenly, a blur appeared in Sebastian's peripheral vision. Before he could react, a pair of hands wrapped around his sister's mouth. The hands were attached to a boy who looked no more than a year or two older than Sebastian and Nina. He had black hair and a few wisps of dark hair on his chin and cheeks.

Nina's cry became muffled, but she squirmed and tried to break free from the hands that squeezed her mouth. The boy merely tightened his grip and moved in as if to wrap his arm around Nina's neck.

Sebastian lunged and grabbed the boy's arm before he could choke his sister, then pulled the arm away as he sidestepped the fallen oak that Nina was sitting on.

"Rook! Stop!" Sebastian shouted.

As Sebastian pulled Rook's arm away from his sister, Rook let her go with his other hand and turned toward Sebastian. The speed at which Rook moved and the darkness prevented Sebastian from blocking or evading Rook's punch. His fist slammed into Sebastian's chest and knocked the boy back.

Sebastian stumbled backwards and fell onto his rear.

Nina rose from the fallen tree with a shriek. "No! Don't hurt him!" she cried.

Rook turned and punched her in the face, sending her sprawling backwards as well. Sebastian sprang to his feet as Nina hit the ground and launched himself at Rook, but Rook grabbed him before he could swing his fist. He pulled Sebastian to the side and pushed him over the fallen tree. Sebastian tumbled onto his back beside his sister, who was still lying on the cold ground with tears running down her face.

Nina's crying had ceased, though only due to the shock of being punched. Before Sebastian could gather his senses and stand up, Rook stepped onto the fallen tree and glared down at them both.

"Stay down, you fool!" Rook whispered. "I'm trying to shut her up since you can't quiet her down!"

Sebastian scrambled to his knees and reached over to protect his sister, thinking Rook was about to attack her again. He glared up at Rook with hate-fueled eyes as he pulled Nina close.

Nina held back her cries, though her breaths remained frantic and ugly.

As if sensing the hateful thoughts bouncing around inside Sebastian's head, Rook balled his hands into fists. "Look, I don't give a damn about you or your sister. I'm in charge here, and if you don't listen to me, I'll beat your face in. The same goes for her." Rook pointed at Nina. "If she starts wailing again, I'll knock her out. And if I have to, I'll break her neck. Yours too if you keep this shit up."

Nina tried to slow her breathing, but between her flowing tears and panicked nerves, all she could do was hold her breath and start to shake. Sebastian wanted to comfort her, but he couldn't take his eyes off Rook.

"If you don't give a damn about us then why did you save us down there?" Sebastian asked, gesturing toward where he thought Verrel was located, though he was unsure which way was which in the darkness of the woods.

"It ... It was an instinct. I don't know. But me getting those two soldiers off you and your sister certainly wasn't an invitation for the two of you to follow me."

A snap of twigs came from the east, behind Sebastian, causing him to realize he had his directions all messed up.

Rook jerked back and stepped away from the fallen tree. "Dammit, they know we're here!" he cursed through his teeth. Before Sebastian could turn around to assess the threat, Rook ran off into the darkness of the thick trees that surrounded the small, partially moonlit clearing.

Sebastian didn't see anyone behind them, but his fear of what may come spurred him into action. He stood up, yanking Nina to her feet, and hopped over the fallen tree, pulling her behind him.

Nina tripped over the tree and fell to the ground on the other side. Sebastian stopped as he felt his sister's arm break from his grasp and turned around to pull her back up.

A second snap of twigs erupted from the east, now straight ahead of him, and this time it sounded much closer. Although the darkness was thick, he thought he saw movement along the tree line, not far away from where the small clearing opened up. With a rush of panic, Sebastian threw himself to the ground next to Nina and slapped a hand over her mouth.

Nina tried to squirm away, but Sebastian grabbed her by the back of the head, pulled himself closer to her, and pushed his back into the fallen tree while keeping his head down and his grip over her mouth.

"Shh!" he said through the gaps of his clenched teeth as he looked at Nina with fear-filled eyes.

Nina understood immediately and tried to calm herself, but she still could not contain her panicked breathing, nor could she stop the tears from running down her face. She curled up next to her brother, keeping her head down, and put her own hands over his hand, which was still over her mouth.

Sebastian wanted to peek over the fallen tree and see where the soldiers were, but his fear of being seen kept his head down. Instead, he held his breath and prayed to his gods that the soldiers would not see him or Nina in the darkness and pass right by them.

The sound of footsteps sent another jolt of fear down Sebastian's spine. They grew louder, sounding as if they were coming directly toward the fallen tree from the other side. Sebastian didn't know what to do. As fear filled his body, he looked at Nina and considered telling her to run.

"Sebastian? Nina?" a female voice said as a bare foot stepped around the fallen tree into Sebastian's view behind Nina.

Sebastian jumped at the voice's emergence, having not realized the soldiers were already upon him and Nina. However, the mention of his and Nina's names gave him pause, wondering how the person knew his name.

The woman was about as tall as Sebastian, and instead of wearing armor she wore only a blood-splattered white wool tunic and brown wool trousers, the same as he, Nina, and Rook wore. She had a boy slung over her shoulder.

He was wearing nothing but a pair of braies and had a great show of blood draining from the back of his head, sticking his semi-long brown hair together in thick strands.

"Help me!" the young woman said as she set the body she was carrying against the fallen tree next to Nina. It took Sebastian a few dumbfounded seconds, his hand still over Nina's mouth, to realize who the person was.

Helena was drenched in sweat and blood, the latter appearing to be the most abundant. Unable to speak, Sebastian stared at Helena with equal parts relief and confusion.

"Please! He's dying!"

Sebastian turned to see whom Helena was speaking of, and upon seeing the person's face, he turned pale in horror.

Carver sat motionless, his eyes shut, propped against the fallen oak, with the palest complexion Sebastian had ever seen. Helena did not need to say another word. Sebastian removed his hand from Nina's mouth and pushed himself to his knees.

"Helena? What happened?"

"He's bleeding too much!" Helena cried. "I don't know how much more blood he can lose. Help me stop the bleeding!"

Not knowing what she expected him to do, Sebastian took Carver's head into his hands and pulled it forward to inspect his wound. A large gash stretched from just above the middle of the back of Carver's head down to just behind his right ear.

"Hold him steady," Helena ordered.

Sebastian looked over at Helena and saw that she was completely exposed from the waist up, her bloodstained tunic in her hands. He looked away immediately, shocked at the sight of his friend's bare chest, but did as she told him. Sebastian held Carver's head firmly in his hands and gave Helena room to work as she tore her tunic in two with a loud grunt, then wrapped a long strip of the torn wool garment tightly around Carver's head. Helena pulled it as tight as she could, then tied it into a knot at the front.

Sebastian thought he saw Carver's eyelids flutter, but it may just have been Carver's face muscles responding to the constricting wool.

Nina scooted herself around her brother to get a proper view of what was going on, and she let out a short gasp when she saw Carver's condition up close. Her tears and short breaths had stopped due to the sudden investment of her attention in Carver, but her panic and fear did not subside in the slightest.

"What is this?" Rook called from behind them, emerging from his hiding spot behind one of the trees.

Helena and Sebastian both turned to face Rook, though Helena followed with more than just a stare.

"Wha—Rook? Rook, get over here and help us!" Helena shouted after she realized who he was.

Rook hesitated for a moment when he saw Helena's bare chest, but as his eyes wandered down to Carver, his attention was immediately turned.

"Is that Carver? By Dema's ass! What are you doing? He's dead!" he shouted, completely forgetting the need to be quiet.

"He's not dead! Get over here and help us!" Helena shouted as she began to tear another strip of wool from the remains of her bloody tunic.

Rook walked up to them but did not get on his knees to help. "Look at him! He's dead, or he will be soon. And look!" Rook pointed to an intermittent trail of blood, barely visible in the darkness of the forest. "He bled all the way through the forest. You've marked a path straight to us, you stupid bitch! They'll follow Carver's blood and kill us!"

Helena dropped the torn stretch of wool and sprang to her feet, then grabbed Rook by the tunic before he could step back.

"I swear to Lilberith, Rook, if you don't help us, and he dies, I'll drag you to those soldiers myself!"

"Get off me, you fool!" Rook spat as he grabbed Helena's wrists and pulled them away from his chest.

Rather than continue to struggle, Helena turned back to Carver and dropped to her knees. As she picked up the torn strip of wool from her tunic, she glared at Rook. "If soldiers were coming, we would see their torchlight long before they arrived. The moment you see fire through those trees, you can run off as far as you'd like, but any sooner than that and I'll pray for dryads to pin your guts to a tree."

Sebastian looked back to his sister with a worried expression, thinking that Helena's threats would spark a series of blows between her and Rook. Nina didn't notice her brother's look, her attention fixed on Carver, watching as his short breaths caused his bare chest to rise while his body rested limply against the fallen tree.

While keeping Carver's bleeding head steady for Helena to apply her makeshift wool bandage, Sebastian looked up at Rook in preparation for what the older boy might do.

To Sebastian's surprise, rather than curse at Helena, leave, or strike out in anger, Rook looked back toward where Helena had arrived from with Carver, then sighed and pulled off his own tunic, tossing it to Helena.

"Put this on, you fool. If I'm to help you, I'd prefer to do so without the distraction of your tits. Now, what do you want me to do?"

Chapter 10

⁓⟲⟋

The manor was eerily silent. The only sound came from the chilly morning wind that blew through the cracks of the closed shutters on the hall's western wall. Accompanying the wind through the thin gaps was the pale, bluish light of the two large moons that brightened the dark hall, aided by wall-mounted torches.

The mixture of cold and warm light illuminated Aellia's path as she walked down the long hall that ended at the large oak double doors with a great bear carved into their face, though the carving was blurred by flickering shadows.

She was tired, and not just because of her restless night. The burning of Verrel only exhausted her physically, which could be remedied by a well-needed rest. It was the situation surrounding the event that drained her the most, both mentally and physically. She rubbed her eyes, pushing away some of her coppery-brown hair, and tried to fight against the rising feeling of exhaustion, as she always did, with the knowledge that for every minute she rested, the Isles continued to head for disaster.

The carving of the great bear came more clearly into view as she neared it and her eyes adjusted to the mixture of natural and unnatural light, but the impressive doors were not her goal. Instead, she turned to the right at the end of the chilly hall and approached a wooden door set in the stone wall. She pushed it open easily and marched through, stepping out onto an elevated loggia that formed a wide square around an inner courtyard situated within the center of the manor, a dozen feet below.

The square courtyard was filled with a garden of flowers and bushes that grew around a handful of small ponds and streams. A four-way path of stone dissected the garden and led to doors at each end of the courtyard, leading into the different sections of the great manor. Up above, the clear sky displayed a smattering of stars, and the two moons, one glowing pale while the other glowed blue, bathed the silent garden waters with soft light. A handful of torches mounted on the loggia's supports gave the courtyard's perimeter an orange glow and revealed the few soldiers who guarded the lower doors.

She paid the pleasant sight of the lower level no mind and marched down the northern side of the loggia until she reached another oak door built into the north wall. She passed through it, leaving the quaintness of the inner courtyard behind.

The room she entered was dark, even with the wall-mounted torches and northern windows that had their shutters wholly open, though little moonlight entered from that side of the manor. She stepped forward and looked over the railing of the wooden balcony on which she was standing.

Down below was a long table surrounded by empty chairs. The room's stone walls were hidden behind several bookshelves, some of which were stuffed with tomes while others were barren and dusty. Two female soldiers stood at attention below, one at each side of the long table, where Julius sat in the centermost chair. His attention was stretched over an open tome and a clutter of loose parchment sheets.

Atop one of the parchments was his silver crown, which appeared as if it were being used as a paperweight. At the sound of the door to the loggia closing, Julius looked up toward the balcony.

"Ah, my marshal has returned," he said as both female soldiers also looked up to the shadowy balcony.

"I was told you wanted to see me as soon as I returned to the city, my lord. Though I must say, I'm concerned that you're still awake at this late hour. Should you not be resting to keep your mind fresh for the coming day?"

"I found that I could not sleep knowing what was happening just beyond the Vellum Hills. So, I decided to await your return in my study so you might tell me of your task once you arrived to quiet my anxious mind."

Aellia took a deep breath through her nose and tightened her grip on the railing without those below seeming to notice. "I see."

She released the railing and walked over to the stairway that led down to the bottom floor. When she reached the bottom, she made her way over to the table so she could face the magistrate.

"Leave us," she said to the guards.

The women looked at each other in confusion, then at Julius. He motioned for them to obey Aellia.

The guards snapped to attention, nodded at Aellia, then marched toward the door directly behind her, which led to the inner courtyard. They closed the door behind them, leaving Aellia and Julius in total silence amidst the flickering orange light of the few burning torches and tabletop candles.

"Please, sit," he said softly as he grabbed his silver crown. He tilted it onto its side, then gently rolled it over to his other hand, which grasped the crown and held it steady. As soon as it rolled off the parchment, the yellowish paper curled into a tube shape.

"I'd prefer to stand."

"As you wish."

They stared at each other for a moment, each waiting for the other to speak. Finally, he nodded at her. "Your crimson surcoat hides the blood well, though not entirely. I assume from those stains that your mission concluded in your favor then?"

She looked down at her surcoat, which indeed had bloodstains that blended in with the crimson-dyed wool. The sight only drained her more and made her wish for a quick end to the meeting. She leaned forward and placed her knuckles on the table. "The mission was a success. With hope, the sovereigns will stay their wrath until we regain control of the larger situation."

"A success? Is that what you'd call it? And how many perished for you to achieve this success?"

Aellia pushed her knuckles into the table. "Of our own, twenty-two. Of Verrel, all but a handful, who fled into Vellum Forest."

"They are all our own!" Julius cried, dropping his silver crown with a clang and leaning forward in his seat. "Every soul in that village was one of us! Every last one! And now they're dead or being hunted in the woods like animals!" His voice filled the room and escaped through the back windows into the night.

Aellia held her tongue as she carefully considered her next words. "I did not give the order to have the survivors pursued," she said finally.

Julius's face lost some of its anger, replaced by confusion. "And why wouldn't you have them pursued? They are Aethi'ziton, after all, enemies of the Sovereign Empire and all the kingdoms within it. Are we to purge this rebel headquarters, only to allow them to escape and build a new one somewhere else?"

"There is no need to inform you as to the details of my decisions. It would only waste both of our time."

Julius sat back and placed his hands on the arms of his chair. "Oh? Have you decided that I'd be better off spared from your complicated tactical decisions?" His words bit at her with each syllable. "Or have you more pressing matters to attend to at so late an hour? I care not for your decision now but for your decisions then. Why did you not prevent the rebels from escaping or chase those who did?"

The authoritative manner in which the magistrate spoke surprised her. Using her knuckles to push herself off the table, she inhaled deeply and adhered to her lord's command. "I withheld the order to pursue those who fled because it was too dangerous and unnecessary."

"Unnecessary? They're criminals, are they not? Rebels, traitors, terrorists, those responsible for the staggering loss of life that befell the market yesterday. What reason can you give for allowing them to flee? Or did you suddenly find yourself doubting Verrel's affiliation with the Lost Seekers and their rebellion, as I did, and try to spare whomever you could at the last moment?"

"I have no doubts about Verrel's affiliation with the Lost Seekers, for I know its inhabitants had nothing to do with today's tragedy, or the Lost Seekers, for that matter."

"What?"

She took a deep breath. "Verrel was not a Aethi'ziton den, nor were any of its villagers aligned with the growing rebellion. They were all innocent."

"What evidence have you of this—"

"Do you think I only deal with petty criminals?" she hissed. "I've been dealing with the Aethi'ziton since my first days in the Caswen Guard, and my time as captain and marshal has seen no less. For years my soldiers and I have striven to eradicate this threat, with little to no help from you or the Queen." Her eyes narrowed angrily at her lord. "And during these efforts I have learned many things about the Lost Seekers, one of which is that they had no ties to that irrelevant little village."

"Then why did you murder its inhabitants?" Julius shouted, slamming his fist on the table, causing the silver crown to move slightly and some loose pages to flutter in the wind created by his arm's movement.

Aellia lost her ability to remain calm and level headed. "I did what I had to! It's you who is responsible for their deaths! You know damn well that the sovereigns will destroy the Isles if they feel they must! One village is a small price to pay for the entire province!"

"The slaughter of Verrel was issued by the sovereigns and implemented by you! I had no part in it!"

"How dare you!" She slammed her hands on the table so hard that her palms stung with pain. "Even now you take no responsibility. It's your duty as magistrate to manage the Isles, not mine, not the queen's, and not the sovereigns'! You put no effort into your governing! You let the Lost Seekers grow larger and more powerful because you feared being harsh on the populace, and look what that did. We have become infested with rebels and terrorists. Every day they grow in number and build their presence within our borders. What few absols and resources we have left after the sovereigns collect their taxes are stolen by these fiends and used against the lands under your charge. The sovereigns see this. They see that your position as magistrate is failing and that you are doing nothing to remedy it! They need to see that we can still handle our duties, that the Isles are not lost to anarchy and rebellion. Verrel paid the price for your incompetent rule. Their deaths will give the sovereigns the illusion that you are getting a grip on the situation here and that we are finally closing in on the Lost Seekers."

"And that's how you plan to prolong our people's lives? By butchering them in droves whenever the Lost Seekers strike? If that is truly your way of saving lives, then why did you allow some of Verrel's villagers to escape into the forest? Why ruin their lives, slaughter their loved ones, and betray their trust under the guise of perpetuating an illusion if you're not even going to end their suffering? Those who escaped your merciful wrath will make their way to the other towns and villages, tell the people what really happened, and tear down the illusion you've hung over this land. And when they do, or even if they don't, they will spend the rest of their days in a pit of sadness so deep that they will think back to the day you tore their lives away from them and wish they never made it to the tree line. And worse still, you tell me that twenty-two soldiers died in the process. How, might I ask, did so many trained men and women fall while burning such a small, defenseless village?"

"You know damn well that Verrel was not a defenseless village. It's widely known that the smaller and more remote human villages practice the old ways of our people more heavily, focusing on our race's tribal custom of a warrior society. Verrel was no exception. I didn't let them escape as a show of mercy. I never intended for any of them to make it out. The assault was supposed to be a quick sacrifice with no possibility for errors."

Julius looked as if he were about to add something, but Aellia gave him no room to do so. "Even still, it was a disaster. While their population remained within our estimate, almost all of the adults were armed, and many fought with the skill of trained soldiers. I ordered groups of cavalry to remain outside the village during the attack to prevent anyone from escaping. But I was forced to call most of them in to aid with the assault once I realized the situation. If I hadn't issued them in, we would likely have lost many more soldiers. It was only due to our greater number and the element of surprise that we managed to succeed without even greater casualties. If I had known Verrel was so rooted in the old warrior ways of our ancestors, I would have brought double the number of soldiers, but I didn't, so I was forced to make the call and prioritize the destruction of the village and the survival of my men and women rather than stopping a few escapees."

Aellia rolled her palms into fists and planted them on the table once more. "And from what we faced in that village, I would be damned if I was going to send anyone after those who fled. It would be nothing short of suicide to chase fighters of near equal skill into the woods, which they are no doubt familiar with. Darkness, confusion, and death waited behind those trees, and I wasn't about to lose any more people chasing after the remains of Verrel. Twenty-two died, but many more were wounded and are in need of aid. Even now we may be losing more. The garrison infirmary is full, and no healers are attending the temples of the Second Children while Cosom's eyes watch the world.

"The sovereigns needed immediate and effective action to be assured that we can still retain a grasp on the situation, and they got it. We will tell the people that no one escaped. Saying otherwise will only lead to the sovereigns finding out and viewing the mission as another failure. Those few who escaped will either fade away and keep their heads down or join the Lost Seekers, in which case nothing they say or do will have any leverage in the eyes of the sovereigns."

She felt out of breath, but that didn't stop her rant. "You need to get off your ass and start fulfilling your role as magistrate before it's too late. When taxes are expected again next August, if the sovereigns see that things haven't changed—or, more likely, have gotten worse—every village, town, hamlet, and farm, along with Caswen, will join Verrel as smoldering ruins."

With that, she removed her fists from the table, turned on her heel, and marched toward the door that the guards had exited through. Her lungs were sore from such a long verbal exertion.

"Aellia ..."

She stopped, but she did not turn around.

A handful of seconds passed as she stared at her fingers, which were wrapped around the wooden door handle. Then she resumed her leave, opening the door and marching into the torchlit darkness of the early morning beyond. No words followed her out even though she left the door open behind her. Aellia turned down the perimeter path that led around the square garden and headed off, wondering if, in her anger, she had said too much, too little, or nothing of sense at all. The only thing she knew for certain was that she was exhausted and needed a rest.

Chapter 11

Sebastian awoke staring up at the blue sky that was visible above the clearing. It took him a few seconds of blinking and adjusting to the light before he realized his back was sore, and his right arm was slightly numb. Tilting his body so it no longer rested atop his right arm, Sebastian allowed himself a few seconds to adjust before he tried to get up.

As he rose from the hard ground, his muscles and bones ached slightly with each movement. After a few stretches and blinks, he looked around the area. He was standing in a small clearing surrounded by trees, forming a messy circle of nature with long shadows stretching to the center of the open space.

At the center of the clearing was the long trunk of a tree that had fallen from the north and invaded the clearing, covering almost half of its width. From the thick moss that clung to much of the bark, Sebastian guessed the tree had fallen long ago, claiming the clearing as its grave.

Sitting atop the fallen tree were Helena and Nina. They had their backs to Sebastian and seemed to be staring at something below. Rook was sitting near the west edge of the clearing with his back against a tree. He was bare chested, Helena still wearing his tunic. Thankfully, the gentle August morning wind was warm, keeping Rook from shivering.

Rook turned toward Sebastian, giving him a displeased look. Before Sebastian could respond, Rook turned back toward the fallen tree.

Sebastian decided to join his sister and Helena. As he stepped over to the fallen tree, he suddenly remembered what had transpired the previous night.

Carver was lying belly down on the grass with his face turned toward the fallen tree and the back of his head angled upwards thanks to a mound of dirt his head rested against. The only clothing he had on was a pair of braies and strips of a bloody wool tunic tied around his head and left leg. His neck-length brown hair was caked in blood, most of it still wet and either clumped together or stuck to his face.

Sebastian would have assumed Carver dead were it not for the faint rising and lowering of his back. The boy was still breathing, despite his condition.

"What are you doing?" Sebastian asked as he stood beside the girls.

Nina glanced at him. "We're waiting to see if he wakes up or stops breathing," she said, her face drained and emotionally weary.

Sebastian looked at Helena, whose eyes had heavy bags beneath and looked even more drained than his sister's, making Sebastian wonder if Helena had gotten any rest during the night.

"Helena, has he gotten any better?" Sebastian asked with an awkward tone, worrying what her answer might be.

Helena turned to face Sebastian. "I don't know. The bleeding has slowed down a great deal, but even with the wrappings, I don't know if it will stop entirely before it's too late." Helena paused and looked at the ground. Her shoulders tensed, and her fingers pushed into the fallen tree's bark. "It's my fault. If I had just paid for that potion instead of leaving it for later, I could save him right now. I'm such a fool."

Sebastian raised an eyebrow. "Potion? What do you mean?"

Helena looked back up at Sebastian. Her eyes seemed redder than they had been moments earlier. "In Caswen. Carver and I ..." Helena paused and sighed. "Never mind. It doesn't matter. All that matters now is that we keep him alive." She returned her attention to Carver's gently breathing body.

"To you, maybe," Rook said before Sebastian could respond. "Who's to say the rest of us value his life more than our own?"

Helena snapped her head toward Rook. "Enough, Rook. We've already discussed this. You helped us with Carver, so you're free to leave whenever you wish."

Rook stood up and stepped away from the tree he was sitting against. "There you go again, speaking like I need your blessing to leave. You talk like you're in control of the situation, but you're not. I stayed and helped you with your dying friend only because our chances of survival are better off in a group for now, not because of your pathetic threats."

Helena leaped to her feet, though she wobbled for a second as her exhaustion hindered her balance. "So you think that you're in charge then, huh? Just because you're two years older than us? And watch your mouth about Carver, Rook, or I'll skip the praying and pin your guts to a tree myself!"

Rook took another step toward her. "Go ahead and try it. I'd be glad to take my tunic back from your corpse."

Knowing what Helena's response would be before she gave it, Sebastian stepped forward and wrapped his arms around her stomach. He struggled to hold her back as she lunged toward Rook, who was only a few feet away.

Rook held still and readied himself if Helena broke free from Sebastian's grasp.

"Let me go!" she snarled, her focus fixed on Rook.

"Stop, Helena!" Sebastian said as she strained to hold her back. "We can't start fighting each other. We need to stay calm and figure out a plan."

Helena tried to get at Rook for a moment longer and then finally ceased her struggling. When Sebastian released her, she spun around to face him. "And what would you have us do, then?" she demanded. "Our village is gone, along with everyone in it!"

Sebastian was unsure why Helena was speaking to him that way. He felt like he was receiving what was meant for Rook. He suddenly regretted holding her back.

"We don't know that it's gone!" he shouted. "We need to go back and see what's going on, if anyone's still there."

"If anyone survived they would have fled into the forest like us," Rook said. "There's no point in going back."

"We need to try," Sebastian said, an unexpected barrage of emotions bubbling to the surface. "People could still be there, hurt or looking for us. And if we don't go back, what should we do? Sit here forever?"

The others remained silent as the wind whistled gently through the trees.

"Dammit," Helena said after a moment. She looked up at Sebastian and sighed. "I'm sorry. I didn't mean to lash out at you like that, it's just that—"

"I know," Sebastian said.

Helena turned toward Nina, who remained sitting on the fallen tree, looking down at Carver with a grieved expression. "Nina," Helena said.

Nina finally tore her eyes away from Carver and looked up at her.

"Can you stay here and watch Carver? Sebastian and I will go see what is left of Verrel."

"No way," Sebastian interjected. "I'm not leaving her here with him." He pointed toward Rook.

"And what's that supposed to mean? You think I'm going to rape her or something?"

"It's fine," Nina said before Sebastian or Helena could respond to Rook. "I'm okay. I'll be fine."

Sebastian gave his sister a concerned look. "Are you sure?"

Nina's back stiffened and her weary face hardened. "Yes. I'm sure."

"Okay, then," Helena said, "watch Carver carefully. If his wounds start bleeding more heavily, or he stops breathing, do what you can."

Helena looked at Rook with a serious expression, but she held her tongue, letting her eyes do the talking.

Rook also remained silent, except what could be interpreted from his unpleasant expression.

Helena gave Carver one last glance, seeing his back rise again ever so slightly as he took another breath, then turned and marched off through the trees to the east.

Sebastian followed after giving his sister one more worried look, then disappeared into the ocean of trees that surrounded the clearing.

✠　✠　✠

The light of the sun slowly became brighter as Helena and Sebastian made their way to the eastern edge of the woods. The trees also began to stand farther apart, leaving wide gaps of space to walk.

Helena hadn't noticed how far she had run into the forest during the night; it had all seemed so fast when it happened. One moment she was carrying Carver up the hill, feeling the heat of her burning village on her back; the next she was blinded by darkness and struggling to avoid hitting every tree she passed. Then, suddenly, she found herself staring down at two of her friends who were hiding behind a fallen tree. The ten minutes of walking so far contradicted her memory of only running through the woods for a minute or two.

Next to her walked Sebastian, who had not said a word since the two of them had departed from the others. He kept up with Helena's brisk pace without complaint. Helena wanted to move quickly, thinking the less time Carver was alone with Rook and Nina the better.

Stepping over exposed roots and curving around the thick trees, the two of them continued to walk in silence until Sebastian came up by Helena's side. "You shouldn't have mentioned Lilberith last night," he said. "We were in a clearing, so the stars could see us. Cosom was watching."

Helena kept her attention on the path as she digested Sebastian's words, then turned to look at the boy, who was only slightly behind her on her right side. "I didn't notice that, with things happening as they were. Do you think he witnessed it?"

Sebastian shrugged as he kept pace with her. "Probably. The clearing let many of his eyes look right down at us. But maybe he was focused on something else when you said it. I don't know. I just thought I'd mention it. It's never a good idea to speak of the Second Children when Cosom is watching."

"I know. Well ..." Helena didn't finish, nor did Sebastian add anything else to the brief conversation. They both returned to silence as they continued their march through the brightening woods.

After only a few more minutes of travel, Helena and Sebastian emerged from the dense forest and stood atop the steep incline where Vellum Forest loomed over their village, or what was left of it.

They stood completely still, each trying to battle their emotions into submission as they gazed down the steep slope.

At the bottom of the hill lay the corpse of Verrel. Collapsed buildings were charred black from a full night of burning. Trails of gray smoke continued to rise into the sky, and a few fires could still be seen as they consumed the last of the unburned wood. Bodies lay stretched throughout the area, leaking out of the village perimeter like spilled grain.

Helena had no strength left to cry. She stepped down the hill without speaking a word, leaving Sebastian at the top, and headed down toward the silent village. She knew the answer to the question in her mind, but she still needed to see it for herself. She walked past the crumbling, charred ruin that was once a small cottage, the heat that destroyed the structure having long since fled the scene.

Helena scanned the carpet of bodies as she entered the ruins of Verrel. Pools of blood around many of the bodies told that the dirt could soak up no more. Much of the grass, drunk from the night of spilled blood, was stained dark red and sticking together in clumps.

It was painful for Helena to see the bodies littering the village, but she forced herself to keep looking while keeping track in her mind.

Not her; she's too short.

Not her either; too tall.

Not her; too young.

No, wrong-colored hair.

No again. Too young. Much, much too young.

No. No. Not her. Not her. Not her. Not—her.

Helena had known the answer, but she needed to see it, though she didn't know why. Falling onto her knees, Helena looked down at her mother's face.

Feira still looked beautiful. Her golden hair was untouched by the blood that covered the rest of her body, spilling from a wound on her side and a deep gash across her left thigh.

Helena strangely found herself hoping that her mother had died before finding Damath, as she had set out to do, because finding him would have only added to her mother's suffering before the end.

✠ ✠ ✠

"Were you seen? Are the soldiers still around? Did they see you?" Rook's words jumped at Helena and Sebastian as they emerged from the trees.

"No. There were no soldiers—or anyone else," Helena replied. Before Rook could ask her anything else, she turned away from him and headed over to Carver. "How is he doing?" she asked as she sat down on the fallen tree next to Nina.

Nina looked like she had not moved from her spot since they had left. "He's still breathing," she said, trying to sound as positive as she could. "Should we roll him onto his back now?"

"No. We should keep his head wound facing up, so the blood has a harder time reaching it."

"But he's not really bleeding anymore."

"That doesn't mean he won't start bleeding again. We don't have anything to stitch him up with, so the wound is still open. If we move him, the wound might start bleeding again. We have to let it heal a little before we can do anything."

"Bullshit!" Rook interjected from behind. He stormed in front of the girls before either of them could turn around. "You want us to just sit here and watch him breathe? What if the soldiers come looking for survivors?"

"I already said there are no more soldiers. They left."

"And how do you know they aren't sneaking about these woods or back in the city getting reinforcements? And even if the soldiers did leave, sitting around waiting for Carver to get better is ridiculous. What are we supposed to eat while we wait, huh? Grass and dirt? It could be days before he wakes up, if he wakes up at all. And then what? Do you think he won't starve either just because he's unconscious? I won't wait around in the woods to starve to death just because he wasn't fast enough to run out of the village."

"I don't think anyone ran as fast as you did," Sebastian said from behind Helena.

Rook's face flushed with anger as his hands curled into tight fists. "Do I need to remind you who got that soldier off your sister, Sebastian? Or who you both followed to safety?"

Helena turned toward Sebastian in confusion and saw the boy's face fill with shame as he turned his face slightly away from the group. Helena turned back to face Rook just in time to receive his next heated words.

"And you. You think you can just show up and make decisions for everyone. I won't be—"

Filled with rage, Helena stood up from the fallen tree before Rook could finish his sentence. "Well then, you can piss right off!" she snarled as she stepped toward Rook, who backed up a half step. "None of us are saying you have to remain with us," she continued, "so by all means, go."

Rook looked like he was about to launch a flurry of angry words at Helena. Instead, he let out a frustrated growl, then stormed off, digging his bare heels into the dirt with each step until he disappeared into the trees that surrounded the clearing.

Helena shot Sebastian a look. "What was he talking about? About you and Nina?"

Sebastian seemed like he didn't want to talk about it, but he forced himself to answer after he looked over Helena's shoulder to see if Rook was really gone. "Rook, he ... he saved us. Nina and I, we ... Two soldiers had us. They came into our home and killed our parents right in front of us, then grabbed me and Nina and dragged us outside. One was holding Nina down and trying to pull her clothes off. The other was dragging me away from her and laughing."

Helena felt sick as she imagined the scene. She looked over at Nina and saw that the girl was focusing on Carver as if she wasn't listening, but the sight of her fingers digging into the tree's bark revealed otherwise.

"That's when Rook appeared," Sebastian continued. "He jabbed a pitchfork into the face of the man on top of Nina. The other soldier let me go and went to attack Rook, but Rook stabbed his pitchfork into the soldier's chest. Rook looked at me then, but he didn't say anything. Then he just turned and ran, leaving his pitchfork in the soldier's chest. I didn't know what to do, so I grabbed Nina, and we followed him out of the village and into the woods."

"Oh," was all Helena could say in response.

A long silence followed as none of the three teenagers knew what to say or what to do. Sebastian looked down at his bare feet, which squished the grass into the dirt, while Helena looked at Carver, who remained breathing but unconscious.

"Rook is right," Nina said softly. "We need to stay in a group if we want the best chance of getting through this. But he's also right that Carver could take days to wake up, if he survives. What are we supposed to do until then? We have no shelter, no food or water, and nothing to protect ourselves from predators. There are vellums, giant spiders, and cougars in this forest. If we just sit here, eventually something will find us and try to kill us."

Helena did not respond. She merely stared down at Carver's body, counting the seconds between each of his faint breaths.

"We can go to Leydes!" Sebastian announced after a handful of seconds went by.

Helena was slightly annoyed by Sebastian's sudden outburst, which caused her to lose track of the time elapsing between Carver's weak breaths.

"What?" she asked, turning to face Sebastian.

Sebastian swallowed, now realizing he was the center of the girls' attention. Helena and Nina stared into his blue eyes. "We can go to Leydes," he repeated. "Our grandfather lives there and runs a fishery, remember? He'll take us in."

"That's a great idea," Nina replied, shifting her position on the fallen tree so she was facing her brother.

Helena looked down at Carver in silent thought as Sebastian continued. "He'll have room for us; I'm sure of it. We can go to Leydes, and he can get Carver help at the Temple of Siyon. All temples of the Second Children have priests devoted to Dema, and they're all trained healers and should have natural healing potions. They can help him."

Helena looked up as Carver took his tenth breath. "I know that Leydes has a temple with healers, but that doesn't change the issue. Carver is in no condition to travel, and Leydes is all the way up on the north coast. It'll take us damn near two days to walk there, three while going through the forest carrying Carver."

"Why would we go through the forest?" Sebastian asked. "You and I saw for ourselves that the soldiers are gone. We don't have to worry about them. It will take less time if we leave the forest and go across the Vellum Hills."

"Because they could come back," Helena said. "If any soldiers are lurking around looking for survivors, we'll be killed. We'll have no chance. The forest will keep us out of sight."

"She's right, Seb," Nina said. "And Vellum Forest stretches right to the southern border of Leydes. It's probably the safest route, all things considered."

The three of them fell silent as they pondered their options. Helena wondered what harm the trip could pose to Carver. Sebastian calculated the method by which they should proceed to Leydes. Nina tried to recall the last thing she had said to her parents before they were killed, but she couldn't remember.

"One day," Helena said finally. "We'll wait one day to allow Carver's wounds to heal a bit more and see if he wakes up. If he doesn't, his wounds should at least be stable enough that we can carry him to Leydes without causing serious harm. And maybe we can find medical supplies back in Verrel that survived the fires. As long as we're careful with him, his injuries shouldn't tear open again."

"What about us?" Sebastian asked.

"We won't starve. We partially live off this forest, remember? We can scrounge up enough food to get by and find a stream or a pond for water. And we'll make a fire to stay warm at night and stave off any beasts."

"Okay," Sebastian agreed, then looked at his sister for her response.

After a couple of long seconds, Nina nodded. "Okay."

Chapter 12

Aellia hadn't felt this angry in a long time.

The crowd below her stared at her with ogling confusion, chattering amongst themselves like a hive of disturbed bees. Handfuls of gray clouds were forming in the sky above Caswen, threatening to rain and further deteriorate Aellia's mood.

"What do you mean he won't come out?" one of the peasants called up to her.

In her exhaustion and frustration, Aellia had messed up her words and admitted that the magistrate would not come rather than spin her words into something more forgiving to Julius's public image. She clenched her jaw and inhaled deeply through her nose before continuing.

"Magistrate Julius very much wished to be here with you all now, but important matters required his attention. I meant to say that he cannot attend, not won't."

"What could be more important than this? First the market, now someplace else," a woman asked, her voice ringing out from the crowd.

"You can see the smoke from Caswen's bridge. Is nowhere safe in this whole damn province?" a man called out.

"Was it a battle? Are we under attack?" someone else asked.

"Be silent, all of you! The marshal of the Isles is speaking!" the male soldier standing next to Aellia on the scaffold shouted.

He was outfitted in the same uniform as the other soldiers standing around the scaffold, the only differences being that his surcoat was black instead of gray and had a red hexagon insignia with three out of six pieces filled in rather than the one or two pieces the other soldiers had showing. His helmet kept his hair hidden but left his pale face—young but aged with black stubble and hazel eyes—exposed to the gawking crowd below.

"Calm down, Harsond. The people's inquiries are just and duly expected," Aellia whispered so the crowd could not hear.

She turned away from Harsond and locked her hands together behind her back, facing the expectant folk. "As I am sure you are all well aware, yesterday the Lost Seekers launched an attack on the market that claimed many lives. I'm also sure that by now most of you have witnessed, or heard from someone who has, the clouds of smoke rising from over the western hills."

Murmurs slithered throughout the crowd. Aellia ignored them.

"On the night of August first, the soldiers of the Caswen Guard launched a strike against a Lost Seekers den rooted in the village of Verrel."

The hive-like buzzing of whispers from the crowd amplified. Aellia felt every last person's eyes on her, awaiting her next words.

"The Lost Seekers, those who steal from the Sovereign Empire and the Kingdom of Terraland, who murder the innocent to advance their goals," a gut-wrenching sensation of anger, sadness, and self-judgement filled Aellia's being as she spoke those words, "corrupted the minds of Verrel's inhabitants and used the village as a central outpost for their treason and villainy throughout the Eastern Isle. We ... we surrounded the village and wiped the Lost Seekers out to the last, torching the village to ash and cinder so as to leave no foundation for those from other cells to return."

Much of the crowd fell silent amidst a few murmurs.

"Not only were the people of Verrel aligned with the Lost Seekers, they were also the force primarily responsible for the attack on Caswen's market. These are somber times, when our own people work against us to steal our resources and slaughter innocents." She paused, the unpleasant feeling intensifying inside her. "But know now that the issue has been resolved, and those villainous terrorists from Verrel will cause no more harm to anyone ever again.

It is our hope, unfortunate though it may be, that the destruction of Verrel will substantially weaken the power of the Lost Seekers within the Isles and that this is the start of real progress toward eradicating this misguided rebellion once and for all from our kingdom and from the mighty Sovereign Empire."

With that, Aellia unlocked her hands from behind her back and turned to face Harsond. "Disperse the crowd," she ordered, then walked past him and down the wood steps behind the scaffold.

She heard the buzzing of whispers from the crowd as she headed off. She knew the words being spoken by the commoners could only be about two things: sorrowful discussions about the events she had just informed them of or the chatter of those who saw through her lies and mistruths. Aellia wondered how many Lost Seekers were in that crowd, how many of them were horrified at what they had caused, and how many of them were clicking their heels in glee at the fact that someone else had taken the punishment for their actions.

Chapter 13

Twenty-four hours passed. Carver did not wake up.

The group's march was slow as they headed north through the thick woods. Helena carried Carver by his legs, while Sebastian hoisted him up by his shoulders. It was a poor way to transport such a gravely wounded person, but they had no alternative.

As painful as it was for her to return, Helena had gone back to Verrel during the day of waiting, this time with Rook, who had returned to the group less than an hour after he had disappeared. He accompanied her, though not to her desire or liking, to scavenge anything they might use or eat. However, the two of them found that Verrel had been almost totally destroyed, with anything that remained taken by the soldiers.

The animals were also missing, having fled or been stolen. What few crops that had yet to be harvested had been burned or trampled, and what hadn't been reduced to ash or buried beneath heaps of collapsed wood had been thoroughly looted.

Naught was left to be taken but the corpses themselves and the clothes off their backs. Rook found the body of a man roughly the same size and shape as him and took the body's tunic to replace his own, which Helena still wore.

Helena spoke against Rook taking the clothes from a dead villager, but after a short argument Rook convinced her to see the situation as it was.

Though she disliked the idea of it, Helena and Rook also gathered four pairs of boots from the bodies around the village.

After nearly two hours of searching, with most of that time spent rummaging through collapsed cottages that still sent thick trails of smoke into the sky, the only things Helena and Rook were able to recover besides the boots and the tunic were from Helena's parents' blacksmith shop.

The first was an arming sword—a double-edged, two-foot iron blade attached to a plain iron guard with a smooth, cylindrical wooden grip above a round iron pommel. The blade was only missed by the looting soldiers because a heavy wooden beam had pushed it into the ground during the structure's collapse. Helena had only found it by luck after deciding to lift the beam during her scavenging. The second item was a chunk of cracked flint, which they found buried amongst a pile of broken bricks that was once the smithy's kiln.

When Helena and Rook had returned to the fallen tree with their scant findings, a heavy cloud of discouragement befell the group.

Every few hours of traveling, Carver's wounds would start to bleed, at which point Helena would call the march to a halt and tend them as best she was able.

Carver's wounds, still wrapped tight in the wool strips of Helena's old tunic, had healed minimally during the twenty-four hour wait. The shrapnel puncture in his left calf had barely begun to scab over, and the deep slash on the back of his head had only been partially stitched shut by Helena. It had taken her hours of the previous day, painstakingly pulling out and then twisting her own hairs together into strands of three and using carefully selected splinters of wood to push through the skin of Carver's scalp. The stitching was not going to hold up, already portions of it had snapped, but it was the best Helena could manage.

Carver's color had improved slightly, though, and his breathing continued to come at a steady, albeit weak, pace.

Rook grumbled each time Helena called for a stop. He complained about their slow pace brought about by Carver's inability to walk and made it clear that he thought the sensible thing to do was to leave Carver behind.

Helena ignored Rook, instead focusing on Carver: monitoring his breathing, inspecting his wounds for reopened scabs, and carefully squeezing the juice from crushed berries down his throat. The group was starving, having eaten only berries and herbs since formulating their plan the day before.

During Helena and Rook's venture to Verrel, Nina left her brother behind to watch Carver and went searching for food in the forest. She found a small pond not far from the clearing and was pleased at the amount of raspberry and blackberry bushes that grew along its shore. She picked the area clean and then brought the bounty back to share with her companions, after slaking her thirst with the pond's cool water.

The berries were not yet ripe and left a sour taste in their mouths, but it was all they had to eat apart from dandelions, plantain leaves, mallow, and clovers that littered the forest floor.

Beyond the group's desire to reach the pond and drink its cool waters, as Nina had, they also had wanted to venture farther into the forest to find something more filling, like an apple tree, bed of carrots, or a patch of potato plants, but the arrival of lurking creatures shortly after Nina's return denied them their desires.

The creatures were short and low to the ground, only slightly larger than the coyotes that also prowled the woods, but instead of fur or hair they were covered in green leathery hide. They walked on four back-jointed legs, each ending in flat, round paws with six short claws protruding from the circumference, looking like flattened Venus flytraps made of thin leather. Their backs and sides were covered in small, thin black spines, each coming to nearly two inches in length. The spines were thickest near the creatures' heads, forming horn-like protrusions that pointed backwards. The creatures' heads themselves looked more amphibian than canine, with black eyes and large mouths that stretched up and down with their movements, their mouths supported entirely with muscle and no bone or cartilage.

These creatures were known by many names, including vellums and goblin wolves, but most commonly as vells. To the denizens of Verrel, they were a familiar sight.

The vells had no doubt marked Nina, who was on her own, as easy prey, but once among the other teenagers, however, Nina was as safe as anyone else in the group. Vellums were cowardly creatures that would not attack a group of humans unless they had double the number or were starving.

Helena counted three of the creatures skulking about the perimeter of their dwelling throughout the day of waiting. She used the iron arming sword she had recovered to sharpen the ends of a handful of thick branches, fashioning them into short, makeshift spears. But even with their weapons, the group did not stray from the clearing for the rest of the day after the vells showed up, leaving them thirsty for the cold water of the pond that only Nina had gotten the chance to drink from.

The vells stalked the clearing's perimeter during that night, forcing the group to remain awake and keep their fire, that had been lit to the group's relief after Helena scraped the chipped chunk of flint against the iron sword for almost an hour, burning as high as they could get it. Only once did the pack set foot within the edges of the firelight, snarling with their strange, vibrating croaks at the frightened teenagers.

Helena and the rest had shouted in unison and thrown hefty stones at the intruders. Any that got too close received a warning slash from Helena's blade. The vells held back for the rest of the night, giving the group a chance to sleep in shifts for the last remaining hours before dawn.

Rook had mostly kept to himself during the day-long wait after returning with Helena from Verrel, only interacting with the others when they were distributing forest rations, be they the berries from Nina's venture or whatever herbs and edible plants the rest of them could find a few feet out into the denser woods without getting too isolated.

The vells followed them as they made their way through the massive forest the following day, rustling the bushes every now and again as they stalked the drained and sleep-deprived group.

During the first hours of their first day on the move, Helena began to think that maybe they should risk moving through the open hills rather than stay in the woods with the vicious beasts. She knew that eventually the pack would sense the group's fatigue, brought on by their lack of proper sleep, hydration, and food, and test their luck again. Helena was unsure whether they could hold the vells back if the creatures fully committed to an attack, and in sufficient numbers.

With Carver occupying Helena and Sebastian's hands during the march, Nina and Rook were tasked with carrying the team's supplies, aside from the remaining flint that Helena kept in her pocket. Nina took charge of the scavenged blade while Rook held onto the three spears, agreeing to the load only after having made a long-winded argument detailing why he, as the oldest and the strongest among them, should be the one to wield the arming sword.

Helena had wanted to wait longer in the clearing after waking, seeing that Carver had not yet regained consciousness, but she had promised her friends, and Rook, that they would leave after one day. She knew that lying on the ground in the middle of the forest and being awkwardly force fed the juice of crushed sour berries was not a good way for Carver to recover, but Helena didn't know what else to do. She knew Carver needed proper aid and that the temple in Leydes could provide it, but she didn't want to hurt him by carrying him through the forest.

When the light of the sun once again vanished beyond the trees, and darkness crept in, the group stopped for their first night away from the clearing. As the two moons rose into the star-filled sky, the summer air chilled more than it had the previous two nights, leaving the group to shiver in their minimal wool clothing until they managed to make a fire after several attempts.

Sebastian did his best to build the fire up to banish the night's chill, despite Nina's constant comments from her seat by the fire's edge, just within the first ring of its orange light, that it was too high and was going to catch the surrounding trees on fire. After the fire needed no more care, Sebastian took the first watch so the others could sleep.

Rook sat closest to the fire, on the opposite side from Nina who lay on her side facing the flames, and didn't speak a word to the others for the whole night.

Helena found herself playing with the idea that the vells would come back and drag Rook into the woods while he slept. Maybe then the beasts would leave the rest of them alone, having full bellies from Rook. The mental image partially amused her, though only for a moment, as she remembered that Rook had given her his tunic to cover herself. She still did not understand why he did, though she had no intention of asking.

Helena was sitting up against a tree, close to the swaying fire, with Carver lying next to her, his head resting on her lap.

Carver's breathing continued at a steady pace, and his skin, though pale, retained some of its color from the previous day. Occasionally, his eyelids would flutter, and his lips would part, emitting a soft sound akin to a groan. Every time this happened, Helena was filled with the hope that he was finally waking up, but it was never the case, and each time she felt more foolish for hoping than the last.

The sight of him in such a state made Helena sick with worry, thinking that at any second his breathing would cease and she would be unable to bring it back. She tried to push away her anxiety by looking up at the two moons, which were just visible through a gap in the dense treetops.

One moon was larger than the other by about two thirds and was partially obscured by the smaller moon, which traveled through the sky a little ahead of it at all times, though they were nearly side by side. Both moons always appeared full in the night sky, never waning or waxing despite the time of month or year. The smaller moon gave off a pale sheen while the larger moon behind it glowed with a bluish hue, creating a gentle mix of pale-blue light that kept the nights of Gaia from being totally dark. Helena had always thought the moons to be the most beautiful yet sad things in the world.

"Do you remember the story of the moons, Carver?" Helena whispered. "I know you never cared much for the legends of the gods, but we're taking you to one of their temples, so if you can hear me in there, you'd better start caring right now. Dema's priests aren't going to be very fond of you if they learn that you don't even know whether Dema is trapped in Xothos or Volmrir."

"Is he awake?" Nina asked, startling Helena.

Helena looked over to see Nina staring at her with wide eyes.

"Oh, no. I'm just talking to myself, really. I'm hoping he can at least hear me, even if he can't respond."

Nina's eyes relaxed, and an expression of pity crossed her face. She pulled her legs in and sat cross-legged, then shuffled closer to Helena. "Can't sleep?"

"Not really."

"Me neither. Even with Sebastian on first watch, I don't feel safe closing my eyes."

Helena didn't have anything to say in return.

"Will you tell me a story?" Nina asked suddenly.

"A story?"

"Yeah."

"Why?"

"To distract us from everything, or at least try to," Nina said. "Besides, you're always reading those storybooks about history. You know more about most stuff than I ever will."

Helena couldn't help the corner of her mouth from grinning. "I've only read a couple of books in my life. You know how hard they are to come by around here. And they weren't really storybooks. It was mostly history stuff that doesn't really work well in story form."

"Well, then tell me about the gods, like you were just doing with Carver."

"But you already know about the gods; we all do."

Nina looked at the dirt. Her short bangs obscured part of her face, but Helena could tell that she was beginning to tear up. "Please, Helena. I can't stop thinking about everything that's happened. Verrel and my parents, and that soldier who was going to—" Nina stopped as if the next word had got stuck in her throat. "I just want to think of something else, even if only for a little bit."

"Nina, I'm sorry." Helena reached forward and placed her hand on Nina's knee. "I didn't mean to be so stubborn about this. Of course I'll tell you a story."

"No, I'm sorry. I'm acting like a stupid child," Nina said through a soft whimper that she tried and failed to hide.

Helena wanted to give Nina a hug, but she didn't want to disturb Carver by moving too much. Instead, she rubbed Nina's knee, then took her hand away and began her tale. "At the start of all time there was only the Void, an infinite blackness that was everywhere and everything."

Nina looked up. Her eyes were red, but she smiled faintly.

"From that great blackness came Cosom, and he was lord over the Void. The stars are his eyes, and with them he could see every inch of the ever stretching nothingness, which was everything."

Nina looked up at the stars, which were partially visible through the tree-tops, and shivered.

"Cosom's power was as mighty as the Void," Helena continued, "and through his great will he created the world of Gaia, though it looked nothing like it does today. Back then the world was a harsh place, a land of rocks, mountains, barren stretches of earth, dark caves, steep crags, and vast chasms leading to untold depths. Cosom desired to have subjects to worship him and entertain his many watchful eyes, so he created the intelligent races of the world: humans, dwarves, goblins, and the tartaruns, all of them known as the First Children, and sent them down to inhabit the world that he had fashioned from his will."

"What about the sovereigns?" Nina asked. "Cosom must have made them too."

Helena sighed. "Yes, I suppose he must have created them too and put them somewhere so far south that we never knew of them until they conquered us."

"Gaia must be huge if the sovereigns weren't known for so long."

"It must be," Helena agreed. "Anyway, so—"

"Oh, sorry for interrupting," Nina said, embarrassed.

Helena smiled. "Don't worry, Nina. I like talking with you."

Nina smiled, sending a much-needed dose of positivity into Helena.

"Gaia was engulfed in the darkness of the Void at all times, with the only light coming from Cosom's distant eyes as he watched the First Children over untold generations. The races of the First Children fought one another with tooth and fist to survive, for Cosom had not created water, plants, or animals to sustain them. The First Children ate each other's flesh and drank each other's blood for survival, and they battled for dominance of the lands, as each of them had the desire to conquer and control due to the spark of their creator residing inside them, and all who died had their souls returned to Cosom in the Void. This was the Age of Darkness, and it stretched for a nearly endless time, with Cosom watching from the Void above with his thousands of eyes."

Helena paused for Nina to interject again, but Nina only cradled her legs and waited patiently.

"Among the races of the First Children, we humans fought the hardest and were the most devout to Cosom, and of all humans, one was most watched by the stars. She was a woman who had won ten thousand battles, whose war cry echoed up into the Void, and who had rallied a vast army of warriors behind her and founded a great tribe in the heart of what would later be called Terraland."

"Dema! That's Dema!" Nina said, looking up excitedly at the largest moon.

Helena nodded with a smirk. "It was Dema. And she became Cosom's favorite living thing, for not only could she fight like no other, she was also beautiful, devout to Cosom, and led her people like a goddess, commanding respect and loyalty from everyone in her tribe. Many of Cosom's eyes followed Dema from battle to battle and watched as each fight made her stronger and more revered among her people. Then, after the largest and bloodiest battle Dema and her tribe fought, Cosom found that he desired her.

"Cosom descended from the Void as a shooting light that struck the world and created a vast crater with his landing. All the stars vanished at that moment as Cosom took physical form and stepped, for the first and only time, onto the world that he had created.

"A darkness the likes of which no one had ever experienced, or has ever experienced since, fell over Gaia, for Cosom's eyes and the light they gave were no longer above the world. Those who witnessed the falling of light that struck Gaia cowered in fear from its blinding power, and those who did not see it felt the whole world shake from the impact and were filled with sudden fear that was no less potent. While none of Gaia's people knew that this was Cosom descending to Gaia, the overwhelming darkness and violent shaking of the world filled all of the First Children with a great dread. As such, the massive crater of Cosom's landing was known as the Crater of Dread.

"Dema's great tribe was one of those that saw the shooting light's descent, and of every gathering of people in the world at that time, they were the closest to where it struck, being at the edge of where the Crater of Dread began its downward slope into the heart of Gaia. They were among the only living things to see the burning white light, akin to starlight and the only remaining light in existence at that moment, that emanated from the massive crater. The light emanating from the depths of the crater called to the souls of those who saw it, but only Dema was brave enough to travel toward the light and descend into the great pit.

"She climbed downwards for many hours until she finally reached the wide bottom. It was there that Dema laid eyes on the chosen physical form of Cosom, who stood in the center of the deep pit, where the ground turned flat and smooth. He was the center of the white light that emanated from the crater. He appeared to her as a human man in pale flesh like that of her people. He was tall and dark haired, robed in swirling starlight that sparked with magical energy. Through all his magnificence, Dema's attention was most drawn to one thing: his eyes. They were as black as the Void, yet his irises were white and glowed with a piercing starlight that seemed separate from the light that filled the crater and made up his clothing yet also the same.

"It was then that Dema realized the light from every star in the Void was shining on her through those eyes and that all of her god's sight was fixated on only her. She knew she was looking at the face of Cosom. At the moment of Dema's realization, Cosom spoke with a voice that came as much from his lips as it did from all around her and from inside her head. Cosom said that Dema was a champion like no other of the descendants of his creations and that he wished for her to return with him to his realm above the world as a living being, one who would be free from the call of death forever, to be his bride.

"Dema could not deny her desire to accept Cosom's offer, but neither could she banish her hesitation, for she already had a husband, Kol, who was a great warrior and who had fathered two children with her, a son named Lok and a daughter named Vail. Dema loved them all deeply. She also loved her tribe, who would be lost without her. Dema was trapped between two choices: abandon everything she loved and ascend to immortality in the Void or defy her god and return to those who loved and depended on her. And it was then that she gave Cosom her two conditions."

"She must have been very brave to give conditions to her god," Nina said, her eyes glittering with fascination.

"Yes. She was very brave, and Cosom, amused that Dema would dare give him conditions but also impressed by her bravery to challenge his offer, listened to her two conditions. Dema's first was that if she were to leave the world, her family, and her people and watch them as an immortal being for all eternity alongside Cosom from the Void, she wanted the power to create in order to help her people and so that she would not truly be abandoning them.

"Cosom agreed to her request with one condition: that everything she created would belong to him, that the wills of her creations could neither match nor surpass those of his own making, and that her creations would remain tied to his will alone. Their souls would have to return to him in the Void upon death.

"To this Dema agreed, and then she gave her second condition: that she be allowed to return to the world at times and provide company to her family and her tribe. Cosom refused, saying that if she were to join him in the Void, she would be his and only his and would not be permitted to set foot on Gaia ever again. Despite this refusal of her second condition, Dema was unable to walk away. Instead, she asked if she might at least return to say goodbye to those she loved before leaving them forever. Cosom agreed to this, showing that he was not without some manner of compassion for his subjects, and Dema, with her terms now met, promised herself to Cosom before she scaled the wall of the crater and returned to her tribe.

"When Dema returned to her people, who all anxiously awaited her at the edge of their cold, barren land not far from the crater's edge, she told them of her interaction with Cosom and informed them of her impending departure from the world. But when she approached her husband and spoke of her imminent departure, a bitter anger filled him. Kol protested his wife's willingness to wed herself to another, regardless of it being Cosom, and a burst of hate clouded his thoughts. In this hate, Kol cursed Cosom openly, only avoiding Cosom's wrath due to the god's attention being contained within the

Crater of Dread, and refused to let Dema say farewell to their children under threat of violence, saying she was no mother to Lok and Vail if she would abandon them in such a way.

"Dema was filled with despair, for she could not sway Kol, nor could she harm the man she still loved in order to see her children one last time. At that moment, Dema may have declined Cosom's offer and healed her relationship with Kol if she had not already promised herself to Cosom, but she would not risk Cosom's wrath on her people for breaking her promise. And so, with deep sadness, she returned to the starlight-filled crater without having said goodbye to her children. She descended into the Crater of Dread and was ascended to the Void with Cosom as his godly bride, and she never again returned to the mortal world or spoke with those she left behind."

Nina shuffled in her spot. "That's so sad."

Helena nodded slightly. "It is."

"And that was the end of the Age of Darkness, wasn't it?"

"Almost. I was getting to that."

"Oh, right. Sorry."

"Cosom stayed true to his word and splintered off some of his godly power and gave it to Dema, granting her the power to create and add to his world as she saw fit for the benefit of her people. But now that Dema was a god and could see all of Gaia from her seat in the Void next to Cosom, she was witness to all of the First Children and their lives and desired to affect them all. In the time that followed, Dema created many things. She created fire so we would have greater light and could keep warm. She created water and placed it in the dips and cracks of the world's rocks, making great rivers, wide lakes, and deep seas so that we no longer needed to drink blood, even filling the Crater of Dread, which afterwards was known as the Sea of Dread. She brought into being trees and plants that bore fruit and vegetables, and animals that we could hunt so we no longer needed to cannibalize our own or battle the other races for the purpose of eating each other, though many battles and wars were still fought for other reasons.

"This was the beginning of the Age of Creation. It lasted for nearly as long as the previous age, now under the care of the Godmother Dema, and the watchful eyes of the Godfather Cosom, to whom every living thing remained bound as their wills and souls were tied to him and were still under his gaze, for all that Cosom sees is his."

Nina looked up at the few stars she could see past the treetops and shivered.

"During the height of the Age of Creation," Helena continued, "Dema bore Cosom three godly children. The first was a son, whom they named Agon. Next was a daughter, named Siyon. The last was another daughter, Lilberith. They were known as the Second Children. The Second Children spent their early lives watching the world from above and marveled at the worship their mother and father received from the First Children. Over time, each of the Second Children wanted their own people to lord over. One by one the Second Children of Cosom asked their father to grant them the power to create and the right to lord over those below, but Cosom denied their request. He had grown bitter and jealous during that age, for as he watched the world progress, he noticed more and more of his creations worshipping Dema rather than him, for she continually added to the world while Cosom merely watched.

"Cosom watched this shift of worship among his First Children with growing displeasure and decided he would never again share his power, as doing so had not only weakened him but also turned his creations toward another despite remaining tied to his will. He told his Second Children that if they wanted the power to create, as their mother did, they could only receive such power from her alone and that they would also obey the same rules Dema did. All their creations would be owned by him alone and have their wills subject to his. Their souls would also return to him upon death, and they could not match or surpass the wills nor mimic the form of the First Children.

"The Second Children obeyed their father and begged their mother for some of her power, and Dema, who loved her children with all her heart, could not refuse their wish. So it was that Dema fractured the power she had received from Cosom in the same manner that Cosom had done for her, and she bestowed these parts of her husband's power to each godly child in equal amounts.

"To her firstborn, Agon, Dema granted mastery of fire and all creatures that took to the air. To her second born, Siyon, she granted mastery of the waters and all creatures that could be found within. To her third born, Lilberith, Dema bestowed mastery over all plant life and insects. The last of her power she kept for herself, still holding mastery over the many animals and beasts that roamed the plains and hills of the world."

"The power meant for the Stolen Child," Nina said.

"Hold on, Nina. I'm getting there."

Nina blushed apologetically.

"With the power gifted to them by their mother, the Second Children descended to the world as gods in flesh, as Cosom had not laid the same restrictions on them about setting foot on Gaia as he had laid on Dema, leaving the Second Children free to travel back and forth between Gaia and the Void as they wished, and they used their fractions of Cosom's power to their own desire.

"Agon, with his mastery over fire, taught the mortal races the art of smithing and forging. Siyon taught the races sailing and how to master the winds so that the seas, lakes, and wide rivers might be traversed. Lilberith brought new plants into existence with magical properties similar to the effects of magic wielded through sorcery and showed the mortals how to craft them into potions.

"In thanks for their new power, the Second Children fashioned great gifts for their mother and delivered them to her upon one of their returns to the Void. Lilberith bestowed upon Dema a dress of vines and flowers that never wilted and would change into new styles and colors to match Dema's desires and moods. Siyon gifted her mother with a tiara of water that kept its form and shape yet flowed like a stream and created the peaceful sounds of a gentle river whenever it was worn. Agon gave his mother a sword he had forged himself of unmatched strength with a blade of bright-red iron that would ignite into flames when drawn. To their father they gave no gifts, and then they returned to Gaia and continued to walk among the First Children as gods.

"So it was that the races of the First Children slowly began to revere and worship the Second Children, along with or even instead of Cosom, just as they did with Dema. The Second Children, being born of the union between Cosom and a human woman, were fond of the human race and even took the form of humans as they walked the lands of Gaia. Of all the lands they spent their time in, Terraland was their favorite because it was the birthplace of their mother and the realm of her people. They began to travel to the other lands less and less, sometimes with hundreds of years between visits. As such, over thousands of years the other lands and races of Gaia began to forget Cosom, Dema, and the Second Children, who had taught them so much.

"The other races, and even other humans in different lands, as it's told, adopted false faiths and legends over time, renaming the gods and losing the true history of the world and becoming ever shunned by Cosom, who resented anyone who turned away from him for any reason. But of all the First Children, the humans of Terraland never strayed from the true gods. Great temples to Cosom, Dema, and the Second Children were erected in the first villages of Terraland and its numerous tribes. The Second Children eventually stopped returning to the Void and grew in pride as each temple dedicated to them was built."

Nina fidgeted as Helena looked at her. "Do you know what this all led to, Nina?"

"The Great Betrayal."

"That's right. See? I told you that you knew more than you thought," Helena said, smiling. Nina blushed at the compliment.

"As the pride of the Second Children grew, so too did their lust for their own realms and people to lord over. After so long spent in the mortal world away from the Void, the Second Children began to think less of their father. They forgot their father's wrath, the power he wielded, and the severity of his claim on all creation. So it was that each of the Second Children disobeyed their father's greatest command and created races of their own design that mimicked the First Children in appearance, intelligence, and will, tied to their individual will alone.

"Agon gave rise to the race of the harpies, Siyon brought forth the race of the naiads, and Lilberith created the race of the dryads. These new races were known as nymphs, also the Third Children, and they each resembled humans mixed with creatures native to their creators' mastery. Despite the Second Children's desire that the Third Children should equal or even surpass the First Children in intelligence and will, their power was not as great as Cosom's, and they failed to achieve such creations, although each harpy, naiad, and dryad was still more similar to the First Children than to any animal or beast.

"This act of disobedience enraged Cosom, and he summoned his Second Children back to the Void. There Cosom said that their power was now forfeit and must be returned to him. Their creations were also to be destroyed because they were not tied to his will, and therefore were unfit to live within his all-seeing sight."

Nina giggled. "Cosom should have chosen different words."

"Careful, Nina," Helena said as she looked up at the partially visible cluster of stars above. "You shouldn't laugh at such things. We may be in Lilberith's realm right now, but you never know when Cosom or his spies can see you."

Nina's pleasant expression dampened slightly. Then she also looked up at the few stars visible through the gaps in the forest's branch and leaf ceiling. "I wasn't making fun," she said to the sky, her voice tinged with worry. She turned back to Helena. "I was just saying. I didn't mean to laugh."

Helena met Nina's gaze with a shrug.

"Please keep going, Helena. I'll try to interrupt less."

"It's okay, Nina, really. Besides, the story is nearly finished."

Nina nodded and waited in silence.

"So, anyway, Agon, Siyon, and Lilberith, well ... they told their father that if he didn't want to see their creations, they would block them from his sight. They each fled from the Void and returned to Gaia with the intent of separating their father from his world and their creations. Lilberith grew many trees into existence in an instant and brought them together to create Gaia's forests, which she had her dryads retreat within. These thick forests blocked her father's view of everything beneath their tops, and Lilberith crowned herself as Lord of the Wood. Siyon dug deep into the rock of Gaia and filled it with her waters, creating the Great Ocean where once much land used to be, and to its embrace she called her naiads. Her ocean was too deep and dark for her father to see to the bottom of, and at the lowest depths of the ocean, she crowned herself Lord of the Deep.

"And Agon, who wanted all the remaining lands that were still within his father's sight, climbed to the highest peak of Terraland's western mountains and harnessed his mastery over fire to create a great ball of flame. The power of this great flame was so much that it set the mountains on fire, burning away everything except the stone. Then Agon hurled this burning sphere into the sky, naming it Aol, though we also know it as the sun in the sovereign tongue. It burned so brightly that it blinded his father from seeing the world and covered all of Gaia with warmth and light, giving Agon lordship over all the fields, hills, and mountains that were touched by Aol's light. The mountains Aol was cast from continued to burn for weeks and since that event have been known as the Mountains of Fire. Then Agon crowned himself the Lord of the Flame, and his harpies made their dwellings and nests in the mountains where they could be closest to their creator's skyward flame.

"Although the sun can only burn in the sky for so long, as it requires much of Agon's strength to keep it burning, so Agon must call Aol back down to the world when he tires. Aol weakens, and Agon hides it in the ocean to the west within his sister's care so as not to leave it in Cosom's sight, where it might be harmed in its diminished state. During Agon's time of rest and the rekindling of Aol comes the night, where the Void becomes visible once again, and Cosom's eyes peer down upon the world for a time before Agon returns Aol to the sky and brings back the day. So was created the cycle of Gaia's days and nights, a constant struggle between a father and his son.

"The event of the Second Children blocking their father's sight is known as the Great Betrayal, and it enraged Cosom. Cosom vowed to murder his Second Children, destroy their creations, and take back the realms of the world that were stolen from him. Dema begged Cosom to stay his wrath, but Cosom was filled with an even greater rage at her words.

"Cosom cursed Dema, saying that if she would side with those who took her power and not with the one who had gifted it to her, she was not deserving of such a gift and must return what little of it she had left so that he might use it to destroy those who had wronged him. But Dema refused, saying she would not relinquish her gifted power, for she was bound by a mother's love to bestow it upon another, her fourth child, who was yet unborn and growing inside her. Cosom said he would not allow Dema to spawn another who would betray him, and with great power he ripped the unborn child from Dema's womb and decreed that she would never see her other children again. This act led to the Cries of the Void that echoed down to the world and were heard by all living things.

"The First Cry came from Dema at the pain of her child being torn from her. This cry was heard by all and brought with it Dema's pain and suffering at the violent loss of her child, which forever tainted childbirth for all creatures and turned it into a painful experience in a mimicry of what Dema felt at that moment. Then came the Second Cry. Cosom had forgotten Dema's strength, for though during the Age of Creation she had adopted the role of caregiver to the First and Second Children, becoming a goddess of healing, nurturing, and protection, she was still the fierce warrior from her past, a past that Cosom had long distanced her from. When Cosom said she would never see her children again, Dema remembered the pain she suffered when her worldly husband, Kol, had told her the same thing.

"Dema would not allow her children to be taken from her again. She turned back into the warrior she had always been, with her dress of vines and flowers erupting into thorns. She drew her sword, which Agon had fashioned for her, and it glowed red with her rage and burned with the flame of its maker. She plunged the blade into Cosom's chest. Cosom let out a great, world-shaking cry of agony as Dema's blade, known forever after as Blood Spiller, pierced his heart.

"Cosom's blood, his godly essence, spilled down to Gaia, carrying with it much of his power, and entwined itself with the very being of the world and entered every living creature. Cosom's essence entering the world and its creatures birthed the power of sorcery and magic, which only some people develop an ability to use, with those people known as sorcerers. Since Cosom's essence coming into our world, only humans and sovereigns have ever shown the ability to wield it through sorcery and channel it into magical spells.

"Cosom survived the wound, though he was forever weakened by it. Many of his eyes closed forever as he lost the power to see through them all. Those stars that remained open became lesser and pulled back from the world, no longer illuminating Gaia as they did in ages past. A great scar was left where Blood Spiller pierced his heart, a scar that forever burns like a fire pushed into his chest due to Agon's enchantment over the weapon. Despite this blow and great loss of his essence and godly power, Cosom managed to strike Dema down with violent fury. It was at that moment when the child that had been ripped from Dema's womb, known only as the Stolen Child, opened its eyes for the first time, and the first thing it witnessed was the violence and rage of its parents.

"The Stolen Child, filled with fear at the sight, let out a cry of terror that echoed down to the mortal world. This was the Third Cry, and with it came a great change to Gaia. For the Stolen Child, unbeknownst to Dema and Cosom, had taken with it upon its removal from its mother's womb the last of her power to create and change the world. As such, the Stolen Child had mastery over every remaining creature that Dema had retained after imparting her power to her other children, but that mastery was misused and corrupted by the violence surrounding the child's birth into the Void. The Third Cry corrupted many animals and creatures throughout the world, changing them into dark beasts and vile things of horror and death. Many new creatures came into being as well, bolstering the ranks of the world's dangers with monsters of all sorts.

"After that, Cosom imprisoned Dema in a sphere of rock, known as Xothos, and placed it above the world for all to see. He did the same with the Stolen Child, entombing the babe in a smaller rock prison, known as Volmrir, beside Xothos in the sky. These prisons are called the moons in the new language. But Dema's resilience was too strong, and her love for her people and her children was too great for her grief to silence her. So, every night when Agon brings Aol down to rest his power, and when the world is left in the darkness of the Void and back in sight of Cosom's remaining eyes, Dema uses what sliver of her power she has remaining to send light to the world amidst the blackness of the night.

"Her power pierces through Xothos and sets the rock aglow with blue light, giving us what little light she can until Agon regains his strength and puts Aol back in the sky. The Stolen Child sees this glow from within Volmrir and imitates its magnificence with what little godly power it can muster, though Volmrir glows pale, for that glow of Dema is all the child has ever known aside from the brutality of its birth and the cold darkness of its prison of rock."

"The Age of Betrayal," Nina said suddenly.

"What?" Helena asked, having gotten lost in the story.

"That was the beginning of the Age of Betrayal. The current age."

"That's right. See? I knew you knew this story well enough. Next time I'll get you to tell it to me instead."

Nina grinned and shook her head. "No way. I couldn't tell it nearly as well as you do."

Helena grinned. "Well, then how about you finish it for me at least. What happened next?"

"Well, um, the Second Children stayed in their stolen kingdoms and started claiming the souls of living things that died in their new realms. Oh, and they also created the seasons to show the First Children that they still had power and influence over Gaia. Lilberith brought spring where everything grows and insects flock to the flowers. Agon created summer with heavy heat and clear skies. And Siyon brought autumn, which brings frequent rains and strong winds from the ocean. But Cosom created his own season to keep his presence in the world. It was winter, and its sole purpose was to attack the creations of the Second Children. Through winter, Siyon's waters freeze, Agon's fires are doused, and Lilberith's plants die."

"What about Cosom's spies?" Helena asked, already impressed with how Nina told the tale.

"Oh, yeah. Cosom created new creatures to spy on the world during the day and within the kingdoms of the Second Children. Cosom made the giant spiders that prowl the woods and also the little spiders that hide in people's homes and always watch from hidden places. He even gave spiders lots of eyes just like him so that they can watch lots of things. Also crows and owls. He crafted crows and made them as black as the Void. They watch from the skies during the day and report back to him in the night. Owls do the opposite, helping him watch the plains and towns at night and sharing their knowledge once the sun—I mean Aol—goes back up. We don't know if Cosom has spies in the depths of the ocean because we don't know what's down there, apart from all kinds of fish, seals, whales, krakens, and naiads." Nina paused suddenly. "Oh, do you know anything about naiads? Were they in any of your books? I heard they're beautiful."

"No. I don't know anything about naiads besides that they're strange water people with tentacles for legs or something."

"Oh well, never mind then. What about the—"

"Nina, we really should try and get some sleep. Especially you, since you're taking the next shift for night watch after your brother."

Nina frowned slightly. "Yeah, I know. Okay, I'll try to get some sleep. But can I ask you one last question, Helena?"

"Okay."

"Do you think that because humans who develop sorcery are rare, but all sovereigns apparently develop sorcery with ease, that sovereigns are Cosom's favorite race?"

Helena didn't know where that question came from so suddenly, nor did she have any clue as to the answer.

"I don't know, Nina. Cosom never intended for magic to enter the world. Those who can wield sorcery into magic spells are technically stealing from Cosom, using his spilled essence as power for themselves. From what is told about Cosom withholding his godly power after sharing it with Dema, I don't think he wants people to use his essence for their own power."

Nina didn't seem entirely satisfied with the answer, but she didn't press further. "Okay, well ... goodnight, then." Nina shuffled back to her spot by the fire, uncrossed her legs, and lay back down facing away from Helena.

"Hey, Helena," she called after a moment without looking back.

"Yes?" Helena replied, fatigue in her voice.

"Thanks for talking with me."

"No problem, Nina. Now try and get some rest."

"Goodnight."

"Goodnight."

Helena looked up at the two moons once again and wondered what Caswen looked like in the light of the moons. The thought of Caswen made her pause. Her last good memory of that place was purchasing the white steel necklace with the winged-horse charm, which she had dropped when the first blast sent her and Carver to the ground. She thought the necklace's loss was a shame since she was just about to put it on when the chaos started.

She bit her bottom lip and wondered how she could feel any significant loss over a trinket after what had befallen her and her companions. She reminded herself that she had lost much more than a piece of jewelry and could potentially lose much more. She tried to stop thinking about it and looked down at Carver's head resting on her lap.

She tried to comb her fingers through his hair but stopped when it became clear to her that the blood had dried and knotted it into hard clumps. *A shame,* she thought, *Carver's hair is normally so soft.*

Chapter 14

❧

Helena felt a rush of fear as she awoke, not remembering why she was not in her bed at home. After a few seconds of looking around at the thick trees, her memory came back to her.

Carver remained unconscious with his head on her lap, steadily breathing in the cool morning air. Sebastian, lying next to the arming sword, was asleep next to his sister near a faintly smoking pile of charred branches and leaves within a circle of small stones. Rook was asleep on the other side of the smoldering pile, facing away from the group.

Helena allowed the quiet moment to linger, taking slow breaths and letting her eyes adjust to the rays of sunlight that came through the dense treetops above. Suddenly, she felt a jolt of panic travel through her body.

The vells! her mind screamed.

Helena carefully moved Carver's head from her lap and onto the ground. Then, leaping up, she darted over to the sleeping siblings.

"Guys!" she yelled as she got to her knees and shook them. "Guys, wake up!"

Both of them woke up immediately, as did Rook a second later due to the commotion.

Nina pulled her head away from Helena, trying to put distance between herself and the cause of her sudden fright.

Sebastian sat up and turned his shocked eyes to Helena while reaching out in the wrong direction for the arming sword. "Wha—what's going on?"

"Everyone's asleep! Why wasn't I woken up for my shift?"

Sebastian pulled his hand back from its blind search for the sword behind him and scanned the immediate area. "Shit! I didn't know I fell asleep. I'm sorry. I was supposed to wake Nina after my shift."

"Wha—we only had a watch for two hours?" Helena's eyes widened further.

Rook jumped to his feet, fury on his face. "You could have killed us all, Sebastian! What were you thinking?"

"I'm sorry!" Sebastian looked from Rook to Helena and then back at his sister. "I was so tired. I was having trouble standing, so I sat down next to Nina by the fire. It was just supposed to be for a minute. I didn't think I would fall asleep. I'm sorry!" Sebastian was clearly scared and ashamed.

Helena immediately regretted the manner in which she assaulted Sebastian with her words. She knew he didn't mean to fall asleep. They were all exhausted, dehydrated, and starving. Keeping their eyes open during their daylight march was strenuous enough. She hadn't even remembered falling asleep herself.

She remembered watching Carver breathe, speaking about the gods with Nina, thinking about the Caswen market, and then nothing. Sleep had snuck up on her, as it no doubt had to Sebastian, and she knew she could not entirely fault him for that. But that meant they had been vulnerable most of the night to an attack from the vells. To Helena's surprise, though, the beasts hadn't come. The fact that she was awake told her that.

"It's fine," she told Sebastian before rising from her knees. "We should get moving. We still have two days before we reach Leydes."

"It's fine?" Rook said in disbelief. "Sebastian could have gotten us all killed, and you say, it's fine?"

Helena turned and glared at Rook. "What happened, happened, Rook! There's no point in fighting about it. We're alive, and the time to get moving is now. So, get yourself ready if you don't want to be left behind." Her tone was angry and unflinching.

Rook glared back at her but didn't say a word. Instead, he turned and made his way behind a collection of trees to relieve himself.

Helena turned back to Sebastian and Nina. Sebastian slowly got to his feet, stretching his back, which generated a multitude of cracking sounds. Sleeping on the ground had left him feeling very sore. His aches only worsened as he arched his back to relieve some of the stress. Nina did the same, with similar results.

Once Sebastian understood that his discomfort was going to stick with him for the rest of the morning, he turned his attention to Helena. "Are we still going to stay in the forest? I thought you were thinking about taking our chances through the hills."

At the sight of Sebastian's stretches, Helena realized she had also had a very uncomfortable sleep. Her back ached from being propped up against a tree all night, and her right thigh was sore after being used as a pillow by Carver for so many hours. She began her own painful stretches before answering Sebastian.

"I still don't know. None of us know why Caswen's soldiers attacked or why they didn't seem to search the forest for survivors. We don't know what their plan is or what they're doing. We don't even know if Verrel was the only place they attacked. Maybe Leydes is gone too. Maybe it's being burned right now, or maybe bands of soldiers are marching across the hills as we speak, on the way there. We can't risk being seen by anyone until we know what's going on."

"But what about the vells?" Sebastian asked, his posture betraying his fatigue.

"I feel our odds are much better against a pack of vells than against a group of soldiers."

"Maybe the vellums are gone," Nina said. "They didn't attack us while we slept, so maybe they aren't following us anymore."

Helena thought hard about her answer before giving it. "I'm not sure why the pack didn't come for us while we slept. Maybe the fire kept them away. But I don't think they would have abandoned potential prey. They most likely found something else to eat and are saving us for later, waiting for our lack of food and proper rest to catch up with us." Helena found it odd how calmly she presented the idea of being killed and eaten by wild animals.

"Which is precisely why we should go across the hills," Sebastian said. "We could probably be at Leydes tomorrow morning if we leave the woods. The pack will most likely not follow us out of the forest, and if we see any soldiers, we can run back in."

Again, Helena thought hard about her answer before replying. "And what if the soldiers see us first? What if they follow us into the woods this time? Armed soldiers are not going to be held back by shouts and sharp sticks, Sebastian."

Helena could tell that Sebastian was thinking hard too. "I don't know," he said finally, apparently not having thought hard enough.

"The only food we have available to us is whatever we find inside the forest, even though we've barely found anything of the sort. If we go across the hills, we certainly won't find anything to keep us going. It's just grass out there. No weeds or herbs grow across the hills, and no berry bushes sprout. There are no ponds or streams between Verrel and Leydes that aren't also in these woods, despite the fact that we haven't found any since the one Nina found."

Helena looked over at Carver's unconscious body and sighed. "Of course the one who knows this forest best between all of us is the one who can't help. If Carver were awake, he would make this so much easier."

Helena kicked the dirt. "Dammit," she cursed under her breath. Then she looked back at the siblings, whose eyes were fixed on her. "The way I see it, it's either two days in here with access to limited food and water, if we're lucky, and the threat of wild animals, or one day out there with nothing but the threat of armed soldiers."

"And why do you get to decide for the rest of us?" Rook called out as he returned from behind a dense cluster of trees across from where Helena was facing. The other three turned toward him.

"I don't, Rook."

"Well, you're certainly acting like you do."

Helena growled under her breath. "I'm simply stating the situation we're in and the dangers of going across the hills. If you want to take your chances out there, go ahead and try it. But when you get spotted by soldiers on horse-back, don't come running back to us."

Rook walked up to the group and pointed a finger in their direction. "You'd like that, wouldn't you, Helena? You'd love it if I just disappeared so you lot could get to Leydes without me and keep me out of the arrangement."

"What arrangement?"

"Their grandfather." Rook gestured to the siblings with an aggressive flick of his wrist.

Helena frowned. "You think you're owed a place at their grandfather's, if he even takes us in at all? You're no friend of theirs, Rook."

Rook's face turned red. "You're damn right I think I'm owed. I saved Sebastian and Nina's lives back in Verrel, Nina's more so since she was going to be raped before she was killed. And for that they owe me. Both of them. What did you do for them, huh? Other than show up with a dying boy who has done nothing but slow us down and keep us in danger."

Helena felt an urge to charge Rook and punch him, but she held herself back. She looked at Sebastian and Nina, who gazed back at her with expres-sions of defeat. She could tell they agreed with Rook, that they felt they owed him a debt for saving them, and Helena had to admit that maybe they were right for feeling that way.

A heavy wave of sadness suddenly came over Helena as she felt her exhaus-tion growing, while her anger seemed to drain away what little energy she had regained from her poor rest.

"Is that how you both feel? Are Carver and I a burden? Are we just slowing you down?"

Sebastian and Nina shook their heads.

"No, of course not," Sebastian said.

"We would never think that, Helena," Nina agreed.

Helena turned her attention back to Rook, feeling sad and angry at the same time. "Maybe you're right, Rook. Maybe you do deserve a place in Leydes more than I or Carver do. And maybe Carver and I are slowing the group down. And maybe, even after all the time and energy we've spent dealing with Carver, maybe he'll still die, and all that I had us do was for nothing. But that doesn't mean I'm going to leave him behind or risk all of our lives by trekking across the open hills just to save us a day of walking."

"Then why don't you stay in these woods and drag him along yourself?" Rook said. "I say we go across the hills. Without Carver weighing us down, we can pick up the pace and be there in no time."

Helena didn't respond to Rook. Instead, she turned her attention back to the siblings and saw that Sebastian and Nina were looking at each other with grim faces.

"What do the two of you think, then? Should we leave and go across the hills? If we split up, we'll just be increasing the odds of the vells getting whoever stays in the woods, especially if only one of us were to try and get to Leydes alone and bring back help. I won't leave Carver behind, and I need help carrying him to Leydes, so I'll go whichever way you all go. And Rook has made it clear that he'll follow you two no matter which route you choose. So, it's up to you guys, then. Choose."

"I don't want to decide," Nina said. "I just want us all to stop fighting and work together. Helena's right that we can't split up without giving the vells even more reason to strike."

"Then pick a way to go, and we'll all go together," Rook said.

"No. I don't want to be responsible for this. I'll go whichever way you three decide," Nina said, looking over at her brother.

Sebastian didn't say anything as he turned away from his sister, only to see that both Helena and Rook were staring at him as well. It immediately became clear to him that if his sister would not choose, he was the one who had to break the tie. Feeling nauseous, he looked away from everyone, staring at a ray of sunlight that passed through the thick treetops above and warmed the cold dirt a few feet away.

Despite turning away, Sebastian felt like he could feel everyone's eyes staring at him as they all silently waited for him to break the tie on what could be a life-or-death decision. In that silence he could barely hear Carver breathing softly on the ground a few feet away. He thought about his answer long and hard before he spoke.

✠   ✠   ✠

The band of teenagers built another small fire during their next night in the woods, during which, between all their night-watch shifts, none of them noted any presence of the vellums.

When Helena awoke the next morning, she thought that perhaps Nina was correct in her prior day's statement that the pack of vellums had abandoned them in search of easier prey.

They were now one day away from Leydes, if their assumptions were correct, and they didn't waste a second of their morning. As the first beams of sunlight found their way down through the treetops, the group resumed their march with high morale, knowing that their time in Vellum Forest was approaching its end, though the boost of their mood died quickly as the pain in their legs, stomachs, and backs and the dryness in their throats soon arrived to burden them.

Carver remained unconscious, forcing Helena and Sebastian to use up what little strength they had left to carry him, though he was now breathing more steadily, and his wounds had mostly scabbed over, thankfully, with no sign of infection.

Rook remained a stone's throw ahead of the group, their slow trudge induced by Carver infuriating him. He had tried again to acquire the arming sword through an argument of how he was the oldest by two years, was the strongest, and felt the least exhausted among the group, but he wound up carrying the three makeshift spears once again.

Nina followed at the back, arming sword in hand, picking as many edible roots and herbs from the ground as their pace allowed, their supply of berries having run out the previous day. The group stopped for more breaks than they had during the previous two days of walking, and each break was lasting longer and longer as none of them wanted to be the one to end the rest and move the group onward, though Helena was always the one to carry that burden in the end, feeling each time like she was directly responsible for everyone's displeasure.

The group continued in an almost trance-like state, induced by their fatigue, hunger, and thirst, which clouded their minds and dulled their senses.

The trees around them began to feel endless, and the idea of ever seeing the end of the woods seemed impossible.

When Nina suddenly screamed from the back of the group, however, those ahead of her snapped out of their trance and turned their heads in a panic. Helena and Sebastian nearly dropped Carver in the process due to their haste and fright.

"Nina!" Sebastian screamed as he released his hold on Carver's shoulders. The side of Carver's head hit against the dirt, sending a deathly shock of dread into Helena's heart. Her immediate instinct was to set Carver's legs down and check if the wound on the back of his head had reopened, but the sight of the vell biting into Nina's face stopped her in her tracks. Instead, Helena let Carver's legs fall onto the dirt.

The vell had Nina pinned to the ground and was biting her face with its frog-like maw, stabbing dozens of tiny teeth into her forehead and left cheek.

Nina flailed violently, kicking and clawing at the beast, but the thin spines on the vell's sides and back cut her hands and punctured her boots, forcing Nina to recoil from each strike. The blade she had been carrying lay by her side. It was within reach, but her panic overwrote her actions and sent her hands toward her aggressor rather than clawing the ground for the dropped weapon.

Sebastian sent his booted heel into the creature's large black eye. The vell croaked furiously, sending a gust of hot breath into Nina's face. It released its hold on Nina, tearing strips of skin from her face as it did, and turned its attention to Sebastian.

Nina broke into a panicked crawl away from the vell the instant it released her. She grabbed at her face, writhing and screaming as blood seeped through her fingers. The arming sword near her was struck by her frantically kicking legs and spun toward her brother.

Before the boy could react or grab the blade, a second vell emerged from the dense foliage and fastened its hanging mouth around Sebastian's right hand. Sebastian shouted in agony as the vell's small but numerous teeth stabbed into his palm. The vell he had kicked in the eye lunged forward and sank its teeth into Sebastian's left ankle just above his boot, mixing the siblings' blood in its mouth.

Sebastian tumbled backwards to the ground, with neither vell releasing his limbs. Feeling the muscles in his hand shred apart, Sebastian thrust three fingers from his free hand into the second vell's large left eye. A gargled snarl exited the vell's mouth as it released Sebastian's hand and jumped back. Sebastian's fingers exited the creature's eye socket as the vell leaped away, leaving a grotesque clump of bloody eye matter behind. The vell collapsed to the ground and kicked its back legs in pain while pawing desperately at its wounded eye with its round, six-clawed paws.

Two more vells sprang from the bushes the moment Helena collided with the one biting Sebastian's ankle. Helena threw her body into the vell's side, tearing it from Sebastian's heel and tackling it to the ground in a desperate lunge that caused the vell to kick and displace the nearby arming sword from Helena's view. She screamed as she felt dozens of the vell's small protective spines stab into her arms and chest.

The vell squirmed and clawed at the ground, trying to get away from Helena, but before it could make any progress, Helena shoved her fingers into the creature's bulbous left eye. The vell snarled with rage and tried to pull its face away as she drove her fingers down to the knuckle into its eye socket.

Helena tore her fingers out from the vell's eye and threw herself to the side to avoid the beast's claws as it spasmed on the ground.

Sebastian fought the urge to faint. The pain in his ankle and his hand threatened to send him into shock, but he managed to hold fast and stay conscious, which allowed him to witness the two new attackers that had emerged from the woods.

The two new vells ran past the first vell, which had retreated farther back amidst the pain in its ruined eye, and attacked Sebastian from his right side. One lunged fast toward his throat, but Sebastian flung his right arm up, shielding his neck. The creature sank its teeth into Sebastian's upper arm instead, the same arm to which Sebastian's chewed and bloody hand was attached. The other sank its teeth into the boy's hip. Together, the beasts began pulling Sebastian away toward the bushes, each yank of their leathery, dark-green heads forcing a howl out of the boy.

Without rising off her knees, Helena grabbed the vell biting Sebastian's hip by the back of its legs and pulled. The vell slid toward her but did not separate from its prey. Instead, it sank its teeth deeper into Sebastian's side.

Helena searched for the dropped blade, but it seemed to have vanished. All she saw was Nina writhing on the ground a short distance away, her blood-covered hands still wrapped over her face.

"Rook!" Helena screamed, looking up to where she remembered him being.

To Helena's dread, she saw that Rook had his back pressed against a wide tree while two vells snapped their boneless jaws at his sides, only held back by Rook's jabbing and thrusting with one of the makeshift spears. The other spears were lying on the ground just a foot away from Rook next to the tree.

"Rook! Kick me a spear!"

Rook looked up at the call, but as he turned his head, the vell to his right lunged forward and attempted to bite into his thigh. Rook's attention was pulled away from Helena by the vell's movement, and he only just managed to thrust his spear to stop the creature's advance. The branch's sharp tip stabbed into the side of the vell's mouth, and the beast jumped away. The second vell on Rook seized the opportunity to lunge and sink its teeth into Rook's upper arm.

Rook shouted in shock and pain as he pulled his arm back, causing the vell's teeth to tear into the skin of his elbow and leave behind multiple lines of ripped flesh. Rook slashed the top of his spear at the vell's face, but it ducked away and stepped back. The vell that Rook had stabbed a moment before scurried to the side and stepped toward Rook's open flank.

Rook stumbled back and put the tree between himself and the two vells, accidentally kicking the two spears on the ground farther from himself in the process. Both vells pursued Rook around the tree, causing him to retreat farther, the remaining spears well beyond his reach behind the charging creatures.

Helena's heart sank at the sight, realizing she was on her own for the moment. The two vells on Sebastian continued to bite into his flesh and tug him away. Helena dug her fingers into the tough, leathery skin of the vell's legs in an attempt to pull its attention away from Sebastian, but the beast did not release its grip on the boy. Instead, it kicked one of its hind legs back at her chest. Helena recoiled with an awkward shuffle.

White-hot pain erupted from Helena's right knee, causing her to look down. She saw that her right knee had been cut horizontally, across its lower end. Blood seeped from her raggedy wool pants and dripped onto the dirt next to the short blade between her legs, which remained pressed against her knee.

Helena cursed her stupidity and lack of perception when she realized what had happened. Without wasting a moment, she removed her right hand from the vell and reached for the arming sword, which had been right beneath her, and scooped it up so fast that when she pulled it off the ground, its sharp edge cut the face of her injured knee again.

The pain sent a surge of anger through Helena that she converted into energy as she clenched her hand around the weapon's grip and stabbed the blade into the vell's exposed flank.

The vell released its grip on Sebastian's hip, shrieking with a reverberating croak as it did, and turned and snapped its flapping mouth at Helena.

She shouted and pulled the vell's leg while simultaneously pushing her right arm forward. The vell was pulled back, and the blade sank deeper into its flank. Blood spilled from the vell's wound and traveled down the blade, coating Helena's hand.

Unable to reach the girl with its boneless jaws, the beast leapt to the side, tearing itself away from the blade before stumbling and collapsing to the ground with another croaking bleat.

Helena turned her attention to the vell that was still attacking Sebastian and attempting to drag him away by the arm. The vell maintained its grip on the boy's right arm, twisting it aggressively. Sebastian was fighting back with a flurry of punches with his free hand. His fist connected with the vell's flat snout again and again, but each strike only prompted the beast to pull harder and bite deeper into Sebastian's arm. It was all Sebastian could do to keep fighting from his awkward angle.

Helena stood up and closed the distance between herself and the vell attached to Sebastian in two quick strides. Seeing her advance, the beast released Sebastian, leaping back, but it did not go far enough. Helena swung the blade with both hands, cutting through the vell's face with a clean swing.

The vell croaked in shock and collapsed to its side, but before it could attempt to escape, Helena dropped to her knees and drove the blade into the beast's side, pinning it to the ground. The vell flailed its limbs in a desperate attempt to flee, but Helena put all her weight into the sword, sending it deeper into the vell's body. The vell went still a moment later as a pool of red quickly formed beneath its body.

Helena pulled the blade from the beast as she stood and turned toward Sebastian, who was struggling to stand up.

"Sebastian, get up! We need you!"

Sebastian barely managed to rise to his knees before he tipped forward and had to push out his arms to stop his fall.

Helena ran to him and wrapped her left arm under his chest. Sebastian leaned into her as she pulled him upwards, focusing less on standing and more on enduring the pain his ascent caused. Just as he managed to get to his feet, Sebastian heard his sister shriek behind Helena.

"Help!"

Helena pulled away and ran toward her.

Without Helena as a crutch, all of Sebastian's weight fell upon his injured ankle. Before he knew it, his back hit the ground.

Sebastian rolled to his side, renewed pain shooting through his body. He tried to push himself back up, but his right arm and hand were too damaged, and his left arm could not handle the burden alone. Collapsing in failure, Sebastian looked at where Helena had run, then paled when he saw his sister's situation.

Two vells lunged and snapped at Nina, who was standing between them and Carver's unconscious body. She was swinging and jabbing a heavy branch at the creatures, but each vell danced away from the branch's short reach. The vells pushed Nina back until her heels bumped into Carver. Then the two creatures tried to flank her, but before they could, Helena showed up.

The vells jumped back as Helena swung her bloody sword from side to side. As the creatures retreated, Nina and Helena advanced. Nina swung her heavy branch toward the vell on the right while Helena attacked the vell on the left.

Sebastian tried again to stand, but his ankle was unresponsive amidst the pain, and his right arm, riddled with teeth marks and bleeding profusely, couldn't bear his weight. All he could do was watch Nina and Helena as the agony from his injuries overwhelmed him. He wanted to call out his sister's name, to shout and be heard, but the pain was too great. Nina disappeared from his vision as darkness swallowed him. The last thing he saw before consciousness failed him was his sister's heavily bleeding face.

Chapter 15

The sudden hard knock on Aellia's door startled her, causing her hand to spasm and the quill she held to create a displeasing stroke across a portion of the paper, ruining some letters.

"Come in," she said with an ounce of annoyance.

The door to her quarters creaked loudly. "I'm sorry to disturb you, Captain, but—"

"Drop the formalities, Harsond. I'm in no mood for such things," she said with a wave of her hand. She did not look up from her writing to acknowledge him; rather, she licked her thumb and attempted to rub away the slash of ink that blotched her letters.

The sound of the door clicking shut told her that he was there for more than a quick exchange.

"Sure thing, Aellia. I just thought I'd check to see how you're doing. We've all noticed that you've been looking stressed these last couple days."

Aellia turned to look at her guest. Harsond wore a similar uniform as the rest of the city soldiers and Aellia, with a few exceptions. He wore a light gambeson covered in a chain hauberk with a matching mail chausses, with a black surcoat overtop displaying the bear emblem of the Isles. His light-brown hide boots were laced, his dark leather gauntlets were tightly fitted, his round iron helmet sat firmly atop his head, and he had an arming sword strapped to his belt. Over his right breast on the black surcoat was a crimson hexagon with three of six pieces filled in.

Harsond was standing just inside the door to Aellia's right, about ten feet away from where she sat at her desk, which was in the center of the square room a little off the north wall. The room was filled with light from the window on the east wall, which allowed the sun's rays to pass by the full bookshelves on the south wall and warm up the brown rug that covered most of the wooden floor.

"Have you all? That's wonderful," she said, her tone contradicting her words. "I'm fine, Harsond, but I do appreciate the concern. I just have a lot on my mind lately."

"The wedding stressing you out that much?" Harsond asked in a light-hearted tone.

Harsond's candid attitude pulled a faint smile out of Aellia. "That's certainly part of it. I still have trouble believing it's real sometimes," she said as she set her writing quill on her desk.

Assuming Aellia's dismissal of the quill to be an invitational gesture, Harsond folded his arms and leaned back against the door. "If it's too stressful, you could always marry me instead. I don't need a fancy ceremony at the fort. We could do it here and now," he quipped with a grin on his stubbled face.

Aellia met Harsond's grin with one of her own, with the addition of a roll of her bright brown eyes. "I'm going to have to deny your request, unfortunately. I don't elope with homeless vagrants, which is exactly what you would become, as it is not permitted for a captain to romance her lieutenants, which means I'd have to fire you here and now in order to grant such a request. And here I thought you enjoyed your pay and lodgings at the garrison above all else."

Harsond unfolded his arms and applauded his captain's wit. "It seems you've thought it all through, then, meaning you have thought about it," he jibed.

Aellia leaned forward over her desk, resting her chin on the back of her hands as she shot Harsond an amused glare. "Not to mention your age. I'm still in my prime while you're getting on in years."

Harsond gave her a look of shock, though it was clear no offense was taken. "Getting on in years? I'm barely pushing thirty-four. That's, what, five years ahead of you?"

"Try nine."

Harsond blushed as he realized his overestimation of Aellia's age could be taken as disrespectful, though her demeanor remained unchanged.

"Am I to continue crushing your fantasies, Harsond, or have you come for anything else?"

With a satisfied sigh, Harsond straightened his posture and removed his helmet, revealing a head of short hair, black to match his stubble beard and moustache and matted with sweat.

"Well, just one other thing. It's about that young soldier, Kieran."

Aellia's joyful sensation evaporated as a cold, harsh feeling of angst filled her. She kept a calm face, however, so as not to reveal her feelings.

Harsond strolled over to the bookshelves to his right and placed his helmet on the middle shelf of the closest one, then turned back to Aellia while leaning on the same bookshelf, completely unaware of his captain's feelings. "Some of the younger lads have been looking for him, apparently, wanting to see how he's faring after that attack at the market, you understand. They couldn't find him here at the infirmary. And they checked the city temples of Agon and Siyon, but he wasn't among the other wounded soldiers being tended to by the Godmother's priests there either. Some of the lads even went to his house, thinking that perhaps the priests had already patched him up and sent him home to recover, but the boy's mother and sister said they haven't seen or heard from him since the market attack. The lads are his friends and all, and they're worried about him, but they're too nervous to ask you directly, so I thought I'd do them a favor. Do you happen to know what happened to Kieran after you took him to see your father that night?"

Aellia flinched.

"Ah, sorry," Harsond said, biting his upper lip.

"Tell those concerned about Kieran not to worry about it," she replied, trying to maintain her calm appearance. "He's with the manor physician."

Harsond lowered his brow and tilted his head in confusion at Aellia's words. The reaction didn't surprise Aellia in the slightest.

"Kieran and I were on our way out of the manor after he informed the magistrate about that Lost Seeker from Verrel who attacked him when he suddenly lost his balance and collapsed in the north hall. I carried him to the manor physician immediately, who told me that Kieran was suffering from a type of lethal poison."

Harsond furrowed his brow even further with an added look of genuine shock.

"It appears that the rebel from Verrel who beat him in the alley also nicked him with some kind of toxin-coated blade. The effects of the poison seem to be slow acting, in which case the physician thinks it can be diluted in the boy's blood through careful administrations of cleansing decoctions and healing potions. I've been checking on Kieran each day, but he is, unfortunately, still unconscious. The poison seems to be stronger than the physician originally thought."

Harsond's worried face tensed with displeasure at the news. "Poor kid. I hope he pulls through. What kind of sick bastard would subject a young man to such a thing? If those Aethi'ziton scum just wanted to steal the tax shipment to finance their villainy, why would they use a poison that doesn't take effect until after they're long gone?" Harsond spat out each word, with growing anger in his tone.

Aellia felt a similar level of irritation and anger, though hers was brought on for entirely different reasons. "I'll be checking on his condition again tonight," she said, trying to discern a way to quickly end the conversation. "Just tell the rest that it's out of their hands for now and that they'll just have to wait and hope for him to recover."

"I'll do that," Harsond said in a melancholy tone. Before he could say anything more, Aellia initiated a dismissal.

"Oh, here, before you go, take this." Aellia grabbed her quill, dipped it in an inkwell, and scribbled the last words onto the bottom of the thin paper she had been writing on.

Harsond watched in silence as Aellia folded the paper and sealed it in an envelope with a red wax seal.

"Here," she said, extending her arm over the desk.

Harsond scooped up his helmet from the bookshelf behind him, then walked over to the desk and took the envelope from Aellia's hand. "What's this?"

"Let's call it a written denial of your previous request," she said, grinning.

Harsond grinned back, though he didn't quite understand what Aellia meant. "Alright, I'll take a peek once I inform Kieran's lads down in the mess hall."

Harsond put his helmet back on and prepared to leave.

"Thanks for the talk," Aellia said, glad it was over.

"Any time. Got to make sure my captain is stable and clear in the head, after all. Otherwise, I might get stuck doing her job," he joked as he shoved the envelope into his surcoat pocket, then opened the door and stepped into the doorway.

Aellia smiled one last time before Harsond disappeared through the doorway, followed by the loud creak and click of the door sealing behind him. Alone once again, Aellia took out a new sheet of paper and applied her inked quill to its surface. Her thoughts kept her from writing, however, as images of Kieran continuously distracted her.

After a handful of unproductive minutes, Aellia set the quill aside and leaned back in her wooden chair, tipping the two front legs off the ground ever so slightly. A wave of stress washed over her, calling for her to break down. She pushed the feeling away by pretending someone else was in the room, watching her for any hint of weakness.

Once the unwanted emotions within her had subsided enough, Aellia tilted forward to plant the legs of her chair back on the floor and stood up. She pushed the chair back and walked over to the door, thinking long and hard before she finally grabbed the handle.

✠　✠　✠

The change in volume as Harsond emerged from the stone stairwell into the garrison's main hall always surprised him. The stairwell did a superb job of buffering out the noise from the rest of the garrison, evident since Harsond hadn't been able to hear more than an echoing murmur from below while in the above room and hallway just a moment ago.

It must get lonely up there, he thought.

He scanned the large rectangular hall. The room was filled with low oak tables, each one hosting a mess of dirty wooden mugs, plates, and bowls. Groups of armored men and women sat on stools on each side of the cluttered tables, some in pairs, while others sat in groups of three or four. Many chatted and ate as normal folk would, but several sat in silence or ate alone.

A waving arm drew Harsond's attention. It belonged to an older soldier with short gray hair and a graying beard and mustache who was sitting at a table on the south side of the room. Helmetless, he was sitting with two clean-shaven younger soldiers, both of whom had concerned looks on their faces.

Harsond reached the table and sat down on a stool beside the older man while receiving an intense stare from the two younger soldiers who were sitting across from him.

"So? What did she tell you?" one of the younger soldiers asked.

Harsond ignored the question at first, instead grabbing a half-filled mug of water from the center of the table and downing it without a thought as to whose it was. Placing the empty mug back on the table, Harsond looked at the two young men across from him.

"She says not to worry about Kieran. He's with the manor physician. Has been since the day of the market attack."

The younger soldiers' faces turned ripe with confusion, but Harsond didn't give them room to ask anything more. "He's been poisoned. That Lost Seeker who beat his face in also nicked him with a poisoned blade or something. Kieran fell unconscious and is being administered doses of certain medicines and potions in an attempt to save him."

"How are we supposed to not worry about him?" the other young soldier blurted. The same question was written on the other's face.

"Because there's nothing you two can do. It's out of your hands, so worrying is pointless." Harsond tilted the empty mug toward himself and looked inside. "He'll either pull through or die in his sleep. Considering how a lot of the others went, you should be grateful Kieran is only faced with the risk of a painless passing. I'd much rather die in my sleep than bleed to death after having both my legs crushed beneath a wagon like Meelin did."

Harsond's response gave the young soldiers little comfort, which was clear from their faces.

"Poison, you say?" the older man next to Harsond said. "Is the captain sure? Because Kieran didn't appear to be suffering from the effects of any poison when I found him and brought him to her. A little dazed and staggered, sure, but he was able to walk by himself and expressed no internal pain."

Harsond turned to face the man. "She's sure. The manor physician explained it to her. Apparently, the poison is a slow-acting one that only becomes apparent after some time has passed. A truly horrid thing, if you ask me. Those Aethi'ziton bastards just needed the absols and supplies from the tax wagons, I don't see why they felt the need to implement a weapon that kills its victim days after the robbery."

"And that's why I'm confused," the older man retorted. "Why would they use it? We've had cases where the Lost Seekers have used lethal poisons before but not during quick skirmishes and not one that is this slow acting. I inspected Kieran when I found him. His armor wasn't pierced, and he didn't have a single wound that looked like it wasn't caused by a fist. The poor chap admitted that he wasn't even able to attack anyone during the massacre, his assailant included, let alone get hit with a poisoned blade in a duel."

"Kieran told you that?" one of the younger soldiers asked.

"He did, and I can't say I blame him. What happened in that market was vile. I'm ashamed to admit that I was a coward that day, but not in the right way. Who knows how many innocents I cut down out of fear that they were Lost Seekers putting on an act, trying to get close to me and drop my guard? And the fact that you three are sitting here means you acted the same way I did, valuing your own lives over those of helpless innocents."

Their table went quiet, as did the chatter directly behind them, the old soldier's voice having been overheard by many of the closer tables. A somber air filled the south side of the mess hall.

Finally, Harsond spoke, but quiet enough so that only his table could hear him. He was uncomfortable with the fact that the older man was speaking so loudly and how the rest of the room seemed to be eavesdropping on their table. "I was not there for the attack. I was stationed at the docks with many others to protect the convoy while it was loaded onto the ships. But—"

"Then you, Lieutenant, are fortunate indeed compared to those of us who were there," the old soldier said.

"But," Harsond clenched his teeth slightly as his tone became harsher, making the two young soldiers across from him nervous, "the way I hear it, there was little else that could have been done. It was horrible, yes, and I'm not wholly sure how I would have handled it if I were there, but I value my life very much, as do most people. So, I wouldn't fault a soldier for defending himself even if innocent lives were lost as a result. The Lost Seekers are who you should be disgusted with, not yourselves or your brothers and sisters in arms. The Lost Seekers knew exactly what they were doing, launching such an attack within the bounds of the market and mixing themselves in with the civilians for protection. It was all part of their strategy to spread chaos amongst the city and breed contempt for the Caswen Guard and the sovereigns."

The older soldier slammed his hand on the table. "We're supposed to protect people from criminals, not kill them because they might be one," he said, raising his voice but not quite to the point of shouting. "People are more scared of the city guards now than they are the Lost Seekers, or even the murderous thugs that prowl the streets at night. The people of Caswen see us as just as much of a threat to their lives as any other lowlife scum."

Harsond stood up, causing his stool to skid slightly on the wood floor. "Look, I have no desire to discuss this further with you. I did as you asked; I got you information about Kieran's whereabouts. If it did not ease your minds, then there's nothing else I can do for you. I'm sure you all have patrols to get back to or posts to man, so I suggest you get to it, or I'll find something else for you to do. The mood in here is shit anyway, so I'm not sure why you'd even want to spend your down time here."

Harsond didn't wait for a response. He turned and made his way toward the exit. He felt himself being eyed by many of the soldiers as he walked through the center of the mess hall, realizing that he hadn't spoken as quietly as he had thought. As he passed the table closest to the door, he overheard part of the conversation a few seated soldiers were having.

"—got what they deserved. How many children died during Verrel's attack on the market? It's only fair that we killed theirs."

Upon exiting the mess hall and the small, four-doored entry room thereafter, Harsond found himself standing in an empty street. The sun's light and warmth was blocked out by the tall brick, wood, and stone buildings surrounding him despite it being high noon. Before the chill from the long shadows could sink in, Harsond began walking down the street to the east, aiming to return to his post in the Port District.

He placed his hands in his surcoat's unbuttoned side pockets, startling himself when his right hand pricked itself against the hard crumpled edge of the envelope that Aellia had given him; he realized he had forgotten the envelope was there. He proceeded to open it, first cracking the red wax seal with a quick bend of the envelope and then pulling open the tabs on the back.

He stopped in the middle of the vacant cobblestone street, still shadowed by the presence of the many buildings, which made it slightly difficult to see the dark letters, but he began reading nonetheless.

> You are cordially invited to the wedding of Aellia Halbear,
> daughter of Magistrate Julius Halbear of the Isles, and Riel
> Togge, son and heir of Magistrate Hester Togge of The
> Coastlands. The ceremony—

A smudge of ink ruined the next few words. It looked like someone had tried to rub the smudge out but only ended up making it worse. As he continued the letter, Harsond realized he was smiling again.

—on December 15, 205, at Fort Audrin, located on the northeast coast of the East Isle, midway between Caswen and Leydes. It is my great hope that you will be able to attend. Aellia Halbear.

Maintaining his smile, Harsond folded the letter and put it in his pocket, tossing the envelope away. He was about to resume his trek when he stopped. His smile disappeared as he turned around and looked back at the garrison. He cursed the fact that the shocking news about Kieran had thrown him off focus, that he had left Aellia's office without telling her the one thing he truly wanted her to know. Feeling a cold wind pass his stubbled face, Harsond opened his mouth and spoke as if Aellia would somehow be able to hear him. "I don't blame you."

Harsond turned around and resumed his walk as his words dissipated, unheard.

Chapter 16

"Is he dead?" Helena called out.

"No," Nina answered. "Is he—"

"No," Helena replied before Nina could finish.

Each of them was tending to the person they cared for most.

Nina held her brother's arm up so the blood would struggle to climb its way up to the many tooth-sized holes that dotted its length and his ravaged hand.

Helena made sure the wound on the back of Carver's head hadn't started bleeding again due to the fact that Sebastian had dropped him earlier. Then she assessed whether any vells had managed to get to Carver. To her relief, he seemed no worse than he was before he was dropped.

"Nina, are you okay?"

Nina looked up from her unconscious brother. The left half of her face was peppered with tooth marks that leaked streams of blood. Her left eyebrow was missing, replaced by a bloody tear that forced her to keep her left eye closed. The worst was a thick cut that spanned from the left side of her mouth, along her cheek, and up to her left ear.

"I'm fine," Nina said, then went back to tending to her brother.

Helena knew Nina was lying, as she herself was anything but okay. She tried to calm herself down, but she could not find a thought to start from. Her mind was hopelessly frazzled. It had all happened so fast. Helena still couldn't fully process what had unfolded. One minute she was carrying Carver with

Sebastian, the next she was grappling with vellums and sticking a sword into their guts. Then, just as quickly as they had arrived, the vells were gone.

Only three vells remained behind, two that Helena had skewered with her arming sword and one that Rook had managed to catch in the throat with his spear, though the spear was now broken in half and lying next to the vell's body.

Rook was sitting against a thick tree with his legs curled up to his chest, cupping his left elbow in his right hand and breathing heavily. His pants were ripped and torn in places, and his left elbow was bleeding profusely under his hand.

Helena heard Nina whimper behind her. Words soon accompanied the girl's expression of agony and despair. "Helena ... what do we do?"

Helena didn't turn around; she didn't want to see Nina's tears. She was too busy holding back her own. Instead, she focused on Carver, watching his eyelids flutter with each steady breath.

"We get Sebastian conscious again and make our way to Leydes; it's our only option."

"What if the vells come back? What if there's more of them?" Nina asked through her sobs.

Helena felt her fatigue sink away into a sea of anger. "Then we'll die," she answered, feeling a wet trail roll down her cheek.

"Great plan! Absolutely great plan, you two. Look what keeping in the forest did for us!"

Helena felt a nearly overwhelming urge to look over at Rook and tell him to shut up, but she couldn't bear the idea of showing him her tears, so she kept her eyes fixed on Carver.

Rook hissed as blood continued to seep through his fingers and drip down onto his lap, but he didn't let his pain stop him from speaking his mind. "I told you both that this would happen. That if we stayed in this cursed forest while being slowed down by Carver we would end up dead!"

Helena gritted her teeth, but she did not look at Rook as she replied. "Well, we aren't dead yet, so just keep your mouth shut!"

Rook hissed again as he applied pressure to his elbow to stop the bleeding. "We will be if we keep this up. You just said it yourself. If those vells try again, we're all screwed!"

"Stop it! Both of you just stop it!" Nina shouted. "We need to get out of here, so stop fighting and help me with Sebastian!"

"No! I've had enough of you all telling me what to do." Rook stood up awkwardly, using his legs to push his back up the tree he had been sitting against. "I'm not going to stay in these woods a moment longer, not with Sebastian now adding to our difficulties. I'm taking my chances through the hills. Follow me or stay in the forest; I don't care. I'll meet you in Leydes or I won't. Good luck with the vells."

Rook scooped up one of the shoddy spears from where he had accidentally kicked them earlier. As he took his right hand off his wounded elbow and grabbed the spear, Helena finally looked over at him. Rook met her gaze, then his eyes trailed away and looked at the arming sword on the ground next to her.

Helena grabbed the weapon, then held it up in a defensive manner, its point facing Rook.

Rook chuckled slightly but he did not respond. Instead, he reached down with his other hand and picked up the second spear, though he clearly struggled with the pain of bending his injured elbow. After arming himself with both spears, he walked over to Nina.

Nina looked up at Rook, not trying to hide her tears. "So that's it? You're just going to abandon us?"

Rook dropped the second spear down by Nina's knees. "By all means, come with me across the hills if you want. But yeah, I'm done sticking to Helena's plan. And you still owe me, Nina. Don't forget that. I'll be waiting for you in Leydes, if you make it there."

Rook didn't leave a moment for Nina to respond before he looked over at Carver to see which way the boy's head was facing, for Rook knew that Carver had been carried with his head pointing south. Then he turned on his heel and began walking what he surmised to be east, based on Carver's placement.

Neither Helena nor Nina said another word to him as he disappeared into the trees. Nina looked over at Helena. "I won't leave you, Helena. And I won't leave Carver either."

Helena wondered if she should tell Nina to take Sebastian and go with Rook. She wondered if Rook had been right all along, that her insistence on saving Carver would lead to their deaths. But Helena stopped herself from speaking these words out loud, knowing that Nina would not listen. Not only would it mean leaving her friends behind, it would also surely mean their deaths in the woods.

"Thank you, Nina. I won't leave you or Sebastian either. We need to stick together if we're going to make it to Leydes."

Nina nodded, the motion causing her to squint as more blood leaked down her cheek and brow. Helena tried to smile at the girl, but the sight of Nina's face and the pain she herself felt from her sliced knee and the many cuts and stabs along her arms and chest from the vells' protective spines prevented her from doing so. Instead, Helena turned back to Carver.

She tried to distance herself mentally from the situation by thinking about something else now that her mind had calmed down enough for her to think properly. She tried to recall the last conversation she'd had with Carver before their lives fell apart, the last thing she had said to him before leaving his room that last night in Verrel, but she couldn't remember. Her memory of that night, of the life she had, felt like it belonged to someone else entirely.

✠ ✠ ✠

The group's pace was terribly slow in the aftermath of the vellum attack. Sebastian had regained consciousness fairly quickly but required Nina to help him walk. His left arm was wrapped around her shoulders, and he hobbled at her side as best he could manage with her help. His right hip and ankle were chewed badly, with the latter being twisted and beginning to swell, making it difficult and very painful for him to move. His right arm, with trails of bright blood running down its length from the many bite marks, hung limp by his side, ending in a torn and bloody hand with ripped skin hanging from the fingers. Sebastian left a light trail of blood as he hobbled forward.

Nina did her best to support her brother and ease his pain despite her own injuries. Her hands bled from the cuts she suffered from the spines of the vell that had grabbed her, her feet hurt from the few times the vell's spines managed to puncture her boots, and her face continued to bleed quite profusely for a time, forcing her to wipe blood from her eyes and out of her mouth after every few uncomfortable steps.

With Rook having left for the hills and Sebastian being in no condition to help, Helena was forced to piggyback Carver, leaving Nina to carry the arming sword. Every couple of minutes, Helena had to stop and put Carver down in order to give herself a break. She was beyond exhausted and felt like her muscles were on fire, the only reprieve from the burning in her arms and legs being when the numbness kicked in, threatening to cause her to collapse on the spot or drop Carver.

Sebastian groaned with each step, and the sound of Nina spitting blood from her mouth accompanied the groans like a rhythm.

Helena almost felt lucky to have come out of the vell attack practically unharmed, her only injuries being a sliced knee, a lightly clawed thigh, and a dozen or so cuts and scrapes from the sharp spines of the vellums along her arms and chest, but she could tell that the pain the siblings endured distracted them from the other feelings in their bodies, the feelings that Helena deluded herself into thinking she would trade for a more serious bodily injury.

The days of almost no food and no water had caught up with her. Her stomach pulsed in agony, feeling as if it were digging through her insides on the hunt for food. Her throat was painfully dry, with each exhausted breath sending a painful tightness down her esophagus. Her knees felt like they were in a vise, with each step screwing them in tighter and tighter. The worst was her headache, which made it strenuous to keep her eyes open. The combination of it all made her feel like vomiting, further distressing her writhing stomach. She felt as though her body was breaking down.

Had the group's injuries and the necessity to reach Leydes not been so great, Helena would have suggested they spend the rest of the day resting and trying to cook the slain vells over a fire, but that luxury was overshadowed by the need for healing from Leydes and the fear of the vells returning to finish them off, as the pack's number was evidently much greater than they had assumed.

To the welcome surprise of everyone, however, they noticed that the trees began to thin out, and that the sunlight was finding larger gaps to shine through the dense green above their heads and illuminate the dark forest. In just under three hours after leaving the site of the attack, the group found themselves standing atop an elevation of earth, looking down at a wide, grassy expanse at the bottom. At the far end of the area was a large town that stretched beyond their view toward the northern coast.

The town's perimeter was made of small brick cottages, all facing inward toward the greater town, with small grassy gaps between. A long, wide dirt road escaped from a large gap between two of the cottages just east of the middle of the southern perimeter and traveled to the southeast a few hundred feet shy of the eastern coast before it disappeared behind a patch of hills stretching farther to the southeast. The group had arrived sooner than they had expected.

"We're here!" Helena shouted. Her voice rang with a relief the likes of which she had never felt before in her young life.

Calling upon their last reservoirs of energy, the group made their way down the slope as carefully as their fatigue and pain would allow.

"Where does your grandfather live?" Helena asked.

Sebastian and Nina both turned to answer, but Sebastian spoke first. "His house is on the east side of town, next to his fishery by the water. Once we get to the main street, we turn right, then take the first left, and his house will be down the street a bit on the right side."

"And the temple?"

"It's just south of the main docks, next to a tavern. Both are at the north end of the market that fills the center of the town. But we need to go to his house first. Our grandfather will have the absols to pay for the healers' services," Sebastian replied.

Upon reaching the bottom of the hill, the wounded group made their way to the dirt road that led into the large town. The road was wide and littered with indents from wagon wheels, horseshoes, and boot soles. Despite the evidence of traffic, the road was empty, with only the group of teenagers stirring up dust.

The relief that washed over each of them when they passed by the first brick cottage was intense. For the first time in four days, they felt safe. Many eyes darted their way as they entered the town, the townsfolk staring in shock at the bloody, wounded bunch of teens. None of the teens paid the looks any notice, as their desperation to finally reach the end of their arduous journey totally took control of their focus, even going as far as to make them forget their concern of being seen by soldiers.

None of Leydes' soldiers were seemingly present, however, and any civilians who were nearest to the group stepped away with concerned looks.

The group's strenuous walk through town was short and unmolested, Sebastian's directions proving to be correct.

"There," he said as Nina guided him around the first left corner, just ahead of Helena, who struggled to keep up with the siblings while keeping Carver steady on her back.

A little ways ahead of them and to the right of the dirt road was a small wooden house with a short, elevated wood porch. The house was built near a much larger wooden structure, a bit back from the house and closer to the water's edge, that resembled a wide, tall barn.

Nina picked up her pace, leading to an unintended boost of suffering from her brother, and nearly pulled Sebastian along with herself toward the porch's two front steps. Sebastian stopped and freed himself from his sister's support as she stepped onto the first step.

Nina didn't seem to notice her brother's detachment and immediately hopped up the second step with a haste that Sebastian would not have been able to match. Sebastian replaced his sister's support with the low porch's wooden railing to his left.

Nina stepped up to the door and smacked her right palm against it three times, sending a loud thud into the home with each strike.

Helena hung back, remaining on the street a few feet away from the porch. She felt Carver's weight beginning to overpower her muscles again, but she clenched her teeth and forced herself to hold on.

Just a bit longer. Just a bit more, she told herself.

After several painful seconds, the door clicked from the inside and was pulled open.

Nina stepped back as a short, blond-haired dwarf woman wearing a brown tunic with matching trousers and a brown apron appeared in the doorway.

Sebastian similarly tilted back in surprise.

"Yes, hel—Craid's hammer! What happened to you?" the dwarf woman said with a gasp at the sight of Nina's bloody face.

Before Nina could digest the fact that those words were probably going to be hurled at her by every new acquaintance for the rest of her life, the dwarf woman looked past the young girl at Sebastian, who was standing behind her.

"And you! Who ... what's going on?" she erupted at the sight of the boy's injured right arm and bloody hand.

"Who are you? Where is Duncan?" Nina asked.

The dwarf woman looked at Nina with an expression of shock and confusion, quickly becoming mixed with worry and fear when she noticed the arming sword gripped in Nina's hand.

"He's in bed, resting. Who are you all? What happened to you, and what do you need with Duncan? If you're in need of aid, you must go to your goddess's temple by the docks. The priests there can help you."

Helena wanted to speak up and try to help the situation, but she could not find the strength to speak as she felt Carver getting heavier, though she knew it was actually her muscles getting weaker. She felt like she was about to faint. *Hold on, dammit!* she screamed at herself within the privacy of her thoughts.

Nina didn't answer the woman. Instead, she pushed past the dwarf and took a step into the house.

"Excuse me!" the dwarf barked as Nina shoved past her. "What are you do—"

"Grandpa! We need help!" Nina shouted.

The dwarf woman turned her gaze to Sebastian, her eyes wide with frustration and confusion. Helena wanted to explain what was going on, but she felt that if she opened her mouth to speak, she would collapse.

"Grandpa, it's Nina!"

"Girl, what do you think you're doing?" the concern in the dwarf woman's tone was no longer present, replaced by sternness. She placed a firm hand on the back of Nina's shoulder.

Before anyone could understand what she was about to do, Nina spun around and punched the dwarf woman just below the left eye.

"Nina!" Helena shouted. Suddenly, her muscles went completely numb, and she felt a huge weight fall from her back. The sight of Nina assaulting the dwarf woman was replaced by dirt as Helena's face crashed into the ground. A welcomed unconsciousness took her.

Chapter 17

❧

The room was as cold as it was dark, and he couldn't see his own feet when he was standing. Hunger pained him but not as badly as the soreness of his face. He found it nearly impossible to sleep with his discomforts, though his thoughts of his mother and sister also made him restless. What did they think happened to him? No doubt they assumed him dead, having been murdered during that terrifying battle at the market. He felt like he was experiencing a night terror that he could not wake up from, and it only got worse with every hour that passed in the dark, windowless room that he found himself in. All he could do was pace back and forth and wait, as he had done for what seemed like days between the hours when he sat on the ground or was able to sleep.

The room itself was only a dozen feet wide in each direction and was made entirely of cold stone. He had tried to find a way out but was met by nothing but stone walls and a locked iron door. He figured he was in some kind of prison cell, though where and why he could not fathom.

The pile of hard bread and dried meat that he had found placed in the corner was nearly depleted, and the last of the few waterskins was nearly empty. The only thing that was increasing in contents was the waste bucket in the adjacent corner, which filled the small room with a sickly odor.

To distract his senses from the horrid smell and suffocating darkness, he thought about his mother and sister, but when the thoughts of them began to make him worry rather than feel calm, he focused on the last moment he remembered in order to try and figure out what was going on.

He had been brought to Caswen manor by his captain and had an audience with the magistrate. The magistrate's chancellor had been there too, as well as two sovereigns who eyed him closely. Then his captain escorted him down the manor's main hall while speaking to him about sacrifices for the greater good. She said she needed to show him something and then took him to a dark stairwell at the back of the manor. She disappeared from his sight as he followed her down the dark stairs. When they reached the bottom, it was like the darkness had swallowed him up and taken him somewhere to rot for eternity.

The sudden sound of a loud click from the far end of the room startled him out of his thoughts. He heard another click, then a louder metallic screech, and then he saw the warm light of fire enter the room from the far corner.

The fire was from a wooden torch held by a woman with coppery-brown hair. She was wearing a plain gray tunic with black trousers, an outfit he had never seen her in before. Without her armor and surcoat, she looked like any common young woman one would see around the city, and quite beautiful too.

"Hello, Kieran," the woman said as she closed the heavy iron door behind her.

"Captain Aellia ..."

Aellia stepped forward and held out the torch so it illuminated most of the room. Kieran saw that her tunic was not simple after all. It had gentle embroideries of silver vine-like lines trailing along the shoulders and collar, while the front was laced up to her breasts so that almost no cleavage was shown, and it was tucked into her trousers, which were secured at her waist with a fine brown belt. Her boots were black like her trousers and laced high, similar to her tunic. Kieran also couldn't help but notice the sword buckled to Aellia's belt.

"To begin, I'm sorry about what I've done to you. I value every member of the Caswen Guard as an equal, and I took no joy in your imprisonment, nor do I take any joy in what we must now discuss."

Kieran didn't know what to say. He was using all his willpower to stop his teeth from chattering due to the cold and his nerves.

"Three people know the truth about Verrel, and you and I are two of them. That number can never increase. It can only stay the same ... or decrease."

Kieran felt his heart booming in his chest as he tried to ignore the meaning of Aellia's words. He tried to think of something else, but all he could do was look at her. Suddenly, he constructed a scenario in his mind to distract himself, one where Aellia was not alluding to his death but instead coming to him in the darkness of the cell and confessing lustful feelings for him, then ordering him to make love to her.

"We need to come to an understanding regarding this situation, Kieran."

The sudden harshness of Aellia's voice tore Kieran's attention away from his delusional coping mechanism. He realized he had unknowingly backed up against the wall farthest from Aellia.

"Where ... where am I? Is this the garrison's dungeon?"

The sudden expression on Aellia's face, glowing orange from the torch-light, told him that his question sounded either arrogant or that she perceived it as an order rather than a timid inquiry.

"No. This is the manor dungeon. Before Caswen was a fully constructed city with a prison and permanent garrison, criminals were kept here beneath the manor. It isn't used anymore—it's too small and poorly built. Now it serves as a forgotten system of crumbling cells and rat nests. No one comes down here since the door leading here is always locked, but I alone have the key, as well as the one for the cells."

"How long have I been in here?" Kieran asked timidly, hoping another question wouldn't be too much to ask in his situation.

"Four days and four nights," she replied calmly. "It's the afternoon of August fifth."

Kieran was taken aback. *Four days ... It's been four whole days and nights ...*

Aellia's voice cut into his head once again, severing his connection to his thoughts like a sharp blade. "This will be your last moment in this cell, Kieran—one way or another. It's up to you to decide which. Your first option is that you can keep quiet about the Verrel issue and lie through your teeth if and when asked about it. You'll walk out of this cell right now, don a fresh new uniform to accompany your promotion for learning the location of a Lost Seekers hideout and suffering injury in doing so, and you'll also have my gratitude. Or," her calm tone turned much colder, "you can reject my offer, hold on to your morals, and have died last night from a slow poison that the manor physician was unable to save you from."

It took Kieran a moment to understand the second option. A long moment of silence passed, giving him ample time to examine every inch of Aellia's face. He wasn't sure, but he thought he could see a hint of sadness or displeasure behind her stern brown eyes.

"I won't say anything. I should never have debated you about Verrel being behind the market attack in the first place. I don't know what I was thinking. I should have just listened to you. I'll tell the others that I don't remember anything about the Verrel boy. I'll say that the beating I took made my memory of the whole day fuzzy. I don't want to die, Captain. Please ..."

"You don't need to claim amnesia. It wouldn't add up with the fact that it was you who recounted the details of the Verrel boy to the magistrate and the sovereigns anyway."

"But please believe me, I won't say anything. I promise. For all I know, Verrel was responsible for the attack. I was wrong to think the boy was telling the truth. I—"

"Kieran, stop. You made it very clear to me what you thought after your sergeant brought you to me. You're reasoning that a simple identification pin was not hard proof that all of Verrel were Lost Seekers was sound, as it was my own thought as well. I must admit that I found your quick conclusion regarding the situation quite impressive. And if what you told me of that boy's final words to you were true, then that only further supports the matter. But the fact was that someone needed to take the blame if the sovereigns were going to be appeased. That boy was simply in the wrong place at the right time. The reason I ordered you to say what you did to the magistrate and the sovereigns was so that others might be saved. One small village is a small price to pay to avoid a purging of the Isles."

Kieran didn't know if he should say anything in reply. He was in total shock at the situation, but he just couldn't stop himself from rambling out of fear.

"I agree with you, Captain. I'm sorry I challenged you before. I should have just listened to you and kept my opinion to myself. I won't say a thing about this or what happened to anyone. I swear by all of Cosom's eyes."

Aellia stared into Kieran's eyes with a look that made him feel like she was looking into his mind and judging if he was being honest with her. Finally, she nodded.

"I believe you."

A long, uncomfortable silence fell over them, though Kieran's heart continued to beat hastily, and its rhythm filled his ears. If Aellia could also hear it, she made no sign of it.

Aellia suddenly closed the distance between herself and Kieran. She stopped only when her chest was nearly touching his own. The heat of her torch was the first comfort Kieran had felt in days. She placed her free hand on his shoulder in a manner that gave Kieran further comfort and leaned toward him, putting her face very close to his. "I can't express how grateful I am for your understanding and cooperation, even though it is not entirely willing. But know this, Kieran. If you break your word, betray my trust, and speak the truth to anyone, you will die, and so will your mother and sister."

Aellia's comforting hand suddenly felt like an iron vise on Kieran's shoulder.

Chapter 18

Helena slowly opened her eyes to a room illuminated with a dim light. She found herself in the comfort of a bed, tucked neatly beneath the sheets. She didn't want to get up yet, so she closed her eyes and nestled her shoulders deeper into comfort.

Suddenly, a feeling hit her, a sensation deep within her gut that something wasn't quite right. She opened her eyes again and pondered what felt off.

Nothing is wrong, she told herself. She was in her bed, in her home, in Verrel.

She turned onto her side to get more comfortable and tried to banish the uneasy feeling.

The wall of her room caught her eye immediately. It was a dark chestnut red with indents dividing its surface into thin panels of wood. It differed greatly from her memory of having a plain, unpainted wooden wall. It wasn't the correct distance from her bed either. The left side of her bed had always been slid up to her room's left wall, so why did it look like she was looking at this strange wall from the center of the room?

Suddenly, the pillow under her head felt harder than she remembered, and the blankets seemed heavier than what she was used to. Helena sat up when the feeling became too strong to try to ignore and was twisting her stomach into a knot. She widened her eyes and took in the whole room.

It was small and looked to be perfectly square. She was in the middle of it, the bed's headboard touching the wall. Then Helena remembered that her bed did not have a headboard, nor was the straw mattress so wide, as if meant for two.

The dim light that illuminated the room came from a trio of candles atop a wooden stool near the door. Helena also noted a large wardrobe against the wall to her right with a small stepping stool beside it.

She didn't have a wardrobe or a stepping stool, and she always kept her candles on her small bedside table, which was missing. She did not understand. This place felt unreal and foreign while at the same time welcoming and comfortable.

Helena attempted to get out of the bed, but she stopped when a sharp pain surged from her right knee.

"Ow!" she hissed as she fell backwards onto the bed.

She grabbed the bedsheets and whipped them off her body to see what was wrong with her knee. To her surprise, she saw that her wool trousers had been rolled up, and the aggressed knee was covered in thick white bandages with a blotchy red "X" staining from underneath.

A rush of cold realization engulfed Helena as her eyes widened.

My parents. Verrel. Vellum Forest. The vells. Leydes. Sebastian. Nina. Carver!

Memories rushed back into Helena's mind, blocking out the pain from her knee as she forced herself into a sitting position on the side of the bed.

"Carver?" she whispered.

She blinked. She did not know why she suddenly said his name out loud.

The dirt street. Strange looks. People. A house. The smell of fish.

Helena's memory kicked in even further, and it was then that she became aware of the few small bandages stuck to her arms.

The door to the room suddenly opened with a quick creak, interrupting Helena's examination of herself, and allowed a bright light to burst into the room, causing her to wince.

"Hello?" a deep voice said from the direction of the intruding light.

It was not a voice Helena recognized. She rubbed her eyes and after a moment was able to look at the person who spoke. A stocky dwarf stood in the doorway.

The porch steps. The front door. The dwarf woman. Nina. Assault.

Helena realized that the dwarf who stood in the doorway was not the same one who had answered the front door. This one was a dark-haired man, though Helena could only tell this by his beard, as his head had no hair at all. He had a thick goatee that grew into patchy sideburns and sent small hairs into the edges of his mouth. His eyes were a similarly dark color.

The dwarf stared at Helena for a second, then looked back over his shoulder. "Charra," he called, then returned his attention to Helena. "How are you feeling?"

His question caught her by surprise. She had not expected the stranger to inquire about her wellbeing.

"Where am I?"

The dwarf took a step into the room. Helena tensed up.

"You're in Leydes. This is the home of Duncan, someone you apparently know. You fell unconscious just outside, and you've been resting here for about an hour," he explained, taking another step closer.

"I fell unconscious? Who are you, and where are my friends?" Her words rang with accusation.

"Relax," the dwarf said, raising his hands, palms out. "I won't harm you. If anything, it's me who should be wary of you after that introduction your friend gave."

"What?"

Another shape appeared in the room's doorway, the dwarf woman from earlier. In her hands was a small wooden tray with a stained wood bowl in its center. She walked past the male dwarf and stopped at the edge of the bed. As she approached, Helena noticed the purple bruise under her left eye.

"It's alright, dear. Here, take this," the dwarf woman said, handing Helena the wooden tray.

Helena looked down at the wood bowl. It contained a gray, soupy liquid with chunks of grayish meat floating in it. A sudden feeling of extreme hunger overwhelmed Helena, and with it came the realization that she could not remember the last time she had eaten anything.

Helena dug her hand into the liquid and retrieved a large chunk of meat, cramming it into her mouth. The soup was hot and burned her hand, and the meat, which tasted like some kind of fish, stung her tongue and the roof of her mouth. Helena didn't care. The fish was plain, and the soup was watery, but it was the best meal she had eaten in days.

"Slow down, girl. Don't spill on our sheets. There's a spoon right there," the man said, pointing to it.

Helena plucked a second chunk of fish from the bowl and shoved it in her mouth before the man's words hit her. She stopped for a moment and saw a wooden spoon next to the bowl.

"Quiet, dear. The girl must be starving. You heard the others. They've been without proper food for nearly four days."

As Helena swallowed the second chunk of fish, her mind told her to take the wooden spoon, but her impulse forced her hand into the bowl again to remove a third piece of fish.

"You can relax, Helena, you're safe here," the dwarf woman said gently.

Helena bit her finger as she placed the third piece of fish onto her slightly burnt tongue. *I didn't tell them my name. Did I tell them my name? How do they know my name?*

"Hough two you low ny mame?" Helena asked through the food in her mouth, sending droplets of hot soup down her chin.

The woman smiled. "Your friends told us. Sebastian and Nina."

Helena opened her mouth to speak, revealing a maw full of chewed fish. The woman held up her hand before Helena could spit her words out. "They're fine, dear. Duncan took them straight to Siyon's temple. They should be with your people's priests as we speak."

"Rud about Carder?"

The dwarf woman maintained her polite smile. "The other boy, the one whom you carried? Duncan took him to the temple too. You were not so badly hurt, so Gorty and I tended to you ourselves. Some simple bandaging with marrowstalk paste was all you needed. Well, and some cleaning up, of course. I'd never seen a person covered in so much blood and dirt."

Helena looked at the bandages on her arm and noted that she could see some of the dark red paste of the marrowstalk plant, which was used as an adhesive as well as a natural healing agent, around some of the bandages.

Helena tried to calm herself and refrain from plunging her hand yet again into the bowl of hot soup. She focused on swallowing the mouthful of fish she had already acquired before speaking again.

"Who are you?" she asked.

"My name is Charra, and this is my husband, Gorty." The woman gestured to the goateed man standing behind her. "We work for Mr. Duncan, Sebastian and Nina's grandfather."

Helena sat still for a moment, trying to process what she'd been told. "Thank you," she said finally. "Thank you for helping us."

Charra widened her smile. "Of course, dear. Even if you didn't know Duncan, we would have helped. We couldn't just leave you kids like that."

"Are you okay?" Helena suddenly asked Charra.

Charra dropped her smile in confusion, then nodded once she realized why Helena asked the question, her hand going to the bruise on her cheek. "Yes, I'm okay. It doesn't hurt much. That girl really hits hard for such a tiny thing."

"Why did she hit you?" Helena asked.

"She was emotional. You all were. She wasn't expecting to find two dwarves living in her grandfather's home. You kids went through a lot getting here, so it's no surprise that she reacted the way she did when I grabbed her shoulder."

"I'm sorry," Helena said softly.

"Don't be. A bruise is nothing compared to what happened to you poor dears. Your friends gave us a quick explanation of what happened before heading to the temple."

The motherly way in which Charra talked made Helena feel even worse about what had happened. Such a kind and caring woman did not deserve to be punched in the face, especially by one of the people who needed her aid.

Helena let the fish settle in her stomach before she ate more, this time using the wooden spoon. Suddenly, droplets of water began to plop into the soup as she ate, followed by the feeling of tears running down her face. They came out of nowhere, a surge of emotion overwhelming Helena.

"Oh, my poor dear," Charra said softly. "It's okay. You've been through so much, and your body is exhausted, but you're safe now. Eat and rest. Gorty and I will be a shout away if you need anything."

Helena was embarrassed for crying in front of these two strangers, despite how friendly they were.

Charra turned and signaled her husband to leave. Gorty followed without another word, looking like he felt embarrassed at the sight of Helena's tears. The two dwarves closed the door behind them.

Helena wasn't sure why she was crying, but she found it impossible to stop. She placed the tray at the foot of the bed. She didn't want to spill on the kind couple's sheets. Her tears already dotted the cozy blankets with darkening splotches.

Helena fell to her side, burying her head in the straw-stuffed pillow to muffle her soft cries. She did not want Charra and Gorty to hear her. Even more importantly, she did not want to hear herself.

After a few minutes, her crying stopped as her exhausted body surrendered to sleep.

When Helena awoke later, her face was still pressed against the pillow, which was now damp. Her eyes were sore, and her left arm was numb from being underneath her while she slept. Though she laid on top of the bedsheets, she still felt warm and comfortable. Inhaling deeply, Helena adjusted her legs and turned over.

A burst of panic filled her as she heard a clink followed by the sensation of her foot hitting something cold and hard near the end of the bed. She yanked her legs back, but it was too late. The bowl of soup tipped over and spilled across the sheets. Helena gasped. She had forgotten she had placed it there.

Charra and Gorty will be furious with me, she thought. But then she remembered how kind they had been to her earlier. Maybe they wouldn't be angry at all.

Helena did not wish to test the dwarves' hospitality, however, so she set the tray and the bowl on the floor. She looked at the bed. It was wet at the top from her tears and soaked at the bottom from the spilled soup. Maybe they would be upset.

Trying to ignore the feeling of guilt that plagued her, Helena unrolled the legs of her trousers to cover the bandage on her knee. Her right pant leg was cut through at the knee and was already beginning to tear further. The vells' claws had also ripped many lines through the left thigh of her trousers.

As Helena finished unrolling her trousers, she noticed that her boots were on the floor at the end of the bed. She grabbed them and put them on. They were still a little uncomfortable, being made for someone else, but they fit well enough.

Hearing voices, Helena got up and pressed her ear to the bedroom door. The mumbled chatter was unintelligible, but she could definitely tell who was speaking: Sebastian.

Overcoming her anxiety, Helena flung the door open. The light from the other side caused her to squint. She blinked for a moment, then fought past the discomfort as she widened her eyes and looked beyond the light.

She found herself staring into the main room of the house. It was barely larger than the bedroom she had emerged from and was filled with warm light from the hearth, which burned brightly in the far-right corner. The center of the room was occupied by a large rectangular wooden table that had an array of candles in the center. Around the table were five individuals, three seated on stools while two stood off to the left.

On one side of the table, Sebastian sat next to a person whose face was half wrapped in bandages. Helena realized with equal parts of relief and shock that it was Nina; this was made clear by her short, dirty-blond bangs, her face mostly obscured behind the bandages.

On the opposite side of the table stood Charra and Gorty. A human man with a short gray beard and a messy mop of gray hair sat on the third stool facing the siblings.

It took Helena a moment to realize that the others had stopped talking and were all staring at her. She did not know who to look at, so she focused on the table between them.

"Helena!" Nina shouted, springing up from her stool. Before Helena could speak, Nina dashed across the short distance between them and crashed into her, embracing her in a strenuous hug.

As Helena hugged back, she noticed Sebastian smiling at her. She also saw that Sebastian's right arm was in a sling and resting on the table. He did not bother standing up.

"Good morning, Helena," he said in a friendly manner, "or I guess I should say, good evening."

Helena looked at him with confusion before she noticed the window behind him. The gaps between the wooden shutters showed darkness.

"How long was I in there?"

"More than a few hours," Gorty said. "It's been dark outside for almost an hour now."

Nina released Helena from the hug and made her way back to her seat. It looked like she was smiling, but it was hard to tell with all the bandages covering so much of her face. As Nina sat down next to her brother, Helena realized the girl's hands were also bandaged, though far more lightly than the left side of her face.

"Gorty, dear, why don't you go get the last stool from the bedroom so Helena has a place to sit?" Charra said.

Helena wanted to say she was okay to stand, but she still felt strange and confused, so she hesitated long enough for Gorty to walk past her into the room. The dwarf emerged in a matter of seconds with the stool and placed it next to the older man, who was now looking at Sebastian and Nina.

"Come sit, dear," Charra said, patting the stool with her hand before stepping away.

Helena hobbled over to the stool, feeling odd with everyone's attention on her.

"Where is Carver?" she asked once she was firmly seated.

"He's still at Siyon's temple," the older man with the gray beard said.

"Is he okay?"

She quickly realized that he was Nina and Sebastian's grandfather. It had been more than two years since she had last seen Duncan during one of his visits to Verrel, and he looked quite different than she recalled. She remembered his beard being thick and bushy and his hair being cut short. Now his hair was a scruffy mess of thick gray. For a second, Helena entertained herself with the idea that Duncan had shaved down his beard and put it on his head. She tensed after she realized how out of place her thoughts were. With what was going on, the last thing she needed to do was think up weird stories about an old man's hair.

"The boy is still alive, but he hasn't woken up yet. The healing priests told us they're doing everything they can to help him, however," Duncan replied.

Helena wanted to pry for more information about Carver's condition, but she could tell that Duncan didn't know much else. Instead, she stood up, her stool screeching as it slid across the wood floor. "Where is the temple? I want to see him."

Charra looked at Helena with the same expression she wore in the bedroom, that of a pitying mother, though now in the light Helena could see that the dwarf woman had piercing blue eyes. "The temple is closed for the night, Helena. You won't be able to see him until the priests get back tomorrow morning."

"Are no healers there with him? They just left him? What if something happens? What if he starts bleeding again?"

Charra cupped the girl's elbow in her hand. The dwarf woman's palm was tough and scratchy. "Please, settle down, Helena. Like Duncan said, your people's priests helped him. He's been freshly bandaged and given potions to aid his healing process. He isn't in any further danger."

Helena looked at the others to either confirm or deny Charra's claims.

Sebastian spoke up first. "She's right, Helena. I was with him when they tended to me."

"Me too," Nina added.

"They cleaned both his wounds and restitched the one on the back of his head," Sebastian continued. "Neither one seemed infected. After they poured some kind of potion down his throat, they told us that we just have to wait."

Helena remained standing. "Do they know when he'll wake up?" she asked, realizing partway through her question that she had to catch herself from saying "if he wakes up," which gave her a chill.

Everyone remained silent. Helena knew why. It wasn't that they were trying to remember what the healing priests had said. They were trying to find a way of saying it delicately. The healers had told them that Carver might never recover. Helena knew that must be the case from the way Sebastian stared at her.

"Soon," Duncan said. "If Carver remains in their care, he should regain consciousness very soon."

Helena almost felt convinced by Duncan's answer. A slight tug at her elbow reminded her that Charra was trying to get her to sit back down. She complied and sat on the stool, scooting it toward the table. She felt awkward after realizing the scene she had just caused.

Everyone at the table continued to watch her as if expecting her to do something else.

"How are you two doing?" Helena directed her question to Nina and Sebastian in an attempt to shift the focus away from her.

"We'll be okay," Sebastian said. "My right arm wasn't broken like I thought, just badly twisted and chewed. The priests said I might not regain some of the feeling in my right hand though. And ..." His voice trailed off into sadness. "They had to cut off my pinkie. Too much of it was missing, and it was never going to heal properly, they said." Sebastian struggled to hold up his wounded arm for Helena to see.

She saw that Sebastian was indeed missing his right pinkie just above the lowest knuckle, leaving a bump with a short line of stitching in its place.

"What about your ankle and hip? The vells got you there too."

"Apart from me not being able to walk properly for a while, there shouldn't be any permanent effects. I got lucky." His words carried a bittersweet tone.

Helena looked over at Nina, who was staring at her brother's bandaged arm. Nina's eyes were full of sadness, no longer gleaming with the joy they showed when Helena had first entered the room.

"Nina," Helena said, trying to get the girl's attention.

Nina turned to look at her. "I'm fine," she said calmly, not at all truthfully by Helena's assumption. Helena detected from Nina's tone and expression that she was desperately trying to prevent a deep sadness from resurfacing.

Helena refrained from inquiring any further about Nina. It was clear that Helena had not been the only one crying that day.

"I've set up a spot in the fishery for you all to sleep," Duncan said. "It's the best I can do for now. I know it won't be ideal, but there isn't room anywhere else."

"It's fine, Grandpa," Sebastian said. "We already told you that. Anything is better than sleeping out in those woods."

Helena wasn't quite sure if she was supposed to say something, as Sebastian seemed to speak for her already. "What about that room?" she asked, pointing to the open door from which she had just emerged.

"That's Gorty and Charra's room," Sebastian replied.

"Oh," Helena said. *Of course that's their room. How can I be so stupid?*

She focused her vision on the two dwarves standing to her left. She realized what she had just said had probably come across as ungrateful or selfish, and nothing could have been further from the truth. Suddenly she felt much worse about the state in which she had left the couple's bed.

"Thank you," she said after a short pause, directing her words to all three adults.

"Think nothing of it," Charra said, placing a hand on Helena's upper arm.

Sebastian straightened his back and turned to Helena. "You came out just in time. Dinner is almost ready."

"By my mind, I forgot!" Charra blurted. She hurried to the far end of the room behind Helena.

Helena turned, realizing she had not noticed the small kitchen that took up the far wall. It reminded her of her kitchen at home. The stone hearth she had noticed upon entering was the start of the kitchen, with a thin chimney leading up through the wooden ceiling. A wide wooden counter stretched from the hearth's side to the other corner of the room. Within the hearth, Helena saw a large lidded iron pot above the fire, held up by cast-iron bars. Streams of water escaped out of the top of the pot and hissed as they poured into the flames.

"I hope it hasn't overcooked," Charra said as she grabbed the iron handles on each side of the large pot.

Helena was shocked at the sight of the dwarf woman reaching inside the hearth and touching the hot metal with her bare hands. She instinctively tensed in preparation for Charra to shriek and drop the pot, spilling scalding liquid all over the floor.

"Phew, that's hotter than a boar's temper in heat," Charra said as she removed the heavy pot from the hearth, seeming only mildly inconvenienced by the heat.

How? Helena wondered. Then she felt foolish, recalling that dwarves had much tougher and thicker skin than humans and could withstand much harsher temperatures. Helena relaxed with the knowledge that Charra was safe from harm, but at the sight of the dwarf woman placing the almost glowing-bottomed pot onto the wood counter, she panicked all over again.

"Wait!" Helena shouted. "It'll burn right into the wood."

Charra turned to Helena, leaving the pot sitting on the counter. Her face did not display the shocked look of realization Helena expected to see. Instead, she looked confused, and then she smiled. "Oh, this isn't wood, dear." She chuckled and gave the counter a hard whack with her palm. "This here is oakstone. Hard as any rock but with the appearance of wood." Charra ran her finger along a dark streak on the counter's front that resembled black wood-grain. "When Gorty and I came over from Dithraine and signed on with Duncan, I insisted that he upgrade his kitchen from wood to oakstone. You won't find a single respectable dwarf's home in any of our kingdoms that uses wooden counters. Too much risk of a fire and far too primitive."

"And far less expensive," Duncan said in an accusative but friendly manner.

Charra shot Duncan a look that a stubborn wife would give her husband but without the seriousness. "For good reason. Proper cooking is crucial for a well-functioning home. Be glad I didn't insist on removing all the wood from this house. Why you humans still build primarily with wood is a mystery to me. Us dwarves shared our advancements with your race for a reason. You humans would be much better off if you used them," she scolded, ending with a calm grin.

A charmed smile surfaced across Duncan's face, but it quickly dissipated into a sorrowful frown. Helena noticed that he looked unwell. The old man had bags under his eyes, and he looked exhausted.

Gorty let out a loud chuckle and smacked Helena across the left shoulder. His strike, though meant as a friendly gesture, caused her to wince. "You should've seen this one gobble down the fish soup earlier!" he announced to the siblings across the table. "Clawed the fish straight from the bowl with her hands, she did."

Rubbing her shoulder, Helena gave her friends across the table a sheepish look.

"I take that as a compliment," Charra said from the kitchen. "If everyone who ate my food scarfed it down like that, all the chefs in the Commonwealth would hound me for my techniques," she added while setting a row of wooden bowls atop the oakstone countertop. Then she pulled the lid off the pot, took a metal ladle from a hook on the wall, and dipped it into the pot. When she pulled the ladle back out, it was dripping with liquid, much like the watery soup Helena had been served earlier. Charra pressed her lips to the edge of the ladle and sipped without blowing on it first.

"Perfect," she said. Then she plunged the ladle in and out of the pot, filling each bowl with a steady rhythm.

The sight of hot food made Helena's body quiver. She felt an urge to dash over to the counter and pour the hot soup directly into her mouth, even with the knowledge that it would burn her badly. Then the urge to feast on more hot fish soup lessened on Helena's mind. Her feeling of contentment passed, overcome by worry and uneasiness.

"Actually," Helena said as she stood up, her stool sending another screech echoing in the small room, "I'm going to go for a walk. I need some fresh air."

All eyes turned on her.

"Have you not had enough of that recently? You've been out there for nearly four days," Gorty said, waving toward the front door. "I'd spend a whole week inside if I had gone through what you five did."

"Five?" Helena turned to Gorty with a confused face.

"Well, yes," Gorty replied. "Sebastian, Nina, you, Carver, and that older boy who arrived shortly after you all did."

"Oh ..." Helena nodded in realization.

"Rook showed up while you were asleep and the rest of us were at the temple. He's in the fishery," Sebastian said, confirming Helena's conclusion.

Helena felt an urge to protest sheltering Rook. She wanted to ask why, after Rook had abandoned them in the forest, he had been taken in and given refuge in the fishery. But then she remembered that Rook had saved Sebastian and Nina at Verrel, a point she was sure Rook led with when introducing himself to Duncan.

Helena found the idea of arguing that they shouldn't help Rook to be tiring, pointless, and even harsh considering how Rook had saved Duncan's grandchildren. "Oh," was all she said in response to the matter. "I'm just going to take a walk through the town. Don't worry."

"Are you sure, dear?" Charra asked as she approached the table with two bowls of soup in her hands. She placed one in front of Sebastian and the other in front of Nina. "At least eat something first."

"That's okay. I'm still full from the soup you gave me earlier," she lied. The smell of the food beckoned her to stay, but Helena shook her head slightly to banish the desire and stepped away from the table. "I'm sorry about your bedsheets, by the way."

Gorty and Charra shot Helena a confused look. Helena merely smiled and then headed for the door.

A splash of cold night air rushed past her, reminding her of the late hour. The chill didn't feel quite the same to her as it had in the woods, however. In Vellum Forest, the wind seemed hostile, another thing trying to grind her down as she tried to survive. Here, however, the cold wind was friendly, seeming to be inviting her along for a quiet stroll through town.

When Helena closed the door behind her, separating herself from the warm common room, she suddenly felt very alone. It was a pleasant feeling at that moment.

Chapter 19

∽⦵⌒

Helena walked slowly down the dirt street. Her right knee hurt with each step, but she endured it. The town itself was filled with a chilled stillness, and the street Helena walked was empty. The men and women who had stared at her when she and her group arrived were all inside their small wood and brick homes, no doubt gossiping about the band of beaten-looking misfits who had wandered into their town that day.

The two moons sat high above the town, giving Helena just enough light to see where she was going. The only problem was, she didn't know where she was going. She stopped in front of the large fishery next to Duncan's house. It was a tall structure, resembling a barn, its back end only two dozen feet away from the water's edge.

Helena walked up to the fishery's large wooden door and placed a hand on the cold metal door handle. She did not pull it. Instead, she held still for a handful of seconds until she released her grip and walked away. She was curious to examine her and her companions' new home, but not now, not with Rook inside. She walked down the wide dirt street under the glow of the moons.

The homes to Helena's left and right all looked similar to the cottages in Verrel, some built with brick while others were made entirely of wood, all with thatched roofs and their windows concealed by wooden shutters. Many of the homes glowed with candlelight from within, the light escaping through the cracks and gaps in the shutters.

Helena wondered if all the homes looked the same as Duncan's on the inside: a cramped square room devoted to a single table and kitchen with two smaller rooms off to the side behind thin doors. Duncan's home seemed to be the only one with a porch, and Helena found herself wondering why that was.

She stopped abruptly as she was faced with a left turn that curved and led farther into town. She turned around and looked down the street she had just walked. She hadn't gone far. Duncan's cottage and fishery were still within view, if a little obscured in the darkness. She didn't want to go back yet, so she continued forward.

The area around her opened up considerably, with the homes now only on her left. To her right was a large open area filled with crates, lumber, and miscellaneous shapes and objects that the darkness concealed from her. Farther beyond the open space were more piles of wood and cargo, and just past that, the sea.

She stopped in the middle of the dirt road, straining to see the far-off water. She saw the shapes of large ships bobbing up and down as unseen waves pushed against their barnacle-covered hulls.

Helena saw that the distant water was getting closer before she understood why. Then she realized she was walking toward the bobbing ships, her curiosity apparently taking control of her legs. As she neared the edge of the town, walking through the large yard of shipping supplies and cargo, the scent of salt and fish became stronger. The smell jolted her muscles, waking her from her daydream-like trance.

She examined the various items scattered around the yard: long spools of rope and twine, large wicker baskets, wooden crates overfilled with tangled fishing rods, and several wide nets, some folded evenly while others were tangled or were draped over crates.

This is their role. The fishing town of Leydes, Helena thought while stepping over a cracked wooden beam. She stopped when she reached the central dock, a long wooden pier that stretched out over the water. Many vessels were tied to it. Some were nothing more than quaint schooners or small boats while others were large fishing ships capable of holding at least a dozen sailors, with room for catch and cargo.

The dark water that rocked the vessels was nearly all Helena could see now. It spanned farther than her eyes could see, vanishing into an eerie blackness that even the glow of the moons and stars could not reveal to her. It made no difference, however, for she knew what lay beyond.

Nothing.

Even in the daylight, nothing but water could be seen past the northern shore. To the north and the west, the ocean was said to go on forever. Many people believed that if one were to sail and never stop, one would hit an invisible barrier of magic, the natural border of the world. Others believed that the ocean simply went on forever and that one would die from old age before finding anything but waves, winds, and currents. Some even believed that if one sailed too far, one would reach the edge and fall off the world, plummeting into the void.

Helena believed otherwise. She wanted to think that somewhere out there, after a hundred years of sailing, land could be found. Land with new and exciting creatures and people. Land that the sovereigns did not lord over, where the populace was ignorant of the existence of the Isles, Terraland, and the rest of Gaia's mainland to the east and south.

The scent of the sea became stronger, and Helena became dizzy from focusing on the miles of swaying dark water, so she turned around and headed back through the shipyard.

The dirt path was still empty once she reached it again. As she continued down the street, however, her lonesome stroll was interrupted by a cavalcade of distant noise.

Completely unaware of how far she had walked into the town, Helena stopped in the middle of the street, this time looking to see where the sounds came from. To her right, which had once been nothing but fishing supplies and cargo crates, was now a large building. From within the building came cries of merriment and chatter. Helena looked up at the open door of the large, noisy building.

"The Fisherman's Port" was painted on the wooden sign hanging above the open doorway of what appeared to be a tavern.

Just as she had approached the docks without understanding why, Helena found herself marching toward the open door. The smell of seawater and fish became less present as she entered the tavern, but it did not vanish entirely, mixing with the smell of alcohol and sweat to create a whole new aroma of strangeness.

Helena had never been inside a tavern before, as Verrel did not have one, but her parents had told her about such places. From her understanding, these establishments were meant to give joy and respite to those who entered, but to her eyes at the moment the place looked more like a large room for drinking, eating, and shouting.

The central room was larger than any room she had ever been in, and it was filled with many low, circular tables, each one with a cluster of people, goblins and humans both, sitting around it with plates of food and mugs of drink. An even light stretched over the tables and patrons from a series of metal fixtures hanging from the ceiling, each surrounded with lit candles. Candles were also burning on the tables and in iron beams sticking out from the walls and support beams.

A sudden anxiety rose up inside Helena as she realized she was still standing in the doorway looking in. The anxiety made her feel as if she were the center of attention or soon would be. But she wasn't. No one was even looking at her; they were totally absorbed in their own business.

Trying to block out the irrational anxiety she felt, Helena made her way farther into the tavern, careful to avoid bumping into anyone and keeping her eyes down so as not to invite attention, though she wasn't entirely sure why. When she finally made it to the center of the room, she noticed a long counter to the far right, in front of which sat a multitude of individuals on tall stools.

Not wanting to sit with a group of strangers, Helena sat on a stool along the counter with empty stools on her right and left. She leaned forward and rested her elbows on the wooden counter and waited, for what she hadn't a clue. She had no idea what she was doing. She was wandering, like she had told her friends, but she also felt like she was doing something wrong.

"Hello, young lady," a loud male voice rang out from behind the counter. Startled by the sudden call, Helena sat up straight.

"Oh, sorry, Miss. Didn't mean to startle you." A large, tall man with wide shoulders stood in front of her on the other side of the counter. He was wearing a long white apron, though it was horribly stained with a plethora of beige splatters. His face was wide and friendly, with thick mutton chops running down the sides that merged into a weighty mustache. Despite his prominent facial hair, the top of his head was utterly bald. He leaned forward and placed his large hands on the counter. "Welcome to the Fisherman's Port. Tie yourself off at the docks and then tie one on in here," he said with a billowy chuckle.

Helena said nothing back. The man gave Helena a puzzled look. "You come straight from gutting some fresh catch? Most sailors I know clean themselves up after working with fish guts."

Helena didn't understand what the man meant, but as she noticed his eyes focusing on her body below the neck, she looked down and examined herself. She felt a jolt of surprise when she saw that her tunic and trousers were stained with blood from where the spines of the vells had pierced her as well as from the vells' own blood from when she ran them through. The stains were somewhat faded, as if someone had taken a wet cloth and tried to scrub them out, but the crimson color was still quite obvious.

Helena looked up quickly. "Yeah, um, working late. I'm a bit of a mess."

"I can see that. And if I didn't know better, I'd think the gulls were picking at your arms for your catch," the man said, giving Helena's bandaged arms a quick glance.

"Oh, no, I—" Helena tried to focus on speaking normally instead of her current flustered tone. "Just had a bit of a fall is all. Scraped up the old arms. I should have cleaned myself up more, but I forgot. Sorry 'bout that, sir."

"Oh, it's no bother. We're all sailors here—well, most of us. A sailor who doesn't come back from the sea with some blood on his clothes probably doesn't have much for the table. The bigger the fish, the more it bleeds, eh?" the man said, finishing with a chuckle.

Upon seeing that Helena did not react to his humor, he halted his casual approach and cleared his throat. "Well, um, can I get you something, Miss?"

Helena shuffled on the stool and straightened her back a little more. "I don't know."

The man's slightly puzzled look returned. "Well, our specialty is salmon. We serve it smoked, boiled, or roasted, though we also serve plenty of cod and haddock. But if you're craving something that ain't from the water, we also have land meats. We get some in every week or so from the local villages and towns through trade, and we also have some of the more exotic stuff shipped here from the Mainland. None of it's as fresh as our town's daily catch, but it's all well preserved, and some of it you won't find anywhere but the Mainland."

The man reached below the counter and pulled out a thick stained menu. He placed it on the counter. "Here, take your pick. Is there something I can get to slake your thirst while you look?"

"No," Helena said, unintentionally bluntly. She could see by the man's face that she was acting strangely despite her honest attempts to appear calm and normal. She still wasn't even sure what she was doing there.

"Well, just holler when you've decided on something," he said, then headed off to serve another person sitting farther down the counter.

Helena felt confused. She swallowed her anxiety and picked up the stained menu. She examined it thoroughly, reading each item with devoted attention.

Slab of salmon with boiled potato – three copper shards.
Pork sausage with bread slices – four copper shards.
Mainland moose cut with tomato sauce – seven copper shards.
Mutton with diced carrots – five copper shards.
Cod stew with bread crusts – two copper shards.

Helena suddenly felt insatiably hungry. Thoughts of returning to Duncan's home for some of the fish stew that Charra had prepared, most likely cod itself, started to blur the menu in her hands. Her anxiety faded as she became lost in the stained parchment, though she had stopped reading it.

The sudden presence of a finger pressing into her right shoulder brought Helena out of her trance. She clenched the menu in her hands, causing it to crumple inward and nearly tear at the center. She turned to see who thought it appropriate to poke her and noticed a man was sitting on a stool adjacent to hers.

The man was large but not in the same way as the bartender. This man was large in the belly and chin, both of which hung like flaps of honey from his body. His dirty brown clothes brought back the stench of fish that Helena had gladly left behind at the docks.

"Ain't chu un 'o those 'un from this mornin'?" the man slurred, poking her again in the shoulder.

Helena pulled away from him. "What?"

The fat man leaned his heavy arm against the counter and snorted loudly. "That group o' folk o' marched in 'ere. You'se was un 'ovem, weren't ya?" he asked as the stench of fish from his attire mixed with his booze-reeking breath. Helena's insatiable hunger was suddenly doused by the smell.

"I'm sorry, do I know you?" she asked, hoping to dissuade the fat man from continuing his inquiry.

He seemed to take Helena's response as a question she wanted answered rather than a rhetorical social breakaway. "Today. Tiss'murnun!" he said, smacking his thick hand on the counter. "You 'nd a couple others. Ye showed up this mornin', scuffed 'nd bloody 'nd all messed up. I'd seen you with 'um, carry'un that boy. Wha' tha hell happened to ya all?"

Helena suddenly realized that any efforts to dissuade the intrusive man would only lead to further prattle, so she decided to speak plainly.

"Vells attacked us in Vellum Forest."

"Vells! Those spiky gublin hounds? In tha forest! Why'ud you lot be trekking through there alone and all?"

Before Helena could think of a quick response, the fat man shouted. "Oh! Uh'wer fleein' from Varral, ain't cha?" he roared with excitement, nearly falling off his stool as he clapped his hands. "What 'appened there? I 'erd there wuz a battle with 'ose rebels. What'er they culled 'gain ... them Seekers o' Lost?"

Helena was finding it harder and harder to understand the fat, drunk, foul-smelling man's ramblings. She didn't wish to hear any more either. She stood up and broke eye contact with him.

As she turned to leave, she felt the man's finger prodding her again, though this time it plunged into her lower back, right along her spine. She spun around and knocked his hand away with a firm swipe.

"Oh, come on, girl. I've gotta place fer ya ta stay, if ya be needing refuge," he said with an ugly smile as he grabbed Helena's crotch.

Helena jerked back a step, but the man's hold did not break. An overwhelming feeling of sickness filled her stomach. Before the man's hand could molest her any further, Helena balled her hand into a fist and smashed it into his right eye.

The fat man released his hold on Helena and let out a cry of pain that filled the tavern.

"Ahrg! Bleedin' whore!" he roared as he fell off the stool and landed his back, covering his eye. "Ahh! You bitch whelp! You—"

His ranting was cut off as Helena kicked him in his large stomach.

The tavern erupted into a cacophony of shouts, laughs, and catcalls. The sounds of stools scraping against the tavern's wooden floor as the patrons stood from their seats seemed never ending.

"Whoa!" a man said right behind Helena as a large hand clamped down on her shoulder. The hand spun her around, stopping her from following through with her next kick into the fallen man's belly. "Hey! What in Siyon's name is going on?" the man barked.

Helena realized that it was the bartender.

"That Verrel bitch attacked me!" the fat man screamed as he stood up, using the counter for support as he cupped his right eye.

"Is she from Verrel?" a woman called out.

"What happened there?" more than one voice shouted at once.

Suddenly, the crowd of patrons gathered around Helena, most of them humans, as the goblins were pushed to the back, all of them squabbling to be heard over each other.

"That's the place that got burned, right?" a man asked from the back.

A woman tugged Helena's tunic. "Was it the Lost Seekers?"

"I heard it was a battle with Caswen soldiers!" a man shouted.

"Nonsense!" another man howled. "Why would Caswen burn one of its own villages?"

"They say Verrel was in league with the Lost Seekers. Ask her! Ask her!" a different voice blurted.

"No! I was told it was the rebels who attacked the village, just like they attacked the capital's market! Aethi'ziton scum, that's what they are!" someone else erupted.

"What happened, girl? Tell us!" another woman said, grabbing Helena's arm.

Helena yanked her arm away from the woman's grasp and pushed through the crowd toward the door. As she did, she felt hands touching her body. One of them found its way to one of her breasts. Another slapped her rear. Helena quickened her pace before anyone else could grab her. She was greeted by one more harsh slap on her rear as she emerged from the crowd and made for the door, followed by frantic shouting.

"Where is she going?"

"She's not from Verrel. She's just some whelp."

"Quite the ass on that one!"

Pockets of laughter erupted amongst the shouting.

Helena was pleased when the sound of stools screeching and cups clanking reached her ears. It meant the crowd was dispersing back to their seats. By the time she walked out into the cold night air, the sounds of questions and footsteps had been replaced with laughing and incoherent yelling. No one followed her outside.

Helena quickly returned to the street, which still remained vacant of any townsfolk. She gave all her groped areas a quick rub, trying to remove the feeling of the crowd's grabby hands. A sudden sensation of coldness covered her left leg, revealing itself to be a large splash of liquid when she looked down at the area. Evidently, someone had spilled a whole mug of ale on her. The wet stain stuck her trouser leg to her thigh, channeling the cold air through the wool with biting ferocity.

The experience left Helena feeling sick and angry. At the same time, she felt tears welling up in her eyes. She wiped them away and told herself that she had cried enough.

To distract herself, Helena started walking down the lonely dirt street, heading farther into the moonlit town.

She only managed to walk a few dozen steps before stopping, still within earshot of the drunken merriment from the tavern behind her. She had stopped in front of a building that was larger than any of the cottages but a bit smaller than the tavern. It seemed to be built entirely of stone, and it had a slanted roof of tile instead of thatch.

Helena read the wooden sign hanging above the wide, dark double doors that led into the strange building. She read it again and again. Each time Helena read the sign, her stomach twisted with dread and anxiety as she spoke the words in her mind.

Temple of Siyon. Temple of Siyon. Temple of Siyon.

Helena approached the double doors and placed her hands against them. The dark wood, almost black in color, was smooth except for a series of carvings along the center of each door. Helena noticed that the markings were actually words carved into the wood. She ran her hands along the letters as she read the words on the left door first.

> In this temple, all the First Children are welcome. A house of worship to the second of the Second Children, Siyon, eldest daughter of the Godfather Cosom and the Godmother Dema. May her waves always carry you to pleasant shores.

Helena moved to the words on the right door.

> Only enter under Aol's light or Siyon's clouds, for these doors are watched at night by the many eyes of the great lord, Cosom, for those who would worship the Second Children over himself. The night is his, as are we all, for we remain his First Children.

Helena removed her hands from the door and stepped back. She looked up at the dark, cloudless sky and the stars that filled it. There were too many stars to count, and she felt as if every last one of them was looking straight at her.

Helena took a deep breath. "I'm not ... I don't ..." She bit her lip as she felt her heart begin to beat faster. "I ... I am not here to worship your Second Children. I just want to see someone. He ... he's one of your First Children, one who has no true love for any of those who betrayed you. I am not betraying you. I have never even been to one of these temples before in my life. I just want to see my friend."

Helena felt silly to think that Cosom would pay attention to only her at that moment and accept her words, but she was scared not to try.

Taking another deep breath, Helena stepped up to the double doors and pushed the left one forward. It slid open, creating a dark gap into the temple.

Helena felt goosebumps arise along her arms and neck, but she stopped herself from looking back up at the star-filled blackness above her. She had already made her choice. She stepped through the gap into the darkness beyond.

Chapter 20

❧

The darkness inside the temple was tenfold that of outside. No windows allowed moonlight to shine in, and none of the candles or lanterns within, if any were indeed inside, were lit. Helena felt like she was trespassing. It made her feel anxious and vulnerable, though she truly had no idea if she was breaking any laws or going to get in trouble if caught. Then she reminded herself that even if she was not supposed to be there at that hour, no one would be inside to notice her anyway.

Helena calmed a bit as her reasoning overruled her nervousness, but she still closed the door behind her just in case someone happened to walk by the temple. As she shut the door, she also shut out the minimal moonlight that had followed her inside. Now in total darkness, Helena stood silently, waiting for her eyes to adjust to the utter lack of light.

It was just as cold inside the temple as it had been outside. Helena folded her arms and tried to warm herself by rubbing them, but her hands were too cold to help much. The wet stain of ale that stuck part of her trousers to her thigh continued to be the coldest part of her, but she tried to ignore it as she waited for her eyes to adjust.

Helena could see that just in front of her was an empty space, so she stepped forward. The darkness was still too thick for her to see properly, so she stretched her leg out to scan for obstacles before she took another step, but as she moved farther in, she continued to find nothing in her way. The large room appeared to be empty. Helena's vision was slowly sharpening, but it remained mostly impaired. Regardless, she continued farther into the temple.

Her hands out in front of her, she shifted her path to the right in an attempt to find a wall, a corner, a support beam, anything to give her some sense of the room's size and shape. Finally, her hand met smooth, cold stone.

At first Helena was startled, but then she realized this was exactly what she was searching for. She placed her hands on the surface and felt around. It was not a wall but an arch, as the stone went upwards and curved over her head toward the center of the chamber. Helena assumed she was near the end of the chamber due to how many steps she had traveled to reach the arch, so she looked to her left as she continued forward.

Helena froze as her eyes picked up the faint outline of a figure up ahead, a person. Helena gripped the archway as fear filled her body. She could not decide what to do, so she stood completely still.

The figure did not approach her, nor did it move away. As the seconds passed, and Helena's eyes continued to adjust to the darkness, she realized the figure was much taller than she was and did not appear to have legs. Instead, its torso seemed to stretch down to the floor.

Helena remained still as she waited for something to happen. Only then did she realize the figure was a statue. She felt a wave of relief followed by a blast of embarrassment.

Removing her hands from the arch, she approached the statue. It was a woman, but a human woman it certainly was not. The head and torso appeared human-like, though with several differences. Her arms were slender and fair, but each stretched nearly a broomstick in length. Her chest had no breasts, and it curved inward rather than outward, like her ribcage was broken, and her eyes were uncomfortably large and lacked irises or pupils. Below the torso there were no legs. Instead, there were four long tentacles that spiraled around the stone base that supported the statue.

At the bottom of the stone base was a flat surface with words carved into it. Helena kneeled down, feeling pain in her right knee as she did, and inspected the writing while also running her fingers over the letters.

> Siyon – Eldest daughter and second born of the union between Cosom and Dema. Goddess of water, winds, storms, sailing, and the creatures of the deep ocean. In her adopted form in the image of her children, the naiads.

Helena looked back up at the figure and felt a chill run down her spine. She did not find the image of Siyon to be pleasing, and it sent her mind to wondering what disturbing appearances the rest of the gods might have.

Helena rose and turned away from the statue, trying to banish her thoughts of the gods. As she had told the stars, she was not there for them.

With renewed initiative Helena combed the walls of the chamber for another door or the entrance to the healing sanctum, which she knew all temples had. It took her some time feeling around in the dark until she found what she was looking for. Halfway back down the chamber along the west wall, she found a wooden door. Unlike the door to the temple itself, this one had no message inlaid into the wood.

Helena opened the door and found herself looking into a chamber of darkness. She stepped inside and immediately bumped into a curtain. She pulled it aside and continued forward. A strong smell hit her. Though she could not see where it came from, the smell was unmistakable.

Blood, and lots of it.

Helena's eyes began to discern the shapes of counters and tables in the far corner of the room. The smell of blood was strong in that direction, so she turned the opposite way, trying to ignore it.

She found herself facing another large curtain that divided the chamber in two. Without a moment's pause, she grasped the curtain and pulled it aside. What seemed to be counters and tables appeared in the darkness, but a moment later she realized they were actually beds, six in all, each spaced a few feet apart against the north wall.

Helena froze, her heart racing as she gripped the curtain so tightly that her fingernails dug into it. On the far-left bed, amidst the overbearing silence and darkness, was the shape of a person.

Helena felt a sudden urge to depart. The thought of seeing what she feared made her want to vomit. But her feet felt as if they weighed a thousand pounds, rooting her in place.

A long minute passed before she built up the will to proceed. Swallowing her fear and doubt, Helena released the curtain and closed the distance between herself and the bed, still fighting the urge to vomit.

She stood at the side of the bed, her heart pounding in her chest. Her knees felt like they would give out at any moment, and her hands began to shake uncontrollably.

"Carver?" she said through trembling lips.

He did not respond.

Helena dropped to her knees beside him. Her injured knee protested in pain, but she didn't pay it any attention.

She placed a hand on Carver's chest. Her urge to vomit was pushed down the moment she felt his chest push up against her hand.

"Carver?" she said, letting the rhythm of his rising and lowering chest calm her.

When he did not respond, she removed her hand from his chest and placed it on his head. She felt the coarse, dry material of fresh bandages wrapped tightly around the top of his head. She also felt his hair, which, to her surprise, had been cut short and washed, no longer stuck together in heavy clumps.

Her feeling of relief turned bittersweet as she removed her hand from his head and wiped the tears from her face.

"Carver?"

Still he did not respond.

She wiped more tears from her face, this time needing both hands. She exhaled loudly, stood up, and with one last look at her friend, walked away from the bed. She began to pull the curtain back into place but then stopped and stared into the darkness where she knew Carver was lying, wondering if she should call his name one more time.

She didn't. Instead, she pulled the curtain shut, doing the same with the other as she passed into the first room. Her memory of the chamber allowed her to pass quickly through the darkness and find the large double doors at the far end. She stepped outside and pulled the door shut behind her.

Wiping more tears away with the back of her hand, Helena began walking down the lonely street again, battling her emotions as she headed back toward Duncan's home, trying to staunch her silent crying.

Chapter 21

Aellia opened her eyes as the sunlight entered her room through the window on the east wall. She heard waves crashing over rocks, followed by the squawking of dozens of seagulls as their shadows occasionally obscured the light on the window's ledge. Aellia wiped her eyes and face, groaned, and tossed off the heavy sheets that gave her comfort. She felt tired and sore, as she did most mornings, but she still managed to force herself out of bed and began her usual morning routine.

First, she walked over to her room's wooden door on the west wall and checked the iron knob to make sure that it was still locked. Once that was confirmed, she began to undress, tossing her brown wool nightwear onto her bed. Once she was free of them, she spent a handful of minutes stretching her limbs in the middle of the room. The warmth her body had maintained after exiting her bedsheets slowly drained through her feet and into the brown fur rug on which she was standing.

Aellia's back cracked as she finished her movements. Then she stepped over to her large oak wardrobe near the window and opened it. Before she looked inside, she turned her head and gazed out the window. The view of the ocean far below stretched forever, with gentle waves moving inland. A gust of wind came through the window and tickled her bare shoulder. She turned her attention back to the wardrobe.

Inside the wardrobe was a range of finely tailored clothing. Tunics ranging in color from gray and brown to faded blue and red hung from wooden pegs. Some were embroidered while others were plain. A few pairs of folded trousers took up the bottom of the wardrobe. Most were gray, black, or brown, though some had some extra flair. In the back corner were two pairs of boots, both of them black and with thick laces. Piled messily atop one of the pairs of boots were a few pairs of gray women's braies. Hanging on more pegs in the back of the wardrobe were a few linen bras.

Aellia took one of the plain brown tunics, a pair of gray trousers lacking any embroidery, one of the gray braies, a linen bra, and a pair of the black boots. She returned to her unmade bed, sat on its disheveled sheets, and dressed herself. She fitted her bra well and laced her open tunic high so as not to show any cleavage, stepped into her trousers, after putting on her braies, and buckled them with a belt she grabbed from where it was hanging off the back of a chair near the bed. She finished by slipping into her black boots and lacing them tightly.

Once she was dressed, she strolled to a small table against the south wall just to the right of the open window. Atop the table was a tall oval mirror in a thin copper frame, in front of which sat a hairbrush, a pair of tweezers, a small wooden jewelry box, and a circular wood container of makeup next to a small feather brush.

Aellia sat on the low stool in front of the table and brushed her coppery-brown hair until she found her appearance acceptable. She placed the hairbrush back in its spot and looked at herself in the mirror. After a few seconds, she stood up and walked over to an armor stand, a series of wooden posts and pegs in the corner of her room adjacent to the wardrobe.

First went on the gambeson, then the hauberk and chausses, then her faded crimson surcoat. After the bulk of the outfit was on, she put on her iron-reinforced leather gauntlets and attached her light iron pauldrons and greaves, then the outer belt with her sheathed arming sword strapped in place. She finished by double checking every inch of the armor that she could see while wearing it.

Aellia walked back across the room, stopping in front of her mirror, and looked herself over for a moment. Satisfied, she headed to her door. After leaving her room it only took her a minute to navigate the halls and exit the building. Once outside, she got her horse from the stable, then rode toward the Caswen garrison in the northwest part of the city.

As her brown horse carried her down the cobblestone street deeper into the city, Aellia thought about her tasks for the day once she reached her destination: distribute the patrols and shifts to the first on-duty soldiers, give Harsond most of the control of the City Guard for the day, then spend the rest of the day going over the stack of reports that had been piling up on her desk over the last few weeks from the other towns and villages throughout the Isles.

Once she completed her other tasks and made it to her office, she decided to take her boots off and get more comfortable for a day of arduous paperwork. Just as she finished unlacing her boots and kicking them off beneath her desk, she heard a series of knocks at her office door.

It was a soldier who informed her that the chancellor had summoned her to his chambers at the manor immediately.

Knowing she could not refuse such a summons even though she wanted to, she slipped her boots back on her feet and went out to get her horse. Aellia's horse didn't seem bothered when she returned and guided it out of the garrison's stable only minutes after it had settled, but Aellia herself felt a headache coming on, provoked by frustration.

The city was in the process of waking up as Aellia trotted her horse back the way she had come. The beams of sunlight that made it over Caswen's high stone walls warmed the back of her neck and glinted off any part of her iron armor that wasn't beneath her faded crimson surcoat.

Human and goblin citizens were slowly filling the city's cobblestone streets. Some were mounted on horses of their own, or donkeys for the shortest of the goblins, but most were on foot. They all seemed oblivious to one another, neither smiling nor greeting passersby.

As Aellia continued her ride back southeast across the city, she noticed that many of the common folk seemed to be tracking her with their eyes. Some stared at her openly while others only glanced at her as she passed. All the common folk kept their distance from her, and she couldn't help but notice that those who walked toward her or noticed her from behind stepped farther to the side of the street than was necessary to let a passing horse go by.

Aellia felt like an outcast in her own city, shunned by the very people whose lives she worked tirelessly to protect. She tried to banish such thoughts and endeavored not to look around at the nearby commoners, but she could not entirely ignore what was happening around her, which only added to her deteriorating mood.

A few minutes later, Aellia found herself riding up a slow incline, with the cobblestone street heading upwards and bending to the east. The street was far less populated and gave her the space to command her horse up the rise with increased speed. Her mount carried her up the gently ascending street until Aellia pulled the reins for it to stop. The beast obeyed and halted where the street leveled out before the massive manor.

It was a large stone structure with a high, slanted wooden roof. The stone walls rose up two stories and sat atop an elevated stone foundation, allowing a full view of the city below from the windows that dotted the manor's north side. The manor had a wide cobblestone roundabout courtyard with many thin cobblestone paths branching out between elevated gardens, leading around, behind, and to different sides of the manor. At the center of the roundabout was a large, raised circular garden packed with flowers and with a single large bush of purple deutzia. The many flowers and flowering bushes that filled the elevated gardens throughout the courtyard were the only things about the manor that Aellia found appealing.

The courtyard and manor themselves were protected on the sloped north and south sides by tall stone walls similar to those that protected the city, while the much steeper east side was protected by a cliff that overlooked the ocean below. The west side was protected by a tall black iron fence of vertical bars held together by two long horizontal bars, one at the base and one at the top just below the tops of the bars, which ended in sharp points. The tall black fence had a large gate in the center, which was open.

The gate was guarded by two soldiers, a man and a woman. Each soldier held an iron-tipped spear and had a sheathed arming sword buckled to his or her surcoat belt. They stared down the long sloped road that led back down to the rest of the city. As soon as the soldiers saw Aellia riding up the hill, they straightened their posture and extended their chins.

"My Lord," the man said, nodding at Aellia.

The woman beside him, whose short, curly black hair was sticking out from under her iron helmet, turned and kicked the man's heel with her boot. "It's Captain, you idiot. She doesn't like—"

Aellia raised her hand and forced herself to smile as she climbed off her horse. "It's fine. I'm technically not the captain of the Manor Guard anyway," she said as she took her horse's reins and walked it toward the gate.

The female soldier nodded slightly. "Well, you still hold the rank of marshal of the Isles above that, and I know you don't like being referred to as—"

Aellia raised her hand again. "Marshal will do fine then."

"My apologies, Marshal Aellia," the male soldier said, adjusting his posture.

"There is no need to fuss over such things," Aellia said, trying to speak in a friendly tone as she approached the gate.

She stopped in front of the woman and handed her horse's reins to her. "Would you mind holding my horse here for a moment? I have important business in the manor, though I doubt it will take long," she said, not wanting to spend time taking her mount to the stables behind the manor.

"Certainly, ma'am. No trouble at all," the woman said.

Aellia smiled gratefully, then headed past the two guards and into the roundabout courtyard.

"It's not like I'm wrong," Aellia heard the man whisper to his partner as she passed by the deutzia bush.

Aellia put her thoughts elsewhere as she rounded the central garden and picked up her pace. As she reached the other side of the middlemost garden, a wooden bench on the other end of the wide cobblestone path came into view. A man was sitting on it reading a tome with a blank cover that blocked his face.

Though she could not see the man's face, he seemed familiar. He was wearing an unbuttoned dark coat over a perfectly white tunic. His trousers were also dark, although the red strips of stitched detail near the bottom of the legs and just below the belt made them more vibrant. His brown, wavy hair was visible above the book that blocked his face.

Aellia stopped as the feeling of familiarity grew even stronger, but then the sound of rustling branches behind her summoned her attention. She spun around and saw the white flowering bush behind swaying as if something large had just moved inside it.

Her instincts kicked in, telling her she was in danger. She took half a step back and reached for her sword, but before she could draw it, the bush shook violently and a person jumped out, snapping many of the bush's branches in the process.

"Surprise!" a young boy's voice screamed.

Aellia squeezed the hilt of her arming sword in fright, but she stopped herself from pulling it out.

"Bo!" The word escaped her mouth like a reflex.

As the small boy ran forward, Aellia released her grip on her sword and dropped to one knee, opening her arms as he reached her. He slammed into her chest and wrapped his thin arms around her. Aellia closed her arms around him in a hug.

"Bo, you're back!"

His response was muffled, his face pressed up against Aellia's surcoat. She leaned back and pulled Bo slightly away from her.

"—nd I wanted to surprise you when I saw you coming through the court-yard," he finished, looking up at Aellia with his blue eyes.

Bo's brown hair was light in color and short in length, though it hung slightly down over his forehead. His clothes, a small white tunic and brown trousers, were stained with dirt at the knees and elbows, and his brown boots were also filthy.

Aellia pulled the boy back in for another hug and then kissed him on the forehead. Bo continued to hug Aellia until she pulled him off and stood up. "Where's our brother? I assume he has returned as well."

Bo immediately pointed past Aellia. As she turned around to follow Bo's direction, she saw that the man sitting on the bench had set his book on his lap and was staring at them. Aellia immediately realized why she had found the man familiar a moment ago, especially when he spoke.

"That I have, sister."

"I told you I'd surprise her!"

"You certainly did," the man said with a faint smile. His face was young and clean shaven, and his eyes were a light brown, much like Aellia's. He set his book onto the bench and stood up.

Aellia started toward him, tugging Bo by the shoulder, so he followed her.

"I'm pleased to see you again, Saelus. You must have just arrived or else I would have run into you both on my way out this morning."

"That we did. Bo and I only just departed from our ship a short while ago."

Aellia looked down at Bo and rubbed the top of his head, messing up his hair on purpose. Bo giggled and stepped away, running a hand through his hair to smooth it down.

"I'm glad the two of you have returned."

"And I'm glad to be home again. I was growing worried about the wellbeing of my little sister being alone with our father for so many months."

Aellia turned her gaze away from Bo and frowned at Saelus. "Don't do that."

"Don't do what?" Saelus asked while leaning against the elevated garden to his right.

"Don't make jokes about my feelings toward him."

Saelus raised his left hand as if to signal that he meant no harm. "I wasn't entirely joking. To be honest, I was hoping that since the two of you would be alone with each other for so long that maybe you'd patch things up. I guess that's not the case, then."

"Patch things up? You mean forget what he did to our mother and act like—" Aellia stopped herself and exhaled through her nose. "I'm tired of this argument, Saelus. And besides, I didn't spend much time at the manor while you were away. Too busy running things and all that." She looked over at Bo, who had wandered to a different elevated garden and was scraping dirt into a mound with his hands.

"I see. And how have your duties been going lately, Guard Captain? Or is it Marshal? I can never remember what your title is. You have so many, after all."

A gust of hot breath escaped Aellia's nostrils as she closed her eyes for a moment. When she opened them, she forced a smile as she turned to face her older brother once again. "Aellia will do fine. So, tell me, how was your journey to the capital?"

"It was incredible!" Bo said, leaping to Aellia's side. "The Mainland is way bigger than the Isles. We got to ride in a carriage across all the provinces and stopped in each provincial capital until we reached the kingdom capital. Then we sailed all the way back. And Keldaria was—"

"We didn't go through all the provinces, Bo. There are five, and we only traveled through three of them. Remember, we talked about this while traveling."

Bo looked up at Saelus. "Oh, yeah. I keep forgetting."

"That's alright. Why don't you name all the provinces to me again, like we practiced before? You can impress Aellia with your knowledge."

Bo's face suddenly lost some of its enthusiasm. Aellia placed a gentle hand on his shoulder. "It's okay, Bo. Give it a shot. I remember having a hard time remembering such things at your age too, so don't be nervous."

Bo looked back and forth between his siblings with slightly worried eyes, but after a quick couple of seconds he began speaking. "Um. The Isles. That's where we live, and it's the newest province."

Aellia smiled at the boy. "That's right, Bo. Good memory."

Bo didn't react to the compliment, too focused on his mental task. "Then, um ... the Coastlands. Then there's Splitland. Oh, and then the Lowlands. That's where the kingdom capital is. And then there's ... uh ..."

"Opposite of lowlands," Saelus prompted.

Bo's face lit up. "Oh! The Highlands. And that's where we didn't go."

Saelus smiled. "That's right, Bo. Very good. I told you that you were smart."

Aellia smiled down at the boy. "You did better than I did when I was your age, Bo. I'm very impressed."

Bo smiled widely and tapped his feet in excitement.

"Our journey went well," Saelus said, "and our time in Keldaria was spent productively with the royal family. Bo even made quite the impression on the queen's youngest daughter."

"Is that so?" Aellia eyed the boy with an arched eyebrow. "I guess it's time to send you back to get married then, Bo," she said, grinning.

Once again Bo's enthusiasm plummeted. "No way. I already told Saelus that I don't want to marry Kerala. She's too bossy when we play."

Saelus chuckled. "You'd best hope that Father gives you the Aellia treatment then."

Aellia turned to Saelus. "The Aellia treatment? And just what is that supposed to mean, brother?"

Saelus chuckled again. "You know exactly what it means. It was you who proposed to that Coastlands boy against father's wishes. If I had tried to marry whomever I wanted, I'm sure that Father would have threatened me with disinheritance."

Aellia clenched her fists slightly, though not enough for either of her brothers to notice. "He's not some Coastlands boy, Saelus. His name is Riel, and he's the heir to that province, much like you are heir to this province. And I don't think you'd appreciate being called that Isler boy, would you?"

"Now, now, sister. I didn't mean to offend you. I was simply speaking casually. I have nothing but respect for Riel. In fact, I even sought him out during our visit to his father's court in New Brienen. I'm actually surprised you haven't asked me about him yet."

Aellia smirked, though not pleasantly. "Very well, Saelus. How was your meeting with my fiancé? Is Riel well?"

"I wouldn't know. I didn't manage to get an audience with him."

"Well, that's very useful then, Saelus. I appreciate you bringing it up."

Saelus held up his right hand again to indicate that he meant no ill will. Aellia ignored the gesture and turned back to Bo, who was staring at them both in silence, appearing somewhat bored.

"Regardless, I'm pleased to have you both home once again," she said. "I must admit that when I received the message to return to the manor, I was irritated, but seeing that the summons was meant to bring me to my brothers has eased my mind."

"A message?" Saelus said. "I didn't send a message for you to return. In fact, I was wondering why you had returned to the manor so early in the morning. I'd thought Bo and I would have to wait until after nightfall to see you."

Aellia tilted her head slightly toward Saelus. "Oh. Well, the message came from Adaman. I suppose he sent it without your knowledge."

Saelus also tilted his head with curiosity, ending his lean against the elevated garden's edge. "Well, that is quite unlike our dear chancellor, acting on his own accord and without instructions. I didn't think the old fool had it in him to think for himself."

Bo let out a laugh.

Aellia shot a look down at Bo, which silenced the boy instantly. "You should not laugh at such remarks, Bo. And you should not say such things about Adaman," Aellia finished, looking back at her older brother.

"My apologies, dear sister. You're clearly not in the mood for jokes. I only meant that it was odd for Adaman to send for you without telling you why and without Bo and I knowing ourselves, if the reason was indeed for a pleasant reunion."

Aellia chewed her lip as her brother's words triggered her memory that the chancellor's message had instructed her to come to his chambers. "Well, brother, I must admit that you have a point, though I'd be surprised if this was all a happy coincidence. I suppose I should go and see the man."

"A smart course of action, sister. Your sharp mind reassures me that the security of our province is in good hands," Saelus said while bowing slightly.

Aellia forced out another grin despite her desire not to, then turned away from Saelus and looked down at Bo, who was staring at some bushes farther off.

"I'll see you again tonight, Bo. And try not to damage the gardens while you're out here, by the way. No more hiding and jumping out of the bushes."

Bo gave Aellia a soft look. "Okay. I won't. But I did surprise you, didn't I?"

Aellia smiled. "Yes, Bo. You sure did."

With that Bo ran off behind a bush-filled elevated garden. Aellia turned back to Saelus with the thought of saying something else, but as she looked back, she saw that Saelus had already returned to his bench and was picking up his book once again. Aellia left it at that and turned to walk toward the great manor.

It only took Aellia two dozen more steps to reach the manor's main door. Another two soldiers, both of them males, stood at attention on either side of the door. Just like the two at the gate, they straightened their backs and nodded at Aellia as she approached.

"Guard Captain," they said, addressing her nearly in unison.

Aellia smiled at the men, then climbed the last few stairs and into the shadow that the wide wooden balcony above the entrance created. She didn't say anything to the two soldiers, and they said nothing further to her as one of them opened the door for her. Aellia nodded in thanks to the man and walked inside.

The central room inside the great manor was wide, high ceilinged, and spacious. Open doorways in the inner stone walls to the north and south led to different rooms and halls, which themselves led to even more rooms, such as a dining hall, several deep and dusty storage closets, a noisy kitchen with a constantly working staff, a cramped, barracks-like living quarters for the manor's soldiers, and other chambers and halls that Aellia did not often visit.

The center of the manor's entrance room was filled by a wide stone staircase that climbed halfway up to the wooden ceiling high above and connected with a second-floor balcony that stretched across the width of the chamber. The balcony led to open doorways on the north and south walls. Another wooden door was in the center of the upper wall, facing east. The few soldiers who filled the room, most on the first floor while only two stood on the second floor looking down, all kept their attention focused on their duty and only gave Aellia the briefest of looks as she entered. Aellia was pleased to see that the soldiers were seemingly focused and watchful.

As the door closed behind her, she walked to the base of the wide stone stairs. She climbed the steps two at a time and reached the inner balcony in a matter of seconds. The balcony had a long red rug that spanned its center, leaving only a small margin of the upper stone floor exposed up to the east wall and the balcony's west edge before a significant drop to the first floor.

Aellia focused on her path and turned to the right, heading across the balcony, through the door at its south end. Upon entering the small hallway with doors along both walls, she chose the second door on the left and entered into a much longer hall with many doors along each wall. The new hall was dim, illuminated only by the sun's light through a window at the far end facing east before the hall made a sharp left and continued north.

Standing guard along the hall at evenly distanced posts between the doors were three soldiers, all of them holding spears at their sides. Each one looked Aellia's way but said nothing. She nodded to each soldier as she passed on her way down the hall. As they nodded back, she couldn't help but notice that their glances seemed uneasy.

Aellia suddenly wondered if the return of her brothers had indeed been coincidental with the chancellor's summons, and what the details of this summons could be seeing as the standing manor guard somehow knew of it already and were upset by the news. The thought had Aellia feeling stressed and irritated all over again as she pondered the possible situation in her mind.

Dema's ass, what could this be? I've yet to go over a single piece of parchment at my office, and already something is wrong. Dammit, Adaman. This had better not be something—

Aellia's distracted mind made her shock ever more severe once she reached the chancellor's door midway down the hall along the south wall and pushed it open without knocking.

Chapter 22

Aellia stood frozen in the chancellor's doorway. Her eyes had at first been drawn to the familiar sight of the chancellor, Adaman, who was standing in the center of the room wearing his usual gray robes, but almost instantly afterwards her gaze became fixed on the back of the towering person the old man was speaking to.

The person stood at least seven feet tall, looming over Adaman with a threatening presence. He wore a set of polished, pearl-colored metal armor with turquoise, white, and silver coloring along the sharp edges and intricate designs along the back, though much of the back's details were blocked from sight by the short red cape that hung down to just above his waist.

Aellia also noticed the person's bald head, gill-like ears, and beige skin. Then her eyes scanned to the bottom and saw the clawed, bone-like "X's" that were the person's feet below the white linen chiton covering much of his legs. Aellia suddenly felt a weight fall on her as her wandering thoughts became fixed on the sight before her.

Only then did she notice the third person standing in the room. He was a middle-aged, dark-skinned human male dressed in unfamiliar garments.

Aellia had been made aware during her childhood education about the grander world of Gaia that humans were not all pale skinned, nor did they only dwell in the north. The knowledge that to Gaia's far south were humans with dark skin and a vastly different culture to those of the north had always enticed Aellia's imagination and wonder as a child, though after living all her years never seeing a human of such distinction, she had long since put such teachings in the back of her mind. Seeing this man now rekindled Aellia's realization that she had experienced so little of the world.

The dark-skinned man was leaning against the east wall between a wardrobe and a desk cluttered with tomes, loose sheets of parchment, and quills and was staring at Adaman and the sovereign with his deep brown eyes. His arms were crossed, and his right leg was raised, pushing his right foot into the wall for support. His face was bearded with heavy stubble, though his upper lip was free of growth, and his dark hair was cut close to his scalp, appearing like heavy stubble itself.

He was armored in a bronze chest piece that extended into a round dip near his waist. Three layers of thick leather strips, ink black with chestnut-red edges, hung from the bottom of his armor and covered most of the man's upper legs, which were garbed in black trousers. More strips of black leather with a red border were attached to the shoulders of his bronze chest piece and covered the man's upper arms down to an inch above his elbows. The rest of his arms were exposed, as were his hands, which had no gauntlets or bracers. Thicker leather strips were attached to the top of his armor's bronze shoulders and connected the front and back of his armor together, along with short buckles and straps at his sides and waist.

Much of the armor's upper portion was obscured under a short yellow cloak, which appeared to be made of linen rather than wool, which was wrapped around the man's neck and ran down the front and back of the bronze armor until it was tied off at the man's right side just above the waist. Also at the man's waist were two weapons in tanned hide sheaths. The sheath on his right side held a long, curved dagger. The one on his left confused Aellia. Although the scabbard stretched about the length of an ordinary arming sword, it was wider than was needed for such a blade and was rectangular in shape. The strange weapon's hilt was also odd, as it appeared to be made of a solid chunk of smooth wood, so thick and fat at the end that it seemed like it could be used as a club. It was curved slightly around a thinner wooden grip as if to shield the wielder's hand.

As Aellia finished her quick observation of the man, she realized the only thing about him that appeared familiar were his boots, which were made of brown leather and laced tightly down the center.

"Ah, Marshal Aellia, please come in. We have been eagerly awaiting your arrival," Adaman said when he noticed her in the doorway.

She hesitated for a moment, battling a wave of nervousness that churned her stomach, but not wanting to show weakness or fear, Aellia bit her tongue and tried to get ahold of herself before stepping into the chamber. The room was illuminated by several candles scattered around the room and a window on the south wall, which let trace amounts of sunlight through.

Before the chamber door clicked shut behind Aellia, the sovereign turned to face her, as did the dark-skinned man. The sovereign's slightly larger-than-human eyes—Aellia couldn't tell if the irises were blue, brown, or dark green—looked her up and down. With the sovereign now facing her, Aellia could see that it was a man and that his face was marked with a similar design to the sovereigns she had met in the magistrate's audience chamber almost a week ago. The design began next to each of his eyes and ran down the sides of his face, while a sharp offshoot jutted out slightly under each eye. The markings that descended the sides of the sovereign's face curved toward his chin and ended in two points that resembled thin blades. From the thickest part of the curve near the chin, the lines ran up over his flat beige lips and ended just below his gill-like nostrils.

Rather than the facial design being entirely black, like those of the sovereigns she had met earlier, this one's was only thinly outlined with black, while the rest was a deep red.

The front of the sovereign's armor was much more intricate than the back, featuring many engravings and grooves, ranging in color from turquoise to silver to pure white. They reached from the sharp, thin pauldrons at his shoulders down to his waist, all of it glinting in the light. Everything about the armor's appearance told Aellia that it was fashioned by a savant of the smithing art and worn by someone of high authority.

Unlike the foreign man, however, the sovereign only had one weapon clearly visible on his person: a long, gently curved blade. It had a lengthy hilt carved from black wood that curved in the opposite direction of the blade, just as gently. It had no hilt guard and ended in a pommel capped with what looked like gold. The weapon was sheathed in a white leather scabbard buckled to his waist.

Aellia bowed her head toward the sovereign.

"So this is the marshal of the Isles and captain of the Caswen Guard," the sovereign said in a deep and somewhat gentle voice.

Aellia lifted her head and looked into the sovereign's large eyes. Dread perforated her body unlike ever before, though she knew she could not let that fact be known.

"I am. And who are you?" She tried to speak bluntly in order to appear confident and calm.

Aellia saw Adaman's eyes widen with worry behind the sovereign, and she assumed he was about to cut in and apologize for her tone, but the sovereign responded almost immediately with something neither Aellia nor Adaman expected: a grin, followed by a brief hum of amusement.

"I'm glad to see you're not as spineless as the chancellor here. I was warned that you were a curt bitch who spoke as she pleased to her superiors," he said, stretching a hand toward Aellia.

Aellia and Adaman were shocked at the sovereign's words, but Aellia's anxiety lessened as she shook the sovereign's hand. It was cold and firm, and his slightly longer-than-human fingers wrapped around the back of her hand like bent twigs. Her hand exploded with pain as the sovereign tightened his grip, his unblinking eyes piercing hers.

Aellia realized what he was doing. He was watching for a reaction from her, looking to see if she would pull away or wince in pain as he crushed her hand within his.

Aellia bit her tongue and kept her stare locked on the sovereign's eyes as she continued to shake his hand without showing any signs of discomfort.

The sovereign grinned again, though faintly this time. "Good."

Aellia suddenly felt the squeezing stop. She lowered her throbbing hand to her side and left it there despite her clawing instinct to rub it.

"Aellia, this is Erol," Adaman said, breaking the tension that filled the chamber. "He—"

"I can introduce myself, Adaman."

The old man twitched and shut his mouth.

"Yes, my name is Erol. I'm here on direct orders from the emperor to monitor the security of the Isles and ensure that the threat posed by these Lost Seekers is dealt with swiftly."

Aellia felt a surge of relief at his words, but as she focused her thoughts and properly digested the sovereign's words, she realized she should not feel entirely relaxed just yet.

"Isn't that my duty both as captain and marshal? Am I being replaced, sir?" she asked with an effort to sound respectful.

"No, you're not being replaced. And yes, that is your duty. But you haven't been very successful in your duty as of late. That's why I'm here. I am to assess the state of this province over the next few months and send reports back to my superiors. You will remain marshal of the Isles and guard captain of Caswen, impressive titles for such a young human, and a female, at that, but now you will report directly to me."

Anger welled up inside Aellia as Erol continued. "I will be staying in the manor during my time here and will be working on my own matters much of the time, both within the city and out amongst the other settlements, but I'll be checking in on you from time to time and will be expecting reports from you personally about the major goings-on throughout the city and the rest of the islands."

Aellia clenched her teeth. "And what about him?" she asked, nodding at the silent man leaning against the wall. He said nothing, and just stared at her.

Erol looked over at the man. "Ah, yes. Why don't you introduce yourself?"

He pushed himself away from the wall. "I am Jaqun. It's a pleasure to finally make your acquaintance, Aellia. I've heard a lot about you."

Aellia did not like the fact that people whom she knew nothing about seemed to know a lot about her. She wondered what Erol and Jaqun had heard about her, both good and bad, and whether she should be worried.

"Jaqun will also be staying in the manor. I hear that you have a great many guest rooms. His tasks, much like my own, will have him moving throughout the city and the rest of the province as well. When not acting on his own, he will be assisting me, though his duties don't require your input. He will be reporting to me and no one else. He is authorized to act on behalf of me and wields my full authority. Jaqun is to be given aid should he request it from you or from anyone else, and he is not to be bothered or hindered by anyone. Do I make myself clear?"

"Yes, sir," Aellia replied, forcing herself to answer calmly.

"Good." Erol stiffened his back, increasing his already grand height by another inch. "Now, I have some other matters that I must attend to before settling in, so I'll be on my way."

"Is it anything I can assist you with, sir?" Aellia asked in an effort to show that she was willing to cooperate.

"No. Jaqun will assist me," Erol said while looking over at Jaqun and nodding toward the door.

Jaqun nodded so softly in reply that Aellia barely detected the movement before he crossed the room, opened the chamber door, and walked out.

"It was good to meet you, Aellia. I intend to stop by the garrison later today and have a more in-depth conversation with you," Erol said as he walked past her, taking long steps toward the chamber door.

Aellia's worry returned as she followed Erol's exit with her eyes.

He ducked to pass through the doorway, then stopped and looked back. "If I take longer than I expect, and I don't arrive, I expect you to come to my chambers before midnight, and we'll talk there. Have a productive day," he said before stepping into the hall while pulling the door closed behind him.

Adaman's room fell eerily silent as he and Aellia stared at each other without moving, each of them wondering who would be the first to speak. After too many seconds of silence, Aellia grew impatient.

"Well, that was certainly a surprise," she said in an accusative tone while crossing her arms.

Adaman didn't say anything in reply, just shrugged and gave her a look that told her exactly what she thought.

"So you knew this sovereign was coming, and I assume the magistrate did as well?"

"Well … yes. We did know."

"For how long?"

"Since the day after the market was attacked. We received notice by carrier pigeon that the sovereigns would be sending someone."

"What? You've known about this for nearly a week, and you didn't inform me! Why?"

"Aellia, please. I was following the magistrate's orders. He didn't want you to know until the sovereign arrived."

"And for what reason would he wish to keep me in the dark about this?"

Adaman raised his hands in a gentle gesture to quiet Aellia down, but she had no intention of doing so.

"He didn't want to distract you with the information. He knows how you can get."

"Knows how … knows how I can get? Are you … distract me with the information?" Aellia frowned, her mouth open as she struggled to maintain her composure. "I can't believe this. I'm the one in charge of the security of the Isles, so I should know when the sovereigns are making decisions regarding it, especially when it involves one taking direct charge over me!"

"Aellia, I—"

"No, I don't want to hear it! I've got things to take care of," Aellia said as she spun around and marched toward the door. As she pulled the door open and stepped through, she turned back. "Would you deliver a message to Wise Magistrate Julius for me the next time you see him? Tell him to go fuck himself." With that, she slammed the door.

Her hand still holding the doorknob, Aellia stood in the hallway, deep in thought. She could see in her peripheral vision that the soldiers down the hall to her right were looking at her, but when she looked over at them, they quickly turned away.

"You met our new guests, I see," a calm, older male voice said from Aellia's left, near the corner of the hall before it continued to the north. She recognized the voice immediately and replied without turning to face it.

"Of course the spymaster would know about an arriving sovereign and his accomplice, but why he would keep me in the dark is not so obvious."

"I did not have enough details. Telling you of their coming would only have distressed you."

"Distressed me!" Aellia released the doorknob and turned to face the man. He was of average height, meeting her angry glare with his brown eyes. His black hair was combed back behind his ears and reached just shy of his long brown leather coat, which he wore overtop of his buttoned black tunic. His demeanor was calm and his expression somewhat flat.

"You bastard, Renneil. Being suddenly summoned to an audience with a sovereign, you know what I th—"

"Stop," Renneil said, raising a hand. "Come with me."

Aellia had no time to respond before Renneil strode past her and headed down the hall toward the door that led to the smaller hall. Aellia ground her teeth together as she turned to follow him without saying another word.

Renneil passed through the doorway without checking to see if Aellia was following him. He guided her down the lesser hall and stopped once he reached the door at its south end facing west. Renneil pulled out a ring of keys from his coat pocket and unlocked the door.

Aellia realized where she was being led.

Another small hall greeted her as she followed Renneil, this one half as long as the previous and with a lone wooden door at its end. Renneil unlocked it with a different key and stepped through, though this time he turned and gestured for Aellia to come through while he held the door open.

Aellia scoffed and then proceeded inside while hearing the door click shut behind her. Before she could turn to look back at Renneil, he had already crossed the room to an oak desk that was pushed up against the west wall, just below a window with closed shutters that would have given a view of the courtyard had they been open.

The room reminded Aellia of her own office. The south wall was lined with bookshelves, all stocked with tomes and thickly rolled parchments standing upright. The area to the north was open, leaving the dark-brown rug mostly visible, save for a few chairs, as it crossed the room, ending at a wall of bookshelves, though with fewer books and scrolls than the others. The wide desk was littered with papers, sealed and unsealed envelopes, a row of inkwells with thick feathers sticking out of each, and a single brown book opened to the middle page.

Renneil flipped the book shut and then turned around and sat on the edge of the desk to face Aellia, who crossed her arms.

"Yes, Aellia, I know what you must have thought when surprised with a visit from a sovereign. A rational assumption given the circumstances. But I also know that you are wrong and that there is no reason for such a thought to be true at present. I am under no impression that anyone, sovereign or otherwise, is aware of anything that could harm you or me."

"Do you view me as a child?"

Renneil raised an eyebrow. "No, I do not."

"Well, if not a child, then perhaps a First District whore who takes cock for coin?"

Renneil frowned while folding his arms. "Aellia, you are too intelligent to believe such ridiculousness."

"Then perhaps a soldier who is too far a fool to solve her problems without hitting them with her sword?"

"Enough, Aellia."

"Well, if not those then what? What am I to you that you can so easily and confidently leave me behind in matters that not only concern the Isles but also me?"

Renneil's frown deepened. "If I must apologize to you for what you deem is an insult or a betrayal of your character, then fine, I'm sorry for not informing you. The recent days have been no less busy for me than they have been for you, and every moment of my time is crucial to things that go beyond what you know."

Aellia scoffed.

"Enough, Aellia. This juvenile display you are putting on must end."

Aellia did not say anything for a time, keeping her arms folded and her eyes fixed on the shutters behind Renneil's head, but after a moment of silence, she sighed and unfolded her arms. "Very well. I don't want to act like such a bitch anyway. I thought what I thought, and it caused me to panic, so I apologize for my harshness."

"There's no need to apologize. You handled yourself well, as I knew you would. You're stronger willed than you give yourself credit for."

Aellia turned back to Renneil. "How did Erol and Jaqun arrive so quickly? Erol wasn't among the sovereigns present during the market attack, and the voyage from Caswen across the Audria Channel to the Coastlands takes at least a day. It's been less than a week since the last sovereigns left, which leaves no such time for them to have sailed to the Coastlands, contacted Erol, and have him sail back across the sea to Caswen. Especially since Erol claims to have been sent by the emperor himself from who knows how far south."

"You sure have thought hard about the details of this sovereign's visit, and so soon after learning of it, no less."

"I find it impossible not to. It doesn't add up. Erol and Jaqun must have already been in the Isles during the market attack and were summoned from whatever they were doing to come to the manor and make themselves known. Why were they already on the islands, and what were they doing? Why lie about being sent directly by the emperor, and why did I, let alone you, not already know about their presence within our borders? Unless you did know and thought it also not worth telling me."

"Aellia ..."

"I'm merely thinking aloud, Renneil."

"If Erol and Jaqun were among the islands before this meeting, I was unaware. And if I'm unaware of something happening in this province, then it is likely not happening at all. I do not think either Erol or Jaqun were here before today. My sources tell me that they both arrived from an arc ship not too long ago."

"An arc ship?"

"Ah, I suppose you've not heard of this type of vessel. They are massive ships built by the sovereigns, usually surrounded by a small fleet of ships, and they can hold thousands of people."

"And this ship is in the port?"

"No." Renneil chuckled. "It's located some distance to the south of the Isles. Such a ship could not find room at Caswen's docks. Erol and Jaqun would have disembarked from the arc ship in a smaller vessel and made port in that. They came to the manor immediately, and Erol requested to see you before Adaman could kiss both of his taloned feet."

"Then I'm at a loss for a rational answer, unless Erol and the emperor were aboard this arc ship, as if expecting to come to the Isles."

"I wouldn't concern myself with such problems if I were you, Aellia. You have enough concerns to take up your time, especially now with your new boss. I'll handle the details of when and where when it comes to Erol and the emperor. The sovereigns are an intelligent people who strive to keep their dealings hidden from us, as you well know, and even I have trouble keeping up with their motives and plans. You should get back to the garrison and focus on keeping Erol appeased for the time being. He strikes me as someone to take seriously, sovereign or not."

"You're ever so wise, oh mysterious spymaster of the Isles," Aellia said with mock courtesy.

Renneil couldn't help but smile at Aellia's ability to transition from furious to sarcastically jovial.

She made to turn toward the door, but before she fully committed to the movement, she stopped and looked back to Renneil.

"Is there something else, Aellia?" he asked so quickly it seemed as if he knew she was going to stop and ask him something else even before she did.

Aellia brushed her tongue against the back of her teeth as she thought for a second. "I'm sure you're aware that my brothers returned today?"

"Yes. Saelus and Bo's ship returned early this morning, and they only just arrived at the manor recently."

Aellia furrowed her brow slightly. "Yes, Saelus told me as much. Do you find it a little odd that my brothers returned home from their diplomatic trip to the Mainland at nearly the same time as Erol and Jaqun arrived?"

The tiny grin near the corner of Renneil's mouth did not escape Aellia's notice. "My, my. You really are a thinker, aren't you, Aellia? It is a little odd, isn't it. But I must conclude that it's merely a coincidence. I was informed that your brothers were making preparations to begin the voyage home well over a week ago, and I suspected that they would arrive either today or tomorrow. News that we were to expect the arrival of a sovereign came after your brothers were already at sea along the Broken Coast."

"Hmm ... a coincidence then," Aellia said. "I suppose this is why we have a word for such an event, after all, or at least a sovereign word."

Renneil sat up a little straighter on the edge of his desk. "I'm sure such a word existed within our people's tongue before Gaia and its kingdoms were sovereignized."

"Perhaps."

"Yes, perhaps."

Aellia gave him a gentle nod. "Well, I shan't take up any more of your time. Good morning, Renneil."

"Good morning, Aellia."

Aellia committed to her turn and went out.

✠   ✠   ✠

"I'm telling the truth," Kieran repeated.

"So you've said before. And I'm telling you that I don't buy it," the male soldier guarding the gate to the manor's courtyard replied.

The female soldier standing next to the male soldier, holding the reins of a brown horse in her left hand, stepped forward and eyed Kieran up and down as if trying to see if his guardsman's uniform and armor were somehow fake.

Kieran stepped back and maintained his hold on the reins of his own brown horse, which was standing calmly beside him.

"What use would the marshal have for a runt like you? With a face like that, maybe you're her practice dummy, but you're not her assistant," the woman said with a laugh.

Out of reflex, Kieran reached up and touched his face. The bruises and welts stung. He pulled his hand away in embarrassment.

The male soldier chuckled heartily along with his comrade as he eyed Kieran more intently. "What even is an assistant to her lordship, anyhow? You fetch her water from the well? Clean her chamber pot? Lace her boots?

Polish her armor? Well, whatever, if any, of that you're going to claim that you do, you still won't be let inside the manor. Now get back to whatever post you're missing from before I run you through."

"Maybe he combs her hair or keeps schedule of when she's due to bleed each month?" The female soldier's laugh got louder with amusement as she slapped her comrade's arm.

"That's enough, soldiers!" Aellia called from the courtyard. Both turned their heads as Kieran looked past them toward the voice.

"Oh, your lordship, we—"

The female soldier kicked her partner in the heel.

"Oh, I mean, Marshal Aellia. We are just keeping out the riffraff."

"I am not riffraff."

Aellia raised a hand toward Kieran. "This young man is my personal assistant. I promoted him last night, so I don't blame you for not knowing. The Manor Guard is often the last to be informed of such things."

Both soldiers stiffened their backs and returned to their places on either side of the courtyard gate.

"My apologies then, ma'am," the male guard said. "I will inform the rest of the manor guard force that this lad is to be allowed entrance to the manor from now on." His partner said nothing, her reddening face fixed on Aellia's horse to hide her embarrassment.

"Come, Kieran, I'm done here," Aellia said as she stepped between the two soldiers and took the reins of her horse from the female soldier's hand.

Kieran stood at attention as Aellia mounted her horse. Only once she was firmly seated in her saddle did Kieran mount his horse and signal it to turn around. Aellia's beast had already begun trotting slowly down the long descending road that led back into the city by the time Kieran had firmly settled himself and ushered his horse to move. He kept himself and his mount a handful of feet behind Aellia as he followed her down the cobblestone road.

"Are you afraid of me, Kieran?" Aellia asked without looking back.

His hands tightened on his horse's reins as he processed her question. He realized he should answer right away, and the fact that he did not caused a sensation of panic to rise in his stomach.

"No ... no, ma'am." His words came out fast and clumsy.

"Then are you planning to stab me in the back?"

Kieran nearly pulled the reins of his horse back as he stiffened up. "What? No! I would never. I gave you my word."

"I meant literally, Kieran. A person who stalks behind someone, though not out of fear, is likely planning some kind of ill will on that person, wouldn't you agree?"

"I'm not planning—Look, I ... I didn't mean to anger you," Kieran said as he kicked his heels into his mount. His horse picked up the pace, trotting next to Aellia's horse before Kieran pulled the reins to slow it down.

"You've not angered me, Kieran. It was those in the manor who ruined my morning."

"Not good news, I take it?" Kieran asked nervously in an attempt to be friendly, while not expecting an actual answer.

"What?" Aellia said so bluntly that Kieran thought he had angered her, though this time he held back from mentioning it.

"Oh, I just mean, well ... When I couldn't find you at the garrison, I asked around and heard that you had been summoned at the manor. It was a bad summons, I guess. That's all I meant, ma'am."

Aellia exhaled hot air up toward her nose. "You have no idea, Kieran."

"Was it to do with a sovereign?"

Aellia stopped her horse and looked over at Kieran. He was so surprised that he didn't manage to stop his own horse until it had taken a few more steps. As he reined it to a stop and looked back at Aellia, he saw that her face, while not seeming angry, was certainly not pleased.

"Oh, I'm sorry, ma'am. I ... I didn't mean to pry. I just—"

"What do you know, Kieran?"

Kieran tensed with nervousness, suddenly upset with himself for getting into such a situation so quickly. "Oh. Nothing, ma'am. I mean ... I overheard those two gate guards talking about it as I rode up. A sovereign arriving at the manor—that is, along with someone else. But they stopped talking once they saw me. I didn't mean to overhear; it just happened."

Kieran felt a bead of sweat run down his bruised right cheek.

"Hmm. I see."

"Ma'am?"

"It was to do with a sovereign. He goes by the name of Erol, since you seem to be so curious."

"Oh! No, ma'am. I didn't mean to seem curious. I'm not at all. I was just … I mean, I was just talking—"

"Kieran! Enough with the nervousness. I'll not have my assistant acting like a timid little boy."

Kieran swallowed and tried to recompose himself. "Yes, ma'am. Sorry. I'll do better."

Aellia rolled her eyes. "Good. Now come along. This whole ordeal has set me back substantially for the day, and I'd like to get back to my work." She kicked her horse gently to encourage it to move.

Kieran watched Aellia pass him for a moment before he remembered that she did not want him following her. He turned in his saddle and urged his horse to move, a little too forcefully, he realized by the huff the beast let out as Kieran dug his heels into its sides. He pulled its reins to slow down once he caught up to Aellia.

Kieran made sure to keep pace with Aellia as they rode down the hill from the manor and followed the cobblestone road leading northwest through the High District.

Chapter 23

As Helena woke up, she felt the cycle play out nearly the same as it had the morning before in Charra and Gorty's bed: a feeling of confusion, a stark realization, a false hope that it had all been a nightmare, a somber recollection, followed by the heart-pounding sickness of grief, and finally, a surge of effort to squash her emotions so she could hold back her desire to cry and get up.

Helena rose off the cold floor of the barn-like fishery and sat up with her back against a stack of crates. She had chosen to isolate herself behind the crates when she had come back in tears after her walk through the town. Her back ached, and her shoulders felt numb. The cold air made her shiver with a series of chilled twitches.

Everything felt like nothing to her, like the world would not continue if she merely continued to sit against the crates and shiver. The idea of standing up and going outside gave her a feeling she wasn't sure she understood. It was equal parts terror, nausea, and grief at the thought of moving from her spot. She saw light coming through the large cracks and holes in the barn's wooden walls, telling her it was morning.

Suddenly, the idea of sitting there any longer repulsed her, making her feel sick with hate, so she stood up, using the wall for support. Another fit of shivers jerked her body, causing her to exhale briefly. Despite her aching body and nausea, Helena opened the door and went out without exploring the area or joining Rook, Sebastian, and Nina, who were sleeping at the back of the barn on the small pile of bedsheets and animal skins that had been left for them.

The morning light hurt Helena's eyes as she emerged from the barn, forcing her to shield her pupils from the early morning sun. She realized she had a splitting headache and that the bright light was making it worse.

"So this is how your father feels, Agon," she muttered under her breath.

The thought of the gods jolted her mind, and a sudden thought overwhelmed her as a result.

The temple.

She nearly forgot about her headache as she hurried forward.

The town's atmosphere was greatly changed from what it had been during the night. The lonely dirt street was filled with people in wool clothing. Most were human, though a few were goblins. Some of the folks were mounted on horses while most others passed by on foot, and some walked alongside small, goat-pulled carts. The previous night's quiet air was filled with squawking seagulls, trotting animals, the clunking of barrels and crates in the backs of carts, and the chattering of locals.

Unlike her last stroll through town during the day, Helena was spared from turned heads and scrutinizing eyes. The absence of her wounded friends allowed her to blend in as if she were a local. Though her attire was still dirty and stained, the blood had mostly dried and faded into dark stains, seeming like nothing more than dirt to anyone who wasn't focusing on them.

Helena still felt out of place, though, and she kept her eyes on the street, avoiding eye contact with the locals.

After a minute of walking with her head mostly down, Helena heard men and women calling orders to each other.

"Bring that over here."

"Set up the riggings properly, you fool."

"Don't tip the catch!"

Helena didn't need to look up to see where she was, but she did anyway. The shipyard and the docks to her right were filled with people, all of whom were loading their boats with supplies or moving crates and barrels around the yard. She looked down again as she passed by.

Helena slowly became accustomed to the slight chill in the air as she maintained her pace through the town. The gulls flying high above continued to squawk and send their shadows across the dirt street. Helena paid the birds no attention and only looked up once she had walked for another minute. When she did, she saw the tavern that she had entered the night before. Though she was no longer cold, she felt a chill crawl up her spine at the sight of it. She looked back down and continued on her way.

Helena knew she was almost at her destination, as she remembered that the temple was just west of the tavern. Her expectations of her surroundings were so strong that when she looked up again, the sight nearly caused her to trip over her feet.

The temple was just ahead of her, exactly as she had calculated it would be, but the two guards standing on either side of the doors were not part of her memory. Each man sported an iron helmet along with a gray surcoat over a suit of chainmail and a light gambeson. Their surcoats had the emblem of a bear's head in profile in the center as well as a red hexagon sewn over their right breast. Each hexagon had only a sixth filled in.

Each man also held a tall, iron-tipped wooden spear and stood as straight and firm as the weapons themselves. The inscribed temple doors between them were open, and warm light emanated from within.

Helena felt a rush of panic rise within her. As soon as she realized that the two men were soldiers, wearing identical uniforms to those who had burned Verrel, she wanted to turn and run, but she felt paralyzed at the same time. Her mind raced with the idea that as soon as one of the soldiers looked her way, they would recognize her and come after her.

"Morning, girl," one of the guards said, having noticed Helena watching him. His voice had a stern yet pleasant tone that matched his grizzled yet clean face. His stubbled chin gave the impression of youth, but he was most likely in his thirties, from what Helena could guess.

"The temple is open, but I'd advise staying out of the healing sanctum unless you are truly in need of aid. There was an assault this morning against one of Dema's priests, so the rest of the healing priests are busy dealing with the Leydes Guard at the moment."

Helena did not answer. Her thoughts were too wrapped up in the realization that the man did not know she was from Verrel. She wondered for a moment if she shouldn't just turn and leave anyway, but after her nerves settled down and she started thinking more rationally, she realized she had nothing to fear, despite fear remaining at the forefront of her mind.

"Okay, thanks," Helena said as politely as she could. Then she swallowed most of her hesitation and entered the temple without looking at either guard, her heart pounding the entire time.

Once inside, Helena saw that the main chamber was no longer dark and empty. In fact, it was exceptionally well lit by large brass rings that hung from chains from the ceiling, though the rings were different from those she had seen in the tavern. Rather than candles, each thick brass ring had a convex rim that spread the light from the small fire held within a brass bowl that hung from chains at its center. Helena had never seen such devices before, and she wondered if they were a dwarf or a sovereign invention.

The large temple chamber was filled with groups of townsfolk, all human, each standing with heads bowed toward the statue of Siyon at the north end. As Helena walked through the chamber, she gazed at the statue. In the light the depiction of the water goddess in naiad form was not as unsettling as it had looked before. It even had a certain beauty to it.

Three individuals, two women and one man, stood silently near the front of the statue, facing toward the other people in the chamber. Each was wearing a brown robe that ended just above their heels, their plain boots just visible.

As Helena continued toward the door on the west wall, she couldn't help but overhear some of what the people around her were saying.

"Beautiful and powerful Siyon, I ask that you treat my boat gently and make my nets heavy."

"Goddess of the great ocean, I beg that my father returns from your kingdom without woe."

"Second of the Godmother, I beg you to hold your clouds at bay and let your brother's flame keep the day bright and warm."

Helena thought about the last time she had prayed and remembered that it had been to Lilberith during their journey through Vellum Forest. She had prayed for a path through the woods free of beasts and with plenty of food, but the goddess of the wood didn't seem to have heard her prayer. Either that or she simply ignored it.

Helena left her thoughts of the past and the gods behind as she reached the door to the temple's adjacent room. The door was open, revealing the white curtain ahead. Light soaked through the curtain from the other side, as did the faint sound of voices. Helena separated the curtain just as she had before and made her way into the temple's healing sanctum.

Just as the main temple chamber had been, the room beyond the curtain was lit with firelight from wide brass rings that hung from the ceiling. The smell of blood that Helena had detected before was now complemented by the red stains that dotted dirty bundles of rags and bandages atop some of the tables.

What truly caught Helena's attention, however, was the soldier who was seemingly standing guard just before the second curtain at the end of the room. The faint voices she had heard were louder and coming from behind the second curtain. She could also see the dark impressions of people's shadows moving about.

The soldier noticed Helena immediately but didn't move from his spot, nor did the spear he held at his side wobble in place.

"Come back later, girl. We're handling a situation here."

Helena suddenly put the situation together in her mind, only then realizing what the soldier outside had said, now that her intense worry had ceased. Panic welled inside her chest. Despite the soldier's words, she dashed across the room and yanked the next curtain aside.

Helena saw two more soldiers, one standing next to the bed where Carver lay and one speaking to a brown-robed woman about three feet in front of Helena. To the far right on one of the beds sat another brown-robed woman whose left cheek was covered by a bandage that was mostly soaked in red and was being inspected by a third brown-robed woman who was kneeling at her side. The three women and the two soldiers all turned in shock toward the sudden intruder.

"Whoa!" the soldier behind Helena blurted as he clamped his gauntleted hand on her left shoulder.

Helena was about to shove his hand away, but the dark green of Carver's eyes made her freeze.

"Helena!" Carver shouted.

Helena could not form any words. The sight of Carver sitting upright with his eyes open was too great a shock for her. She didn't even hear the spear drop to the floor behind her or feel the soldier's hands grab her arms.

"Hold on!" the soldier restraining Helena barked while pulling her back a step.

Finally noticing the soldier's grip, she twisted her body around in an attempt to break free, but the soldier only tightened his hold on her.

"Let me go!" Helena shouted, her eyes fixed on Carver as she struggled.

"Helena!" Carver shouted again at the sight of her struggle.

His voice was followed by a barrage of thuds and clinks as well as a bout of fatigued grunting. It was then that Helena noticed that Carver's hands were manacled to the wooden bedframe, keeping him from getting off the bed.

"He's at it again!" the robed woman closest to Helena shrieked. "Get this girl out of here."

"Hold on!" Helena's restrainer said. "They know each other."

Carver's grunting suddenly halted as the soldier next to his bed punched him in the side of the head. Carver's eyes fluttered for a brief second before shutting tight, followed by him collapsing backwards onto the bed.

"Stop!" Helena shrieked, continuing to pull and tug against the soldier's hold.

"Calm yourself, dammit!" the soldier barked as he threw her to the ground.

"Restrain her!" the woman aiding the wounded woman shouted.

"No! For Dema's sake, everyone calm down!" the soldier who had been speaking to the closest woman shouted while stepping forward and spreading his arms out to prevent the other two soldiers from advancing toward Helena. The man's order was adhered as a moment of silence reigned over the room, and no one moved.

All was quiet except for Helena's heart, which beat madly inside her chest from stress and fear. Just as Helena was about to stand up, the soldier who had told the others to calm down spoke up again. "Listen here, girl," he said, pointing a finger sternly at Helena, "you've just barged into our business, so unless you want to be beaten and manacled, I suggest you calm down and do as I say."

Helena froze and looked up at the man in charge. She noticed that the hexagon insignia over his right breast had four of six pieces filled in, while those around him only had one each. She stared into his eyes for a moment before she mustered the confidence to speak.

"Don't hit him again."

"I'll have my men refrain from it, but he isn't exactly cooperating."

"I'm sorry, Werner. She ran right past me before I could stop her," the other soldier said while picking his spear up from the floor.

"It's fine. Now, hush."

The soldier pressed his lips together and returned to where he had been standing when Helena had come in.

"So, girl, now you know my name, and I understand that yours is Helena," Werner said in a stern yet calm tone. "Since we've been introduced to each other, how about you tell me what you're doing, charging in here like this? I assume it pertains to this lad." He gestured toward Carver, who was still unconscious from the blow.

Helena felt more anxious than she had in the tavern the night prior, though her feelings told her to persist rather than flee this time. After a moment of careful thought, she adjusted her position on the ground to get somewhat comfortable and spoke clearly.

"I'm sorry for bursting in here. I was worried about my friend. I was told there was an assault in the healing sanctum, so I panicked with the thought that something had happened to him."

Werner let out an amused chuckle. "To him? Ha. He's not the one who had a knife stabbed through his cheek, although he does seem to have a fair amount of his own injuries."

"What?" Helena asked with rising worry.

Werner's amused tone became stern once again. "Your friend, upon waking this morning, burst into an aggressive frenzy. These humble priests of Dema tried to calm him, but he continued to shout and act violently. As they tried to subdue him, he grabbed a small knife and stabbed it through this poor woman's cheek." Werner gestured toward the priest, which was the unisex title given to both men and women of the practice, sitting on the far bed. "It was only due to the boy's injuries that he wasn't able to cause more serious harm before he was restrained."

Helena wasn't sure what to say. She wanted to tell Werner the whole story, that Carver was probably in a state of panic when he regained consciousness, causing him to lash out in fear for his life, but she didn't know Werner or his men apart from their uniforms, and she no longer trusted soldiers.

"We were attacked," Helena blurted once she realized that thinking for too long would draw suspicion. "We ..." She looked from person to person, soldier to priest, all of whom stared at her with uninterrupted attention. "We were returning from Caswen by wagon to our village after the tax deliveries when ... when we were ambushed by bandits."

Werner's face filled with interest as she continued. "They killed all but a few of us and then took us to their hideout in Vellum Forest. They wanted to ransom us or something, but a few of us managed to escape during the night and made our way north until we got here. The bandits nearly killed Carver during our escape. He's been unconscious ever since. That's why he attacked the temple healers. The last thing he remembered was fighting for his life. He would have thought the priests were bandits upon waking, I'm sure. He was scared and only trying to protect himself."

Werner stared at Helena for a moment, causing her to tense up and pray silently to Dema for her tale to be believed.

"Bleeding tits!" Werner broke the silence and turned to the other soldiers. "First we have Verrel working with those Aethi'ziton rebels—"

The hairs on the back of Helena's neck pricked up.

"—and now we've got outlaws ambushing travelers from the forest."

Helena felt a rush of relief run through her body, but what Werner had said about her home left her with a feeling of confusion and deep worry.

"You two head back to the garrison and inform the lieutenant about these brigands in the woods. He'll ensure the word is spread. We're going to have to keep an eye on Vellum Forest's northern edge."

"But, Captain," the soldier standing next to Carver said, "what about the boy?"

"I'll handle the rest. Now go. That's an order."

The two soldiers nodded to Werner, then made their way toward the door. They both paid Helena no attention as they passed, though she glared at the soldier who had struck Carver.

Werner beckoned the two non-injured priests over to him, and the three of them spoke in hushed tones for a moment.

Feeling the tension in the room dying down, Helena felt it appropriate to stand up, her cut knee pulsing with pain as she did. Once she was up, she waited for Werner to finish his conversation with the priests and return his attention to her. Thirty seconds later, Werner did just that. Turning away from his secretive dialogue, Werner dismissed the robed women with a wave and walked over to Helena.

"Under the circumstances, I find it hard to justify locking the boy up, but I can't ignore what he did to the priest, who will be scarred for life."

Helena looked over at a counter that had a number of vials atop it filled with dark-red liquids. Potions, she surmised. Recalling her interaction with Paalen, she also assumed they were not amplified with sorcery and thus, while they could heal, it was slower and would not prevent scarring.

"So, what I'm going to do is tell you to take your friend away from here once he wakes up. I can't have the town's temple healers terrified for their lives while they're tending to the sick and injured. So, when he's up, take him back to Duncan's, where you'll tell that fisherman he owes the temple a visit to discuss the cost of this incident."

Helena felt every muscle in her body freeze as a cold fear ran up her spine. Werner knew more than she had assumed.

Shit! Helena thought in panic. Then she remembered that Charra had told her that Duncan was the one who had brought the others to the temple and paid for their treatments. The idea that Duncan or any of the others might have already told the priests something about how they had been injured jumped to the forefront of her mind, and Helena realized that her neglect of that idea potentially threatened the narrative she had spun for Werner.

"Do I make myself clear, young lady?"

"Yes," Helena replied.

"Good." Werner clapped his gauntleted hands together, startling one of the priests behind him. "Now, while you wait for your friend to wake up, I'd like to ask you some questions about your village and your relationship with Duncan."

Helena filled with intensified anxiety.

✠　✠　✠

Carver's vision was blurry at first, but it slowly came into focus as he opened his eyes a bit more. The seemingly blinding light was the first thing he detected as the swimming blur dissipated from his perception. He tried to bring his hands up to shield his eyes but found that he was unable to. The burning from the light was countered by the cold tightness he felt around his wrists. A wave of confusion struck him as he tried to move his arms again, followed by a burst of panic when he felt them being held back by some sort of solid apparatus. His emerging senses picked up the sound of rattling behind his head as well as a rising soreness in his arms and shoulders.

"Werner!" a woman shrieked from his left.

The shout caught him off guard, further increasing his panic. He now had enough of his perception back to properly register his surroundings. He saw that he was lying on a bed with more beds to his left. The room was small and rectangular, with one of the walls appearing to be a white curtain.

"Werner!" the voice said again, though this time it was much louder.

His frightened confusion turned into fearful rage as he continued to flail his arms about, unable to free them from whatever device held them out of view. A surge of pain rippled through his midsection as he writhed his entire body. When he looked down at where the increasing pain was emanating from, he started to panic even more.

He saw that he was wearing only a pair of braies and that a large portion of his torso was heavily bruised, but the bandages wrapped around the middle of his left leg drew his attention far more. He opened his mouth to yell, but before a frightened wail or an angry shout could come forth, the curtain in front of him flew to one side, revealing two individuals. One was a man in a surcoat, and the other was a young girl with her left hand still gripping the white curtain.

While he did not recognize his whereabouts or the situation that brought him there, he absolutely recognized her.

The girl gripped the curtain in her fist, not letting go despite the thin barrier now being out of the way, nor did she take even a single step forward, instead remaining nearly motionless as she stared at Carver with a face that displayed a wide mixture of emotions.

The desperate shout that climbed up his throat evaporated almost immediately, giving way to something else.

"Helena ..."

"Hi, Carver," she said in a soft voice that signaled she had no idea what to say in such a moment.

A strange silence enveloped the room as the two of them stared at each other, neither one knowing how to proceed. Then, just as Carver was about to speak, Helena released her hold on the curtain and walked toward him.

"Are you okay?" she asked.

Before Carver even had time to think of something to say, Helena had already reached him and planted herself on her knees beside the bed.

"Helena ... what's going on?"

Helena's demeanor of shock and uncertainty seemed to give way to calmness and clarity. "I'll tell you everything soon, Carver, but right now we need to go."

"What's going on?" he asked again despite Helena's answer, this time with more confusion and worry in his tone.

"Please, just stay calm, and do what Werner says."

"Who's Werner?" Carver asked as he tried to sit up properly while fidgeting against whatever held his arms in place.

"I'm Werner," the man said, walking up behind her. Carver had forgotten about him due to the impact of seeing Helena.

Upon seeing Werner approach, and noticing his armor and insignias, Carver tensed up and pulled his legs in.

Helena placed a hand on Carver's right leg, "It's okay, Carver. He's not going to hurt you."

"As long as you don't do anything to make me hurt you," Werner warned.

Helena tensed with discomfort at Werner's words, but she quickly calmed when she saw Carver begin to ease.

"Your friend here is going to take you away now, but only once I'm convinced that you won't attack anyone else on the way out," Werner said, gesturing to his right.

Carver was confused by Werner's words, but as his eyes followed Werner's gesture, he suddenly remembered. A middle-aged woman in a brown robe sat on a nearby bed staring at him with terror in her eyes as she held a thick wad of bandages against her left cheek.

Carver looked away from the woman and back up at Werner. He wasn't sure what he was supposed to say or if he should say anything at all.

"Carver?" Helena said, summoning his attention from the side.

Carver still had very little understanding of what was going on around him, but he trusted Helena.

"I'm okay." His voice was more relaxed, but it still carried a level of confusion and fear.

Helena removed her hand from Carver's leg and looked up at Werner, who was focused intently on the boy. Another moment of silence passed before Werner finally spoke up.

"Alright, but there are no further chances, do you understand?" He dug a small iron key from his surcoat pocket and unlocked Carver's shackles. Carver brought his hands forward and rubbed his wrists, which were chafed and red. A sensation of dizziness hit him as he sat up, making him feel like he was falling. Helena saw this and grabbed Carver by the shoulders, holding him up as the blood rushed around in his bandaged head.

"The priests said that he will still need plenty of time to fully recover," Werner said as Helena helped Carver stand up. "The potions they administered will shorten his body's healing process from months to a few weeks, though only if he ingests more every few days. Duncan can speak to them about purchasing some of their stock if he wishes. You will still need to let him rest and keep him away from any physical strain while his body heals. He's suffered extreme injuries, so keep a close eye on him."

"Thank you," Helena said over her shoulder.

As Helena helped Carver toward the door, he lost his balance and leaned into her for aid. Helena did her best to support Carver as she guided him past the curtain and through the healing sanctum's main room.

"Helena, where are we?" Carver asked, looking around. "What happened to Ve—"

"Hush, Carver! I'll explain once I get you to Duncan's."

"Duncan's?"

"Just focus on walking right now, okay? I promise everything will make sense later."

Carver groaned slightly but kept his mouth shut.

As Helena brought Carver nearer to the next divider curtain, she noticed the female priests were staring at them. The women's eyes followed the pair with looks of worry, anger, and sadness as they passed through the room.

Helena had felt all three of those emotions just moments before, but now that she was leading Carver out of the temple, she felt a huge sensation of relief.

Chapter 24

◦◦

"What do you mean he attacked a priest?" Gorty spouted, his eyes widening with disbelief.

"I mean exactly that," Helena said firmly as she closed the front door once Sebastian and Nina had come through.

The siblings made their way to the center of the room and stood next to the table where Duncan, Charra, Gorty, and Rook were seated, eagerly awaiting Helena's next words. Charra gave her seat to Sebastian as soon as she noticed him having a hard time standing on his injured leg.

Helena stepped away from the door and stood in front of the window's closed shutters. "I need to know what everyone knows about what happened and what any of you told the priests at the temple about it."

Helena's audience looked at each other, then returned their attention to her. Charra was the first to speak up. "I don't understand your wording, dear. What are you talking about?"

Helena rubbed her forehead. "I mean what Sebastian and Nina told you all about Verrel and what you all told the priests at the temple about it," she said.

"We told them what happened," Sebastian replied, gesturing to Duncan and the dwarves. "We told them that soldiers from Caswen attacked us and drove us into Vellum Forest, then how we got here and the stuff about the vells. After that we left you here with Charra while Gorty and Duncan took us to the temple and paid for our healing."

Helena shifted her focus from Sebastian to the others, waiting for them to add to his words. She saw that everyone was clearly uncomfortable, especially Duncan, who looked like he hadn't slept in days.

"Did anyone tell the priests that we're from Verrel?"

Sebastian looked like he was going to speak again, but his grandfather beat him to it. "No. Those at the temple don't know, or at least they shouldn't. I told everyone here to keep quiet about what happened. Word of Verrel's burning reached Leydes before you five did, though the details were muddled with rumor. Gossip still abounds about whether the razing of Verrel was the work of the Aethi'ziton, bandits, or soldiers. Once Sebastian and Nina told us the true story, I made sure your connection to Verrel was unknown. The soldiers here may be linked to whatever is going on, so we need to hide your true origin from them for the time being."

"It's true," Gorty said. "Duncan and I were the ones who brought Sebastian, Nina, and Carver to your people's healing priests. We told them that we didn't know what happened to you or who you all were and that you all just appeared on our doorstep, which wasn't far from the truth, if I might say. The priests didn't pry; it's not their business to. They don't care about who or why, just that their fee is met so they can restock their healing supplies for others. We planned on figuring out a story once you'd all had a rest and calmed down."

"Well, now there's a story as well as another fee to be paid." Helena's words made those sitting at the table lean forward. "Carver woke up before I got there this morning. He panicked and stabbed a knife into a priest's cheek before they could settle him down."

Everyone's eyes widened while Charra's mouth opened slightly in shock.

"Everything's fine," Helena said as she raised her hands. "The priest is fine, but now Duncan needs to pay for the supplies used to heal her."

Everyone seemed to calm a bit at her words, though not entirely.

Helena lowered her hands as she continued. "The problem is that the incident called soldiers to the temple. That's when I got there. Carver was manacled to the bed, and the soldiers were questioning the healers about him.

That's why I needed to know what you told the priests, to make sure that their story doesn't clash with my story."

"Your story?" Duncan said a moment before Gorty could.

"A soldier named Werner questioned me. I needed to explain who we were and why Carver acted the way he did. It was the only way to stop him from arresting Carver and taking him away."

"What did you tell him?" Duncan asked.

"I said we were from a small village southeast of Gale. It's a large town on the south side of Keldrid Lake."

"I know where Gale is," Duncan said, waving his hand dismissively.

"I told him we were traveling home from Caswen after the tax deliveries and that we were ambushed by bandits and abducted to their camp in Vellum Forest with the intent of ransoming us. I said we managed to escape after some time in captivity but that we had to fight to get away, which is how Carver received his injuries, and that we ran north to Leydes because it was the closest settlement. I also mentioned the vell attack."

Duncan raised a finger and opened his mouth to speak, but Helena cut him off before he could. "I told Werner that we came to Duncan's because our village had done some trading with him before and that he was very kind to us. I know it isn't the best reasoning, but I had to come up with it on the spot. Werner asked me how we knew Duncan and why we came to him before I was ready."

The room was quiet for a moment while everyone appeared to be deep in thought.

"Did he believe you?" Nina asked.

"I think so." Helena felt sad again when she saw Nina's face, or rather, the bandages that hid large portions of it.

"So, you spoke to Werner, and you're sure it was him?" Duncan asked bluntly, severing Helena's focus from his granddaughter's appearance.

"Yes, he seemed to be the one in charge. They called him Captain."

"Therein lies our problem with the story you spun for him. Werner is indeed the captain of the guard here in Leydes. He's a good man—a nice man, I should say. He even has folks around here call him by his name rather than his title to make him more approachable. But he's also an intelligent man and one who takes his duty to the Crown seriously." Duncan paused and rubbed his chin before continuing. "I think that sooner or later Werner will connect your presence with the events of Verrel and come looking for you for another round of questioning. If not by his own deduction, the presence of Sebastian and Nina will lead him to that connection. He knows I have two grandchildren by those names and that they lived in Verrel, as do many others in this town, though none know their faces, I should think. However, if he learns that Sebastian and Nina were part of the injured group that came into town, he's sure to figure out the true details and be on us immediately."

The room fell silent once again as everyone's nerves tensed with newfound worry.

Helena opened her mouth to speak but was cut off by Duncan. "Werner came by a few days ago," he said, sounding weak and defeated. "He asked me about my family and what I knew about Verrel. I was so confused. That was how I first heard about what happened, through what little information he provided. I thought you were both gone, along with my dear Lidia ..." his voice broke off as he looked at the twins.

At the mention of her name, Helena suddenly remembered Lidia, Sebastian and Nina's mother. She realized it was not only Lidia's children who suffered from her death but her father, Duncan, as well.

Charra placed a hand on Duncan's shoulder, her own expression rife with sadness.

"I just wish I knew why ... Why did they take her from us?" Duncan asked softly to no one in particular.

"I ... I know why," Helena said. Everyone's attention was turned to her once again. She felt nervous and sad all at once, her own emotions creeping up at the sight of Duncan's plight and the memory of her own family, which she had not yet had the time to properly mourn. "Werner, he ... I heard him say that Verrel was working with the Aethi'ziton, that rebel group who fights against the sovereigns. And last night, while I was walking through the town, I also heard people talking about how the Aethi'ziton were somehow involved with what happened to Verrel. It seems everyone thinks Verrel was working with the Lost Seekers."

"That's not true!" Sebastian shouted.

Nobody replied, as everyone else was mired in a miasma of deep thought.

Helena felt tears building up behind her eyes. It took everything she had to keep them at bay. But when Nina suddenly burst into tears, Helena's eyes reddened, and she began to tear up.

Without another word, Helena left her position by the window and marched over to Charra and Gorty's bedroom, closing the door behind her.

The bedroom was much darker than the main room, with the only light coming from a small grouping of candles set on the stepping stool near the wardrobe across the room. The tiny flames were fading, making the wardrobe and bed nearly invisible within the encroaching dark.

"Helena?" Carver said, his alarmed voice sounding from the darkness that had overtaken the bed.

Helena did not answer. Instead, she sat on the edge of the bed, cradling herself in her arms as she tensed and shuddered in a failing effort to suppress her emotions. Her increasing whimpers and heavy breathing were answer enough.

"Helena, what's wrong? What just happened?" Carver's voice was much closer now, sounding weak and tired.

"Nothing, Carver."

Helena did not look at where she knew Carver's eyes were. She felt extremely uncomfortable; she didn't want him to see her like this, but for whatever reason her instincts to hide her tears from the rest of the group had driven her there.

She heard rustling and felt the sheet beneath her move.

"Carver, don't. You need to rest."

Carver didn't listen. He was sitting up before Helena could say it again.

"What's going on?"

"Nothing. Nothing's going on."

"Stop lying to me!" Carver suddenly gasped in pain.

"Carver?" Helena turned toward him in concern. She saw that he was propping himself up with his left arm and clutching a bruised area across his lower ribs with his right hand.

"It hurts ..." he wheezed.

Carver looked strange to Helena, the dim light offered by the fading candles making his dark-green eyes look browner than usual, and his recently cut hair, though mostly tucked underneath bandages, made him look like a different person.

"Lie down, and don't raise your voice, Carver. You're going to hurt yourself," Helena ordered, not noticing that her tears had ceased for the moment.

Carver complied, lying back down until his face became obscured in the darkness beyond the candlelight's reach. The act of moving seemed to generate a great deal of pain for him, however.

Silence joined the darkness as Carver focused on the sharp pain in his lower ribs and Helena struggled to calm her thoughts. Finally, Carver spoke.

"Please, Helena, talk to me. I don't understand. What's going on? Where are we? What happened to Verrel?"

Helena wasn't sure what to say or where to start, so she began by asking her own question. "What's the last thing you remember?"

It took Carver a moment to reply, his recollection slowed by pain. "I remember fire. I woke up and there was fire and smoke everywhere. I crawled outside. Everything hurt, but then it didn't. I saw my mother. She was fighting. I wanted to go to her, but my father ... He ... I ... I found him ..." Carver's voice started to break. "They killed him ... then my mother ... she ..." He sounded as if he were struggling to form his words. "She gave me something. I think ... A potion ... It was so fast ... I drank it ... She said it would help me, but it made me lose control of myself. I ... I left her. She was dying on the ground, and I just left her there ... By Cosom ... I abandoned her to die ..."

"I'm sorry, Carver," Helena said, sliding closer and placing a hand on his left leg, which was beneath the sheet.

"I could have saved ... If I hadn't lost control, I could have helped her ... I left her ... She watched me leave her ..."

Helena suddenly heard whimpers coming from the head of the bed, followed by sobs. Her own sadness crept back as Carver's words triggered thoughts of her family and her home once again.

"I'll never see them again," Carver said, his sobs becoming louder and more frequent.

The creeping sadness that Helena felt charged into her heart, overtaking her. Her tearful sobs and gasps filled the breaks between Carver's, creating a painful rhythm of despair and defeat.

For what seemed like a long while, the two of them cried together on opposite ends of the bed, feeling utterly alone and helpless despite each other's company.

"Helena ... I'm so sorry ..." Carver said suddenly, breaking their despairing symphony. His apology confused Helena, making her look his way for clarity. She could no longer see his face, the candles having died out amidst their sorrows, leaving the two emotionally broken teens in total darkness.

Carver's next words were horribly broken up and displaced by his sobs. "I ... your father ... He ... I—"

"I know, Carver," she said. "I found him next to you ... at the schoolhouse. They killed him too. Probably the same person who nearly killed you." She was choking her words out through a series of sharp breaths and tears.

Carver's heart sank. He wanted to tell her, to finish his explanation, but he couldn't. Instead he held his tongue, hoping desperately that it was the right thing to do, both for her and for him.

"It's all gone, Carver. Verrel, they ... they razed it to the ground. Nothing's left. Others may have escaped, but if they did then we have no idea who or where they are."

"Did your mom make it out?"

"No."

Helena felt dizzy and exhausted, and her crying was only making it worse. She laid down near the foot of the bed next to Carver's legs. She closed her eyes and tried to focus on her breathing, but her sporadic sobs made it difficult.

The passing of time escaped Helena's notice, and before long she and Carver both began to quiet down. The darkness of the room was indiscernible from the darkness of her closed eyelids, further disconnecting her from her senses. The minutes passed by uncounted as the two teens slowly succumbed to a fatigued sleep.

✠ ✠ ✠

Carver was the first to open his eyes.

The darkness of the room was not so overwhelming now that his eyes had become accustomed during his sleep, allowing him to look around in confusion before he remembered where he was. His recollection of his situation and his surroundings sent a feeling of despair through his body, but before the sensation could crush him under its weight, the faint sound of movement near his feet summoned his attention.

Carver looked down and saw that Helena was still asleep next to his legs. He tried to pull his legs away and sit up slightly without waking her, but the moment he moved, her eyes flew open.

She shook for a split second before she pulled her limbs in and looked around quickly. Before Carver could say something to calm her, Helena pushed herself into a sitting position, right on his legs.

Carver hissed as a sharp pain erupted from his left calf. He pulled his legs away from Helena in a reflex that caused her to shift and tip over. Catching herself, she looked over at the source of the movement and, upon seeing it was only Carver, visibly relaxed.

Carver readjusted himself now that his legs were free and sat up properly. "Hey, Helena."

"Oh, uh. Hi, Carver."

They stared at each other for a moment before the feeling of awkwardness became too great and they looked away. Helena rubbed her eyes and then pushed herself off the bed while Carver removed the sheet and rotated so his legs hung over the edge.

A chill hit Carver's skin as he realized he was still only wearing a pair of braies besides the bandages wrapped around his leg and his head. He would have felt awkward to be seen by Helena in such little clothing had he not felt so sore and exhausted. Ignoring the chill, Carver tried to stand up.

The moment he arched his back to push off the bed, a terrible pain spread across his torso, emanating from one of his lower ribs. He groaned and sat back down, then took a deep breath and tried to hold still until the ache faded away.

"No, Carver. You need to rest. The priests said you're still badly hurt and need lots of time to recover."

Carver clenched his teeth. "How long?"

"They said it would be a few weeks, and only if Duncan can get you more healing potions. Otherwise, it might be a month or two."

"I'm not going to just lie here for a few weeks or months, Helena. I can handle myself. I walked here from the temple, didn't I?"

"Barely. I'd say I dragged you more than you walked."

"Then drag me!"

Helena stepped back from the bed, but even with the added distance, she could see the shock on Carver's face.

"No. I mean ... I'm sorry, Helena. I didn't mean to say that. It's just ..." Carver placed a hand on the side of his head and squinted. "My head feels strange. I didn't mean to snap at you. Helena, I—"

"No, Carver. It's fine," she said as she stepped toward the bed. "If you want to get up, then how about I help you a little, walk you to the table in the other room?"

Carver moved his hand away and opened his eyes fully. "No, I don't want you to feel responsible for me. I can handle it myself."

"But Carver. I—"

"No, Helena! I said—"

Carver placed a hand on his forehead and groaned as a wave of dizziness washed over him, and a sudden tingling sensation spread through his arms and legs.

"Okay, Carver. Just calm down," Helena said softly, as the feeling that something was not right increased within her.

"Helena, I ..." Carver suddenly found it difficult to breathe. "I can't ... Something's—"

Filled with panic, he forced himself to his feet without noticing any pain in doing so. His vision swam, and before he could do anything else, he felt his knees buckle and he collapsed to the floor on his right side.

"Carver!"

Helena's voice barely made it into Carver's ears as his vision and his hearing seemed to falter. Carver suddenly found himself on his back as his arms and legs stiffened and spasmed in quick, erratic bursts. He barely had time to notice that he was shaking before he lost all feeling throughout his body and could only stare up at the ceiling.

Helena threw herself onto her knees next to Carver and grabbed his arms. She squeezed them tight, but she could not stop him from shaking.

The sight of Helena kneeling above him jumped out at Carver so suddenly it was as if Helena had simply appeared out of thin air. He could see that her mouth was moving, but he couldn't hear what she was saying.

Then the sight of Helena's horrified face disappeared as blackness enveloped Carver's vision.

Chapter 25

Carver awoke in the same bed as before, wrapped in the same sheet and staring up at the ceiling. His vision was foggy, taking time to focus despite being already adjusted to the darkness of the room.

Carver felt strangely tired, accompanied by a feeling of confusion and déjà vu. He scanned the room for Helena but saw that this time he was alone. He thought for a minute about what had happened but realized he could recall nothing recent save for the memory that he had been speaking with Helena in that room about something that he also could not remember.

After another minute of lying there thinking, Carver removed the thick sheet and sat up, giving himself a once-over. Seeing the bruises across his torso and the bandages around his left leg no longer startled him, nor did the presence of the bandages around the top of his head.

His entire body felt sore, and an incessant ache plagued the back of his head. But worst of all was his stomach, which groaned with hunger, feeling as though it were twisting in place to let him know how empty it was.

Listening to his body, Carver rotated his legs over the edge of the bed and slowly stood up. He wobbled at first due to a pain in his left calf and the strain on his torso, but he stabilized with some effort. After a moment of standing to ensure he was okay to move, Carver took a deep breath and walked toward the door.

The act of walking caused his muscles to ache and some of his wounds to protest with pain, but it was manageable for the moment.

The next room was also dark, though a bright light emanated from the left end, which summoned Carver's attention instantly. He squinted as he turned to face it.

"You're awake," an old voice said from within the sphere of illumination.

Startled, Carver saw that the light was coming from a fat flame atop a wide, flat, circular metal object at the center of a wide wooden table. The object also had an iron handle, almost as thin as a sheet of paper, stretching off one side and looping back slightly below.

An older-looking man in a dirty gray coat was sitting at the far side of the table on a wooden stool, looking at him. The man's face seemed weary and sullen.

"Do you know who I am?" the man asked.

Carver shook his head, but then became concerned that his nonverbal response would make him look stupid or scared. "No," he added.

"My name is Duncan. I'm Sebastian and Nina's grandfather. And you are in my home in the town of Leydes."

Carver remained stationary near the bedroom door. Duncan patted the stool beside him. "Come sit, Carver. It's not safe for you to be standing on your own."

Carver accepted Duncan's offer and calmly walked up to the table and took the closest seat at the opposite end from him.

"How do you feel?"

"I ... I'm okay. Sore and hungry but I think I'm okay."

Duncan smiled. "No doubt you're hungry, young man. Your appetite is a whole day behind your friends, and they were famished when they arrived."

"My friends?"

"Did Helena not tell you yet? The two of you arrived here alongside my grandchildren."

"Sebastian and Nina are alive?"

"That they are. As is another Verrel boy by the name of Rook, who arrived shortly after you four did."

Carver's excitement decreased slightly, though mostly only due to confusion. "Rook is here? Why? He's no friend of ours."

"Yes, I'm aware of that. Helena and Sebastian made that fact clear to me shortly after his arrival. However, it was also made clear to me that Rook saved both of my grandchildren during the attack on Verrel."

Carver's confusion heightened. "He saved them? How?"

"The specifics do not matter," Duncan replied. "The fact is, without him, my grandchildren would be dead or worse, which would have left Helena to fend for herself while dealing with you in the forest. I doubt Helena would have been able to save you and get you both to Leydes by herself, so I would also go as far to say that Rook's actions saved you two as well." Duncan leaned over the table and clasped his hands together. "So, friend or not to you all, Rook has a debt of gratitude from me, and I'd say from all of you as well."

Carver found it difficult to disagree with Duncan's reasoning, but he kept that to himself.

Suddenly, Duncan looked over Carver's shoulder at something. "Charra, would you mind fetching Carver some of that terrific stew you made earlier?"

Carver turned around on the stool and was surprised to see the kitchen behind him where a short woman was standing and staring at him with a wooden bowl in one hand and a rag in the other. He hadn't noticed the kitchen earlier, his eyes fixed on the light.

"Oh, of course," she said, then smiled at Carver.

Carver smiled back, though it was purely a polite reflex.

Charra placed her bowl and rag on the countertop and then filled a wooden bowl with some of the contents of a large black pot sitting in the hearth, coals glowing faintly red beneath it.

Charra grabbed a thick wooden spoon from the counter and marched over to the table, setting the bowl and the spoon in front of Carver.

Carver rotated in his seat and grabbed the spoon the moment Charra had taken her hands away. The sudden urge to eat overwhelmed him, and all manner of politeness fell to the back of his mind. The stew was warm and watery, more like a soup than a stew, and was filled with stringy chunks of floating gray fish along with soggy carrots and barely detectable pepper seasoning, but it was absolutely delectable to Carver's starving stomach.

"Well, look at that," Charra said with a smile. "I was betting he would follow Helena's approach and dunk his hand right in."

Carver looked up from the bowl, not sure what she meant. Only then did he realize Charra was not merely a short woman.

Picking up on Carver's thoughts through his facial expression, she smiled pleasantly. "No, your eyes don't deceive you, dear. I'm a dwarf, and so is my husband, Gorty. I'm sure you'll meet him later. He's out at the tavern right now."

Carver felt slightly embarrassed that his thoughts were so easily read, but he quickly forgot his embarrassment when his stomach grumbled once more. He resumed his eating and did not look up again until Duncan spoke to him.

"How's your head?"

Carver quickly swallowed a chunk of warm fish. "It hurts but not like before."

"I would hope not. You gave us all quite a scare when you started shaking like that, especially Helena."

"Shaking?" Carver asked, another spoonful of soup held halfway to his mouth.

"You don't remember?" Duncan asked as he shot a concerned look at Charra.

Carver followed Duncan's look with his eyes and saw that Charra had a worried look on her face.

"Well," Duncan continued, "as it was told to me by Helena, after you awoke a few hours ago, you started acting strangely before you collapsed and began shaking uncontrollably on the floor."

Carver nearly dropped the spoon into the bowl. "What? I don't remember that. Why would I do something like that?"

"I don't know. Helena called for help, and Charra here responded, but after a minute or two of you shaking and not responding, you just stopped and fell unconscious."

Carver looked over at Charra, who nodded. "It's true, dear. I've never seen anything like it. You were shaking as if being engulfed by an invisible flame, and then you just stopped all at once. I moved you back into our bed and kept a watch over you with Helena for a long while until we felt that you were okay, at least for the time being. Mind you, I was just as worried for Helena the whole time. She was going through a fit of panic unlike I've ever seen. I'm grateful to Kailianeth that I was able to calm her."

"Kailianeth?" Carver asked.

"The goddess of the mind. Sorry, dear. I often forget that you humans are not as well versed with the dwarf gods as we are with yours."

"Oh, I see. Uh, well, where are Helena and the others?" Carver asked, turning back to face Duncan.

"Helena's next door at the fishery—or fish barn as you teens keep calling it."

"She wanted to sit by you until you woke up again," Charra cut in, "but I told her that you needed privacy and rest. She'll be ecstatic to see that you're feeling better."

Carver tried to refocus on eating again, but his eyes became fixated on the burning object in the center of the table. He studied it for a few seconds, trying to determine what it was.

Charra seemed to detect Carver's puzzlement. "Is something wrong, dear? You seem stuck."

Carver shook his head. "No, I just, uh, what is that thing? It's not like any candle I've ever seen."

"Oh, the lantern? What, you've never seen one before?"

"No, I don't think I have."

"My, Verrel must have been very, um ... traditional."

Carver knew what she had almost said, though he did not take any offence.

"Lanterns are quite common in the Commonwealth. They hold oils and burn for a long while and can be lit and unlit with ease as the wick is soaked in fuel as well."

Carver turned back to the lantern. "Oh. Sounds useful."

"They are, dear. Though you must be careful with them. They're filled with oil, as I just said, so if you tip or spill them, they can ignite into a terrible fire. Best always to make sure the lid is secure and to hold the lantern with a steady hand."

Carver nodded, then began eating again until the splashing sound of the spoon hitting the gray liquid changed into the clink of it hitting the bottom of the bowl. He sat up straight and inhaled deeply, feeling the relief in his stomach immediately. Before Carver could ask, Charra offered him a second helping, which he happily agreed to and thanked her for. He finished the second bowl much quicker than the first as no words were spoken while he ate.

"Thank you," he said to Duncan as he placed the spoon in the once again empty bowl, "and you too," he added, turning to Charra.

They both smiled, Charra more brightly than Duncan, then Charra took the bowl and spoon from Carver and carried them to the kitchen, wiping them with the rag she had been holding earlier.

"Listen, Carver, I know you must be eager to go see the others, but there are some things we must discuss first," Duncan said. The tone of his voice worried Carver, giving him the feeling that troubling news was about to follow. Duncan leaned forward and put his elbows on the table. Looking suddenly very serious, he stared straight into Carver's eyes. "While you were unconscious, we all had a long discussion about our situation and our next steps. No one in town can know you all are still here. We don't know why, but the word spreading around town is that your village was involved with the Lost Seekers."

Carver frowned in confusion, causing Duncan to raise his hand to prevent the boy from interrupting him. "None of us know why that is, and we all know it isn't true, but that doesn't matter. The fact is that if anyone learns you and your group are from Verrel, they'll label you all as rebels and terrorists, and then the town soldiers will arrest you, torture you all for information you don't have, and then most likely have you all hanged at the market gallows for the whole town to see."

Carver's worry increased exponentially, but he remained silent.

"The immediate problem we face is that dozens of townsfolk and soldiers witnessed your little group hobble into town yesterday, and your incident at the temple this morning only furthered the gossip about you all. Sooner or later, people are going to start asking questions and connecting your group to the attack on Verrel. Helena tells me that some folks were already claiming that she was from Verrel last night in the tavern. Luckily, these people were mostly all drunks, and their shouts were muddled with many other claims and weren't given much credit. I imagine that many of them forgot the whole idea the next morning, but that kind of luck won't last forever and can't be relied upon."

Duncan rubbed his mouth without taking his eyes off Carver. "I found and apologized to the captain of the Leydes Guard today about your assault on the priest and paid for the healing supplies needed to treat her. I also explained to him that I was only planning on patching you all up before I send you on your way. I made it clear that I wasn't planning on sheltering a bunch of teenagers who only knew me by merit of my trading with their village and that I would be returning you to your village southeast of Gale. So, tomorrow morning you, Helena, and my grandchildren are going to be seated in the back of my wagon, and I'll take you out of town for everyone to see."

"What about Rook?" Carver asked.

"I'm getting to that. I'll be taking you four a good distance out of town down the coast. Once I feel that we're far enough away and out of sight from any road patrols, we'll make camp down by the shore and wait for Gorty, Charra's husband, who will arrive by sea in one of my fishing boats and take you all back to the fishery under cover of night and sneak you inside. Then I'll ride the rest of the way to Gale and then head back so everything seems accurate.

"From then on, or at least until we can figure something else out, you, Helena, and my grandchildren are going to be staying in the fishery. It's spacious and secure, and most importantly, it will keep you all hidden from outside eyes. Rook will be the only one who can come and go from the fishery since he arrived separate from your group without much injury and didn't need to go to the temple's healing sanctum. I'm going to have him work with Gorty and me during the day, and I'll make it known that he is merely some new hired help.

"During Rook's time out of the fishery I'll have him bring the rest of you things you'll need from the house or the market: food, blankets, clothes, and whatever else. A small sleeping area has already been set up inside the fishery with some sheets and furs from the house. What's there isn't much right now, and you'll have to share for a while as we can't go and buy a bunch of bedding and clothing from the market so soon after your arrival without drawing suspicion to ourselves, but soon we'll make it more comfortable for you all. I know it isn't the most ideal situation, but it's all we have available to us right now, so it will have to do."

Carver was unsure what to say. The information was not entirely pleasant, but he also understood that this was probably the best he could hope for given the current situation.

"Thank you," he said as sincerely as possible.

Duncan responded with a sad smile. "Night has already fallen, so you may go to the others if you're ready. Just let me make sure that no people or patrols are in the street. The fewer people who see you the better." Duncan rose from his seat. "But take these first." He grabbed a pile of clothing from the stool next to him and placed it in front of Carver on the table.

Moving slowly so as not to aggravate his hurts, Carver put on every item he was handed without complaint, including a brown wool tunic that was a little too big, gray wool trousers that hung a little too long, a worn-out belt, and two old boots that didn't quite squeeze his feet enough and gave off the aroma of seawater.

While Carver got dressed, Duncan opened the front door and looked outside.

"Alright, the street is empty for the moment. You should be clear to get to the others. The fishery is next to the house, to the right and a bit back by the water. Go before any patrols round the corner."

Carver was about to step outside when Duncan put out an arm to stop him. "Wait, there's one other thing, Carver."

Carver stopped and looked up at Duncan, his face a mixture of worry and confusion.

"Your head ... What happened earlier ..." Duncan seemed troubled about how to continue. "I asked the temple healers about it. That large gash on the back of your head, it's from a sword slash. They cleaned it, fed you a healing potion, bandaged it along with some marrowstalk poultice, and stitched it up, but ..."

Carver's body began to prickle with fear.

"They said your skull was cracked and that the blade may have cut into your brain."

Carver felt his skin freeze.

"They told me that such an injury might have damaged your mind and that they were not sure if potions or time could heal such an injury, potentially leading to unknown problems. It's my guess that your collapse and fit of shaking was a result of this potential injury to your brain."

Carver broke eye contact with the man and stared out into the street, losing himself in his thoughts. "What do I do?" he asked, finally turning back to Duncan.

"I don't think there's anything you can do other than hope whatever issues arise aren't lifelong, I suppose. The fact that the blade didn't kill you is a miracle."

Duncan leaned out the door and looked up at the sky. Carver followed Duncan's gaze and saw a black sky filled with stars.

"The blow happened during the night, under Cosom's watch," Duncan said as he brought his gaze back down to Carver. "It seems to me that Cosom intervened and kept you from death that night, which means you have his favor, a rare thing for any person to have after the Great Betrayal. Why Cosom protected you that night, I don't know, but I do know that you should be wary, for the Lord of the Void does not interact with the world unless for his own gain."

Carver continued to stare up at the stars, Cosom's thousands upon thousands of eyes. He suddenly felt small and vulnerable beneath those distant, twinkling specks, like each one was focused on him. Wishing to get away from his terrified thoughts, he thanked Duncan for everything and then stepped out the door.

The air outside was chilly as Carver made his way toward the fishery. Once inside, he discovered it was one massive room. It was dark, with the only light coming from what little the two moons could send through the cracks and gaps of the old wooden walls and ceiling. The chilly air seeped in through the same cracks, giving the place an unwelcoming aura. The powerful odor of fish and seawater also assaulted Carver from every direction.

"Carver?" a familiar male voice called from the far side of the room.

"Sebastian?"

Four shadowy figures rose near the back of the fishery and approached until the gentle moonlight revealed their identities.

"Carver!" Nina shrieked with joy and ran up and hugged him.

Carver's lower ribs and gut tensed in pain as she pressed her body against his bruised torso. "Hi," he wheezed as he gently pushed Nina away by the shoulders.

Nina released Carver and stepped back, suddenly aware of his pain by the groan that escaped his lips. "Oh, I'm sorry."

He was about to tell Nina that it was alright, but when Nina stepped back, he realized that half of her face was covered in bandages. Noticing the look on Carver's face, her childlike joy drained immediately. Carver realized he was staring, so he quickly turned away and looked past her at the others.

"Hey, Carver," Helena said, giving him a small wave. She appeared to be exhausted and quite drained of emotion.

Carver waved back, then looked at the boy beside her.

"Hi, Sebastian."

"We were worried you'd never wake up," Sebastian said, his smiling face streaked with beams of moonlight.

Carver saw that Sebastian was leaning against a crate and that his right arm was in a sling. "Are you okay, Sebastian?"

Sebastian looked at his injured arm, then back at Carver, still smiling. "I'm fine. I'm sure Helena has already told you about the vell attack."

Carver tilted his head slightly, his face worried. "The vell attack?"

Sebastian looked at Helena and then back at Carver. "Oh, I guess not then. Well, we can fill you in in the morning. It's a long story," Sebastian said as his smile faded.

Carver looked over at Rook and wondered if he should say something to him. He thought of thanking him for supposedly helping get everyone to Leydes or acknowledging that he had apparently saved the lives of Nina and Sebastian, but Rook turned and walked back to the far end of the fishery without saying a word before Carver could say anything.

"Don't concern yourself with him," Sebastian whispered. "He hasn't said a word to any of us since we caught him crying earlier today. He likes to have us think he's handling things better than we are."

Sebastian pushed himself away from the crate. As he did, Nina reached out to support him. Sebastian gave her a frustrated look but did not object as she helped him turn and walk back to where they had come from, leaving Helena and Carver alone near the door.

"How are you feeling?" Helena asked, looking slightly nervous, as if expecting him to fall and start shaking again.

"Better. Things still hurt, but I walked here from the house on my own without falling, and I don't feel dizzy anymore."

"That's good."

"How are you?"

Helena did not answer right away. "I don't know. I feel okay, but then I don't. I don't know what I feel anymore."

Carver closed the distance between them and placed a hand on Helena's arm. "It's going to be okay, Helena, I won't let them get away with this."

Helena was confused by his words. "Get away with what? Who?"

"I'm going to kill them all. Every last person who had a hand in destroying Verrel and killing our families."

His cold tone sent a shiver up Helena's spine.

Chapter 26

❧

The next two months crawled by.

Each day seemed to move at a snail's pace from within the confines of the fishery. After being taken far out of Leydes the morning after Carver came to the fishery, then being smuggled back by Gorty on a small fishing boat under a layer of sails and fishing nets during the night, the group of teens spent the first few days resting and recovering from their wounds, both physical and emotional.

The next few days after that, they explored the first and second floor of the building and talked amongst themselves until their jaws were sore. Carver and Helena told the group about the Caswen market attack and the appearance of the sovereigns, after which everyone told Carver the events of their trek through Vellum Forest.

Sebastian and Nina were the most invested in the details of Carver and Helena's experience at the Caswen market, while Rook seemed uninterested and focused more on bringing up how the group had made a mistake in marching through Leydes so openly.

The interest in the events at the market and the sovereigns and the argument of who was to blame for exposing them to the town soon faded, however, as their mood once again became somber.

The smell of fish never left. Day after day the group awakened from their uncomfortable sleep and nightmares to the unwelcoming stench of fresh marine life, continually brought in by Gorty and Rook and eventually Duncan, after he returned to Leydes a few days later.

Rook had been summoned from the fishery three days after Duncan's return, and from that point on he spent most of his time working with Duncan and Gorty out on the water or helping Charra gather supplies from the town market for his younger companions.

The task of gutting, scaling, preserving, and storing the catch was bestowed upon the four teens confined to the fishery. At first they performed the duties with the displeasure of a chore, though they never expressed it openly, but over time they eagerly anticipated the activity, which broke up their many hours of boredom and turned their minds away from dark thoughts.

Over time the second floor of the fishery, mainly used as rented storage for old and surplus boating and fishing gear, became the teenagers' sleeping quarters. More hefty blankets were brought in, allowing them all to have their own private sleeping space.

Sebastian and Nina shared a spot on the north side of the second floor, tucked against the north wall, as Nina feared sleeping anywhere near the large rectangular gap that separated the top floor into a "U" shape, allowing the ground floor to be seen and hopped down to, though the stairs were always used.

Rook resided on the same side as the siblings, making his sleeping setup in the corner farthest from them along the west wall near the door.

Carver and Helena took up the south end of the upper floor, close to each other in the center of the south side, separated by a small, overturned fishing boat that was smothered beneath a heavy pile of tangled nets and ropes.

The nights inside the fishery grew colder as August turned to September and then October. Time became a blur for the group as each new day ended up a near copy of the one before.

Their wounds continued to heal as summer changed to autumn, though the speed at which they healed was faster than normal thanks to the few non-magical healing potions Duncan had purchased on the day of their arrival, which they sipped at regular intervals until they ran out.

Sebastian found it easier and easier to walk as his leg and hip healed, and after some time he was able to take his arm out of the sling and use it normally again, though much of the feeling in his right hand and remaining fingers did not return.

Nina eventually removed the bandages from her face, revealing a large, hideous scar that stretched from the left side of her mouth up under her left ear as well as another wide scar that trailed horizontally across her left eyebrow and ran down around her eye. These two scars drew attention away from the many smaller, less prominent scars that remained around her chin, the left side of her forehead, and her left cheek.

Helena's minor injuries healed up nicely. The many cuts and punctures she'd received from the vells' sharp spines along her arms and chest faded into pale white marks, as did the X-shaped cut on her knee, the only sign of it being a faint pink scar.

The bruises along Carver's lower ribs disappeared, though an area near one of his lowest ribs on his right side still occasionally flared up with pain if he bent certain ways, but even that was lessening with time. The deep puncture in his left calf had also scarred over and no longer troubled him enough to affect his ability to walk.

Much like Nina, however, Carver realized he was probably going to be stared at by strangers for the rest of his life, though he was at least lucky enough that he would not see them doing it. Made visible by his short hair, the back of his head showcased a nasty scar that was slightly sunken into his head. The mark could be seen from a distance within the fishery, forcing the others to either stare or look away quickly whenever Carver turned his back.

The grotesque wound also made itself known by the strange fits it would occasionally send Carver into. Every few days he would suddenly tense up and fall to the floor before breaking out into a bout of uncontrollable shaking.

The first few times it happened the other teens were terribly frightened and did all they could to hold Carver still, but after multiple failed attempts, and seeing that Carver always stopped by himself after a short time, they switched their approach and merely tried to clear the area and keep Carver from hitting his head on anything. They also became aware of some of the signs that indicated he was going to fall into a shaking fit. Sometimes he would suddenly seem to lose focus during a conversation, stare off into nothingness for a moment, or get dizzy and begin struggling to breathe. Whenever they witnessed Carver beginning to show these signs, they would grab a blanket and a straw-stuffed pillow to soften the area around him for the duration of his shaking. Each time Carver awoke from one of his fits, he would be exhausted and have little to no memory of what had happened. Over time, however, his fits became less frightening to the others and even him. They also reduced in frequency until he was only having one per month.

After two weeks had passed since his last episode, Carver began to hope that maybe he had healed enough to be rid of the fits forever, thinking that his brain had healed along with the rest of his body. Sebastian and Nina also hoped that was true, but Helena was skeptical.

With Carver's fits seemingly at an end, and with no sign of them being found out by Werner or the Leydes soldiers, the group's mood improved, and everyone started sleeping a little better. However, none of them had come to terms with what had happened to them, nor had they reached peace in their minds. Helena was the furthest behind in the emotional healing process, and for a very specific reason.

What Carver had said to her after his arrival at the fishery many weeks earlier remained strong in her mind and kept her up longer than it should have most nights. She wanted to speak to him about it, but even when she was alone with him, and the others were out of earshot, she was still unable to bring it up.

Helena desperately wanted to ask Sebastian or Nina for their thoughts on how, or even if, she should bring it up with Carver, or to ask if maybe she was wrong in believing Carver was truly capable of acting on such a statement. But each time she had the opportunity to bring it up with either sibling, she became quiet and anxious.

It wasn't until a cold night in mid-October that Helena finally found the guts to confront Carver.

"Carver, are you awake?" she asked from her side of the boat that separated them.

"Yes," Carver whispered from the other side.

It took Helena a few seconds to figure out what to say and how to say it. "Are you serious about what you said?"

"About what?"

"When you first came in here. What you said about the people who attacked us. You said you were going to kill them."

Now it was Carver who seemed to be struggling with what to say.

"Carver?"

"Yes."

Helena wanted to think that Carver was only responding to the call of his name, but she could not convince herself that that was the case. "I don't understand."

"How can you not understand? They deserve to die. All of them. I won't let them get away with what they did."

The fear that Helena had felt on the night when Carver first spoke those words crept back into her heart. "But that's not something you can do, Carver. As much as I agree that those people are monsters and should suffer for what they did, there's nothing we can do about it."

"I don't believe that. I won't. No one else will do it. No one else will get revenge for our families, so it has to be us."

Helena felt eerily cold beneath her light blanket, more so than usual. The moonlight cast her sleeping area in a dim, bluish glow that was just bright enough for her to see the piles of miscellaneous fishing gear and crates that surrounded her.

"That's what scares me, Carver. I don't want you to go back to Caswen or try to avenge our parents. You'll die. I've already lost everyone I cared about, and I already thought I'd lost you—twice. I don't want to lose you again. Not for real."

Carver did not reply, leaving Helena with naught but the sound of creaking wood and the distant gentle crashing of ocean waves against the pier behind the fishery.

"I'm sorry," Carver said suddenly.

Helena didn't know what to say in reply. She didn't know if she had achieved anything by bringing the topic up or what he meant by his apology. The whole situation felt wrong to her.

They lay in silence for a long while, listening to the sound of the ocean.

Helena knew she needed to say something, but she couldn't figure out the right thing to say at that moment.

"Carver ... do you think it would have been better if we had died in Verrel ... if we never made it out?" she asked finally.

"I don't know, Helena. Maybe."

☩   ☩   ☩

Helena awoke the next morning to birds chirping a vibrant melody. She opened her eyes and looked at where the peaceful sounds were coming from in the hopes of spotting the cheery birds, but she was immediately disappointed when she saw nothing but a dusty wood wall, which reminded her as to her whereabouts and situation.

She was sore and stiff, and the cool air began to slowly make itself known once again. Despite her discomfort, however, Helena remained beneath her blanket with her head on her pillow. She listened intently to the birds, wondering what they looked like, until the chirping halted suddenly, replaced by the fluttering of tiny wings.

With the quaint birdsong gone, Helena stood up and stretched the kinks and sore spots created from sleeping on a wood floor with only a thin animal hide to separate her from it. As she glanced over the boat that separated her sleeping area from Carver's, she realized he was gone.

Helena scanned the large upper floor, but all she saw were crates, barrels, old fishing and sailing gear, and cobwebs. Her ears suddenly picked up the faint sound of voices below, indicating that the others were already awake. She scooped up a set of clothes from a crate to her right and made her way over to the southeast corner of the floor.

There, in an isolated section, some crates were stacked in a square, creating a sectioned-off space that the group had designated as an area to wash themselves.

Helena placed her fresh clothes atop one of the crates, then picked up a blanket and hung it over the two nails behind her so it hung like a curtain between the two top crates.

Helena glanced down at a wooden pail filled with water by her feet. The pail sat next to a hole in the floor that was barely the size of her fist. Looking through the hole, she saw a larger pail down below, ready to catch whatever water fell through.

Helena listened for a moment, trying to hear if the voices from below were coming up the stairs. Deducing that she was in the clear, she removed the clothes she had slept in and tossed them to the side, then undid the long braid that hung down her back, allowing her hair to fall freely down past her shoulders.

Then Helena picked up the pail and, after a moment's hesitation, tipped it toward her, emptying the water over her body.

The water was cold, causing Helena to tense up, but she held firm and continued pouring. Once the pail was empty, she set it down, then whipped her head back and forth, flinging her hair out of her face. She ran her fingers through her hair to remove the knots, wiping streaks of water from her face and eyes every few seconds.

After a few moments of shivering and combing her soaked hair back behind her ears, Helena dried herself off with her previous day's clothes. Her hair still dripping, she put on her clean clothes and emerged from the secluded area while holding the wet, dirty clothes in her arms.

After stashing her dirty clothes in her sleeping area, Helena went downstairs. She spotted the tops of Sebastian and Nina's heads, though the loud creaking of the stairs muffled their voices. Only when she reached the ground floor did Nina's voice become clear.

"Other kinds? What other kinds?"

Charra responded quickly, which surprised Helena. "Well, kinds might not be the right word. You and them are still all human, after all."

Helena rounded a stack of crates and saw that Charra, too short to be seen from the other side, was speaking to the siblings, who were each leaning against the crates behind them.

When the dwarf woman noticed Helena, she smiled pleasantly. "Good morning, dear. I was wondering when you and Carver would wake up."

Helena smiled back. "But Carver's already—"

"Oh, crap!" Nina said, turning to Helena. "I should have woken you. Charra has been telling us about the Mainland. Sorry, Helena. I know how much you like history stuff."

"Technically, she's not telling us history," Sebastian said, "just what it's like over there."

"She's telling us about the other kinds of humans who live on Gaia's mainland. Come listen," Nina said.

"Other kinds?" Helena asked, immediately captivated with the topic.

"Well, like I said, other kinds is a bit too strong of a term. They're the same as you lot, just with some differences, is all."

"What kinds of differences?" Nina asked.

"Skin color mostly, but also some facial features."

"How many different kinds are there?" Nina asked, her excitement growing.

"Again with the kinds." Charra touched her forehead and smirked. "Well, the most common of you humans living in the Commonwealth and Terraland is, well, you, the pale-skinned of your kind. You all come from Mainland Terraland, which is called as such because the old dwarf word for your kind was terran. To the east of Terraland is where the second bunch of you humans come from. Their skin is a bit darker than yours or mine, and their eyes are slightly smaller, more squinted, if I'm describing it right. Orienterrans is what they're called, since the old dwarf word for east was orient. Your people's name was changed to Boreaterran once the Orienterrans were discovered, meaning North Human, since we had to be able to refer to two groups of you. But you were all still terrans."

"Wait. East of Terraland? I thought the only other human kingdom was south," Nina said.

"Oh, I didn't explain that right. Here, let me ask you something first. Do you three know how your kingdom came to be?"

Sebastian and Nina both looked at Helena. She felt a pinch of anxiety, but she pushed it away. "Um, Keldar made it—conquered it, I mean. He conquered all the human tribes and brought them together into one kingdom."

Charra frowned slightly. "Ha! You say it as if Keldar did it all by himself. Keldar had most of the Dwarven Commonwealth aiding him during his unification of your people."

"Yes, well, we know that. But Keldar was a great warrior. He was a descendant of Dema's mortal children and second in battle to only Dema herself. We learned the tale of Keldar at our schoolhouse."

"Oh, your village had a schoolhouse? Then you were a fortunate bunch. From what I've heard and seen, most smaller human settlements don't have schoolhouses. Even Leydes doesn't have a schoolhouse. Absurd, I say. In the Commonwealth, schools, which were a dwarven creation, I proudly remind you, are as common as temples. The knowledge and ways of life that we dwarves shared with you humans, and how much of it seems to be unused or forgotten, is maddening."

Charra shook her head slightly and smiled at the three of them. "Well, anyway, that brings me back to what I was saying before. Keldar was allied with the kings and queens of the Dwarven Commonwealth who helped him conquer the tribes of Terraland. After Keldar proclaimed himself king, the dwarf kingdoms also shared their knowledge and advancements with him and his people to help build the kingdom up."

"But what about the Ori-uhm, Orienterrans?" Sebastian asked.

"I'm getting to that, dear. The land of the Orienterrans, the Highlands, as it's called today, was already somewhat unified into one nation, though no one person held the title of king or queen, leaving the nation as more of a collection of independent parts which made up a greater whole. The Orienterrans also had a very different culture and faith to your own people's and Keldar's. And Keldar didn't move his army to the Highlands until after Terraland was formed. The Orienterrans were not outright conquered by Keldar, but rather, hmm ... how do I describe this?" Charra bit her lip, deep in thought. "The various independent chieftains of the Highlands' tribes came to an agreement with Keldar to have their land be brought into the kingdom of Terraland as a province, but their province would remain mostly independent, self-governed, and would hold to their people's culture and faith. They had to pay taxes and supply soldiers to Terraland's army during times of war, however. You Boreaterrans were permitted to build settlements within their borders, and their people were free to migrate west. It's more of an allied, tributary nation than a vassalized province, if that makes any sense to you all."

"How do you know so much about all this?" Helena asked.

"We dwarves value history. All of us take pride in knowing the history of the world and our families. Our kings and queens are also our greatest historians, leading our people to the future with an iron-clad knowledge of the past. To record the past is to create a permanent source of knowledge."

Sebastian looked at Helena. "Sounds like you'd be a good dwarf, Helena."
Nina chuckled and Helena grinned.

Charra also grinned at Sebastian's remark before she continued. "Over the years, Orienterrans have migrated to the rest of Terraland and throughout the Dwarven Commonwealth, though not many. Those who live away from the Highlands are shunned by their homeland people, I hear, as the culture is heavily rooted in tradition and heritage. Gorty and I only saw a handful of Orienterrans while we lived in our home kingdom of Dithraine, and I imagine the farther south you go the less of them you'll see. That's the same for you Boreaterrans too, actually. It's the Meriditerrans who are more common down south."

"Meriditerrans?" Nina and Sebastian asked in unison before Helena had a chance to.

"Does meridi mean south in the old dwarf language then?" Helena asked before Charra could address the siblings.

Charra smiled. "That it does, dear. You catch on fast. When the sovereigns arrived from the south, coming up through Beldar and across Mishil and Hathrak, as it is told, the Meriditerrans were a large part of their army. They were the first people that the sovereigns conquered, or so it is said. Their skin is dark, and their hair seems to only grow black. Unlike the two terran groups to the north of the Commonwealth who had no name for themselves and so adopted the dwarf word of terran as their own, the Meriditerrans called themselves humans, and so the sovereigns did also. Once the sovereigns discovered the rest of you lot, they unified your race under the name human. Boreaterran, Orienterran and Meriditerran are still used to distinguish you, but only in the context of your diverse kinds. Oh, now I'm saying kinds." Charra slapped her forehead and chuckled.

All the teens had questions, but Nina was the first to speak up. "Are there other kinds of dwarves too?"

"No. We're all just as light-skinned as you Boreaterrans. What led your race to these differences or why you humans seem to come from every direction in Gaia is still a mystery."

"Why didn't the Terraland humans have their own name for themselves in their own language?" Sebastian asked.

"Well, dear, your ancestors, and those of the Orienterrans, had no written language. Their dialect was minimal and lacked words for a great many things. As such, the Boreaterrans adopted the dwarf language over time, with the Orienterrans adopting the language shortly after. I mean no offence to you or your people, but you humans were hundreds of years behind us dwarves before we uplifted you."

"Well, it sounds like we needed it," Sebastian said, grinning.

"How do you know these old dwarf words, Charra?" Helena asked. "The sovereigns wiped out the old languages when they converted everyone to their language."

"You know what, Helena? You would make a good dwarf," Charra said, laughing. "That they did indeed. Though most, if not all, of the world's texts and histories were preserved by being translated into the sovereign tongue, the original languages they were written in are dead and gone. A great defeat to dwarves and humans—goblins too. But some aspects of the old languages managed to find their way into the sovereign tongue. Since the sovereigns had no words to address each human group individually, they adopted the dwarf words and integrated them into their own language.

"This is why we know that borea means north, orient means east, and meridi means south. It's the history behind the words regarding the locations of your peoples. The old dwarf word for west, however, is forgotten. If only there were another group of humans to the west, then one more word would have survived. An extra piece of our history would still be here." Charra seemed sad as she finished.

"I prefer terran," Nina said. "The word human makes it sound like we're all men because man is in it."

Sebastian chuckled and poked his sister with his heel. "No, it doesn't. It's the same as the sovereign word, woman. That has man in it too."

Charra chuckled. "It is odd that the Meriditerrans' own name for themselves was so close to the sovereign words for the genders, but we digress. What matters is that the final name for your race is human. However your features might differ and whether your skin is pale, tinted, or dark, you are one single race. One people."

The teenagers were quiet as they digested the information.

"Are there many Meriditerrans in the Commonwealth or Terraland?" Helena asked.

Charra shook her head. "Not many in Terraland, no. But farther south, like I said earlier, yes. I've not seen many of them myself, as they are still not too common within Dithraine, but I hear that there are many Meriditerrans living in Hathrak, Dulengar, and Yodmere, and also within Beldar and the Mahkouan Colony Kingdoms. The kingdom of the Meriditerrans is called Xaidar, if I remember correctly. Xaidar is said to be far across the Urubinon Desert, somewhere near the sovereign kingdom, as the rumor goes, but I know next to nothing about the lands beyond the Urubinon Mountains. All I know for sure is that after the sovereigns conquered the northern lands of Gaia, many of the Meriditerrans who made up their vast army remained up here, and apparently, over time many more have continued to migrate northwards."

"Wow, you know a lot," Sebastian said.

Charra blushed. "Well, being from the Mainland means I know a thing or two about it. However, I need to be going now. The horses need to be fed and groomed, and the house chores won't do themselves. I'm glad I could teach you kids something, though. If you ever have questions about anything else, don't hesitate to ask."

Helena, Nina, and Sebastian all thanked Charra and watched her stroll out of the fishery. Afterwards, the three of them remained in silence, each thinking over what they had just learned.

Sebastian looked over at Helena. "Looks like Charra is going to be your new best friend, what with all the history you two can talk about. Carver's going to be jealous."

Nina's cheeks blushed as she looked at Helena and giggled. Helena frowned at the implication.

Sebastian stood up straight and stretched his arms. "Anyway, you should go wake him up, Helena. We should probably get to work on cleaning and gutting yesterday's catch."

"He's already up," Helena said.

Sebastian tilted his head in confusion and looked up at the second floor. "Why hasn't he come down then? I know Carver doesn't care about history, but even he might have found this interesting."

Helena's brow furrowed in confusion. "Carver did come down. I mean, I thought he did. He wasn't in his spot when I woke up, and I didn't hear or see him up there."

The siblings searched each other's faces for an explanation.

"Oh," Sebastian said as he turned away from his sister and peered around the area. "Carver?" he called out somewhat quietly so as not to be overheard from outside.

"Carver?" Helena called when no response came.

The three of them spread out, searching for him.

"Where is he?" Nina asked, a hint of panic in her voice.

"I don't know," Sebastian said, his voice revealing his discomfort as well.

Helena felt panic rising within her, though she refrained from expressing it verbally.

"He's not here," Sebastian announced after looking behind every last crate in his area.

"Check upstairs. Maybe he started shaking again and he's unconscious," Nina suggested.

Helena was already halfway up the stairs.

"We would have heard him bumping into stuff or thumping the floor if that were the case," Sebastian said with a harsh tone.

"Well, I don't know then!" Nina said in a raised voice brought on with her worry.

Helena left the bickering siblings behind and searched upstairs. When she couldn't find Carver, she tried desperately to remember where the other thing she was looking for was, or rather, where she hoped it still was. She followed her memory to a cluster of wooden barrels near the large gap that separated the upper floor.

This is it. It's here somewhere.

As she searched through them, one of the empty barrels tipped and fell over the edge, crashing down on the lower floor with a loud crack as it split open on one side.

"Whoa! Helena, what are you doing up there?" Sebastian called out from below.

Helena did not answer because just then something caught her eye: a faint horizontal mark stretched a quarter of the way across a barrel's lower half, a mark that filled Helena with as much hope as it did dread.

"What are you doing, Helena?" Nina asked, slightly out of breath after running up the stairs to find her.

Again, Helena did not respond. Instead, she gripped the top of the marked barrel and pulled on the wooden rim until it popped off. Helena tossed it away with no care as to where it landed.

"It's gone!" she cried.

The sound of Sebastian's boots heading up the stairs indicated his arrival.

"What's gone?" Nina asked.

Helena turned to Nina just as Sebastian jogged up, stopping beside her. His eyes widened slightly. "Wait, isn't that where we hid—"

"The arming sword!" Helena cried.

The sudden sound of the fishery door opening seized the group's attention. All three of them looked down the massive gap in the second floor and saw Charra enter the building.

She looked around until she spotted the three of them above her.

"Did you three hear anything outside last night near the south wall?"

Sebastian and Nina looked at Helena, whose sleeping spot was the closest to that wall, aside from Carver's. She shook her head.

"Charra, what's wrong?" Nina asked.

"One of Duncan's horses! It's been stolen!"

Chapter 27

❦

"Whoa," Carver commanded while tugging on the reins. The horse hesitated at first, but after a second tug, it complied and brought its legs to a halt.

Carver sat as still as a statue, trying to focus as his thoughts and emotions pulled back and forth on his weary mind. The long ride through the night had left him drained and groggy, and he suspected his horse was even more tired than he was.

Carver had stopped the horse about every hour during their trek over the Vellum Hills in order to give the animal some time to rest, during which the horse would relax and chew on the cold damp grass that blanketed the hills. The horse, perhaps thinking this stop was one of those instances, began to sweep its nose over the ground in search of food.

The dew-speckled grass glistened as the early morning sunlight stretched across the land. Despite the sun having risen an hour earlier, the chill that pinched Carver's skin did not lessen. The biting wind reminded him that winter was fast approaching and would soon bring heavy snow to the Isles. He did not mind the October winds at the moment, as they had been a great boon in preventing him from falling asleep in the saddle and kept his attention somewhat sharp during his moonlit ride.

Now, however, Carver hardly seemed to notice the chill. His perception of the temperature was brushed to the side by his scrambling mind as the sight before him called forth every drop of his attention.

Appearing from over the last hill that he and his mount had climbed, the sight struck Carver with a cold truth: Verrel. He recognized it immediately, though many things were not as before.

Some cottages were missing, replaced by massive piles of debris. Of the many cottages that were still standing, most of their roofs had collapsed. Of the few buildings that remained standing with their roofs intact, they all had the same thing in common with the less fortunate structures: each was charred black and veiled in ash.

Carver felt an urge to look away, but he was unable to turn his head. All he could do was stare down at his former home.

The horse suddenly broke Carver's trance as it shuffled its hooves slightly and let out a loud sneeze. With his mind snapped back into focus, Carver shivered, then squeezed his legs together to signal his horse to move down the hill.

The horse huffed and then trotted down toward the abandoned village without any understanding that something was wrong about the destination. Carver, on the other hand, understood far too well.

The horse carried Carver into the village on the side of the archery range, though no one would call it that anymore. The range's painted targets were gone, as were the roped stands that held them up. Now it was nothing but an empty field, the range a distant memory.

The horse continued on, walking across the field like it did to any other flat expanse of grass. Before Carver could dwell on his memories of the range, he was confronted by a large wooden structure, its roof and one of its walls having collapsed. The village schoolhouse had not been a place Carver enjoyed apart from his classes in fighting, but he felt sad nonetheless to see it in this way.

He took a deep breath and then looked at the area on the west side of the building. There, stretching a few dozen feet from the burned husk of Verrel's schoolhouse, was a round patch of flattened dirt that had been used as a training yard for combat exercises. Two of the straw training dummies were still standing on their thick poles. The other six were either lying on the ground or missing entirely.

That training yard held some of Carver's best memories, but those memories were now drowned by one memory alone.

The memory was so clear, so real in his mind, that he felt he could almost relive it if he thought hard enough. It was because of his clear recollection, the pain that it brought him, and the constant presence it maintained in his mind that Carver felt such confusion and worry at the sight of the flat stretch of dirt.

The body's gone ... his inner voice said.

As he wondered what could have happened to it, he froze, suddenly realizing something else.

They're all gone ...

Not a single human body could be seen in any direction. Confusion swept over Carver as he came to this realization, followed by a burst of dread. He was frozen once again, not from the cold but by his bitter observations and unpleasant thoughts.

Carver was snapped away from his thoughts by a noise. At first his mind told him that it was just his horse again, but then his mind corrected itself with the rationale that horses didn't speak.

The voice that reached his ears was faint and far away, finding its way around the burnt cottages from somewhere deep inside the village to the south.

Carver was unable to link the voice to a specific gender or age, as his senses only managed to detect the tail end of the sound. Regardless of the details, the voice's arrival made him uneasy. He placed a firm hand against his horse's neck and issued it forward with a squeeze of his legs. The horse hesitated against Carver's order, and just as before, it required a second effort to comply.

Carver pointed his left ear forward as his mount carried him deeper into the village. As he passed a few ruined cottages, hearing nothing else, he began to wonder if he had only imagined the sound. His doubts were quashed when the voice returned, almost seeming to speak up in response to them. Carver stopped his horse again. The voice was female and much closer than before, though its age still eluded him.

Hidden behind one of the many burned cottages, Carver sat and listened. Almost immediately, he heard another voice, a male this time, and it seemed to come from the same direction as the female's had.

Carver quietly dismounted, planting his boots on the ground just in time for another voice to reach his ears. His sense of worry began to rise as he wondered how many people were actually there. He still didn't understand why anyone would be there at all. Helena had told him there wasn't anything left in Verrel to be taken by looters or scavengers, and the village was certainly in no state for new occupants.

Trying to clear his head, Carver took a deep breath. Suddenly, his horse let out a grumbling snort and turned as if about to wander off. Carver quickly grabbed the reins.

"Horse!" he whispered through his teeth while giving the reins a firm pull.

He wished he knew the horse's name, thinking it would make commanding the animal much easier. The nameless horse resisted Carver's pull for a moment, but after a second and third yank, it turned back toward him and settled down. After giving the animal a few gentle pats on the head and whispering kindly for it to stay put, Carver released the reins and reached his hands between the fat saddle and the left side of the horse.

Feeling some straps and buckles, Carver unfastened the makeshift knot he'd tied to remove the prize that was hidden there. Careful not to bother the horse with the item's cold faces or sharp edges, he removed the arming sword and hefted it in his hand.

Despite his growing fear and worry, Carver turned and advanced toward the voices, leaving Duncan's horse hidden behind the cottage.

As Carver inched down the narrow grassy lane alongside the charred and collapsed cottages, the speakers remained out of sight behind the structures. Carver tried to settle his fear and anxiety as he advanced, but his efforts bore little fruit. Each step he took only added to his rising sense of worry. His mind was begging him to turn back, but his will forced him onwards.

The blackened row of cottages that Carver kept to his right quickly began to near its end, finishing at a wide grassy gap that turned left, leading out toward the hills, and right leading toward the center of the village. Carver's mind searched frantically for a plan for once he made it to the end of the path, but no plan came. As he reached the corner of the last ruined cottage, he planted his feet in the ground and pressed his back against the wall of the charred structure. A cloud of dark ash trickled down from the outer wall, covering Carver's shoulders and back.

Carver mustered the courage to peer around the corner, but already he could get a picture in his mind of the situation from the noises he heard. The sound of boots squishing wet grass; the faint crackling of a fire, apparently small enough not to create an obvious trail of smoke visible from the hills surrounding the village; a fit of hoarse coughing and persistent sniffling; and a handful of voices.

It was a mixture of males and females, at least six people, from what Carver could tell, and the voices went back and forth. Being so much closer now, Carver was able to hear some of what the strangers were saying.

"Someone come help me gather firewood."

"Get Jess to go. She's been asking for something to do."

"Anyone have any squirrel left?"

"It's mine. Go snare one yourself if you've stooped to begging."

"This chill is worse than my cocking hemorrhoids."

"Enough, you! There are children listening."

Hearing the mention of children being present calmed Carver a great amount, but not fully. He figured that if children were around, these people could not be bandits or thugs, and that lowering of risk allowed him to finish mustering the nerve to peek around the corner.

Carver saw much more than he expected to see. At least a dozen or more people—men, women, and a few children—mingled around the open area at the center of the village or stood near the beginnings of the grassy avenues that led elsewhere in Verrel while others sat on half-cut logs around a small fire.

Carver eyed each person thoroughly, trying to assess the threat, if any, each might pose. The people wore brown and gray wool clothing that looked plain, dirty, and well-worn. Other than a few adults with knives tied to their belts, most were not visibly armed, though Carver kept his suspicion up. They all seemed occupied either in conversation, handling the children, or struggling with the cold brought on by the wind. None of them seemed to notice his presence.

Carver felt strange observing these people. Not because he was spying but because of where he was. He felt like an intruder, sneaking around and spying on villagers in their home. But then he reminded himself that this was his village, his home, and these people were the intruders, not him. Ever since he had awoken in Leydes so many weeks ago, nearly everything about his current situation had felt wrong and backwards, but this moment struck him the hardest.

He reflected on his life and all the changes that had occurred in such a short time. He felt like he was living someone else's life, that everything that had happened to him wasn't real. Carver wished that were true and that he could find a way to return to his former life, but part of him held on and stayed tied to the reality of his situation. As much as he wanted to deny and forget, to come up with a theory to make it all better, he couldn't fool himself.

Once again lost in thought, Carver became disconnected from his goals and surroundings. He continued to peek around the corner at his village's new guests, but he no longer truly took in anything that he saw. Then something caught his eye, and his instincts sent a surge of panic through his body, pulling his attention out of its mental purgatory.

Carver suddenly realized he was staring at a child who was standing a few feet away from the adults who were sitting around the fire. The child was wearing a small, ragged brown coat along with gray wool pants and a knit wool cap. A brown scarf was also wrapped around the child's neck and mouth. The scarf made it impossible for Carver to discern the child's gender, but the more pressing matter, Carver quickly realized, was that the child was looking straight at him.

Carver ducked back behind the cottage so fast that his nose scratched against the wall. He didn't feel a thing, however, as his worry and his racing heartbeat completely suppressed the brief flash of pain.

Shit! Did he see me? Carver's mind blurted, guessing that the child was a boy. *Of course he saw me; he was looking right at me!*

Carver's instincts told him to stay still, but another part of him urged him to flee back to his horse. He did neither. Instead, he tightened his grip on the arming sword and peered back around the corner, fighting off the alarms in his mind.

Maybe he didn't see me. Maybe he's not there anymore. Maybe he—

Carver's nerves pinched as he locked eyes with the small child again.

The child hadn't moved and continued to stare straight at him, removing any doubt that Carver had been spotted. Suddenly, the child raised a hand and waved at him.

Carver pulled his head back behind cover, though not before he saw one of the adults, a brown-haired woman in brown wool clothing, notice the child waving. Carver's panic rose, and his grip on the hilt of the arming sword tightened further. He felt certain that he had only moments to act before he was caught, though what being caught would mean still escaped him. He looked to his left, far down the grassy lane toward his horse.

The fussy animal hadn't wandered too far off. Just as he was about to bolt toward it, he froze, suddenly remembering why he was there and, more importantly, what he wanted to know.

Carver pressed his back against the cottage wall again and took a deep breath as more ash trickled down on him. He remained still for a handful of seconds as he took control of his unsteady breathing. Then, after a continued struggle with his instincts, he turned and stepped out in full view of the intruders.

Carver was immediately startled by the close proximity of the woman who had seen the child waving. She was now standing only a few feet away from him, seeming to be on her way to investigate the corner. The woman was also startled, jumping back and gasping as Carver popped out from behind the charred cottage. Her eyes went wide with shock as they met his and then darted down to his sword.

The woman let out a strange, timid squeal as she stumbled back. "Gregory!" she shouted as she backpedaled away from Carver, her eyes still on his sword.

Carver did not advance toward the woman, nor did he lower his blade. He stood firm, knowing his horse was only a brief sprint away and that nothing was in the way of his retreat.

The rest of the people sitting around the fire sprang to their feet, and the ones wandering about the open area turned Carver's way. Some pulled their children close. Others retreated a handful of steps, and a few pulled out weapons; nothing more than some knives and a couple small axes, but weapons nonetheless.

"Dad, who's that?" a young voice asked.

"Hush!" a much-older voice responded.

Carver realized he should say something, but despite his best efforts, all he could manage was to stand where he was while darting his eyes amongst the armed strangers.

"Get back, Natalee," a broad-shouldered man with a thick beard ordered as he dashed up behind the woman and pulled her to the side, nearly knocking her over. He held a large knife in his right hand and had it pointed at Carver.

"Who are you, boy?"

Carver took a moment to scan his surroundings one last time, making sure no one was flanking him. Confident that he was clear of danger, at least for the moment, Carver turned his full attention toward the man.

"Where is everyone?"

The people behind and around the man looked at one another in confusion. The man, however, did not take his gaze off Carver. "What are you talking about? Who are you, and what do you want?"

"I'm nobody," Carver said, still holding his sword in a defensive stance.

Judging from the looks on the people's faces, Carver could tell that his answer was not well received, but he didn't care. Instead, he decided to seize the initiative. "Where are all the bodies?"

"Ha! The boy's a scavenger!" a different man said from the back of the small crowd, the others chuckling in response.

The man who had questioned Carver adjusted his posture and furrowed his brow, his eyes remaining locked on Carver as he did so. "You're far too late to get anything here. Them city soldiers picked this place clean after they cleared it of that rebel lot, and what's left is ours. We got here first."

Rage grew inside Carver in response to the man's words, but he tried to keep himself calm.

"Where are the bodies?" Carver asked more aggressively, despite his efforts to stay relaxed.

"Ha!" a woman's voice rang out. "This kid isn't too smart, is he?"

Another round of chuckling arose.

"Quiet, you lot!" the man barked over his shoulder. The chuckles faded away in response.

Carver began to feel incredibly nervous as he noticed the man size him up, as if estimating his chances.

"Listen here, boy," the man said in a much harsher tone than before, "if you want to pick through bones and ash, be my guest. We dragged the bodies to the south side of the village and burned them near some ruined stables. Go dig around there if you wish, but don't even think about prowling these cottages. Anything left in them is ours now. We've taken this here land as our own."

Carver felt like he had just been punched in the gut. His anger grew, but it was quickly diluted by sadness. He felt like he should say something else or inquire more, but all he wanted to do was leave the situation as quickly as possible. Not turning his back on the hostile man or the moderately armed crowd behind him, Carver backed up and then vanished behind the same cottage he had emerged from.

Carver sprinted toward his horse, but instead of mounting it immediately, he stopped and turned around to see if he was being followed.

He didn't see anyone, but he knew that could change at any moment. He didn't feel safe. The presence of children in the group had at first given him the impression that these folks might have been hospitable, despite his nervousness, but after their territorial manner and aggressive attitude, Carver was second-guessing the potential threat they posed to him. Because of this, he kept his arming sword firmly in his grasp rather than stowing it.

"Let's go," Carver said as he mounted the horse, then grabbed the reins with his left hand and squeezed his legs together, urging the horse forward.

The horse once again ignored his order, forcing Carver to wind up the reins in his left hand and give them a strong tug to the side. Only after the second yank and a strike on the side from Carver's knee did the horse give in and start to move forward, albeit slowly.

Carver guided the fussy horse north to the partially collapsed school-house, then west along the outer edge of the empty archery range, until he finally turned the horse south and guided it toward the other end of the village via the gap between the base of the hill that led to Vellum Forest and the westernmost cottages. Carver wanted to give the center of the village and the people who were camped there a wide berth.

The horse walked slowly past the ruined cottages to its left, not giving a care to anything but the rhythm of its hooves. Carver was not nearly as complacent. Each cottage that the horse brought him past only amplified his heart rate, not merely due to the sight of the burned homes and the memories they stirred up but because he dreaded seeing their end if what the man said was true.

Carver struggled to get the horse to stop, not because of the animal's persistent fussiness, but because he could barely muster the will to pull the reins or squeeze his legs together. The horse stopped regardless, perhaps sensing that something was wrong, or perhaps it was simply tired of conveying the boy who had stirred it awake in the middle of the night and forced it along through many hours of moonlit darkness. Whatever the reason, the horse stood still and calm, allowing Carver a steady, clear view of the heap of burned bodies a few dozen feet ahead of him.

Carver's own body went numb at the sight. All he could feel was the beating of his heart and the smooth wood of his sword's hilt sliding down his palm. The round iron pommel passed through his fingers, and the weapon fell from his grip before he could react. It clanged as the flat of the blade struck the horse's front right hoof.

Though harmless, the blow spooked the horse into a clumsy shuffle. Carver's reaction was too slow, and he found himself sliding awkwardly from the saddle. He hit the ground before he realized he was falling.

The pain that shot through Carver's left arm and hip was harsh and instant. It took him a moment to deal with the shock, along with the fit of coughing caused by having the wind knocked out of him.

By the time he recovered, the horse had settled itself and eyed Carver curiously from a few feet away. He wanted to smack the beast across the face for its constant faults, but he held himself back after taking a deep breath. He did, however, walk over to the beast and grab the reins so it wouldn't take off.

Adhering to Carver's command after a second tug, the horse lowered its head and stepped closer. Carver did not remount the animal, however. Instead, he bent down and scooped up his sword, then turned around and walked toward the pile of corpses, leading the horse along beside him.

As Carver got closer, he realized how sick he was feeling. The smell was revolting and made him nauseous, though not as strongly as his understanding of what he was looking at did. He fought to suppress the overbearing sickness, but it continued to rise the closer he got.

Finally, the feeling became too much to bear, stopping Carver dead in his tracks. He barely managed to stab his blade into the ground before he fell to his knees and vomited a mess of watery bile onto the grass.

Carver tipped forward and planted his hands on the ground as he vomited a second time. This time, however, nothing but a loud, coarse grunt came out, followed by a second heaving grunt and then a third. His dry heaving continued, as did the pain in his gut with each new convulsion, until he was finally able to regain control of himself. Carver leaned back on his knees and looked at the pile of bodies just a few feet in front of him.

It was a mess of skeletons, most of them charred black and veiled in gray ash, though how many bodies there were, Carver could not tell. Many of the skeletons were interlocking and mangled together. Others were missing crucial parts or broken in too many places to maintain their shape. Many were lost under the others, and some were completely buried beneath the gray ash that formed the base of the pile. A few of the skeletons still had portions of skin, muscle, and even clothing clinging to their bones, having survived the fire and not yet rotted off or been picked away by animals, though all of this too was mostly charred black and dirtied with ash.

Carver couldn't identify a single one of the bodies. All he could distinguish was which were children and which were adults based on their size, but even that was difficult due to the manner in which they were piled. Carver had no idea if the skull he was staring at belonged to his neighbor, someone he didn't know, or his own mother or father, and that was what pained him the most.

"Well, would you look at that! A sword and his own horse!"

Carver sprang to his feet and spun around, sword in hand. His horse neighed loudly, startled by his sudden movements. Carver's eyes focused on three individuals, two men and one woman, approaching from where the last southern cottages ended near the wide-open field before the ruined stables.

"Shut up! We had the drop on him, you idiot!" the woman barked at the man to her left.

"It don't matter, he's only one, and we're three."

The woman scoffed, clearly expressing what she thought on the matter.

The three of them took a few more steps forward until they stopped a good distance away from Carver. The two men looked remarkably similar in age and appearance. Both had unkempt brown hair, patchy black beards, and pale, wrinkled faces that looked weathered with age, though they couldn't have been more than twenty-five.

The woman also appeared to be in her mid-twenties, though she looked much closer to her actual age. Her skin was even paler than that of the two men, and her face was smooth and wrinkle free. Had her long blond hair not been tangled up in a ratty mess, she would have looked quite pretty, Carver noted subconsciously.

Their garb was similar to Carver's; simple wool tunics, trousers, and hide boots that offered little in the way of protection, though they were more weathered and dirtier than his own. Also similar to Carver, they were all armed. The woman held an iron-headed woodsman's axe with an arm's-length wooden haft while the man to her right removed a sword, only a few inches shorter than Carver's, from its sheath. The man to the woman's left appeared to be the least equipped. He was holding a wooden club that seemed to be a singed table leg with a cluster of bent and broken nails poking out from the top.

"Alright, kid," the man with the sword said. His beard was slightly thicker than the other's. "Drop the sword and walk away from the horse. We don't want to hurt you."

"But we will if you don't listen," the woman spat.

Carver's horse seemed to feel the threatening energy of the strangers and began whining and shifting in place. Carver looked at the horse but had no way of comforting it, so instead he ignored the animal and looked back at the three individuals.

"Go away or I'll kill you," Carver said, blunt and aggressive, almost without thinking as he raised his weapon and angled it toward the new threat.

All three of the strangers looked slightly surprised by Carver's response, but then they looked at one another and began laughing.

"You really are that bleedin' stupid!" the man with the club said between laughs. "First you come to loot a spot that's two months old, then you go to pick through a literal pile of bones and ash, and now you think you can threaten us off by yourself? Oh! It's so pathetic it's almost sad!"

The man with the sword finally quieted his laughter. "Look, kid, this is real, okay? We're serious. Drop the weapon and piss off outta here."

Carver thought hard and fast about his options, but with all the grief and anger swirling through his mind, only one option made sense to him.

"Go away," Carver took a short breath, "or I'll kill you."

None of them laughed this time.

The two men looked at each other and nodded, though what was communicated, Carver could not discern.

"Well, you heard him," the woman said. "Let's kill the foolish brat."

The two men looked at the woman between them.

"You sure you want to kill him?" the man with the sword whispered, though Carver still managed to hear his words. It gave Carver a small boost of confidence to know that at least one of them seemed hesitant to act.

The woman eyed Carver intently. "There's no soldiers around here. We have nothing to worry about."

"What if he ain't alone? He isn't acting like he's alone. Someone of his might be watching us," the man with the club said.

"Enough!" the woman shouted, her eyes still locked with Carver's. "By Agon's wrath, you two are pathetic. He's obviously by himself, and there ain't a soldier patrol for miles. Now help me gut the whelp, or neither of you will get between my legs ever again."

With that, the two men looked at each other once again, nodded, then turned toward Carver. The three of them moved forward. The woman advanced in a straight line while the men branched off in wide arcs toward Carver's flanks.

Carver remained where he stood, snapping his eyes from person to person as they came closer. He felt like he should say something else, threaten them or warn them one last time, but he found himself holding back, almost wanting them to keep coming.

The fear he felt before was gone, replaced with a calm sense of focus. All his anxiety and hesitation seemed to slip away despite the gravity of his situation. Instead of panic, he was focused. Instead of doubt, he felt clarity. And instead of fear holding him back, he felt an insatiable rage urging him toward violence.

The man with the club was now directly to Carver's left, and the other man was to his right. The woman remained in front of Carver and continued to creep closer, her axe now held firmly in her pale, slender hands.

Carver's horse let out a series of uncomfortable whines and grunts and began to back away from Carver and the three strangers, who approached him from three of four sides. Carver's back was protected by the mound of bones and ash that still assaulted his nostrils with the scent of death and rot. The smell no longer added to his emotional sickness, though. Now it only reminded him of what filled him with hate for the world, a hate that gave him a surge of newfound energy.

Carver noted the men's positions as they finally stepped beyond his peripheral vision. Keeping his eyes on the woman and his ears on the men, Carver tightened his grip on his sword and took a deep breath through his nose. Cool air filled his lungs until he couldn't hold any more. Then, as he calmly exhaled through his nose, he closed his eyes and thought about the soldiers who had murdered his family.

Immediately, Carver heard the crunching sound of quickening boots to his left. He opened his eyes and half turned to face the approaching attacker, bringing his blade up.

The man with the club stopped dead in his tracks only a few feet from Carver. His face flushed with shock, but then he smiled as his eyes looked past Carver's shoulder. Carver knew exactly what gave the man such confidence, and he spun around to face it.

The man with the sword was already within striking distance of Carver, swinging his weapon toward Carver's head. The angle and haste with which the man swung his blade left Carver no time to block, but he didn't need to. He merely lowered his right shoulder and leapt to the left. The man's blade cut through nothing but air as Carver turned to face the man's right side.

Before the man could react, Carver was slicing his blade up through the man's unprotected right arm. Both of them let out a cry—Carver's due to rage and the man's due to pain.

The man leaped instinctively away from Carver without looking to see what was near, causing him to stumble and crash into the pile of death just behind him. Skeletons smashed together as the man collided with them, creating a symphony of sickening clunks and cracks as bones shifted and snapped under his weight, though the sounds of clattering bones did little to muffle the shouts of the man himself. Dropping his blade and clutching just below his right shoulder with his left hand, the man let out a series of horrid wails. Dark blood erupted through his fingers and flowed down his arm.

"Oh, shit! No! Help me!"

Carver wanted to lunge forward and finish the man off, but he had other things to worry about.

He turned away from the man to face the ratty-haired woman, who was nearly upon him. She let out an angry shout as she prepared to swing. Carver had just enough time to raise his sword in defense. He turned his sword horizontal and tensed his muscles as the woman's axe plummeted down and smashed against his bloody blade. The impact sent a loud ring of metal into the air. The head of the woman's axe slid up and jutted over Carver's blade as he struggled to hold his ground.

"I can't move my arm! I'm dying!" the wounded man cried. Carver felt an urge to look at him, but he kept his focus entirely on his struggle with the woman.

They contested for control of the situation, each pushing and angling their weapons in the hope of breaking past their opponent's guard and opening up for a killing strike. Then the man with the club appeared behind her. He smiled widely as he wound up for a swing that was aimed for Carver's exposed left side.

Carver realized the woman was not trying to overtake him, as he thought, but was actually holding him in place for her ally's strike. He quickly shifted his right leg behind him for more balance and then lifted his left leg and kicked his heel as hard as he could into the woman's right knee.

The woman shrieked as her right knee buckled. Carver pushed as hard as he could, forcing the woman to divert all her weight onto that same leg. She slipped and fell over backwards.

With the woman out of the way, albeit for what would only be a moment, Carver turned to face the second man, raising his blade. It connected with the table leg, deflecting it off course.

As he knocked his assailant's weapon aside, Carver realized his own legs had not yet caught up with his quick spin. He attempted to step back, finish his spin, and line up his feet to stabilize, but instead he stumbled backwards, struggling to regain his balance.

Carver's attacker saw his vulnerable state and tried to seize the opportunity, releasing his own weapon, which fell to the ground beside him.

Realizing what the man was attempting, Carver tried desperately to regain his footing and raise his blade, but the man was too quick. He dove at Carver, grabbing him by the neck with both hands.

They crashed to the ground. Carver's head smacked hard against the ground. Though it was only grass and dirt, the pain that erupted across the back of his head made it feel like he was striking solid stone. The surge of pain forced his eyes shut.

Carver suddenly wondered if this was it, if this was where he would die. He also realized that should his head hitting the ground trigger another seizure, he would be unable to defend himself and would surely die.

All within the same second, the back of his head filling with a cloudy pain, Carver felt the man's hands tighten around his neck, followed by a warm liquid splashing onto his face. Carver opened his eyes and saw that the man was staring down at him, his eyes wide with shock and his mouth splattered with blood, which was now covering the better part of Carver's face.

"No!" the woman screamed.

The man continued to stare down at Carver for a moment. Then he let out a sickening groan as fresh blood spilled out of his mouth and onto Carver's chin and chest.

Carver's head was still throbbing, but it didn't seem to be sending him into a seizure as he had feared. He raised his head slightly and looked down toward his feet. There he saw the cause of his attacker's state and the reason for the woman's scream.

Held firmly above his stomach with both hands was the hilt of his sword, the hilt angled toward the sky. Carver could only see a fraction of the blade as the rest was hidden within the stomach of the man on top of him.

The man let out another groan, followed by a third burst of blood from his mouth. This time, however, his grip loosened around Carver's neck.

Mustering his strength and fighting to ignore the pain in his head, Carver pushed the hilt of his sword up, sending what remained of the blade farther into the man's gut and twisting it for good measure. The man would have screamed if he were not vomiting up blood.

The next splatter of blood that covered Carver's chest was also the last as he heaved the man to the side. The man slumped to the ground.

Now free from his assailant, Carver had a full view of his surroundings.

The first man was still lying against the pile of corpses, clutching his upper arm. The blood continued to flow at a substantial rate, draining into the grass. His wailing had ceased, replaced by a fit of quick, short breaths as his face turned pale. He made no indication of rejoining the fight.

The woman, on the other hand, was quite the opposite. Her face was red with emotion as she charged toward Carver.

Still on his back, Carver released the hilt of his sword, which was still embedded in the man's gut to his right, and scrambled backwards, but the woman reached him almost immediately. With a hateful roar, she hopped over her dying ally and swung her axe at Carver's legs.

Carver rolled to the left and heard a thump as the woman's axe hit the ground. As she raised it for another strike, Carver rolled out of the way again. This time when she swung, the thud he heard was much closer to his head.

Not wishing to try his luck a third time, Carver reversed his roll and reached blindly toward where he had heard the last thud. His hands met the round wood of the weapon's shaft, and he grabbed it as the woman made to pull the axe out of the dirt. Carver pulled as hard as he could from his prone position.

The woman's face twisted with rage as she struggled against him. Her hateful expression distracted him from seeing the kick she sent into his stomach. The sudden shock of the blow nearly forced Carver to release the axe, but his adrenaline kept him from doing so.

The second kick Carver did see coming, and he managed to tense his muscles in preparation for the impact. Though less powerful than before, the kick sent a spike of pain into his gut.

Carver held onto the wooden shaft with all the strength he could muster, but he could feel it slipping from his grasp. He knew that he couldn't win the struggle from his angle, and the sight of the woman winding up a third kick told him he needed to think of something fast.

Carver tried to rotate his body and put his legs between himself and her, but his quivering arms could not manage the extra distance caused by the movement. Instead, he used every last morsel of his strength to pull the axe down toward himself. The axe lowered a few inches in Carver's favor, but the victory was short-lived. The woman's boot struck him once again, this time hitting his side.

Pain exploded throughout Carver's lower-right ribs as the woman's boot connected. He felt the last of his energy begin to fade as the shaft of the axe began to rise away from him. In a last desperate act, Carver surrendered to the pull and allowed the woman to haul her weapon up. Rather than letting go, however, he held on and arched his back upwards as the woman pulled not just her axe from the ground but Carver as well.

When she had dragged him almost into a sitting position, Carver released his grip on the weapon and wrapped his hand around the woman's left wrist.

Before she could react, he clamped his jaw around the second knuckles of her left hand.

Shrieking in pain, the woman released the weapon and tried to pull her fingers back. She was too late, however. As her fingers straightened and pulled away, Carver bit down hard and trapped them inside his mouth. The woman howled in pain as his teeth tore through skin and ripped apart ligaments.

With a horrid cry of agony, the woman sent another desperate kick into Carver's stomach. The blow turned Carver's jaw into a vise as his gut twisted in pain and breath exploded between his teeth. The woman let out another scream as she suddenly became free of Carver and stumbled backwards, falling to the ground.

Carver fell back as well, returning to his prone state. His insides felt like they were on fire, and he could barely feel his elbows after so much strain. His bodily grief was suddenly interrupted as he felt something large hit the back of his throat, sending him into a fit of choking. Carver rolled to his side and erupted into a series of wet gags and coughs.

His eyes widened when he saw two fingers fly from his mouth and land in the grass along with a spray of dark blood.

Carver suddenly heard a much more potent scream from the woman. Her screams continued as he painfully and hastily got to his knees while struggling to stop coughing.

Once Carver was stabilized, he saw that the woman was on the ground a few feet away. She was writhing erratically and holding her left hand. At that same moment, Carver also realized he was holding her axe upside down in his left hand.

Seeing his chance, Carver pushed himself to his feet and transferred the axe to his right hand while looking around for any approaching danger.

The man with the sword was quiet and motionless, blood still gushing from his upper-right arm. The other man had likewise gone completely still, his eyes wide in a blank stare toward the sky and his mouth splattered with blood. All that still moved was the ratty-haired woman, who was slowly getting to her knees amidst her wailing.

Carver didn't wait a second more. The woman rose to her knees, still cupping her left hand, and rotated around just in time to witness Carver charging toward her. Her eyes went wide in horror as he raised the axe.

"No, please! Wait! Wai—"

Silence filled the air.

Carver felt as if time had stopped, like he was frozen in the moment. Neither he nor the woman moved a muscle. His adrenaline faded, his pain became lost, his breathing calmed, and his rapid thoughts came to a stop. Everything became second to the shock of relief that held his senses in place. He heard nothing but the wind around him, felt only the axe's wooden shaft in his hands, and saw nothing but the woman's face below him.

Her mouth hung open, and her eyes stared, her expression that of a brain-dead sheep.

Carver released his hold on the axe as the first streaks of dark red ran down the woman's face. Her lips barely managed a quiver before she slumped to the ground, taking the axe embedded in her forehead down with her.

Carver looked away from her lifeless body as the passing of time returned to his senses. The chilly wind picked up, causing him to shiver, and the pain in his head, stomach, and side returned to his attention. Carver fell to the grass, landing hard on his rear. He wrapped an arm around his gut and side in an attempt to suppress the pain, but he achieved no such effect. The pain swirling around the back of his head was intense, but it was manageable.

Cold, alone, and in pain, Carver sat in the field that had once been the stable area of his village, now surrounded by even more death.

"Are you dying?" a young boy's voice called out from afar.

The sound startled Carver. He looked up but remained sitting on the grass, with his left arm wrapped around his gut and right side. He saw no one at first, just the body of the woman and the ruined cottages farther off to the north.

"Did they get you?" the young voice sounded again.

This time Carver homed in on the voice's direction. What he saw was the eyes of a young child in a knit cap spying on him from around the corner of a house. The child looked familiar, though he wasn't immediately sure why.

It wasn't until a moment later, when the child stepped out from behind the house, revealing his scarf-covered face, that Carver realized it was the same one who had spotted him earlier. The young boy's eyes expressed nervousness, and his hands fidgeted together, but he stood his ground and continued to look straight at Carver.

It took Carver a moment to realize the boy was waiting for him to respond.

"No," Carver coughed out. "I'm not dying."

The boy continued to stare at him. Carver was unsure what was going on, and he felt uneasy. He broke his stare with the boy and turned his head from side to side, looking to see if anyone else was watching. He saw no one else, though, just the burned cottages and green hills that surrounded him.

"That was amazing."

"What?" Carver asked, turning his head back toward the boy.

"I watched the whole thing. You were amazing! How do you fight so good?" the boy asked as he pulled his scarf down to speak more clearly, also revealing that his nervous face was glowing with excitement.

Carver wasn't sure what to say. The whole situation felt so strange, and his pain was taking up most of his attention. "Are you by yourself?"

"Yeah. We all saw those three come this way after you disappeared, but no one wanted to get involved. Papa said they would do what they would, and if they died it'd be less mouths to feed. I didn't understand, so I snuck away and followed them to watch. I get what Papa meant now. I'm glad you killed Thomas. He ate so much." The boy pointed to the impaled man's corpse.

Carver was surprised by how the boy so quickly and openly told him the information. He spoke with such carelessness and pride that Carver knew he was telling the truth. He felt a great calm wash over him with the knowledge that the boy was alone and that he wasn't about to be ambushed, with the child acting as some kind of distraction.

"How do you fight so good?" the boy asked again.

The compliment within the question made Carver grin slightly. "My village taught me, and my parents." His grin vanished as he completed his answer.

"What village are you from?"

Carver thought for a moment about how to respond. The pain in his head was beginning to fade, allowing him to focus more clearly on his thoughts and situation.

"I'm from here."

"This one?"

"Yeah, this one."

Carver pushed himself to his feet. The pain in his gut had leveled out to a manageable level as long as he refrained from leaning or applying pressure to the muscles.

"Papa said that soldiers came and killed everyone here, even the kids like me. That's all of them in that pile." The boy pointed to the heap of corpses behind Carver.

Carver didn't turn to look. Instead, he walked over to the man whom the boy had referred to as Thomas and bent down. The ache in his body flared as he did so, but he didn't let it stop him. He wrapped his hands around the hilt jutting out from the man's stomach and placed a foot on his chest. A heavy spray of blood burst forth from the man's stomach as Carver pulled the blade out.

"Are you a Ashi'zaton?"

"What?" Carver turned away from Thomas and faced the boy.

"Papa said the city's soldier boss gave a speech about how the people here were Ashi—uh ... Ashi'zaton. The same ones who attacked a market."

Carver felt a return of anger inside as the boy spoke so casually about the situation that had destroyed his life. "The person who said that is wrong. Whoever he is, he—"

"The boss of the soldiers is a girl. People call her lots of names for some reason. Aellia, Marshal, and Cap—"

"It doesn't matter! It's not true. We had nothing to do with the Aethi'ziton." Carver emphasized the name to correct the boy's pronunciation. "I was at the market when it was attacked. I saw who attacked too; they were people from Caswen, not from Verrel."

The boy did not seem bothered by the sudden harshness of Carver's tone. Instead, his eyes filled with interest.

"Whoa! How did you get away?"

"I killed the people who tried to kill me. And then I ran."

"What about here? How did you get away from here?"

"The same way. Except ..." Carver's voice trailed off as he became fixed in thought. "I didn't run ... I ... I didn't get away ... Helena. She ..."

"Who's Helena?"

"She ..."

Carver suddenly closed his mouth and shook his head, clearing his thoughts while also accidentally adding to the pain in his head. He squinted and palmed the side of his head with his free hand, the other holding the dripping sword.

"Is she from here too?"

"Enough!" Carver barked, letting the pain in his head influence his words.

The boy took a step back.

Carver felt bad for frightening the boy, so he took a deep breath and gently rubbed the back of his head. "Sorry. Look, don't worry about it, okay? Or me, for that matter."

The boy eased slightly. He looked like he wanted to ask another question, or several, but he remained silent, his eyes fixed on Carver.

The young boy's silent stare began to frustrate Carver. He wasn't sure what to say next and ended up just standing and staring at the child. The moment of awkward silence dragged on until Carver realized he didn't care any longer. Without a word, he turned away from the boy and lowered himself to his knees adjacent to Thomas's body, then began rifling through the dead man's pockets.

Carver was met with disappointment when he found nothing but fresh blood. He grabbed his sword and stood up, realizing now his hands were completely stained in blood. He began to wipe one of them on his trousers, but in doing so noticed they were already sprayed in blood, as was the front of his tunic. After giving himself a quick look over, Carver realized that much of his attire was stained in sprays and splashes of red.

"It's on your face too."

Carver looked over at the boy for a moment, then wiped the back of his right arm across his cheek, creating a fresh red smear down his arm as a result. Carver looked back down at his gory clothing. He knew he couldn't be seen like that, that any soldiers would arrest him the moment they saw his blood-splattered face and clothing.

He looked down at Thomas's body and eyed his clothing. It was just as bloody and in no better condition than Carver's, worse even with the hole going through the front and back of the tunic.

Carver let out a sigh as he turned away from Thomas and walked over to the man near the corpse pile. The man was no longer gripping his slashed arm, which allowed Carver to see how effective his initial strike had been. The man's arm was nearly severed. The intense bleeding had slowed, but the damage was done. His front was soaked in the blood he had tried to staunch. The red ran down his body, trailed across his legs, and soaked into the ground.

Realizing those clothes were also too far gone to be of use, Carver searched through the man's pockets but once again found nothing.

"Whoa! That scar! What happened to your head?"

Carver cringed at the boy's outburst, realizing it was probably going to be the first of many identical occurrences. He turned to face the boy and saw that his face was equal parts fascination and disgust, both of which made Carver angry.

"It's nothing. I got hurt. Nothing to talk about."

The boy picked up on Carver's mood and refrained from inquiring further.

Carver sighed again as he looked away from the boy. He brought his gaze to the last body, the woman who was now a dozen feet away, and examined the condition of her clothing as he walked over to her resting place. He was met with some relief once he saw how little the woman's attire suffered from the fight. Her bloodiest parts were her hands and face. The rest of her appeared quite untouched.

Carver thought for a moment about his options. Then he came to a realization. He remembered one of the first things the boy had divulged to him: that he had snuck away from his father and the group. While at first Carver had been thrilled by the information, knowing that it meant the boy was not being followed by the rest of the group, he realized that someone would soon notice the child's absence and start looking for him.

With this in mind, Carver ended his mental calculations and set forth acting on them. He took a quick breath and stabbed his sword firmly into the ground beside the woman. He heard a quick gasp come from the boy, who perhaps thought he was going to stab the woman's corpse. Then Carver dropped to his knees, wiped his bloody hands as best as he could over the wet grass, and began tugging at the woman's clothes.

"What are you doing?"

Carver ignored the boy and focused on his grisly task. It was difficult and awkward, but he managed to get both of the woman's limp arms through the sleeve holes before he shifted his body around her head. He tugged the tunic toward himself. He felt resistance, then heard a tear.

Carver looked to see what tore and instantly saw the problem. The axe embedded in the woman's face was holding the tunic's neckline in place. In his haste, he had entirely forgotten the axe was there.

Carver felt foolish for such an oversight, but he didn't let it stop him for long. He stood up, placed a booted foot over the left half of her face, then grabbed the axe handle and heaved. He heard a loud, suction-like pop as the axe head came free of the woman's forehead.

Carver stumbled back due to momentum and then tossed the weapon aside and knelt by the woman's head. Blood was flowing heavily from the large crevasse separating her eyes. It poured over her ears and hair as Carver quickly tilted her head back to prevent any more from staining the tunic.

Lifting her upper back with one hand and pulling the tunic with the other, Carver wrestled the dirty garb over the woman's head and past her shoulders.

"What are ... Are you—"

"No! I just need her clothes. Nothing more!" Carver barked at the boy while removing his own tunic and replacing it with the woman's.

The new tunic, which was standard peasant garb, fit him well enough, though it was a little tight. Carver rolled his shoulders in adjustment and then stepped over to the woman's feet. He pulled her boots off with little effort before unfastening her thin and nearly ruined belt.

Despite his intentions and rationale, Carver was beginning to feel uncomfortable as he yanked the woman's trousers farther and farther down her legs. He tried to remind himself that he needed the clothes for practical reasons, that this woman tried to kill him, and that she was not his first choice for stripping down. His reasoning only did a little to help him banish the feeling of wrongness.

With one last heave, the trousers passed over the woman's pale feet, her hoisted-up legs falling to the ground as Carver released them. He did his best not to look at the woman as he kicked off his boots and unfastened his own belt, but he couldn't help his eyes from wandering.

Her body was thin and lined with curves, though the visible protrusion of ribs through her pale skin indicated her slim figure was not a healthy one. A stained layer of brown, bandage-like wrappings covered her breasts.

Carver bit his tongue and looked away before his eyes could wander any lower, turning his attention fully to switching his trousers. Just like the tunic, the new trousers fit fine enough and gave no indication that they were weaved for a specific sex. Once he had the trousers on, Carver felt around in the pockets after realizing he had not checked them and was surprised to feel something both soft and hard in the left one. Carver pulled the object out and saw that it was a brown pouch that clinked from within. He untied the string that kept the pouch closed and poured out its contents.

Three iron-framed coins rolled out onto his palm. Two were entirely filled with ten thin triangular copper shards each, while one was mostly an empty frame and held only two copper shards. Carver dropped them back into the pouch, then shoved it into his pocket. Then he started to fasten his new trousers with his original belt.

"Is that all you're taking?"

Carver pinched his finger under the belt buckle as he looked up and saw that the boy had gotten closer and was staring at the woman's nearly naked body. He looked as if he were disappointed. Carver was shocked as he understood what the boy seemed to be eagerly anticipating.

"You're sick, kid," Carver said as he put on his boots.

The boy looked genuinely surprised by Carver's remark. "I ..."

Carver picked up his sword and turned away before the boy could find his words, though in doing so Carver found himself facing the pile of burned corpses once again. The sight struck him with just as much impact as it had before, causing his stomach to twist and churn in sickening grief.

Carver saw that Duncan's horse had retreated a fair way behind the heap during the fight and was now meandering about. His instincts urged him to get to the animal and ride fast and far away, but he had one thing left to do before he left.

Lowering his eyes to view as little of it as he could, Carver walked over to the pile of death once again. He stopped in front of the newest addition to the pile and reached down toward the scabbard strapped to his belt. A few buckles and knots were all that resisted, and in no time at all, Carver had the scabbard attached firmly to his own belt.

After testing the scabbard's fitting with a few twists and stretches, Carver took up his arming sword and made to sheath it. He was met with failure, however, when his blade stopped before it was fully sheathed.

Pulling the blade out with a grunt of frustration, Carver searched the ground until he spotted the man's sword lying next to its owner. Carver grabbed it and then wiped the blade over the man's shoulder, leaving behind as much of the man's blood as possible before sliding the new weapon into the sheath.

Carver noted that the new sword's hilt was different from his own. The iron tang was partially exposed underneath the dark leather wrappings that encased it, and the pommel was not weighted properly. Both these features gave the sword a less comfortable grip and weight than Carver's own sword, which had a properly weighted pommel and a sanded wooden grip that fully encased the tang.

With the shorter blade sheathed and his own sword in hand, Carver took another deep breath and then walked a wide berth around his family and fellow villagers.

The horse shied away as Carver approached but did not continue once Carver grasped its reins.

Carver mounted the disinterested horse while keeping his blade in one hand. That and the new weight of the sheathed sword made it awkward to do, but he settled in the saddle well enough.

He looked back the way he had come and saw that the young boy was still staring at the woman's body.

"Hey."

The boy snapped his attention toward Carver.

"If you're curious, my name's Bran. I'm heading to Quinredal, to the west. Bye."

Carver immediately turned his horse west toward the large hill with Vellum Forest at its top. With a soft kick, he commanded the horse to climb the hill. When he reached the top, he had to give a second light kick with his heels to issue the beast into the arms of the forest itself.

"You're not supposed to ride a horse through the woods!" Carver heard the boy shout.

Carver didn't indicate that he had heard the boy's warning and focused on guiding his horse into the trees. After allowing the horse to take a few steps into the woods, Carver pulled gently on the reins. The horse stopped, then at Carver's next calm pull, slowly turned itself around.

Carver slid off the horse and walked back to the tree line. He pressed himself up against one of the last trees before the hill and peered around its girth. Far below, the boy was still there, staring up at the forest. He seemed to be scanning the tree line, but the expression on his face was lost to Carver due to the distance.

Carver waited until the boy stopped scanning the trees and turned back toward the woman.

Get out of here, you brat! Carver shouted in his head.

He started to think he might be stuck there for a while, or at least until it was too late, but after a painfully long minute, the boy turned away from the woman and ran back into the village.

Carver waited a few more seconds, then ran back to the horse and climbed up into the saddle so fast that he almost dropped his arming sword.

The instant he found his balance in the saddle, he squeezed his legs together and commanded the animal toward the tree line.

Before the horse's rear had even left the shade of the trees, Carver tried to order the animal into a gallop down the hill, despite the danger that provided. The horse disobeyed him, feeling unsafe, and only descended the steep hill at a pace it was comfortable with. Once it reached the bottom however, Carver successfully got the beast into a gallop.

The sight of his fight quickly passed from his view, as did the outer cottages of Verrel behind a series of low hills. Carver tightened his hold on the reins and steered the horse southeast.

His senses each locked on a single thing as the horse carried him away: the feeling of cold wind whipping against his face, the sound of hooves stamping into dirt, the taste of blood in his mouth, the smell of it on his hands, and the sight of blurred green blotches as each hill passed.

After a few minutes at breakneck speed, Carver brought the horse to a light canter, then slowed to a brisk trot. He could tell the horse was tired and in need of a break after such harsh exertion. The animal's head hung slightly lower than normal, and its breathing sounded heavy.

"Soon, boy. Just another few minutes. I'm sorry."

The horse made no indication of understanding, merely continuing at a diminishing pace.

Carver looked back. All he could see was countless hills that obscured the husk of Verrel. He felt confident that his attempt at misdirection would work, but he was still nervous. He banished his lingering fears, though, and focused on the path ahead.

A couple of minutes later, a massive lake came into view from over the hills.

"There we go."

The horse, now slowed to a walk, made its way down the last hill toward the lake without protest. Carver scanned the immediate area for signs of danger. He didn't see any people or animals, but he knew that could change shortly.

Keeping his eyes open, Carver led the horse to the lake's edge and dismounted. The horse immediately walked forward and began drinking the cold water. Carver likewise walked up to the water's edge, but he did not drink. He dropped his sword to the grass beside him and sat down. His descent stopped halfway down as the tip of his new sword and scabbard hit the ground first and jabbed the weapon's hilt into his hip. Before Carver could catch himself, he stumbled over toward the horse and fell awkwardly onto his rear. The horse seemed not to notice his clumsy descent and kept on drinking from the lake.

Carver burned with frustration at his mishap but then thought about how if Helena had seen it, she would've laughed hysterically. Carver wasn't sure why he suddenly thought of Helena, but the image of her teasing him made him smile and almost chuckle to himself.

A moment later, though, his thoughts of Helena turned sour. He realized that by now she was probably awake and had noticed his absence. He knew what his departure would do to her, and the thought of it made him feel sick. He tried to stop thinking about it by focusing on his next task.

Minding his new weapon, Carver scooted to the water and leaned forward. His reflection in the water's surface made him wince. His face and neck were caked in blood, as were his hands and lower arms. He plunged his hands into the water and started scrubbing them. The water began to discolor as his hands slowly returned to their normal pale appearance. Once they were mostly clean, Carver moved to a new area of untainted water, cupped his hands together, and scrubbed his face. Looking back into the lake, Carver saw that his face and neck were no longer red, but that his hands were once again. A final scrub under the water, now up to his elbows, removed the last of the blood from his skin. What little amounts of red still stained his new clothes were diluted after a series of dips and rubs from his wet fingers.

When he was done, Carver sat back and reached for his arming sword. It too was a mess, splattered in blood from tip to pommel. Carver submerged it beneath the water and wiped his hand along the flat sides of the blade.

As he attended to the sword, he found that his efforts to stop thinking about Helena were failing. The image of her distraught and panicking over his disappearance was all he could see. The thought made it hard for him to rationalize his actions.

Feeling regret, sadness, and self-hatred, Carver lost his focus on cleaning the arming sword.

"Ahh!" Carver cried as he suddenly felt a sharp pain surface across his fingers. He pulled his hand out of the water so fast the splash hit his nose. Looking down at his right hand, he saw a fresh cut across his index and middle fingers. A light stream of bright blood ran over his palm, dripping into the water.

"Shit."

Carver dunked his hand back into the water and swished it around, letting the water deal with the fresh blood, then pulled the sword from the water and placed it beside him. After a few moments of waiting for the stinging and bleeding to stop, while also feeling quite foolish, he wiped his wet fingers on his tunic and stood up.

"I guess I shouldn't waste any more time here anyway," he said to the horse, which was now standing a few feet away.

Before mounting the horse, he placed his arming sword back between the saddle and the harness, which he used to tie the blade firmly in place. After he was finished, content with his appearance and his equipment, Carver mounted the horse and issued it into a relaxed trot and headed east along the lake's northern edge.

Chapter 28

◦~◯✓~

"It's half a copper sol per day," the man told Carver.

"What? Five shards for just one day?"

"Uh-hm, or a single silver shard for two," the man confirmed as he placed his elbows on the wooden counter between him and Carver. The man was quite thin and had a thick brown beard that grew up his cheeks into his messy mop of light-brown hair.

"All you're doing is keeping my horse in your stable. You don't need half a copper absol to do that," Carver said in a frustrated tone.

"All I'm doing is keeping it here? A horse is not a wagon, boy. It doesn't just take up room. Horses eat, shit, and need space to move. Who do you think feeds them and shovels the shit? I don't, but my workers do, and not for free either. Besides, this is a business, lad. If you don't agree with my prices, then by all means, leave your horse somewhere else."

The man leaned over the counter. The old wood creaked in a way that seemed to travel up the wooden beams on its sides and into the ceiling of the semi-outdoor stable office. "But I'll tell you what: you won't find a cheaper rate inside the city's walls. And if you don't leave your beast in a stable, between all the thugs and Lost Seekers skulking around here, you definitely won't find it when you return."

Carver frowned. "Well, what does one day mean? Will you boot my horse out once night hits or the next morning?"

"One day means till noon the next day. But I won't boot the animal out. If you don't show by an hour past noon, it won't be your horse anymore; it'll be mine."

Carver's frustration deepened at how the man spoke to him; he was feeling like the man was trying to sound unfair. Carver wanted to debate further, but he knew it probably wasn't going to get him anywhere. Instead, he pulled out the small pouch of absol coins and quickly recounted the amount in his head.

Two full copper absols, so twenty shards, and then two extra shards. Twenty-two copper shards worth of absols.

Carver tied the pouch shut and put it back in his pocket without removing any of its contents, then turned around to his horse, which was standing calmly behind him. Carver unbuckled the arming sword and then turned back to the stablemaster.

"What about this?"

The stablemaster's eyes widened with surprise as the blade clanged atop the wooden counter. "Well, would you look at that, a horse and two swords." His eyes glanced from the arming sword on his counter to the shorter arming sword sheathed to Carver's belt.

"You're quite well armed for someone your age. What are you doing here anyway, alone with two swords?"

"I'm here to visit some people."

The man ran his right hand along the face of the blade, then examined the smooth wooden hilt and touched the iron pommel. "This sword is fine quality. With what I might be able to trade it for, hmm ... I'll tell you what: this'll get you a week. Plenty of time to visit whoever you'd like in this fair city. And if you throw in two copper shards, we'll give your beast a decent grooming."

Carver thought for a moment, wanting to make his money stretch as far as it could, then shook his head. "No. Just the week will do for now."

"Then that's what you'll get. Your horse will be safe and tended to while it's here, but remember, if you're not here an hour past noon exactly seven days from now, don't bother coming back."

"Yeah, I got it."

Carver turned and made to exit the stablemaster's office.

"Hold on a minute, young man."

Carver turned back, a pang of worry shooting through him.

"What's your name, and the beast's, for that matter? I need to write down who's picking up which animal."

"My name is Bran. And the horse is named ... Thomas."

"Well, alright, Mr. Bran. Thomas will be waiting for you here. Don't be late."

Carver nodded, then turned and walked past the wooden beams that held up the slanted thatch roof of the stablemaster's outdoor office.

As he followed the dirt path around the stable, he heard his horse neigh and snort. When he looked back, he saw two men guiding the horse through a large door leading into the stable proper. Carver turned away and continued on his way.

After a minute of walking, the path branched into three directions. The path forward, to the north, led into an expansive system of wooden cottages and, every so often, a small brick structure. To the left, heading west, the path led to a similar sight, though Carver could see the beginning of the Vellum Hills farther beyond the roofs of the numerous small buildings. To the right, east, the road passed by some cottages and shops, and at its end was a low stone bridge. Beyond that loomed the high stone walls that surrounded the city of Caswen.

Carver stood at the crossroads, turning over the many possibilities in his mind as well as his actions and the events that led him here, and he tried to banish the dark thoughts that aggressed his emotions. Finally, he took a short breath of cool air and turned down the east path straight toward Caswen.

✠　✠　✠

The bright sun was beginning to fade from view behind the city's high stone walls and tall towers. Wide shadows stretched across the cobblestone streets and filled the tight alleys between the many wood, brick, and stone buildings. Evening was approaching, and with it, Carver's heart began to pound in his chest. He tried to distract himself by continually walking through the streets, turning down random avenues, and staring at people's feet as they passed. It did little to quell his anxiousness, but he had no other ideas at the moment.

The air was getting colder as the sun's light and warmth struggled to pass over the city's stone walls. Carver shivered as a gust of wind swept over his arms and neck. He heard voices all around him. They came from up high on tower balconies, from around the corners of houses, and from the handfuls of human and goblin pedestrians who filled the street. The constant commotion of the city felt strange to him after having spent the last few weeks in such silence and solace.

In his efforts to ignore and block out the strangeness he felt, along with his lingering thoughts on what made him so nervous, Carver did not pick up on the fact that the voices around him were steadily increasing in number. With his eyes on the street and his hands in his trouser pockets, he continued to walk without a true destination.

His brow perked in confusion when he noticed the cobblestone street suddenly widen into a massive, round courtyard. His stressing heart and wandering thoughts were blanketed in silence as he looked up and found himself standing in one of the four openings to the city's main market.

Goblin and human citizens strolled about the area in great abundance, going from one merchant's stall to the other. Some carried their purchases in small crates, others in animal-hide bags, and others in small wagons pulled by goats or small horses.

Carver felt his legs trying to lead him somewhere else, but he stopped his impulse and remained still, staring into the hive of commerce with his hands in his pockets and trying to discern what it was his mind was telling him to do. His thoughts crawled back to his last experience there and how its horror followed him back home. This place was the beginning of his dramatically changed life, and that fact caused Carver to freeze on the market's perimeter, staring into it like a child looking at some monstrous creature.

The sight and sounds of the market seemed mostly unchanged, the only difference being that he could see shallow craters scattered around the cobblestone ground, some being quite small while others were a few feet wide. The adults walked around the craters while groups of children hopped in and out of some like it was a game.

Carver's skin began to cool even more as his lack of movement allowed the chilly air to hold him tightly. The discomfort the wind brought helped Carver make his decision faster, and before he knew it, he was stepping farther into the busy market courtyard.

The sun's light continued to withdraw from the market, and many of the stall owners began to pack up their wares. The crowds within each ring of stalls started to thin out as well. The chatter died down to an ignorable amount, and the merchants who remained vigilant behind their stalls beckoned the remaining customers over, trying to get what little extra business they could before the sun disappeared behind the city walls.

Carver ignored the calls and gestures from the remaining merchants who saw him wandering about alone. He kept to himself and only wandered near the stalls, never actually approaching any specific one. All of what he saw was disheartening. Like the last time, everything looked old and worn, even the food. The merchants didn't look much better, nor did their customers. Those selling looked stressed and frustrated, while those buying showed desperate eyes and sad expressions.

Carver tried to stop himself from staring at the people's faces and instead focused his attention on what was being advertised at the stalls: an assortment of wooden tableware, a dusty tome with faded lettering on the cover, a row of grayish dried meat hanging from a metal rod, wooden trays of bruised fruits and dark-green vegetables, a white chain necklace with a charm, and a blue vase with a thin crack around its circumference.

Carver froze in place as his thoughts caught up with his eyes. Then he stepped backwards and looked toward the previous stall. There, amongst the cluttered stock, a specific item jumped out at him. Hanging from an empty clay bottle was a thin rope of white steel that was weighed down by a flat charm depicting a winged horse of the same color.

The man running the stall was nearly bald and had a fat chin covered in gray stubble. Carver avoided making eye contact with him as he examined the necklace from a few feet away, then decided to get closer.

"Greetings, young lad. Do some of my wares catch your interest?"

"Yeah, um, that necklace." Carver was standing directly in front of the stall now with his hands in his pockets.

"Oh," the merchant said, somewhat surprised.

Picking up on the balding man's tone, Carver furrowed his brow. "What?"

"Oh, nothing."

Carver's brow furrowed further.

"It's just that, well, nobody's so much as looked at that charm since it's been on this counter. Jewelry isn't on many people's minds lately, what with the hard times and all, and with winter coming, if you can't eat it or drink it, or it doesn't keep you warm, people don't seem to see it these days."

Carver couldn't deny the man's words. His own stomach grumbled with discomfort every few minutes, and his lips were uncomfortably dry, having not eaten or drank since he entered the city many hours earlier. He hadn't noticed how much the hunger and thirst bothered him, his mind was so focused on his situation and goal, but suddenly the needs of his body seized his attention.

"Then why even try to sell it at all?" he asked, wearing his curiosity on his sleeve.

"Oh! Don't get me wrong. I'm not trying to tell you not to buy it. Sorry, um ... It's a very fine piece of jewelry."

Carver nearly smirked as the merchant desperately backpedaled on his approach, but he managed to keep the edges of his lips from rising.

"Go ahead, hold it. See for yourself," the merchant said with forced enthusiasm as he lifted the necklace off the bottle and held it out to Carver.

Carver took the necklace and laid it on his palm. It was just as he remembered, a thin spiral of white metal leading down to a charm of a running horse with wings.

"That there is what's called a pegasus, or pegasi in groups. A majestic and mighty type of horse that you can only find on Gaia's mainland."

Carver looked up at the merchant with sudden interest. "That can't be true. The Mainland actually has horses that can fly?"

"It sure does, though I've never seen one myself. But I've never seen a naiad either, and we all know they're true. If blue-scaled water folk with tentacles for legs exist, then why not horses with mighty wings? Them pegasi aren't too common on the Mainland, though, or so I've heard. They come from the aptly named Pegasus Mountains on the eastern border of the Highlands, as far east as Terraland can go. As such, only them Highland tribes, those humans who look different from us and worship their own gods, or so I hear, are the ones known to tame and ride the creatures."

Carver pictured Helena riding atop such a creature.

"If you have a special woman in your life, that there bauble will lift her lips into a smile like a pegasus lifts its wings off the ground. Maybe even lift her tunic for you too."

The mental picture of Helena riding the pegasus morphed into her riding it topless. Carver shook his head to banish the image.

"It won't cost you no fortune neither, not like some other jewelry dealers here in the market. That right there will only cost you—"

"Six copper shards."

The merchant paused. "How ... yes. Yes, that's right. How did you know that?"

Carver rubbed his thumb over the pegasus charm. The metal was smooth and bumpy at the same time.

"I remember from when my friend bought it two months ago. Right before the attack," Carver said casually, not fully grasping how odd his words would come across as he eyed the white necklace in his palm.

"You ... you bought it? So you were here when they ... when it happened, then?"

Carver looked up and made eye contact with the man, realizing his statement had left the man in complete shock. The merchant's eyes were opened wide, and he was leaning over the counter a bit more, anxiously awaiting Carver's next words.

"Yeah, um ... my friend, Helena, and I, we came to the city to deliver our village's taxes. She saw this necklace and bought it from a lady. But the attack started before she could put it on," Carver finished while looking away.

The merchant followed Carver's gaze and saw the small black crater that he was staring at. He opened his mouth, but no words came out. He just stared in silence at the crater until he and Carver turned back to face each other.

The merchant's confusion remained evident on his face, but then it shifted to something else. He looked down, and his mouth closed as sadness took hold of his features. Carver wasn't sure what to do, so he just stood there, the necklace still in his palm.

"That woman was my eldest daughter," the merchant said, his eyes facing the merchandise strewn about his counter, the top of his balding head pointing at Carver.

Carver stopped playing with the necklace and focused his attention on the man's balding head. He didn't know if he was supposed to say something or what he could say, if anything, to comfort the man. The situation had developed so suddenly that he was completely lost for words.

"Her name was Grenna," the merchant continued. "It was her necklace to begin with, but absols have been tight as of late, so she added it to our wares to help us get by. She manned the stall for me most days ..." The merchant concluded with a tone that seemed more bitter than sad as he tensed his shoulders.

Carver grew increasingly uncomfortable, feeling like he had brought a great deal of anguish to the merchant. His feeling of discomfort grew as the silence between them dragged on, the only sounds around being footsteps and distant murmured chatter.

"I'm sorry if she died," Carver said, unsure if such words were appropriate.

The merchant looked up, revealing a face that was stricken with emotion. "She did, lad. And so did many others. Many who witnessed the slaughter did not live to tell of it. Unless they were the ones responsible. Damn sovereigns and those Aethi'ziton rebels, may Agon flay them all with whips of fire. They always—" The merchant stopped himself from continuing, but his anger and sadness continued to show through his face. "Well ... you were there. You saw what happened."

Again, Carver realized he may have said too much without thinking. The necklace and the memories it stirred had distracted him, and his mind had allowed his tongue to wander without thought, saying things he did not intend to reveal.

"Yes. I was," Carver said slowly, trying to limit what he revealed as he unknowingly closed his fingers around the necklace.

"And you made it out. How?"

Carver tightened his grip around the necklace, feeling the charm dig into his palm.

"I ran. I protected myself, and I got away," he said, feeling on edge about having such a conversation in public.

"Then you're one of the lucky ones. Perhaps Agon was watching out for you that day," the merchant said as he looked up at the diminishing rays of sunlight.

"Someone else said that Cosom is the one who watches over me."

The merchant tensed. "Boy, it's not wise to speak of him while under the light of Agon. Aol may be waning as it returns to its master, but it is still in the sky for some time yet."

Carver nodded apologetically.

"The market's shutting down now, boy. I ought to pack up and return home, as should you. Your parents are probably wanting you back safe before nightfall."

Carver felt his chest tighten. "Yeah," was all he could say in reply.

The merchant let out a heavy sigh. "Look, kid, I believe you when you say that your friend already paid for the necklace. But the fact is that the absols never reached me. In fact, most of my stock was destroyed or looted by the time the market cleared, and I arrived to save what was left. It's a blessing from Agon that I found that necklace among what remained. So, if you want it, I must still ask for payment. Six copper shards. My remaining children and my daughter's children still need to eat."

Carver considered bargaining with the man, then thought how easy it would be to simply run, since the necklace was already in his hand, but he didn't have the heart to do that. Instead, he set the necklace on the counter, took out his money pouch, and poured the three absol coins into his hand. Carver took the absol frame with only two copper shards and placed it next to the necklace. Then he held a full absol coin over the counter and pushed four copper shards out of its thin iron frame, one at a time. The shards hit the wooden counter and rattled for a moment before they stilled. He placed his remaining absols back in the pouch and then grabbed the necklace and slid it inside as well.

Carver stuffed the pouch back into his trouser pocket. Then he nodded to the merchant as the man tallied up the six shards and deposited them into his own trouser pocket. As Carver turned to walk away, thinking the transaction was complete, the merchant grabbed him by the shoulder.

Carver spun around with a surge of worry, though the moment he faced the merchant the man released his shoulder, and Carver saw that his face and posture gave no indication of threat.

"You be careful, now," the merchant said. "Whether it involves bandits or street thugs, the Lost Seekers, the sovereigns, or the soldiers meant to keep order, it's always us common folk who get caught in the middle of things and suffer the most. Each day is a gamble, so keep those who you love close, and don't squander the time you have with them. You could lose them any day or any time, or they could lose you. Make the most of what you have with whomever you have before you don't have anything left."

Carver didn't have any idea of what to say in response as the merchant's expression seemed to crumble into despair. Rather than standing there in silence, Carver turned and walked off without giving any indication that he had heard a word the man had said. However, as he hurried away from the stall and exited the market, the merchant's last words burrowed into his mind.

As the last of the sun's light pulled out of the market and left Carver walking in a fresh stretch of shadow, he squeezed the pegasus charm in his pocket through the coin pouch so tightly that the grooves of the horse's wings slightly indented his palm.

Chapter 29

❧

Night had fallen quickly over the coastal city, bringing with it an unforgiving cold and blanketing darkness. The light from the two moons illuminated the streets a little, but the darkness was still dominant. Carver sat with his legs pulled in and his back against the wall of a small tavern that stood in the middle of one of Caswen's many darkened streets. The brick wall was cold and uncomfortable on his back, and the cobblestone street beneath caused him to readjust every now and again to prevent his rear end and his legs from getting sore. The orange light coming out of the tavern's low open windows and the warmth it signified beckoned to him, but Carver held himself back.

While inside the tavern, Carver had felt anxious and out of place, feeling as though he had everyone's attention or was the topic of their drunken conversations. Sitting at the long wooden counter while waiting for his food and drink had been the most mentally arduous, as Carver knew for a fact that the scar on the back of his head was still quite visible. So, when the barmaid had arrived with his order, Carver handed her the payment and took it outside, preferring to be cold rather than surrounded by prying eyes and curious strangers.

The half loaf of bread Carver had obtained for two copper shards was hard and tasteless, but it did lessen his hunger as he ate it. The clay tankard of ale, also costing him two copper shards, was bitter and did not quench his thirst like he thought it would. As Carver reluctantly drank the unpleasant liquid, he wondered if he was not supposed to have taken the tankard out of the tavern. He quickly dismissed that worry as he finished the last of the drink and set the tankard to the side, thoroughly disappointed with his first experience with alcohol. The bitter taste of the beverage lingered on Carver's tongue, and he enjoyed his tasteless bread even less as he continued to break off brittle pieces. After filling himself with the bread, he noticed a faint sensation of warmth emerge from within his stomach and spread through the rest of his body.

The warmth aided against the chill for a time, but when Carver finished the last bite of bread, the pleasant sensation began to fade. He shivered as he wiped the crumbs from his lips and stood up. His legs feeling sore from sitting on the hard ground for so long, Carver set out down the empty street. After only a few steps, he stopped and looked up at the stars that were emerging from the infinite blackness far above.

"I know I've never … talked to you before. And I know I've never shown much interest in your story or the other gods—I mean, those who betrayed you. But if you really are watching me, Cosom—if it was you who kept me alive that night in Verrel and led Helena to save me—and if you truly have some purpose for me that I don't know yet, like Duncan said, then I ask that you watch over me again tonight. And if I survive, then know that I will be yours to serve you in whatever purpose you have for me."

Carver let out a long breath and turned his attention back to the street. He walked until he reached a small brick house. The structure was seemingly abandoned, which was apparent due to its crumbled left wall and lack of a front door, which was why he had checked it out earlier when the city was still blessed with sunlight.

Carver walked around the corner of the building, stepping over a pile of bricks, and walked down the tight alley between the abandoned building and the brick building next to it. He stopped halfway down the alley, facing some semi-deconstructed wood scaffolding. What the scaffolding was doing there, Carver did not know, but he had been looking around the city all day for a method of getting up to a roof once he'd constructed his plan, and he hadn't found a better method than this.

The thick darkness of the alley made it hard to climb what remained of the scaffolding, which was leaning over the partially crumbled building, but before long, Carver reached the highest level of the scaffolding that seemed stable, and from there he managed to reach the edge of the brick building's flat roof.

Once on the roof, Carver lay on his back and rested for a moment, breathing heavily from the climb. After a few seconds, he flipped onto his belly and pushed himself into a crouched position. He scuttled to the other side of the roof, stopping near the opposite side.

The alley was narrow, and across from it was a tall cottage made of brick. The building was slightly taller than the one Carver was on, and its roof was triangular and constructed of clay tiles. The highest point of the roof was on the right side, near Carver.

He took a deep breath and launched himself across the small gap between the buildings. He slammed into the clay tiles and grabbed onto the apex of the roof. The thud Carver made upon hitting the tiles caused him to freeze in fear, as he thought it would reveal himself to anyone nearby. Holding still and breathing carefully, Carver looked around for any indication that he had been heard or seen. After a brief period of holding himself in place and waiting, it appeared the sound hadn't alerted anyone. The cold wind and dark sky kept the people of Caswen sheltered in their homes or at the nearest tavern, leaving the partially torchlit streets empty save for those drunkenly heading home from said taverns or the night patrols of shivering soldiers. But even should someone, soldier or otherwise, pass by under Carver, their eyes were unlikely to detect him as the blackness of the night grew even thicker above the dancing flames of the infrequently placed street torches.

The darkness assailed Carver in the same manner, however. The yellow-and-orange glow from the street torches did nothing to illuminate his surroundings, but they did reveal enough of the streets that should any patrolling soldiers come by, Carver would see them easily.

Thanks to the two moons, he was able to see the closest buildings and rooftops from where he was, but even then it was still difficult to judge the actual distance from each building to the next. This fact made Carver's heart pound. He had not thought about how dark it was going to be so far off the ground.

His thoughts ran wild with speculation and doubt as he scanned the moonlight-diluted darkness around him. He knew the route, and he knew exactly how many leaps it was going to take, but the darkness made him feel like his planned route had completely changed.

It's no different, he thought, trying to reassure himself. *It's the same as when I figured it out today. Just a handful of leaps and some climbing, and I'm there.*

Despite his rationale, Carver still felt like the darkness had turned his plan upside down. He continued to hang with his belly pressed firmly into the clay tiles, reevaluating his plan. Soon, however, his arms and hands began to feel numb from the cold air and the even colder tiles, making it difficult to hang on.

The feeling of numbness in his fingers made Carver panic, as did the sensation of his stomach sliding down the tiles. He pulled himself up over the peak of the roof, then quickly adjusted his legs to stop himself from sliding down the other side and wrapped his left elbow over the peak behind him for support. The short arming sword buckled to his belt caught on the tiles, but Carver shifted his waist to free it.

He looked ahead and saw another tall building as well as a wide pit of blackness between him and it. He knew the gap wasn't as large as it looked. His earlier examination from below had placed the alley's width at only four or five feet across, but the darkness seemed to amplify the distance. Carver swallowed his fear and steadied himself on the slanted roof, planting his boots flush with the angled tiles and holding onto the roof's peak behind him.

He wanted to leap across, but he was frozen by fear and doubt, his mind also distracted by what the merchant had said to him earlier. It angered him to know that his confidence and drive could be so easily shaken by a single conversation with a stranger.

Carver told himself that he knew what he was doing; he was sure of it. Nothing mattered more to him than killing those responsible for his suffering and the suffering of his friends. But then, as it did every time Carver remembered it, the thought of those he left behind in Leydes made him question his actions.

Carver shook his head with frustration as he felt his doubt taking over, as well as the creeping numbness in his fingers. Fueled by his frustration, he released his hold on the peak, leaned back, and shuffled down the incline until his feet nearly protruded off the edge. Then he launched himself forward, both arms extended. He passed over the dark gap and collided with the slanted roof on the other side.

Carver was filled with panic as his grasping hands failed to grasp anything, and he felt himself sliding down the roof toward the gap behind him.

Carver was filled with relief just as quickly when his right hand wrapped around a clay tile that was sticking up higher than the rest, which allowed him to stabilize his feet beneath him and dig them firmly into the sides of more tiles. His relief was short-lived, however, as his hands and feet began to slip. He lunged for the roof's peak, but he wasn't quite able to grab it.

Again, Carver felt himself sliding down the roof. Like a desperate animal, he scrambled and lunged, reaching out into the darkness to grab anything that would stop him. His heart pumping at the speed of an insect's wings, Carver finally managed to halt his slide and pull himself to the top of the roof, flinging both elbows over the peak and locking himself in place.

Carver's fingers were no longer numb from the cold, having flooded with warmth from his panicked scaling of the roof. His heart continued to race, and his breathing was quick and erratic. Forcing himself to calm down, he closed his eyes and tried to slow his breathing.

As Carver's body began to relax, the air seemed to get colder as it touched his adrenaline-heated skin. He saw that the next building was lower than the one he was on, which helped him cope with the idea of jumping again.

Hearing voices below, Carver looked down toward the street and saw a moving circle of orange light with three soldiers marching within it. Unable to discern what the soldiers were saying, Carver held his breath and kept himself as still as possible while the trio walked past. He remained in place until the soldiers were no longer in sight and then a few seconds longer. Then he pulled himself over the peak and shuffled down the other side.

Once again, he used his legs to propel himself to the next building. He was able to grab the roof, but he nearly lost his grip as his body crashed against the hard clay tiles with more force than he expected. He managed to hold on, though, taking a moment to secure himself.

Then Carver wondered if his thud into the roof could be heard by those beneath. The thought led him to press forward, just in case.

Again and again, Carver hopped from roof to roof. Some required a bit of scrambling to traverse while others were no challenge at all. Some roofs had clay tiles missing due to age and decay, providing him with handholds and footholds, while some were constructed of thatch and wood rather than clay tiles, giving Carver a much easier time finding something to grab on to. After each leap, he would scan the dark streets below, looking for any indication of patrols.

Only once more did Carver have to pause and hold his breath as a group of patrolling soldiers traveled down the street below, causing him to wonder what would happen if they spotted him. The soldiers didn't appear to have bows, so they couldn't threaten to shoot him down. He also wondered how he would get away, being trapped atop the buildings as he was with no quick or easy way down. Carver stopped himself from thinking about such things as the soldiers disappeared into the darkness.

Carver did his best to keep aware of his surroundings, but the darkness made it difficult. Even with his eyes being somewhat adjusted to the night, and the full moons picking up some of the slack, his vision remained limited. He pressed on despite this, however, using his memory of the city during the daytime to guide him across the rooftops.

A handful of leaps and climbs later, Carver found himself peering down at his goal. The buildings and structures that made up Caswen's garrison were only partially visible in the all-consuming darkness. The main building had a flat roof and was made of stone with wooden framing. The building was longer than it was wide, and several smaller rooms extended from its sides. A courtyard on the garrison's north side connected to a few smaller buildings with flat stone roofs. The main structure also had a second story that rose gradually from the west end until it formed a pointed arch at the east end.

Carver couldn't see any guards, and no light came through the windows. Just below the second-floor arch, facing east, was a window. Unlike the other windows that dotted the lower floor and adjoining chambers, which all had their wooden shutters closed, this window was made of clear glass. Carver had never seen a glass window before. He knew of the substance, though, including that it was expensive and rare. This led him to believe that the room must belong to someone important. Seeing as the room was also the highest room in the garrison, Carver surmised that the person who occupied it was the captain of the Caswen Guard, the woman of many names whom he had heard about from the boy at his ruined village and from the few people he had questioned during his time in Caswen when the sun still warmed the back of his neck.

Carver told himself that if anyone was to blame for the recent events of his life, including the burning of Verrel and the murder of its people, it was her.

Carver maneuvered himself close to the edge of the roof he was on. He was right above the garrison's southwest corner at the back of its main building, where the west wall of the courtyard branched off from the building's flat-roofed extension.

Carver took a deep breath to calm himself as he turned and stepped backwards over the edge of the roof while holding onto the edge. He lowered himself as far as he could go while still maintaining a firm hold. The drop to the flat stone roof of the main building was not far, but it was far enough to fill him with hesitation and anxiety, especially with the edge above the courtyard so near to where he needed to land. Carver clenched his teeth and closed his eyes as he tried to psych himself up, and then he forced himself to let go and push off.

Carver's mind filled with fear as the air beneath him gave way, then almost as quickly as he realized that he was falling, his rear end slammed onto the roof's stone surface and he flopped onto his back.

A gasp escaped Carver's mouth as he realized he had made it. He rolled onto his side and let out a quiet groan as the pain and discomfort began to catch up with him once the immediate shock had fled his senses.

His rear end and his lower back burned with pain, and his left arm pulsed as well after having been rolled on, as did the spot where his sword's hilt had pushed into his side. Carver groaned again as he readjusted his limbs and gave himself a moment to settle while at the same time listening for any sign that he had been heard.

Still not quite convinced he was safe, Carver assumed a crouched position and continued to listen, his ears met by nothing but silence.

He looked up at the stars. He opened his mouth as if to speak but then closed it and began moving toward the rising slant of the roof to the east. He stayed partially crouched while listening for any sounds of alarm either from the streets around him or from the chambers beneath his feet. But Carver's ears detected only his own careful footsteps as he reached the east end of the roof. He got on his stomach and peered over the pointed arch.

The street below was the closest it had been since Carver had first climbed up the wooden scaffolding nearly thirty minutes earlier. He could still see the wind-dancing flames of street torches illuminating portions of the distant streets, but the garrison itself was mostly isolated in moonlit darkness, and no soldiers could be seen within the flickering glow of the distant fires.

Carver had heard from the few locals he spoke to during Caswen's daylight hours that the garrison wasn't usually guarded from the outside during the night, nor during the day either. He hadn't fully believed them, and he didn't pry beyond the most basic questions about the subject for fear of seeming suspicious, but now it seemed to him that the folks had been correct. The garrison did seem lacking in security from the outside, though Carver assumed some soldiers still kept vigil inside, guarding the prison cells or waiting to relieve their patrolling comrades.

Deeming this moment his best chance, he hung over the east side of the building next to the glass window. His sword dragged and caught on the edge of the roof, but Carver tilted his hip and got the weapon clear.

With his right hand holding the edge of the roof above him and his left hand flat against the stone wall facing east over the street behind him, Carver planted his boots on a small ledge below the window and steadied his balance. Once stable, Carver pressed himself against the cold glass and peered inside.

It was dark beyond the glass, but Carver was able to see clearly enough that the room was not a bedroom. From what he could tell, the chamber beyond the glass was an office of sorts, with furniture disguised as dark shapes by the lack of light, though nothing appeared to him in the shape of a bed or a human.

Carver had assumed such would be the case. In fact, it was crucial for his plan to work, but his situation of being barely able to fit his feet on a lip of stone more than a dozen feet above the hard ground with patrolling soldiers possibly nearby kept his relief at bay.

Now that he was so close to it, Carver saw that the window was not a solid glass pane but instead two large panes of glass held together at the center by a flat metal bar. He ran his left hand over the bar and felt a thin crease running from the top to the bottom, which indicated that the bar was also two separate pieces.

Carver used the same free hand to lightly push against the center of the window, but neither the glass nor the metal bars that held the panes together pushed inward, nor did either pull outward like any wooden shutters would have as Carver tried to use his fingernails to pull the window out from within the thin gap of the flat metal bars, though each attempt did cause the window to rattle slightly in place.

Carver suddenly felt his balance slipping, so he quickly placed his free hand against the wall. After securing himself, he inspected the glass for any sign of weakness. After some strained squinting, he spotted a small hook on the other side of the window, holding the panes in place.

Again, Carver felt some relief, though it didn't last long. He removed his left hand from the wall and reached for the hilt of his sword. After turning his head to the side to make sure no patrolling soldiers were approaching, Carver drew the sword quickly and struck the glass with its iron pommel.

A sharp bang echoed as the glass cracked, but it did not break. After reestablishing his center of gravity, he struck the glass again. A louder bang sounded as the cracked section of glass broke, sending a few shards into the room and others tumbling down to the street below, creating a fist-sized hole to the right of the flat metal bars.

Carver's heart began to race again. The noise from the window breaking had been louder than expected, and the hole was larger and more noticeable than he wanted. Nearly losing his balance, Carver shoved his blade back into its sheath and then put his left hand through the hole in the glass. Pushing through the pain created by his wrist scraping on the sharp edges of the glass, he undid the latch. Then he placed his fingers against the interior side of the glass and pulled. The right side of the window popped free and gently opened toward him. Wasting no time, Carver turned sideways and climbed into the dark room.

The broken glass crunched beneath his boots as he stepped through the windowsill. Carver ignored the sound and turned to close the window as soon as he was fully inside. He pulled the damaged glass pane closed and heard it click shut. He did not relock the window, however, in case he needed to flee.

Carver looked through the glass toward the city streets beyond to see if his break-in had gone unnoticed. After a minute of watching, he believed he was safe. He saw neither lights nor movement, and he didn't hear any voices from outside or from another room inside. He turned away from the damaged window and walked a few steps deeper into the room.

It was much darker inside than it was outside, the only light to be had coming from the trace amounts of moonlight that snuck through the window, which was now accompanied by a chill as the cold air seeped in through the hole in the glass.

Carver held still for a moment to give his eyes time to adjust, but even as the room's layout and furniture began to take form, he struggled to perceive most of the details.

To his right he detected the shape of a large desk with a chair situated behind it. To his left was a few feet of open space, the floor appearing to be covered in a wide rug, which ended at a wall lined by three wide bookshelves. A few long strides in front of him, across the large rug and at the adjacent wall from the window, was the outline of a door.

Carver felt another short burst of relief as he confirmed he was indeed in an office and not an occupied bedroom, but he knew he needed to be certain that this office was the correct one before he relaxed too much.

He crept toward the desk and examined its surface. A stack of papers, three rolled parchments, an inkwell holding a feathered pen, a thick book, and an extinguished lantern nearly identical to the one at Duncan's were all neatly placed atop the desk.

Carver pulled the chair away from the desk, lifting it slightly so as not to scrape its legs across the portion of the wooden floor that was not covered by a rug behind the desk, then sat down. He grabbed the thick book and opened it to a random page in the middle. He leaned forward and squinted at the words, due in part to the darkness and in part to his lack of practice reading.

The book contained a list of names and detailed routes throughout many of Caswen's streets. Carver turned the page and saw that the next contained more of the same, as did the next few pages.

The book was a ledger, he realized, with each page seeming to be a single day's record of patrols throughout the city, along with the names and the ranks of the soldiers who performed them. As Carver finished skimming the page he was currently on, he noticed that at the bottom was a finely inked signature, and as he read it in his mind he felt his chest tighten.

Captain Aellia Halbear.

Carver read the name again in disbelief, then flipped back to the pages he had previously skimmed and saw that the same signature was at the bottom of each one. Carver closed the ledger and pushed it across the desk. His mind spiraled through shock and worry at the knowledge of whom he had come to kill, increasing the severity of the situation, for despite his disinterest in the world's history and politics, one thing he did know was the surname of the Isles' ruling family.

The captain is nobility. She's a Halbear, the same as the magistrate ...

His understanding of the gravity of his intentions suddenly escalated, and his heart began to race, causing him to look over to the window. He found himself suddenly desiring to flee, to abandon his efforts and escape the city before it was too late.

No! No! It doesn't matter who she is, Carver told himself as he jerked his eyes away from the window. *She ruined everything. She ordered the deaths of my family and nearly everyone I know. She deserves to die.*

He felt a sudden anger at his cowardice, an anger that mostly pushed away his fear, which had grown after learning who exactly he was planning to murder. He let his anger fester as he sat in the dark room thinking about his situation and his upcoming actions. He had nothing left to do but wait for the captain to walk into her office in the morning, unsuspecting and vulnerable.

It was a simple plan, and one that Carver knew could easily get him killed even if he succeeded. He also knew that the escape was going to be the most dangerous part: somehow getting to the street below and fleeing the crowded city in broad daylight after murdering such a high-profile figure. His escape was the part of his plan that he had thought about the least, mainly because every time he did he only saw one outcome—being cut down in the streets—so he tried not to think about it and told himself he would figure it out when the time came.

✠   ✠   ✠

Time passed slowly for Carver as he sat in the wooden chair. He had no idea how long he had been waiting. It could have been one hour or three. His eyes had adjusted quite well to the dark, and he was now able to see the bookshelves with more clarity.

They were nearly full, their shelves packed with all manner of thick, parchment-bound books and scrolls. Most of the books' spines were unlabeled, and those that were could not be discerned from a distance.

As time passed, Carver grew increasingly bored and anxious. His angry thoughts had kept him occupied at first, but when his anger faded, he began to obsess over his plan rather than his memories. His constant analyzing of his plan and his future actions distracted him for a time, though the thoughts caused him much stress, but even that only lasted so long.

His boredom and his anxiety grew over the next two hours, which felt like four, sending his eyes around the room in search of something to distract him. He saw no such distraction, however, only a wide room with not much to interest him.

Carver felt an urge to go over and see what was in the books and scrolls across the room, but he dismissed the idea of snooping around as foolish and potentially dangerous. He forced himself to ignore the urging of his youthful mind, which called for him to find some kind of distraction, and remained sitting in the chair. Soon, however, Carver couldn't stand the waiting any longer.

He grabbed the ledger again and opened it to the first page. He was surprised to see that the earliest entry was March first, the beginning of spring and the first day of the year.

Carver wondered if a new ledger was started every year. He looked up at the bookshelves and wondered if 204 similar ledgers could be found there. Quickly deciding that wasn't possible, he examined the ledger's first page in more detail, then started going through the rest of the pages in order.

As he got closer to the current date, he noticed more and more patrols were taking place in the First District, in the north part of the city. He also noticed that those patrols, more often than in the other districts, it seemed, encountered some kind of trouble: suspicious individuals, failing architecture, scuffles with criminals, run-ins with potential Lost Seekers, and even the presence of bodies in the streets.

Carver had heard that the First District was the most run down and impoverished, which spoke volumes considering his observations of the central portion of the city, but the ledger told him that the First District was far worse than he had imagined.

After nearly fifteen minutes of flipping through the pages, Carver grew bored. He closed the heavy book and slid it back to its original spot on the desk. Glancing over at the window, he noted it was still dark outside. He wondered how long he had been waiting and how much longer it would take, while at the same time he felt anxious at the thought of the sun rising and somewhat desired it to delay.

Sensing his doubts returning and his mind wandering into paranoia and fear, he attempted to combat his faltering nerve with further distractions. He reached for the short stack of papers near the left corner of the desk and started shuffling through them.

Most were uninteresting or too complex for him to understand—armor and weapon requisitions from local blacksmiths; new recruit forms from men and women, both local and foreign; recent arrests and the charges applied; concluded and ongoing interrogations; executions, both public and private and the scheduling of each; correspondences with other towns and villages throughout the Isles; and a few documents detailing the deaths of soldiers in recent days. Each sheet of paper had Aellia's signature at the bottom, and those that didn't had a clear space for where it would be inked eventually.

Carver returned the papers to their spot and leaned back in the wooden chair, only a few minutes having passed. Searching for another distraction, he turned his attention to the base of the thick desk. To the right of his knees were two small drawers. Carver slid the top drawer open. Inside were inkwells and quill pens beside a short, dull knife with dried wax caked over much of its blade.

He slid the drawer shut and opened the one beneath it. He expected to find something similarly uninteresting, but instead he found a parchment-bound book. His curiosity nudged ever so slightly, Carver lifted it out of the drawer and set it on the desk. It was clear immediately that it was no simple tome but rather a twine-laced portfolio, though he did not know that name for it.

Just as he was about to undo the coarse twine that bound its thick parchment flaps together, he noticed something else in the drawer: a small tome that had been beneath the portfolio, as if hiding.

Carver pulled it out. Its cover was made of tough leather, unlike the rest of the books and tomes he had seen, which all had covers and bindings made from thick parchment. He saw no title or label on the cover as he turned the book over in his hands. Wondering what could be inside, Carver opened it to the first page. After reading the first few lines, he realized what the book was: a diary.

> May 12, 197.
> Today is the first of many great days, and this diary will be the record of my new life; my original was nearly full anyways. I did it. I finally did it. My bastard of a father said I can now serve in the Caswen Guard. After spending

most of my seventeenth year sneaking out to patrol the streets after dark and spending my days with the soldiers at the garrison, I will no longer be dragged back to the manor and told to stay there. My private lessons with Spymaster Renneil are to thank for my father's change of mind. After I disarmed the soldier assigned to keep me in my room and broke his nose before running back to the garrison, my father understood that he was not going to keep me from my goal. Let my brothers stay in that manor and rule when father is gone. My life is my own, and I will live it how I choose.

Carver flipped past dozens of pages before stopping again.

February 9, 199.

I can't believe how much has changed in just two years. Me, captain of the Caswen Guard. Never had I dreamed of reaching such a status in so short a time, especially being only nineteen, but the men and women of the Caswen Guard respect me despite my youth. To be honest, when I volunteered for the position after the sudden deaths of Captain Darious and Lieutenant Goedfri at the hands of the Lost Seekers, I didn't expect to be chosen since I was only a few months into my promotion to sergeant. But thanks to Renneil's support and endorsement, Marshal Audicas chose me for the position.

I'm aware that many will see my rise in rank as a consequence of my birth, and I cannot fault them for thinking such. I must admit that such thoughts trouble my mind too. After all his years of protest regarding my joining of the ranks, would my father suddenly use his influence to have me promoted? But I will show my soldiers, and indeed those wretched sovereigns, that I am deserving of this station and that I will take it with the utmost seriousness. Never will a soldier die needlessly under my command, and brief will be the danger of these Lost Seekers.

Renneil even told me that I would make an excellent marshal of the Isles one day. But that is something too distant to consider, as Marshal Audicas is far from an old man.

Uninterested with the ramblings of the woman he detested, Carver closed the diary. Then he turned his attention to the thick parchment portfolio, untied the twine that held it shut, and let it fall leftward onto the desk. Carver brought his face in closer and squinted as he read the first inked line of the top paper.

You are cordially invited to the wedding of Aellia Halbear, daughter of Magistrate Julius Halbear of the Isles, and Riel Togge, son and heir of Magistrate Hester Togge of the Coastlands. The ceremony will take place on December 15, 205, at Fort Audrin, located on the northeast coast of the East Isle, midway between Caswen and Leydes. It is my great hope that you will be able to attend. Aellia Halbear.

Carver did not recognize the groom's name, nor did the name of the fort ring any bells for him. He lifted the finely inked invitation and placed it on the desk, looking at the next piece of writing beneath. It was another invitation, and so were the next seven papers thereafter. Each had been carefully written in black ink and signed at the bottom with the captain's full name.

Carver was about to stop going through the papers, assuming the portfolio's contents to be nothing but unsent invitations, when he saw that the next letter was different. It was, in fact, not a letter at all but rather a detailed list consisting of placements for tables, flowers, decorations, and other furnishings and decor.

Carver flipped the page over and saw that more was written on the paper beneath with regard to food, drinks, and the costs and shipping details of their gathering.

He flipped to the next page and saw that similar details continued, with page after page of lists and notes detailing the captain's wedding arrangements, the confirmed guests, detachments of soldiers for security, and the schedule of events.

Continuing on, Carver found himself examining a series of sketches and maps for what he assumed to be the location of the wedding, which seemed to be a fort of some kind.

From the diagrams and sketches, Carver could see that the fort had a watchtower, a large central structure with many rooms and a dungeon underneath, a spacious yard all around it, and a high stone wall encircling it, with the southeast and northwest portions of the wall having wide arches that allowed access. One of the maps also revealed that the fort was built on the edge of a high cliff overlooking the ocean.

The sketches and maps indicated not only where the fort was, but also where the guards would be stationed, what hallways were connected to what chambers inside the large central building, and the stations set up for the ceremony. It was all catalogued in great detail and telling of a woman who had meticulously planned every aspect of her wedding.

Carver noted that what he was examining would be a great boon to anyone who was planning an attempt on Aellia's life, but he quickly dashed the notion from his mind, telling himself that it didn't matter. He was already there and committed to his plan, and he knew there would be no second chance should he fail.

Carver continued to go through the papers until he reached the end. Then he put them all back in the proper order. His attention was so focused on putting the portfolio back together and the plethora of new information he had just read that the clicking sound from the door to his far right went completely unheard. It was only when the door flew open and a bright light filled the chamber that Carver realized he was caught.

Chapter 30

Carver's first instinct was to look directly toward the light, but he winced and turned his face away, the many hours spent sitting in the dark having made his eyes overly sensitive.

He leaped to his feet, knocking the chair over backwards, and wrapped his right hand around the leather-bound grip of his arming sword. He drew the weapon so quickly that the tip of the blade struck the flat iron lantern that was sitting on the right corner of the desk and knocked it over the edge. It hit the floor with a crash, and oil splashed in every direction as its lid came off, with most of it pooling within the stretch of wood flooring between the front of the desk and the thick rug that covered the center of the room.

Carver's mind barely registered the lantern's fall as his attention was fully locked on the open doorway where two figures stood amidst the light. Both were men, and they entered the room side by side. One of them was wearing the standard uniform and armor of a Caswen soldier while the other was barefoot with a gray tunic and brown trousers. The soldier was holding an arming sword in one hand and a lantern in the other. The other man was also holding an arming sword, which he pointed at Carver.

"Stop right there!" he shouted. His beard and mustache were the same color as his short, combed-back yet messy black hair.

Carver complied with the man's order, though not by force of will. He merely stood still because he was frozen in fear.

"Lieutenant, what do we do?" the soldier asked. His voice sounded much younger than that of the man standing next to him. He looked younger too, his face lacking any facial hair.

"Quiet! Hold that light up and stay in the doorway!" the man addressed as Lieutenant barked while scanning the room before looking back at Carver. "Drop that weapon, kid. You're under arrest for burglary." He glanced at the open portfolio on the desk. "And for rifling through the private documents of the marshal of the Isles and captain of the Caswen Guard. I suggest you don't make things worse for yourself and come quietly."

Carver raised his sword, holding it in both hands, and pointed it at the men, keeping the desk between them as his mind scrambled for some idea of what to do next.

The lieutenant stepped forward, then looked down at the pool of oil that was now soaking into the rug. He stepped over it easily and continued his slow approach toward the left side of the desk.

As the lieutenant moved closer, Carver shifted his footing to keep the desk between them, but he quickly realized that he was cornering himself by not making a move.

It was too late now, however, as the lieutenant was now standing in front of the window, and the other man was blocking the doorway. Carver was trapped.

"I'm not messing around, boy. Put your sword down, or we'll be forced to put you down."

Carver began to panic. He had no idea what to do other than surrender or attack, and each option seemed certain to lead to his death. He held his tongue and continued to dart his eyes back and forth between the two men. As he did, the lieutenant began to creep forward.

His sword still raised, Carver backed up until he hit the wall behind. He knew that he would need to move toward the man blocking the doorway if he wanted to keep away from the lieutenant, but he suspected that was exactly what the man wanted him to do.

Carver held his position as the lieutenant came within a foot of the desk's left side. His stomach churned with fear as he felt his options dwindling and his likelihood of escape fading. Before he could think it through, Carver hopped onto the desk.

The lieutenant lunged and swung his weapon at Carver's legs, but Carver jumped before the blade could connect and landed awkwardly on the other side of the room.

Carver spun around, prepared for an attack, but instead he saw the lieutenant still standing beside the desk and the other man still blocking the doorway, sword and lantern in hand. The fat flame twisting around atop the flat iron lantern seemed to have dimmed drastically, though Carver was sure it was merely that his eyes had adjusted.

"He's a quick one," the lieutenant said, glancing toward his comrade. "Leave the lantern on the desk. Take this and lock me in with the boy." He fished a ring of keys out of his trouser pocket. "Go get whoever's on duty below and bring them up here."

The soldier looked confused at first, but then he placed the lantern on the desk, coincidentally where the unlit one had been.

Carver considered lunging forward and striking the somewhat distracted soldier, but the distance between them was too great; doing so would allow the lieutenant to attack his exposed right side.

The lieutenant tossed the ring of keys at his comrade, who caught it and then ran out, slamming the door behind him and leaving Carver and the lieutenant alone in the dimly lit room. Two fast, loud clicks came from the other side of the door, signaling that they were now locked in.

Carver turned his full attention toward the lieutenant, whose smile was revealed by the warm light emanating from the lantern on the desk.

"That's it, kid. Just you and me now, though in a moment there will be a whole group of soldiers here to take you down. You can try to unlock the door from this side and run, but I'll strike you down before you do. I suggest you drop your weapon and surrender. You'll only make things worse for yourself if you keep this up."

Carver knew that the man was right. Things were indeed going to get worse for him if he didn't do something fast.

The lieutenant backed up slightly until he was blocking the window on the east wall. He kept his sword pointed at Carver, but he did not advance.

Carver panicked as he realized his opponent was simply trying to keep him in place until it was too late. He darted his eyes around the room for any options other than trying to kill his assailant and fleeing out the window, but nothing he saw replaced that option. Carver didn't doubt his ability with a blade, as he had already proved he could handle himself when outnumbered, but the idea of fighting one on one with someone who had risen to the rank of lieutenant among Caswen's soldiers seemed like a duel best avoided.

Telling himself that he had no choice, and psyching himself up to fight with everything he had to slay or get past the man, Carver was about to attack when he noticed something.

Thanks to the warm illumination of the lantern on the desk, he noticed the oil that had spilled from the other lantern had formed a pool near the front of the desk. What hadn't soaked into the north edge of the rug stretched out with narrow black tendrils toward Carver and the bookshelves. Glancing from the bookshelves to the lieutenant to the flame, Carver burst into action.

He grabbed the top of the middle bookshelf and pulled it forward. It tipped over, spilling the tomes and scrolls it contained onto the floor before it slammed onto the floor itself with a resounding thud. As the bookshelf struck the floor, it created a gust of wind that blew the open portfolio and much of its contents off the desk and onto the floor near the north wall.

The lieutenant was about to advance toward Carver, but before he could commit to a lunge, Carver stepped onto the fallen bookshelf and grabbed the top of the next shelf nearest to the east wall.

"Stop! What are you—"

The second bookshelf crashed down in front of the lieutenant before he could finish, causing him to jump back to avoid his bare feet being crushed. More tomes and scrolls scattered across the floor. The lantern's glow revealed the lieutenant's face, rife with fury.

He stepped up onto the second fallen bookshelf, intending to strike at Carver before he could do any more damage to the room, but Carver hopped backwards before his enemy could step within striking distance.

Carver dashed toward the desk, hopping over the pool of oil. Spinning around to face the lieutenant, who was still standing on the second fallen bookshelf, Carver slid his boot into the heaviest portion of the spilled oil and splashed it over the fallen bookshelves, the clutter of tomes and scrolls, and the lieutenant's trousers.

"That's enough, you brat!" the lieutenant roared as he instinctively held up a hand to block the spray from his eyes, though none of it came near his face. "You'll hang tomor—"

The lieutenant's face switched from anger to horror as Carver grabbed the lantern and hurled it across the room. It crashed at the lieutenant's feet, the thumb-sized flame erupting into a fireball.

The thick trail of oil leading across the room morphed into a river of fire, with the many thin tendrils of oil becoming its hellish tributaries. The fire traveled down the burning river of oil like red and orange sails. As it touched the shallow pool of blackness near Carver's feet, the pool transformed into a lake of tall flames.

Carver jumped back as the space ahead of him filled with fire faster than he had anticipated. Despite his fast reaction, however, the flames ignited his left boot, which was also splattered in oil from the kick. He felt the heat, but his attention was still focused on the lieutenant.

The lieutenant cursed as the flames struck him from below. He tried to jump back, but the speed at which the flames erupted outmatched him. The oil that dotted the lieutenant's trousers ignited, and flames shot up to his knees. He cursed again with a voice nearly broken with fright and fell backwards while dropping his sword. The blade clanged as it struck the hard wood of the overturned bookshelf, but the lieutenant's shouts nearly drowned it out.

"Ah! Cosom, no!" he shouted as he scrambled backwards away from the fire while smacking the flames along his legs. When his back hit the wall, he continued to smack and swipe his hands at the flames, which were quickly crawling up his trousers.

The thick rug was rapidly swallowed by fire, and the flames stretched over the edges of the fallen bookshelves, beginning to swallow them while also devouring any loose tomes or scrolls that were nearby. Some of the flames reached up high enough to lick the wooden beams along the ceiling, leaving faint black dots wherever the tips of fire happened to strike. Whatever oil had filled the tight spaces between the floorboards had also given birth to fire, and many of the boards became obscured in dancing flames.

At that moment, black smoke burst from the flames, seeming to come from every corner of the room at once. It leaped up toward the ceiling and spread throughout the room, which was glowing red and orange from the flames.

His vision obscured by the thick smoke, Carver's mind turned to his memory of Verrel. Fear assaulted his mind as he backed up a few more steps before a sudden hot sting of pain attacked his left foot. Realizing his boot was still on fire, he slammed his foot into the desk again and again, but the fast-spreading flames did not vanish. So, Carver dropped his sword and reached down to pull the burning boot off his foot. The hot teeth of fire bit his fingers as he ripped the boot from his foot and tossed it into the spreading smoke. Only then did Carver snap out of his fear and look for a way out.

His eyes leaped to the window, which was still visible through the smoke. Suddenly, the lieutenant's screams reached his ears once again, sending a sickening chill through Carver's body. Forcing himself to ignore the lieutenant's cries, he left his sword behind and dashed toward the window. Upon reaching it, Carver shoved both panes open, sending a wave of cold air into the room. All at once the thick black smoke above his head ignited into a burst of flame, swallowing the entire ceiling in fire. The force of the blast nearly knocked Carver out the window, but he managed to grab the sides and hold himself steady.

He hoisted himself up into the windowsill and then stepped out onto the thin ledge beyond. He readjusted his hold on the window's edges and turned around so he could prepare to reach up for the roof, but as he did, he got another look inside the burning room, which caused him to pause.

Thick smoke obscured nearly all the flaming ceiling and the far end of the room, but as some of the smoke escaped through the window, requiring that Carver duck slightly so as not to receive smoke to the face, a portion of the room was still visible to him.

He saw the lieutenant frantically crawling toward the door. His trousers were still on fire, the exposed skin beneath them terribly burned. The lieutenant disappeared into the smoke again, howling in panic and agony. Nearly everything was on fire or obscured in swirling black smoke, including the desk.

Through the smoke and flames, Carver glimpsed the thick parchment portfolio and much of its contents scattered on the floor behind the desk, the flames having yet to reach that area. As such, the portfolio and its contents jumped out at him like a gem amongst boulders. Before Carver could truly assess the risks, he heaved himself back into the office.

Staying low to avoid the worst of the smoke, he dashed around the desk, picked up the wooden chair and tossed it away to give himself space, and then grabbed the portfolio and as much of its scattered contents as he could. Some papers were spilled out onto the floor as Carver picked it up, and some were too close to the approaching flames to save. Carver barely noticed the loss, and he slammed the portfolio shut and tightened his hand around the opening side.

A hot gust of air suddenly blew past Carver toward the west wall. As he looked up, he caught a glimpse of the office door swinging open before the heavy smoke swallowed the sight up once again.

Carver spun around and darted back toward the window. Stepping back onto the ledge and turning himself around, he stretched his right arm up toward the roof's edge. Once his fingers wrapped over the stone edge, he stepped to the side toward the lower area of the roof where he had come from.

He immediately realized that the right windowpane was in his way, so he rotated and grabbed the narrow edge above with his left hand as best as he could while still holding onto the portfolio. He brought his right hand down and grabbed the top of the right windowpane, then arched his back out slightly as he tried to shut it.

As his back extended out to give the window enough room to pass by his torso, Carver felt his balance shift, and his left foot slipped backwards. He pushed the knuckles of his left hand into the stone edge of the high roof, his fingers still mostly wrapped around the portfolio, and tried to hold himself steady, but his left hand's grip was not enough, and Carver's knuckles scraped off the roof's high edge.

His entire left side went along with the momentum of his left foot, swinging back and causing his balance to shift completely. Carver tightened his right hand's grip on the thin glass of the windowpane and pushed his right foot, still inside a boot, which added support, down into the thin windowsill's edge. Now hanging over the cobblestone street, Carver's heart launched into a flurry of powerful beats.

Before he could steady himself or pull his left side back toward the ledge, his right hand slipped a few inches down the smooth edge of the windowpane. His body tilted backwards over the street, and the muscles in his right leg strained painfully as they stretched to maintain the distance between his body and his right foot, which was still pushed into the thin edge of the windowsill.

His hand continued to slide down the windowpane's edge as more of his weight shifted downwards. Carver turned his head and looked down at the cobblestone street, wondering if he should simply jump.

Just as Carver gauged the fall to be about fifteen feet and determined he didn't want to try it, his right palm slid past the last inch of smooth glass, leaving nothing but his fingers holding onto the bottommost portion of the open window.

Carver pulled his right leg off the windowsill just as his fingers slid off the glass. In doing so, he was just able to shift the angle of his body, so he fell feet first rather than upside down. The descent lasted barely a second, and he hit the ground well before he was ready for the impact.

He landed on his left leg first, which shot to the side at an awkward angle as his body came crashing down on top of it. The feeling of his left arm and shoulder getting crushed into the cobblestones beneath his weight came next, just before Carver found himself lying on his chest. The portfolio remained clamped in his left hand only because it was pinned between his chest and the street.

Carver's instinct was to shout and curse as the impact sent pain throughout his entire body, but only a shallow gasp came out of his mouth, the wind having been knocked out of him.

Lying prone on the street, Carver coughed painfully and tried to gather his breath and collect his senses. He used his right arm to push himself up enough to unpin his left arm from beneath him, but as he did, a burst of pain exploded from his left ankle. Carver hissed through his teeth at the sudden escalation of pain and awkwardly turned himself onto his back to see what was wrong. His heart skipped a beat when he saw that his left foot was pointing sideways.

"Oh no ... No, no, no, no."

Carver sat up, leaving the portfolio on the ground, and grabbed his crooked foot with both hands in an attempt to turn it upright and assess the damage. The moment he moved his foot, a surge of pain exploded from his ankle. The pain nearly tipped him onto his back again, but he used his arms to stop his fall.

"Shit! Ahh fu—ow! Damn it!"

Panic overwhelmed Carver as the pain in his ankle increased in intensity. He didn't know what to do except stay sitting upright, but he wasn't making much progress. The pain was getting worse by the second, even managing to block out the minor pain he felt in other parts of his body, and all he could do was curse through his teeth.

Carver tried to curl his left leg inwards, but the movement triggered too much pain from his ankle, so he kept the leg still as he continued to curse and gasp. Some of the flames from the office above now stretched out the window, reaching up toward the sky and partially illuminating Carver in an orange glow that grew out over the dark street akin to the rising sun.

His mind filled with the realization that he was done for, that he was going to die in the streets of Caswen, and he could do nothing to prevent it. The pain in his ankle was only increasing, and severely reducing his options of escape.

Glancing around to take in his surroundings, he saw that the wide street was empty of people. The street extended to Carver's right, north, toward a series of branching side streets that disappeared behind stone buildings and brick or wood homes. To his left, south, the street opened up into a wide square with three main roads branching off to the east, south, and west.

Clenching his teeth, Carver rolled himself over and positioned himself on his hands and knees, facing north. The action of lifting his left leg over his right made his eyes water with pain.

Carver reached for the portfolio, which was only a foot away from him. Despite his urgency to escape, he couldn't leave the item behind. Then, without waiting another moment, he launched himself into a crawl.

He barely managed to crawl a few feet before he had to stop due to the pain in his ankle. His attempts to move his left knee forward caused his ankle to drag along the cobblestone street and flare with pain, and if he tried to lift his leg instead, his ankle hung down, which was just as painful.

Carver dropped onto his stomach and lifted his left leg over his right, then set it down. The effort caused him great pain, and his ankle still hung slightly above the ground, but it was all he could think of at the moment. With his left leg resting on his right, Carver threw his arms forward and pulled himself along using his elbows.

Inching forward across the cobblestone street, grunting as each pull strained his muscles and caused his left ankle to move slightly despite his efforts to keep it still, he fought against pain and fatigue as he drew closer to the nearest buildings. He bit his lip as he forced himself on, using all the strength in his arms to pull his body forward while also using his right leg to push in any way he could.

The empty scabbard attached to his belt dragged and scraped along the cobblestones, slowing Carver down and making it harder to move. Not thinking to unbuckle the scabbard and leave it behind or even recalling that he had abandoned his weapon within the burning office, he arched his back and angled himself onto his right side to prevent the scabbard from impeding his movement.

Carver heard the roaring and crackling of the uncontrolled fire as it ravaged the office behind him, but he didn't look back. He kept his attention on his goal, which was a shadowy alleyway between the closest brick house and its neighbor. Suddenly, however, Carver heard something that forced him to look back.

"Fire! Fire at the garrison!" a man shouted a good distance behind him.

Carver stopped crawling and turned back, his eyes greeted by the sight of four soldiers running across the open square. The soldiers all had their eyes fixed on the high window, which was now vomiting orange light onto the street and bright embers into the night sky. None of the four soldiers appeared to notice Carver, who was about two dozen feet away from them and only a handful of painful pulls away from reaching the shelter of the narrow alley.

Carver turned his attention back to his crawling. He heaved his weight toward the alley's dark embrace with everything he had, but his strength was waning. He was able to fight through the burning strain in his arms far better than he could the thumping pain in his ankle.

"Fire!" someone else cried, though the voice was more distant than before.

With a final heave, Carver pulled himself into the shadow of the alley between two small brick homes. He used what little strength he had remaining to push himself into a sitting position. His back hit the brick wall of the southern building with a thud as he seated himself in the dark.

Carver tried to stay silent, but as he curled his left leg closer to himself, his ankle pulsed with pain, causing him to groan through his clenched teeth. He wanted to keep moving, to continue dragging himself down the alley and get as far from the area as he could, but he needed a moment to rest and try to block out the pain coming from his crooked ankle.

As Carver struggled to keep his composure, he heard many footsteps approaching from around the corner. His mind screamed for him to crawl away from the alley opening, but his exhausted arms and his fear of amplifying his ankle's torment made him hesitate. Instead, he held his breath and kept as still as he could in the hope that whoever was approaching would pass him by.

The noise of running footsteps took form as two female soldiers appeared from around the corner of the alley's north building. They ran straight past the alley without noticing Carver.

"Fire! Don't let it spread! We need water!" one of the soldiers screamed as she and her fellow vanished from Carver's view past the alley's south building, the sound of their footsteps diminishing as they ran down the street.

The light of the fire now reached far and wide down the street and climbed up the base of the nearby homes and buildings. The warm glow of the strengthening flames almost penetrated the darkness of the alley but stopped just shy of where Carver sat in the sheltering blackness. Despite his better judgment, he leaned his head out from the alley and looked back toward the garrison to see what was transpiring, and what he saw shocked him.

The street was full of orange light from the flames, which were now bursting from sections of the main structure's roof that were not directly above the office where the fire had started. Thick black smoke spilled from the office window as well as from portions of the roof where the wooden supports were cracking apart from the heat. A handful of soldiers near the base of the burning building's east side were shouting at each other, seemingly in a panic.

"What happened?"

"We need to get to a well!"

"The nearest one is south! Come follow me!"

"Find buckets. Wake up anyone nearby!"

A few of the soldiers ran off toward the open square and disappeared from view while the others ran to neighboring homes and started pounding on doors.

Carver pulled his head back into the alley once he saw the soldiers spreading out across the street. A moment later, he heard a thud, like a wooden door striking a brick wall.

"Cosom's wrath! What's happening?" a woman shouted.

"Ma'am! Grab any buckets you have and get to a well! Hurry!"

Carver heard the woman run back into her house. Then from around the alley's right corner, he heard another door thudding into a brick wall.

"You there, sir! Find us—"

Carver turned his attention away from the commotion and looked down the narrow alley to his right. His muscles were still aching with fatigue, but he knew that if he spent any more time sitting there, he would be noticed sooner or later. The pain in his left ankle continued to grow, and his watering eyes sent tears down his face, but Carver managed to tip himself over into a crawling position. Before he started moving, he lifted his left leg over his right and then lowered himself onto his stomach.

He tried to keep his throbbing ankle steady, but the pain still came in waves. Carver groaned as he lifted his stomach slightly off the ground and arched his shoulders up. Then, this time more loudly despite his efforts to keep his voice down, he started dragging himself deeper into the alley's dark embrace.

The process was slow and painful, and Carver had no idea where he was going or how he would get back to Leydes. His only desire was to get as far from the garrison as possible.

The sounds of the roaring fire and the shouting soldiers began to fade as Carver pulled himself down one of the alley's branching paths behind some tall buildings. After heading down a second branching alley and then a third, the commotion was much harder for him to hear.

Carver's sense of direction quickly became nonexistent as he made his way through the maze-like system of alleys and streets within Caswen's tight clusters of residences, crawling around corner after corner. He couldn't tell if he was heading north or south, west or east, or even if he had looped around and was heading back toward the garrison. He just kept dragging himself with the hope that he was at least creating distance between himself and those who would harm him.

The tall buildings blocked out most of the light granted by the two moons, forcing Carver to crawl in near total darkness, though he could still make out the outlines of closed doors and shuttered windows as he pulled himself past inward-facing abodes. Each door that Carver's eyes managed to detect sent a jolt of fear into his heart, as his mind worried that it would open and he would be caught.

Though the pain in Carver's left ankle remained constant and intense, his eyes had stopped watering, and he no longer groaned in anguish with each pull of his arms. Having adjusted slightly to his pain, he became more aware of his environment despite the lack of light.

The surface on which he crawled had turned from cobblestones to dirt, and every so often he felt grass between his fingers. The smell had also changed to a foul and constant odor of filth. Though Carver was unfamiliar with Caswen's layout and was completely lost, he felt that he had a pretty good idea of where he had ended up: the city's northern district.

A wave of grief filled Carver at the realization that he had traveled deeper into the city. Not that he had been trying to maintain a certain direction, lost and panicked as he was, but he had still hoped he was at least heading west or south, somewhat toward Caswen's only exit by road. With his error sinking in and the pain in his ankle seeming endless, he was hit with a feeling of complete defeat and hopelessness.

Carver stopped his crawl and laid still on the ground, using his elbows to keep his face out of the dirt. His eyes stung with tears due to the pain and the sudden feeling of despair. Then he felt warm droplets landing on his tired arms and hands.

He tried to think of what he could do, if anything, to fix his situation, but the pain that rocked his ankle and the utter hopelessness that squeezed his heart prevented him from properly gathering his thoughts. He was lost in the city and now in his own mind, swimming in confusion and despair with no clear goal to focus his thoughts.

Carver's sadness and hopelessness suddenly began to mix with anger, with much of it directed at himself. He looked at the portfolio that was still held tightly in his right hand and clenched his teeth. He regretted taking it, thinking immediately that if he had left it to burn, his left hand would have kept hold of the thin ledge above the office window and he would not have fallen.

Tears began to run down Carver's face, his sudden hate for himself and his actions pushing them out harder than his physical pain could, and his body shook with emotion; he felt like he was losing control of himself.

"Ahhhhh!" Carver screamed as he threw the portfolio into the darkness, scattering the papers in every direction.

His cry of rage bounced off the wooden buildings on either side of the alley and echoed into the night. Carver felt a near overwhelming urge to scream again, but he resisted and instead clenched his fists and planted his forehead into the dirt.

The dirt was hard, and it cooled Carver's warm forehead slightly as a few blades of grass brushed against his cheeks and tickled his nose. He paid the physical sensations no mind, however, as he cried angrily into the ground.

He regretted everything. He regretted taking the portfolio as he tried to flee. He regretted coming to Caswen by himself in the first place, and he regretted leaving the only friends he had without saying a word. Everything was wrong, and he knew he could only blame himself.

The sound of soft thuds suddenly reached Carver's ears – thuds that he barely detected due to his fit of angry tears. He pulled his head off the ground and listened carefully, his tears ceasing as his instinct toward self-preservation overruled his emotions. Carver quickly realized he was hearing footsteps from behind him.

"Lookit. I said I heard someone," a gravelly yet high-pitched voice said.

Carver hastily pushed himself up on his elbows and then, using his left arm to support him, reached down for his sword. His heart skipped a beat when his fingers felt nothing but the top of an empty scabbard.

"Not so quick!" a different voice barked at Carver from behind, also high pitched yet gravelly.

Suddenly, something slammed down onto his upper back. The impact pushed Carver's chest into the ground and knocked the breath out of him. As the force continued pushing into him, he realized that what he was feeling was two boots digging into his back and that someone was standing on him.

Carver attempted to push himself up. After crawling so far, he was exhausted, but surprisingly, the weight of whoever was standing on his back was not enough to keep him down. Carver's chest began to rise off the ground.

"Keep 'im down, Marn!"

"I'm tryin'!"

Carver felt the resistance on his back increase for a moment, and then the weight vanished entirely. A second later, both boots slammed into his back just below the shoulders, driving him into the ground.

"Yeahhaha! Like that!"

Before Carver could readjust himself, the boots pushed into his back again, suddenly disappeared, then came crashing down. Carver clued in that the person addressed as Marn was jumping up and down on his back.

Carver coughed as Marn's boots sank into his back for the third time, but now that Carver understood that Marn was apparently going to keep jumping on his back to keep him down, he quickly formulated a response. As soon as Carver felt Marn's boots push off his back for another jump, he shoved his elbows into the cold dirt and flipped himself over. Before he could fully roll to his back, Marn's boots came back down, slamming into Carver's right shoulder. The unexpected movement caused Marn to flip to the side and fall to Carver's right.

Before Marn could recover, Carver reached out and grabbed whatever he could. Immediately, he realized that Marn was oddly shaped: short, thin, and with proportions that didn't seem right for a human.

"Wah! Let go!"

At that moment, he realized his attacker was not a human but a goblin.

Marn looked to be no more than four and a half feet tall and was thin and lanky. His head was dark green, as was the rest of his skin, which was visible through the holes in his raggedy brown trousers and torn-up white tunic. The top of his round head was bald, and on each side of it was a long green ear that stretched firmly outwards nearly half a foot in length. He had a fat green nose nearly twice the size of Carver's that tilted downwards, hiding the nostrils. His mouth was wider than a human's or a dwarf's and was filled with small teeth, and his eyes were large like a sovereign's, looking right at Carver in panic with yellow sclera and fat, oval-shaped pupils.

Carver didn't let the surprise of Marn's appearance cause him any hesitation. Instead, he doubled down on his efforts to subdue the goblin, tightening his grip on Marn's body and pulling him toward himself.

Marn squirmed like a drowning rat and kicked his legs as Carver dragged him through the dirt.

Carver raised his face to avoid Marn's kicks and moved his right hand from Marn's waist to his throat. Marn's face contorted, making his already large eyes bulge even more as Carver lifted himself over the goblin and squeezed his green throat, putting his body's weight onto his hand.

A pair of hands wrapped around Carver's right arm and pulled it back. Carver looked over his shoulder and saw that another goblin was standing next to him. The goblin's pull forced Carver to loosen his grip on Marn's neck and allowed Marn to take a loud breath.

Carver struggled to shake off the second goblin, but with his strength already drained, his other arm focused on keeping Marn's arm pinned, and while also trying to block out the pain in his ankle, he couldn't keep up the fight for long.

After a moment of resisting, Carver's right elbow bent out and his hand slipped off Marn's throat. The second goblin jumped back and pulled Carver's arm along with him while at the same moment Marn, now free to breathe, managed to roll out from under Carver.

Carver's balance shifted, and his left arm gave out under his own weight, causing him to fall onto his chest again while the other goblin continued to pull his right arm back. Before Carver could readjust himself, the goblin pulling his right arm jumped over his legs to his left side, kicked his foot into Carver's lower back, and held it there, yanking his right arm behind his back.

Carver felt the muscles in his arm stretch painfully, and his elbow burned like it was going to pop, but he couldn't muster the strength to pull his arm away at the angle he was at, and with the goblin's foot pushing into his lower back from the left Carver could not roll into the pull of his arm.

"Kick 'im in the nog already!" the goblin pulling Carver's arm shrieked.

Marn pushed himself to his feet and took a fast step toward Carver from the right. Carver tried to move his head away, but his neck could only stretch so far to the left. The tip of Marn's left boot struck him in the side of the head, smearing mud across his cheek and ear.

Dizziness assaulted Carver in place of the pain he expected from the kick, a dizziness that also somewhat numbed the pain in his right arm and left ankle for a second.

"Again! Again!"

Carver's dizziness faded slightly as a throbbing ache emerged from the right side of his head. The ache brought a new surge of panic into Carver's being that sent him into a frenzy as he struggled to escape, which was why he was unprepared when Marn's boot slammed into the side of his head for a second time.

Carver felt no pain from the second kick. Instead, the dizziness returned, only much stronger. It made it hard for Carver to focus on his struggle, and for a split second he lost track of what he was trying to do.

"Do it right!"

"I am!"

The goblins' voices sounded strangely distant to Carver, like they were echoes coming from other alleys. He tried to hold onto his thoughts and attempted to lift his head off the ground, but he could not focus hard enough to tense the muscles in his neck. Then the darkness of the alley seemed to push into his mind and everything went black.

Chapter 31

◯◯◯

Carver opened his eyes to the sight of Cosom's many twinkling eyes staring down at him from the dark sky. The stars seemed oddly blurry and appeared to move gently in place like flower petals floating on a pond. Suddenly, a strong headache emerged from the back of Carver's mind and ruined the beautiful sight. Along with the strange headache came a spell of dizziness and nausea, followed by a general sense of confusion. A series of gentle tingles ran across his forehead, and with each one he had to close his eyes for a moment and focus on not throwing up.

After a few seconds of his mind and stomach being bombarded with odd sensations and unpleasant feelings, the strange aura of grogginess holding Carver's mind captive started to fade, allowing the rest of his body to communicate with him. His right arm suddenly ached, and the soreness around his head began to localize on the right side. Worst of all, however, was a steadily increasing discomfort coming from his left ankle.

The discomfort turned into a throbbing pain that pushed away the last of the fog inside Carver's head like cold water being poured over his face. It was then that his thoughts began to connect to one another and allowed him to make sense of what he was seeing and feeling.

Carver quickly realized that the stars were not moving in place but that he himself was moving. Then, with a slow turn of his head to the right and left,

Carver realized that not only was he lying on a flat wooden surface, he was surrounded by a wooden wall no more than three feet high.

None of his next thoughts made sense as he tried to remember where he was and what had happened. The image of the burning office was the first thing that returned to his mind with any clarity. Then Carver recalled that he had gotten far away from the garrison, though he was not sure how, and that he had been traveling through darkness. He remembered crawling but could not remember why he did not simply walk. Holes began to form in his recollection, and he wondered if he was dreaming or if his memories had been a dream.

The wooden floor he was lying on suddenly tilted and Carver felt his body slide backwards. The quick movement ignited a strong feeling of nausea, but before he could truly feel sick, his head smacked into something hard. He winced and attempted to move his hands up to grab his head, but his arms wouldn't budge.

Carver looked down his body as he realized his arms were pushing into something, and only then did he notice not only was there another small wooden wall a little ways beyond his feet, he was covered in a raggedy blanket as well. The blanket bulged in some areas like other objects were underneath it, and a sour smell seemed to be woven into the material.

The unpleasant smell didn't bother Carver for a second, as his attention was immediately drawn to the fact that he couldn't move his arms or his legs. Though he could not see what constrained him beneath the blanket, the feeling was unmistakable, and Carver realized what the problem was: his arms were bound to his sides with rope, and his legs were tied together.

His dizziness and nausea faded as his mind continued to sharpen and the pain in his left ankle began to climb to unbearable levels. The pain and discomfort led Carver to groan. The moment he did, the wooden floor tilted back again, and his head smacked into something hard, turning his groan into a sharp grunt.

"Is he awake?" a gravelly, high-pitched voice asked from behind Carver's head.

The floor stopped moving.

Almost like someone had shown him a painting, Carver suddenly recalled the image of the two goblins attacking him in the alley. In a panic, he closed his eyes and went still.

A loud creak of wood came from where the voice had.

"Nah. He's still out. Just making sleep sounds is all."

Carver remembered Marn's voice.

"Well, keep your eyes at him. We're almost back, and I ain't want him to come clear and run off after all that work."

"He ain't going no place, Avin. Tied up good 'nd great. But sure, if you're gunna steer the wagon on your own then I'll eye him."

Marn and Avin, Carver thought, repeating the names in his mind.

The wooden floor started to move again, though now Carver knew he was actually in the back of a small wagon. He wanted to open his eyes, but he knew that Marn' must be looking down at him now from the front seat. Carver kept still and tried to focus on making his breathing look natural. He didn't know what else he could do.

The rocking of the wagon made it difficult to keep his composure as his head continually thudded into the wooden barrier separating him from the drivers. Carver's ankle pulsed with pain and threatened to overwhelm him at times, but his fear of being killed by the goblins should he awaken kept him from reacting. Each time the wagon rocked and bumped along the uneven terrain, Carver allowed his body to wiggle and used the few seconds of movement to struggle his arms around, hoping he might eventually break free of the ropes that restrained him.

After his sixth bout of concealed struggling, with the bumpy ride acting as his cover, Carver felt the rope over his arms beginning to loosen, but before a seventh bump in the road, the wagon came to an abrupt stop.

"Keep a stare on him, Marn. I'm a get the lads inside."

"Yep."

Carver contemplated trying to attack Marn, now that the goblin was alone, but he couldn't think of how he would do it while tied and injured. The sudden ruckus of a door opening and many footsteps approaching told Carver that he would not have had the time to act anyway.

"He's in the wagon," Avin said.

Carver tried to discern how many pairs of footsteps he was hearing, but he was unable to focus enough to figure it out.

"What use do we have for a human lad?" a third, higher-pitched gravelly voice asked.

"It depends on what's the deal of these papers, Kip."

Carver noted that name as well.

"They were scattered next to him in the alley when we found him. People with papers are usually important. Here, you're the best at reading."

Carver heard the shuffling of papers.

"Most of these sovereign words ain't the ones I know. I ain't some dwarf scholar to be tossed a book and told to read. Besides, these letters is inked funny. Whoever wrote is to blame."

"What about that word?" Carver heard Marn ask. "Ael ... Aelli ... Aellia. It's on a bunch of the papers. Sometimes twice."

"Don't be staring your eyes over my shoulder, Marn. I read that word myself and forgot to tell. And that's the name of the guard captain."

"I thought her name was Marshal?" a new voice said.

"That's her bigger title. She's the boss of lots a things."

Carver couldn't keep up with who was saying what anymore as many new voices joined the mix.

"So, does that mean those papers are hers then? Why's this terran human got them for?"

"It's just human or terran you fool. Yer sayin' human human when you say terran human."

"I know that! Shut that mouth!"

"I told you, boss! I told you! Them papers are special. Belonging to Ellya they do."

"Not Ellya, you daft fool. A-laya is how you say it."

"He must be her page boy then. Carrying her letters round the city."

"No page boy moves at dark. And this one had a scabbard and was crawling through the mud. He's a page thief is what he is."

"What kinda thief thieves pages?"

"Click your teeth together, you fools. I've figured it all out," Kip said, his voice rising to silence the others. "What's the only humans who move around in the dark that also read good and carry scabbards for swords?"

"Soldiers! They do."

"No! They wear armor, and this one has none. Rebels, you idiot. Aethi'ziton! This human is working with them Lost Seekers. It's obvious."

"You shit idiots! What were you thinking attack-napping a Aethi'ziton? We do business with them. This will ruin our trade if they find out what you two did!"

"It's not our fault! We couldn't see. It was dark and muddy. Let's just put him back before he sees us."

"He already eyed you two. We can't risk it. We should kill him and dump the body off the docks."

Carver tensed up but kept still.

"If he's a rebel, he might have sorcery! We should slit his neck before he casts magic fire on us!"

"He didn't use magic on us when we found him. Besides, he's tied. What spells can he cast without his hands?"

"Let's take his hands then. He can't for sure if he hasn't those."

Carver started trying to wriggle his arms and hands free of the ropes despite his worry of being caught.

"That could make it worse. Let's just put him back where we found him."

"No! Be quiet, you fools! All of you! Listen and don't touch him. This is absols, it is. Absols and lots of 'em!"

Carver stopped moving and listened closely.

"Whatcha mean, boss?"

"Don't you lot see? This human's a Lost Seeker on a stealing mission. He stole these from the captain and was takin' 'em to his rebels. That means the Lost Seekers want the papers, which means they're valuable, which means the Lost Seekers will toss plenty of sols for them and this boy."

"Ah. So, ransom."

"Yes, but that's only half. We contact the Lost Seekers and get a meet to happen, tellin 'em we have their thief and pages. They come and pay us for both, then while they're handing over the sols and shards, we tell the soldiers and get them all caught. The soldiers will pay us for the rebels and the return of their boss's papers."

"Won't a ransom make them Aethi'ziton angry, boss? They could say no and stop buying our goods."

"They can stomp harder than a quake from Craggon for all I care. They rely on us. Them lot need us to bring them their weapons and supplies from the Mainland. Without us they wouldn't be no rebels here at all. They'll have no choice but to listen."

"But if we sell them out to the soldiers, they'll stop buying for sure. They'd burn down the warehouse with spells if they found out."

"We wouldn't be crossing all of them. Just those who come to deal. There's plenty of Aethi'ziton on these islands. Plenty to buy our goods. And the rest won't find out. I've got it all planned. We'll tell the soldiers about the deal while it's happening. The armored lads will show up as the rebels leave without their absols and take them then. We won't be near when it happens. Afterwards, we get paid in soldier sols. For sure we will. And the Aethi'ziton will be none the wiser. It's a sure thing, it is."

"That's mighty smart, boss. Twice paid and no smuggling work to be done. We'll be rolling in sols and shards after this."

"I'm the boss for a reason. Don't you lot forget that. Now, all of you, take the human and bind him in the back of the warehouse. Check 'im for injuries and make it so he doesn't die from them. We need him alive for the most sols."

"You got it, boss."

Carver heard footsteps come near to where his feet were, followed by the sound of metal latches and a creak and a bang. His instincts told him to look, but he didn't want to let it show that he was awake and aware. He knew that if the goblins thought he had heard them they would kill him for sure.

Instead, Carver decided he would feign unconsciousness until his kidnappers either undid his bindings to move him or became less numerous, though how he would get away with his ankle in its current state, he wasn't sure.

"Pull half of 'im out and steady the legs on my shoulders, then grab him by the shoulders, and we'll take 'im from there."

The blanket covering Carver was yanked off, and a pair of hands wrapped around each of his ankles and pulled hard. The sudden pain was too much for Carver. He shouted in agony, and a second later, he felt the hands around his ankles disappear, causing his legs to surrender to gravity and pull the rest of him along. His shout of pain barely had time to end before his back hit the hard ground, followed by his head, filling his mind with a sudden fuzziness.

Carver closed his eyes for a brief second as he lost track of his thoughts while at the same time he tried to free his arms from the rope, running purely on instinct and a surge of panicked energy.

"You fools woke him! Shut him up, quick!"

Carver opened his eyes and saw a group of goblins standing around him. They were all green skinned, bald, large eared, and yellow eyed, and each stood somewhere between four-foot-five to four-foot-ten. However, the goblins seemed blurry and out of focus, as if he were looking at them from underwater.

Carver pulled his right arm up, barely feeling the coarse rope burn against his skin, and managed to free it. He raised his right arm to defend himself, but suddenly he forgot how to control it. His awareness of his left arm also disappeared despite his efforts to wriggle it free also.

Carver felt a new surge of panic as he realized what was happening and what was going to happen. As he tensed up, his entire body spasmed.

The goblins quickly closed in around him. One grabbed Carver's right arm and slammed it to the ground while another dove onto his legs to keep them pinned. Carver wanted to fight against the goblins, but as quickly as the thought crossed his mind, he felt a strong jerk in his neck, and he suddenly lost his idea of what was going on around him. His legs began to shake and pull in sharp movements, causing the goblin atop his legs to wobble.

"What's he doing?" one of the goblins howled.

Carver didn't hear a response, suddenly feeling like he was suffocating. He opened his mouth to breathe, but instead he let out a long groan that sounded as if he was trying to vomit.

A third goblin dropped to his knees next to Carver's head and slapped a hand over Carver's mouth, partially shoving his palm inside. Carver's sick groan became muffled for a moment until another jolt shot through his neck and caused his jaw to slam shut.

The goblin smothering Carver screamed as Carver's teeth pierced his hand. He tried to pull away, but Carver's jaw had tightened like a vise and refused to let go. The goblin howled again and pulled his hand away once more, this time with enough force to separate his hand from Carver's teeth. The goblin shrieked and jumped back, his hand now bleeding profusely as much of its skin remained between Carver's teeth.

"Choke him out! Choke him!" another goblin called from behind.

Before Carver could taste the blood in his mouth, a different goblin leaped onto his chest and wrapped his green hands around his neck. Carver continued to shake in place despite the other goblins holding him down, and he remained unable to think straight or fight back as his throat tightened up.

A pressure began to build up in Carver's forehead, and he felt his eyes pulsing in their sockets. He wanted to gasp for air, but he could not figure out how to relax his jaw, nor could he properly perceive that a goblin was sitting on his chest and strangling him.

The last thing Carver noticed was the stars fading into darkness.

Chapter 32

❧

Aellia's horse carried her quickly through the cobblestone city streets, causing her hastily donned chainmail to announce her approach to anyone nearby with metallic clinks.

The sun was still a few hours from rising, but Caswen was already beginning to wake. Soldiers marched down the streets and civilians peered out their doors and windows. Aellia paid them no mind. In no time at all, thanks to her obedient steed, she reached her destination and pulled the reins to bring her mount to a halt.

Despite being told of the situation after she had been unexpectedly awoken by a series of rapid knocks on her bedroom door in her manor chambers, the sight still hit her with shocking force.

The east wall of the city garrison's main structure had collapsed out onto the street, revealing an interior of charred wood and cracked rubble. The contents of Aellia's office were mixed in with the debris. Shattered bookshelves, a charred oak door, and part of her desk were half buried in stone and blackened support beams, all of which had gray smoke emanating from them, trailing up into the dark sky. The entire office had collapsed through the floor, taking the east wall of the mess hall along with it, leaving the long chamber open to the elements along with its many tables now covered in dust and chunks of stone.

Dozens of soldiers, as well as a group of civilians, were standing around the debris. Many were holding buckets, some empty and some full of water. A few held burning torches and paced around the immediate area while many others sat on the ground panting with exhaustion.

The sight left Aellia speechless and sitting idle in her saddle in shock, but then she brought herself under control. Giving her brown horse a pat on the neck for running so vigorously so early in the morning, Aellia unhooked her boots from the saddle straps and dismounted. Her armor, still not properly fastened and with buckles and straps hanging in some places, jangled and shuffled as she marched toward a male soldier who was standing apart from the group.

"You, soldier, what happened here?"

The soldier nearly jumped with surprise as he spun around. He was holding a wooden bucket of water that leaked steadily from the bottom in fat drips.

"Guard Captain. You're here."

"Yes. Now tell me what happened!"

The soldier looked around with confusion on his face. "I ... I don't rightly know, ma'am. I was on patrol at the other end of the Low District when I heard shouting from the northwest. My patrol and I followed the commotion, and we found the place burning, with other soldiers all around. We stirred the populace awake and sent for water to extinguish the flames, but truth be told it did very little. The main fire only ceased due to the collapse that happened about ten minutes ago. We only just managed to finish putting out the debris itself."

"How did the fire start?"

"I'm sorry, but I don't know, ma'am. I wasn't here when it started. You'll need to ask someone else."

"Where is Lieutenant Harsond?"

"I don't know, ma'am."

Aellia grunted and pushed the man aside as she brushed past him. She stepped over a pile of debris and made her way toward a crowd of soldiers.

"Who here has seen Lieutenant Harsond?"

The small crowd of male and female soldiers looked Aellia's way, as did many of the civilians, but they all turned away quickly. The manner in which the soldiers looked around and eyed each other told her that they were also clueless.

"Guard Captain!" a voice shouted from Aellia's left.

She turned and saw Kieran fast approaching. He was unarmored, wearing only a brown wool shirt and trousers with old leather shoes. His beaten face had healed, and his short blond hair bounced as he ran toward her, as did the bucket he carried, spilling water over the edges with each hurried step the young man took.

"Slow down, Kieran. The fire is out."

Kieran skidded to a halt just before Aellia. His eyes widened with shock. "By ... it's collapsed!"

"Do you know what happened here, Kieran?"

"No, ma'am. I was off duty tonight. I live close by, though, and I was awakened by the commotion. I've been running to and from the closest well and waking up anyone along the way."

Aellia wiped some of her stray hair away from her face, having not been able to brush it before she headed out due to the urgency of her summons, and sighed. "Do you know where Harsond is? He resides at the garrison's barracks, so he should be here."

"I haven't seen him, ma'am. I've been focused on the fire the whole time."

"Guard Captain!" a female voice called from the other side of Aellia.

She turned to see a female soldier, fully armored and not one of the members of the group Aellia had addressed just seconds earlier, was standing behind her with a worried expression on her face.

"What is it, soldier?"

"I overheard you. Lieutenant Harsond ... he ..."

Aellia stepped toward the woman. "Yes? Where is he?" she demanded, having lost much of her patience.

The soldier recoiled slightly but maintained eye contact with Aellia. "He's in the infirmary, ma'am. He's been badly hurt."

"What? What happened?"

The soldier opened her mouth to speak, but before she could form a word, Aellia turned and ran off toward the south wall of the main structure. Kieran dropped his bucket, letting the water spill out into the cracks of the cobblestone road, and followed his captain.

Aellia reached the door at the south end of the building, flung it open, and marched inside. The room she found herself in was laid out like a cross, with a door at each end of a small hallway. As soon as she entered, she heard the painful cries of a man coming from the door down the left protrusion of the cross.

Aellia strode down the left hall and pushed the door open. The cries of pain became much louder. The room was the garrison infirmary, a rectangular chamber filled with beds, low counters, and wooden shelves containing a range of medical supplies. Her attention was immediately drawn to a man writhing in the middle-most bed. He was being held down by a male soldier while a female soldier was attempting to bandage his legs.

The man being restrained appeared to be horribly burnt. His tunic was charred and riddled with holes, revealing a torso covered in red skin and blisters, while his hands were almost entirely pink with blisters. If he had had a beard or any hair before, both were now gone, along with his eyebrows, causing his face to look strange. Worst of all were the man's legs, both of which were exposed, as his trousers were mostly burnt away while whatever remained had been cut to allow the female soldier to tend to his skin.

Each leg had suffered intense third-degree burns from the ankle up to the thigh, after which second and then first-degree burns continued up his body. The meat of his legs was dark red in most areas and black in others, all of it surrounded with bright-pink skin and melted blisters. Blood trailed down and soaked into the bed from almost every inch of the man's legs, and as the female soldier attempted to apply thick bandages around his legs, the hot blood would immediately soak through the wrapping.

With each touch the man would howl in pain and slap his blistered hands against the bed in violent protest, all while fighting against the male soldier who was holding him down by the shoulders from behind the bed.

Aellia's face paled when she finally recognized the man's face.

"Harsond!"

He looked toward Aellia but responded only with a groan of exertion.

Both of the soldiers also looked toward her. "Guard Captain," they said hurriedly as they continued to deal with their patient.

"By the stars!" Kieran spouted from behind Aellia as he too entered the infirmary.

Aellia walked toward the bed and stood at its end. "What happened to him?"

The female soldier looked up from Harsond's badly bleeding legs. "He was caught in the fire that filled your office, Captain. We barely arrived in time to unlock the door and pull him out. Any longer and he would have burnt to death."

Harsond hissed through his clenched teeth as the woman finished wrapping his right leg. The bandages were stained red and only covered a portion of his leg.

Aellia looked at Harsond's hairless face and saw the agony that spoke through it. Then she looked down at his other burnt leg, yet to be bandaged.

"Have you given him any potions?" Aellia asked as she looked over at the cupboards and counters to the left and right of the room.

"We poured some healer's potion across his legs, but we don't have enough stock to apply to every wound," the female soldier said. "And it takes at least an hour for the pain to lessen."

Aellia stormed over to the nearest cupboard and pulled its doors open, revealing three wooden shelves with medical supplies lined up from left to right, with only two small bottles of dark-red liquid, each marked with a label that said "Healing Potion."

Harsond screamed again.

Aellia growled and slammed the cupboard doors closed as she turned back to the female soldier who was now beginning to apply bandages to Harsond's other leg.

"Healer's potion won't do shit for this! We need something stronger, rage-whirl or something!"

The female soldier looked back to Aellia. "We checked and we don't have any! We—I'm not a medic, ma'am, I don't know what we should do!" she said with far more panic in her tone than had been noticeable previously.

Aellia stopped herself from reaching over and checking the next cupboard. Instead, she turned around to face the others, hesitating as her thoughts raced from one idea to the next, but as the female soldier touched Harsond's other leg with the new bandages and he screamed in pain, Aellia snapped out of her hesitation.

"We don't have the means of dealing with these injuries here. We need to get him to the healers at Agon's temple. They'll have the potions and skills to treat this better than us."

Kieran stepped farther into the room and stood next to Aellia. "But Captain, the temple will still be shut. Aol isn't up yet. Cosom is still—"

Aellia turned and backhanded Kieran across the face, sending him stumbling back into a wooden table, causing the medical supplies atop it to fall to the floor.

"I don't give a damn if Cosom is watching! If this man dies, you'll suffer my wrath, not Cosom's!"

Kieran rubbed his cheek, which was now red and stinging, though he was immediately thankful that Aellia was not wearing her gauntlets, else he was sure his cheek would have split open from the blow. "Captain, I—"

"I'll do it myself!" Aellia barked. She took one step toward the door before she stopped and stared at a tall figure blocking her path.

Kieran gasped when he saw the figure and stepped backwards until he was against the back wall of the infirmary on the other side of the table.

Erol ducked his head as he entered, then stood up straight and looked down at those in the room. "So, you would compare your power to that of your all-seeing god? And here I thought you humans were entirely slaves to your superstitions."

Aellia stared up at Erol, frustration building into a headache behind her eyes. "Get out of my way, Erol. I need to get Harsond proper aid!"

Aellia could not see it, but the faces of those behind her filled with shock at her words. Erol simply grinned, keeping his stare locked on her.

"Proper aid? You mean those weak potions and poultices you make from weeds that your leaders of superstition keep tucked away in their temples?"

He smirked. "If you humans could understand how primitive your methods are, you'd be far more grateful to my kind for the tools we provide."

Aellia balled her hands into fists. "You know damn well why our potions are not as strong as they could be! And I don't see you providing any tools to compensate for that right now. So if you want gratitude from me, someone so low to a mighty one like yourself," she said through clenched teeth, "then move out of my way so I can help my lieutenant."

Erol's grin faded. "I understand from what I heard that your lieutenant was here when the fire began and that he might know what started it."

"Yes, he was here, but—"

"I was here," Harsond grunted. "Ah! I saw him. Mmmpf! I can talk!" He struggled to get each word out between his frantic breaths.

Erol strode past Aellia without a glance and walked to the end of Harsond's bed. The soldiers who were tending to him stopped what they were doing and stepped away from the bed, avoiding eye contact with Erol. Kieran, on the other hand, could not take his eyes off the towering sovereign.

Erol placed himself where the female soldier had been bandaging Harsond's legs and kneeled next to the bed. Harsond continued to writhe and twist as his right leg bled through the bandages and the blood from his left leg continued soaking into the straw-stuffed bedding.

Erol looked into Harsond's eyes, and Harsond tried to stare back without the pain breaking his focus. Aellia turned around and watched the sovereign with suspicious scrutiny.

"This is going to hurt a lot, Harsond. I would give you something to lessen the pain, but it would slow your mind, and I need you to speak clearly and recount the events of the fire accurately once this is over. Do you understand?"

Harsond nodded despite not understanding a thing, his face contorting in pain as he tried to deal with his current agony.

Erol turned to Kieran and Aellia. "Both of you, come hold the man in place." Then Erol looked over at the other soldiers standing in the corner, who were watching silently. "You two. Be gone."

"Yes, sir," the soldiers said in unison, then scurried out the door.

Aellia and Kieran positioned themselves on either side of Harsond and placed their hands on his chest and shoulders while trying to avoid touching his burns. Harsond continued to twist and fight against the hands keeping him down despite his desire to cooperate.

Erol quickly removed the blood-soaked bandages from Harsond's legs, pulling bits of charred, sticky flesh with them, sending Harsond into a fresh round of writhing and cursing.

Kieran felt sick at the sight, and the rancid smell of burnt flesh made it no easier to control his stomach, but his intense fear of messing up in front of not only Aellia but also Erol kept him from vomiting.

Erol examined Harsond's legs like someone evaluating how much dust had built up on an old shelf. Then he looked up at Kieran and Aellia. "Be ready. Keep him still and do as I say."

Erol looked into Harsond's eyes. "Deep breath now, Lieutenant."

Erol suddenly grabbed the middle of each of Harsond's legs, wrapping his long beige fingers around the bloody flesh like he was gripping a weapon. Harsond screamed and tried to pull his legs away, but Erol tightened his grip and held them in place.

"Stop! Stop!" Harsond cried as the pain overpowered his self-control. He tried desperately to force himself up, but Aellia and Kieran kept him pinned to the straw mattress.

"Hurry up, Erol!" Aellia shouted as she strained to keep Harsond still.

Erol did not respond or even look at her. Instead, he stared intensely at his hands wrapped around Harsond's legs. Nothing was happening apart from Harsond squirming and howling in agony, and Aellia was furious at the sovereign's apparent lack of concern. Then she noticed, as did Kieran, that the air around Erol's hands was beginning to change, seeming to take form, like the air one can see at the end of a long stone road during a hot summer day.

The seemingly visible air around Erol's hands began to move like rippling water. Harsond screamed even louder and struggled much harder as the air around Erol's hands continued to distort and sway.

Then the flesh of Harsond's legs next to Erol's hands began to move as well, rising up and seeming to stretch out like spilled honey spreading itself over the floor. The moving and contorting flesh covered the red and pinkish meat of Harsond's legs, and the bits of charred skin began to sink into new, soft flesh. The speed at which the newly forming flesh advanced was steady, and soon the effects reached all the way up to Harsond's knees.

As the flesh grew and spread, Harsond's original skin tone began to return to the burned areas, with no scarring left behind. The blisters on his hands and torso thinned out and vanished while the pink and red skin around them faded into a paleness. Harsond continued to fight against Aellia and Kieran, however, shouting a mixture of pleas and demands to stop, but after another minute, the entirety of Harsond's legs were healed as if nothing had happened to them, and he suddenly stopped shouting.

"Done," Erol said in a casual tone as he released Harsond's legs and stood up.

Aellia and Kieran also released their hold on Harsond. The moment he was free, Harsond sat up and feverishly inspected his legs.

"By the gods! The pain, it's … it's gone. It's actually gone. And my legs, they're—"

The sight of his legs being hairless and almost totally smooth was nearly as odd to Harsond as seeing them no longer charred and bloody.

"There's no scars. How … how can that be?"

"Rejuvenancy does as it implies," Erol said, "though it cannot heal scars once they have set in naturally. You're lucky I was able to treat you before your legs healed on their own, if you had survived at all. It would have been a ghastly sight otherwise. Your hair will grow back with time."

Harsond eyed his legs in silence. Then he examined his hands and looked over the rest of his body. His face showed a mixture of disbelief and joy as he moved his hairless legs around on the bed. He gave no indication that anything felt wrong. Then he locked eyes with Erol.

"Thank you, sir. You're truly a most generous lord."

"Do not thank me. I did this not out of care or generosity but out of need for your words to be calm and your memory to be unhindered by pain. Now, tell us what happened tonight." Erol's tone was flat and demanding, sending a chill down Harsond's spine.

"Yes, of course," Harsond said with less excitement as he looked over at Kieran and Aellia.

Aellia nodded and made her way next to Erol, Kieran following close behind but keeping on the side of her away from Erol.

With all their eyes on him, Harsond suddenly felt a great deal of shame, for now his failure would be known to all three of them. Swallowing his pride and readying himself for their disappointment and perhaps anger, he sat up more comfortably in the bed and cleared his throat.

"First, I would like to tell you just how sorry I am. Both of you," Harsond motioned his eyes from Aellia to Erol, "for my failure. This whole situation was escalated by my own error. I should have been able to stop it."

Aellia folded her arms and frowned. "Harsond ..."

Harsond readied himself for his captain's words.

"You're my most trusted soldier, my lieutenant, and my friend. If you could not prevent whatever happened, then I doubt anyone could have."

Harsond was taken aback by his captain's words, so much so that he didn't know how to continue.

"You have a forgiving captain, it seems, Harsond," Erol said, "so cease with the apologies and speak plainly of what transpired."

Harsond saw how Erol's words angered Aellia, who shot Erol a look that went unnoticed by the sovereign.

"Yes, well ..." Harsond cleared his throat. "I was asleep in my private chambers in the barracks when a young male soldier knocked on my door. I questioned him immediately on why he had left his post and why he was disturbing me at so late an hour, and the lad told me that he stepped over some shards of glass while passing by the east wall of the mess hall during his patrol.

"While at first he thought nothing of it, he later wondered why glass, being uncommon around these parts, would be broken on the street. He convinced his fellows to return with him to the spot. That's when he noticed that the captain's office window, which is the only glass window aside from those you can find at the manor, by my understanding, was right above the shards of glass. He told me that he and his patrol concluded that someone had thrown a stone at the window, so they did not deem it something to report until morning."

"Is this tale going to arrive somewhere?" Erol asked coldly.

"Yes, sir. Sorry, sir. The lad later felt uneasy as he thought about it. Apparently, he began to worry that he and his fellows would get in trouble for not reporting the act of vandalism immediately, and then he worried it might be more than just a stone. So, he left his patrol and came to my door, apparently at the ridicule of his comrades, to report what he assumed was the aftermath of an angry commoner throwing a stone at the captain's office window.

"After he explained this to me, I decided to err on the side of caution and armed myself before taking the lad with me to investigate the office. Inside, we found a boy, probably no more than seventeen, going through the captain's things in the dark."

"A Lost Seeker?" Erol furrowed his prominent, hairless brow.

"I assume so. The boy drew a sword as soon as we entered. I had the lad who followed me lock me in the room and leave to gather support and manacles. My intent was to keep the intruder in place until aid arrived."

Erol folded his arms. "Are you saying you could not kill this boy alone? That you needed aid?

"My intent was not to kill him, sir. I wanted answers. I assumed this boy to be a Aethi'ziton—a Lost Seeker, I mean—, I beg your pardon, one sent to steal information from the captain's quarters. I wanted to interrogate him to discern what information he was looking for, why, and where his fellow rebels were hiding. This boy was angry and full of fear; I could tell from how he moved and the look in his eyes. As such I suspected he would not go down without a serious wound or being killed outright if I attempted to restrain him myself, so I sent for aid."

Erol remained silent and waited for more. Harsond looked at Aellia and wondered what she was thinking, as she had been silent since his tale began.

"The boy ... he ... well ... Ah, screw it. He bested me. The little shit danced around the room faster than I could follow and pulled the bookshelves down."

"He pulled down my shelves?" Aellia exclaimed. "What for?"

"At first I thought he was simply trying to create a barrier between himself and me, but I was wrong. I did not understand what he was actually doing until his plan was already in action.

"There was already oil spilled across the room from the captain's desk lantern, which the boy had knocked over. I had brought a lantern to the room, and the boy knocked it over, igniting the oil on the floor. A fire erupted, and the flames spread like a swarm of flies, creating a barrier between me and the boy. The little shit also kicked oil onto my trousers a moment before, which caused the flames to spread up my legs almost instantly."

Harsond looked back at his healed legs. "It all happened so fast after that. If those soldiers hadn't arrived when they did and pulled me out of the room, I would have burned to death."

Harsond's audience remained silent as they considered the information. Erol rubbed his sharp chin before speaking.

"This boy, the supposed Lost Seeker, tell me about him in detail. Everything."

"Yes, sir. He ... um, he was young, a little younger than Kieran here, I'd guess, judging that he had no facial hair at all. He was wearing simple commoner clothes, nothing special. It was too dark for me to see the color of his eyes, but his hair ... it was short and brown. And that scar ..."

"What scar?" Aellia asked before Erol could, regaining some charge over the questioning.

Harsond thought for a moment before looking at his captain. "When he first crossed the room, I saw that there was a wide scar going down the back of his head at an angle. The skin around it was mostly hairless, so it stood out immediately."

Aellia turned to Erol. "I'll put out a bounty for this scar-headed boy. If the scar is as noticeable as Harsond remembers, it shouldn't be hard to find him."

Erol did not respond or even look her way, he merely stared at Harsond, apparently deep in thought. Aellia did not like to be ignored, especially not in view of her soldiers, so she pushed her presence.

"Erol."

He finally turned and looked at her. A moment of silence occurred, which made Kieran feel nervous as he watched.

"Come with me, Guard Captain. Outside," was all the sovereign said before he turned and left the infirmary.

Aellia looked at her soldiers, but neither had words for her, so she turned and left. She headed through the cross-shaped chamber and made her way outside to where Erol was standing next to an isolated section of the building's south wall, only slightly within the illumination of a distant torch struggling to pierce the darkness.

Aellia walked up to him and stood firm, waiting for whatever words Erol had that required a change in location.

"You seem to have the respect of your soldiers, and having their respect makes them loyal to you more than if without, so I do not wish to lessen their view of you."

"So you decided to scold me away from their eyes, like a child pulled from her siblings and sent to her room? Is that it?"

"Do not be petty with me, Aellia. I am not your enemy."

Erol's tone sounded almost friendly, but she didn't drop her guard.

Erol paused and looked off down the empty street for a moment as if thinking about something, but he quickly turned his attention back toward Aellia, his tone serious once again. "Not more than two months have I been in this island city and already I see the failings of your command."

Aellia couldn't help but clench her hands into fists, an action that did not go unnoticed by Erol.

"Get angry all you like, Aellia, but not another word from you while I'm speaking. When I was assigned to monitor the Lost Seekers threat here, I was told that you were a stubborn, defensive, strict woman, all traits that should be of benefit to someone in your position, but all I have seen from you so far is inaction and failure. One rebel—a young boy, no less—was able to break into your private quarters and learn who knows what from your letters and records. And not only did he escape, he nearly killed your lieutenant in the process."

Erol looked over at the collapsed section of the building. Aellia kept her stare directly on him.

"Evidence of this disaster is piled behind you, making it clear to the whole city who bested who in this midnight exchange. These rebels rely on momentum to operate. They need victory after victory to seed doubt into the people and make them think they actually have a chance. The attack on the market was crippling to the authority and image of the Caswen Guard, and now an attack on your own garrison pulled off by a boy. Pathetic. Slaughtering some insignificant village will not get you out of this."

Aellia's eyes widened. "Verrel was—"

"Quiet!" Erol stamped his right foot into the ground. His foot's four bone-like talons pierced the cobblestone street, scattering specks of stone. Then he lowered his voice back to a somewhat calm level, though each new word still carried more bite than usual.

"Do you think I'm a fool? Some Terraland commoner who you can trick with lies? I know very well that Verrel, that insignificant little blot on the map, had no ties to the Lost Seekers, their actions, or their leadership. Your plan worked despite its brutality and quelled some of my peers' and superiors' tempers surrounding the situation on these islands, but that kind of desperate misdirection will not have the same effect if done again. You can trust me on that, Aellia.

"You must turn all your focus to the heart of the issue, the strong Lost Seekers presence in this city and this city alone. Start by finding this boy with the scar, interrogate him until he has nothing left to tell, then execute him publicly. And I expect to be there when you have him. I will not tolerate another failure to happen under your command."

Before Aellia could think of a response, Erol pulled his talons out of the ground and marched past her. He strode down the street, given a wide berth by the few commoners and soldiers he passed, then disappeared around the corner of the building's collapsed wall.

Aellia didn't move as she watched Erol leave. Anger enhanced her heartbeat, and her head was pounding from stress.

"Not getting along with the new boss, I see," a male voice called from her right.

Aellia turned toward it. "Do you often spy on me, Renneil? Am I such a failure that I need two people watching my every move?"

Renneil stepped out from a small side street between two brick homes. The darkness of the night veiled his appearance almost entirely, but Aellia knew it was him. He casually crossed the cobblestone street toward her. As he neared her, the light from the nearby torches revealed his aged face as well as his black cloak, which hung down to his shins, and his equally black hair, which was combed back behind his ears.

"I was keeping tabs on Erol as much as I was you, my dear. It's my job to know what's happening around here, after all."

Aellia looked around and saw that no one, either soldiers or civilians, were within earshot before looking back to Renneil. "It seems you know more about my actions than I'd like. I assume it was from either you or my father that Erol learned the truth about Verrel?"

"Why would you assume I told the sovereign anything about your decision regarding Verrel? Or that I myself know about it? You never spoke to me about such matters."

"Don't mess around with me. I never told you the details, but I know that you know. Like you said, it's your job to know things. My father then, that spineless bastard. He's bent over fully for Erol and is telling him everything, it seems."

"I wouldn't be so sure that your father is to blame. I'm not the only one with a spy network on these islands. The sovereigns have eyes and ears everywhere, though they'd prefer us not to know that. Besides, Erol is an intelligent man. I've no doubt he has uncovered much during his time secretly digging into our affairs."

Aellia took a breath through her nose and wiped some of her hair from her face. "Well, that's a pleasant thing to hear. It seems I'll not have privacy anywhere I go then."

Renneil turned slightly and looked past Aellia toward the collapsed wall. Most of the recently woken civilians had left the area or were watching from a good distance, while many of the soldiers were beginning to clear the debris from the street as others held torches for light. Finally, Renneil turned his attention back to Aellia and took a sharp breath.

"It could be so, unfortunately. Even here at your place of duty, it would seem, if what you were told of what transpired here is to be believed."

Aellia shot Renneil a curious look. "What, you think Harsond was lying? I won't have you in—"

Renneil raised a hand to signal that he meant no insult. "I'm flattered that you think I'm everywhere at once, but I have to admit I only just arrived here.

If you spoke with your lieutenant, I am unaware of it or what you discussed. But if your little spat with Erol was regarding information given by Harsond, then trust me when I say I am not calling Harsond a liar. I am merely wondering how accurate the information is."

"So, who then? You think this was done by someone who wasn't acting on behalf of the Lost Seekers?"

Renneil nibbled his lip. "I'm not saying I think anything yet. I'm merely evaluating. But if this was orchestrated by someone in the Aethi'ziton—and I'll find out if it was—then I'll see to it that those who ordered it suffer greatly."

"Oh, really. And how do you intend to do that? If we knew who their leaders were or where they were hiding then they would all be hanging by their necks right now."

Renneil laughed softly and waved his hand toward Aellia. "I'm merely speaking of intent, my girl. Seeing what has happened here troubles me greatly, I admit, for I dread to think of something ill befalling you, such as an Aethi'ziton assassin waiting for you inside your office chambers."

Aellia looked over at the debris stretching over the cobblestone street. "Yes, well, not much chance of that happening now." She turned back to Renneil. "Enough of this. Handling this disaster is going to require more of my time than I'm capable of giving, so I need to get started right away. And by the way, I'd prefer if you didn't spy on me, at least not for the rest of today."

"Very well. My apologies if my presence has disturbed you, Aellia." He bowed, turned to head down the street, and then stopped. "Oh. Just one more thing, Aellia."

"What?"

"If you have a problem with spying eyes and eavesdropping ears, you might want to have a word with that new assistant of yours." Renneil turned and pointed to the door Aellia had come from.

Aellia followed the gesture and just managed to catch the sight of the door closing. She looked back at Renneil, but he was already walking down the street opposite of the way Erol had gone, whistling a soft tune like he was walking through a sunny field. Aellia scoffed and rolled her eyes before she turned and approached the door.

She was not surprised to find Kieran standing on the other side.

"I'm sorry, ma'am. I didn't mean to be intrusive. I was just keeping close, like you told me to do. I didn't hear a thing."

"Kieran, shut up. And don't lie to me. I don't care one bit if you were listening in. I have bigger things to worry about right now. How is Harsond doing?"

"He left, ma'am. Said he felt as good as new and went to get a change of clothes."

"Good. Then you and I have work to do. I want you to get into uniform and then go to the printing house in the High District and talk to the people there. If they're still asleep, wake them up. I want them on those printing presses making some bounty notices immediately. Male, short brown hair, no facial hair, seventeen to twenty years old, and don't forget the scar on the back of his head. I want that boy found as soon as possible. Tell them to set the bounty at five silver absols, and make sure it says wanted alive, not dead. I'm going to find and question the soldier who was with Harsond, then those who helped battle the fire and see if they saw the boy. I'll have the bounty description changed later if I find out more, but I want to get an immediate start on this for now."

"Yes, ma'am. But, uh, pardon me, ma'am, but um ... shouldn't you have asked the spymaster for aid too? He was just with you, after all."

"No, Kieran. I don't need his help, and I sure as shit don't need Erol's. I'll find this Lost Seeker with only the aid of the people and my soldiers. Meet me back here once you finish your task."

"Yes, ma'am. I'll get to it right away." Kieran nodded and made his way past her to get to the door.

"And Kieran."

He stopped halfway outside and looked back.

"If Erol comes poking around again and questions you about anything—anything, you understand me—tell him you don't know shit and play dumb. I want that sovereign out of my damn business."

Chapter 33

Duncan's fishery continued to be a place of little comfort for those living inside, especially during the cold mid-October nights.

In the current moment, sitting silently on the ground floor within the faint illumination of four burning candles near his outstretched feet, Sebastian felt as though he was cut off from his surroundings, like he was isolated on a small island of light amidst an ocean of blackness.

The sense of isolation was further enhanced by the silence, so quiet that all Sebastian could hear was the steady rhythm of chewing coming from the older boy who was sitting on the other side of the lonely island of light.

"Hey, Rook."

"Yeah?" Rook looked up from the mostly devoured chicken drumstick in his hands, still chewing.

"I ... Never mind," he said softly as he lifted up his own, mostly intact, drumstick and took a bite. Rook didn't seem to care enough to prod, and looked away to chew in peace.

Sebastian looked up at the fishery wall. The pale blue glow of the dual moons that normally seeped through the cracks in the wall was missing, blocked by a thick layer of clouds high in the night sky.

Sebastian swallowed his mouthful of meat and proceeded to take another bite. He noticed that Rook's drumstick was showing more bone than cooked flesh now, a problem that Rook was addressing with his filleting knife, which each of them had for gutting and cleaning out fish, cutting and scraping the last bits of meat from the bone.

Sebastian looked at his own dinner and realized he had barely touched it. He was hungry, and he wanted to eat, but he found himself sitting and thinking more than he did taking bites. The quality of the food didn't help his appetite either. The chicken was cold and stringy, and the bone was poorly cut, leaving each drumstick with sharp, broken ends. Sebastian assumed that the butcher Rook had purchased the meat from didn't strive for quality.

"Rook, are you really not bothered at all by what happened?"

Rook looked up from his near-finished dinner and locked eyes with Sebastian. "You mean about Carver? What's there to be bothered about? It's one less person to have to share our food with. That's not something I'm bothered by."

"You really are a jerk, you know. Carver was my friend, and Nina and Helena's too. I know you didn't like him, but you shouldn't be glad about him dying."

Sebastian thought he saw Rook smirk for a second, but the fading candle-light made it hard to tell.

"So, you're telling me that if I suddenly disappeared or died, you three wouldn't immediately start thinking about the benefits to yourselves?"

"You help bring us what we need from outside, so no, we'd be a little upset."

Rook frowned, an expression that was clear enough for Sebastian to see even in the dim light, but he didn't follow it with a response. Instead, he tossed his meatless drumstick next to a similarly broken and chipped bone by his feet, placed his fillet knife down to his other side, then reached over to a small pot between himself and Sebastian that was just outside the circle of candlelight. He lifted the lid and pulled out another drumstick.

"Say what you will, but I wouldn't be having this third piece if Scar-head was here."

Sebastian stopped himself from responding, knowing that anything he could say wasn't going to get him anywhere. Instead, he lifted his own drum-stick to his mouth to take another bite, but the sudden sound of creaking wood from behind him reached his ears before the food reached his mouth. Sebastian lowered the drumstick and turned around.

Though he couldn't see her, his eyes followed her descent through the darkness as each stair creaked under her step. Her soft, dirty-blond hair was the first thing to catch his eye, though next was the deep scar trailing from the left side of her mouth over her cheek and up to just below her left ear, as well as the prominent scar stretching over where her left eyebrow should have been. The rest of her facial scarring was too difficult to see in the darkness.

Sebastian had mostly gotten used to seeing Nina's face, but every now and again he would forget the extent of the damage and cringe at the sight.

"How is she?" he asked as his sister stepped into the dim island of light.

Nina sat down beside her brother. "She's not coming down. She says she's not hungry."

"You hear that, Seb?" Rook said, smiling. "Even more for us tonight."

"What?"

"Ignore him, Nina."

Nina frowned at Rook and then peered at the pot beside him. She was about to ask him to hand her some food, but then she thought better of it and served herself.

"Is she any better?" Sebastian asked.

Nina waited until she had finished chewing what was in her mouth. "I'm not sure. She's not crying anymore, but now she's ... well ... she's just ..."

"What?"

"Defeated."

"Defeated?"

"Yeah. That's the best way I can describe her right now. She's just sitting up there against a crate. I tried talking to her about it more, but I couldn't get her to say much, and when she did it was almost like she was whispering." Nina's tone carried both sadness and frustration. "She thinks it's her fault, that if she hadn't brought up what Carver told her that night he wouldn't have left. Like he had forgotten and only remembered because she started talking to him about it. I tried to tell her that it isn't her fault, but she seems so determined to blame herself."

Sebastian let out a deep sigh. "I'm worried about her, Nina. It's been four days, and it doesn't feel like she even wants to get better."

Nina placed a hand on Sebastian's shoulder. "I know. I'm worried about her too."

"I'm not."

Nina felt her brother's shoulder tense, but before she could react, he sprang to his feet.

"We know you aren't! You've made it very clear that you'd rather we had all died in Verrel or the woods! Well, we didn't. We're here. Trapped in this stupid, freezing barn filled with stinking fish and a miserable bastard like you!"

"Sebastian," Nina said quickly, tugging at her brother's arm.

"No, leave it, Nina!" Sebastian barked as he pulled away from her grasp. "You may have saved our lives back in Verrel, but we got you through Vellum Forest just as much as you got us through it, and it's thanks to us that you've had a place to live for the last two months. We've more than repaid our debt to you, so now I'll say with no guilt that you need to shut up and stop chiming into conversations just to be an asshole!"

"Sebastian!"

At first Sebastian assumed it was Nina again, but the voice sounded different, and it didn't come from beside him. He turned around toward the old set of stairs, hearing footsteps coming down. Helena's face looked furious as she stepped into the light.

"Stop shouting!" she said in a whispered shout of her own.

"I—"

"Someone is going to hear you and report us to the town soldiers, you idiot!" she hissed.

Before Sebastian could choose his response, Rook piped up. "Look who decided to come down."

Sebastian saw Helena's furious stare shift from him to Rook. He was expecting her to send some whisper-shouts Rook's way but was surprised to see her hold back. Sebastian felt Nina tug his arm once again, and this time he allowed her to coax him into a sitting position.

As Sebastian got seated, he noticed that Nina looked worried, and the worry seemed directed at him. He wanted to say something to her, to try and explain his sudden lashing out and apologize for how he had spoken to her, but shame kept his mouth shut. Nina didn't say anything either. She kept a hand against his shoulder and her blue eyes on his, only looking away when Helena sat down.

"Are ... are you okay, Helena?" Nina asked cautiously. The air was tense, and Helena's expression filled Nina with concern.

"Don't you ever talk about him like that again."

"I ..." It took Nina a second to realize that Helena was addressing Rook.

Rook's face twisted with anger as he lowered his drumstick. "I'll talk about him however I damn well please."

Neither of the siblings said anything, each watching as Helena's furious expression hardened.

"I can't believe how foolish you three are," Rook continued. "You defend Carver even though he abandoned you to chase some suicidal revenge fantasy. He clearly didn't care about any of you enough to stay. Otherwise, he would still be here."

"Rook. Enough." Sebastian said, finally finding his voice.

"No. He runs out, takes the sword from wherever you all hid it, steals one of Duncan's horses, and rides off to, as Helena tells us, kill all of Caswen's soldiers. Yet here you are, four days and nights later, feeling sorry for him and hoping he's okay."

"Stop it, Rook. We don't want to hear it!" Nina raised her voice but kept it quiet enough to avoid outside ears.

"I know you don't want to hear it! All of you and your double-standard bullshit. When I want to ditch Carver because he's slowing us down and we're starving with vells at our throats, I'm the bad guy, but when he ditches all of you to go on some delusional quest for revenge, he's the good guy."

"Maybe you're right, Rook," Helena said.

Sebastian and Nina turned to face her with utter disbelief in their eyes. Even Rook looked at Helena with surprise on his face.

"Maybe Carver didn't care about us as much as we thought. Maybe he's delusional, even suicidal. Maybe all of those things. The point is, he was our friend. We cared about him, and we still care about him."

Helena spoke in a cold, almost lifeless manner, but everyone watching could see her body shaking with rage.

"Nothing you say is going to make us hate him like you do, Rook, so stop. Don't talk about him. Don't mention him. Don't even say his name. And if I overhear you referring to him as Scar-head ever again, I swear to Cosom I'll kill you."

No one said a thing. Everyone just sat silently and stared at Helena.

"Now, Rook," Helena said through the silence with the same lifeless tone as before, "would you please hand me a piece of food?"

"Sure," Rook said casually as he reached into the pot and pulled out a fresh drumstick. As he held it out toward Helena, he met her eyes with his. "Here you go. You can have Carver's share."

Before anyone could react, Helena launched herself forward and wrapped her hands around Rook's neck.

Rook let out a panicked gasp as his back hit the floor, with Helena on top of him.

"Helena!" Sebastian and Nina blurted.

Helena ignored them entirely as Rook shoved his palms into her face while also attempting to jab his knees into her sides, but Helena's grip around his throat only tightened.

"Helena! Stop!" Sebastian yelled. Then he and Nina grabbed her by the shoulders and pulled.

Rook continued to squirm on the floor as Helena fought against Sebastian and Nina's efforts to pull her off him. He swung his fists at her head, but she managed to keep her face out of his reach.

"I'm sorry, Helena," Sebastian said from behind her. Then he slammed his knee into her exposed left side.

Helena growled violently as the knee sent a sharp spike of pain into her body. The sudden shock and force of the blow caused her grip on Rook's throat to falter, giving the siblings their opening. With a mighty heave, they peeled Helena off Rook. Helena growled with rage as they yanked her to her feet and prevented her from advancing toward Rook.

Rook sounded off into a fit of hoarse gasps and aggressive coughs as he struggled to his feet.

Before Nina or Sebastian saw it coming, Rook wound up and sent his fist straight into Helena's stomach.

"Hey!" Sebastian roared, giving no thought to the loudness of his voice as he released his hold on Helena and stepped forward. He shoved his palms into Rook's chest, pushing the older boy back with a surge of force.

Rook stumbled back, only stopping once his flailing hands gripped the side of a nearby stack of crates.

Sebastian stepped toward Rook, holding his arms out. "Enough! Rook, it's ove—"

Rook lunged forward and punched Sebastian in the side of the head.

Sebastian's vision swam, and he stumbled back. He tripped over the cluster of candles, extinguishing two of them with his boot, and tumbled to the floor, slamming his head into the corner of a crate.

"Sebastian!" Nina cried as she watched her brother's body go limp.

Rook stepped forward, winding up for another punch as he neared Helena.

Helena managed to break free from Nina's hold but slipped and tumbled to the floor in doing so, landing on her hands and knees. Her right hand slid into something hard just outside the realm of the candlelight, and in a rage-blind panic, she reached into the darkness to grab it. It was smooth, and it fit her hand well. Without knowing what it was, she sprang to her feet.

As she did, she saw Rook entering the candlelight, his fist flying toward her. Without thinking, she lunged toward him and swung whatever she was holding at his head.

Rook's fist hit her square in the right eye. Helena collapsed backwards just outside the remaining candlelight. Her vision swam, making the high ceiling of the fishery appear as if it was rising and falling as she struggled to keep her eyes open.

She knew that Rook was doubtlessly about to follow up his attack, whether through a kick, another punch, or strangling her, so she told herself that she needed to get up and defend herself.

Helena closed her eyes to ease her dizziness and pushed herself into a sitting position. With one arm propping her up, she stretched her other arm out to deflect Rook's next strike, whatever it may be. When Helena opened her eyes to witness Rook's imminent attack, she froze in shock.

Rook was not looming over her or in mid swing like she had anticipated but instead was slowly walking backwards while clutching the left side of his neck. Dark-red liquid was seeping through his fingers and pouring over the backs of his hands. His eyes were locked on Helena's, and his mouth opened and closed as if he were trying to speak, but only short breaths and wet gurgles escaped his lips.

Rook suddenly ran out of space to walk backwards and collided against a stack of three wooden crates, creating a reverberating thud that echoed through the fishery. His knees buckled, and he slid down against the crates. When his rear hit the floor, he let out a long choking sound as trails of red liquid ran over his bottom lip and onto his legs. His eyes, still locked in a stare with Helena, were filled with disbelief and terror.

Rook's expression perfectly emulated Helena's own feelings as she watched him struggle and gag. She couldn't move or say anything. All she could do was sit there and watch in shock.

Rook suddenly removed a hand from his throat and pointed at Helena. The hand was coated in red and dripped all over his outstretched legs. With his hand removed from his neck, Helena could clearly see the filleting knife stuck into the side of his throat.

Still unable to move a muscle, Helena watched as Rook's pointing hand slumped down to his side. He continued to struggle, kicking and shifting his legs as he choked and gurgled. Blood continued to pour from his neck, and his breaths began to slow, but he kept his eyes fixed on Helena.

She maintained his gaze, watching as he took a long, weak breath, then a short weak breath, then stopped breathing entirely. Helena felt her blood chill as Rook's eyes broke their stare and slowly trailed off toward the floor.

She wanted to stand up, but she couldn't. She felt immobilized, like her muscles were frozen. All she could manage was to look away from the motionless boy, turning her gaze to where Nina was spastically shaking her brother's limp body on the floor.

"Sebastian! Are you okay? Wake up!"

Helena felt utter dread at the sight, fearing the worst. She wanted to go and help the girl, but she still couldn't shake free from the grip of shock that pinned her down. She was met with some relief, however, though not nearly as much as Nina felt, when she heard a groan from Sebastian's lips and saw his eyelids flutter faintly.

"Sebastian!" Nina choked with joy as she pulled him close.

"What ... I ..." Sebastian croaked as he struggled to regain his senses.

"Shh, it's okay. You hit your head after Rook hit you. But it's okay. You're alright."

"I ... Rook, he ..." Sebastian's eyes opened more fully. "What happened, what's going on?"

"Sebastian? Are you listening?" Nina asked as she ended her hug and held her brother by the shoulders. "You hit your head. Just take it easy for a moment."

Sebastian didn't make it clear if he had heard a word his sister had said. His head wobbled, and his eyes darted between the same two locations over and over again. He looked completely incoherent. Then, out of nowhere, he bent forward and vomited all over Nina's chest.

She recoiled out of instinct but didn't let Sebastian go. She held firm to his shoulders, keeping him propped up in a sitting position while rancid liquid and shredded bits of meat splashed across her clothing. Helena cringed at the sight but didn't look away.

"Helena, Rook, Sebastian's hurt. Someone get him some water," Nina called out without taking her eyes off her brother, who was staring at the floor and groaning softly, thick drool hanging from his lips. When no one responded, she steadied Sebastian and glanced over her shoulder. "Guys? Hello? What's going o—" Her expression changed from worry to utter shock. "By the stars ..." Nina struggled to look away, but after a bout of dumbfounded blinking, she managed to turn toward Helena.

Helena wanted to look away, Nina's eyes aligning with hers making her feel wholly unpleasant, but just as she could not stand, she could also not break her stare from Nina's.

"He's ... Helena ... You ..."

Helena's lips started to move before she knew what to say. "I ... I didn't mean ... It just ... I ..."

Helena's babbling was interrupted as Sebastian let out another sickening groan and threw up over his sister's legs.

"Ugh ... I'm sorry, Nina," Sebastian said more clearly as his self-awareness started to return.

Nina turned back to him. "It's okay ... Can ... um, can you stand?"

After a pause, Sebastian nodded, then tried to do so.

"Whoa. Hold on, Sebastian. Take it slow. Let me help you. You're not well."

Sebastian allowed Nina to help him to his feet, leaning on the stack of crates he had struck his head on for balance.

Nina turned her attention away from her brother and fixed her stare on the haunting scene a few feet away.

"By the gods, Helena ... What happened?"

Helena felt as if her legs were anchored to the fishery's cold wood floor, preventing her from standing, but she managed to shift herself into a sitting position. "I don't know. I just grabbed it and swung. I wasn't thinking. It happened so quickly. I didn't mean for that. I didn't know ..."

"I can't believe you really ... I mean ... I know you said you wou—"

"I know what I said! And I meant it! I just ... I didn't—"

"By the stars ..." Sebastian's weary voice returned.

Both girls looked over to see that he had shifted himself around and was staring at Rook's body, his eyes wide and his mouth agape. "Rook ... You killed him."

"Stop it! Both of you. Please. I didn't mean to. It was an accident."

Silence filled the fishery as the three of them dealt with their individual shock, each of them keeping their eyes glued to the body and the pool of red quickly spreading around it. The two remaining burning candles were fading fast, and as the light receded, it took Rook's figure along with it, leaving behind only the faint outline of his body in the increasing darkness.

The darkness did little to ease Helena's feelings of sickness and shock as she stared blankly into the blackness. The silence ended when she heard two sets of footsteps approaching her.

Nina attempted to aid her brother's balance as they neared Helena, but he waved her off. They sat down on either side of Helena. The three of them were quiet for a time, each waiting for someone else to speak first.

"We need to do something about this," Nina said, tired of waiting.

Sebastian and Helena turned toward her.

"What do you mean?" Sebastian asked.

"We need to ... get rid of him. It's not like we can just leave him there."

Helena felt sick and didn't want to speak, but she forced herself to anyway. "We need to tell Duncan. He'll know what to do."

Neither of the siblings responded right away, giving Helena the inkling that something was wrong with her suggestion, but after a moment Nina stood up.

"I'll sneak over to go get him. You two stay here."

The candlelight had died further, making it impossible for Nina to read the expressions of her peers once she was standing, but as neither Helena nor Sebastian spoke in protest, she deemed them to be both in agreement. Nina walked to the fishery's large front door and put her ear to it, waiting for a moment in silence. After she felt sure no one was about, she cracked the old wooden door open and slipped into the chilly night.

Once again, silence returned to the dark fishery. Helena began to feel horribly awkward for not saying a word to Sebastian while they waited for Nina to return, but she couldn't think of anything to say.

"Was it really an accident?"

Helena nearly jumped at Sebastian's sudden question. It took her a second to settle herself before she answered with unthinking haste. "Of course it was."

"You don't have to lie if it wasn't."

"You think I planned on killing him?" she asked in disbelief, turning to face Sebastian.

"No, I don't think you planned to. But ... I don't know. I guess it doesn't really matter. Never mind. I'm sorry."

Helena paused, feeling a great sorrow fill her chest.

"I don't know, Sebastian ... Maybe I did."

Sebastian turned toward her in surprise. "I—"

"It happened so fast. I just lost it. All I could think about was how much I wanted him to suffer. I couldn't stop myself, but I don't know if I actually tried to stop myself either. I was in control the whole time, Sebastian. I was. I don't know how to explain it. It was like I wasn't me. Like I was someone else who wanted him dead. I only grabbed the knife because my hand happened to touch it. I didn't even know it was a knife; I just swung it without thinking. I don't know what to say. I feel like I'm going crazy."

Now Sebastian was the one who felt awkward and was lost for words. He stared at her, but Helena's eyes remained fixed on the floor.

"You're not going crazy, Helena. If Nina had disappeared instead of Carver, and Rook said what he did about her instead of him ... I probably would have lost it too."

Helena felt some small comfort at Sebastian's words but also a deal of sadness.

"I don't know, Sebastian."

"I'll tell you one thing, though. He was right."

"Who was? Rook? About what?"

"As much as I'm trying not to, I can't help but think about the benefits Rook's death might bring us."

Chapter 34

Carver opened his eyes to the sound of seagulls squawking. His body attempted to force out a yawn, but the balled-up rag stuffed in his mouth, which was held in place by another rag wrapped over his mouth and tied behind his head, made that impossible. Carver gagged on the filthy rag as he fully opened his eyes to take in the thin beams of sunlight that came through the cracks in the boarded-up windows on the western and northern brick walls.

Once he was fully aware, he proceeded to perform his morning routine: stretching his legs as best as he could while attempting to keep his swollen left ankle still, fidgeting his wrists in their tight rope bindings, which kept him tied to the thick wooden beam behind him, and trying to push the rag out of his mouth with his tongue. None of the actions were successful, and they only managed to enhance his discomfort.

Carver felt wholly fatigued as each day that passed left him increasingly drained of energy. He had watched what few rays of sunlight he could see coming through the boards on the windows make their hours-long journey across the floor and finally vanish in place of night three times since he had first opened his eyes and found himself bound to the support beam in the back of a cluttered warehouse.

He was surrounded by dusty crates and old barrels, and the hard wooden floor offered no comfort to his rear end or his legs. His surroundings left him feeling utterly isolated despite the sounds he heard around him.

On top of the racket of many seagulls from outside, which Carver assumed to mean he was somewhere close to the water in the Port District, he also heard the occasional sound of wagons, horses, footsteps, and mumbled chatter. During the first day of his captivity, he had tried calling for help, but his cries only left him with fresh bruises and the rag being forced into his mouth. Afterwards, Carver stopped trying to draw attention to himself.

Since being silenced, he had done nothing but think of how to escape, but even after three days of silent calculation, he hadn't come up with anything other than waiting for an opportunity to arise. His goblin captors would periodically check up on him and ungag him to give him a bit of bread and water, and the gag would usually return before Carver could finish his hand-fed meal, after which they also checked his bindings.

Carver had learned that there were five goblins in total: Marn, Kip, Avin, Swaa, and Dren, with Kip being the leader of the group. From what Carver understood of his captors, they were smugglers, secretly sailing stolen or untaxed goods across the ocean to Caswen from mainland Terraland to the east and the goblin realms of the Mahkouan Peninsula to the south.

Of all his captors, Carver hated Kip the most. He was the cruelest of the bunch, often insulting Carver and mocking his situation, all while showing a wide, toothy smile. Kip had also taken his pouch of absols, along with the white pegasus necklace stored inside. Most aggravating of all, Kip wore the necklace around his thin green neck and flaunted it in front of Carver whenever he could. Carver could do nothing to satisfy his burning rage except bite down on the rag and growl at his captors as they passed.

During the three long days and mostly sleepless nights, through eavesdropping and the loose lips of the goblins, Carver learned that his actions at the garrison were the talk of the city. Bounty posters had been posted in all four districts calling for his capture.

The news was that he was one of the Lost Seekers who had attempted to steal important documents from the City Guard. It seemed the young rebel thief with a large scar across the back of his head was on everyone's lips, which pleased the goblins because it meant Carver's bounty was higher than they had expected.

Advertised across most of the city was that five silver absols, the equivalent of five hundred copper shards, was up for grabs to whomever brought Carver in alive, and only alive.

Carver felt a little relief when he first heard that the bounty was only for his capture, not his death, but that relief vanished once he overheard the goblins say that the punishment for most crimes under sovereign law was public execution. He assumed he was only wanted alive so that he could be interrogated, possibly under torture, for information about the Lost Seekers and their rebellion against the Sovereign Empire's hold on Gaia, after which he would surely be executed.

Carver tried to stop thinking about his potential torture and execution as he finished his morning stretches and straightened his back against the wooden beam behind him. Then he focused his mind and tried to steady his rattled nerves. Today was going to be important, and he wanted to be ready, for he knew that soon he might get his only chance to escape.

The previous day, he had overheard from Swaa, a loud and obnoxious goblin, that they had finally managed to get in touch with their contacts inside the Lost Seekers sect operating within the Isles. This information was followed with the news, spoken in excited and hushed voices, though still perceptible by Carver, that a deal had been made to trade Carver, who they still assumed to be the sect's fellow rebel and thief, alongside Aellia's documents, for a great deal of absols.

Carver waited anxiously for hours, with nothing to do but watch the thin rays of daylight slowly move from one side of the large warehouse to the other as the sun crossed the sky. At what Carver guessed to be around noon, he heard a commotion stirring at the north end of the warehouse.

The vast clutter of crates and barrels in front of him blocked his view, but the shifting footsteps and hushed whispers were clear. Suddenly there was a loud series of thuds against wood from the same direction as the hushed voices. Carver realized the thuds were knocks.

His body tensed up despite his mind's insistence that he be relaxed and focused. He wanted to be calm and appear docile so as not to raise suspicion, expecting that his only chance to break free and escape was to be underestimated by those around him.

There was a moment of silence, followed by more knocking and a flurry of nearby whispers, which ended in Kip's voice rising above the others.

"Put your teeth together. We keep the plan. It's too late to change ideas now. Dren, get the door."

Carver heard movement, then the sound of a heavy door pulling open. Footsteps entered—how many, he could not discern—and in a moment the sound of the door clicking shut reached his ears.

"I hear we have some business together," a male voice said.

Though Carver didn't recognize the voice, he was glad that it sounded like a human and not a goblin, though he immediately realized that wouldn't make much difference considering the situation.

"Who is you two? You both ain't the regulars. Where's Griff an' Horrak?" Kip asked.

"They're both occupied elsewhere today. We've come in their place."

"Well, how do I know that you both are from the right group?"

Carver heard a sigh.

"Because we're meeting with you at the disclosed place during the disclosed time. Now do you have something for us or not?"

There was a brief pause.

"Yeah. Yeah we do. Stick your weapons at the door 'nd show us the absols first. Fore we show you at all, I wanna see proper coin."

"Here," Carver heard a woman's voice say. She also sounded human.

There was a moment of silence.

"Feh, what's this? Seven silver sols."

"The price your emissary negotiated with us," the male voice said. "Five hundred shards for our man, as posted on the bounty, and two hundred for the documents."

"Amasearry? I don't know what you say about that, but I didn't give my man no boss status to talk cost. And your man is no man but a boy. And most of all, these absols are not many enough. Too few. You lot ain't paying the bounty. If we wanted the bounty, we'd go to them soldiers. If you want him eez-illby costing ya at least seven on his ownsome. And them documents is special. We want three silvers for the lot of 'em. A full gold sol you'll show, or you can both get nogged."

The woman's voice suddenly kicked back in. "Listen here, you greedy little—"

"Enough, Shiala. I'll handle this."

Carver tried to stretch his neck to see over the clutter of crates and barrels, but he was bound too tightly to the post.

"If the details of price have changed, we can surely come to a new agreement. But I will not part with a single copper shard more until we see him and these documents with our own eyes."

"Fine. You can see him. And you can look at them pages, but only three! I'll not have you sneak reading them all so you'se don't be paying in full. You follow by our say if you want us to keep smuggling for yer group."

"Agreed."

"Swaa. Go get three of them pages, and take the green-face lady with ya. I'm showing him the boy."

"Yes, boss."

Carver readied himself and steeled his nerve in preparation for whatever might happen next, but then something caught his notice and distracted him. Out of the corner of his left eye, he detected movement, and when he looked over, he was stung with shock and confusion.

A goblin was standing on his left. Unlike the ones he had been in the company of these last three days, this goblin was a woman. She was crouched over, but Carver figured she must have been about four-foot seven.

Her nose, though slightly more pointed, was much smaller than the males', similar to a human's. She had long blades of black hair that hung down the sides of her face and dangled near the top of her chest, the rest of her hair hidden under a gray hood along with her large ears, which were pushing into the hood's material from within. The hood continued into a buttoned gray cloak that covered her entire body, save for her bare clawed feet. Carver noticed that each green foot had only four toes.

The goblin looked over at Carver with large black pupils in the center of large yellow eyes. Carver held completely still, utterly lost for words and actions, not that he had the ability to do or say anything.

The goblin woman suddenly smiled at Carver. Her grin was wide and showed many small teeth, her canines being especially large. Then she lifted her right hand and held her index finger over her thin, dark-green lips. Carver understood the meaning but not the reason.

She turned away from Carver and fit herself through a tight gap between two large wooden crates and disappeared.

The sudden sound of wood dragging against the floor from nearby startled Carver, and he turned to face the source of the noise.

"There's your lad," Kip said as he finished pushing a crate out of the way.

Carver could now see the rest of the room as well as those who occupied it. Standing next to Kip was a human man with brown eyes. He was pale skinned and brown-haired with a short, thick beard. He looked aged but not enough to be considered past his prime. He was wearing a black tunic underneath an open-fronted dark brown coat. His leggings were that of standard gray wool pants, though his brown boots stood out, composed of fine leather and seemingly immaculately polished. He also had on leather bracers with iron studs circling around in three evenly distanced rings.

Behind Kip and the human man, Carver could also see the rest of the goblins as well as the woman he heard addressed as Shiala.

Shiala was quite tall for a woman, at least five feet ten inches, and wore thick wool pants, light brown in color, with a thick belt holding a few pouches, along with a dark-brown leather jerkin that left her muscular arms entirely exposed. The leather jerkin had gray animal fur, seemingly from a wolf, woven into the leather around the shoulders and waist, giving the attire an intense aura. Her short brown hair was messy and barely passed over her ears.

Her face was also pale but stood out due to the green marking, somewhat similar to the markings Carver had seen on the faces of the sovereigns at the Inner Market so long ago, which displayed itself over the left side of her face.

To Carver, the green-inked design looked like a smooth, curved blade of grass that thickened as it descended from her left temple down her cheek until it thinned out again just below her cheekbone. From the center of the design, a separate blade jutted inwards over her cheekbone just under her brown left eye, giving the impression of a sickle cupping her eye.

Shiala was standing near a small table by the north window where Swaa was showing her a collection of papers from the thick portfolio, which he held firmly behind his back in his other hand.

Dren and Avin were scrutinizing her and the human man, their hands ready over their daggers, while Marn was nowhere to be seen.

Carver looked up at the human man who was now staring down at him and waited for something to happen.

"So, now you've eyed him, and she's eyed them papers. It's the true thing. The price stands."

"Ungag him," the man said. "I want to speak with him."

"No. I want to see the more absols first. The rag stays in."

The human man did not look at Kip. Instead, he kept his stare on Carver. He seemed to be thinking intensely about something, but Carver could not discern what it could be.

"These papers seem genuine. I'd say we have what we need," Shiala said.

The man nodded. "I'd have to agree."

"What'er you two pale skins jabbering abo—"

The man suddenly slapped his left palm into the center of Kip's chest. Before a full second could pass, a flash of white light blinked into existence beneath the man's palm. Kip flew backwards off his feet and crashed into a stack of barrels near the east wall a few feet to Carver's right. The stack collapsed, burying Kip in a manner of seconds as his high-pitched, gravelly voice wailed throughout the room.

Dren and Avin drew their daggers. Dren dashed toward the man's back while Avin darted toward Shiala, who was holding Swaa by the throat and arm and smashing his head into the sharp corner of the wooden table.

The goblin woman suddenly emerged from a cluster of crates behind Dren and Avin, and in each of her hands she was holding a long, curved dagger, a few inches longer than what the other goblins had.

The goblin woman ran forward and leapt in between Dren and Avin. As she did, both goblins heard her and turned. The female goblin slashed one of her long daggers at the side of Dren's head before he could react and raised the other to protect herself from Avin.

Dren fell to the ground, his long right ear landing next to him in a splash of dark blood. He shrieked while dropping his weapon and grabbing at his head. Avin was about to strike his attacker, but he hesitated for a second too long, and the man standing next to Carver shot a blast of bluish-white energy from his outstretched left hand toward him. The blast struck Avin's right leg and froze it solid. Avin screamed in fear and pain before the female goblin lunged forward and slashed the frozen leg with both daggers. The leg shattered into large bloody chunks of frozen meat as Avin fell backwards to the floor.

The female goblin stepped over Avin and stuck her left dagger into his throat, then leapt back, spinning 180 degrees in the air and then plunging both her blades into Dren's back as he was trying to stand up.

Dren and Avin shrieked, spasmed, then went still.

Swaa had gone completely limp in Shiala's hands as the heavy flow of blood running down his head spilled over the table and pooled onto the floor. Shiala threw his body to the side.

The barrels that had collapsed onto Kip were now rolling around the room and banging into other barrels and crates, one of which rolled into Carver. As he glanced over it, he noticed that Kip was alive and struggling to stand. His ragged tunic was completely burnt through where the man had struck him, and his chest beneath had a smoldering burn mark roughly the size of the man's handprint.

Looking dazed and hurt, Kip managed to stand up and pull a long knife from his belt. He locked eyes with Carver for a moment before he scanned the rest of the warehouse. His large yellow eyes bulged in their green sockets and then he flew back to Carver.

Carver tried to call out, but the rag in his mouth restricted him to a long, muffled hum, and before anyone could react, Kip ran behind Carver. Carver tried to pull his head away, but Kip grabbed him by the hair and brought his knife to his throat. Carver filled with panic as he felt the knife's edge push against his throat, cutting slightly into the skin.

"No one move, or I'll kill your thief!"

"Stop! If you want to live, you'll drop that knife," the man warned.

Carver tried to speak, to shout, to say anything that might save himself, but all that came out was muffled grunts.

No one in the warehouse moved or said anything for a moment, though to Carver the seconds felt like minutes.

"Liar! You double-crossers will kill me both ways! I know it! But you won't get yer wants!" Kip shouted, then pulled his knife across Carver's throat.

Carver's eyes bulged as he felt a sharp pain shoot across his throat and a warm wetness run down his neck.

Kip dropped the knife and released Carver's hair as he bolted off amongst the scattered crates.

The man lunged forward and dropped to his knees in front of Carver. He grabbed him by the throat with both hands and squeezed.

Carver squirmed violently as he felt his hot blood spilling from his neck and seeping through the man's fingers. His heart beat faster than it ever had in his life, and he was filled with more fear than he thought possible.

"Hold still, boy!" the man shouted as he tightened his grip on Carver's throat.

Carver suddenly felt an intense burning sensation over top of the pain in his throat. It made the skin around his neck feel as if it were moving and pulling together. His eyes watered intensely, and he kept kicking his legs out of sheer instinct to flee his quickly approaching death. He knew it was over. He knew he was going to die right there, tied to a post in a dirty warehouse away from everyone he knew or cared about.

In that brief moment before his end, Carver's thoughts raced over many things. He thought of his village. He thought of his mother and father. And he thought of Helena. He regretted leaving her at Leydes without saying goodbye. He regretted the pain he knew he must have caused her by secretly and suddenly leaving. And he felt a burst of heart-numbing despair at the idea that she would forever hate the memory of him once he never returned.

"There. It's done."

Carver didn't notice the man pull his hands off his throat, nor did he clue in that the sensation of blood running down his neck and chest had stopped. Carver was locked in a bout of panic and terror that made him oblivious to everything else in the world.

"Settle down, boy! It's over. You're healed."

Carver heard the man's words but didn't understand them amidst his thoughts of home and those he had left behind. Finally, the man slapped Carver across the face. He stopped writhing and fell into a fit of erratic coughing, though the rag in his mouth turned the coughs into chokes.

The man reached behind Carver's head and pulled the rag off, allowing him to yank the soggy ball of cloth out of his mouth. Carver let out a flurry of coughs and gasps.

"You're no longer dying, boy. I've healed you. Calm yourself."

Carver heard the man's words more clearly this time and began to realize he was indeed still breathing. He finished his coughing and settled in place. He looked down at his chest and saw that blood had stained the collar of his tunic and ran down to his stomach in red trails.

"That goblin didn't even manage to cut your throat properly. It would have taken you awhile to bleed out."

The man's words did not make Carver feel any better.

He looked up at the man, then he scanned the warehouse for the two women.

Shiala was standing over by the table, placing the three papers back into the portfolio along with some others that had fallen out while she had been bashing Swaa's head in. The goblin woman appeared to be going through the pockets of Kip, who currently had both the goblin woman's long, curved daggers sticking into his back as he lay motionless a dozen feet to Carver's left.

As the goblin woman pulled the seven silver absols from Kip's right pocket, she noticed the necklace hanging around his neck. She stashed the absols into her trouser pocket and then quickly unhooked the necklace and pulled it free from Kip's neck, lifting his limp head ever so gently.

"Don't touch that! It's mine!" Carver shouted without thinking.

The goblin woman turned to Carver with a look of surprise, though instead of responding, she turned her attention back to the necklace, inspecting it with her big yellow eyes. As she did, she lifted her thin chin, which caused more of her long black hair to loosen out of her gray hood and fall to the sides of her face.

"We have what we came for. Are we ready to go, Farren?" Shiala asked the man as she approached from behind, the portfolio tucked under her muscular arm.

"Almost. I want to have a chat with him first."

"A chat? The kid's not one of us. It's the documents we wanted, not him. Someone's sure to have heard the fighting, so we should get out of here before any soldiers arrive."

"I give the orders, Shiala. You and Vie go watch the windows. I don't want any surprises."

Shiala frowned but then turned around and headed toward the boarded-up window on the north wall.

The goblin woman, Vie, put the necklace into her cloak's inside pocket, shooting Carver a wide toothy smile as she did, then turned and made her way over to face the poorly boarded-up window on the west wall.

Carver kept his mouth shut about the necklace and looked over at the man he now knew as Farren.

"You healed me ... with sorcery?"

"I did."

Carver felt lost. He did not know what to say, if anything. "Thank you."

Farren got down on one knee, resting his crossed arms on the other leg, and looked Carver in the eyes. "My companion is incorrect in saying that we came here just for the papers. In truth, when I learned of this deal, I was far more interested in meeting the person who has caused so much stir throughout the city. But she was right about one thing: that we must leave with haste to avoid detection by soldiers. So, answer quickly and truthfully, and I might just take you with us."

Carver almost spoke up about how the city soldiers would already be tipped off by now as a result of the goblin smugglers' planned treachery, but he held his tongue, thinking that revealing that information could trigger the group to depart immediately and leave him tied to the post.

"Take me with you?"

"Or I can leave you here to rot or be arrested. Or maybe I should turn you in for the bounty on your head. Five silver absols isn't nothing, after all."

"No! Wait. I'll tell you whatever you want to hear."

"No. You'll tell me the truth, regardless of if it's something I want to hear or not. Who are you, and what was your motive for stealing that portfolio from the marshal's office?"

"My name is Carver. I'm from Verrel. And I didn't go there to steal those documents. I went there to kill her."

Farren raised his eyebrows with interest. "To kill the marshal? By yourself? My, that is a weighty goal, indeed. I would ask why you would want her dead, but you've already told me. So, you're from Verrel, huh? That small village west of the city. After what happened to your village under her orders, I can't blame you for wanting her head. But if your intent was to kill her, why steal her private documents?"

"I ... I don't know. I messed it up. I got caught and had to run. I started the fire, and in the chaos I just grabbed them. I didn't want to leave empty handed. I wanted something that I might use to find her later. But that was a mistake. I lost my grip because of that stupid thing holding the papers. If I had just left it behind, I wouldn't have fallen from the window and broken my ankle, and I wouldn't have been taken by those goblins and brought here."

"To find her later? You really are a committed young lad. And what made you think a handful of random papers would lead you to her? After all, you must know that she is almost always in the city, either at the city garrison commanding her soldiers or in the manor with her family. What good could some papers do?"

Carver got the impression that Farren was not asking him these questions for his own sake but rather to analyze and judge his answers.

Shiala seemed to get this impression as well while she looked through the cracks of the boarded-up window. "Stop toying with the runt and finish up. We need to leave before it's too late."

Farren turned to face her. "This runt broke into the marshal's office alone, escaped while burning part of the garrison to the ground, and all anyone saw was the back of his head. If that doesn't merit a proper inquisitive conversation, I don't know what does. Be silent." Farren turned back to Carver. "Please continue, Carver. But be quick."

Carver noted the friendly manner in which Farren spoke, but he did not feel comforted by it in the slightest. Farren was looking for something in his words, Carver saw that, but exactly what he was searching for and why he wanted it remained a mystery.

"The pages aren't random. They are everything she has about her wedding. She's getting married in ... I can't remember when. But it's soon, and it's in those pages. Everything is. Where it's happening. Maps of the building. Where the guards will be. Everything. I thought I could use it to get to her then."

Farren pondered Carver's words in silence without breaking his stare, then suddenly looked over at Carver's left ankle.

"It doesn't look that bad to me. Broken, maybe, but no bones are sticking out."

"Can you heal it?"

"Ha! I most certainly could. But why? Mustering up rejuvenative magic takes effort and skill. Why should I waste more than I already have on you? What use are you to me?"

Suddenly feeling extremely nervous, Carver chose his next words carefully. "You said it yourself. I'm impressive to you. You're with the Lost Seekers, who fight against the sovereigns and their empire. The marshal—Aellia—she works for the sovereigns, so that means I fight against them too. If she were to die, it would help your cause, so you and I are the same. I could join you, help you. I could be of use."

There was a long pause between Carver and Farren. Carver did not know what else he could say or if what he had said was enough. He felt like he was losing the conversation and that he was missing his only chance of ever seeing his friends again. He felt his chance to escape shrinking as each second went by that he was still tied to the post. Such thoughts filled Carver with anger, an anger that quickly molded into an intense hatred for the man staring him in the face.

Why should this stranger get to decide if I'm worth saving? Why should he need to be swayed so that I might live?

Carver's skin turned hot with anger, and he decided that if this was his last chance to get free, he would give it everything he had.

"Fuck you! Fuck all three of you! I don't need you to tell me if I'm useful or not. I was in the middle of your attack on the market, and I made it out. I killed to get away. When my village was burned that same night, I crawled out of my burning home, and I killed again to survive."

Bits of saliva sprayed from Carver's teeth as he continued. "On my way to this rotten city, I was attacked by thugs in the ruins of my village. I was outnumbered three to one, but I still killed them all. I broke into Caswen's garrison without anyone's help, and I left it burning behind me, and even though I was unable to walk, I still got away. I would have escaped from this warehouse too, even if you three hadn't arrived. You know why? Because I'm not going to die until I've made the woman who killed my family suffer!"

When Carver finished, he was short of breath, beads of sweat running down his right cheek. He held back his tongue and took a series of deep breaths as he stared into the calm eyes of his judge.

Farren remained quiet, his expression unchanged. Then he grinned.

"You won't be any use to anyone if you can't walk. Hold still."

He grabbed Carver's left foot and jerked it toward himself. Carver barely had time to scream before Farren twisted the foot so the toes faced upwards instead of slightly left. Carver cried out in both pain and anger as he tried to pull his foot away from Farren's grasp, but Farren kept his hold on it with his left hand while he wrapped his right hand around Carver's ankle and squeezed. Carver tried to recoil his left leg while letting out another sharp cry of pain, but Farren held his leg still and his ankle in place.

The air around where Farren's hand gripped Carver's ankle began to take form and sway as if it were a kind of clear smoke. A sharp, burning discomfort spread through Carver's ankle, somehow separate from the other pain, and before long it morphed into an intense pain that almost matched the rest. Carver felt as though the bones and muscles in his ankle were shifting into place.

A loud pop from his ankle was accompanied by a burst of pain. Carver continued his instinctual efforts to pull his leg away from Farren's grasp, but Farren lost no ground in the struggle and continued to squeeze tightly.

The swelling around the ankle began to quickly shrink away, as did the redness of the skin, and soon Carver's pain began to fade as well. Then, almost immediately, all the pain was gone as if it had never been there to begin with.

Farren pulled his hands away and stood up, leaving Carver to stare in awe at his freshly healed ankle.

"Vie, come cut Carver free. We're leaving. And give him his necklace, would you?"

"Aww. But it's so pretty. And shiny too."

Vie's feminine voice was also slightly high pitched and gravelly, though it sounded far more pleasant to the ears than the male goblins' voices. Carver also noticed that she spoke properly rather than how his captors spoke.

"Enough with that, Vie. Let's go, everyone."

Vie ran over from the west window, pulling her blades from Kip's back as she passed by him, and slashed the rope that kept Carver's wrists tied behind the thick wooden beam in one clean motion.

Carver pulled his hands to his chest and rubbed them. His wrists were chafed and red and the skin was peeling from the coarseness of the rope, but it was nothing compared to the relief he felt from his ankle being healed and the fact that he was finally free.

After Vie sheathed her long daggers under her cloak, she reached into her cloak's inner pocket and pulled out the necklace, the pegasus charm dangling before Carver's eyes. "You know, it's rude to take jewelry from a lady," she said with a wide, toothy grin. Carver reached out and snatched the necklace from her small green hand. Vie scrunched her face at him and then turned away. "Hmph. And here I thought I was going to like you."

Carver stuffed the necklace into his trouser pocket and stood up, feeling greatly relieved to have no pain shoot through his ankle as he did. Farren picked up a dagger from the floor, the blade Avin had dropped, and turned to

Carver, holding it out with an open palm. "Take this. If your captors robbed you of anything else, you must leave it behind. We don't have time to search for your things. Be thankful you recovered your necklace and follow us."

"It's not for me," Carver said as he took the crude iron dagger.

Farren strode across the room and reached the door at the far end. Carver followed close behind and saw that at the door there was a large one-handed axe that was clearly not made for woodcutting and a sword buckled in its sheath leaning against the wall next to the door.

Farren picked up the sword and buckled it to his belt. Then he handed the axe to Shiala, who walked up behind him next to Carver. Shiala tucked the portfolio into the back of her trousers, keeping it half exposed above her belt, which she used to keep it secure against her back, before she took the weapon from Farren and held it with a relaxed hand.

Vie was standing off to the side, staring at Carver with a look that made him uncomfortable.

"Don't fall behind, Carver," Farren said as he reached for the door handle.

As Carver looked behind him at the goblins' bodies, a sensation of relief filled him, but then he realized something was off. There were only four goblin bodies, not five.

After a quick glance around the warehouse, Carver froze, his relief gone. He remembered.

"Wait!"

All three of Carver's new acquaintances turned to face him with surprised expressions.

"What is it now, boy?" Shiala asked in exasperation.

"The goblins—" Carver glanced at Vie out of instinct. "They sold you out—sold us out. Marn isn't here. The fifth one. He's bringing soldiers for a reward."

Carver's fatigue and dehydration left him unable to react in time as Shiala dropped her axe and strode toward him. The green tattooed woman grabbed Carver's arms and swung him around. His back crashed into the wall next to the door, and he dropped his dagger in shock.

"You knew this, and you kept silent about it? You little shit!"

Carver struggled to focus. "You would have left me!"

"You're damn right we would have!"

"Shiala, that's enough! If this is true, then we have no time. We must leave now."

Farren opened the door and strode outside without another word. Vie ran after him, though not without shooting Carver a strange glance from her large eyes as she passed. Shiala let out a short growl of frustration as she released Carver, letting him drop to the floor, then took her axe and followed Vie. Carver hurried after them.

Chapter 35

❧

The full might of the sun hit Carver as he stepped outside of the dimly lit warehouse, forcing him to raise his hand to his forehead and squint as he ran to keep up with the others. Despite the sudden glare burning his eyes, he could see that the area outside the warehouse was a wide dirt square that was surrounded by brick and wood buildings with two tight streets leading out, one going southwest and the other heading northwest. Carver suddenly wondered just how far he was from where he had been crawling nights before.

The thought evaporated from his mind as he saw the three Lost Seekers come to a quick halt ahead of him. Carver tried to stop in time, but he stumbled into Shiala's back, the force of the impact knocking him back onto his rear.

A little disoriented as to what had just happened, Carver stood up and looked beyond Shiala and the others. The first thing he saw was a horse gallop into the empty square from the southwest dirt street at the far-left corner. Then another horse charged into view from the tight street leading to the northwest. Each horse came to a halt at the behest of their human riders, who were armored and holding crossbows, which they pointed at Carver and the others.

Then two more riders entered the square, one from each obscured street, and halted next to the first two to form a line. One of the riders wielded a long spear, and the other had an arming sword.

Carver heard the hiss of steel as Farren pulled his sword from its sheath. Vie also drew her long, curved daggers and crouched low to the ground, kicking up some dirt as she did. Carver reached to his belt for the dagger he had been given but realized with dread that he had forgotten to pick it up after Shiala pushed him into the wall.

"Stop where you are!" a fifth rider shouted as she rode in from the southwest street on a brown horse. Despite her iron helmet keeping most of her long, coppery-brown hair secured, much of it still trailed behind her in the wind as she pulled her horse's reins and stopped just ahead of the other soldiers. Her sword was ready at her side. A goblin was sitting behind her in the saddle. Carver recognized him immediately.

"That's them! That's them!" Marn shouted and pointed from behind the leading woman.

"None of you move!" the woman demanded as she pointed her polished blade at the Lost Seekers and Carver.

The Lost Seekers held out their weapons and kept steady while Carver sought an escape but found none.

"You four are under arrest for treason against Terraland and the Sovereign Empire! We have the neighboring streets surrounded. Drop your weapons and surrender!"

Farren kept his weapon steady and motioned with his other hand for those behind him to stay still. "Have you and your sovereign masters still not learned that punishing all crime with execution does little in the way of coercing surrenders?"

"Those who surrender will be given a chance to trade ample information for their lives. Resist, and you will all be run down like rabid dogs here and now."

Carver was unaware that revealing information could potentially spare one from execution, or if it were true, but regardless, he knew he had no information to give for his life. His only chance to survive was to somehow get away.

"The only dogs I see are the ones the sovereigns let off their leashes," Farren said. "If anyone is responsible for treason against Terraland and humanity, it is those who allow those creatures to oppress this land and its people."

Carver looked back at the warehouse. The door wasn't that far. He calculated that he could probably run back inside, thinking that the horses wouldn't be able to catch him in time, and the crossbowmen might miss their shots or keep their weapons aimed at the others. If he could get inside, he might be able to pry open the boards on the north window and escape down a different street.

Even if the woman was being truthful in saying that the surrounding area was being watched for runners, Carver felt those odds would be better than waiting where he was.

His heart racing, he felt short of breath. He looked back at the others and saw that Vie was staring at him with a concerned face.

She mouthed a single word with her thin green lips that Carver understood quite clearly.

"Wait."

Vie used her eyes to redirect Carver's attention. He followed her signal and ended with his eyes fixed on Farren's back. It was then that Carver noticed that Farren had one hand slightly behind his back and was holding a small, strange-looking metal object. It was round and gray, with a bit of what looked like rope sticking out of a flat silver ring on top. Carver suspected that something was about to happen, and whatever that something was, he did not want to be caught in the middle of it.

"This is your last chance. Drop your weapons, or we will put you down. Those who resist and survive will talk under torture before their execution. Those who comply will be spared to serve their sentence behind bars."

"Your sovereign masters claim to spread security and order to all kingdoms within their empire, but all they do is hold us back and keep us down. How much of our history and culture has been subject to their meddling? How many young human sons and daughters, who have only just begun to experience life, have been snatched away from their homes and families, never to be seen or heard from again, for the apparent crime of developing sorcery, something they have no control over? These sovereigns, who you blindly serve, seek to ruin us and make us slaves to their tyrannical dominion."

Farren paused for a moment, and in that brief period of silence Carver thought he saw the mounted woman's mouth twitch as if about to give the order to attack, but then Farren spoke up again, and the woman's face went still.

"Do you remember the defeat you and your masters experienced at the market and the great blasts of flame that left those smoldering craters? Contrary to what the oppressors might have you believe, those blasts were not created through sorcery but through progress. Progress attained not from any boon gifted to us by the sovereigns but from human, dwarf, and goblin minds. Minds free of foreign subjugation. The market was a brief show of how great our peoples can be if not under the taloned feet of the sovereigns."

Carver saw a flicker of flame spark from Farren's fingers and catch onto the nub of rope sticking out of the metal ball in his hand.

"Now witness that progress again."

Farren swung his left arm out from behind his back and threw the metal sphere at the mounted soldiers. It struck the ground just ahead of the woman's horse and bounced beneath the mare's long legs before stopping between the two horses carrying the crossbow-wielding soldiers behind her.

Carver heard a sizzle, a click, and then a loud bang that filled the whole area. A large cloud of gray smoke snapped into existence behind the woman, who fell off her horse to the side, along with Marn, as the beast's back legs blew apart amid a heavy spray of dirt that flew in every direction.

The horses carrying the crossbowmen shrieked and fell to the ground, taking their riders with them. The horse on the far left cried in fear and bolted back the way it had come as its spear-wielding rider was thrown from the saddle. The horse on the far right spasmed and collapsed to the ground as shards of metal stuck into its side and underbelly, pinning its rider's leg beneath its heavy body.

Carver barely had time to register the cacophony of human and horse screams before he was snapped out of his shock by Vie, who was tugging his belt. Carver spun around to see that Vie had already released him and was running toward the doorway of the warehouse they had just come from.

Carver broke into a sprint as a burst of adrenaline filled his system. Once inside the warehouse, he hopped over the goblin bodies, banked to the left, and made for the window on the north wall.

Carver reached the window and began to frantically pull at the boards. The old wood bent and creaked from the strain. He heard a pop from the center of the closest board, but none of them gave way to his efforts.

"Carver! This way!"

He turned and saw Farren looking at him from just inside the warehouse. A crossbow bolt was sticking out of his left shoulder, and he was leaning on Shiala for support. Shiala still had the portfolio secured against her lower back by her belt, but her axe was gone.

"But this is the only other way out!" Carver cried as he continued to heave and pull at the boards.

Shiala left Farren to lean against a nearby crate. Then she started sliding other nearby crates in front of the door.

"No!" Farren shouted as he reached up to grab the bolt that pierced his left shoulder, wincing with pain as he did, and yanked it from his flesh. "It isn't!"

The wails of horses continued to emanate from outside the closed door just behind Farren and Shiala, as did the horrid screaming of at least two men among fits of coughing and shuffling.

"Vie! Where is it?"

"Over here, boss."

Carver looked toward the voice but could not see the goblin woman. Her voice had come from behind a cluster of barrels and crates near the post where Carver had been bound.

Farren grunted as he clasped his hand over the growing red stain under his coat and headed toward her.

Shiala pushed another heavy crate next to the two already blocking the door and then ran over to Farren's side. She gave Carver a quick glare as she crossed the room.

"Now is not the time to freeze, runt," she remarked with a bitter tone before following Farren into the back of the warehouse.

Carver let go of the boards and ran over to the others, then stopped and ran back to grab his dagger.

"After them!" Carver heard the lead woman's voice shout over the pain-racked cries of the animals and fits of coughing from the soldiers.

Carver panicked and spun back around, the dagger gripped firmly in his right hand, and ran to join the others just in time to see Vie opening a hatch in the wood floor, revealing a steep ramp of wooden planks that traveled down to an eastward-facing tunnel with wooden boards for a floor. Vie leapt down, followed by Farren, though he struggled to descend the steep slant due to his shoulder injury.

"How did you know this was here?"

Shiala looked at Carver. "We've done business with these goblins long enough to learn where their smuggling tunnel was. How do you think Vie snuck in here?"

Shiala slid down the planks before Carver could respond.

A loud crash summoned Carver's attention. He looked back and saw the warehouse door being forced inward, the crates that were blocking the door sliding backward from the force of the blows.

With no time to lose, Carver descended the slanted planks into the darkness below. He thought about closing the hatch only after he had descended too far down to reach it. Cursing his stupidity, he turned to go back up and correct his error, but just then he heard a loud crash from up top.

"We're in. Find them!"

Carver turned to run after the others, who were already obscured in the total darkness that filled the tunnel. As he ran, he heard footsteps fill the room above and approach the hatch.

"There's a tunnel! Alert the others! I want this entire district under lock-down until we have them!"

Carver picked up his speed despite his inability to see more than a few inches ahead of himself.

The tunnel was wide and had thick beams of wood supporting the dirt walls and ceiling. It was tall enough that Carver did not need to duck as he ran, though the darkness forced him to run with his hands forward to protect him from running into a wall should there be any sharp turns. He encountered none, however, as the tunnel proved to be straight and level for the most part. He stumbled a few times over a bump or a piece of wood sticking up from the floor, but he managed to maintain his footing and his momentum.

The footsteps of the others ahead of him remained distant but did not leave him behind. The footsteps behind him, however, sounded like they were gaining ground. Carver did not look back, not that the darkness would have allowed him to see how far back his pursuers were. He kept running as fast as he could despite his instinct telling him to slow down due to the lack of visibility.

After less than a minute of blind running, a light crept into view up ahead. It was faint and broken into thin beams, telling Carver that it was coming through some kind of blockage. As he maintained his panicked pace, the light suddenly enlarged and filled the tunnel. He realized he was not nearly as far behind the others as he had thought.

The light continued to grow as Carver approached until he suddenly found himself standing outside the tunnel. Shiala, Farren, and Vie had all stopped once free from the tunnel's embrace, so Carver also took the opportunity to stop and catch his breath.

He looked around as he inhaled the fresh air into his burning lungs. He and the others were standing on a wide area of dirt and mud that stretched out to the open sea a handful of feet ahead.

The water was calm and lapped gently at the land's edge with foamy splashes. Around Carver were a series of thick wooden beams that grew upwards into the bottom of a wooden ceiling about six feet above his head that spanned a few dozen feet over the water beyond where the dirt and mud stopped. Carver realized he was beneath a pier. He could hear footsteps and voices up above and saw shadows flashing over the cracks in the wood.

A grunt from behind pulled his eyes away from his new surroundings. Carver turned around and saw Vie struggle to lift a thick wooden pallet out of the mud and then tip it toward the tunnel's exit. The heavy pallet thudded against the stone foundation that surrounded the tunnel's opening, covering the dark hole almost entirely.

"That won't do anything, Vie. Stand back."

Farren pulled the pallet off the wall with his right hand. It slammed to the ground and sank slightly into the mud, sending a light spray of wet dirt over everyone's feet and legs. Farren reached both hands toward the tunnel and stood still for a moment. Carver felt the urge to run, fearing their pursuers would be on them at any moment, but the sudden presence of swirling air around Farren's hands caught his attention and kept him watching.

The air continued to swirl and ripple as Farren held himself still and focused. Then at the center of each hand there was a sudden flash of light, and a ball of spiraling flame manifested just above each of his palms. He pushed the two vibrating flames together and they melded into a great sphere nearly the size of a human man's head.

Carver could feel waves of heat emanating off the swirling ball of flame, and the light of it illuminated a fair distance down the dark tunnel. Then Farren grunted and pushed his arms forward.

The ball of flame shot down the tunnel. Faster than Carver's eyes could follow, the glowing orb smashed into the left wall and erupted into a spray of flames with a resounding boom.

The nearest two wooden beams blew apart, and the dirt around them collapsed, pulling the ceiling down and sending a great blast of dust and dirt toward Carver and the others. A loud rumble echoed through the tunnel, and within a few seconds all Carver could see was a wall of dirt and rock where the opening once was.

Farren spun around and faced the others. His face was pale and sweat poured down his forehead. His left shoulder continued to leak dark red, which had stained his coat much of the way down to his chest on the left side.

"We need to go. Now," he said with great effort and then suddenly stumbled to the side.

Vie held him steady, her arm wrapped around his waist, before he collapsed.

Shouts and quickened footsteps sounded above their heads. Carver looked up to see dozens of shadows flashing over the gaps in the wooden pier in much greater speed and number.

"Everyone, listen up. Carver! Pay attention."

Carver looked back at Farren.

"We split up. Shiala, you take Carver out of Caswen. Everyone is looking for him in this city, so go to Quinredal and find a ship to take you both to Rudenhull. Vie and I will return to the nearest northern safehouse with the documents."

"What?" Shiala protested. "I'm not babysitting this boy! You need me here."

"Silence, woman! Do as I order and now. We must be gone from here before the soldiers manage to lock down the district. I will send word to our brothers and sisters in Rudenhull of your arrival," Farren said as he leaned forward and took the portfolio from Shiala.

Farren looked down at Vie, who was still supporting him from the side. "Vie, give Carver your cloak. He needs to keep the back of his head covered."

Vie gave Farren an annoyed look. "What? But I like this cloak, and it's far too small for the human anyway."

"Vie!" Farren barked, though in his effort to shout he stumbled again. He looked faint and utterly exhausted.

Vie kept hold of Farren for a moment until he seemed able to stand firm. Then she released him and pulled her cloak over her head. As she did, her long black hair became fully visible, revealed to have no braids or ties, and her long green ears sprang up with a slight jiggle. Beneath her cloak she was wearing black trousers, a tight brown tunic laced up the front and showing no cleavage, nor much presence of breasts at all, with leather-reinforced shoulder pads and a belt where her blades were sheathed.

Vie handed the hooded gray cloak to Carver. He put it on as best he could, undoing the buttons and leaving them undone, for it was too small to fit properly and only covered halfway down his back. However, the hood did cover the scar on the back of his head, and due to the tight fit, it gave no indication of falling off.

"Now off with you two, and make haste. Let's hurry, Vie."

Although he still looked a little woozy, Farren started jogging along the water's edge toward the north with the portfolio clutched in his right hand.

Vie shot Carver a look that reeked of worry and then ran after Farren.

Carver turned toward Shiala, but before he could face her, she was on his other side and pulling him by the shoulder in the opposite direction of Farren and Vie. Carver stumbled and nearly dropped his dagger as he struggled to keep up.

"Hurry, runt, or I'll leave you behind."

Carver didn't doubt Shiala's words, and he broke into a sprint to match hers. He followed her down the length of the muddy coast below several piers toward the south until they reached the end of the stone wall to their right and rounded the corner, keeping the water to their left.

Once around the corner, Carver saw that the water stretched farther toward the south than his eyes could see.

A series of docks and piers bordered the water, with dozens of ships floating next to them. Farther out to sea were stretches of elevated rocks with seals sitting atop them, basking in the sun, while seagulls circled above in the hopes of stealing a fish or two from the seals' clutches.

Many more ships were visible at a distance. Some were small and bobbed up and down even on the calm ocean waters, while others were massive with three sets of sails and didn't so much as sway as they cut through the sea.

The size and scale of the port dwarfed the one at Leydes, and Carver was slightly in awe at the sight. He did not have time to stare, however, as he had to keep up with Shiala, who did not slow down.

Shiala kept a good distance ahead of him despite his efforts to keep up with her. She hopped over rocks and piles of discarded rotten timber, bobbed between the posts and supports of the piers and docks, all without looking back or saying a word to Carver.

The commotion on the piers and docks above continued, and Carver was even able to see up top from time to time. The sight was nearly the same as what he had seen through the cracks of the fishery's old wooden walls at Leydes, though on a much grander scale. Folk scurried about the wharves and walkways, going onto and off ships, carried crates up and down steps, or rolled barrels up and down ramps. The area reeked of marine life and saltwater, and the cries of gulls filled the gaps of silence between voices and the scraping of wood.

"Up here, boy!" Shiala barked as she started up a stairway carved into the stone wall to her right.

Carver hurried up behind her. The stairway was steep and shallow, and it was covered in seaweed and barnacles, which caused him to lose his footing and slide down three steps. His right leg dragged along the rough stone and barnacles, and Carver cursed under his breath as he felt some of his skin scrape away under his trousers.

Carver pulled himself up and raced up the rest of the steep steps, Shiala having already disappeared over the top. As he reached the top, he saw Shiala running through a crowd of surprised fishermen and dock workers a few feet up ahead. Carver ran into the gap she had created in the crowd before they could finish scowling at her, thus receiving a barrage of frowns and insults.

Carver kept Shiala in sight as she ducked and weaved through the bustling port until they reached a series of brick buildings far from any dock. Shiala entered an alley between two of the buildings, and Carver followed. The port's wooden walkway changed into a floor of compressed dirt as the buildings shadowed him from the sun's noontime light.

Carver felt a chill run down his spine, his current situation feeling all too familiar: running through the tight alleys and shaded side streets between the many buildings of Caswen with no idea where he was headed while the threat of death was all around him.

Shiala eventually slowed her pace, allowing Carver to catch up. Then as they approached a branching split at the end of the current alley, Shiala stopped suddenly and stretched out her right arm, causing Carver to smack into it and come to a sudden halt.

Before he could step back, Shiala grabbed his bloodstained tunic and hauled him to the side, slamming his body into the alley's left wall. She released him and pressed her back against the wall beside him.

"Quiet," she hissed through her teeth.

As the seconds passed, Carver saw trails of sweat running down Shiala's forehead and over her green face markings. He listened carefully to see if he could determine what was around the corner that worried Shiala, but all he

heard was distant chatter and the racket of boots and wooden wheels traversing a cobblestone street.

Shiala peeked around the corner and then looked back at Carver. "We're
nearing another loading dock that's sure to be packed and busy. We're going to
find a horse and take it as discreetly as we can, then make for Caswen's gate."

"How do you know where we are? This place is a maze."

"Close your mouth, runt. You're going to follow my lead and do exactly
as I say, or you'll be left behind. Now keep silent, and hand me that dagger."

Shiala grabbed the dagger before he could fully open his hand, but Carver
kept his mouth shut and let her take it. Then before he could even think,
Shiala vanished around the corner.

Carver felt a surge of worry fill his chest, and his breathing suddenly
became very apparent to him as he followed her.

Shiala was speed walking down an alley that opened up to a busy cobblestone street before a wide area that was filled with dozens of people and all
manner of horse-drawn wagons. At the far end, Carver saw the open ocean,
dotted with a variety of ships.

Initially, Carver thought Shiala had been taking him away from the water,
but now he realized they had only traveled to a different part of Caswen's vast
Port District.

Shiala had the crude goblin dagger tucked into a chest strap over her thick
leather jerkin, which kept the blade mostly concealed from non-prying eyes.
She marched calmly but quickly and did not let her eyes stray from her path.
Carver, on the other hand, scanned the area with quick glances as he followed.

Hundreds of people filled his vision in nearly every direction. The area was
a mess of people and wagons passing by each other, coming on and off the ships
that were docked along the many wharfs. Carver saw several horses too, most of
them pulling wagons or carrying riders through the clusters of people and cargo.

Carver couldn't understand how he and Shiala were supposed to steal a horse
and ride away with so many eyes and obstacles around, but he didn't mention his
concern to her and just focused on keeping up with her and appearing calm.

Shiala was fast approaching a wide wooden canopy that stood a few
dozen feet away from the land's quick decline to the water. The canopy was

surrounded with crates and dock workers as well as two wagons a stone's throw to the right, each with two horses hitched to the front.

Carver realized this was it.

Shiala didn't look at the dock workers as she went straight toward the horses. She immediately started unfastening the left-most horse from the buckles, clasps, and straps that connected it to the wagon.

The horse huffed and snorted but remained mostly calm. Shiala worked quickly. As Carver arrived at her side, the third-to-last clasp came apart and its metal buckle fell to the cobblestones with a clank.

"Hey. What are you—what's going on?" an old-looking man with a short white beard asked as he emerged from behind the wagon. He was wearing a wide-brimmed hat and a dirty brown tunic with gray trousers.

Shiala looked away from the second-to-last clasp, though she continued undoing it, and smiled at the man. "The Caswen Guard have ordered these wagons to be moved."

"Moved? What for? And how does unhitching my horses move the wagons? Stop that right now," the man demanded as he approached Shiala.

Carver looked around and saw that the old man's angry voice had summoned the attention of a few nearby dock workers.

The second-to-last clasp keeping the horse in its harness fell to the ground, taking the thick strap around the horse's flat saddle along with it.

"Just following orders, sir. Go ask the patrol if you have questions."

"Piss on your orders, lady. You don't look like any soldier I've ever seen."

The old man grabbed her left forearm to prevent her from undoing the last clasp. "Get away from my—"

He choked on his last word as Shiala slammed her left fist into his face so abruptly that all Carver saw was a blur. The old man's wrinkled hand released its grip on Shiala's forearm, and he stumbled backwards into a barrel, catching it to prevent a fall.

Carver heard a series of gasps and raised voices. More than a few dock workers and sailors had stopped what they were doing and were either staring at him and Shiala or approaching with worried or angry faces.

"Assault! Thief!" an angry voice cried. As Carver turned to face it, he was surprised to find that it came from the old man, who was lunging at Shiala rather than fleeing as Carver had assumed he would.

The old man grabbed Shiala's leather jerkin and tried to pull the tall woman away from his animal, but Shiala turned and slammed her fist into his stomach. The old man stumbled back, a crude dagger sticking out of his belly, causing Carver to realize that the second blow was no punch at all.

The old man didn't make it more than two steps backwards before his legs gave out, and he collapsed to the ground, letting out a shout that ended in a gasp.

Carver stepped back in shock and bumped into the corner of a wooden crate. The edge jabbed his hip, sending him recoiling forward. As soon as the jolt of pain arrived in his hip, his ears were met with shouts and screams.

Carver spun around and saw that many of the people who had been approaching had backed up, their eyes wide. Handfuls of them were shouting, which was quickly calling the attention of those who had not seen what happened, while many more were scurrying away from the scene.

"Guards! Guards!" someone shouted.

"Murder! Someone's been killed!" another screamed.

A hand grabbed Carver by the shoulder from behind. He spun around to meet it and saw Shiala glaring at him.

"Are you deaf? Grab that dagger, and let's go!"

Carver barely registered Shiala's command before she released his shoulder and pulled herself onto the horse, which was now unhitched. The animal itself was neighing loudly and stamping its hooves in displeasure at the sudden movements and rising commotion all around it, as were all the other horses.

Carver was hit with a rush of adrenaline as the realization set in that if he didn't act immediately, he would definitely be left behind. He darted over to the old man, who was still alive despite the calls of "murder," which had now multiplied across multiple voices, and reached down toward the dagger in his gut.

The old man, with blood running over his sides and weak gasps escaping his mouth, looked up at Carver with a face dominated by anguish and fear, and he reached out with a hand in a gesture of begging.

Carver's mind was hit with a strong sense of discomfort, which caused him to hesitate. The old man's eyes looked into Carver's in a way that Carver thought expressed both that he was afraid of him and hoping for his aid at the same time. The desire to help the poor man manifested inside Carver for the briefest of seconds, but before it could settle, fear took hold and drove him to act nearly without awareness.

Carver reached down past the man's extended arm and pulled the dagger from his belly. A thick spurt of blood followed the short blade, spraying Carver's boots.

The man let out a pain-riddled cry that pierced Carver's ears, making him realize what he had just done, but he forced himself to separate the man's suffering from his own action as he spun away and closed the distance between himself and Shiala.

Shiala reached down to grab Carver's extended arm and heaved him onto the horse. He steadied himself behind her, wrapping his arm around her for support. Not a second later, she shouted as she kicked the horse in the sides with her booted heels.

The horse broke into a run so suddenly that Carver would have fallen off had he not been holding onto Shiala. The horse darted around a pile of barrels and leaped over a mess of fishing nets.

Shiala kicked the beast again and pulled its reins to the left. The horse grunted in displeasure but turned with the tug. Again, Carver nearly fell off, squeezing Shiala even tighter to stay seated while at the same time he tightened his grip around the bloody dagger in his right hand.

A fresh round of shouts and commotion struck Carver's ears as the horse galloped through the quickly separating crowds up ahead and away from the cries of alarm behind. Carver wanted to look back to see if he and Shiala were being chased, but he felt like the act of turning would loosen his grip on her, so he just closed his eyes and held on, keeping his ears open for any further instructions that Shiala might give.

No instructions came, however, as the only things Carver heard from Shiala was heavy breathing and shouts at the horse. After a minute of riding, he opened his eyes and looked ahead. There was no sign of the ocean, and the crowded dockyard had been replaced with a wide cobblestone street with half as many people traversing it.

Many of the human and goblin pedestrians shot Carver and Shiala panicked looks as their galloping horse left them with little time to react or move out of the way. Despite the speed at which the horse continued to carry them, Carver could feel that its gallop had slowed ever so slightly. He also noted that the shouts calling for guards from behind had ceased.

Everything was happening too quickly for him to process. He couldn't tell if he'd had his eyes closed for a minute or ten seconds. The only thing that seemed clear to him was that he was completely reliant on Shiala to get him out of the city, though if that would lead him to safety, he did not know.

Carver kept his eyes open as Shiala guided the galloping horse down one wide cobblestone street to the next. He suddenly realized he was feeling incredibly nauseous and dizzy due to the sudden turns she took, making his stomach seem to twist more and more.

Carver fought the urge to vomit and tried to quell his dizziness by focusing on the back of Shiala's neck. The struggle to hold himself together and stay seated drained all his attention away from his surroundings, and soon he had lost all semblance of distance and time.

"Seekers! Seekers!" Shiala's voice suddenly broke Carver's focus.

He looked up from Shiala's neck and saw a familiar sight. The grand portcullis of Caswen hung open at the end of the wide cobblestone street, with many people passing under it in both directions. The handful of soldiers wielding tall spears caught Carver's attention immediately after.

A soldier was standing on either side of the tall archway leading out of Caswen, and four more were stationed under the archway, five feet apart from each other. Carver saw all the soldiers' eyes look his and Shiala's way as the distance between them and the gate rapidly decreased.

"Lost Seekers at the docks! An attack from the sea!" Shiala screamed so loudly that her voice hurt Carver's ears.

A situation of panic overtook the area as people exiting the city started running and kicking their horses into gallops while those entering and already inside ran for the gate or to their homes. The soldiers started shouting and trying to calm the panicked crowd, but the chaos was too much for them to control. The soldiers underneath the portcullis were forced out of the way by the fleeing people and horses and soon had their backs up against the city's stone wall so as not to get knocked over or trampled.

Shiala kicked her heels into the horse again and sent it charging under the portcullis and out into the wide-open area just outside the city.

The horse ran over the narrow stone bridge that led into the outer town of Caswen. The folk there were coming out of their wood and brick homes in concern as the shouting and commotion from the city gate began to reach them.

Shiala did not slow down. She kicked the horse's sides yet again and urged it down the town's main street.

Before long, Carver and Shiala were clear of the outer town and galloping down the wide dirt road toward green hills and fields. Then Shiala turned the horse off the road and headed over the sun-covered Vellum Hills to the southwest.

Chapter 36

❧

Carver dunked his hands into the water and cupped as much of it as he could up toward his lips before it drained through his fingers. He drank the small amount he was able to hold, then dunked his hands into the cool water again and repeated the motion. He had no idea just how thirsty he was until the waters of Lake Keldrid came into view over the cluster of sunbathed green hills. The sight of the gentle lake had stirred a desperation within him, and he had barely waited for Shiala to stop the horse before he hopped off and ran to the lake's edge.

The horse itself was drinking farther down the shore, panting between sips. The animal was exhausted after galloping out of the city and running for the better part of the short journey across the Vellum Hills.

Shiala was standing next to the horse, holding it by the reins to ensure it did not abandon them, as she watched Carver drink from the lake, a displeased expression on her face.

"Hurry up and drink your fill, Carver. We'll be heading off again in a moment."

Carver was surprised to hear Shiala call him by name rather than "boy" or "runt." He sucked back more of the water draining from his cupped hands and then turned on his knees to look at Shiala. "Can't we rest here for a bit? The horse has been run to exhaustion, and we're far from the city. No soldiers followed us."

Shiala's displeased expression intensified. "That we managed to flee Caswen so easily was a blessing from Agon," she said as she glanced up at the sun, then turned her attention back to Carver. "Those soldiers by the gate will have reported what they saw by now after realizing there was no attack in the Port District. The higher ups will connect the dots, if they haven't already, and send riders out looking for us."

Carver turned away and scooped up more water from the lake.

"We'll ride the horse until exhaustion takes it. With luck it will last us to the town of Gale, where we can find a new animal to take us the rest of the way."

Carver wiped his mouth and then looked at Shiala. "The rest of the way?"

"Did you not hear Farren's orders, boy? We're going to Quinredal on the west coast. There we'll take a ship to Rudenhull, a large town on the eastern shore of the West Isle."

"What? Why are you taking me there?"

Shiala gave a befuddled look. "Because you're wanted, you stupid boy. Your description is on bounty posters all around Caswen, with great attention on that nasty scar you've got, and your actions are on everyone's lips. The whole city will be on watch for you, and within a few days the whole Grand Isle will be too. You need to leave this island and lie low if you're to survive the week."

"But ... for how long? When will I be back?"

"Be back? Dema's tits, you really don't get it, do you? I doubt you'll ever be coming back, nor should you want to if you're looking to keep your neck away from the headsman's axe or the hangman's rope."

Carver suddenly realized the gravity of his situation. "No. I can't. I can't just leave. I have people here. Someone who needs to know I'm alive. I can't disappear forever. Not after ... I need to get back to her."

"You, stupid, ignorant, selfish little brat!" Shiala's loud voice startled the horse, but its exhaustion and its thirst kept it from moving away from the water. "You don't just do what you did at Caswen's garrison and then go back to your life as normal. The night you broke into the guard captain's office and set it aflame was the night you separated yourself from your normal life.

Were you left to your own abilities, you would be dead or in a dungeon right now, but you got lucky. Instead of soldiers or someone with enough smarts to turn you in for the bounty, you got caught and kept alive by those stupid, greedy smugglers who thought themselves more important to our cause than they were anywhere close to being. Even luckier is that your actions managed to catch the attention of Farren, who only saved you because he thinks you will be useful to our cause and can aid in our fight for freedom against the sovereigns. You've gotten into something bigger than yourself, whether you wanted to or not, and after that shitshow outside the warehouse with the guard captain herself, you're not—"

Carver felt a sharp chill run up his spine. "Wait. The guard capt—"

"No! You keep quiet, runt. In fact, you don't need to understand or agree at all beyond this point. You're the one who convinced Farren to save you, not me. If it were up to me, we'd have left you to your fate and avoided that whole mess you just put us through. But Farren made the call, and now my orders are to get you to our people in Rudenhull and then await further instructions, so that's what I'm going to do. Now pick up your dagger and get mounted. We're moving on."

Shiala tugged the horse away from the lake by its reins and mounted the animal with little effort.

Carver turned away from Shiala and stared into the calm lake. The water where he had dunked his hands just moments ago was now still and returned the image of his reflection. He looked into his reflection's eyes and struggled to form words. "That wom ... that woman ... she was ... that was her ... that ... the captain ... that was Aellia ..."

A deep rage began to build inside Carver as he stumbled over his words, and his reflection looked back at him with a face that was void of emotion. Everything hit him all at once: the reality of how close he had come to death over the last few days; the image of the woman with the coppery-brown hair and the realization of who she was; the sick feeling as he pulled the dagger from the old man's gut before leaving him to die; the pile of charred skeletons and corpses on the outskirts of his destroyed village; and the idea of being taken away and never getting the chance to see Helena again or tell her he was sorry.

All these thoughts circled through Carver's head again and again like an angry maelstrom, filling him with grief, regret, and a burning fury. In the background of these thoughts was the memory of the instance that had led to them all.

The attack on Caswen's Inner Market.

That singular, potent memory assaulted Carver's mind with such force that his knees began to shake. He realized that event was what started it all, kicking off the series of incidents that had led him to where he was that very moment. That conclusion screamed inside his skull so loudly that he felt it wasn't birthed from his own thoughts but by another voice coming from inside his head. The voice shouted at Carver about who had launched the attack that had put him on a collision course with so much pain and loss.

The Lost Seekers.

It was the Lost Seekers who had attacked the market, and it was their actions that led to Verrel taking the blame, as Helena had told him. The voice in Carver's head told him that it was as much the Lost Seekers' fault as it was Aellia's that his family was dead and his home was gone.

As Carver's thoughts latched onto this idea, he recalled all the things he had experienced with the Lost Seekers. He thought about how he had to almost beg for Farren to save him, how easily Shiala had stabbed the innocent dock worker, and how vicious and violent the Lost Seekers seemed to be.

"But we're supposed to leave civilian bodies behind."

Carver's memory suddenly singled out what he had heard while sitting next to the Lost Seekers who were robbing the overturned wagon during the market assault.

"Only us working within the guard are! Now help us get these out of here, you fool!"

Carver felt as if something suddenly clicked in his mind. The Lost Seekers wanted to cause chaos and kill innocents during the attack, to make the soldiers look responsible, apparently having infiltrated the soldiers' ranks.

The voice inside Carver's head directing his thoughts suddenly became his own again, and he took control of what he was thinking about.

I could have been one of them. If a Lost Seeker dressed as a soldier had gotten near me, they would have killed me. They say they want to save us from the sovereigns, but they don't care about anyone but themselves. Only their cause matters to them, whatever the cost of innocent life, of the lives they claim to be fighting for. They're liars and murderers. They got my family killed. They ruined everything.

Carver looked away from the lake. Shiala approached him on the back of the horse and turned the animal to face south.

"Get your blade, and get on, Carver."

He took a deep breath and got to his feet. He nodded to Shiala and then stepped over to where he had discarded the dagger in the grass when his desire to drink overtook him. After picking it up, he looked at the bloody blade for a moment before turning to the horse and reaching up with his free arm for Shiala to help him up.

"The ride to Gale will take some time, if the horse makes it that far. We'll have to walk the rest if it—"

Carver stuck his dagger deep into Shiala's lower-right side.

She let out a sharp scream as she tumbled off the horse and struck the ground on her back with a thud.

The horse let out a panicked cry and shuffled away from Shiala while Carver reached forward and grabbed the reins.

Shiala screamed a second time as she overcame her sudden shock from the fall and looked down at the dagger sticking through the back of her leather jerkin at an angle, the tip of the blade sticking out of her gut and pushing the leather jerkin out into a hard point just above her belly button.

Shiala grabbed the dagger's hilt as blood started to run over the blade and down her back and right hip. She shouted in pain again as she looked up at Carver with a face full of agony and rage. "You stupid bastard! I'll tear your damn eyes out!"

Carver ignored Shiala's wails and curses as he pulled himself forward in the saddle and secured his feet in the stirrups. He kicked his heels into the horse's sides and it broke into a run, neighing loudly.

"Get back here, you runt!" Shiala bellowed, followed by a long, horrible cry of anger infused with pain.

Carver did not look back as he urged the horse over the closest hill. The animal raced up the slight incline and then descended the other side much faster. Carver forced the horse to continue running over the next two hills before he reined it to stop.

Shiala's shouts and cries echoed over the hills, but the grassy mounds to the south blocked her from sight.

Carver pulled the horse's reins to the left and bade it to head north at a canter. He forced the horse to continue for a minute before he allowed it to slow down to a trot.

Even maintaining a trot seemed too strenuous to the exhausted animal, but Carver buried his empathy with the knowledge that he needed to put as much distance as possible between himself and Shiala and the soldiers who were no doubt following them as Shiala had said. However, Carver understood that if he pushed the beast too hard it could collapse from exhaustion, so he kept it to a trot despite his intense desire to travel as fast as he could.

It was going to be a long ride back to Leydes.

Chapter 37

Aellia's newly acquired horse, a black stallion rather than a brown mare, as her previous horse was, carried her up the cobblestone street that ascended toward the manor. The animal made uneasy noises along the way, almost as if it could sense its rider's thoughts.

Aellia did not address the two soldiers stationed by the iron gate as she trotted past them into the garden courtyard. The horse followed the narrow cobblestone path to the right, around the circular dais of bushes and flowers, and brought Aellia to the stable against the far south corner of the courtyard near the stone wall.

The stable workers all bowed at her arrival, though they wore expressions of worry and concern when they saw her appearance.

Aellia's hair, now without her helmet covering most of it, was a mess of knots and nonconforming strands, covered with dust and dirt. Her face was also smeared with dirt where she had tried to wipe it away, and her surcoat and armor were filthy, like she had just crawled through a stretch of mud. Mixed in with the dirt, mud, and dust were bloodstains, most of it on her upper back and lower surcoat, the latter seeming to be a result of her wiping her hands.

Aellia didn't address the stable workers as she slipped off her horse, dismissing them with a wave as her boots hit the ground, her chainmail clinking and her sheathed sword rattling at her waist. Aellia left her horse to be tended to without giving the handlers any instructions, her mind elsewhere.

She walked along the trail from the stable back into the courtyard and made her way toward the steps that rose to the manor's entrance. She rounded a patch of abelia bushes and was about to ascend the steps when she noticed something and stopped. She stared at the abelia bushes' many pink flowers, seeing more clearly now that one bush's thin branches had been snapped and was hanging by a string of wood fibers. The faint wind jostled the broken branch, shaking the tiny pink petals from side to side.

Aellia watched for a moment as the broken branch twisted and brushed against the rest of the bush. It seemed pleasant to her. Pink had always been her favorite color of flower, and the way the petals vibrated in the wind struck her with a sense of beauty. She reached out and pulled the branch from the bush.

The branch detached with a wet snap, causing the bush to jiggle around for a moment. Aellia lifted the branch up to her face and rubbed the tiny flowers along her right cheek. The petals were soft, and they tickled Aellia's skin as their faint scent filled her nostrils. She smiled and took a deep breath. Then she dropped the branch and turned away. The moment had calmed her, but she needed to move on.

She made her way through the front door, which was opened for her by one of the two soldiers stationed out front, both of them seeming just as worried as the stable workers when they saw her. Then she made her way past the soldiers on guard inside, each of whom greeted her with respectful nods and polite smiles despite the shocked looks on their faces.

By the time Aellia reached the second floor and turned down the north hall beyond the door, she had entirely lost the pleasant feeling she had felt in the garden.

She walked down the dimly lit hall in silence. The chirping of birds entered through the open windows in the high part of the left wall, as did the fading beams of sunlight as evening approached.

Aellia stopped at the old wooden door at the end of the hall to her right, opened it, and stepped through onto the wooden loggia that stretched across the inner courtyard like a bridge along the north side. She crossed the walkway above the inner courtyard's garden, pond, and quiet streams, heading past the door on her left that led to the manor's large study, and arrived at the door directly across of where she had entered. Aellia passed through the door and entered a tight, somewhat dim hall much like the one she had traversed to attend her unusual summons with Adaman and Erol many weeks ago.

Along the left wall was a series of wooden doors that ran down nearly to the end, about ten feet between each, until the hall turned sharply to the right and continued to the south. Each door led to nearly identical rooms that were used to accommodate visiting dignitaries and important guests, though they were not often filled.

Aellia headed down to the end of the hall. When she arrived, she realized no soldiers were standing guard in that part of the manor. She wondered for a moment if she should be worried, but before she could decide, she reached the final door on the left wall.

Instead of worrying about the lack of soldiers and the reason they may not be on duty, Aellia raised her hand to knock on the door, only to stop when she heard a deep laugh from the other side, which surprised her.

What surprised her even more was that she recognized the laugh to be Erol's. Despite never having heard the sovereign laugh before, the deep tone of the chuckle was unmistakable. Aellia waited and listened, hearing another voice inside the room as well, though she could not hear what it was saying.

Aellia tensed her shoulders when she realized she was eavesdropping, something she found unprofessional and childish, so she broke her moment of silence by banging her knuckles on the door three times.

"Enter," Erol's deep yet smooth and fair-sounding voice called from within.

Aellia grabbed the wooden handle and pushed the door open, then entered the room in two long strides and pushed the door shut behind her in a smooth, elegant motion.

The room was almost perfectly square and spacious enough not to feel stuffy. It had a large window on the north wall, its wooden shutters pushed wide open, offering a northern view of Caswen's eastern side toward the ocean.

A wide bed filled about a fifth of the room. The rest was furnished by a tall wooden dresser, a long table with two chairs on one side, a brown rug that covered most of the wooden floor, and a thick desk against the east wall that supported a network of tall candles, though at the moment the chamber was only lit by the sunlight that entered through the window, giving the room a dim natural light.

Sitting at the desk was Erol, though he had the chair facing away from the desk and sat facing toward a dark-skinned human man in the center of the room. Aellia had almost forgotten about Jaqun's presence in Caswen, as she had only seen him on three occasions after their initial meeting, and during none of those brief sightings did the man speak to her beyond a formal greeting.

Jaqun was wearing the same outfit he always seemed to be wearing when Aellia saw him: a light jerkin of black leather with a bronze chest piece overtop, adorned with more strips of black leather inked with chestnut-red edges; a yellow linen cloak that wrapped around his neck, covered his shoulders, and descended his back; tight-fitting black trousers; and deep-brown boots that were always polished and immaculate. Jaqun was also equipped with his usual weapons, his large, curved dagger and seemingly rectangular arming sword with its round, club-like grip, although Aellia still had not seen either of these weapons drawn from their tanned-hide sheaths.

However, Jaqun's face was still the most unchanged thing about him. His heavily stubbled chin and cheeks, along with his hair of near matching texture and length, seemed so identical to past meetings that Aellia had to assume the man trimmed every single dark hair each morning without fail.

Erol, however, looked quite different. Instead of being adorned in his usual exquisite, pearl-colored armor with turquoise grooves and the short red cape that ran down his back, he wore an outfit almost as foreign looking as Jaqun's. The outfit included an intricately embroidered white chiton robe that hung from his shoulders down to his knees. It was tied at the waist, leaving his strange, bone-like taloned feet visible, as always. Wrapped around his torso and also hanging nearly to his knees, beginning from a strap fastened around his right shoulder, was a long red toga, though Aellia did not know the true name of that attire, having never seen its likeness before.

Jaqun and Erol turned to face Aellia as she entered. Erol was still smiling after having laughed at whatever Jaqun had just said. The sight of Erol's wide smile was strange to Aellia, as she had never seen him show any kind of pleasant emotion, beyond a slight grin, since her first interaction with him around two months earlier.

Aellia couldn't help but look at Erol's teeth, which were revealed as his thin, almost non-existent lips pulled back to accommodate his laugh. She noticed that his teeth looked no different from a human's or dwarf's. Aellia was unsure why she made the observation or why she was surprised to see little distinction between Erol's teeth and her own, so she quickly banished the torrent of thoughts from her mind and focused on standing up straight. However, she could not ignore the strange feeling she felt upon seeing Erol appear so casual and pleasant, given her past experiences with him.

As Erol fixed his gaze on Aellia, his smile disappeared, and his expression returned to one of scrutiny and seriousness, the look she was used to seeing on his face.

Now looking into the sovereign's larger-than-human eyes from across the room, Aellia was still unsure if his irises were blue, brown, or dark green, as both their shade and color seemed to change depending on the light.

"Ah, Aellia. As always you arrive sooner than I expect. A good quality, despite things. I like a soldier who reports quickly, not even bothering to clean up first," Erol said gently as he eyed her up and down.

Aellia twitched her mouth to speak, but before she could form a word, Erol looked over at Jaqun and spoke to him instead. "I'd like the room with Aellia, Jaq. You and I can finish our conversation later."

Jaqun nodded with an expression that did not indicate he was the kind of person who could make anyone laugh, but Aellia did not doubt what she had heard through the door. As Jaqun walked past Aellia, he gave her a look that she detected was one of evaluation, a look she had felt was being cast her way quite often these days.

Aellia did not take her attention off Erol as Jaqun left. As soon as the door clicked shut, Erol sat up straighter while placing his elbows in a relaxed position on the chair's thin wooden arms. The sovereign looked like he was about to speak, but Aellia spoke up first, taking the slightest degree of control away from him.

"Why are there no guards in the northeast hall? There should be at least two at all times."

"I had them dismissed to guard elsewhere. I dislike having those I don't trust within earshot of my chambers."

"You don't trust the manor's soldiers?" Aellia asked without showing much emotion. "The Manor Guard is made up of only the finest and most loyal soldiers, handpicked by me or the spymaster."

Erol gently clasped his long-fingered hands together. "Yes, I know. But who's to say I trust your or Renneil's judgment yet?"

Aellia felt a prickle of irritation run down her neck, which she assumed was no doubt intended by Erol.

"Besides, I doubt anyone wishing me harm could infiltrate the manor, and if they did, I don't think they'd find my hospitality to unwanted guests very agreeable. But enough of such things. I assume you know why I summoned you here?"

"To berate me without my soldiers present."

Erol sighed. "To keep your soldiers' opinion of you from lessening, yes, that is part of it. But not all, and I am not going to berate you. I want to be filled in on what happened today. I know about the conflict in the Port District."

"Surely you already know the details. Your sovereign spies must keep you informed far better than any human woman like I could."

Erol rose out of his chair so quickly that it tipped over backwards and hit the floor. "Do not play these childish games with me, Aellia! I'm in no mood for your juvenile bitterness."

Aellia nearly flinched from Erol's sudden animation, but she managed to keep herself steady and didn't show any sign of fear or weakness.

"Do you see sovereigns marching around the city's streets? Has your spymaster found or reported any other of my kind among this backwater province of islands? I very much doubt it, because I'm the only one here. Those who report to me, who are separate from your council, are humans, goblins, and dwarves. They gladly serve the empire because they know it is not their enemy. I am not your enemy, Aellia. I was sent here to help you, not hinder you. I want to see the Isles return to peace as much as you surely do, and to achieve such peace I am working in my own way to aid you, even if you don't see it."

Aellia let herself cool down for a moment after Erol finished his intense yet still somewhat calm rant. His final words had hit her unexpectedly and, as such, her planned response evaporated along with some of the wall she always had raised when conversing with the sovereign.

"I'm not sure that the Isles has ever known peace, to be honest, sir," Aellia said with less hostility to her tone, though she kept it from being pleasant.

Erol stared at Aellia for a moment. It seemed like he was analyzing her response to see if it carried any sarcasm or snideness, but then he surprised her again by chuckling. "So it seems," he said with an almost undetectable grin as he turned away from Aellia and stepped toward the window overlooking the northeastern side of the city and the ocean beyond. "In my studies of you humans, specifically you Boreaterrans and the history of your kingdom, I have learned much about your past conflicts, and this insignificant little chain of islands always seems to be somehow involved in those conflicts despite its irrelevance. The raids and skirmishes launched from these shores into mainland Terraland by the Old Goblin Empire before it fell apart, though I use the term empire very loosely. The battles your people faced against your old enemy, the tartaruns, trying to liberate the islands from their grasp, and the struggles the inhabitants here suffered after the province's annexation into Terraland. Then that civil war that Keldar began against his sister. And now these traitorous rebels."

"Keldrid, sir."

"What?" Erol turned around to face her.

"It was Keldrid who started the civil war against Keldria. Keldar was their father."

"Ah, my mistake. You Boreaterrans don't make it easy for someone to follow your history. Keldar, Keldrid, Keldria, Terraland's capital of Keldaria. Such similar names breed confusion. But I did not call you here to talk about your people's ancient history. I want to hear about today. And I want to hear it from you regardless of what I may already know from others. Now please, begin." Erol leaned against the wall next to the window and tilted his head to look out at the ocean.

Aellia cleared her throat and adopted a more relaxed stance. "The situation began around noon. I was leading some daily training exercises in the garrison's courtyard when one of my soldiers arrived with a goblin at his side. The goblin quickly began spouting details about how he and his fellows had caught the scar-headed Lost Seeker, along with some documents the boy had apparently stolen, and that other Lost Seekers were arriving to collect both. He spat out a list of convoluted instructions about how we should arrest the arriving traitors and where we needed to do it, as well as a persistent demand that we pay for each rebel on top of the posted bounty for the boy with an extra bonus thrown in for the documents. I understood immediately what was going on."

"And what was going on, Aellia?"

"Well," she turned and began to pace back and forth between the room's bed and desk, "if this goblin was to be believed—and I was skeptical at first—then he and his fellows had captured the Lost Seeker boy and could have turned him in for the bounty for easy absols. Instead, they apparently arranged some kind of trade with the Lost Seekers themselves, no doubt thinking to double their coin by selling the boy to them first and then having us pay a grand sum of absols for the lot of them."

"That seems like a logical plan, though greedy and dangerous, and one that lessens the funds of the Lost Seekers while sending them into your hands. What went wrong?"

"We were given no time to act, is what went wrong. The greedy goblin arrived with this information while the deal was apparently already underway in the Port District. I was forced to rally what few soldiers I had around me and ride out for the meeting place immediately to ensure we arrived before it was too late.

"I sent some of my soldiers to find other nearby patrols in order to set up a perimeter throughout the Port District in case things got out of hand, as I did not anticipate a clean ambush, nor did I know even how many Lost Seekers would be present at this supposed meeting, though time was not on their side either. The goblin refused to indicate the meeting place, however, insisting that we only ambush the Lost Seekers once they were far enough away from the location of the trade."

"A strange insistence from someone who's only motivation is absols."

"I agree. The whole situation stunk of manipulation and illegal activity, and in the Port District, illegal activity is usually tied to smuggling rings. Regardless, I forced the information from the goblin, and he led me and four other soldiers to a warehouse close to the harbor. Once we arrived, we stationed ourselves out of sight and waited for the Lost Seekers to exit the building with the bounty target."

"Why not go in and apprehend them immediately? What if they did not exit that way or had already left?"

"They hadn't left yet. We passed no one in the alleys and streets that led to the warehouse entrance, and two riderless horses were hitched right before the turn into the secluded area that led to the building. From those observations I gathered that we had a possibility of dealing with four rebels if two shared each horse, with a fifth being the bounty target.

"Including me, we had five soldiers, not counting the goblin, who I kept in the saddle with me, so I did not feel comfortable leading us into a direct assault with the possibility of our opponents' numbers being so near to ours and with no understanding of the building's layout. The goblin stressed that only two Lost Seekers were to be arriving for the trade, but I wasn't going to put my trust and the lives of my men in his words. Better to wait and assess the odds further once the rebels came out, I thought."

"A sound decision given the circumstances. What then?"

Aellia stopped pacing and stood next to the overturned chair beside the cluttered desk. "After a few minutes of waiting they came out, four in total: a human man, a human woman, a female goblin, and a teenage human boy who fit the description Harsond gave perfectly, though I could not see the back of his head to identify the scar. We moved in immediately and cornered them. I wanted to take them alive for interrogation, especially the boy, so I gave them a chance to surrender.

"I allowed the adult man, who I assumed to be their leader, to give his little speech, as cornered Lost Seekers often do, only because we had crossbows aimed at the group and could easily run them down before they had the time to channel magic."

Erol turned his head to face Aellia. "A well-informed understanding of sorcery, Aellia. Have you had much experience with illegal sorcerers?"

Aellia felt that Erol's words meant something more than what was plain to hear, though she wasn't absolutely sure. "Some. At times the Lost Seekers indeed have harbored sorcerers working for their cause."

Erol rubbed two fingers along the side of his sharp chin. "Yes, I have seen how these Lost Seekers use sorcery for acts of terrorism. It is a troubling thing to have to wonder if an enemy might suddenly wield magic against you. It is a good thing you know enough about sorcery and magic to be prepared for it, like how you seemed to know what I was doing before my sorcery manifested into magic when I healed your lieutenant, calling for me to hurry up, as you did so brazenly."

Aellia was uncomfortable with the way Erol's eyes burrowed into her. She felt a sudden desire to look at the floor to escape the sovereign's stare, but she forced herself to maintain eye contact. Aellia's quick inner battle forced out an anxious half grin despite her lack of any positive emotion at the moment.

"Yes, well, unfortunately, despite my knowledge and preparation, I did not see what the lead Seeker was doing until it was too late. He cast a small object forward that created a deafening sound and blew the legs out from under my mount. It sent the other horses into a panicked frenzy or crippled them as well."

"A small object? Describe it."

"I didn't get a good look at it before I was knocked from my horse and the smoke emerged, but it looked like a round metal stone, no bigger than two fists wrapped together. Right before the man tossed it, he spoke of the attack on the market and the blasts of flame that were used to sow such chaos there. He said it was not sorcery but progress that created the blasts and that he would show me that progress again."

Erol turned away from Aellia and looked out the open window once again. He kept silent for a moment, with his hands clasped behind his waist, until he finally spoke without turning to face Aellia.

"I have heard of this type of weapon used before elsewhere in Gaia. From what little we know, it is some kind of powder that when touched with flame ignites into a wave of force and fire, similar to some spells in the School of Elementancy. However, I have only heard of this new weapon used in its base form or within large containers such as barrels, just as these Lost Seekers used when they attacked your market and raided the province's taxes. But now you tell me they wield it in throwable metal stones, and with such potency. Most concerning."

"If you've heard of this weapon before then you must know where it comes from or how it's made."

Erol turned back to Aellia with a look of interest. "Must I? The blasts leave little behind to be studied, and I am no alchemist. There are those serving the empire who are looking into this substance, but if they have learned anything substantial, I have not been told. Though it seems that these rebels are advancing this strange weapon faster than we anticipated. The first report that reached my ears of this weapon was barely over a year ago. I will report on this news in my next letters. Now, fill me in on what transpired next."

"There isn't much left to say. Only one of my soldiers was wounded from the blast, having his leg crushed by his fallen horse. I had one man stay behind to help him while I took the other two with me after the Seekers who had run back inside the warehouse. We pushed our way past their makeshift barricade and found that they had fled through a hatch in the floor that led to an underground tunnel."

"So you were right about the goblin and his fellows. Smugglers and thieves."

"Yes, it seems so."

"If the rebels escaped your grasp, then what of the goblins? Surely you didn't leave them to continue their business."

"The goblin sharing my saddle was crushed by my horse and killed. The rest were all dead inside the warehouse. It seems the deal had gone sour before we arrived."

"Hmm. As I said, greedy and dangerous."

Aellia nodded. "Regardless, though, we lost the targets down the tunnel when they collapsed the exit, whether through sorcery or another container of this strange powder, I am not sure, which caused a collapse of the whole tunnel that me and my two men narrowly escaped. Despite my efforts to lock down the district, the lack of time and communication between my soldiers and me allowed the bastards to slip through and disappear before we could properly organize.

"I received a report soon after that a human woman and teenage boy fled through the city's gate on horseback while shouting about an attack in the Port District. The description of the pair matches those who I saw outside the warehouse. I have already sent out scouting bands to search for any trace of them, and I've issued extra patrols throughout the city for the other two, though I have significant doubts about the success of either venture."

"That is not the attitude I like to hear. Especially not from someone in charge of the province's military and security."

Aellia took a deep breath, then clasped her hands together behind her back. "Then you will be pleased by what I have to say next. I am resigning from my duties."

"What?" Erol's tone expressed shock, making him appear vulnerable to Aellia for the first time.

"It's just that simple, sir. I'm stepping down from my roles as captain of the Caswen Guard and marshal of the Isles," Aellia said with calm focus and a clear, steady voice.

Erol seemed taken aback by her words. He stood in silence for a moment, his only movement being the occasional blinking of his large, piercing eyes.

"Why?"

Aellia took another deep breath, letting her chest fill with air as she brought her hands back to her sides. "Because I'm finished, sir. I have proven unable to staunch the growing chaos caused by these rebels, and my efforts to stabilize the realm have only added to its decline."

Erol took a long stride forward. "You've proven? Proven to whom? You have not proven anything to me yet."

"To myself, sir." Aellia tried to keep herself calm and confident under Erol's scrutiny. "Over these last few months I have failed in my duties time and time again, and each time it is others who suffer for it. I had not anticipated the attack on the market, and that failing alone cost a great many lives. I ordered an entire village to be burned to the ground and its inhabitants killed just to create the illusion of retaliation against the Lost Seekers, though that drastic effort seems to have done more harm than good. And a single rebel boy has made a fool of me twice while nearly killing those under my command each time, with the incident today being a direct failing of my command. I am unfit to lead Caswen's soldiers, let alone the province's entire military."

"So you'll just give up? You'll throw away your rank and titles in the face of defeat and hide in this manor with your family while your lands fall to the enemy? These aren't the actions of the woman I was told about. You, who at seventeen years of age joined the City Guard in defiance of her father's wishes. You, who rose to the rank of city captain and then marshal of all the Isles in only a few years. You, who lead your soldiers from the front and do not shy away from battle. The Aellia I was told about would not cower from her responsibilities in the shadow of failure like a spoiled noble child crying for her mother."

Aellia's calm demeanor quickly sank into anger, and she unintentionally balled up her fists. "Don't you speak about my mother, you sovereign bastard! You don't know anything about her or me! You, who look down on me and my people and treat all other races like ignorant children! You think I give a damn about what you think of me? A sovereign? You should be grateful I didn't join the Lost Seekers myself after you stole my mother from me! I have nothing but contempt for you and your whole kidnapping race. You—"

Erol dashed toward Aellia in three long strides and grabbed her by the throat, slamming her into the wall next to the desk. He grabbed her right wrist as well, keeping her hand away from her sword.

Aellia felt her feet leave the ground as Erol slid her up the wall with strength she did not expect him to have. She choked loudly as Erol held her off the ground with her back pushed into the wall. She grabbed at Erol's arm and tried to push it away, but her efforts had no effect on the sovereign.

"Those words sound awfully similar to those I've heard spoken by many Lost Seekers before they meet their ends at the gallows. I have already told you that I am not your enemy, Aellia, and I strongly advise you not to become mine."

Aellia tried to kick and squirm out of Erol's grip, but the sovereign's strength was too great. She felt completely incapable in his grasp and could only listen and choke for breath as a tight pressure built up behind her eyes.

"I am not the embodiment of the Sovereign Empire. The actions of my peers and superiors are not my own, and I will not have you putting whatever distrust or anger you have for them onto me. If you only knew, you stupid girl, the true scale of the things that exist beyond your small kingdom and its mountains. You humans, dwarves, and goblins are treated as ignorant children because that is exactly what you are, ignorant beings who are lucky if you live even a fifth of a sovereign lifetime and who can never experience the knowledge that so many years bring."

Erol's grip tightened around her throat and upper-right arm. Her desire to breathe turned more desperate, and her strength to break away began to drain as a result, but she did not look away from Erol's eyes as she continued to struggle.

"If I could have things happen differently, I would. But it is not up to me. The reigning emperor decides our methods, and it is through the will of the Council that those methods are enforced through the chain of command. There are things at stake far greater than your province of islands, the whole of Terraland, and all of you humans scattered throughout this world."

Erol stopped his rant and gave Aellia a long glare with his large eyes, then he suddenly let her go and turned away.

Aellia slid down the wall and fell to her hands and knees. She gasped for air, but a fit of frantic coughing prevented her from taking a full breath. When she finally regained control of her breathing, she pushed herself up to her feet.

Erol was already on the other side of the room staring out the window, his hands pressed against the wall on each side.

"Maybe you're right, Erol. Maybe I am ignorant to the greater dealings of the world, whatever they may be." Aellia coughed once more. "But I don't give a damn about any of that. I have someone special to me, someone I am to marry come winter. I love him, but I have continually pushed him away to focus on my duties here, something I regret having done for so long. I wanted to be with him while protecting my home and my people, but in attempting to do both I have succeeded in doing neither."

Aellia rubbed her aching neck with her left hand. "I forfeit my rank and titles not to cower with my family in this manor but to start a new life away from this place with the man I have brushed aside for too long out of a sense of pride and duty. Well, fuck my pride and duty. Fuck the Isles. Fuck Caswen. Fuck the Lost Seekers. Fuck the Empire. And fuck my bastard of a father. I wash my hands of it all!

"After my wedding at Fort Audrin I will sail away with my love to the Coastlands and leave all this behind me. My time spent trying to protect others is over. I am going to finally start caring about myself for a change and seek the happiness I rightly deserve." Aellia finished with a final cough.

Erol kept his back turned to Aellia as he stared out at the slowly darkening city. The ocean's waves crashed against the visible portion of the Port District with greater strength, and with each splash came a bounty of white foam that was quickly pulled back into the water by another wave.

Aellia didn't know what to do or say next as she stood and stared at Erol's back. She wondered if she should have said all she had and also why she had let it all out in the first place.

"Aellia," Erol said without facing her. She kept silent. Erol turned around and unfolded his arms. His demeanor had returned to a calm and collected state, and the look in his eyes seemed almost apologetic. "You do not need to explain such personal matters to me. Go. Find your happiness in whatever form you wish. I know you performed your duties here to the best of your abilities, despite what you might think. If only we had more human leaders like you serving the empire, this land could achieve so much. I am greatly disappointed to see you step down, but I respect your wishes and know that you will have chosen only the best replacements for your positions."

Aellia was hit with an uncomfortable feeling in response to Erol's sudden kindness. "Thank ... um ... thank you, sir. I have only chosen the new captain.

However, the title of marshal is assigned by the magistrate and his council, not me. And I apologize for my earlier outburst. You have been nothing but fair to me since your arrival, and you did not deserve such disrespect. I should not blame you for what happened to my—"

Erol waved his hand dismissively and turned back to stare out the window. "You may go now, Aellia. Retire to your chambers and get some rest. I sense you desperately need it. I will make my rounds tomorrow morning and get acquainted with the new captain of the Caswen Guard, though I suspect I have already done more than meet him. And I suppose I will simply have to wait and see who your father and his council assign as the new marshal in the days to come. I wish you luck in finding the happiness you seek."

Aellia did not know how to respond or even if she should carry on the conversation at all, so she merely nodded, despite the fact that Erol was once again facing away and couldn't see the gesture, which made her feel silly, and turned to walk for the door. As she pulled it open, Erol's voice suddenly caught her.

"One more thing, actually, Aellia. Before you go."

She stopped and looked back. "Yes, Erol?"

Erol turned away from the window and locked eyes with Aellia once more. "My current duties have kept me away from my studies of this place for longer than I would like. So, I would like to ask you a question to satiate my current lack of knowledge about your province. A proper city's port is meant to have a wall farther inland to defend against those who would invade by sea. Why then is this city, with such high stone walls around so much of it, lacking not only an eastern wall to section off the port, but also fortifications of any kind along its exposed eastern side?"

Aellia thought for a moment before replying, her hand on the door. "Caswen's wall did span across the east at one point, a few hundred years ago when Prince Keldrid returned from his years missing in the west of the Great Ocean and turned Caswen from the goblin port town it was into the province capital it is today."

"Years missing? Is it normal for your princes to go missing at sea? And where was he sailing to so far west of the Isles?"

"I don't know. Nothing lies west of the Isles save for endless water, and to my knowledge there are no official records of Keldrid giving an explanation for his departure. From what I recall the legend is that our goddess, Siyon, saved him alone from a terrible storm that destroyed his ship, and she kept him in her kingdom beneath the sea for a long while for reasons unknown. Or so the legend claims. But the stories and translated records of the time after tell that upon Keldrid's return, he built Caswen into a great city, apparently very quickly considering its scale, and surrounded it with the great stone wall it has today.

"But after his civil war against his sister, Keldria, for the throne of Terraland ended with his defeat and death at Victory Fields, Keldria ordered the eastern portion of Caswen's wall, which divided the Port District from the others, to be destroyed so that the city would always be vulnerable to an attack from the Mainland. It was to discourage another civil war from being launched by Keldrid's supporters, as the province's capital was then exposed and mostly defenseless to the queen's armies. It's the same as Old Brienen."

"Old Brienen?"

"Oh, well. It was an old city in the Coastlands. It used to just be called Brienen and was built at the west end of the Valley of Aol, the narrow pass from Splitland to the Coastlands between the Terran Mountains and the Mountains of Fire. During Keldrid's civil war, he took control of Brienen and fortified it. He also built the Towers of Betrayal in the valley. The only way for Keldria's armies to reach the Coastlands by foot was through that valley, and since Keldrid had taken the Coastlands, he had control over most of Terraland's navy, so his sister couldn't reach him by sea around the Broken Coast either. Keldrid had a nearly impenetrable position."

Erol turned his body fully away from the window and leaned against the wall, giving Aellia his full attention. Upon seeing the sovereign's action, Aellia realized she was probably going on too long, so she tried to quickly wrap up her answer, suddenly feeling a little strange to be talking to Erol so casually after what had just transpired between them.

"Anyway, when Keldrid and his host were eventually defeated, the queen forbade the Coastlands from having a city at the western exit of Aol's valley since it created too great a defense for any enemy attacking from the west. So, Brienen was abandoned, and its people moved north to build a new city near the Brienen lake. They called it New Brienen, and the original city has been dubbed Old Brienen ever since."

Aellia stood in silence and watched Erol for any sign of emotion. Finally, he grinned. "You know quite a deal about this land's history, Aellia. Perhaps you should have gone to a dwarven historium and became a historian or a scholar instead of taking up a military career."

Aellia smiled out of forced politeness, though she did feel flattered from the comment. "I appreciate the compliment, but I only know what I was forced to learn. I never really had much interest in history, but being a noble I had to endure the lessons all the same. Thankfully, having one kingdom meant that the lessons in my kind's history were not too complicated."

"You speak as if you Boreaterrans are all alone in this world. Have you forgotten about the others of your kind? Those of your race to the east once had their own kingdom, did they not? And Jaqun is living proof that another human kingdom existed far to the south."

Aellia felt a degree of levity within herself. She was surprised to find herself enjoying the conversation with Erol, despite his previous assault, and felt it agreeable to continue talking.

"The Orienterrans were never a true single kingdom. Our records say they were still somewhat of a fractured people before Keldar incorporated their land into Terraland as a province, if our texts remain correct after their translations into your people's language. And I must admit that I often forget about the Meriditerrans, as Jaqun is the only one I have ever seen. From the things he wears I would guess that his kingdom is a beautiful place. But you said existed. Did something happen to Jaqun's kingdom?"

Aellia thought she picked up a sudden shift in Erol's posture, though she wasn't sure.

"My apologies. I misspoke. I said existed in the context of the kingdom's time before being joined into the Sovereign Empire. The kingdom of the Meriditerrans is known as Xaidar. It lies far to the south, across the Urubinon Mountains and the desert of the same name, though I know little of that realm aside from that it is nothing like your own and is free from the blight of these Lost Seekers."

Erol's words were suddenly quick and less calm than they usually were. He moved away from the wall and picked up the chair he had knocked over near his desk. "I have enjoyed our discussion, but I must return to my work. Goodbye, Aellia. I wish you luck in your desired life." he said bluntly as he sat at his desk and began busying himself with the scattered papers atop its surface.

"Oh ... um, yes, sir," Aellia responded with a renewed sense of unease at the sudden shift in Erol's mood. The sovereign had a knack for switching his demeanor, a trait that made her unsure of him.

Aellia kept her thoughts to herself as she exited Erol's chamber.

Chapter 38

⚜

The town of Leydes came into view beyond a long stretch of plains as Carver's horse carried him over the last hill. The waterside town was veiled in the darkness that had arrived alongside the two moons after the sun had vanished beyond the high western trees of Vellum Forest some hours ago. The wood and brick homes around the perimeter of Leydes had dim, pulsing candlelight emanating from behind their closed wooden shutters and from the cracks beneath their locked doors. The sight of the settlement filled him with relief and anxiety.

Carver commanded his horse to keep moving with a gentle squeeze of his legs, and the beast obeyed without protest. The horse had relaxed greatly under its new rider's care. Once he had felt he was comfortably ahead of any dangers that could be following, he had let the animal continue at a pleasant walk for the rest of the long journey.

Carver, however, was more exhausted than before, having stayed in the saddle from the beginning of the sun's descent to the arrival of the harrowing gaze from the stars above. He had nearly fallen out of the saddle during some of the steeper hills due to his lack of energy and strength, but now his hunger and thirst, creating a constant discomfort in his stomach and throat, banished all his weariness due to his lack of proper sleep over the last few days and made him determined to reach his destination without stopping for a break.

Carver's horse walked through the field of tall grass that led to the town with no further instruction from its rider. Carver was too wrapped up in his thoughts about his next actions to focus on guiding the horse, and so the animal started to meander away from its initial path where it would have joined with the southern dirt road that led into the quiet town.

Carver thought about what he should say first, and to whom. First, he wondered if he should apologize immediately or if he should explain himself beforehand. Then he wondered if he should wait until sunrise to make his entrance so that his companions and hosts would all be awake and in a more relaxed mood. If so, he wondered where he could spend the night without attracting both notice and attention. Lastly, he thought about the reactions he would get from each circumstance and which would be the most unpleasant.

"Hey, you. Stop there!" a firm male voice commanded from Carver's right.

Carver jolted in the saddle and looked at where the voice had come from. At first he could not see anyone in the darkness, but then he realized that one of the nearby windows emanating candlelight was not a window at all but a man approaching with a round wooden disk topped with five candles in his left hand.

Carver stopped his horse and turned it to face the man, giving him a much better look at the stranger.

Carver's heart began to race. The man's armor jumped out immediately, followed by the arming sword in the man's other hand.

"Why are you riding into Leydes at this hour? Honest folk don't travel under starwatch."

Carver felt a surge of panic. He looked down and saw that the bloodstain from his briefly sliced throat was still visible across the collar of his tunic and chest where Vie's cloak didn't cover, and even fresher bloodstains were on the right thigh of his trousers from when he stabbed Shiala, which Vie's cloak did not cover either. Carver also quickly realized that he had no weapon, having left his dagger stuck into Shiala's side, and that he was apparently on bounty posters, which could have easily reached Leydes in the days he had been bound in the smugglers' warehouse.

Just as Carver felt that he had no other option but to kick his horse into a gallop and flee back into the hills, he came up with a half-baked plan that his anxiety shoved out of his mouth in an instant.

"Messenger business! Oh, uh, I mean, messenger business, sir." Carver tried to calm himself down and not make a scene.

The soldier stopped and frowned. "What kinda messenger works at this hour? And travels away from the road, at that?" he asked sternly as he turned and pointed his sword at the dirt road leading into the town farther back. Then he turned back to Carver and lowered his blade.

"Oh, that. Yes, well ..." Carver straightened his posture and rolled his shoulders forward in order to shift the hood of Vie's gray cloak over his forehead, hoping to obscure as much of his face as possible without appearing to be doing so.

"I came from Caswen, so I thought I could save time by getting off the road and cutting more directly northwest through the hills. But I got myself turned around and became lost. Also, my horse tired itself out from all the ups and downs of the steep hills, so I had to ride slower. You know how it is." Carver tried to sound friendly without seeming too cheerful.

The soldier took another few steps forward, which allowed Carver to see the thick moustache that covered his upper lip and extended onto his slightly pudgy cheeks.

Carver tensed slightly and hoped to the stars that the soldier did not get close enough to spot the dark red stains on his right thigh or the upper portion of his tunic.

"To save time? Only a fool would think those hills could beat the road. You came from Caswen, did you? On whose business?"

Carver began to worry that he was going to trap himself in answers he didn't know the true details behind if pressed further, so he tried to come up with something vague that couldn't be checked immediately. "Oh, well, on the business of Aellia—Captain Aellia, I mean. She sent out many messengers this evening to spread word about the changes to the bounty being posted through Caswen."

"Bounty? What bounty?"

Carver felt a wave of relief wash over him.

"Oh, yes, well, that's exactly why she sent us out. Some places don't even know about the bounty, let alone the new information. There's been some recent incidents with rebels in Caswen lately, and the captain has put out a bounty for the ones responsible. I'm supposed to spread the word through the tavern and shipyard here, and then I'll be on my way, though I suppose due to my foolishness and late arrival I'll have to wait till morning to do my job."

The soldier kept silent for a moment, apparently weighing the truth of Carver's story while furrowing his thick moustache. Suddenly, he took a heavy breath through his nose that shook his mustache. "Can't believe the marshal would hire such a rock-headed fool. Well, alright then, ride on. But follow the road, and do so from now on if you want to keep your job in the future. You can get yourself a room at the tavern if it ain't full, which it usually isn't, to wait out the night. It's in the center of town, just past the market."

"Thank you, sir. I'll do that."

The soldier had already turned around and was walking back to his post before Carver could finish speaking. Carver felt a great sense of relief at his success and took a quiet moment to relax before he instructed his horse along and followed the soldier's trail, though he kept a fair amount of distance from the man as he headed toward the wide dirt road that led into Leydes from the south. Once the horse's hooves touched the road, Carver turned the animal toward Leydes and pushed it into a light trot.

The soldier was just returning to his duty by the road's left side, leaning against the corner of a brick house, and he gave Carver an unpleasant look as he passed by.

Carver kept his eyes straight ahead to avoid any further problems. Once the horse brought him past the first set of old houses along the town's southern border, he guided the animal around the road's first right turn and then allowed it to continue down the main street at a more relaxed pace.

As Carver rode down the street, he saw many more homes with candlelight escaping from the cracks in their shutters and doors and heard the faint sounds of activity inside. The warm light and pleasant sounds from within the buildings did little to calm Carver's mood. Despite being totally alone and seeing no one ahead or behind him, he felt like he had many sets of eyes on him and that if he made any kind of suspicious movement or mistake, he would be caught.

Carver attempted to remind himself that his current situation was nothing like it had been in Caswen, trying to tell himself that if the soldier guarding the road didn't know anything about the events in Caswen or the bounty on his head, then perhaps no one in Leydes did.

His reasoning did little to relax his mind, as the past few days had left him paranoid and anxious. Before he could attach his thoughts to any specific worry about what could happen, he reached another turn. It led to the left around a large wooden structure that looked to be a blacksmith's shop or a craftsmen's workshop. Carver ignored his impulse to look the building over and guess what it might be, his mind too occupied with other things.

As the horse continued to carry him down the next street at a relaxed gait, he saw an orangish-yellow light appear up ahead. The light forced his distracted mind to focus, only to see two soldiers come into view.

One soldier was a man holding a torch. The other was a woman, her hands stuffed into her surcoat pockets. They were walking side by side down the road toward Carver with their swords sheathed at their hips. They were occupied in humble chatter, but when they noticed Carver, they both stopped and eyed him curiously.

Carver adjusted himself in the saddle to turn his front away from the soldiers, trying to hide the bloodstains, then smiled and nodded as his horse carried him past them, which caused both soldiers to nod and smile back, though neither soldier's look seemed truly genuine. They did not say a word to Carver, and the moment he rode past them, they returned to their conversation as they walked leisurely down the street.

Carver fought against his instincts telling him to look back at the soldiers, feeling a worry that they might still be watching him or trying to trick him into acting suspicious. Instead of succumbing to his paranoia, Carver took a deep breath and kept an eye out for his goal. After a few more seconds of riding, he looked to his right and saw that he was directly in front of Duncan's wooden home, the tall, barn-like fishery standing off to the left a little ways farther down the road near the water's edge and separated from the house by a long patch of grass.

Carver pulled the horse's reins and bade it to walk even slower, though he did not command it to stop or turn toward Duncan's dwelling. Instead,

Carver focused his attention on the distant noise of the patrolling soldiers' chatter, but he still didn't dare turn around in case they were watching him.

Carver let a handful of seconds pass as his horse carried him farther north down the road, enough that the soldiers would either be gone around the corner or far enough that should he turn his head slightly toward them, they would not be able to detect the motion.

As Carver glanced back, he saw that, sure enough, the orange glow of the torchlight had vanished, along with the two soldiers.

He steered his horse back toward Duncan's house, then led it between the house and the fishery, where he was soon greeted by the sight of two-dozen feet of grassy ground that ended in a short stretch of sand. Beyond the sand was the eastern reaches of the Great Ocean, known as the Audria Channel, which spanned out into the darkness farther than Carver could see and separated the Isles from Gaia's nearest shore.

The sight of the far-reaching waters and the low waves that rhythmically struck the beach gave Carver a sense of peace, but after a few seconds of watching the cold waves retreat and then return from the sea, he realized that he was stalling by letting the motions distract him. He suddenly felt very anxious about continuing any farther.

Despite his feelings, Carver forced himself to look away from the seemingly endless waters, which were complemented by the seemingly infinite darkness of the night, and guided his horse over to the small stable built into the back of Duncan's house. One horse was already within the stable and watched the new arrivals with calm eyes. Carver wondered if he had awakened the animal or if it had yet to fall asleep.

Carver led his animal to the stable, dismounted with slow and troubled movements brought forth by his fatigue, hunger, and thirst, then opened the gate. His horse wandered in and was greeted by the other animal with a snort, a sniff, and soft whinny.

Carver saw that the trough in the stable's far corner had plenty of water and that it was surrounded with hay, so he pushed his concern for the overworked animal out of his mind and closed the gate.

Carver looked back out at the dark waters that spanned the land's edge from the east to the north and took several deep breaths to calm himself. Then he reached into his trouser pocket and pulled out the necklace, rubbing the pegasus charm between his fingers. The charm was smooth, slightly bumpy where the wings and legs were detailed, cold to the touch as the metal soaked in the night's chill, and glimmered in the light of the two moons.

Carver squeezed the charm with his fingers and closed his eyes. After a moment of anxious thought, he opened his eyes and put the necklace back in his pocket before he stepped forward and headed to the front of the fishery.

Quicker than he was hoping for, Carver found himself standing in front of the fishery's front door. He took another deep breath as he put his hand on the iron handle, then turned his head and looked for any sign of onlookers or patrolling soldiers, but nothing except darkness surrounded him.

Carver opened the squeaky door and stepped inside, then closed it with a loud thud echoing throughout the fishery as the door fit tightly into place.

He stayed utterly still while facing the door, his hand pressed against the cold wood as he tried to calm his nerves, but his pounding heart refused to slow.

Suddenly, he heard a creak above and behind him.

"Hello?" a hushed female voice called out.

Carver felt like he was going to throw up. He didn't answer, nor did he turn around. His worry about the impending confrontation kept him frozen in place.

There was another creak of old wooden planks being stressed, but it came from lower down than before.

"Sebastian, is that you?"

Carver kept silent.

"Nina? Which one of you went out? What were you doing?"

Carver forced himself to turn around and pull his gray hood back.

There was another creak of wood, followed by the sound of approaching footsteps.

The fishery was dark, and the light of the two moons only partially pierced the cracks and holes in the walls and ceiling, blessing small areas of the interior with pale bluish light. The most well-lit portion of floor inside the fishery was near the entrance, as the door and the wall it was a part of had the most holes and cracks for the light to creep through.

"Hello? Answer me. I can see you just standing th—"

Carver's arms and neck pulsed with goosebumps as Helena walked into the dim ring of moonlight and stopped dead in her tracks.

"Hi, Helena ..."

He immediately regretted leading with that.

Helena didn't flinch or say a word. She merely stood a few feet away from Carver, partly obscured by darkness, but her face was visible enough for Carver to see that her brown eyes were wide in shock.

"Helena ... Look ... I—"

Helena's expression morphed into an ugly scowl of rage. Before Carver could speak another word, she lunged forward and punched him in the jaw.

Carver stumbled backwards into the door, and he flung his arms out to catch himself, but his hands slid across the wall, and he fell with an awkward crash.

A burst of pain shot through Carver's jaw as he tried to collect himself. He leaned against the wall and pulled himself to his feet, but just as he was beginning to straighten his knees, a booted foot slammed into his stomach.

Carver let out a hoarse grunt and bent over as the impact knocked the wind out of him, causing him to tip forward and collapse onto his hands and knees. He held out his hand and waved it frantically.

"Helena! Stop! Let me just—"

Helena's boot slammed into Carver's left side.

The force of the kick rolled him onto his back while forcing a sharp gasp from his lips. As his body filled with pain, Carver covered his stomach and exposed side with his hands. He looked up to Helena, who was standing next to him with her teeth bared in rage. He was about to try and speak again in the hopes of calming her down, but before he could form a word, he noticed that despite Helena's rage, her eyes were running with tears.

Before Carver could banish his hesitation at the sight, she let out a bestial grunt through clenched teeth and wound up for another kick.

Carver stretched his arms out to block it, so Helena kicked his out-stretched hands instead. He cursed and pulled his hands away as her boot sent a shockwave down his arms and into his elbows. He quickly tried to push himself away from her, but he only managed to crawl a few feet before he bumped into a large wooden crate.

"Helena! Stop! What are you doing?"

She crossed the distance Carver had created and kicked at his feet the moment they were within reach.

"You piece of shit! You, selfish, stupid, bastard!" she cried, kicking at his legs with each curse and insult.

Carver kicked out with his right leg as Helena went to kick him again, and his booted foot connected with hers. His kick absorbed the force of hers and sent her off balance, stumbling toward the door. Helena swung her arms out to stop her fall, but before her hands could grasp anything, her back collided with the wall next to the door, and her knees gave out in the same manner Carver's had moments before. She slid down the wall, and her rear end smacked onto the floor.

"Helena! Just listen! I don't know what you're doing!" Carver shouted in desperation, totally unsure of what he was supposed to do in this situation, especially if Helena kept at it.

To Carver's surprise, however, she did not continue her assault, nor did she try to stand. Instead, she curled her legs up to her chest, keeping her back pressed up against the wall, and planted her face on her knees.

"You left us! You left me! How could you do that? How could you just disappear without a word? Who the hell are you, Carver? I thought you were my friend! I thought you cared!" Tears streamed from Helena's eyes with each word.

Carver had never felt so ashamed of himself. Seeing Helena in such a state tore him up inside more than he imagined possible. None of his assumed ideas of how she might react to his return came anywhere close to this reality.

He pushed himself into a sitting position, leaning against the crate behind him and curling his legs toward his chest, similar to Helena. He was just about to speak when he heard voices from his right.

"Helena! What's going on?"

Sebastian ran into view from around the corner of some crates, followed by his sister. Both of them skidded to a halt when they saw Helena sitting against the wall crying, but when they saw Carver, they both froze in nearly the same manner that Helena had earlier.

"Carver?" Nina shouted, sounding as if she were unsure if he was really there in front of her.

"Carver ... you're alive ..." Sebastian added after coming to grips with his own shock.

Carver felt the pain from Helena's strikes emerging more aggressively now that the situation had settled and his panic was subsiding, but he tried to ignore the pain and focus on his words despite the distraction.

"Yes. I'm back."

Helena looked up from her fit of angry sobs and glared at Carver with freshly reddened eyes. "Oh, you're back. You say it as if you just returned from a walk to the market! You've been gone for five days, Carver! And then you just show up in the middle of the night and act like nothing happened?"

Sebastian stepped forward and raised his hands, casting a worried glance between Carver and Helena. "Please, both of you, keep it quiet. You're going to draw attention from outside if you both keep shouting like this," he said in a hushed voice.

"I didn't act like nothing happened! I—I'm not acting like anything. You attacked me before I could even say anything," he continued in a quieter tone, though not nearly as quiet as Sebastian had hoped.

"I don't want to hear what you have to say. I can't believe you," Helena said, her voice still well above a whisper.

"Would you rather I had not returned? Did you want me to die?"

"No. Of course not. I wanted ... You shouldn't have—" Helena cut herself off with an angry growl and leaped to her feet. Before anyone could say anything, she stormed off into the darkness and disappeared. A moment later, the sounds of the stairs creaking reached their ears.

Carver looked at Sebastian and Nina, who were staring at him in silence. "What was I supposed to do?" he asked. "What does she want me to say?"

"Carver ..." Sebastian was the first sibling to speak up. "Where were you? What happened?"

"Helena told us you went to kill all the soldiers who attacked Verrel. Is that true? Did you do it?" Nina asked.

"No. No, of course I didn't. I mean ... I ... yes, I left to ... but I didn't ... No. Never mind all that."

Carver readjusted himself and used the edge of the crate to pull himself up to his feet. The tight cloak restricted his movements, and he tore it off in frustration.

Nina gasped when she noticed the dark red on Carver's tunic as well as the similar stain covering the better part of his trousers on his right thigh. "Wait. Carver, is that blood? Are you hurt?"

Carver placed a hand on his side to relieve some pain. "Yes, I'm hurt. Helena saw to that." He looked down and was reminded of the state of his clothing. "Wait, no, that's not my blood." He looked back up at Nina and Sebastian. "Or ... well, yeah, I guess most of it actually is ... but it's not—Ah, damn it! I can't explain this right now. Get out of my way."

Carver pushed past the siblings and headed toward the stairs.

"I think she needs some time away from you, Carver," Sebastian said from behind.

"That's exactly what caused this whole stupid problem!" Carver shouted back from the darkness, entirely forgetting the need to stay silent as his frustration pushed to the forefront of his mind.

Carver raced up the stairs, the boards creaking loudly under his hurried footsteps.

"Go away. I don't want to see you!" Helena called out as he reached the last stair.

"I have to talk to you, Helena. Please, just listen to me," he replied as he proceeded. He didn't know where she was, but it sounded like she was somewhere in the far-right corner behind a pile of seafaring junk and wooden containers.

Carver ignored the pain in his jaw and lower torso as he maneuvered through the obstacles until he finally spotted Helena curled into a sitting position much like she had been down below.

"What could you possibly have to say to me that I don't already know?" Helena asked, sending another tear-stained glare at Carver as he stopped in front of her. "That you're sorry? That you're selfish and abandoned us all here to foolishly chase after revenge? That you want me to forgive you and to forget each horrible hour I spent in this place thinking you were dead?"

"I'm sorry, Helena. I know you think you know that already. But I'm sorrier than you know."

"Oh, shut up! You're sorrier than I know? That's what you have to say to me?"

Carver pressed his palms against his forehead and closed his eyes. "I don't know what you want from me, Helena. I thought you'd be happy to see me. I thought you'd be relieved to know that I'm not dead."

"I am happy to see you!"

"Well then what in Cosom's name is all this?" Carver flung his arms out to his sides in frustration.

Helena sprang to her feet and lunged toward Carver. He stepped back and tried to raise his hands in defense against her incoming attack, but Helena grabbed his wrists before he could ready himself. He flinched in anticipation of a strike, but instead of hitting him, she pulled him toward her.

A rush of shock shot through Carver's body as Helena's lips pressed against his, and a powerful tingling sensation exploded within his stomach and sent even more goosebumps up the back of his neck and down his arms. Despite the bombardment of feelings and sensations, Carver felt the sudden and unexplained desire to ignore everything and kiss her back.

He let himself be taken by the strange moment and surrendered to the kiss, but then Helena pushed him away and stepped back.

"Shit. I'm sorry. I don't ... Dema's ass, what did I ..."

As Helena stepped away, Carver was too shocked to move, the sudden pleasant sensation that had filled his whole body having abruptly vanished. Everything felt so unbelievably strange all of a sudden.

"Helena, I ..."

"No. Don't," Helena held up her hand and looked away. "I'm sorry, okay? I don't know what I'm doing anymore."

She continued to back up until she bumped into the wall.

"No, Helena. I'm sorry. You don't have to apologize for anything. I'm the one who messed everything up. I'm the one who left without telling you. I don't know what I was thinking. I'm sorry. I'm really, really sorry. Please don't hate me. Please. I ... I can't lose you because of myself."

Carver took a few steps toward her. Helena looked at Carver with wide, tear-filled eyes. Her lips quivered as if she was about to speak, but instead she stepped forward again and grabbed him in a hug.

Carver stumbled back but managed to support Helena, who was leaning into him more than standing on her own, and wrapped his arms around her as well. He felt a sudden wetness spreading over his right shoulder where Helena had planted her face.

"I was scared, Carver. And so angry. I thought you were never coming back. I thought I would never see you or talk to you again. It made me feel crazy. It made me ... I ..." Helena looked up to him with tears running down her cheeks. "I killed Rook. He made me snap, and I stabbed him in the throat. Carver ... I murdered him."

"Helena ... I ... I'm so sorry. I didn't know ..."

"I feel like a crazy person, Carver. What's wrong with me?" Helena planted her face back onto his shoulder.

Carver squeezed her and pressed his head against the side of hers. "You're not crazy, Helena. It's my fault. I put you through this. I never should have left."

He pulled back and placed his hand under Helena's chin, tilting her head up so he could look into her eyes. She was surprised to see tears running down Carver's face as well. "Look, Helena. I got you this," he said as his lips tried to form a gentle smile. He reached into his pocket and pulled something out, then uncurled his fingers, revealing the necklace with the pegasus charm resting atop its coiled chain. "I found it in Caswen. Can you believe it? Here."

He pushed the trinket into Helena's hand.

Helena looked down at the necklace in silent disbelief, then she looked up at Carver in bewilderment. "Carver ... How did you ... This is the same necklace I found at the Inner Market."

Carver smiled again, and this time it had less sadness surrounding it. "Yes, it is. I found the same stall while I was there. The man who sold it to me, he was … well, that doesn't matter. What matters is that I want you to have it. I remembered you were buying it just before the attack, and I knew I needed to get it for you the moment I saw it again. I couldn't stop thinking about you while I was gone, and seeing this necklace helped me realize I should never have left in the first place. This isn't meant to make up for what I did, but please … please don't hate me."

Helena looked back down to the necklace. She managed a smile as another tear ran down her cheek. Then she gripped the necklace tightly and swung her arms back around Carver and kissed him again. This time she didn't pull away when he kissed back. Her soft lips rolled over his, and her hot breath mixed with his own.

Carver felt a sensation of happiness that he had never felt before, and he surrendered himself to it entirely. He grabbed Helena by the lower back and kissed her more.

Helena suddenly broke away, pulling her head back. He looked into her eyes, realizing no more tears were running down her face.

"I'm sorry I beat you up, Carver."

Carver chuckled and then kissed her again.

Chapter 39

∼⁀

Carver awoke to the racket of birds chirping and whistling outside the fishery. He opened his eyes and was hit by the pleasant sunlight that illuminated most of the fishery's interior, save for a few dark corners and areas not near the cracks in the old wooden walls.

He yawned, then groaned as the motion provoked a soreness in his jaw. He rubbed his chin as he recalled why it hurt. Then he looked to his right, which prompted a bout of confusion.

The space next to him was empty, with nothing but a dirty, creased blanket between him and an overturned dinghy. The sight of the dinghy being on his right side had Carver realize that he was on the wrong side of it, sleeping in Helena's spot rather than his own. His confusion vanished as he finally recalled what had happened. Carver looked up to the ceiling and told himself that nothing was the matter. Helena must have woken earlier and was sure to be downstairs.

Carver stretched his limbs and waited for the feeling of lethargy from waking to dissipate. He sat up and waited for his mind to clear, then rose to his feet.

As he stood up, he felt an unpleasant, cold stickiness on his chest and down his right thigh. Carver looked down mid-stretch and saw where it was coming from. He was still wearing his clothes from the day before, as he and most folk did in order to stay warm during the night, and the blood from himself and Shiala that stained the wool so heavily caused his clothes to stick to his skin.

A sense of disgust hit Carver, causing him to pull the bloody clothing away from his skin. The sensation that the pull created was worse than the feeling before, and he suddenly realized he needed to change his clothes if he were to ever feel comfortable again.

Carver rounded the overturned dinghy and felt a surge of regret at the sight of his own sleeping area, which looked like it hadn't been touched since he left, as the realization set in that it was probably one of the first things Helena saw after he left so suddenly.

The idea of the grief he had caused her hit him once again, so he turned away from the messy pile of bedding and scooped up his stack of spare clothes, which were coated by a thin layer of dust. Carver shook them out, then tore off his dirty clothes and put on the clean garments.

As he finished tightening his belt, he realized that he should probably have washed himself before getting dressed. The thought of taking his clothes off again, going to the corner where the bucket of cold water was kept, and giving himself a quick clean crossed his mind, but the growing desire to head downstairs and see everyone climbed higher in his list of priorities.

The sunlight from outside was more prevalent near the stairs and the entire ground floor in general, which allowed Carver to get a clear view of the lower area. The sight was the same as he remembered, a vast clutter of crates and barrels with small boats and piles of netting in between, though he quickly told himself that there was no reason for it to look any different after only five days. The sight reminded Carver of the goblin warehouse, with its messy array of seafaring gear and cargo containers. He tried to banish the connection from his mind as he made his way down the steep wooden stairs.

The area immediately below, a wide square space that the young group used primarily as an eating area and a place to sit and talk, had four clay bowls sitting around an iron pot with a circular lid as well as four wooden tankards, one beside each bowl. Three of the bowls looked like they had just been used, while one remained clean. The clean bowl was the only one that had its nearby cup filled with what looked like water.

Just as Carver stepped off the last stair, he heard a faint thud from behind. He turned around and noticed that Sebastian, Nina, and Helena were all working behind a long table some distance behind the stairs in the back half of the fishery in the shadow of the upper floor.

The three of them were working with fish, sockeye salmon and cod, pulling out the innards, slicing off the scales, and then after a brief clean, placing the fish into buckets of salt. Each of the young workers performed the actions in silence.

Carver also noticed that Helena was wearing the pegasus necklace.

Suddenly, he felt strangely nervous as he watched his friends working in silence. Finally, he approached them, leaving the tankard of water alone despite his desire to drink it.

"Hey, guys," Carver said in a manner that he immediately thought sounded too casual given the circumstances.

The three of them looked up from the table of dead fish.

"Hello, Carver," Sebastian said.

"Morning, Carver," Nina said immediately after.

Helena gave Carver a quick, awkward smile before she looked back down and continued her work. The oddness of her manner only added to Carver's discomfort.

He tried to ignore his sense of uneasiness as he approached the table and stopped on the side across from the others. "You all starting early today?"

Sebastian finished pulling the bones out of a small fish and looked back up to Carver. "No. It's almost noon, actually. We thought we'd let you sleep in. Figured you needed some extra rest."

"Oh, um, sorry about that, guys. Well, thanks, I guess."

"We already ate what Charra brought in this morning, but we left you a clean bowl by the pot. The pot's still got stew inside, though it might have gotten a little cold by now. There's water too."

Carver looked over at Helena, who kept her eyes fixed on the large cod she was gutting. He got the feeling that something was wrong.

"Oh, yeah. I saw that back there ... Um. Thanks. So, uh, why so quiet?"

Nina looked up from the sockeye salmon she had been filleting. "We didn't want to wake you. Felt you needed the sleep, you know."

"Oh, yeah. That's right. Thanks again," Carver said awkwardly as he looked back at Helena. He got another strange feeling that told him the three of them were not staying quiet for him. He looked back at the siblings, who were both still looking at him, with fish guts draped over their knuckles.

"So, um, I guess I should talk to you two ... about what happened."

Helena gave Carver a panicked look.

"About me leaving, I mean," Carver quickly added.

He immediately detected the relief in Helena's eyes before she returned to gutting the cod.

Sebastian and Nina shifted uncomfortably, though Carver did not notice, his attention fixed on Helena.

"You should wait," Sebastian said. "Duncan said that if you returned, he wanted to speak to you immediately. He's been out fishing with Gorty since before we all woke up, but he should be back in a few hours. Charra knows that you're back and said she'll let Duncan know when he returns. I imagine he'll want to hear what you're about to tell us as well, so maybe it's better to wait and do all the talking at once later tonight."

"Oh. Okay. Yeah, that makes sense," Carver said as he looked back at Helena, who still seemed entirely focused on gutting the same fish, although he realized he had never seen her take so long to do such a simple chore before then.

"Hey, guys. Could you two give Helena and me a minute, please? I want to talk to her about something."

Helena didn't look up, but Carver detected the sudden movement of her shoulders tensing.

Sebastian and Nina looked at each other, then put their fillet knives down and wiped their bloody hands on their trousers.

"Sure," Sebastian said as he followed his sister, who was already rounding the table.

They headed over to the eating area and then went a little farther, until they were obscured by the distant clutter of dusty crates. Carver watched the siblings go with unease building in his stomach, as he felt he could sense that they knew what was going on.

Carver turned back to Helena, who was still looking down and working on gutting the same fish. "Helena."

She stopped what she was doing and looked up at him. She didn't have her usual aura of levity, so Carver decided to try and lighten things up. "I see you're wearing the necklace. You like it, huh?" he said, following up with a nervous smile.

Helena looked down at the necklace and touched it with her fingers. The pegasus charm spun gently and shook before resting calmly against her chest just below her collarbone. A light smear of fish blood was left behind over the pegasus's hind legs.

"Yeah. It's really nice. Thanks for finding it again, Carver," she said in a pleasant tone, though he detected a level of unease behind her words.

"No problem. Um ... Yeah, it was crazy that I managed to stumble upon it like that. I thought it was gone for good, you know. But um, well you know ... I, um ..."

"Carver."

He exhaled and rubbed his arm. "Okay. Sorry. I know. I can tell something's up, and I'm pretty sure I know why. I figure we should talk about what happened. Last night, I mean."

Helena looked over Carver's shoulder to see where Sebastian and Nina had gone. Upon seeing no sign of the twins, she turned her gaze back to Carver. "Look, I was a mess last night, and I acted stupid. I shouldn't have started hitting and kicking you. And I'm sorry for just suddenly kissing you. I was just—"

"No. Don't be sorry. I mean ... I kissed you too. I thought that ... Well, that we ... I mean you were—"

"I don't know what I was doing. I got confused and lost control."

"You ... oh. So then ... we, um. Look, I'm really confused right now. I don't know what to say or do, but I can tell you don't feel happy about what we did."

Helena tensed her shoulders further and took a deep breath. "Carver, I ... I didn't mean to just throw that kind of ... to just act on you like that."

"No, no. It's fine. I didn't stop you. I liked it. I mean ... ah, damn it."

Carver ran a hand through his hair in frustration and nervousness. "Look, Helena. We kissed, alright? We kissed a lot and slept next to each other under the same blanket. It happened, and we both liked it, at least I thought we both did. But—"

"Carver, I—"

"Wait, Helena. I'm just trying to say that I don't know what happens now. What are we after that? I can tell you're ... well, I don't know exactly how you're feeling right now, but I can tell it's not good."

"I'm not feeling not good, Carver. I just ... I don't want to ..."

Helena let out a grunt of frustration and stabbed her filleting knife into the table. The thud of it startled Carver. "I don't want to force this."

"This? What do you mean?"

Helena gripped the edge of the table with both hands and squeezed. "This! Us! You and me, Carver. Dema's ass, have you seriously never thought about this before?"

"Thought about kissing you? No—I mean ... okay, I have. Like only once or—I mean ..." Carver sighed. "Helena, you're my friend. I didn't think ..."

"Didn't think what?"

"I don't know. I didn't think about it seriously. I didn't know you wanted us to be like that."

"It's not that I want us to be like that. I just thought it could happen. I've noticed how you sometimes look at my body when you think I'm not looking, and I know that during some of our sparring sessions that turned to wrestling in the past you got an erection, which is why you suddenly stopped sometimes."

Carver took a step back and went red in the face. His stomach filled with queasiness, and his cheeks suddenly felt very warm. "Helena! I don't—I mean, I've looked, but it's just by accident. And I never got—"

"Carver, don't lie to me. And I don't care about that stuff. But I noticed, alright? And I assumed that it meant you might like me more than you were showing. I didn't make a big deal of it, though. I assumed that if you liked me that way you would tell me at some point."

"I mean, okay, I guess I've thought about it before, a little bit. But I thought it would be weird. I didn't want to mess things up between us."

"That's the point, Carver. I feel like I messed things up between us. I threw myself at you last night and rushed everything."

"You didn't force it, Helena. I didn't stop you."

"I know that, Carver. But I didn't want it to happen like that. Like this. I wanted it to happen naturally. I wanted ... Dema's—" Helena cut herself off with another frustrated grunt and then gestured her hands between herself and Carver. "This is what I mean. Look at what we're doing right now. I messed the whole thing up."

"So, then let's just forget about it. Let's just say it didn't happen and go back to the way things were."

"But it did happen, Carver. We can't just pretend it didn't."

"Why not?"

"So that's all you want then? To just forget it happened and move on? That's it?"

"I don't know, Helena. Damn it, I feel like we're talking in circles."

"Then let's just stop talking about it. It didn't happen. We're back to being friends, and that's that," Helena said in a more aggressive tone than before and straightened her posture.

"Helena ... I didn't mean—"

"No, Carver. I don't want to talk about this anymore. Go get Sebastian and Nina, and let's get to work," Helena said bluntly and looked back down to the table. She pulled her filleting knife out of the table and began slicing the cod's scales off.

Carver wanted to say something more and try to fix the damage he felt he had caused, but he couldn't think of anything to say that wouldn't make things worse. So, instead of forcing the situation further he turned and walked off to find Sebastian and Nina.

He found the siblings talking quietly behind a tall stack of empty crates. As soon as they heard Carver's approach, they both stopped speaking. Carver pretended he hadn't heard the subject of their gossip.

"Hey, guys. Sorry about that. Let's get back to it." He gestured toward the way he had come.

Nina nodded quickly and made to pass by him and return to the table, but Sebastian remained where he was and looked at Carver in silence. Carver felt a growing discomfort until Sebastian suddenly spoke.

"Are you two okay, Carver? We could hear some of it from here, and we're worried about both of you."

Carver frowned. "It's fine, Sebastian. Don't worry about it."

"You two didn't have ... well ... you know? Because last night, Nina and I overheard some noises that—"

"What? No! Of course not. We only—actually, just keep out of the whole thing. It's none of your business anyway, so drop it," Carver said, frustration driving his tone.

"Okay, sorry. I didn't mean to upset you. I'll drop it," Sebastian said, making his way around Carver to follow his sister.

Carver remained where he was for a moment, feeling an intense mixture of anger and confusion at his situation. Most of the anger was directed toward himself, feeling that once again he had messed everything up.

Not wanting to let the others know how upset he was, Carver pushed his emotions down before he turned to return to them. He hoped the rest of the day would not be so strange and terrible.

⊠　　⊠　　⊠

The rest of the day passed quickly, though that did little to improve Carver's mood. After his unsuccessful discussion with Helena, he ate the remaining stew in the pot and then drank the cup of water. Once he had nourished himself with what was available, though he remained hungry and slightly thirsty after having been without proper food or drink for so many days, Carver joined his friends in the task of gutting, scaling, and salting the fish that had been acquired from Duncan and Gorty's long fishing excursion the previous day.

The group worked in silence for the most part, aside from awkward attempts from Nina to get a conversation going. However, each of Nina's attempts were met with disinterest from everyone but her brother, leading to short-lived conversations until she eventually stopped trying.

Many hours later, once Duncan had returned from his day of fishing off the coast and learned from Charra of Carver's return, Carver spent a great deal of time explaining himself and the events of the last week to Duncan and the others within the fishery. After Carver had spun his tale, he spent almost as long answering the old fisherman's questions. The questions involved how many Caswen soldiers had seen his face, if he had been followed out of the city, if he had been seen entering Leydes, and many other such things, which spoke of Duncan's worry and his concern for the safety of his grandchildren and the others in his hospitable care.

The information that Carver's described likeness was on bounty notices around Caswen did not please Duncan, nor did Carver's revelation that his escape from the city was violent and seen by many.

At the end of the questioning, Carver was crushed when Duncan said he wanted him to leave. Soldiers searching for him might discover Duncan's grandchildren, and the risk was far too great for the old fisherman to leave to chance.

It was only after the incessant pleading of those same grandchildren, as well as from Helena, Carver, and Charra, despite her husband taking Duncan's side, that Duncan submitted and allowed Carver to remain.

Although Carver understood Duncan's reasoning, he now had a deep distrust of the man, but he kept his opinion to himself.

After the threat of being banished from Duncan's protection had passed, Carver spent the evening eating with his young companions in a slightly less awkward though still silent atmosphere as Sebastian and Nina questioned him more about his time in Caswen. He answered their excited questions despite his desire to no longer speak of the experience, his mind still greatly troubled by the week's events.

Helena kept silent and only listened as she ate her dinner beside the others. Whenever she and Carver happened to lock eyes, they would look away almost immediately.

Carver spent the night by himself, on his side of the overturned dinghy and under his own blanket. He could hear Helena's movements on the other side of the vessel, but he didn't engage her in conversation.

The next day was more of the same, gutting and cleaning fish, tidying the fishery, organizing the gear Duncan and Gorty would need for their next trip out to sea, and breaks spent sitting on the floor with the others while eating whatever food Charra brought to them throughout the day.

During all these activities, Carver and Helena were not the same with each other. Their shared glances continued to be awkward and brief, and their conversations were short and clumsy.

Each day that came eased the tension between the two a little more, though neither of them brought up the passionate moment they had shared on the night of Carver's return. Both of them wanted to speak of it again, but neither Carver nor Helena wanted to be the one to initiate the conversation, so the topic was left ignored despite its constant presence in their minds.

After a week they began to talk more, and they no longer avoided eye contact throughout the day. The teens' mood eventually became lighter, and the time they spent eating together in the cleared-out area near the stairs slowly filled with more chatter and laughter.

Tension still existed between Carver and Helena, but both of them avoided acknowledging it. Sebastian and Nina could tell that they were not the same with each other despite the pair's attempts to push the awkwardness under the rug.

Eventually, Sebastian attempted to talk to Carver, and Nina to Helena, about what had transpired between the two of them.

Carver responded to Sebastian with anger for bringing the situation up, while Helena told Nina that everything was dealt with and there was nothing to worry about regarding her and Carver.

The siblings were not fooled by either of them, but they understood that their meddling was not helping, so they left the subject alone and ignored it just as Helena and Carver seemed to want.

After the second full week had passed since Carver's return, most of the interactions between the group had returned to normal, and the days became a regular pattern of work, chores, and levity when spirits happened to be up.

Carver and Helena continued to be friendly to each other, although at times it felt forced. Both of them knew that their friendship had been shaken due to their actions and their inaction on the subject, but they each still waited for the other to bring it up, each hoping they would not have to be the one to initiate and chance another blow to their relationship.

Neither of them spoke of it, and each day that passed only increased Carver and Helena's hesitation to return to that moment, eventually leading them to think they had waited too long to try, that they had missed their chance to address it, and that bringing it up after so long would only start the whole problem over again and make it worse.

After the third week, the issue was buried underneath an impenetrable layer of anxiety, indecision, and fear.

Life returned to normal for the group, as normal as their lives could be, and each day moved along as it had before Carver had left, when the days were nothing more than interchangeable blurs of working, eating, and talking with each other to try and distract themselves from the events that still haunted their thoughts and dreams.

This cycle continued through the fourth and fifth week after Carver's return, until the group's sleep was suddenly interrupted by the loud ringing of a bell during a cold November night.

Chapter 40

‿◦‿

Carver woke up in a panic. Torn from his sleep by the sudden chime of the bell, Carver looked around frantically, but he saw only darkness and the familiar pale blue light from the moons that crept in through the walls and ceiling near his sleeping area.

The ringing continued, so Carver kicked off his blanket and forced himself to his feet. As he did, he noticed Helena doing the same on the other side of the barrier.

"Carver, what's going on?" she asked in a startled voice.

"I don't know. Isn't a bell supposed to be the town alarm? Something must be happening outside."

Helena nodded and then made for the stairs. "Come on!" she called back over her shoulder.

"What in Cosom's watch is going on?" Sebastian asked as he and Nina also appeared at the top of the stairs. "Guys, what's happening?"

"I don't know," Carver said, "neither of us do. We just woke up from the noise, same as you."

Sebastian shot a quick look at his sister before they followed Carver and Helena down the stairs.

Carver reached the bottom a few seconds after Helena, who was already jogging toward the fishery's front door.

"Helena, don't go out there."

"I'm just going to look through the cracks. I want to see what's going on," she said without slowing her pace.

Before Helena reached the door, however, it opened. She skidded to a halt, as did the other teens behind her.

The light of the two moons illuminated the fishery as Charra stepped inside and let the door swing open slightly behind her. The dwarf woman looked distraught as she met the group's startled looks with panic-filled eyes.

"Charra, what's going on?" Helena asked.

"Please, all of you, you need to come to the house right away. There are people. Humans. They want Carver and the rest of you right now," Charra said in a frantic, winded voice.

"What?" Helena asked as she turned and looked back at Carver, her eyes wide with worry.

"Who are they?" Carver asked. "Is it soldiers? We should get out of here before they catch us!"

"No! Carver, please, don't run. None of you can run. They said if you don't all show up immediately, they'll kill Duncan and Gorty."

"What?" Sebastian and Nina called out in unison.

"Please, all of you, come quickly. They can't think I'm helping you escape." Charra turned and ran out of the fishery without waiting for a response.

Carver looked at Helena again. He wanted to say something, but he had no idea what. He didn't understand what was going on, but he felt like he had an idea of what it could be, that something very bad was going to happen, and that once again he was the cause of it.

"Come on, you two! We have to help them!" Sebastian shouted as he and Nina charged past Carver and Helena before disappearing through the doorway into the moonlit night.

Helena looked away from Carver and then broke into a sprint to follow the siblings.

Carver hesitated for a second, then bolted toward the doorway. "Helena, wait!" he called as his legs carried him outside and the moonlight pressed onto his shoulders.

He needn't have called to her, however, as Helena had already halted and was staring toward the north.

Carver stopped and followed Helena's gaze toward the empty street, where he saw three great spires of black smoke rising into the moonlight-diluted darkness of the star-filled sky from where the town's large port was. The sight was accompanied by a bright orange glow that peeked over the distant houses and pushed the night away, as if the sun were rising straight out of Leydes.

The bell continued to ring, sounding as if it were coming from the west end of Leydes.

Carver's peripheral vision suddenly picked up nearby movement, yanking his eyes away from the smoke. It took him only a half second to register that the movement was Helena running toward Duncan's house.

"Helena!"

She skidded to a stop and spun around. "What, Carver? Didn't you hear Charra? We need to go now!"

Carver kept silent. He felt words trying to force their way out of his mouth, but he couldn't get himself to release them. Helena turned, about to resume her run, but Carver felt a sudden jolt of fear fill his body as he realized he was about to miss his chance. The sensation overruled his nerves, and he blurted out his words before Helena could take a step.

"Run with me!"

Helena stopped and turned back to face Carver. "What?"

"Run with me. It's soldiers from Caswen. It has to be. They know I'm here, and now they're attacking the town looking for me. They'll arrest us and execute us all. There's no reason to go into that house; it won't change anything if we do. We should go. Right now. You and me, Helena. Before they come outside and see us."

The loud bell chimed again at the trail end of Carver's words.

"Carver ... I ... We can work it out with them. We'll tell them that Verrel had nothing to do with the Aethi'ziton. We'll explain everything. They'll listen. They have to. We can figure this out."

Carver quickly closed the distance between himself and Helena. She didn't move as Carver approached, stopping right in front of her. "No,

Helena, we can't. They won't listen. Especially not after everything that happened in Caswen. I screwed us out of ever claiming not to be involved with the Lost Seekers. We can't go in there. We'll die. Please, let's just run. You and me. I don't want to die, Helena, and I don't want you to die either. Especially not because of me."

Carver stepped closer to her and grabbed her arms. "Helena, I'm sorry for everything I've done and how I've acted. I never should have left for Caswen, and I shouldn't have let what happened between us the night I returned cause so much wrongness. I just didn't know what to say or how to make things better."

"Carver. That ... This isn't the time for that. We need to get in there. They'll think we ran, and then they'll kill the others!"

Helena tried to turn and run for the house, but Carver tightened his grip on her arms and pulled her back.

"No, Helena! This is the only time. I didn't know what to say because I was scared of messing things up more. Because I didn't want to push you even further away than I already have. Because ..."

Carver felt like he was losing his ability to breathe. "I'm in love with you, Helena. I think I have been for a long time. I just never knew how to act on it. I can't let it all end like this. Please. Let's run. We can get away and hide together somewhere else. We can leave the Isles and go far away, somewhere no one will be looking for us. If Gaia is as big as people say it is then there must be somewhere we can go and be safe. Please, Helena. I'm begging you. Run with me right now."

Helena looked at Carver with eyes wide in utter shock. "Carver ... I—" She cut herself off with a gasp as her eyes darted to something over his right shoulder.

Before Carver could react, a blur of movement entered his peripheral vision from his right and then something hard struck him in the side of the head.

Carver released his grip on Helena's arms and tumbled to the ground.

"I don't think so, runt!" a female voice barked.

Carver tried to get onto his knees in order to stand, but a boot kicked him in the side, just under his right arm, which forced him back down to the ground on his back.

With his eyes now facing upwards, Carver saw a human woman standing over him. She had a large axe with a long, thick wooden shaft in her hands and a green marking going down the left side of her face.

Filled with panic, Carver tried to stand, but before he could rise more than a few inches, Shiala thrust the butt end of her axe's wooden shaft into his forehead. His vision swam as he collapsed back to the ground. The stars above him seemed to shake in place, and everything else in his vision blurred.

"Stop! Get off me!" Helena's voice suddenly pierced Carver's ears.

Carver struggled to snap out of his daze as he tried to roll over and stand up. His spinning vision made him stumble and slip, but he managed to force his knees into the dirt and then stand up.

"Don't move a muscle!" Shiala warned from just out of his dizzy sight.

Carver paled when he saw Helena gripped tightly around the torso by Shiala's left arm and the heavy blade of Shiala's axe held against the side of her neck.

"Come at me or make a run for it, and I'll cut your girl's pretty little neck from ear to ear. And unlike yours, Farren won't be healing it shut," Shiala said, each word filled with anger and spite.

Carver held perfectly still, though his heart raced inside his chest. "Stop! What do you want?"

Shiala squeezed Helena around the chest with her muscular arm as she glanced around the area before refocusing on Carver. "Get yourself into that old fisherman's house right now before anyone sees us and calls the guards. Do it now or this one dies."

Carver held his hands up a short distance from his chest. "Don't! Please! Okay, I'll go, alright? Just don't hurt her."

Shiala followed Carver's movements with a keen stare while keeping the blade of her hefty axe pressed against Helena's neck. Helena looked at Carver with fear-filled eyes as she struggled to keep her panicked breaths from expanding her throat into the weapon's sharp edge.

"I'm sorry, Helena. I'll get you out of this. I promise," Carver said as he backed toward Duncan's front porch, not taking his eyes off Helena and Shiala.

"Shut your mouth, runt. Get inside. Now."

Shiala pulled the axe away from Helena's throat and pushed the girl forward. Helena stumbled but managed to catch herself from falling.

Carver turned away from Helena and stepped onto the wooden porch. The door to the house was closed, but Carver could see light coming from inside through the cracked frame. As he opened the door, he glanced back at Helena, who was just stepping up onto the porch with Shiala right behind her.

"Ah, there he is," a male voice said from inside the house.

A chill ran down Carver's spine as he recognized it immediately. When he looked into the room, although he saw many people inside looking at him, his attention was drawn to one person.

Farren was seated at Duncan's dining table, facing the door, his arms across the table with his hands clasped together in a comfortable manner. He was wearing the same open-buttoned brown coat over a black tunic as the last time Carver had seen him. His trousers and boots also appeared to be the same, but above his neck was where Carver noticed the differences from his last meeting with the man five weeks earlier.

Farren's once-thick beard had been replaced with dark stubble, and his short brown hair had grown nearly to his ears. However, the most noticeable difference was that his left eye was covered by a round leather patch. It was light brown and was held in place by two thin leather straps that wrapped around the back of his head.

Duncan was seated to Farren's left, near the edge of the table. A man was standing behind him who had a short knife in his right hand. Gorty and Charra were standing in the back corner of the room, near the gently burning hearth. A woman was standing near them, resting an arming sword on her shoulder while staring at Carver.

Sebastian and Nina were standing near the door on the south wall that led into Gorty and Charra's room, a man leaning against the wall right beside them. The man held no weapon, though the unsheathed arming sword buckled to his belt was plain for all to see.

Carver heard Helena and Shiala approaching from behind him, so he stepped inside the house while keeping his attention fixed on Farren.

Farren gave Carver a calm grin and patted his right hand on the table. "Come, Carver. Take a seat. I'd like to have a word with you."

Carver tried to remain calm as he crossed the short distance from the door to the table and took a seat on the empty stool directly across from Farren. As he sat down, he heard the front door slam shut behind him.

Farren looked over Carver's shoulder. "I trust no townsfolk or guardsmen saw you collecting these two?"

"Nobody that I saw," Shiala replied, "though I'd suggest you hurry up and get on with it before things have a chance to settle down out there."

"Don't worry, Shiala. This will go much smoother than our last interaction with the boy." Farren looked back to Carver. "For us, at least."

Carver felt another chill run down his spine. He wanted to look at Helena, but he forced himself to keep his attention on Farren.

Farren interlaced his fingers on the table once again. "I trust you saw the smoke coming from the port, Carver? I dislike setting fire to the ships of honest fishermen and traders, but I needed to get the town's eyes away from this house."

"You could have just had us all go inside the fishery! You didn't need to burn people's ships!" Gorty barked from the corner.

"Hush, Gorty! Keep out of this," Charra said as she pulled on her husband's arm.

Farren chuckled and turned his head to face the two dwarves. "No, I find it far more agreeable to be in here. A house is better suited for a meeting than an old barn that reeks of fish." He turned back to Carver. "Now, Carver. Oh boy, you really upset me, you know. You betrayed my trust. Running off like that after I saved your life and gave you a place in our ranks was bad enough, but leaving Shiala in those hills after giving her such an injury, an injury she would have surely died from had she not been in possession of some potent magical potions, I might add. Well, now ... that is something I can't forgive without punishment."

Carver leaned forward and placed his hands on the edge of the table. "Look, I'm sorry. I know I betrayed your trust and ran, but I wasn't trying to kill Shiala. If I wanted to, I would have—" He stopped, realizing his current approach was not going to do him any good. "I mean ... I was just trying to leave, but I knew that—"

Carver stopped again, realizing he was trapped in the conversation with no real way to explain himself. Whether he kept silent or tried to apologize, he knew he wasn't going to get anywhere.

Farren pulled his arms off the table and sat up straight, as if he were about to speak, but Carver preempted him with one last idea that he thought might possibly do more good than harm.

"Wait! It was just me, okay? Nobody here had anything to do with my actions against you or Shiala. They didn't even know where I was or if I was even alive. You have to let them go. They didn't do anything to you."

"I have to, do I?"

"No, that's not what I meant—"

"Silence. I know how you meant it, boy," Farren snapped before looking over at Shiala, who was standing beside Helena near the door. "Do I even need to ask why these two arrived so late after their friends and needed you to escort them in?"

"Just like I said would happen, sir. The runt tried to make a run for it. He even tried to convince his little sweetheart here to run with him." Shiala tapped the end of her axe into Helena's lower back.

Carver felt compelled to look over at Sebastian and Nina, who were staring at him with widened eyes. Sebastian's look was accompanied by an expression of disbelief and animosity, while his sister's face seemed to be filled with sadness.

Carver felt a rush of shame as he realized that not only had he so quickly decided to sacrifice the lives of everyone in the room for his and Helena's chance for escape, but that they all now knew it as well.

"So this is the person you meant," Farren said, regaining Carver's attention. "Shiala told me everything that happened after you two went off on your own. How you told her you needed to let someone know you were alive and such. After hearing it, I figured it was a girl." Farren stopped and squinted his right eye at Helena. "And I see you weren't lying when you told me that necklace wasn't for you. A gift for your girl. No wonder you got so angry when Vie tried to take it."

Carver's anger began to build as the man spoke, causing him to lose some of his caution. "What do you want? If you've come for me, then take me, but leave Helena and the others out of this."

"Ha! He calls her by name but refers to the rest as others. My, my, he does care for this lass more than the rest. Good. That'll make things much easier."

Carver leaped up and slammed his palms onto the table, his fear and anger finally getting the better of him. "Stop this! What do you want from me?"

The other Lost Seekers stepped forward in response to Carver's sudden movements and raised voice. Farren looked up at him, unimpressed by his outburst, and leaned back in his stool as if he were getting more relaxed.

"I want what you want, Carver. I want that bitch Aellia dead. Though she is no longer the captain of the Guard or the marshal, I still deem her a threat to our cause and cannot forget the part she has played in keeping the sovereigns in power over her own kind."

"If you want her dead, then kill her. You have all these Lost Seekers working for you and that book thing filled with information about her wedding. Everything you could want for an assassination is in those pages."

"Portfolio. It's called a portfolio, Carver."

"I don't care what it's called! You have it, and that's all you should need."

"Things are not that simple, Carver, though I wish they were. If the only factor was me wishing her dead, then I could have her ambushed at any time during her travels through Caswen. For Dema's sake, the woman doesn't even ride with an escort most of the time."

"Well, why don't you, then?" Carver asked.

Farren took a deep breath and leaned forward to put his elbows on the table. "You see, Carver, I lead the Aethi'ziton here in the Isles, but I'm not the one leading them or the entire rebellion everywhere else. The reach of our cause stretches throughout all the kingdoms of the world, and our members fight for freedom, indeed our lost freedom, against the sovereigns and their oppressive empire on a thousand fronts at once. I follow the orders of my superiors just as my subordinates follow mine, and many of the orders I receive entail what I can do and when I can do it. And one of these orders is that no one under my command is to harm a single coppery-brown hair on Aellia's head."

"What? Why? You just said she's a threat to your cause."

"She is. She has done much damage to our efforts over the years and has been responsible for the deaths of many who fight against the Sovereign Empire. But despite this, my orders remain unchanged year after year. Why this is the case has eluded me thus far, but the whys and whats are not your concern, Carver. The fact is that I want Aellia dead, but I cannot do it myself or order those under me to do so in my place. But an infamous criminal who has his own reasons for wanting the woman dead, now that is something entirely out of my control."

Carver's anger turned to dread as he realized what Farren was getting at. Farren reached into his coat and pulled out the portfolio, dropping it on the table. Feeling his knees weaken, Carver sank back down onto his stool.

"I trust you're smart enough to know what I want here, Carver. You've already shown an aptitude for skills that would make you able to reach her and end her life, and your recent actions have painted you as a menace to the Isles and the Sovereign Empire outside the ranks and orders of the Aethi'ziton rebellion. The fact that most people think you actually are an agent of the rebellion at this point matters little, since those I report to now know full well that you are not part of my cell. In fact, your stabbing Shiala and leaving her for dead helped me convince my superiors that you are not under my charge and did not infiltrate the city garrison under my orders, since they were quite adamant that was the case at first. So, thanks for that."

Carver heard Shiala grumble behind him, but he did not look away from Farren.

"So, you'll study this portfolio, as I have these last few weeks. You'll learn the layout of the location, the routes of the workers, the patrols and positions of the guards, and anything else that you might need to know. Then, on the day of that bitch's wedding, you're going to slip in and end her life for me."

Carver looked around the room at his friends and saw expressions of intense shock and fear on their faces. He turned back to Farren and swallowed before speaking. "I can't do that. I failed in Caswen and got caught afterwards. I'm not the person you seem to think I am. I messed up in thinking I could kill her, and even though I still wish I could take her life, I know I never can. I can't do it."

"You will do this, Carver, because—"

"Please, I can't. I'm not some assassin or expert fighter. I'll get caught or killed. You're better off hiring someone from far away. Just do what you want with me, but let everyone else—"

Farren rose from his seat and slammed his fist on the table, silencing Carver and creating a thud that echoed through the dimly lit room. "Silence, boy! You didn't let me finish. You will do this because if you don't, then those you care for will die, starting with her." He pointed at Helena.

Carver saw that Helena was looking at him with fear and sadness in her eyes. He turned back to Farren. "No. Don't do this. I'm sorry I betrayed you. I wasn't—"

"I said silence! And if you fail and are captured or killed, then that is your fate and the punishment for your actions against me after I saved your life and offered you a chance to fight for your race's freedom from sovereign oppression. Should you succeed and survive, we will find you, and I will return your lover unharmed."

Farren looked over Carver's shoulder and nodded. "Take her."

"No!" Carver shouted, losing his sense of caution once more as he rose from his stool in a panic and turned around just as Shiala grabbed Helena around the waist and brought her axe up to her neck.

"Sit back down, Carver!" Farren demanded.

Carver turned back to Farren with grinding teeth and shaking hands but did not sit back down.

"This is how it's going to be, Carver. Refuse me, and you'll all die right now, or do as I say and guarantee that nobody dies tonight. Succeed in the task I am giving you, and you will see this girl again. Fail, and you will meet the fate Shiala wishes I gave you right now. It isn't a hard choice for someone in your position."

Carver looked back at Helena and saw that her eyes had reddened, though no tears ran down her face. The sight made him feel sick to his stomach. At that moment, all Carver wanted to do was scream and launch himself across the table at Farren in a desperate rage, but he held back.

"Okay. Okay, I'll do it. I'll kill Aellia for you. But please don't take Helena. Just let everyone go, and I'll still do it. I'll come with you, and you can help me with the portfolio's information and make sure I have the tools to get the job done."

Farren grinned. "That's not how this works, Carver. You're smart enough to know that. If I took you with us again and helped you, I'd be drawing the attention of my superiors. Good luck."

Farren rose from the stool and turned to look at the three other armed humans standing at the ready behind him. He gave a quick gesture with his hand toward the front door.

"Let's go, you three. The town is sure to be getting a handle on the fires by now."

Farren stepped around Duncan, who had kept silent in his seat with his head down the whole while, and rounded the table toward the door near where Shiala held Helena, but Carver stepped to the right, blocking Farren.

"Wait. Please don't—"

Farren grabbed Carver's right arm and the side of his head, then yanked Carver's head to the side as he pulled his arm outwards. Before Carver could react, his head slammed down onto the table with a resounding thud. He closed his eyes as a wave of dizziness swelled inside his head before he was suddenly pulled back up and pushed backwards. He tried to stand his ground, but his feet hit the stool behind him, and he toppled over it with a crash.

Before Carver could regain his bearings, Farren lifted him up by the collar of his tunic. Carver wrapped his hands around Farren's arms, but he was too disoriented to act fast enough, and Farren slammed his back into the nearby wall.

"Listen here, you stupid boy! I should be killing you right now for what you caused! Look at me!" Farren removed one hand from Carver's tunic and grabbed the boy's face to hold it steady. "Look at my face. I've been maimed, thanks to you. It was because of you that I found myself face to face with Aellia and her soldiers outside the smugglers' warehouse. She was there for you, just as I was. And only by my actions did we escape her clutches. Those actions, however, cost me dearly."

Farren released Carver's face and brought his hand to the patch covering his left eye. Then he pinched the leather patch at the bottom and pulled it up toward his forehead, revealing his empty eye socket. Farren released the patch and it fell back down into place, covering the dark hole into his head with its sun-bleached leather.

"I had my fucking eye pulled out! You know why? Because among my actions to save my life and the lives of Shiala, Vie, and you, Carver, I was forced to harm Aellia. I knew the explosion wouldn't kill her, and collapsing the tunnel was necessary for our escape, but my reasons didn't matter. I was held down and a knife was brought to my eye. It was removed entirely so that I couldn't heal it. Rejuvenancy can only go so far, Carver. It can't restore what has been removed from the body."

Farren gripped Carver's tunic even tighter in rage. "Throughout all my investigations over the years, I've never figured out why Aellia, or her whole sovereign-serving family, for that matter, is off limits to retribution for the crimes they have committed against their own people, but I've had enough of it. I want that bitch dead, Carver, even more than I want you dead right now. So, instead of succumbing to my desire to reopen your throat and watch you bleed to death like I could have in that warehouse, I'm showing you a great mercy. I'm giving you a chance to heal my opinion of you and to sway me to forgive you for the hurts you have caused me. You should have heard the things Shiala said she was going to do to you once we found you, but because of me none of her acts of torture will befall you. You should be thanking me! Do you hear me? Thanking me!"

Farren threw Carver to the floor and looked back at Duncan, who had finally looked up and was watching the situation unfold. "I trust that you and those in your company will keep this midnight meeting to yourselves, fisherman. After all, I'm sure you don't want the town guards to learn of your actions in harboring such a wanted individual."

Duncan rose from his seat and lifted his hands up to his chest. "I won't say anything. None of us will."

"Good. I also recommend giving Carver some help in his mission, since I won't be able, nor willing, to do anything from my end. I'm sure you understand."

"Yes, sir. I'll do whatever I can. Just please, don't hurt anyone."

"Good. Good. But you know, I like to make sure that the people I'm working with are committed."

Farren looked over at the three Lost Seekers who were heading toward the door.

"Both of you," he said, pointing at the two males. "Grab one of his grandchildren. Either one will do."

"No!" Duncan shouted.

Farren's men turned and marched over to Sebastian and Nina, who were both backing toward the kitchen with terror on their faces. Sebastian, however, forced Nina behind him as the men approached. As Nina fell to the floor, the men grabbed Sebastian by the arms and yanked him away from his sister.

"Don't touch him!" Nina cried as she tried to quickly stand up, but by the time she got to her feet, the men had pulled Sebastian across the room near Shiala and Helena.

Charra ran forward and grabbed Nina around the waist before the young girl could move. Nina only struggled for a moment before she gave up and held still in Charra's firm grasp.

"I thank you for your hospitality, Duncan," Farren said as he looked over at Carver with a suddenly calm demeanor. "And I look forward to hearing of your actions at Aellia's wedding, Carver, whatever the outcome might be."

Farren opened the door, then stepped aside to allow Shiala and the others to exit first, along with Helena and Sebastian, who both were led along by pulls and shoves. Helena was taken from the room first by Shiala and given no time to look back at Carver. Sebastian, however, glared at Carver the whole way with a look of burning hatred on his face. Carver met Sebastian's rage-filled stare with a look of utter helplessness. Before Carver could even think about trying to say something to him, Sebastian was pushed out the door and into the night.

As Farren stepped out onto the porch, he turned once more and looked at Carver. "I'm giving you quite the chance here, Carver. Don't waste it. For their sake at least. And if I hear or see this door open behind me, then one of those two won't be making it to our horses." Farren slammed the door behind him.

The moment it was closed, Carver ran over to the window to the left of the door.

"Carver! Don't!" Nina shouted from behind him.

Carver ignored her and pressed his face against the wooden shutters, finding a crack that gave him the best degree of vision of the street beyond.

He watched in boiling rage as Shiala, Farren, and the other Lost Seekers forced Helena and Sebastian over to five horses just off to the side of the house. The Lost Seekers unhitched the horses and then leaped on. Sebastian was forced to climb into the saddle behind one of the male rebels while Helena shared the saddle with Shiala, though she sat in front of the woman.

Farren was the last to mount. As he settled into his saddle, he let out a sharp whistle. The horses turned in response to their riders' pulls and then galloped down the street and into the darkness. The echoes of their hooves vanished soon afterwards.

Carver pulled himself away from the window and looked back at the others. Charra and Gorty had come to the table and were sitting where Duncan and Farren had been, both in silent shock, while Duncan held Nina in a tight hug away from the table as she cried into his shoulder. Carver didn't know what to say or do. He could only watch as their grief consumed the entire room.

He knew he was to blame for all of it. All of the suffering that his friends and hosts had gone through since his arrival in Leydes had been because of him. This realization made Carver want to collapse to the floor in grief, but he stopped himself from shutting down with the image of Helena and Sebastian being stolen away on horseback. The image filled him with fury, and he suddenly began to shake without control. Carver told himself that he needed to save them, that he couldn't let them suffer because of his mistakes.

A burst of energy struck him, and he darted over to the table. He grabbed the portfolio and then turned to run for the door.

"Carver! Wait! Where are you going?" a voice called from behind him, but he couldn't focus enough to even discern whose voice it was.

He ran outside and dashed toward the fishery. As he ran, he looked up and saw the dark clouds of smoke continuing to ascend into the star-filled sky. The massive orange glow at the base of the smoke spires continued to pulse and radiate.

The loud chime of the town bell suddenly reached his ears once more, having not ceased for a moment but having been totally forgotten by Carver during the situation in Duncan's home.

He looked away from the signs of the distant fires ravaging the port and ran inside the fishery. He entered the building so quickly that he tripped over the wood that jutted up in the doorway and crashed onto the cold floor with his arms extending, the portfolio sliding from his grasp.

Carver leaped up, grabbed the portfolio, and then ran to the empty space near the stairs where his group so often relaxed to eat their meals. The cluster of recently replaced candles situated in the center of the space were all unlit, having been extinguished many hours ago, but Carver dropped to his knees beside them and slapped the portfolio down on the floor right next to them. He pulled the portfolio apart with such haste and force that the twine that kept it closed snapped as the thick parchment swung open, knocking over a candle.

He grabbed one of the other candles, hunting around for something to ignite its cold wick, but then realized he would find no such flame within the cold confines of the old fishery.

Carver threw the candle to the side and pushed the portfolio across the floor until it entered a small patch of pale moonlight that stretched through a crack in the wall facing the ocean.

The faint light barely did anything to illuminate the details of the papers, but in Carver's desperation and panic, he couldn't think of any other alternative besides using the light within Duncan's house, and he could not stomach the idea of showing his face to anyone back there after what he had done to them.

"Carver!" a voice called from behind. He turned his head and saw that Nina was standing in the open doorway of the fishery. Much of her appearance was obscured by the surrounding darkness, but as she walked toward Carver, he saw tears running down her scarred face. An intense sorrow filled his body as he watched her approach.

"I'm so sorry, Nina. I didn't mean for any of this to happen. But I'll fix this. I'll get your brother back. And Helena. I won't let those bastards hurt them. I promise. I—"

Before Carver could finish, Nina dropped to her knees in front of him and gripped him in a tight hug. He lost his ability to speak, overcome with surprise and confusion.

"I don't blame you, Carver. I can't blame you," Nina said gently into his right ear. "After Helena told me that you had left Leydes to kill every soldier responsible for burning our village and killing our families, I felt angry. Not because you left us without saying goodbye but because you didn't offer me a chance to go with you. I've prayed to the Starfather each night since we got to Leydes that everyone who had a hand in our suffering would have suffering brought upon them. And when you were gone, I prayed to all the gods that you would succeed. I pleaded with Dema and the Second Children each day, and I begged Cosom each night, to help you avenge our families and then bring you back safely to us. That you came back at all is a blessing from the gods, whichever one listened to my prayers. But I'm not going to just sit around and pray anymore. I won't let you do this alone."

Nina released Carver from the hug and looked into his eyes. Although she still had tears running down her face, her expression of deep hate surprised him.

"I'm done letting other people destroy my life and take the ones I care about away from me, and I'm finished doing nothing about it. Let me help you kill this woman and save Sebastian and Helena. Then, once we're done, we'll make Farren and those bastards wish they had never come to my grandfather's doorstep."

END OF PART ONE

Lightning Source UK Ltd.
Milton Keynes UK
UKHW020206090223
416652UK00003B/836